AMERICAN SCIENCE FICTION

FOUR CLASSIC NOVELS 1953–1956

AMERICAN SCIENCE FICTION

FOUR CLASSIC NOVELS 1953–1956

The Space Merchants • Frederik Pohl and C. M. Kornbluth
More Than Human • Theodore Sturgeon
The Long Tomorrow • Leigh Brackett
The Shrinking Man • Richard Matheson

Gary K. Wolfe, *editor*

THE LIBRARY OF AMERICA

The paper used in this publication meets the
minimum requirements of the American National Standard for
Information Sciences—Permanence of Paper for Printed
Library Materials, ANSI Z39.48—1984.

Distributed to the trade in the United States
by Penguin Group (USA) Inc.
and in Canada by Penguin Books Canada Ltd.

Library of Congress Control Number: 2011937585
ISBN 978-1-59853-158-9

Second Printing
The Library of America—227

Manufactured in the United States of America

Contents

The Space Merchants
by Frederik Pohl and C. M. Kornbluth 1

More Than Human
by Theodore Sturgeon 157

The Long Tomorrow
by Leigh Brackett 367

The Shrinking Man
by Richard Matheson 585

Biographical Notes 777

Note on the Texts 783

Notes 789

Online Companion

The Library of America has created an online companion to this volume. For more on 1950s science fiction and these works and writers, including jacket art and photographs, additional stories, author interviews, new appreciations of the novels by Michael Dirda, Neil Gaiman, William Gibson, Nicola Griffith, James Morrow, Tim Powers, Kit Reed, Peter Straub, and Connie Willis, and more, go to loa.org/sciencefiction.

THE SPACE MERCHANTS

Frederik Pohl and C. M. Kornbluth

1

AS I DRESSED that morning I ran over in my mind the long list of statistics, evasions, and exaggerations that they would expect in my report. My section—Production—had been plagued with a long series of illnesses and resignations, and you can't get work done without people to do it. But the Board wasn't likely to take that as an excuse.

I rubbed depilatory soap over my face and rinsed it with the trickle from the fresh-water tap. Wasteful, of course, but I pay taxes and salt water always leaves my face itchy. Before the last of the greasy stubble was quite washed away the trickle stopped and didn't start again. I swore a little and finished rinsing with salt. It had been happening lately; some people blamed Consie saboteurs. Loyalty raids were being held throughout the New York Water Supply Corporation; so far they hadn't done any good.

The morning newscast above the shaving mirror caught me for a moment . . . the President's speech of last night, a brief glimpse of the Venus rocket squat and silvery on the Arizona sand, rioting in Panama . . . I switched it off when the quarter-hour time signal chimed over the audio band.

It looked as though I was going to be late again. Which certainly would not help mollify the Board.

I saved five minutes by wearing yesterday's shirt instead of studding a clean one and by leaving my breakfast juice to grow warm and sticky on the table. But I lost the five minutes again by trying to call Kathy. She didn't answer the phone and I was late getting into the office.

Fortunately—and unprecedentedly—Fowler Schocken was late too.

In our office it is Fowler's custom to hold the weekly Board conference fifteen minutes before the regular opening of the business day. It keeps the clerks and stenos on their toes, and it's no hardship to Fowler. He spends every morning in the office anyway, and "morning" to him begins with the rising of the sun.

Today, though, I had time to get my secretary's summary

off my desk before the meeting. When Fowler Schocken walked in with a courteous apology for his tardiness I was sitting in my place at the foot of the table, reasonably relaxed and as sure of myself as a Fowler Schocken Associate is ever likely to be.

"Good morning," Fowler said, and the eleven of us made the usual idiot murmur. He didn't sit down; he stood gazing paternally at us for about a minute and a half. Then, with the air of a day-tripper in Xanadu, he looked carefully and delightedly about the room.

"I've been thinking about our conference room," he said, and we all looked around at it. The room isn't big, it isn't small: say ten by twelve. But it's cool, well-lighted, and most imposingly furnished. The air recirculators are cleverly hidden behind animated friezes; the carpeting is thick and soft; and every piece of furniture is constructed from top to bottom of authentic, expertized, genuine tree-grown wood.

Fowler Schocken said: "We have a nice conference room here, men. As we should have, since Fowler Schocken Associates is the largest advertising agency in the city. We bill a megabuck a year more than anybody else around. And—" he looked around at all of us, "I think you'll agree that we all find it worth while. I don't think there's a person in this room who has less than a two-room apartment." He twinkled at me. "Even the bachelors. Speaking for myself, I've done well. My summer place looks right over one of the largest parks on Long Island. I haven't tasted any protein but new meat for years, and when I go out for a spin I pedal a Cadillac. The wolf is a long way from my door. And I think any one of you can say the same. Right?" The hand of our Director of Market Research shot up and Fowler nodded at him: "Yes, Matthew?"

Matt Runstead knows which side his bread is oiled on. He glared belligerently around the table. "I just want to go on record as agreeing with Mr. Schocken—one hundred per cent—all the way!" he snapped.

Fowler Schocken inclined his head. "Thank you, Matthew." And he meant it. It took him a moment before he could go on. "We all know," he said, "what put us where we are. We remember the Starrzelius Verily account, and how we put Indiastries on the map. The first spherical trust. Merging a whole subcontinent into a single manufacturing complex. Schocken Associates pioneered on both of them. Nobody can say we were floating with the tide. But that's behind us.

"Men! I want to know something. You can tell me truthfully —are we getting soft?" He took time to look at each of our faces searchingly, ignoring the forest of hands in the air. God help me, mine was right up there too. Then he waved to the man at his right. "You first, Ben," he said.

Ben Winston stood up and baritoned: "Speaking for Industrial Anthropology, no! Listen to today's progress report—you'll get it in the noon bulletin, but let me brief you now: according to the midnight indices, all primary schools east of the Mississippi are now using our packaging recommendation for the school lunch program. Soyaburgers and regenerated steak"—there wasn't a man around the table who didn't shudder at the thought of soyaburgers and regenerated steak—"are packed in containers the same shade of green as the Universal products. But the candy, ice cream, and Kiddiebutt cigarette ration are wrapped in colorful Starrzelius red. When those kids grow up . . ." he lifted his eyes exultantly from his notes. "According to our extrapolation, fifteen years from now Universal products will be broke, bankrupt, and off the market entirely!"

He sat down in a wave of applause. Schocken clapped too, and looked brightly at the rest of us. I leaned forward with Expression One—eagerness, intelligence, competence—all over my face. But I needn't have bothered. Fowler pointed to the lean man next to Winston. Harvey Bruner.

"I don't have to tell you men that Point-of-Sale has its special problems," Harvey said, puffing his thin cheeks. "I swear, the whole damned Government must be infiltrated with Consies! You know what they've done. They outlawed compulsive subsonics in our aural advertising—but we've bounced back with a list of semantic cue words that tie in with every basic trauma and neurosis in American life today. They listened to the safety cranks and stopped us from projecting our messages on aircar windows—but we bounced back. Lab tells me," he nodded to our Director of Research across the table, "that soon we'll be testing a system that projects direct on the retina of the eye.

"And not only that, but we're going forward. As an example

I want to mention the Coffiest pro—" He broke off. "Excuse me, Mr. Schocken," he whispered. "Has Security checked this room?"

Fowler Schocken nodded. "Absolutely clean. Nothing but the usual State Department and House of Representatives spy-mikes. And of course we're feeding a canned playback into them."

Harvey relaxed again. "Well, about this Coffiest," he said. "We're sampling it in fifteen key cities. It's the usual offer—a thirteen-week supply of Coffiest, one thousand dollars in cash, and a week-end vacation on the Ligurian Riviera to everybody who comes in. But—and here's what makes this campaign truly great, in my estimation—each sample of Coffiest contains three milligrams of a simple alkaloid. Nothing harmful. But definitely habit-forming. After ten weeks the customer is hooked for life. It would cost him at least five thousand dollars for a cure, so it's simpler for him to go right on drinking Coffiest—three cups with every meal and a pot beside his bed at night, just as it says on the jar."

Fowler Schocken beamed, and I braced myself into Expression One again. Next to Harvey sat Tildy Mathis, Chief of Personnel and hand-picked by Schocken himself. But he didn't ask women to speak at Board sessions, and next to Tildy sat me.

I was composing my opening remarks in my head as Fowler Schocken let me down with a smile. He said: "I won't ask every section to report. We haven't the time. But you've given me your answer, gentlemen. It's the answer I like. You've met every challenge up to now. And so now—I want to give you a new challenge."

He pressed a button on his monitor panel and swiveled his chair around. The lights went down in the room; the projected Picasso that hung behind Schocken's chair faded and revealed the mottled surface of the screen. On it another picture began to form.

I had seen the subject of that picture once before that day, in my news screen over my shaving mirror.

It was the Venus rocket, a thousand-foot monster, the bloated child of the slim V-2's and stubby Moon rockets of the past. Around it was a scaffolding of steel and aluminum, acrawl with tiny figures that manipulated minute, blue-white welding flames. The picture was obviously recorded; it showed the rocket as it had been weeks or months ago in an earlier stage of construction, not poised as if ready for take-off, as I had seen it earlier.

A voice from the screen said triumphantly and inaccurately: "This is the ship that spans the stars!" I recognized the voice as belonging to one of the organ-toned commentators in Aural Effects and expertized the scripts without effort as emanating from one of Tildy's girl copywriters. The talented slovenliness that would confuse Venus with a star had to come from somebody on Tildy's staff.

"This is the ship that a modern Columbus will drive through the void," said the voice. "Six and a half million tons of trapped lightning and steel—an ark for eighteen hundred men and women, and everything to make a new world for their home. Who will man it? What fortunate pioneers will tear an empire from the rich, fresh soil of another world? Let me introduce you to them—a man and his wife, two of the intrepid . . ."

The voice kept on going. On the screen the picture dissolved to a spacious suburban roomette in early morning. On the screen the husband folding the bed into the wall and taking down the partition to the children's nook; the wife dialing breakfast and erecting the table. Over the breakfast juices and the children's pablum (with a steaming mug of Coffiest for each, of course) they spoke persuasively to each other about how wise and brave they had been to apply for passage in the Venus rocket. And the closing question of their youngest babbler ("Mommy, when I grow up kin I take *my* littul boys and girls to a place as nice as Venus?") cued the switch to a highly imaginative series of shots of Venus as it would be when the child grew up—verdant valleys, crystal lakes, brilliant mountain vistas.

The commentary did not exactly deny, and neither did it dwell on, the decades of hydroponics and life in hermetically sealed cabins that the pioneers would have to endure while working on Venus' unbreathable atmosphere and waterless chemistry.

Instinctively I had set the timer button on my watch when the picture started. When it was over I read the dial: nine minutes! Three times as long as any commercial could legally run. One full minute more than we were accustomed to get.

It was only after the lights were on again, the cigarettes lit, and Fowler Schocken well into his pep talk for the day that I began to see how that was possible.

He began in the dithering, circumlocutory way that has become a part of the flavor of our business. He called our attention to the history of advertising—from the simple handmaiden task of selling already-manufactured goods to its present role of creating industries and redesigning a world's folkways to meet the needs of commerce. He touched once more on what we ourselves, Fowler Schocken Associates, had done with our own expansive career. And then he said:

"There's an old saying, men. 'The world is our oyster.' We've made it come true. But we've eaten that oyster." He crushed out his cigarette carefully. "We've eaten it," he repeated. "We've actually and literally conquered the world. Like Alexander, we weep for new worlds to conquer. And *there*—" he waved at the screen behind him, "*there* you have just seen the first of those worlds."

I have never liked Matt Runstead, as you may have gathered. He is a Paul Pry whom I suspect of wire tapping even within the company. He must have spied out the Venus project well in advance, because not even the most talented reflexes could have brought out his little speech. While the rest of us were still busy assimilating what Fowler Schocken had told us, Runstead was leaping to his feet.

"Gentlemen," he said with passion, "this is truly the work of genius. Not just India. Not just a commodity. But a whole planet to *sell.* I salute you, Fowler Schocken—the Clive, the Bolivar, the John Jacob Astor of a new world!"

Matt was first, as I say, but every one of us got up and said in turn about the same thing. Including me. It was easy; I'd been doing it for years. Kathy had never understood it and I'd tried to explain, with the light touch, that it was a religious ritual—like the champagne-bottle smash on the ship's prow, or the sacrifice of the virgin to the corn crop. Even with the light touch I never pressed the analogy too far. I don't think any of us, except maybe Matt Runstead, would feed opium derivatives to the world for money alone. But listening to Fowler

Schocken speak, hypnotizing ourselves with our antiphonal responses, made all of us capable of any act that served our god of Sales.

I do not mean to say that we were criminals. The alkaloids in Coffiest were, as Harvey pointed out, not harmful.

When all of us had done, Fowler Schocken touched another button and showed us a chart. He explained it carefully, item by item; he showed us tables and graphs and diagrams of the entire new Department of Fowler Schocken Associates which would be set up to handle development and exploitation of the planet Venus. He covered the tedious lobbying and friend-making in Congress, which had given us the exclusive right to levy tribute and collect from the planet—and I began to see how he could safely use a nine-minute commercial. He explained how the Government—it's odd how we still think and talk of that clearinghouse for pressures as though it were an entity with a will of its own—how the Government wanted Venus to be an American planet and how they had selected the peculiarly American talent of advertising to make it possible. As he spoke we all caught some of his fire. I envied the man who would head the Venus Section; any one of us would have been proud to take the job.

He spoke of trouble with the Senator from Du Pont Chemicals with his forty-five votes, and of an easy triumph over the Senator from Nash-Kelvinator with his six. He spoke proudly of a faked Consie demonstration against Fowler Schocken, which had lined up the fanatically anti-Consie Secretary of the Interior. Visual Aids had done a beautiful job of briefing the information, but we were there nearly an hour looking at the charts and listening to Fowler's achievements and plans.

But finally he clicked off the projector and said: "There you have it. That's our new campaign. And it starts right away—*now*. I have only one more announcement to make and then we can all get to work."

Fowler Schocken is a good showman. He took the time to find a slip of paper and read from it a sentence that the lowest of our copyboys could deliver off the cuff. "The chairman of the Venus Section," he read, "will be Mitchell Courtenay."

And that was the biggest surprise of all, because Mitchell Courtenay is me.

2

I LINGERED with Fowler for three or four minutes while the rest of the Board went back to their offices, and the elevator ride down from the Board room to my own office on the eighty-sixth floor took a few seconds. So Hester was already clearing out my desk when I arrived.

"Congratulations, Mr. Courtenay," she said. "You're moving to the eighty-ninth now. Isn't it wonderful? And I'll have a private office too!"

I thanked her and picked up the phone over the desk. The first thing I had to do was get my staff in and turn over the reins of Production; Tom Gillespie was next in line. But the first thing I *did* was to dial Kathy's apartment again. There was still no answer, so I called in the boys.

They were properly sorry to see me go and properly delighted about everybody's moving up a notch.

And then it was lunch time, so I postponed the problem of the planet Venus until the afternoon.

I made a phone call, ate quickly in the company cafeteria, took the elevator down to the shuttle, and the shuttle south for sixteen blocks. Coming out, I found myself in the open air for the first time that day, and reached for my antisoot plugs but didn't put them in. It was raining lightly and the air had been a little cleared. It was summer, hot and sticky; the hordes of people crowding the sidewalks were as anxious as I to get back inside a building. I had to bulldoze my way across the street and into the lobby.

The elevator took me up fourteen floors. It was an old building with imperfect air conditioning, and I felt a chill in my damp suit. It occurred to me to use that fact instead of the story I had prepared, but I decided against it.

A girl in a starched white uniform looked up as I walked into the office. I said: "My name is Silver. Walter P. Silver. I have an appointment."

"Yes, Mr. Silver," she remembered. "Your heart—you said it was an emergency."

"That's right. Of course it's probably psychosomatic, but I felt—"

"Of course." She waved me to a chair. "Dr. Nevin will see you in just a moment."

It was ten minutes. A young woman came out of the doctor's office, and a man who had been waiting in the reception room before me went in; then he came out and the nurse said: "Will you go into Dr. Nevin's office now?"

I went in. Kathy, very trim and handsome in her doctor's smock, was putting a case chart in her desk. When she straightened up she said, "Oh, Mitch!" in a very annoyed tone.

"I told only one lie," I said. "I lied about my name. But it is an emergency. And my heart is involved."

There was a faint impulse toward a smile, but it didn't quite reach the surface. "Not medically," she said.

"I *told* your girl it was probably psychosomatic. She said to come in anyhow."

"I'll speak to her about that. Mitch, you know I can't see you during working hours. Now please—"

I sat down next to her desk. "You won't see me any time, Kathy. What's the trouble?"

"Nothing's the trouble. Please go away, Mitch. I'm a doctor; I have work to do."

"Nothing as important as this. Kathy, I tried to call you all last night and all morning."

She lit a cigarette without looking at me. "I wasn't home," she said.

"No, you weren't." I leaned forward and took the cigarette from her and puffed on it. She hesitated, shrugged, and took out another. I said: "I don't suppose I have the right to ask my wife where she spends her time?"

Kathy flared: "Damn it, Mitch, you know—" Her phone rang. She screwed her eyes shut for a moment. Then she picked up the phone, leaning back in her chair, looking across the room, relaxed, a doctor soothing a patient. It took only a few moments. But when it was all over she was entirely self-possessed.

"Please go away," she said, stubbing out her cigarette.

"Not until you tell me when you'll see me."

"I . . . haven't time to see you, Mitch. I'm not your wife. You have no right to bother me like this. I could have you enjoined or arrested."

"My certificate's on file," I reminded her.

"Mine isn't. It never will be. As soon as the year is up, we're through, Mitch."

"There was something I wanted to tell you." Kathy had always been reachable through curiosity.

There was a long pause and instead of saying again: "Please go away," she said: "Well, what is it?"

I said: "It's something big. It calls for a celebration. And I'm not above using it as an excuse to see you for just a little while tonight. Please, Kathy—I love you very much and I promise not to make a scene."

". . . No."

But she had hesitated. I said: "Please?"

"Well—" While she was thinking, her phone rang. "All right," she said to me. "Call me at home. Seven o'clock. Now let me take care of the sick people."

She picked up the phone. I let myself out of her office while she was talking, and she didn't look after me.

Fowler Schocken was hunched over his desk as I walked in, staring at the latest issue of *Taunton's Weekly*. The magazine was blinking in full color as the triggered molecules of its inks collected photons by driblets and released them in bursts. He waved the brilliant pages at me and asked: "What do you think of this, Mitch?"

"Sleazy advertising," I said promptly. "If we had to stoop so low as to sponsor a magazine like Taunton Associates—well, I think I'd resign. It's too cheap a trick."

"Um." He put the magazine face down; the flashing inks gave one last burst and subsided as their light source was cut off. "Yes, it's cheap," he said thoughtfully. "But you have to give them credit for enterprise. Taunton gets sixteen and a half million readers for *his* ads every week. Nobody else's—just Taunton clients. And I hope you didn't mean that literally about resigning. I just gave Harvey the go-ahead on *Shock*. The first issue comes out in the fall, with a print order of twenty million. No—" He mercifully held up his hand to cut off my stammering try at an explanation. "I understood what you meant, Mitch. You were against *cheap* advertising. And so am I. Taunton is to me the epitome of everything that keeps advertising from finding its rightful place with the clergy, medicine, and the bar in our way of life. There isn't a shoddy trick he wouldn't pull, from bribing a judge to stealing an employee. And, Mitch, he's a man you'll have to watch."

"Why? I mean, why particularly?"

Schocken chuckled. "Because we stole Venus from him, that's why. I told you he was enterprising. He had the same idea I did. It wasn't easy to persuade the Government that it should be our baby."

"I see," I said. And I did. Our representative government now is perhaps more representative than it has ever been before in history. It is not necessarily representative *per capita*, but it most surely is *ad valorem*. If you like philosophical problems, here is one for you: should each human being's vote register alike, as the lawbooks pretend and as some say the founders of our nation desired? Or should a vote be weighed according to the wisdom, the power, and the influence—that is, the money—of the voter? That is a philosophical problem for you, you understand; not for me. I am a pragmatist, and a pragmatist, moreover, on the payroll of Fowler Schocken.

One thing was bothering me. "Won't Taunton be likely to take—well, direct action?"

"Oh, he'll try to steal it back," Fowler said mildly.

"That's not what I mean. You remember what happened with Antarctic Exploitation."

"I was there. A hundred and forty casualties on our side. God knows what they lost."

"And that was only one continent. Taunton takes these things pretty personally. If he started a feud for a lousy frozen continent, what will he do for a whole planet?"

Fowler said patiently, "No, Mitch. He wouldn't dare. Feuds are expensive. Besides, we're not giving him grounds—not grounds that would stand up in court. And, in the third place . . . we'd whip his tail off."

"I guess so," I said, and felt reassured. Believe me, I am a loyal employee of Fowler Schocken Associates. Ever since cadet days I have tried to live my life "for Company and for Sales." But industrial feuds, even in our profession, can be pretty messy. It was only a few decades ago that a small but effective agency in London filed a feud against the English branch of B.B.D. & O. and wiped it out to the man except for two

Bartons and a single underage Osborn. And they say there are still bloodstains on the steps of the General Post Office where Western Union and American Railway Express fought it out for the mail contract.

Schocken was speaking again. "There's one thing you'll have to watch out for: the lunatic fringe. This is the kind of project that's bound to bring them out. Every crackpot organization on the list, from the Consies to the G.O.P., is going to come out for or against it. Make sure they're all for; they swing weight."

"Even the Consies?" I squeaked.

"Well, no. I didn't mean that; they'd be more of a liability." His white hair glinted as he nodded thoughtfully. "Mm. Maybe you could spread the word that spaceflight and Conservationism are diametrically opposed. It uses up too many raw materials, hurts the living standard—you know. Bring in the fact that the fuel uses organic material that the Consies think should be made into fertilizer—"

I like to watch an expert at work. Fowler Schocken laid down a whole subcampaign for me right there; all I had to do was fill in the details. The Conservationists were fair game, those wild-eyed zealots who pretended modern civilization was in some way "plundering" our planet. Preposterous stuff. Science is *always* a step ahead of the failure of natural resources. After all, when real meat got scarce, we had soyaburgers ready. When oil ran low, technology developed the pedicab.

I had been exposed to Consie sentiment in my time, and the arguments had all come down to one thing: Nature's way of living was the *right* way of living. Silly. If "Nature" had intended us to eat fresh vegetables, it wouldn't have given us niacin or ascorbic acid.

I sat still for twenty minutes more of Fowler Schocken's inspirational talk, and came away with the discovery I had often made before: briefly and effectively, he had given me every fact and instruction I needed.

The details he left to me, but I knew my job:

We wanted Venus colonized by Americans. To accomplish this, three things were needed: colonists; a way of getting them to Venus; and something for them to do when they got there.

The first was easy to handle through direct advertising.

Schocken's TV commercial was the perfect model on which we could base the rest of that facet of our appeal. It is always easy to persuade a consumer that the grass is greener far away. I had already penciled in a tentative campaign with the budget well under a megabuck. More would have been extravagant.

The second was only partly our problem. The ships had been designed—by Republic Aviation, Bell Telephone Labs, and U. S. Steel, I believe, under Defense Department contract. Our job wasn't to make the transportation to Venus possible but to make it palatable. When your wife found her burned-out toaster impossible to replace because its nichrome element was part of a Venus rocket's main drive jet, or when the inevitable disgruntled congressman for a small and frozen-out firm waved an appropriations sheet around his head and talked about government waste on wildcat schemes, our job began: we had to convince your wife that rockets are more important than toasters; we had to convince the congressman's constituent firm that its tactics were unpopular and would cost it profits.

I thought briefly of an austerity campaign and vetoed it. Our other accounts would suffer. A religious movement, perhaps—something that would offer vicarious dedication to the eight hundred million who would not ride the rockets themselves. . . .

I tabled that; Bruner could help me there. And I went on to point three. There had to be something to keep the colonists busy on Venus.

This, I knew, was what Fowler Schocken had his eye on. The government money that would pay for the basic campaign was a nice addition to our year's billing, but Fowler Schocken was too big for one-shot accounts. What we wanted was the year-after-year reliability of a major industrial complex; what we wanted was the colonists, and their children, added to our complex of accounts. Fowler, of course, hoped to repeat on an enormously magnified scale our smashing success with Indiastries. His Boards and he had organized all of India into a single giant cartel, with every last woven basket and iridium ingot and caddy of opium it produced sold through Fowler Schocken advertising. Now he could do the same with Venus. Potentially this was worth as much as every dollar of value in existence put together! A whole new planet, the size of Earth, in prospect as rich as Earth—and every micron, every milligram of it ours.

I looked at my watch. About four; my date with Kathy was for seven. I just barely had time. I dialed Hester and had her get me space on the Washington jet while I put through a call to the name Fowler had given me. The name was Jack O'Shea; he was the only human being who had been to Venus—so far. His voice was young and cocky as he made a date to see me.

We were five extra minutes in the landing pattern over Washington, and then there was a hassle at the ramp. Brink's Express guards were swarming around our plane, and their lieutenant demanded identification from each emerging passenger. When it was my turn I asked what was going on. He looked at my low-number Social Security card thoughtfully and then saluted. "Sorry to bother you, Mr. Courtenay," he apologized. "It's the Consie bombing near Topeka. We got a tip that the man might be aboard the 4:05 New York jet. Seems to have been a lemon."

"What Consie bombing was this?"

"Du Pont Raw Materials Division—we're under contract for their plant protection, you know—was opening up a new coal vein under some cornland they own out there. They made a nice little ceremony of it, and just as the hydraulic mining machine started ramming through the topsoil somebody tossed a bomb from the crowd. Killed the machine operator, his helper, and a vice-president. Man slipped away in the crowd, but he was identified. We'll get him one of these days."

"Good luck, Lieutenant," I said, and hurried on to the jetport's main refreshment lounge. O'Shea was waiting in a window seat, visibly annoyed, but he grinned when I apologized.

"It could happen to anybody," he said, and swinging his short legs shrilled at a waiter. When we had placed our orders he leaned back and said: "Well?"

I looked down at him across the table and looked away through the window. Off to the south the gigantic pylon of the F.D.R. memorial blinked its marker signal; behind it lay the tiny, dulled dome of the old Capitol. I, a glib ad man, hardly knew where to start. And O'Shea was enjoying it. "Well?" he asked again, amusedly, and I knew he meant: "Now all of *you* have to come to *me*, and how do you like it for a change?"

I took the plunge. "What's on Venus?" I asked.

"Sand and smoke," he said promptly. "Didn't you read my report?"

"Certainly. I want to know more."

"Everything's in the report. Good Lord, they kept me in the interrogation room for three solid days when I got back. If I left anything out, it's gone permanently."

I said: "That's not what I mean, Jack. Who wants to spend his life reading reports? I have fifteen men in Research doing nothing but digesting reports for me so I don't have to read them. I want to know something more. I want to get the feel of the planet. There's only one place I can get it because only one man's been there."

"And sometimes I wish I hadn't," O'Shea said wearily. "Well, where do I start? You know how they picked me—the only midget in the world with a pilot's license. And you know all about the ship. And you saw the assay reports on the samples I brought back. Not that they mean much. I only touched down once, and five miles away the geology might be entirely different."

"I know all that. Look, Jack, put it this way. Suppose you wanted a lot of people to go to Venus. What would you tell them about it?"

He laughed. "I'd tell them a lot of damn big lies. Start from scratch, won't you? What's the deal?"

I gave him a fill-in on what Schocken Associates was up to, while his round little eyes stared at me from his round little face. There is an opaque quality, like porcelain, to the features of midgets: as though the destiny that had made them small at the same time made them more perfect and polished than ordinary men, to show that their lack of size did not mean lack of completion. He sipped his drink and I gulped mine between paragraphs.

When my pitch was finished I still didn't know whether he was on my side or not, and with him it mattered. He was no civil service puppet dancing to the strings that Fowler Schocken knew ways of pulling. Neither was he a civilian who could be bought with a tiny decimal of our appropriation. Fowler had helped him a little to capitalize on his fame via testimonials, books, and lectures, so he owed us a little gratitude, and no more.

He said: "I wish I could help," and that made things easier.

"You can," I told him. "That's what I'm here for. Tell me what Venus has to offer."

"Damn little," he said, with a small frown chiseling across his lacquered forehead. "Where shall I start? Do I have to tell you about the atmosphere? There's free formaldehyde, you know —embalming fluid. Or the heat? It averages above the boiling point of water—if there were any water on Venus, which there isn't. Not accessible, anyhow. Or the winds? I clocked five hundred miles an hour."

"No, not exactly that," I said. "I know about that. And honestly, Jack, there are answers for all those things. I want to get the feel of the place, what you thought when you were there, how you reacted. Just start talking. I'll tell you when I've had what I wanted."

He dented his rose-marble lip with his lower teeth. "Well," he said, "let's start at the beginning. Get us another drink, won't you?"

The waiter came, took our order, and came back with the liquor. Jack drummed on the table, sipped his rhine-wine and seltzer, and began to talk.

He started way back, which was good. I wanted to know the soul of the fact, the elusive, subjective mood that underlay his technical reports on the planet Venus, the basic feeling that would put compulsion and conviction into the project.

He told me about his father, the six-foot chemical engineer, and his mother, the plump, billowy housewife. He made me feel their dismay and their ungrudging love for their thirty-five-inch son. He had been eleven years old when the subject of his adult life and work first came up. He remembered the unhappiness on their faces at his first, inevitable, offhand suggestion about the circus. It was no minor tribute to them that the subject never came up again. It was a major tribute that Jack's settled desire to learn enough engineering and rocketry to be a test pilot had been granted, paid for, and carried out in the face of every obstacle of ridicule and refusal from the schools.

Of course Venus had made it all pay off.

The Venus rocket designers had run into one major complication. It had been easy enough to get a rocket to the moon a quarter-million miles away; theoretically it was not much harder to blast one across space to the nearest other world, Venus. The question was one of orbits and time, of controlling the ship and bringing it back again. A dilemma. They could blast the ship to Venus in a few days—at so squandersome a fuel expenditure that ten ships couldn't carry it. Or they could ease it to Venus along its natural orbits as you might float a barge down a gentle river—which saved the fuel but lengthened the trip to months. A man in eighty days eats twice his own weight in food, breathes nine times his weight of air, and drinks water enough to float a yawl. Did somebody say: distill water from the waste products and recirculate it; do the same with food; do the same with air? Sorry. The necessary equipment for such cycling weighs more than the food, air, and water. So the human pilot was out, obviously.

A team of designers went to work on an automatic pilot. When it was done it worked pretty well. And weighed four and one half tons in spite of printed circuits and relays constructed under a microscope.

The project stopped right there until somebody thought of that most perfect servo-mechanism: a sixty-pound midget. A third of a man in weight, Jack O'Shea ate a third of the food, breathed a third of the oxygen. With minimum-weight, low-efficiency water- and air-purifiers, Jack came in just under the limit and thereby won himself undying fame.

He said broodingly, a little drunk from the impact of two weak drinks on his small frame: "They put me into the rocket like a finger into a glove. I guess you know what the ship looked like. But did you know they *zipped* me into the pilot's seat? It wasn't a chair, you know. It was more like a diver's suit; the only air on the ship was in that suit; the only water came in through a tube to my lips. Saved weight . . ."

And the next eighty days were in that suit. It fed him, gave him water, sopped his perspiration out of its air, removed his body wastes. If necessary it would have shot novocaine into a broken arm, tourniqueted a cut femoral artery, or pumped air for a torn lung. It was a placenta, and a hideously uncomfortable one.

In the suit thirty-three days going, forty-one coming back. The six days in between were the justification for the trip.

Jack had fought his ship down through absolute blindness: clouds of gas that closed his own eyes and confused the radar, down to the skin of an unknown world. He had been within a thousand feet of the ground before he could see anything but swirling yellow. And then he landed and cut the rockets.

"Well, I couldn't get out, of course," he said. "For forty or fifty reasons, somebody else will have to be the first man to set foot on Venus. Somebody who doesn't care much about breathing, I guess. Anyway, there I was, looking at it." He shrugged his shoulders, looked baffled, and said a dirty word softly. "I've told it a dozen times at lectures, but I've never got it over. I tell 'em the closest thing to it on Earth is the Painted Desert. Maybe it is; I haven't been there.

"The wind blows *hard* on Venus and it tears up the rocks. Soft rocks blow away and make the dust storms. The hard parts—well, they stick out in funny shapes and colors. Great big monument things, some of them. And the most jagged hills and crevasses you can imagine. It's something like the inside of a cave, sort of—only not dark. But the light is—funny. Nobody ever saw light like that on Earth. Orangy-brownish light, brilliant, *very* brilliant, but sort of threatening. Like the way the sky is threatening in the summer around sunset just before a smasher of a thunderstorm. Only there never is any thunderstorm because there isn't a drop of water around." He hesitated. "There is lightning. Plenty of it, but never any rain . . . I don't know, Mitch," he said abruptly. "Am I being any help to you at all?"

I took my time answering. I looked at my watch and saw that the return jet was about to leave, so I bent down and turned off the recorder in my briefcase. "You're being lots of help, Jack," I said. "But I'll need more. And I have to go now. Look, can you come up to New York and work with me for a while? I've got everything you said on tape, but I want visual stuff too. Our artists can work from the pix you brought back, but there must be more. And you're a lot more use than the photographs for what we need." I didn't mention that the artists would be drawing impressions of what Venus *would* look like if it were different from what it was. "How about it?"

Jack leaned back and looked cherubic but, though he made me sweat through a brief recap of the extensive plans his lecture agent had made for his next few weeks, he finally agreed. The Shriners' talk could be canceled, he decided, and the appointments with his ghost writers could be kept as well in New York as in Washington. We made a date for the following day just as the PA system announced that my flight was ready.

"I'll walk you to the plane," Jack offered. He slipped down from the chair and threw a bill on the table for the waiter. We walked together through the narrow aisles of the bar out into the field. Jack grinned and strutted a little at some ohs and ahs that went up as he was recognized. The field was almost dark, and the glow of Washington backlighted the silhouettes of hovering aircraft. Drifting toward us from the freight terminal was a huge cargo 'copter, a fifty-tonner, its cargo nacelle gleaming in colors as it reflected the lights below. It was no more than fifty feet in the air, and I had to clutch my hat against the downdraft from its whirling vanes.

"Damn-fool bus drivers," Jack grunted, staring up at the 'copter. "They ought to put those things on G.C.A. Just because they're maneuverable those fan-jockeys think they can take them anywhere. If I handled a jet the way they—*Run! Run!*" Suddenly he was yelling at me and pushing at my middle with both his small hands. I goggled at him; it was too sudden and disconnected to make any kind of sense. He lurched at me in a miniature body block and sent me staggering a few steps.

"What the hell—?" I started to complain, but I didn't hear my own words. They were drowned out by a mechanical snapping sound and a flutter in the beat of the rotors and then the loudest crash I had ever heard as the cargo pod of the 'copter hit the concrete a yard from where we stood. It ruptured and spilled cartons of Starrzelius Verily rolled oats. One of the crimson cylinders rolled to my toes and I stupidly picked it up and looked at it.

Overhead the lightened 'copter fluttered up and away, but I didn't see it go.

"For God's sake, get it off them!" Jack was yelling, tugging at me. We had not been alone on the field. From under the buckled aluminum reached an arm holding a briefcase, and through the compound noises in my ears I could hear a bubbling sound of human pain. That was what he meant. Get it off them. I let him pull me to the tangled metal, and we tried to heave it. I got a scratched hand and tore my jacket, and then the airport people got there and brusquely ordered us away.

I don't remember walking there, but by and by I found that I was sitting on someone's suitcase, back against the wall of the terminal, with Jack O'Shea talking excitedly to me. He was cursing the class of cargo 'copter pilots and blackguarding me for standing there like a fool when he'd seen the nacelle clamps opening, and a great deal more that I didn't get. I remember his knocking the red box of breakfast food from my hand impatiently. The psychologists say I am not unusually sensitive or timorous, but I was in a state of shock that lasted until Jack was loading me into my plane.

Later on the hostess told me five people had been caught under the nacelle, and the whole affair seemed to come into focus. But not until we were halfway back to New York. At the time all I remembered, all that seemed important, was Jack's saying over and over, bitterness and anger written on his porcelain face: "Too damn many people, Mitch. Too damn much crowding. I'm with you every inch of the way. We *need* Venus, Mitch, we need the space . . ."

3

KATHY'S APARTMENT, way downtown in Bensonhurst, was not large but it was comfortable. In a homey, sensible way it was beautifully furnished. As who should know better than I? I pressed the button over the label "Dr. Nevin," and smiled at her as she opened the door.

She did not smile back. She said two things: "You're late, Mitch," and, "I thought you were going to call first."

I walked in and sat down. "I was late because I almost got killed and I didn't call because I was late. Does that square us?" She asked the question I wanted her to ask, and I told her how close I had come to death that evening.

Kathy is a beautiful woman with a warm, friendly face, her hair always immaculately done in two tones of blond, her eyes usually smiling. I have spent a great deal of time looking at her, but I never watched more attentively than when I told her about the cargo nacelle near-miss. It was, on the whole, disappointing. She was really concerned for me, beyond doubt. But Kathy's heart opens to a hundred people and I saw nothing in her face to make me feel that she cared more for me than anyone else she had known for years.

So I told her my other big news, the Venus account and my stewardship of it. It was more successful; she was startled and excited and happy, and kissed me in a flurry of good feeling. But when *I* kissed *her*, as I'd been wanting to do for months, she drew away and went to sit on the other side of the room, ostensibly to dial a drink.

"You rate a toast, Mitch," she smiled. "Champagne at the least. Dear Mitch, it's *wonderful* news!"

I seized the chance. "Will you help me celebrate? Really celebrate?"

Her brown eyes were wary. "Um," she said. Then: "Sure I will, Mitch. We'll do the town together—my treat and no arguments about it. The only thing is, I'll have to leave you punctually at 2400. I'm spending the night in the hospital. I've a hysterectomy to do in the morning and I mustn't get to sleep too late. Or too drunk, either."

But she smiled.

Once again I decided not to push my luck too far. "Great," I said, and I wasn't faking. Kathy is a wonderful girl to do the town with. "Let me use your phone?"

By the time we had our drinks I had arranged for tickets to a show, a dinner table, and a reservation for a nightcap afterwards. Kathy looked a little dubious. "It's a pretty crowded program for five hours, Mitch," she said. "My hysterectomy isn't going to like it if my hand shakes." But I talked her out of it. Kathy is more resilient than that. Once she did a complete trepan the morning after we'd spent the entire night screaming out our tempers at each other, and it had gone perfectly.

The dinner, for me, was a failure. I don't pretend to be an epicure who can't stand anything but new protein. I definitely am, however, a guy who gets sore when he pays new-protein prices and gets regenerated-protein merchandise. The texture of the shashlik we both ordered was all right, but you can't hide the taste. I scratched the restaurant off my list then and there, and apologized to Kathy for it. But she laughed it off, and the show afterwards was fine. Hypnotics often give me a headache, but I slipped right into the trance state this time as soon as the film began and was none the worse for it afterwards.

The night club was packed, and the headwaiter had made a mistake in the time for our reservations. We had to wait five minutes in the anteroom, and Kathy shook her head very decisively when I pleaded for an extension on the curfew. But when the headwaiter showed us with the fanciest apologies and bows to our places at the bar and our drinks came, she leaned over and kissed me again. I felt just fine.

"Thanks," she said. "That was a wonderful evening, Mitch. Get promoted often, please. I like it."

I lit a cigarette for her and one for myself, and opened my mouth to say something. I stopped.

Kathy said, "Go ahead, say it."

"Well, I was going to say that we always have fun together."

"I know you were. And I was going to say that I knew what you were leading up to and that the answer still was no."

"I know you were," I said glumly. "Let's get the hell out of here."

She paid the tab and we left, inserting our antisoot plugs as we hit the street. "Cab, sir?" asked the doorman.

"Yes, please," Kathy answered. "A tandem."

He whistled up a two-man pedicab, and Kathy gave the lead boy the hospital's address. "You can come if you like, Mitch," she said, and I climbed in beside her. The doorman gave us a starting push and the cabbies grunted getting up momentum.

Unasked, I put down the top. For a moment it was like our courtship again: the friendly dark, the slight, musty smell of the canvas top, the squeak of the springs. But for a moment only. "Watch that, Mitch," she said warningly.

"Please, Kathy," I said carefully. "Let me say it anyhow. It won't take long." She didn't say no. "We were married eight months ago—all right," I said quickly as she started to speak, "it wasn't an absolute marriage. But we took the interlocutory vows. Do you remember why we did that?"

She said patiently after a moment: "We were in love."

"That's right," I said. "I loved you and you loved me. And we both had our work to think about, and we knew that sometimes it made us a little hard to get along with. So we made it interim. It had a year to run before we had to decide whether to make it permanent." I touched her hand and she didn't move it away. "Kathy dear, don't you think we knew what we were doing then? Can't we—at least—give it the year's trial? There are still four months to go. Let's try it. If the year ends and you don't want to file your certificate—well, at least I won't be able to say you didn't give me a chance. As for me, I don't have to wait. My certificate's on file now and I won't change."

We passed a street light and I saw her lips twisted into an expression I couldn't quite read. "Oh, damn it all, Mitch," she said unhappily, "I *know* you won't change. That's what makes it all so terrible. Must I sit here and call you names to convince you that it's hopeless? Do I have to tell you that you're an ill-tempered, contriving, Machiavellian, selfish pig of a man to live with? I used to think you were a sweet guy, Mitch. An idealist who cared for principles and ethics instead of money. I had every reason to think so. You told me so yourself, very convincingly. You were very plausible about my work too. You boned up on medicine, you came to watch me operate three times a week, you told all our friends while I was sitting right in the room listening to you how proud you were to be married to a surgeon. It took me three months to find out what you meant by that. Anybody could marry a girl who'd be a housewife. But it took a Mitchell Courtenay to marry a first-class rated surgeon and *make* her a housewife." Her voice was tremulous. "I couldn't take it, Mitch. I never will be able to. Not the arguments, the sulkiness, and the ever-and-ever fighting. I'm a doctor. Sometimes a life depends on me. If I'm all torn up inside from battling with my husband, that life isn't safe, Mitch. Can't you see that?"

Something that sounded like a sob.

I asked quietly: "Kathy, don't you still love me?"

She was absolutely quiet for a long moment. Then she laughed wildly and very briefly. "Here's the hospital, Mitch," she said. "It's midnight."

I threw back the top and we climbed out. "Wait," I said to the lead boy, and walked with her to the door. She wouldn't kiss me good night and she wouldn't make a date to see me again. I stood in the lobby for twenty minutes to make sure she was really staying there that night, and then got into the cab to go to the nearest shuttle station. I was in a vile mood. It wasn't helped any when the lead boy asked innocently after I paid him off: "Say, mister, what does Mac—Machiavellian mean?"

"Spanish for 'mind your own God-damned business,'" I told him evenly. On the shuttle I wondered sourly how rich I'd have to be before I could buy privacy.

My temper was no better when I arrived at the office next morning. It took all Hester's tact to keep me from biting her head off in the first few minutes, and it was by the grace of God that there was not a Board meeting. After I'd got my mail and the overnight accumulation of interoffice memos, Hester intelligently disappeared for a while. When she came back she brought me a cup of coffee—authentic, plantation-grown coffee. "The matron in the ladies' room brews it on the sly," she explained. "Usually she won't let us take it out because she's afraid of the Coffiest team. But now that you're star class—"

I thanked her and gave her Jack O'Shea's tape to put through channels. Then I went to work.

First came the matter of the sampling area, and a headache with Matt Runstead. He's Market Research, and I had to work with and through him. But he didn't show any inclination to work with me. I put a map of southern California in the projector, while Matt and two of his faceless helpers boredly sprinkled cigarette ashes on my floor.

With the pointer I outlined the test areas and controls: "San Diego through Tijuana; half the communities around L.A. and the lower tip of Monterrey. Those will be controls. The rest of Cal-Mexico from L.A. down we'll use for tests. You'll have to be on the scene, I guess, Matt; I'd recommend our Diego offices as headquarters. Turner's in charge there and he's a good man."

Runstead grunted. "Not a flake of snow from year's end to year's end. Couldn't sell an overcoat there if you threw in a slave girl as a premium. For God's sake, man, why don't you leave market research to somebody who knows something about it? Don't you see how climate nulls your sigma?"

The younger of his stamped-out-of-tin assistants started to back the boss up, but I cut him off. Runstead had to be consulted on test areas—it was his job. But Venus was my project and I was going to run it. I said, sounding just a little nasty: "Regional and world income, age, density of population, health, psyche-friction, age-group distribution and mortality causes and rates are seven-place sigmas, Matt. Cal-Mex was designed personally by God Himself as a perfect testing area. In a tiny universe of less than a hundred million it duplicates every important segment of North America. I will not change my project and we are going to stick to the area I indicated." I bore down on the word "my."

Matt said: "It won't work. The temperature is the major factor. Anybody should be able to see that."

"I'm not just anybody, Matt. I'm the guy in charge."

Matt Runstead stubbed out his cigarette and got up. "Let's go talk to Fowler," he said and walked out. There wasn't anything for me to do except follow him. As I left I heard the older of his helpers picking up the phone to notify Fowler Schocken's secretary that we were coming. He had a team all right, that Runstead. I spent a little time wondering how I could build a team like that myself before I got down to the business of planning how to put it to Fowler.

But Fowler Schocken has a sure-fire technique of handling interstaff hassles. He worked it on us. When we came in he said exuberantly: "There you are! The two men I want to see! Matt, can you put out a fire for me? It's the A.I.G. people. They claim our handling of the PregNot account is hurting their trade. They're talking about going over to Taunton unless we drop PregNot. Their billing isn't much, but a birdie told me that Taunton put the idea into their heads." He went on to explain the intricacies of our relationship with the American Institute of Gynecologists. I listened only half-heartedly; our "Babies Without Maybes" campaign on their sex-determination project had given them at least a 20 per cent plus on the normal birthrate. They should be solidly ours after that. Runstead thought so too.

He said: "They don't have a case, Fowler. We sell liquor and hang-over remedies both. They've got no business bitching about any other account. Besides, what the hell does this have to do with Market Research?"

Fowler chuckled happily. "That's it!" he crowed. "We throw them a switch. They'll expect the account executives to give them the usual line—but instead we'll let you handle them yourself. Snow them under with a whole line of charts and statistics to prove that PregNot never *prevents* a couple from having a baby; it just permits them to *postpone* it until they can afford to do the job right. In other words, their unit of sale goes up and their volume stays the same. And—it'll be one in the eye for Taunton. And—lawyers get disbarred for representing conflicting interests. It's cost a lot of them a lot of money. We've got to make sure that any attempt to foist the same principle on our profession is nipped in the bud. Think you can handle it for the old man, Matt?"

"Oh, hell, sure," Runstead grumbled. "What about Venus?"

Fowler twinkled at me. "What about it? Can you spare Matt for a while?"

"Forever," I said. "In fact, that's what I came to see you about. Matt's scared of southern California."

Runstead dropped his cigarette and let it lay, crisping the nylon pile of Fowler's rug. "What the hell—" he started belligerently.

"Easy," said Fowler. "Let's hear the story, Matt."

Runstead glowered at me. "All I said was that southern California isn't the right test area. What's the big difference between Venus and here? Heat! We need a test area with continental-average climate. A New Englander might be attracted by the heat on Venus; a Tijuana man, never. It's too damn hot in Cal-Mex already."

"Um," said Fowler Schocken. "Tell you what, Matt. This needs going into, and you'll want to get busy on the A.I.G. thing. Pick out a good man to vice you on the Venus section while you're out, and we'll have it hashed over at the section meeting tomorrow afternoon. Meanwhile—" he glanced at his desk clock, "Senator Danton has been waiting for seven minutes. All right?"

It was clearly not all right with Matt, and I felt cheered for the rest of the day. Things went well enough. Development came in with a report on what they'd gleaned from O'Shea's tape and all the other available material. The prospects for manufacture were there. Quick, temporary ones like little souvenir globes of Venus manufactured from the organics floating around in what we laughingly call the "air" of Venus. Long-term ones—an assay had indicated pure iron: not nine-nines pure and not ninety-nine nines pure, but absolute iron that nobody would ever find or make on an oxygen planet like Earth. The labs would pay well for it. And Development had not developed but found a remarkable little thing called a high-speed Hilsch Tube. Using no power, it could refrigerate the pioneers' homes by using the hot tornadoes of Venus. It was a simple thing that had been lying around since 1943. Nobody until us had any use for it because nobody until us had that kind of winds to play with.

Tracy Collier, the Development liaison man with Venus Section, tried also to tell me about nitrogen-fixing catalysts. I nodded from time to time and gathered that sponge-platinum "sown" on Venus would, in conjunction with the continuous, terrific lightning cause it to "snow" nitrates and "rain" hydrocarbons, purging the atmosphere of formaldehyde and ammonia.

"Kind of expensive?" I asked cautiously.

"Just as expensive as you want it to be," he said. "The platinum doesn't get used up, you know. Use one gram and take a million years or more. Use more platinum and take less time."

I didn't really understand, but obviously it was good news. I patted him and sent him on his way.

Industrial Anthropology gave me a setback. Ben Winston complained: "You *can't* make people want to live in a steam-heated sardine can. All our folkways are against it. Who's going to travel sixty million miles for a chance to spend the rest of his life cooped up in a tin shack—when he can stay right here on Earth and have corridors, elevators, streets, roofs, all the wide-open space a man could want? It's against human nature, Mitch!"

I reasoned with him. It didn't do much good. He went on telling me about the American way of life—walked to the window with me and pointed out at the hundreds of acres of rooftops where men and women could walk around in the open air, wearing simple soot-extractor nostril plugs instead of a bulky oxygen helmet.

Finally I got mad. I said: "*Somebody* must want to go to Venus. Otherwise why would they buy Jack O'Shea's book the way they do? Why would the voters stand still for a billion-and-up appropriation to build the rocket? God knows I shouldn't have to lead you by the nose this way, but here's what you are going to do: survey the book-buyers, the repeat-viewers of O'Shea's TV shows, the ones who come early to his lectures and stand around talking in the lobby afterwards. O'Shea is on the payroll—pump him for everything you can get. Find out about the Moon colony—find out what types they have there. And then we'll know whom to aim our ads at. Any arguments, for God's sake?" There weren't.

Hester had done wonders of scheduling that first day, and I made progress with every section head involved. But she couldn't read my paper work for me, and by quitting time I had six inches of it stacked by my right arm. Hester volunteered to stay with me, but there wasn't really anything for her to do. I let her bring me sandwiches and another cup of coffee, and chased her home.

It was after eleven by the time I was done. I stopped off in an all-night diner on the fifteenth floor before heading home, a windowless box of a place where the coffee smelled of the yeast it was made from and the ham in my sandwich bore the taint of soy. But it was only a minor annoyance and quickly out of my mind. For as I opened the door to my apartment there was a *snick* and an explosion, and something slammed into the doorframe by my head. I ducked and yelled. Outside the window a figure dangling from a rope ladder drifted away, a gun in its hand.

I was stupid enough to run over to the window and gawk out at the helicopter-borne figure. I would have been a perfect target if it had been steady enough to shoot at me again, but it wasn't.

Surprised at my calm, I called the Metropolitan Protection Corporation.

"Are you a subscriber, sir?" their operator asked.

"Yes, dammit. For six years. Get a man over here! Get a squad over here."

"One moment, Mr. Courtenay. . . . Mr. *Mitchell* Courtenay? Copysmith, star class?"

"No," I said bitterly. "Target is my profession. Will you kindly get a man over here before the character who just took a shot at me comes back?"

"Excuse me, Mr. Courtenay," said the sweet, unruffled voice. "Did you say you were *not* a copysmith, star class?"

I ground my teeth. "I'm star class," I admitted.

"Thank you, sir. I have your record before me, sir. I am sorry, sir, but your account is in arrears. We do not accept star-class accounts at the general rate because of the risk of industrial feuds, sir." She named a figure that made each separate hair on my head stand on end.

I didn't blow my top; she was just a tool. "Thanks," I said heavily, and rang off. I put the *Program-Printing to Quarry Machinery* reel of the Red Book into the reader and spun it to Protective Agencies. I got turndowns from three or four, but finally one sleepy-sounding private detective agreed to come on over for a stiff fee.

He showed up in half an hour and I paid him, and all he did was annoy me with unanswerable questions and look for nonexistent fingerprints. After a while he went away saying he'd work on it.

I went to bed and eventually to sleep with one of the unanswered questions chasing itself around and around in my head: who would want to shoot a simple, harmless advertising man like me?

4

I TOOK my courage in my hands and walked briskly down the hall to Fowler Schocken's office. I needed an answer, and he might have it. He might also throw me out of the office for asking. But I needed an answer.

It didn't seem to be the best possible time to ask Fowler

questions. Ahead of me, his door opened explosively and Tildy Mathis lurched out. Her face was working with emotion. She stared at me, but I'll take oath she didn't know my name. "Rewrites," she said wildly. "I slave my heart out for that white-haired old rat, and what does he give me? Rewrites. 'This is *good* copy, but I want better than *good* copy from *you*,' he says. 'Rewrite it,' he says. 'I want color,' he says, 'I want drive and beauty, and humble, human warmth, and ecstasy, and all the tender, sad emotion of your sweet womanly heart,' he says, 'and I want it in fifteen words.' I'll give him fifteen words," she sobbed, and pushed past me down the hall. "I'll give that sanctimonious, mellifluous, hyperbolic, paternalistic, star-making, genius-devouring Moloch of an old—"

The slam of Tildy's own door cut off the noun. I was sorry; it would have been a good noun.

I cleared my throat, knocked once, and walked into Fowler's office. There was no hint of his brush with Tildy in the smile he gave me. In fact, his pink, clear-eyed face belied my suspicions, but—I *had* been shot at.

"I'll only be a minute, Fowler," I said. "I want to know whether you've been playing rough with Taunton Associates."

"I always play rough," he twinkled. "Rough, but clean."

"I mean very, very rough and very, very dirty. Have you, by any chance, tried to have any of their people shot?"

"Mitch! *Really!*"

"I'm asking," I went on doggedly, "because last night a 'copter-borne marksman tried to plug me when I came home. I can't think of any angle except retaliation from Taunton."

"Scratch Taunton," he said positively.

I took a deep breath. "Fowler," I said, "man-to-man, you haven't been Notified? I may be out of line, but I've got to ask. It isn't just me. It's the Venus Project."

There were no apples in Fowler's cheeks at that moment, and I could see in his eyes that my job and my star-class rating hung in the balance.

He said: "Mitch, I made you star class because I thought you could handle the responsibilities that came with it. It isn't just the work. I know you can do that. I thought you could live up to the commercial code as well."

I hung on. "Yes, sir," I said.

He sat down and lit a Starr. After just exactly the right split second of hesitation, he pushed the pack to me. "Mitch, you're a youngster, only star class a short time. But you've got power. Five words from you, and in a matter of weeks or months half a million consumers will find their lives completely changed. That's power, Mitch, absolute power. And you know the old saying. Power ennobles. Absolute power ennobles absolutely."

"Yes, sir," I said. I knew all the old sayings. I also knew that he was going to answer my question eventually.

"Ah, Mitch," he said dreamily, waving his cigarette, "we have our prerogatives and our duties and our particular hazards. You can't have one without the others. If we didn't have feuds, the whole system of checks and balances would be thrown out of gear."

"Fowler," I said, greatly daring, "you know I have no complaints about the system. It works; that's all you have to say for it. I know we need feuds. And it stands to reason that if Taunton files a feud against us, you've got to live up to the code. You can't broadcast the information; every executive in the shop would be diving for cover instead of getting work done. But—Venus Project is in my head, Fowler. I can handle it better that way. If I write everything down, it slows things up."

"Of course," he said.

"Suppose you *were* Notified, and suppose I'm the first one Taunton knocks off—what happens to Venus Project?"

"You may have a point," he admitted. "I'll level with you, Mitch. There has been no Notification."

"Thanks, Fowler," I said sincerely. "I *did* get shot at. And that accident in Washington—maybe it wasn't an accident. You don't imagine Taunton would try anything without Notifying you, do you?"

"I haven't provoked them to that extent, and they'd never do a thing like that anyhow. They're cheap, they're crooked, but they know the rules of the game. Killing in an industrial feud is a misdemeanor. Killing *without* Notification is a *commercial offense*. You haven't been getting into any of the wrong beds, shall I say?"

"No," I said. "My life's been very dull. The whole thing's crazy. It must have been a mistake. But I'm glad that whoever-it-was couldn't shoot."

"So am I, Mitch, so am I! Enough of your personal life. We've got business. You saw O'Shea?" He had already dismissed the shooting from his mind.

"I did. He's coming up here today. He'll be working closely with me."

"Splendid! Some of that glory will rub off on Fowler Schocken Associates if we play our cards right. Dig into it, Mitch. I don't have to tell you how."

It was a dismissal.

O'Shea was waiting in the anteroom of my office. It wasn't an ordeal; most of the female personnel was clustered around him as he sat perched on a desk, talking gruffly and authoritatively. There was no mistaking the looks in their eyes. He was a thirty-five-inch midget, but he had money and fame, the two things we drill and drill into the population. O'Shea could have taken his pick of them. I wondered how many he had picked since his return to Earth in a blaze of glory.

We run a taut office, but the girls didn't scatter until I cleared my throat.

"Morning, Mitch," O'Shea said. "You over your shock?"

"Sure. And I ran right into another one. Somebody tried to shoot me." I told the story and he grunted thoughtfully.

"Have you considered getting a bodyguard?" he asked.

"Of course. But I won't. It must have been a mistake."

"Like that cargo nacelle?"

I paused. "Jack, can we *please* get off this subject? It gives me the horrors."

"Permission granted," he beamed. "Now, let's go to work—and on what?"

"First, words. We want words that are about Venus, words that'll tickle people. Make them sit up. Make them muse about change, and space, and other worlds. Words to make them a little discontented with what they are and a little hopeful about what they might be. Words to make them feel noble about feeling the way they do and not foolish. Words that will do all these things and also make them happy about the existence of Indiastries and Starrzelius Verily and Fowler Schocken Associates. Words that will do all these things and also make them feel unhappy about the existence of Universal Products and Taunton Associates."

He was staring at me with his mouth open. "You aren't serious," he finally exclaimed.

"You're on the inside now," I said simply. "That's the way we work. That's the way we worked on you."

"What are you talking about?"

"You're wearing Starrzelius Verily clothes and shoes, Jack. It means we got you. Taunton and Universal worked on you, Starrzelius and Schocken worked on you—and you chose Starrzelius. We reached you. Smoothly, without your ever being aware that it was happening, you became persuaded that there was something rather nice about Starrzelius clothes and shoes and that there was something rather not-nice about Universal clothes and shoes."

"I never read the ads," he said defiantly.

I grinned. "Our ultimate triumph is wrapped up in that statement," I said.

"I solemnly promise," O'Shea said, "that as soon as I get back to my hotel room I'll send my clothes down the incinerator chute—"

"Luggage too?" I asked. "Starrzelius luggage?"

He looked startled for a moment and then regained his calm. "Starrzelius luggage too," he said. "And then I'll pick up the phone and order a complete set of Universal luggage and apparel. And you can't stop me."

"I wouldn't dream of stopping you, Jack! It means more business for Starrzelius. Tell you what you're going to do: you'll get your complete set of Universal luggage and apparel. You'll use the luggage and wear the apparel for a while with a vague, submerged discontent. It's going to work on your libido, because our ads for Starrzelius—even though you say you don't read them—have convinced you that it isn't quite virile to trade with any other firm. Your self-esteem will suffer; deep down you'll *know* that you're not wearing the best. Your subconscious won't stand up under much of that. You'll find yourself 'losing' bits of Universal apparel. You'll find yourself 'accidentally' putting your foot through the cuff of your Universal pants. You'll find yourself overpacking the Universal luggage and damning it for not being roomier. You'll walk into stores and in a fit of momentary amnesia regarding this conversation you'll buy Starrzelius, bless you."

O'Shea laughed uncertainly. "And you did it with words?"

"Words and pictures. Sight and sound and smell and taste and touch. And the greatest of these is words. Do you read poetry?"

"My God, of course not! Who can?"

"I don't mean the contemporary stuff; you're quite right about that. I mean Keats, Swinburne, Wylie—the great lyricists."

"I used to," he cautiously admitted. "What about it?"

"I'm going to ask you to spend the morning and afternoon with one of the world's great lyric poets: a girl named Tildy Mathis. She doesn't know that she's a poet; she thinks she's a boss copywriter. Don't enlighten her. It might make her unhappy.

> 'Thou still unravish'd bride of quietness,
> Thou foster-child of Silence and slow Time—'

That's the sort of thing she would have written before the rise of advertising. The correlation is perfectly clear. Advertising up, lyric poetry down. There are only so many people capable of putting together words that stir and move and sing. When it became possible to earn a very good living in advertising by exercising this capability, lyric poetry was left to untalented screwballs who had to shriek for attention and compete by eccentricity."

"Why are you telling me all this?" he asked.

"I said you're on the inside, Jack. There's a responsibility that goes with the power. Here in this profession we reach into the souls of men and women. We do it by taking talent and—redirecting it. Nobody should play with lives the way we do unless he's motivated by the highest ideals."

"I get you," he said softly. "Don't worry about my motives. I'm not in this thing for money or fame. I'm in it so the human race can have some elbow room and dignity again."

"That's it," I said, putting on Expression Number One. But inwardly I was startled. The "highest ideal" I had been about to cite was Sales.

I buzzed for Tildy. "Talk to her," I said. "Answer her questions. Ask her some. Make it a long, friendly chat. Make her share your experiences. And, without knowing it, she'll write lyric fragments of your experiences that will go right to the hearts and souls of the readers. Don't hold out on her."

"Certainly not. Uh, Mitch, will she hold out on me?"

The expression on his face was from a Tanagra figurine of a hopeful young satyr.

"She won't," I promised solemnly. Everybody knew about Tildy.

That afternoon, for the first time in four months, Kathy called me.

"Is anything wrong?" I asked sharply. "Anything I can do?"

She giggled. "Nothing wrong, Mitch. I just wanted to say hello and tell you thanks for a lovely evening."

"How about another one?" I asked promptly.

"Dinner at my place tonight suit you?"

"It certainly does. It certainly, certainly does. What color dress will you be wearing? I'm going to buy you a real flower!"

"Oh, Mitch, you needn't be extravagant. We aren't courting and I already know you have more money than God. But there *is* something I wish you'd bring."

"Only name it."

"Jack O'Shea. Can you manage it? I saw by the 'cast that he came into town this morning and I suppose he's working with you."

Very dampened, I said: "Yes, he is. I'll check with him and call you back. You at the hospital?"

"Yes. And thanks so much for trying. I'd love to meet him."

I got in touch with O'Shea in Tildy's office. "You booked up for tonight?" I asked.

"Hmmm . . . I *could* be," he said. O'Shea was evidently learning about Tildy too.

"Here's my proposition. Quiet dinner at home with my wife and me. She happens to be beautiful and a good cook and a first-rate surgeon and excellent company."

"You're on."

So I called Kathy back and told her I'd bring the social lion about seven.

He stalked into my office at six, grumbling: "I'd better get a good meal out of this, Mitch. Your Miss Mathis appeals to me. What a dope! Does she have sense enough to come in out of the smog?"

"I don't believe so," I said. "But Keats was properly hooked by a designing wench, and Byron didn't have sense enough to stay out of the venereal ward. Swinburne made a tragic mess out of his life. Do I have to go on?"

"Please, no. What kind of marriage have you got?"

"Interlocutory," I said, a little painfully in spite of myself.

He raised his eyebrows a trifle. "Maybe it's just the way I was brought up, but there's something about those arrangements that sets my teeth on edge."

"Mine too," I said, "at least in my own case. In case Tildy missed telling you, my beautiful and talented wife doesn't want to finalize it, we don't live together, and unless I change her mind in four months we'll be washed up."

"Tildy did miss telling me," he said. "You're pretty sick about it, seems to me."

I almost gave in to self-pity. I almost invited his sympathy. I almost started to tell him how rough it was, how much I loved her, how she wasn't giving me an even break, how I'd tried everything I could think of and nothing would convince her. And then I realized that I'd be telling it to a sixty-pound midget who, if he married, might become at any moment his wife's helpless plaything or butt of ridicule.

"Middling sick," I said. "Let's go, Jack. Time for a drink and then the shuttle."

Kathy had never looked lovelier, and I wished I hadn't let her talk me out of shooting a couple of days' pay on a corsage at Cartier's.

She said hello to O'Shea and he announced loudly and immediately: "I like you. There's no gleam in your eye. No 'Isn't he cute?' gleam. No 'My, he must be rich and frustrated!' gleam. No 'A girl's got a right to try anything once' gleam. In short, you like me and I like you."

As you may have gathered, he was a little drunk.

"You are going to have some coffee, Mr. O'Shea," she said.

"I ruined myself to provide real pork sausages and real apple sauce, and you're going to taste them."

"Coffee?" he said. "Coffiest for me, ma'am. To drink coffee would be disloyal to the great firm of Fowler Schocken Associates with which I am associated. Isn't that right, Mitch?"

"I give absolution this once," I said. "Besides, Kathy doesn't believe the harmless alkaloid in Coffiest is harmless." Luckily she was in the kitchen corner with her back turned when I said that, and either missed it or could afford to pretend she did. We'd had a terrific four-hour battle over that very point, complete with epithets like "baby-poisoner" and "crackpot reformer" and a few others that were shorter and nastier.

The coffee was served and quenched O'Shea's mild glow. Dinner was marvelous. Afterward, we all felt more relaxed.

"You've been to the Moon, I suppose?" Kathy asked O'Shea.

"Not yet. One of these days."

"There's nothing there," I said. "It's a waste of time. One of our dullest, deadest accounts. I suppose we only kept it for the experience we'd get, looking ahead to Venus. A few thousand people mining—that's the *whole* story."

"Excuse me," O'Shea said, and retired.

I grabbed the chance. "Kathy, darling," I said, "It was very sweet of you to ask me over. Does it mean anything?"

She rubbed her right thumb and index finger together, and I knew that whatever she would say after that would be a lie. "It might, Mitch," she lied gently. "You'll have to give me time."

I threw away my secret weapon. "You're lying," I said disgustedly. "You always do this before you lie to me—I don't know about other people." I showed her, and she let out a short laugh.

"Fair's fair," she said with bitter amusement. "You always catch your breath and look right into my eyes when you lie to me—I don't know about your clients and fellow-employees."

O'Shea returned and felt the tension at once. "I ought to be going," he said. "Mitch, do we leave together?"

Kathy nodded, and I said: "Yes."

There were the usual politenesses at the door, and Kathy kissed me good night. It was a long, warm, clinging kiss;

altogether the kind of kiss that should start the evening rather than end it. It set her own pulse going—I felt that!—but she coolly closed the door on us.

"You thought about a bodyguard again?" O'Shea asked.

"It was a mistake," I said stubbornly.

"Let's stop by your place for a drink," he said ingenuously.

The situation was almost pathetic. Sixty-pound Jack O'Shea was bodyguarding me. "Sure," I said. We got on the shuttle.

He went into the room first and turned on the light, and nothing happened. While sipping a very weak whisky and soda, he drifted around the place checking window locks, hinges, and the like. "This chair would look better over there," he said. "Over there," of course, was out of the line of fire from the window. I moved it.

"Take care of yourself, Mitch," he said when he left. "That lovely wife and your friends would miss you if anything happened."

The only thing that happened was that I barked my shin setting up the bed, and that was happening all the time. Even Kathy, with a surgeon's neat, economical movements, bore the battle scars of life in a city apartment. You set up the bed at night, you took it down in the morning, you set up the table for breakfast, you took it down to get to the door. No wonder some shortsighted people sighed for the spacious old days, I thought, settling myself luxuriously for the night.

5

THINGS WERE rolling within a week. With Runstead out of my hair and at work on the PregNot–A.I.G. hassle, I could really grip the reins.

Tildy's girls and boys were putting out the copy—temperamental kids, sometimes doing a line a day with anguish; sometimes rolling out page after page effortlessly, with shining eyes, as though possessed. She directed and edited their stuff and passed the best of the best to me: nine-minute commercial scripts, pix cutlines, articles for planting, news stories, page ads, whispering campaign cuelines, endorsements, jokes-limericks-and-puns (clean and dirty) to float through the country.

Visual was hot. The airbrush and camera people were having fun sculpturing a planet. It was the ultimate in "Before and After" advertising, and they were caught by the sense of history.

Development kept pulling rabbits out of hats. Collier once explained to me when I hinted that he might be over-optimistic: "It's *energy*, Mr. Courtenay. Venus has got *energy*. It's closer to the sun. The sun pours all that energy into the planet in the form of heat and molecular bonds and fast particles. Here on Earth we don't have that level of tappable energy. We use windmills to tap the kinetic energy of the atmosphere. On Venus we'll use *turbines*. If we want electricity on Venus we'll just build an accumulator, put up a lightning rod and jump back. It's an entirely different *level*."

Market Research–Industrial Anthropology was at work in San Diego sampling the Cal-Mex area, trying Tildy's copy, Visual's layouts and films and extrapolating and interpolating. I had a direct wire to the desk of Ham Harris, Runstead's vice, in San Diego.

A typical day began with a Venus Section meeting: pep talk by me, reports of progress by all hands, critique and cross-department suggestions. Harris, on the wire, might advise Tildy that "serene atmosphere" wasn't going well as a cue phrase in his sampling and that she should submit a list of alternatives. Tildy might ask Collier whether it would be okay to say "topaz sands" in a planted article which would hint that Venus was crawling with uncut precious and semiprecious stones. Collier might tell Visual that they'd have to make the atmosphere redder in a "Before" panorama. And I might tell Collier to lay off because it was permissible license.

After adjournment everybody would go into production and I'd spend my day breaking ties, co-ordinating, and interpreting my directives from above down to the operational level. Before close of day we'd hold another meeting, which I would keep to some specific topic, such as: integration of Starrzelius products into the Venus economy, or: income-level of prospective Venus colonists for optimum purchasing power twenty years after landing.

And then came the best part of the day. Kathy and I were going steady again. We were still under separate cover, but I was buoyantly certain that it wouldn't be long now. Sometimes she dated me, sometimes I dated her. We just went out and had fun eating well, drinking well, dressing well, and feeling that we were two good-looking people enjoying life. There wasn't much serious talk. She didn't encourage it and I didn't press it. I thought that time was on my side. Jack O'Shea made the rounds with us once before he had to leave for a lecture in Miami, and that made me feel good too. A couple of well-dressed, good-looking people who were so high-up they could entertain the world's number one celebrity. Life was good.

After a week of solid, satisfying progress on the job I told Kathy it was time for me to visit the outlying installations—the rocket site in Arizona and sampling headquarters in San Diego.

"Fine," she said. "Can I come along?"

I was silly-happy about it; it wouldn't be long now.

The rocket visit was routine. I had a couple of people there as liaison with Armed Forces, Republic Aviation, Bell Telephone Labs, and U. S. Steel. They showed Kathy and me through the monster, glib as tourist guides: ". . . vast steel shell . . . more cubage than the average New York office building . . . closed-cycle food and water and air regeneration . . . one-third drive, one-third freight, one-third living space . . . heroic pioneers . . . insulation . . . housekeeping power . . . sunside-darkside heat pumps . . . unprecedented industrial effort . . . national sacrifice . . . national security . . ."

Oddly, the most impressive thing about it to me was not the rocket itself but the wide swathe around it. For a full mile the land was cleared: no houses, no greenhouse decks, no food tanks, no sun traps. Partly security, partly radiation. The gleaming sand cut by irrigation pipes looked strange. There probably wasn't another sight like it in North America. It troubled my eyes. Not for years had I focused them more than a few yards.

"How strange," Kathy said at my side. "Could we walk out there?"

"Sorry, Dr. Nevin," said one of the liaison men. "It's a deadline. The tower guards are ordered to shoot anybody out there."

"Have contrary orders issued," I said. "Dr. Nevin and I want to take a walk."

"Of course, Mr. Courtenay," the man said, very worried. "I'll do my best, but it'll take a little time. I'll have to clear it with C.I.C., Naval Intelligence, C.I.A., F.B.I., A.E.C. Security and Intelligence—"

I looked at Kathy, and she shrugged with helpless amusement. "Never mind," I said.

"Thank God!" breathed my liaison man. "Excuse me, Mr. Courtenay. It's never been done before so there aren't any channels to do it through. You know what *that* means."

"I do indeed," I said, from the heart. "Tell me, has all the security paid off?"

"It seems so, Mr. Courtenay. There's been no sabotage or espionage, foreign or Consie, that we know of." He rapped a knuckle of his right hand solemnly on a handsome oak engagement ring he wore on the third finger of his left hand. I made a mental note to have his expense account checked up on. A man on his salary had no business wearing that kind of jewelry.

"The Consies interested?" I asked.

"Who knows? C.I.C., C.I.A. and A.E.C. S.&I. say yes. Naval Intelligence, F.B.I. and S.S. say no. Would you like to meet Commander MacDonald? He's the O.N.I. chief here. A specialist in Consies."

"Like to meet a Consie specialist, Kathy?" I asked.

"If we have time," she said.

"I'll have them hold the jet for you if necessary," the liaison man said eagerly, trying hard to undo his fiasco on the tower guards. He led us through the tangle of construction shacks and warehouses to the administration building and past seven security check points to the office of the commander.

MacDonald was one of those career officers who make you feel good about being an American citizen—quiet, competent, strong. I could see from his insignia and shoulder flashes that he was a Contract Specialist, Intelligence, on his third five-year option from the Pinkerton Detective Agency. He was a regular; he wore the class ring of the Pinkerton Graduate School of Detection and Military Intelligence, Inc. It's pine with an open eye carved on it; no flashy inlay work. But it's like a brand name. It tells you that you're dealing with quality.

"You want to hear about Consies?" he asked quietly. "I'm your man. I've devoted my life to running them down."

"A personal grudge, Commander?" I asked, thinking I'd hear something melodramatic.

"No. Old-fashioned pride of workmanship if anything. I like the thrill of the chase, too, but there isn't much chasing. You get Consies by laying traps. Did you hear about the Topeka bombing? Of-course-I-shouldn't-knock-the-competition-but those guards should have known it was a setup for a Consie demonstration."

"Why, exactly, Commander?" Kathy asked.

He smiled wisely. "Feel," he said. "The kind of thing it's hard to put over in words. The Consies don't like hydraulic mining—ever. Give them a chance to parade their dislike and they'll take it if they can."

"But *why* don't they like hydraulic mining?" she persisted. "We've got to have coal and iron, don't we?"

"Now," he said with pretended, humorous weariness, "you're asking me to probe the mind of a Consie. I've had them in the wrecking room for up to six hours at a stretch and never yet have they talked sense. If I caught the Topeka Consie, say, he'd talk willingly—but it would be gibberish. He'd tell me the hydraulic miner was destroying topsoil. I'd say yes, and what about it. He'd say, well can't you *see*? I'd say, see what? He'd say, the topsoil can never be replaced. I'd say, yes it can if it had to be and anyway tank farming's better. He'd say something like tank farming doesn't provide animal cover and so on. It always winds up with him telling me the world's going to hell in a handbasket and people have got to be made to realize it—and me telling him we've always got along somehow and we'll keep going somehow."

Kathy laughed incredulously and the commander went on: "They're fools, but they're *tough*. They have discipline. A cell system. If you get one Consie you always get the two or three others in his cell, but you hardly ever get any more. There's no lateral contact between cells, and vertical contact with higher-ups is by rendezvous with middlemen. Yes, I think I know them and that's why I'm not especially worried about sabotage or a demonstration here. It doesn't have the right ring to it."

Kathy and I lolled back watching the commercials parade around the passenger compartment of the jet at eye level.

There was the good old Kiddiebutt jingle I worked out many years ago when I was a trainee. I nudged Kathy and told her about it as it blinked and chimed Victor Herbert's *Toyland* theme at us.

All the commercials went blank and a utility announcement, without sound effects, came on.

> *In Compliance With Federal Law, Passengers Are Advised That They Are Now Passing Over The San Andreas Fault Into Earthquake Territory, And That Earthquake Loss And Damage Clauses In Any Insurance They May Carry Are Now Canceled And Will Remain Canceled Until Passengers Leave Earthquake Territory.*

Then the commercials resumed their parade.

"And," said Kathy, "I suppose it says in the small print that yak-bite insurance is good anywhere except in Tibet."

"Yak-bite insurance?" I asked, astonished. "What on earth do you carry that for?"

"A girl can never tell when she'll meet an unfriendly yak, can she?"

"I conclude that you're kidding," I said with dignity. "We ought to land in a few minutes. Personally, I'd like to pop in on Ham Harris unexpectedly. He's a good kid, but Runstead may have infected him with defeatism. There's nothing worse in our line."

"I'll come along with you if I may, Mitch."

We gawked through the windows like tourists as the jet slid into the traffic pattern over San Diego and circled monotonously waiting for its calldown from the tower. Kathy had never been there before. I had been there once, but there's always something new to see because buildings are always falling down and new ones being put up. And what buildings! They're more like plastic tents on plastic skeletons than anything else. That kind of construction means they give and sway when a quake jiggles southern California instead of snapping and crumbling. And if the quake is bad enough and the skeleton does snap, what have you lost? Just some plastic sheeting that broke along the standard snap grooves and some plastic structural members that may or may not be salvageable.

From a continental economic viewpoint, it's also a fine idea not to tie up too much fancy construction in southern California. Since the H-bomb tests did things to the San Andreas fault, there's been a pretty fair chance that the whole area would slide quietly into the Pacific some day—any day. But when we looked down out of the traffic pattern, it still was there and, like everybody else, we knew that it would probably stay there for the duration of our visit. Before my time there had been some panic when the quakes became daily, but I'd blame that on the old-style construction that fell hard and in jagged hunks. Eventually people got used to it and—as you'd expect in southern California—even proud of it. Natives could cite you reams of statistics to prove that you stand more chance of being struck by lightning or a meteorite than you do of getting killed in one of their quakes.

We got a speedy three-man limousine to whisk us to the local branch of Fowler Schocken Associates. My faint uneasiness about Market Research extended to the possibility that Ham Harris might have a tipster at the airport to give him time to tidy up for a full-dress inspection. And that kind of thing is worse than useless.

The receptionist gave me my first setback. She didn't recognize my face and she didn't recognize my name when I gave it to her. She said lazily: "I'll see if Mr. Harris is busy, Mr. Connelly."

"Mr. Courtenay, young lady. And I'm Mr. Harris's boss." Kathy and I walked in on a scene of idleness and slackness that curled my hair.

Harris, with his coat off, was playing cards with two young employees. Two more were gaping, glassy-eyed, before a hypnoteleset, obviously in trance state. Another man was lackadaisically punching a calculator, one-finger system.

"*Harris!*" I thundered.

Everybody except the two men in trance swiveled my way, open-mouthed. I walked to the hypnoteleset and snapped it off. They came to, groggily.

"Mum-mum-mum-mister Courtenay," Harris stuttered. "We didn't expect—"

"Obviously. The rest of you, carry on. Harris, let's go into your office." Unobtrusively, Kathy followed us.

"Harris," I said, "good work excuses a lot. We've been getting damn good work out of you on this project. I'm disturbed, gravely disturbed, by the atmosphere here. But that can be corrected—"

His phone rang, and I picked it up.

A voice said excitedly: "Ham? He's here. Make it snappy; he took a limousine."

"Thanks," I said and hung up. "Your tipster at the airport," I told Harris. He went white. "Show me your tally sheets," I said. "Your interview forms. Your punchcard codes. Your masters. Your sigma-progress charts. The works. Everything, in short, that you wouldn't expect me to ask to see. *Get them out.*"

He stood there a long, long time and finally said: "There aren't any."

"What have you got to show me?"

"Finalizations," he muttered. "Composites."

"Fakes, you mean? Fiction, like the stuff you've been feeding us over the wire?"

He nodded. His face was sick.

"How could you do it, Harris?" I demanded. "*How—could —you—do it?*"

He poured out a confused torrent of words. He hadn't meant to. It was his first independent job. Maybe he was just no damn good. He'd tried to keep the lower personnel up to snuff while he was dogging it himself but it couldn't be done; they sensed it and took liberties and you didn't dare check them up. His self-pitying note changed; he became weakly belligerent. What difference did it make anyway? It was just preliminary paperwork. One man's guess was as good as another's. And anyway the whole project might go down the drain. What if he had been taking it easy; he bet there were plenty of other people who took it easy and everything came out all right anyway.

"No," I said. "You're wrong and you ought to know you're wrong. Advertising's an art, but it depends on the sciences of sampling, area-testing, and customer research. You've knocked the props from under our program. We'll salvage what we can and start again."

He took a feeble stand: "You're wasting your time if you do that, Mr. Courtenay. I've been working closely with Mr. Runstead for a long time. I know what he thinks, and he's as big a shot as you are. He thinks this paperwork is just a lot of expensive nonsense."

I knew Matt Runstead better than that. I knew he was sound and so did everybody else. "What," I asked sharply, "have you got to back that statement up with? Letters? Memos? Taped calls?"

"I must have something like that," he said, and dived into his desk. He flipped through letters and memos, and played snatches of tape for minutes while the look of fear and frustration on his face deepened. At last he said in bewilderment: "I can't seem to find anything—but I'm *sure*—"

Sure he was sure. The highest form of our art is to convince the customer without letting him know he's being convinced. This weak sister had been indoctrinated by Runstead with the unrealistic approach and then sent in on my project, to do a good job of bitching it up.

"You're fired, Harris," I said. "Get out and don't come back. And I wouldn't advise you to try for a job in the advertising profession after this."

I went out into the office and announced: "You're through. All of you. Collect your personal stuff and leave the office. You'll get your checks by mail."

They gaped. Beside me, Kathy murmured: "Mitch, is that really necessary?"

"You're damned right it's necessary. Did one of them tip off the home office on what was going on? No; they just relaxed and drifted. I said it was an infection, didn't I? This is it." Ham Harris drifted past us toward the door, hurt bewilderment on his face. He had been *so* sure Runstead would back him up. He had his crammed briefcase in one hand and his raincoat in the other. He didn't look at me.

I went into his vacated office and picked up the direct wire to New York. "Hester? This is Mr. Courtenay. I've just fired the entire San Diego branch. Notify Personnel and have them do whatever's necessary about their pay. And get me Mr. Runstead on the line."

I drummed my fingers impatiently for a long minute, and then Hester said: "Mr. Courtenay, I'm sorry to keep you waiting. Mr. Runstead's secretary says he's left for Little America on one of those tours. She says he cleaned up the A.I.G. thing and felt like a rest."

"Felt like a rest. Good God almighty. Hester, get me a New York to Little America reservation. I'm shooting right back on the next jet. I want to just barely touch ground before I zip off to the Pole. Got it?"

"Yes, Mr. Courtenay."

I hung up and found that Kathy was staring at me. "You know, Mitch," she said, "I've been uncharitable to you in my time. Kicking about your bad temper. I can see where you got it if this has been a typical operation."

"It's not typical," I said. "It's the worst case of flagrant obstructionism I've ever seen. But there's a lot of it. Everybody trying to make everybody else look bad. Darling, I've got to get to the field now and bull my way onto the next Eastbound. Do you want to come too?"

She hesitated. "You won't mind if I stay and do a little tourist stuff by myself?"

"No, of course not. You have a good time and when you get back to New York I'll be there."

We kissed, and I raced out. The office was clear by then and I told the building manager to lock it until further notice when Kathy left.

I looked up from the street and she waved at me from the strange, flimsy building.

6

I SWUNG OFF the ramp at New York, and Hester was right there. "Good girl," I told her. "When's the Pole rocket shoot off?"

"Twelve minutes, from Strip Six, Mr. Courtenay. Here are your ticket and the reservation. And some lunch in case—"

"Fine. I did miss a meal." We headed for Strip Six, with me chewing a regenerated cheese sandwich as I walked. "What's up at the office?" I asked indistinctly.

"Big excitement about you firing the San Diego people.

Personnel sent up a complaint to Mr. Schocken and he upheld you—approximately Force Four."

That wasn't too good. Force Twelve—hurricane—would have been a blast from his office on the order of: "How dare you housekeepers question the decision of a Board man working on his own project? Never let me catch you—" and so on. Force Four—rising gale, small craft make for harbor—was something like: "Gentlemen, I'm sure Mr. Courtenay had perfectly good reasons for doing what he did. Often the Big Picture is lost to the purely routine workers in our organization—"

I asked Hester: "Is Runstead's secretary just a hired hand or one of his—" I was going to say "stooges" but smoothly reversed my field "—one of his confidants?"

"She's pretty close to him," Hester said cautiously.

"What was her reaction to the San Diego business?"

"Somebody told me she laughed her head off, Mr. Courtenay."

I didn't push it any harder. Finding out where I stood with respect to the big guns was legitimate. Asking about the help was asking her to rat on them. Not that there weren't girls who did. "I expect to be right back," I told her. "All I want to do is straighten something out with Runstead."

"Your wife won't be along?" she asked.

"No. She's a doctor. I'm going to tear Runstead into five or six pieces; if Dr. Nevin were along she might try to put them back together again."

Hester laughed politely and said: "Have a pleasant trip, Mr. Courtenay." We were at the ramp on Strip Six.

It wasn't a pleasant trip; it was a miserable trip on a miserable, undersized tourist rocket. We flew low, and there were prism windows at all seats, which never fail to make me airsick. You turn your head and look out and you're looking straight *down*. Worse, all the ads were Taunton Associates jobs. You look out the window and just as you convince your stomach that everything's all right and yourself that it's interesting country below, wham: a sleazy, oversexed Taunton ad for some crummy product opaques the window and one of their nagging, stupid jingles drills into your ear.

Over the Amazon valley we were running into some very interesting stuff, and I was inspecting Electric Three, which happens to be the world's biggest power dam, when, wham:

BolsterBra, BolsterBra,
Bolsters all the way;
Don't you crumple, don't you slumple;
Keep them up to stay!

The accompanying before-and-after live pix were in the worst possible taste, and I found myself thanking God again that I worked for Fowler Schocken Associates.

It was the same off Tierra del Fuego. We went off the great circle course for a look at the whale fisheries, vast sea areas enclosed by booms that let the plankton in and didn't let the whales out. I was watching with fascination as a cow whale gave suck to her calf—it looked something like an aerial refueling operation—when the window opaqued again for another dose of Taunton shock treatment:

Sister, do you smell like this to your mister?

The olfactory went on, and it was the very last straw. I had to use my carton while the ad chirped:

No wonder he's hard to get! Use Swett!

and one of those heavenly-harmony trios caroled in waltz time:

Perspire, perspire, perspire,
But don't—kill off his desire—

and then a gruff, prose, medical pitch:

DON'T TRY TO STOP PERSPIRATION.
IT'S SUICIDE. DOCTORS ADVISE
A DEODORANT AND NOT AN ASTRINGENT

and then back to the first line and the olfactory. This time it made no difference; I had nothing more to give.

Taunton's was great on the gruff medical pitch; you'd think they invented it.

My seatmate, a nondescript customer in Universal apparel, watched with a little amusement as I retched. "Too much for you, friend?" he asked, showing the maddening superiority people who suffer from motion-sickness know too well.

"Uh," I said.

"Some of those ads are enough to make anybody sick," he said, greatly encouraged by my brilliant riposte.

Well, I couldn't let that get by. "Exactly what do you mean by that remark?" I asked evenly.

It frightened him. "I only meant that it smelled a little strong," he said hastily. "Just that particular ad. I didn't mean ads in general. There's nothing wrong with *me*, my friend!"

"Good for you," I said, and turned away.

He was still worried, and told me: "I'm perfectly sound, friend. I come from a good family, I went to a good school. I'm in the production end myself—die-maker in Philly—but I know the stuff's got to be sold. Channels of distribution. Building markets. Vertical integration. See? I'm perfectly sound!"

"Okay," I grunted. "Then watch your mouth."

He shriveled into his half of the seat. I hadn't enjoyed squelching him, but it was a matter of principle. He should have known better.

We were held up over Little America while a couple of other tourist craft touched down. One of them was Indian and I mellowed at the sight. That ship, from nose to tail, was Indiastry-built. The crewmen were Indiastry-trained and Indiastry-employed. The passengers, waking and sleeping, paid tribute minute by minute to Indiastry. And Indiastry paid tribute to Fowler Schocken Associates.

A tow truck hauled us into the great double-walled plastic doughnut that is Little America. There was only one check point. Little America is an invisible export—a dollar trap for the tourists of the world, with no military aspects. (There are Polar military bases, but they are small, scattered, and far under the ice.) A small thorium reactor heats and powers the place. Even if some nation desperate for fissionable material were to try and get it, they wouldn't have anything of military value. Windmills eke out the thorium reactor, and there's some "heat pump" arrangement that I don't understand which ekes out the windmills.

At the check point I asked about Runstead. The officer looked him up and said: "He's on the two-day tour out of New York.

Thomas Cook and Son. His quarters are III–C–2205." He pulled out a map of the place and showed me that this meant third ring in, third floor up, fifth sector, twenty-second room. "You can't miss it. I can accommodate you with a nearby room, Mr. Courtenay—"

"Thanks. Later." I shoved off and elbowed my way through crowds chattering in a dozen languages to III–C–2205 and rang the bell. No answer.

A pleasant young man said to me: "I'm Mr. Cameron, the tour director. Can I help you?"

"Where's Mr. Runstead? I want to see him on business."

"Dear me. We try to get away from all that—I'll look in my register if you'll just wait a moment."

He took me to his office-bedroom-bath up the sector a way and pawed through a register. "The Starrzelius Glacier climb," he said. "Dear me. He went alone. Left at 0700, checked out in electric suit with R.D.F. and rations. He should be back in five hours or so. Have you arranged for quarters yet, Mr.—?"

"Not yet. I want to go after Runstead. It's urgent." And it was. I was going to burst a blood vessel if I didn't get my hands on him.

The slightly fluttery tour director spent about five minutes convincing me that the best thing for me to do was sign on for his tour and he'd arrange *everything*. Otherwise I'd be shifted from pillar to post buying and renting necessary equipment from concessionaires and then as like as not be turned back at checkout and not be able to find the concessionaires again while my vacation was ticking away. I signed on and he beamed. He gave me a room in the sector—plenty of luxury. It would have been twelve by eighteen if it hadn't been slightly wedge-shaped.

In five minutes he was dealing out equipment to me. "Power pack—strap it on *so*. That's the only thing that can go wrong; if you have a power failure take a sleepy pill and don't worry. You'll freeze, but we'll pick you up before there's tissue damage. Boots. Plug them in *so*. Gloves. Plug them in. Coveralls. Hood. Snowglasses. Radio direction finder. Just tell the checkout guard 'Starrzelius Glacier' and he'll set it. Two simple switches plainly labeled 'Out' and 'In.' Outward bound it goes 'beep-*beep*'—ascending. Inward bound it goes '*beep*-beep'—descending. Just remember, going *up* the glacier, the tone goes *up*. Going *down* the glacier, the tone goes *down*. Distress signal—a big red handle. You just pull and immediately you start broadcasting. The planes will be out in fifteen minutes. You have to pay expenses for the search and rescue, so I *wouldn't* yank the handle just for a ride back. It's always possible to rest, have a sip of Coffiest, and keep on going. Route-marked map. Snowshoes. Gyrocompass. And rations. Mr. Courtenay, you are equipped. I'll lead you to checkout."

The outfit wasn't as bad as it sounded. I've been more heavily bundled up against the lakeside winds in a Chicago winter. The lumpy items, like the power pack, the R.D.F., and the rations, were well distributed. The snowshoes folded into a pair of staffs with steel points for ice climbing, and went into a quiver on my back.

Checkout was very thorough. They started with my heart and worked through my equipment, with particular emphasis on the power pack. I passed, and they set the R.D.F. for Starrzelius Glacier, with many more warnings not to overdo it.

It wasn't cold, not inside the suit. For a moment only I opened the face flap. *Wham!* I closed it again. Forty below, they had told me—a foolish-sounding figure until my nose felt it for a split second. I didn't need the snow shoes at the base of the towering plastic doughnut; it was crust ice that my spike-soled shoes bit into. I oriented the map with the little gyrocompass and trudged off into the vast whiteness along the proper bearing. From time to time I pressed my left sleeve, squeezing the molded R.D.F. switch, and heard inside my hood a cheerful, reassuring "Beep-*beep*. Beep-*beep*. Beep-*beep*."

There were some score people frolicking in one party I passed and waved cheerily at. They seemed to be Chinese or Indians. What an adventure it must be for them! But, like indifferent swimmers hugging a raft, they did their frolicking almost under the shadow of Little America. Farther out there were some people playing a game I didn't know. They had posts with bottomless baskets set up at either end of a marked-off rectangular field, and the object was to toss a large silicone ball through the baskets. Still farther out there was a large skiing class with instructors in red suits.

I looked back after trudging for what seemed only a few

minutes and couldn't see the red suits any more. I couldn't see details of Little America—just a gray-white shadow. "Beep-*beep*," my R.D.F. said and I kept going. Runstead was going to hear from me. Soon.

The aloneness was eerie but not—not unpleasant. Little America was no longer visible behind me, not even as a gray-white blur. And I didn't care. Was this how Jack O'Shea felt? Was this why he fumbled for words to describe Venus and was never satisfied with the words he found?

My feet plunged into a drift, and I unshipped and opened the snowshoes. They snapped on, and after a little stumbling experiment, I fell into an easy, sliding shuffle that was a remarkably pleasant way of covering ground. It wasn't floating. But neither was it the solid jar of a shoe sole against a paved surface—all the walking I had known for thirty-odd years.

I marched the compass course by picking landmarks and going to them: an oddly-recurved ice hummock, a blue shadow on a swale of snow. The R.D.F. continued to confirm me. I was blown up with pride at my mastery of the wild, and after two hours I was wildly hungry all at once.

What I had to do was squat and open a silicone-tissue bell into which I fitted. Exposing my nose cautiously from time to time I judged the air warm enough in five minutes. I ravenously gulped self-heated stew and tea and tried to smoke a cigarette. On the second puff the little tent was thoroughly smoked and I was blinded with tears. Regretfully I put it out against my shoe, closed my face mask, stowed the tent, and stretched happily.

After another bearing I started off again. Hell, I told myself. This Runstead thing is just a difference of temperament. He can't see the wide-open spaces and you can. There's no malice involved. He just thinks it's a crackpot idea because he doesn't realize that there are people who go for it. All you've got to do is *explain* it—

That argument, born of well-being, crumbled at one touch of reason. Runstead was out on the glacier too. He most certainly could see the wide-open spaces if, of all the places on earth he could be, he chose the Starrzelius Glacier. Well, a showdown would shortly be forthcoming. "Beep-*beep*."

I sighted through the compass and picked a black object

that was dead on my course. I couldn't quite make it out, but it was visible and it wasn't moving. I broke into a shuffling run that made me pant, and against my will I slowed down. It was a man.

When I was twenty yards away, the man looked impatiently at his watch, and I broke into the clumsy run again.

"Matt!" I said. "Matt Runstead!"

"That's right, Mitch," he said, as nasty as ever. "You're sharp today." I looked at him very slowly and very carefully, phrasing my opening remarks. He had folded skis thrust into the snow beside him.

"What's—what's—" I stammered.

"I have time to spare," he said, "but you've wasted enough of it. Good-by, Mitch." While I stood there dumbly he picked up his folded skis, swung them into the air, and poleaxed me. I fell backwards with pain, bewilderment, and shamed rage bursting my head. I felt him fumbling at my chest and then I didn't feel anything for a while.

I woke thinking I had kicked the covers off and that it was cold for early autumn. Then the ice-blue Antarctic sky knifed into my eyes, and I felt the crumbly snow beneath me. It had happened, then. My head ached horribly and I was cold. Too cold. I felt and found that the power pack was missing. No heat to the suit, gloves, and boots. No power to the R.D.F. coming or going. No use to pull the emergency signal.

I tottered to my feet and felt the cold grip me like a vise. There were footprints punched into the snow leading away —where? There was the trail of my snowshoes. Stiffly I took a step back along that trail, and then another, and then another.

The rations. I could thrust them into the suit, break the heat seals, and let them fill the suit with temporary warmth. Plodding step by step I debated: stop and rest while you drink the ration's heat or keep moving? You need a rest, I told myself. Something impossible happened, your head is aching. You'll feel better if you sit for a moment, open a ration or two, and then go on.

I didn't sit. I knew what that would mean. Painful step after painful step I fumbled a Coffiest can from its pocket with fingers that would barely obey me, and fumbled it into my suit. My thumb didn't seem strong enough to pop the seal and I told myself: sit down for a moment and gather your strength. You don't have to lie down, pleasant as that would be . . . my thumb drove through the seal and the tingling heat was painful.

It became a blur. I opened more cans, and then I couldn't work them out of their pockets any more. I sat down at least once and got up again. And then I sat down, feeling guilty and ashamed of the indulgence, telling myself I'd get up in one more second for Kathy, two more seconds for Kathy, three more seconds for Kathy.

But I didn't.

7

I FELL ASLEEP on a mountain of ice; I woke up in a throbbing, strumming inferno, complete with red fire and brutish-looking attendant devils. It was exactly what I would have consigned a Taunton copysmith to. I was confused to find myself there.

The confusion did not last long. One of the attendant devils shook my shoulder roughly and said: "Gimme a hand, sleepy. I gotta stow my hammock." My head cleared and it was very plain that he was simply a lower-class consumer—perhaps a hospital attendant?

"Where's this?" I asked him. "Are we back in Little America?"

"Jeez, you talk funny," he commented. "Gimme a hand, will ya?"

"Certainly not!" I told him. "I'm a star-class copysmith."

He looked at me pityingly, said "Punchy," and went away into the strumming, red-lit darkness.

I stood up, swaying on my feet, and grabbed an elbow hurrying past from darkness to darkness. "Excuse me," I said. "Where is this place? Is it a hospital?"

The man was another consumer, worse-tempered than the first. "Leggo my yarm!" he snarled. I did. "Ya want on sick call, ya wait until we land," he said.

"Land?"

"Yah, land. Listen, Punchy, don't ya know what ya signed up for?"

"Signed up? No; I don't. But you're being too familiar. I'm a star-class copysmith—"

His face changed. "Ahah," he said wisely. "I can fix ya up. Justa minnit, Punchy. I'll be right back wit' the stuff."

He was, too. "The stuff" was a little green capsule. "Only five hunnerd," he wheedled. "Maybe the last one on board. Ya wanta touch down wit' the shakes? Nah! This'll straighten ya out fer landing—"

"Landing *where?*" I yelled. "What's all this about? I don't know, and I don't want your dope. Just tell me where I am and what I'm supposed to have signed up for and I'll take it from there!"

He looked at me closely and said: "Ya got it bad. A hit in the head, maybe? Well, Punchy, yer in the Number Six Hold of the Labor Freighter *Thomas R. Malthus.* Wind and weather, immaterial. Course, 273 degrees. Speed 300, destination Costa Rica, cargo slobs like you and me for the Chlorella plantations." It was the rigmarole of a relieved watch officer, or a savage parody of it.

"You're—" I hesitated.

"Downgraded," he finished bitterly, and stared at the green capsule in the palm of his hand. Abruptly he gulped it and went on: "I'm gonna hit the comeback trail, though." A sparkle crept into his eye. "I'm gonna introduce new and efficient methods in the plantations. I'll be a foreman in a week. I'll be works manager in a month. I'll be a director in a year. And then I'm gonna buy the Cunard Line and plate all their rockets with solid gold. Nothing but first-class accommodations. Nothing but the best for my passengers. I always kept her smooth on the Atlantic run. I'll build you a gold-plated imperial suite aboard my flag ship, Punchy. The best is none too good for my friend Punchy. If you don't like gold I'll get platinum. If you don't like—"

I inched away and he didn't notice. He kept babbling his hophead litany. It made me glad I'd never taken to the stuff. I came to a bulkhead and sat down hopelessly, leaning against it. Somebody sat down beside me and said "Hello there" in a cozy voice.

"Hello," I said. "Say, are we really headed for Costa? How can I get to see a ship's officer? This is all a mistake."

"Oh," said the man, "why worry about it? Live and let live. Eat, drink, and be merry is my motto."

"Take your God-damned hands off me!" I told him.

He became shrill and abusive, and I got up and walked on, stumbling over legs and torsos.

It occurred to me that I'd never really known any consumers except during the brief periods when they were serving me. It occurred to me that I'd casually accepted their homosexual component and exploited it without ever realizing what it reduced to in reality. I wanted very badly to get out of Number Six Hold. I wanted to get back to New York, find out what kind of stunt Runstead had pulled and why, get back to Kathy, and my friendship with Jack O'Shea, and my big job at Fowler Schocken. I had things to do.

One of the red lights said Crash Emergency Exit. I thought of the hundreds of people jammed in the hold trying to crowd out through the door, and shuddered.

"Excuse me, my friend," somebody said hoarsely to me. "You'd better move." He began to throw up, and apparently containers weren't issued aboard labor freighters. I rolled the emergency door open and slid through.

"Well?" growled a huge Detective Agency guard.

"I want to see a ship's officer," I said. "I'm here by some mistake. My name is Mitchell Courtenay. I'm a copysmith with the Fowler Schocken Associates."

"The number," he snapped.

"16–156–187," I told him, and I admit that there was a little pride in my voice. You can lose money and health and friendship, but they can't take a low Social Security number away from you . . .

He was rolling up my sleeve, not roughly. The next moment I went spinning against the bulkhead with my face burning from a ham-handed slap. "Get back between decks, Punchy!" the guard roared. "Yer not on an excursion and I don't like yer funny talk!"

I stared incredulously at the pit of my elbow. The tattoo read: "1304–9974–1416–156–187723." My own number was buried in it, but the inks matched perfectly. The style of lettering was very slightly off—not enough for anybody to notice but me.

"Waddaya waitin' for?" the guard said. "You seen yer number before, ain't ya?"

"No," I said evenly, but my legs were quivering. I was scared—terribly scared. "I never saw this number before. It's been tattooed around my real number. I'm Courtenay, I tell you. I can prove it. I'll pay you—" I fumbled in my pockets and found no money. I abruptly realized that I was wearing a strange and shabby suit of Universal apparel, stained with food and worse.

"So pay," the guard said impassively.

"I'll pay you later," I told him. "Just get me to somebody responsible—"

A natty young flight lieutenant in Panagra uniform popped into the narrow corridor. "What's going on here?" he demanded of the guard. "The hatchway light's still on. Can't you keep order between decks? Your agency gets a fitness report from us, you know." He ignored me completely.

"I'm sorry, Mr. Kobler," the guard said, saluting and coming to a brace. "This man seems to be on the stuff. He came out and gave me an argument that he's a star-class copysmith on board by mistake—"

"Look at my number!" I yelled at the lieutenant.

His face wrinkled as I thrust my bared elbow under his nose. The guard grabbed me and snarled: "Don't you bother the—"

"Just a minute," said the Panagra officer. "I'll handle this. That's a high number, fellow. What do you expect to prove by showing me that?"

"It's been added to, fore and aft. My real number is 16–156–187. See? Before and after that there's a different lettering style! It's tampering!"

Holding his breath, the lieutenant looked very closely. He said: "Umm. Just barely possible . . . come with me." The guard hastened to open a corridor door for him and me. He looked scared.

The lieutenant took me through a roaring confusion of engine rooms to the purser's hatbox-sized office. The purser was a sharp-faced gnome who wore his Panagra uniform as though it were a sack. "Show him your number," the lieutenant directed me, and I did. To the purser he said: "What's the story on this man?"

The purser slipped a reel into the reader and cranked it. "1304–9974–1416–156–187723," he read at last. "Groby, William George; 26; bachelor; broken home (father's desertion) child; third of five sibs; H-H balance, male 1; health, 2.9; occupational class 2 for seven years; 1.5 for three months; education 9; signed labor contract B." He looked up at the flight officer. "A very dull profile, lieutenant. Is there any special reason why I should be interested in this man?"

The lieutenant said: "He claims he's a copysmith in here by mistake. He says somebody altered his number. And he speaks a little above his class."

"Tut," said the purser. "Don't let that worry you. A broken-home child, especially a middle sib from the lower levels, reads and views incessantly trying to better himself. But you'll notice—"

"That's enough of that," I snarled at the little man, quite fed up. "I'm Mitchell Courtenay. I can buy you and sell you without straining my petty cash account. I'm in charge of the Fowler Schocken Associates Venus Section. I want you to get New York on the line immediately and we'll wind up this farce. Now jump, damn you!"

The flight lieutenant looked alarmed and reached for the phone, but the purser smiled and moved it away from his hand. "Mitchell Courtenay, are you?" he asked kindly. He reached for another reel and put it in the viewer. "Here we are," he said, after a little cranking. The lieutenant and I looked.

It was the front page of the *New York Times.* The first column contained the obituary of Mitchell Courtenay, head of Fowler Schocken Associates Venus Section. I had been found frozen to death on Starrzelius Glacier near Little America. I had been tampering with my power pack, and it had failed. I read on long after the lieutenant had lost interest. Matt Runstead was taking over Venus Section. I was a loss to my profession. My wife, Dr. Nevin, had refused to be interviewed. Fowler Schocken was quoted in a ripe eulogy of me. I was a personal friend of Venus Pioneer Jack O'Shea, who had expressed shock and grief at the news.

The purser said: "I picked that up in Capetown. Lieutenant, get this silly son of a bitch back between decks, will you please?"

The guard had arrived. He slapped and kicked me all the way back to Number Six Hold.

I caromed off somebody as the guard shoved me through the door into the red darkness. After the relatively clear air of the outside, the stink was horrible.

"What did you do?" the human cushion asked amiably, picking himself up.

"I tried to tell them who I am . . ." That wasn't going to get me anywhere. "What happens next?" I asked.

"We land. We get quarters. We get to work. What contract are you on?"

"Labor contract B, they said."

He whistled. "I guess they really had you, huh?"

"What do you mean? What's it all about?"

"Oh—you were blind, were you? Too bad. B contract's five years. For refugees, morons, and anybody else they can swindle into signing up. There's a conduct clause. I got offered the B, but I told them if that was the best they could do I'd just go out and give myself up to the Brink's Express. I talked them into an F contract—they must have needed help real bad. It's one year and I can buy outside the company stores and things like that."

I held my head to keep it from exploding. "It can't be such a bad place to work," I said. "Country life—farming—fresh air and sunshine."

"Um," said the man in an embarrassed way. "It's better than chemicals, I guess. Maybe not so good as mining. You'll find out soon enough."

He moved away, and I fell into a light doze when I should have been making plans.

There wasn't any landing-ready signal. We just hit, and hit hard. A discharge port opened, letting in blinding tropical sunlight. It was agony after the murky hold. What swept in with it was not country air but a gush of disinfectant aerosol. I untangled myself from a knot of cursing laborers and flowed with the stream toward the port.

"Hold it, stupid!" said a hard-faced man wearing a plant-protection badge. He threw a number plaque on a cord around my neck. Everybody got one and lined up at a table outside the ship. It was in the shadow of the Chlorella plantation, a towering eighty-story structure like office "In-and-Out" baskets stacked up to the sky. There were mirrored louvers at each tier. Surrounding the big building were acres of eye-stabbing glare. I realized that this was more mirrored louvers to catch the sun, bounce it off more mirrors inside the tiers and onto the photosynthesis tanks. It was a spectacular, though not uncommon, sight from the air. On the ground it was plain hell. I should have been planning, planning. But the channels of my mind were choked by: "From the sun-drenched plantations of Costa Rica, tended by the deft hands of independent farmers with pride in their work, comes the juicyripe goodness of Chlorella Proteins . . ." Yes; I had written those words.

"Keep moving!" a plant-protection man bawled. "Keep it moving, you God-damned scum-skimmers! Keep it moving!" I shaded my eyes and shuffled ahead as the line moved past the table. A dark-glassed man at the table was asking me: "Name?"

"Mitchell Court—"

"That's the one I told you about," said the purser's voice.

"Okay; thanks." To me: "Groby, we've had men try to bug out of a B Contract before this, you know. They're always sorry they tried. Do you know what the annual budget of Costa Rica is, by any chance?"

"No," I mumbled.

"It's about a hundred and eighty-three billion dollars. And do you happen to know what the annual taxes of Chlorella Corporation are?"

"No. Damn it, man—"

He broke in: "About a hundred and eighty billion dollars. From that, a bright fellow like you will conclude that the government—*and courts*—of Costa Rica do just about what Chlorella wants done. If we want to make an example of a contract-breaker they'll do it for us. Bet your life. Now, what's your name, Groby?"

"Groby," I said hoarsely.

"First name? Educational level? H-H balance?"

"I don't remember. But if you'll give them to me on a piece of paper I'll memorize them."

I heard the purser laugh and say: "He'll do."

"All right, Groby," the man in dark glasses said genially. "No harm done. Here's your profile and assignment. We'll make a skimmer out of you yet. Move on."

I moved on. A plant protection man grabbed my assignment and bawled at me: "Skimmers that way."

"That way" was under the bottom tier of the building, into light even more blinding, down a corridor between evil-smelling, shallow tanks, and at last through a door into the central pylon of the structure. There was a well-lit room which seemed twilit after the triply-reflected tropical sun outside.

"Skimmer?" said a man. I blinked and nodded at him. "I'm Mullane—shift assignment. I got a question to ask you, Groby." He peered at my profile card. "We need a skimmer on the sixty-seventh tier and we need a skimmer on the forty-first tier. Your bunk's going to be on the forty-third tier of the pylon. Frankly, which would you rather work on? I ought to mention that we don't have elevators for skimmers and the other Class 2 people."

"The forty-first-tier job," I told him, trying to make out his face.

"That's very sensible," he told me. "Very, very sensible." And then he just stood there, with seconds ticking away. At last he added: "I like to see a sensible man act sensible." There was another long pause.

"I haven't got any money on me," I told him.

"That's all right," he said. "I'll lend you some. Just sign this note and we can settle up on payday without any fuss. It's just a simple assignment of five dollars."

I read the note and signed it. I had to look at my profile card again; I had forgotten my first name. Mullane briskly scrawled "41" and his initials on my assignment, and hurried off without lending me five dollars. I didn't chase him.

"I'm Mrs. Horrocks, the housing officer," a woman said sweetly to me. "Welcome to the Chlorella family, Mr. Groby. I hope you'll spend many happy years with us. And now to work. Mr. Mullane told you this draft of crumbs—that is, the present group of contractees—will be housed on the forty-third tier, I think. It's my job to see that you're located with a congenial group of fellow-employees."

Her face reminded me faintly of a tarantula as she went on: "We have one vacant bunk in Dorm Seven. Lots of *nice, young* men in Dorm Seven. Perhaps you'd like it there. It means so much to be among one's *own kind* of people."

I got what she was driving at and told her I didn't want to be in Dorm Seven.

She went on brightly: "Then there's Dorm Twelve. It's a rather rough crowd, I'm afraid, but beggars can't be choosers, can they? They'd like to get a nice young man like you in Dorm Twelve. My, yes! But you could carry a knife or something. Shall I put you down for Dorm Twelve, Mr. Groby?"

"*No*," I said. "What else have you got? And by the way, I wonder if you could lend me five dollars until payday?"

"I'll put you down for Dorm Ten," she said, scribbling. "And of course I'll lend you some money. Ten dollars? Just sign and thumbprint this assignment, Mr. Groby. Thank you." She hurried off in search of the next sucker.

A red-faced fat man gripped my hand and said hoarsely: "Brother, I want to welcome you to the ranks of the United Slime-Mold Protein Workers of Panamerica, Unaffiliated, Chlorella Costa Rica Local. This pamphlet will explain how the U.S.M.P.W.P. protecks workers in the field from the innumable petty rackets and abuses that useta plague the innustry. Yer inishiashun and dues are checked off automatically but this valable pamphlet is an extra."

I asked him: "Brother, what's the worst that can happen to me if I don't buy it?"

"It's a long drop," he said simply.

He lent me five dollars to buy the pamphlet.

I didn't have to climb to Dorm Ten on the forty-third tier. There were no elevators for Class 2 people, but there was an endless cargo net we could grab hold of. It took a little daring to jump on and off, and clearance was negligible. If your rump stuck out you were likely to lose it.

The dorm was jammed with about sixty bunks, three high. Since production went on only during the daylight hours, the hotbed system wasn't in use. My bunk was all mine, twenty-four hours a day. Big deal.

A sour-faced old man was sweeping the central aisle lackadaisically when I came in. "You a new crumb?" he asked, and looked at my ticket. "There's your bunk. I'm Pine. Room orderly. You know how to skim?"

"No," I said. "Look, Mr. Pine, how do I make a phone call out of here?"

"Dayroom," he said, jerking his thumb. I went to the dayroom adjoining. There was a phone and a biggish hypnoteleset and readers and spools and magazines. I ground my teeth as the cover of *Taunton's Weekly* sparkled at me from the rack. The phone was a pay phone, of course.

I dashed back into the dorm. "Mr. Pine," I said, "can you lend me about twenty dollars in coin? I have to make a long-distance call."

"Twenty-five for twenty?" he asked shrewdly.

"Sure. Anything you say."

He slowly scrawled out an assignment slip and I signed and printed it. Then he carefully counted out the money from his baggy pockets.

I wanted to call Kathy, but didn't dare. She might be at her apartment, she might be at the hospital. I might miss her. I dialed the fifteen digits of the Fowler Schocken Associates number after I deposited a clanging stream of coins. I waited for the switchboard to say: "Fowler Schocken Associates; good afternoon; it's *always* a good afternoon for Fowler Schocken Associates and their clients. May I help you?"

But that isn't what I heard. The phone said: "*Su número de prioridad, por favor?*"

Priority number for long-distance calls. I didn't have one. A firm had to be rated a billion and fast pay before it could get a long-distance priority number in four figures. So jammed were the world's long lines that an individual priority in any number of figures was unthinkable. Naturally all that had never worried me when I made long-distance calls from Fowler Schocken, on the Fowler Schocken priority number. A priority number was one of the little luxuries I'd have to learn to live without.

I hung up slowly. The coins were not returned.

I could write to everybody, I thought. Write to Kathy and Jack O'Shea and Fowler and Collier and Hester and Tildy. Leave no stone unturned. Dear Wife (or Boss): This is to advise you that your husband (or employee) who you know quite well is dead is not really dead but inexplicably a contract laborer for Costa Rican Chlorella and please drop everything and get him out. Signed, your loving husband (or employee), Mitchell Courtenay.

But there was the company censor to think of.

I wandered blankly back into the dorm. The rest of the Dorm Ten people were beginning to drift in.

"A crumb!" one of them yelled, sighting me.

"Court's called to order!" another one trumpeted.

I don't hold what followed against any of them. It was traditional, a break in the monotony, a chance to lord it over somebody more miserable than themselves, something they had all gone through too. I presume that in Dorm Seven it would have been a memorably nasty experience, and in Dorm Twelve I might not have lived through it. Dorm Ten was just high-spirited. I paid my "fine"—more pay vouchers—and took my lumps and recited the blasphemous oath and then I was a full-fledged member of the dorm.

I didn't troop with them to the mess hall for dinner. I just lay on my bunk and wished I were as dead as the rest of the world thought I was.

8

SCUM-SKIMMING wasn't hard to learn. You got up at dawn. You gulped a breakfast sliced not long ago from Chicken Little and washed it down with Coffiest. You put on your coveralls and took the cargo net up to your tier. In blazing noon from sunrise to sunset you walked your acres of shallow tanks crusted with algae. If you walked slowly, every thirty seconds or so you spotted a patch at maturity, bursting with yummy carbohydrates. You skimmed the patch with your skimmer and slung it down the well, where it would be baled, or processed into glucose to feed Chicken Little, who would be sliced and packed to feed people from Baffinland to Little America. Every hour you could drink from your canteen and take a salt tablet. Every two hours you could take five minutes. At sunset you turned in your coveralls and went to dinner—more slices from Chicken

Little—and then you were on your own. You could talk, you could read, you could go into trance before the dayroom hypnoteleset, you could shop, you could pick fights, you could drive yourself crazy thinking of what might have been, you could go to sleep.

Mostly you went to sleep.

I wrote a lot of letters and tried to sleep a lot. Payday came as a surprise. I didn't know two weeks had slipped by. It left me owing Chlorella Proteins only eighty-odd dollars and a few cents. Besides the various assignments I had made, there were the Employee Welfare Fund (as closely as I could figure that one out, it meant that I was paying Chlorella's taxes); union dues and installment on the initiation fee; withholding tax (this time my own taxes); hospitalization (but try and get it, the older men said) and old age insurance.

One of the things I faintheartedly consoled myself with was the thought that when—*when*, I always said firmly—I got out I'd be closer to the consumers than any ad man in the profession. Of course at Fowler Schocken we'd had our boys up from the ranks: scholarship kids. I knew now that they had been too snobbish to give me the straight facts on consumers' lives and thoughts. Or they hadn't cared to admit even to themselves what they had been like.

I think I learned that ads work more strongly on the unconscious than even we in the profession had thought. I was shocked repeatedly to hear advertising referred to as "that crap." I was at first puzzled and then gratified to see it sink in and take effect anyway. The Venus-rocket response was, of course, my greatest interest. For one week I listened when I could to enthusiasm growing among these men who would never go to Venus, who knew nobody who would ever go to Venus. I heard the limericks we had launched from Fowler Schocken Associates chuckled over:

A midget space-jock named O'Shea
Loved a girl who was built like a dray—

Or:

A socially misfit machinist
Asked his sweetheart: "Dear, what's come between us?"

Or any of the others, with their engineered-in message: that Venus environment increased male potency. Ben Winston's subsection on Folkways, I had always said, was one of the most important talent groups in the whole Schocken enterprise. They were particularly fine on riddles: "Why do they call Venus the Mourning Star?", for instance. Well, it doesn't make sense in print; but the pun is basic humor, and the basic drive of the human race is sex. And what is, essentially, more important in life than to mold and channel the deepest torrential flow of human emotion into its proper directions? (I am not apologizing for those renegades who talk fancifully about some imagined "Death-Wish" to hook their sales appeals to. I leave that sort of thing to the Tauntons of our profession; it's dirty, it's immoral, I want nothing to do with it. Besides, it leads to fewer consumers in the long run, if they'd only think the thing through.)

For there is no doubt that linking a sales message to one of the great prime motivations of the human spirit does more than sell goods; it strengthens the motivation, helps it come to the surface, provides it with focus. And thus we are assured of the steady annual increment of consumers so essential to expansion.

Chlorella, I was pleased to learn, took extremely good care of its workers' welfare in that respect. There was an adequate hormone component in the diet, and a splendid thousand-bed Recreation Room on the 50th tier. The only stipulation the company made was that children born on the plantation were automatically indentured to Chlorella if either parent was still an employee on the child's tenth birthday.

But I had no time for the Recreation Room. I was learning the ropes, studying my milieu, waiting for opportunity to come. If opportunity didn't come soon I would make opportunity; but first I had to study and learn.

Meanwhile, I kept my ears open for the results of the Venus campaign. It went beautifully—for a while. The limericks, the planted magazine stories, the gay little songs had their effect.

Then something went sour.

There was a downtrend. It took me a day to notice it, and a week to believe it could be true. The word "Venus" drifted out of the small talk. When the space rocket was mentioned it was in connection with reference points like "radiation poisoning," "taxes," "sacrifice." There was a new, dangerous kind of Folkways material—"Didja hear the one about the punchy that got caught in his space suit?"

You might not have recognized what was going on, and Fowler Schocken, scanning his daily precis of the summary of the digests of the skeletonized reports of the abstracts of the charts of progress on Venus Project, would never have the chance to question or doubt what was told him. But I knew Venus Project. And I knew what was happening.

Matt Runstead had taken over.

The aristocrat of Dorm Ten was Herrera. After ten years with Chlorella he had worked his way up—topographically it was down—to Master Slicer. He worked in the great, cool vault underground, where Chicken Little grew and was cropped by him and other artisans. He swung a sort of two-handed sword that carved off great slabs of the tissue, leaving it to the lesser packers and trimmers and their faceless helpers to weigh it, shape it, freeze it, cook it, flavor it, package it, and ship it off to the area on quota for the day.

He had more than a production job. He was a safety valve. Chicken Little grew and grew, as she had been growing for decades. Since she had started as a lump of heart tissue, she didn't know any better than to grow up against a foreign body and surround it. She didn't know any better than to grow and fill her concrete vault and keep growing, compressing her cells and rupturing them. As long as she got nutrient, she grew. Herrera saw to it that she grew round and plump, that no tissue got old and tough before it was sliced, that one side was not neglected for the other.

With this responsibility went commensurate pay, and yet Herrera had not taken a wife or an apartment in one of the upper tiers of the pylon. He made trips that were the subject of bawdy debate while he was gone—and which were never referred to without careful politeness while he was present. He kept his two-handed slicer by him at all times, and often idly sleeked its edge with a hone. He was a man I had to know. He was a man with money—he *must* have money after ten years—and I needed it.

The pattern of the B labor contract had become quite clear. You never got out of debt. Easy credit was part of the system, and so were irritants that forced you to exercise it. If I fell behind ten dollars a week I would owe one thousand one hundred dollars to Chlorella at the end of my contract, and would have to work until the debt was wiped out. And while I worked, a new debt would accumulate.

I needed Herrera's money to buy my way out of Chlorella and back to New York: Kathy, my wife; Venus Section, my job. Runstead was doing things I didn't like to Venus Section. And God alone knew what Kathy was doing, under the impression that she was a widow. I tried not to think of one particular thing: Jack O'Shea and Kathy. The little man had been getting back at womankind for their years of contempt. Until the age of twenty-five he had been a laughable sixty-pound midget, with a touch of grotesquerie in the fact that he had doggedly made himself a test pilot. At the age of twenty-six he found himself the world's number one celebrity, the first man to land a ship on Venus, an immortal barely out of his teens. He had a lot of loving to catch up on. The story was that he'd been setting records on his lecture tours. I didn't like the story. I didn't like the way he liked Kathy or the way Kathy liked him.

And so I went through another day, up at dawn, breakfast, coveralls and goggles, cargo net, skimming and slinging for blazing hour after hour, dinner and the dayroom and, if I could manage it, a chat with Herrera.

"Fine edge on that slicer, Gus. There's only two kinds of people in the world: the ones who don't take care of their tools and the smart ones."

Suspicious look from under his Aztec brows. "Pays to do things right. You're the crumb, ain't you?"

"Yeah. First time here. Think I ought to stay?"

He didn't get it. "You *gotta* stay. Contract." And he went to the magazine rack.

Tomorrow's another day.

"Hello, Gus. Tired?"

"Hi, George. Yeah, a little. Ten hours swinging the slicer. It gets you in the arms."

"I can imagine. Skimming's easy, but you don't need brains for it."

"Well, maybe some day you get upgraded. I think I'll trance."

And another:

"Hi, George. How's it going?"

"Can't complain, Gus. At least I'm getting a sun-tan."

"You sure are. Soon you be dark like me. Haw-haw! How'd you like that?"

"Porque no, amigo?"

"Hey, *tu hablas español! Cuando aprendiste la lengua?*"

"Not so fast, Gus! Just a few words here and there. I wish I knew more. Some day when I get a few bucks ahead I'm going to town and see the girls."

"Oh, they all speak English, kind of. If you get a nice steady li'l girl it would be nice to speak a li'l Spanish. She would appreciate it. But most of them know 'Gimmy-gimmy' and the li'l English poem about what you get for one buck. Haw-haw!"

And another day—an astonishing day.

I'd been paid again, and my debt had increased by eight dollars. I'd tormented myself by wondering where the money went, but I knew. I came off shift dehydrated, as they wanted me to be. I got a squirt of Popsie from the fountain by punching my combination—twenty-five cents checked off my payroll. The squirt wasn't quite enough so I had another—fifty cents. Dinner was drab as usual; I couldn't face more than a bite or two of Chicken Little. Later I was hungry and there was the canteen where I got Crunchies on easy credit. The Crunchies kicked off withdrawal symptoms that could be quelled only by another two squirts of Popsie from the fountain. And Popsie kicked off withdrawal symptoms that could only be quelled by smoking Starr cigarettes, which made you hungry for Crunchies . . . Had Fowler Schocken thought of it in these terms when he organized Starrzelius Verily, the first spherical trust? Popsie to Crunchies to Starrs to Popsie?

And you paid 6 per cent interest on the money advanced you.

It had to be soon. If I didn't get out soon I never would. I could feel my initiative, the thing that made me *me* dying, cell by cell, within me. The minute dosages of alkaloid were sapping my will, but most of all it was a hopeless, trapped feeling that things were this way, that they always would be this way, that it wasn't too bad, that you could always go into trance or get really lit on Popsie or maybe try one of the green capsules that floated around from hand to hand at varying quotations; the boys would be glad to wait for the money.

It had to be soon.

"Como 'sta, Gustavo?"

He sat down and gave me his Aztec grin. "*Como 'sta, amigo Jorge? Se fuma?*" He extended a pack of cigarettes.

They were Greentips. I said automatically: "No thanks. I smoke Starrs; they're tastier." And automatically I lit one, of course. I was becoming the kind of consumer we used to love. Think about smoking, think about Starrs, light a Starr. Light a Starr, think about Popsie, get a squirt. Get a squirt, think about Crunchies, buy a box. Buy a box, think about smoking, light a Starr. And at every step roll out the words of praise that had been dinned into you through your eyes and ears and pores.

"I smoke Starrs; they're tastier. I drink Popsie; it's zippy. I eat Crunchies; they tang your tongue. I smoke—"

Gus said to me: "You don't look so happy, Jorge."

"I don't feel so happy, amigo." This was it. "I'm in a very strange situation." Wait for him, now.

"I figured there was something wrong. An intelligent fellow like you, a fellow who's been around. Maybe you can use some help?"

Wonderful; wonderful. "You won't lose by it, Gus. You're taking a chance, but you won't lose by it. Here's the story—"

"Sst! Not here!" he shushed me. In a lower voice he went on: "It's always a risk. It's always worth it when I see a smart young fellow wise up and begin to *do* things. Some day I make a mistake, *seguro*. Then they get me, maybe they brainburn me. What the hell, I can laugh at them. I done my part. Here. I don't have to tell you to be careful where you open this." He shook my hand and I felt a wad of something adhere to my palm. Then he strolled across the dayroom to the hypnoteleset, punched his clock number for a half-hour of trance and slid under, with the rest of the viewers.

I went to the washroom and punched my combination for a ten-minute occupancy of a booth—bang went another nickel off my pay—and went in. The adhesive wad on my palm opened up into a single sheet of tissue paper which said:

A Life Is In Your Hands

This is Contact Sheet One of the World Conservationist Association, popularly known as "the Consies." It has been passed to you by a member of the W.C.A. who judged that you are (a) intelligent; (b) disturbed by the present state of the world; (c) a potentially valuable addition to our ranks. His life is now in your hands. We ask you to read on before you take any action.

Facts About the W.C.A.

The Facts: The W.C.A. is a secret organization persecuted by all the governments of the world. It believes that reckless exploitation of natural resources has created needless poverty and needless human misery. It believes that continued exploitation will mean the end of human life on Earth. It believes that this trend may be reversed if the people of the Earth can be educated to the point where they will demand planning of population, reforestation, soil-building, deurbanization, and an end to the wasteful production of gadgets and proprietary foods for which there is no natural demand. This educational program is being carried on by propaganda—like this—demonstrations of force, and sabotage of factories which produce trivia.

Falsehoods About the W.C.A.

You have probably heard that "the Consies" are murderers, psychotics, and incompetent people who kill and destroy for irrational ends or out of envy. None of this is true. W.C.A. members are humane, balanced persons, many of them successful in the eyes of the world. Stories to the contrary are zealously encouraged by people who profit from the exploitation which we hope to correct. There are irrational, unbalanced and criminal persons who do commit outrages in the name of conservation, either idealistically or as a shield for looting. The W.C.A. dissociates itself from such people and regards their activities with repugnance.

What Will You Do Next?

That is up to you. You can (a) denounce the person who passed you this contact sheet; (b) destroy this sheet and forget about it; (c) go to the person who passed you the sheet and seek further information. We ask you to think before you act.

I thought—hard. I thought the broadside was (a) the dullest, lousiest piece of copysmithing I had ever seen in my life; (b) a wildly distorted version of reality; (c) a possible escape route for me out of Chlorella and back to Kathy.

So these were the dreaded Consies! Of all the self-contradictory gibberish—but it had a certain appeal. The ad was crafted —unconsciously, I was sure—the way we'd do a pharmaceutical-house booklet for doctors only. Calm, learned, we're all men of sound judgment and deep scholarship here; we can talk frankly about bedrock issues. Does your patient suffer from hyperspasm, Doctor?

It was an appeal to reason, and they're always dangerous. You can't trust reason. We threw it out of the ad profession long ago and have never missed it.

Well; there were obviously two ways to do it. I could go to the front office and put the finger on Herrera. I'd get a little publicity maybe; they'd listen to me, maybe; they *might* believe enough of what I told them to check. I seemed to recall that denouncers of Consies were sometimes brainburned on the sensible grounds that they had been exposed to the virus and that it might work out later, after the first healthy reaction. That wasn't good. Riskier but more heroic: I could bore from within, playing along with the Consies. If they were the worldwide net they claimed to be, there was no reason why I shouldn't wind up in New York, ready and able to blow the lid off them.

Not for a moment did I have any doubts about being able to get ahead. My fingers itched for a pencil to mark up that contact sheet, sharpening the phrases, cutting out the dullness, inserting see-hear-taste-feel words with real sock. It could use it.

The door of the booth sprang open; my ten minutes were up. I hastily flushed the contact sheet down the drain and went out into the day room. Herrera was still in the trance before the set.

I waited some twenty minutes. Finally he shook himself, blinked, and looked around. He saw me, and his face was immobile granite. I smiled and nodded, and he came over. "All right, *compañero?*" he asked quietly.

"All right," I said. "Any time you say, Gus."

"It will be soon," he said. "Always after a thing like that I plug in for some trance. I cannot stand the suspense of waiting to find out. Some day I come up out of trance and find the bulls are beating hell out of me, eh?" He began to sleek the edge of his slicer with the pocket hone.

I looked at it with new understanding. "For the bull?" I asked.

His face was shocked. "No," he said. "You have the wrong idea a little, Jorge. For me. So I have no chance to rat."

His words were noble, even in such a cause. I hated the twisted minds who had done such a thing to a fine consumer like Gus. It was something like murder. He could have played his part in the world, buying and using and making work and profits for his brothers all around the globe, ever increasing his wants and needs, ever increasing everybody's work and profits in the circle of consumption, raising children to be consumers in turn. It hurt to see him perverted into a sterile zealot.

I resolved to do what I could for him when I blew off the lid. The fault did not lie with him. It was the people who had soured him on the world who should pay. Surely there must be some sort of remedial treatment for Consies like Gus who were only dupes. I would ask—no; it would be better not to ask. People would jump to conclusions. I could hear them now: "I don't say Mitch isn't sound, but it was a pretty far-fetched idea." "Yeah. Once a Consie, always a Consie." "Everybody knows that. I don't say Mitch isn't sound, mind you, but—"

The hell with Herrera. He could take his chances like everybody else. Anybody who sets out to turn the world upside down has no right to complain if he gets caught in its gears.

9

DAYS WENT by like weeks. Herrera talked little to me, until one evening in the dayroom he suddenly asked: "You ever see *Gallina*?" That was Chicken Little. I said no. "Come on down, then. I can get you in. She's a sight."

We walked through corridors and leaped for the descending cargo net. I resolutely shut my eyes. You look straight down that thing and you get the high-shy horrors. Forty, Thirty, Twenty, Ten, Zero, Minus Ten—

"Jump off, Jorge," Herrera said. "Below Minus Ten is the machinery." I jumped.

Minus Ten was gloomy and sweated water from its concrete walls. The roof was supported by immense beams. A tangle of pipes jammed the corridor where we got off. "Nutrient fluid," Herrera said.

I asked about the apparently immense weight of the ceiling. "Concrete and lead. It shields cosmic rays. Sometimes a *Gallina* goes cancer." He spat. "No good to eat for people. You got to burn it all if you don't catch it real fast and—" He swung his glittering slicer in a screaming arc to show me what he meant by "catch."

He swung open a door. "This is her nest," he said proudly. I looked and gulped.

It was a great concrete dome, concrete-floored. Chicken Little filled most of it. She was a gray-brown, rubbery hemisphere some fifteen yards in diameter. Dozens of pipes ran into her pulsating flesh. You could see that she was alive.

Herrera said to me: "All day I walk around her. I see a part growing fast, it looks good and tender, I slice." His two-handed blade screamed again. This time it shaved off an inch-thick Chicken Little steak. "Crumbs behind me hook it away and cut it up and put it on the conveyor." There were tunnel openings spotted around the circumference of the dome, with idle conveyor belts visible in them.

"Doesn't she grow at night?"

"No. They turn down the nutrient just enough, they let the waste accumulate in her just right. Each night she almost dies. Each morning she comes to life like San Lázaro. But nobody ever pray before *pobrecita Gallina*, hey?" He whacked the rubbery thing affectionately with the flat of his slicer.

"You like her," I said inanely.

"Sure, Jorge. She does tricks for me." He looked around and then marched the circuit of the nest, peering into each of the tunnel mouths. Then he took a short beam from one of them and casually braced it against the door to the nest. It fitted against a cross-bar on the door and against a seemingly-random groove in the concrete floor. It would do very well as a lock.

"I'll show you the trick," he said, with an Aztec grin. With a magician's elaborate gesture he took from his pocket a sort of whistle. It didn't have a mouthpiece. It had an air tank fed by a small hand pump. "I didn't make this," he hastened to assure me. "They call it Galton's whistle, but who this Galton is I don't know. Watch—and listen."

He began working the pump, pointing the whistle purposefully at Chicken Little. I heard no sound, but I shuddered as the rubbery protoplasm bulged in away from the pipe in a hemispherical depression.

"Don't be scared, *compañero*," he told me. "Just follow." He pumped harder and passed me a flashlight which I stupidly turned on. Herrera played the soundless blast of the whistle against Chicken Little like a hose. She reacted with a bigger and bigger cavity that finally became an archway whose floor was the concrete floor of the nest.

Herrera walked into the archway, saying: "Follow." I did, my heart pounding frightfully. He inched forward, pumping the whistle, and the archway became a dome. The entrance into Chicken Little behind us became smaller . . . smaller . . . smaller . . .

We were quite inside, in a hemispherical bubble moving slowly through a hundred-ton lump of gray-brown, rubbery flesh. "Light on the floor, *compañero*," he said, and I flashed it on the floor. The concrete was marked with lines that looked accidental, but which guided Herrera's feet. We inched forward, and I wondered vividly what would happen if the Galton whistle sprang a leak . . .

After about two thousand years of inch-by-inch progress my light flashed on a crescent of metal. Herrera piped the bubble over it, and it became a disk. Still pumping, he stamped three times on it. It flipped open like a manhole. "You first," he said, and I dived into it, not knowing or caring whether the landing would be hard or soft. It was soft, and I lay there, shuddering. A moment later Herrera landed beside me and the manhole above clapped shut. He stood up, massaging his arm. "Hard work," he said. "I pump and pump that thing and I don't hear it. Some day it's going to stop working and I won't know the difference until—" He grinned again.

"George Groby," Herrera introduced me. "This is Ronnie Bowen." He was a short, phlegmatic consumer in a front-office suit. "And this is Arturo Denzer." Denzer was very young and nervous.

The place was a well-lighted little office, all concrete, with air regenerators. There were desks and communication equipment. It was hard to believe that the only way to get in was barred by that mountain of protoplasm above. It was harder to believe that the squeak of inaudibly high-frequency sound waves could goad that insensate hulk into moving aside.

Bowen took over. "Pleased to have you with us, Groby," he said. "Herrera says you have brains. We don't go in a great deal for red tape, but I want your profile."

I gave him Groby's profile and he took it down. His mouth tightened with suspicion as I told him the low educational level. "I'll be frank," he said. "You don't talk like an uneducated man."

"You know how some kids are," I said. "I spent my time reading and viewing. It's tough being right in the middle of a family of five. You aren't old enough to be respected and you aren't young enough to be the pet. I felt kind of lost and I kept trying to better myself."

He accepted it. "Fair enough. Now, what can you do?"

"Well . . . I think I can write a better contact sheet than you use."

"Indeed. What else?"

"Well, propaganda generally. You could start stories going around and people wouldn't know they were from the Co— from us. Things to make them feel discontented and wake them up."

"That's a very interesting idea. Give me an example."

My brain was chugging nicely. "Start a rumor going around the mess hall that they've got a way of making new protein. Say it tastes exactly like roast beef and you'll be able to buy it at a dollar a pound. Say it's going to be announced in three days. Then when the three days are up and there's no announcement start a wisecrack going. Like: 'What's the difference between roast beef and Chicken Little?' Answer, 'A hundred and fifty years of progress.' Something like that catches on and it'll make them think about the old days favorably."

It was easy. It wasn't the first time I'd turned my talent to backing a product I didn't care for personally.

Bowen was taking it down on a silenced typewriter. "Good," he said. "Very ingenious, Groby. We'll try that. Why do you say 'three days'?"

I couldn't very well tell him that three days was the optimum priming period for a closed social circuit to be triggered with a catalytic cue-phrase, which was the book answer. I said instead, with embarrassment: "It just seemed about right to me."

"Well, we'll try it at that. Now, Groby, you're going to have a study period. We've got the classic conservationist texts, and you should read them. We've got special publications of interest to us which you should follow: *Statistical Abstracts, Journal of Space Flight, Biometrika, Agricultural Bulletin*, and lots more. If you run into tough going, and I expect you will, ask for help. Eventually you should pick a subject to which you're attracted and specialize in it, with an eye to research. An informed conservationist is an effective conservationist."

"Why the *Journal of Space Flight?*" I asked, with a growing excitement. Suddenly there seemed to be an answer: Runstead's sabotage, my kidnaping, the infinite delays and breakdowns in the project. Were they Consie plots? Could the Consies, in their depraved, illogical minds, have decided that space travel was antisurvival, or whatever you call it?

"Very important," said Bowen. "You need to know all you can about it."

I probed. "You mean so we can louse it up?"

"Of course not!" Bowen exploded. "Good God, Groby, think what Venus means to us—an unspoiled planet, all the wealth the race needs, all the fields and food and raw materials. Use your head, man!"

"Oh," I said. The Gordian knot remained unslashed.

I curled up with the reels of *Biometrika* and every once in a while asked for an explanation which I didn't need. *Biometrika* was one of the everyday tools of a copysmith. It told the story of population changes, IQ changes, death rate and causes of death, and all the rest of it. Almost every issue had good news in it for us—the same news that these Consies tut-tutted over. Increase of population was always good news to us. More people, more sales. Decrease of IQ was always good news to us. Less brains, more sales. But these eccentrically-oriented fanatics couldn't see it that way, and I had to pretend to go along with them.

I switched to the *Journal of Space Flight* after a while. There the news was bad—*all* bad. There was public apathy; there was sullen resistance to the shortages that the Venus rocket construction entailed; there was defeatism about planting a Venus colony at all; there was doubt that the colony could do anything if it ever did get planted.

That damned Runstead!

But the worst news of all was on the cover of the latest issue. The cutline said: "Jack O'Shea Grins As Pretty Friend Congratulates With Kiss After President Awards Medal Of Honor." The pretty friend was my wife Kathy. She never looked lovelier.

I got behind the Consie cell and pushed. In three days there was a kind of bubbling discontent about the mess hall chow. In a week the consumers were saying things like: "I wish to hell I was born a hundred years ago . . . I wish to hell this dorm wasn't so God-damned crowded . . . I wish to hell I could get out on a piece of land somewheres and work for myself."

The minute cell was elated. Apparently I had done more in a week than they had done in a year. Bowen—he was in Personnel—told me: "We need a head like yours, Groby. You're not going to sweat your life away as a scum-skimmer. One of these days the assignment boss will ask you if you know nutrient chemistry. Tell him 'Yes.' I'll give you a quickie course in everything you need to know. We'll get you out of the hot sun yet."

It happened in another week, when everybody was saying things like: "Be nice to walk in a forest some day. Can y'imagine all those trees they useta have?" and: "Goddamn salt-water soap!" when it had never before occurred to them to think of it as "salt-water soap." The assignment boss came up to me and duly said: "Groby! You know any nutrient chemistry?"

"Funny you should ask," I told him. "I've studied it quite a bit. I know the sulfur-phosphorus-carbon-oxygen-hydrogen-nitrogen ratios for chlorella, I know the optimum temperatures and stuff like that."

Obviously this little was much more than he knew. He grunted, "Yeah?" and went away, impressed.

A week later everybody was telling a dirty joke about the Starrzelius Verily trust and I was transferred to an eight-hour job inside the pylon, reading gauges and twisting valves that controlled the nutrient flow to the tanks of chlorella. It was lighter and easier work. I spent my time under Chicken Little—I could pass through her with a Galton whistle almost without cringing—rewriting the Consies' fantastically inept Contact Sheet One:

> CAN YOU QUALIFY FOR *TOP-LEVEL* PROMOTION?
>
> You and *only you* can answer these important questions:
>
> Are you an intelligent, forward-looking man or woman between the ages of 14 and 50—
>
> Do you have the drive and ambition needed to handle the really BIG JOBS tomorrow will bring—
>
> Can you be trusted—*absolutely trusted*—with the biggest, hopefulest news of our time?
>
> If you can't stand up and shout YES! to *every one* of these questions, please read no further!
>
> But if you *can*, then you and your friends or family can get in on the *ground floor* of. . . .

And so on. Bowen was staggered. "You don't think that appeal to upper-level IQs limits it too much, do you?" he asked anxiously. I didn't tell him that the only difference between that and the standard come-on for Class 12 laborers was that the Class 12s got it aurally—they couldn't read. I said I didn't think so. He nodded. "You're a natural-born copysmith, Groby," he told me solemnly. "In a Conservationist America, you'd be star class." I was properly modest. He went on, "I can't hog you; I've got to pass you on to a higher echelon. It isn't right to waste your talents in a cell. I've forwarded a report on you—" he gestured at the communicator, "and I expect you'll be requisitioned. It's only right. But I hate to see you go. However, I'm pulling the strings already. Here's the Chlorella Purchasers' Handbook . . ."

My heart bounded. I knew that Chlorella contracted for raw materials with a number of outlets in New York City.

"Thanks," I mumbled. "I want to serve wherever I best can."

"I know you do, Groby," he soothed. "Uh—say, one thing before you go. This isn't official, George, but—well, I do a little writing too. I've got some of my things here—sketches, I guess you'd call them—and I'd appreciate it a lot if you'd take them along and . . ."

I finally got out with the handbook, and only fourteen of Bowen's "sketches." They were churlish little scraps of writing, with no sell in them at all that I could see. Bowen assured me he had lots more that he and I could work on.

I hit that handbook hard.

Twisting valves left me feeling more alive at the end of a day than scum-skimming, and Bowen made sure my Consie labors were as light as possible—to free me for work on his "sketches." The result was that, for the first time, I had leisure to explore my milieu. Herrera took me into town with him once, and I discovered what he did with those unmentioned week ends. The knowledge shocked, but did not disgust me. If anything, it reminded me that the gap between executive and consumer could not be bridged by anything as abstract and unreal as "friendship."

Stepping out of the old-fashioned pneumatic tube into a misty Costa Rican drizzle, we stopped first at a third-rate restaurant for a meal. Herrera insisted on getting us each a potato, and insisted on being allowed to pay for it—"No, Jorge, you call it a celebration. You let me go on living after I gave you the contact sheet, no? So we celebrate." Herrera was brilliant through the meal, a fountain of conversation and bilingual badinage with me and the waiters. The sparkle in his eye, the rapid, compulsive flow of speech, the easy, unnecessary laughter were like nothing so much as the gaiety of a young man on a date.

A young man on a date. I remembered my first meeting with Kathy, that long afternoon at Central Park, strolling hand in hand down the dim-lit corridors, the dance hall, the eternal hour we stood outside her door. . . .

Herrera reached over and pounded me on the shoulder, and I saw that he and the waiter were laughing. I laughed too, defensively, and their laughter doubled; evidently the joke had been on me. "Never mind, Jorge," said Herrera, sobering, "we go now. You will like what I have for us to do next, I think." He paid the check, and the waiter raised an eyebrow.

"In back?"

"In back," said Herrera. "Come, Jorge."

We threaded our way between the counters, the waiter leading the way. He opened a door and hissed something rapid and Spanish to Herrera. "Oh, don't worry," Herrera told him. "We will not be long."

"In back" turned out to be—a library.

I was conscious of Herrera's eyes on me, and I don't think I showed any of what I felt. I even stayed with him for an hour or so, while he devoured a wormy copy of something called *Moby Dick* and I glanced through half a dozen ancient magazines. Some of those remembered classics went a long way toward easing my conscience—there was actually an early "Do You Make These Common Mistakes in English?" and a very fine "Not a Cough in a Carload" that would have looked well on the wall of my office, back in Schocken Tower. But I could not relax in the presence of so many books without a word of advertising in any of them. I am not a prude about solitary pleasures when they serve a useful purpose. But my tolerance has limits.

Herrera knew, I think, that I lied when I told him I had a headache. When, much later, he came stumbling into the dorm I turned my head away. We scarcely spoke after that.

A week later, after a near-riot in the mess hall—sparked by a rumor that the yeast fritters were adulterated with sawdust—I was summoned to the front office.

A veep for Personnel saw me after I had waited an hour. "Groby?"

"Yes, Mr. Milo."

"Remarkable record you've made. Quite remarkable. I see your efficiency rating is straight fours."

That was Bowen's work. He kept records. He had taken five years to worm himself into that very spot. "Thank you, Mr. Milo."

"Welcome, I'm sure. We, uh, happen to have a vacancy approaching. One of our people up North. I see his work is falling off badly."

Not his work—the ghost of his work; the shadow on paper

of his work; the shadow carefully outlined and filled in by Bowen. I began to appreciate the disproportionate power that Consies could wield.

"Do you happen to have any interest in purchasing, Groby?"

"It's odd that you should ask, Mr. Milo," I said evenly. "I've always had a feel for it. I think I'd make good in purchasing."

He looked at me skeptically; it was a pretty standard answer. He began firing questions and I respectfully regurgitated answers from the Chlorella manual. He had memorized it twenty-odd years ago, and I had memorized it only a week ago. He was no match for me. After an hour he was convinced that George Groby was the only hope of Chlorella Protein, and that I should be hurled into the breach forthwith.

That night I told the cell about it.

"It means New York," Bowen said positively. "It means New York." I couldn't keep back a great sigh. Kathy, I thought. He went on, heedlessly: "I've got to tell you some special things now. To begin with—the recognition signals."

I learned the recognition signals. There was a hand sign for short range. There was a grand hailing sign of distress for medium range. For long range there was a newspaper-ad code; quite a good one. He made me practice the signs and memorize the code cold. It took us into the small hours of the morning. When we left through Chicken Little I realized that I hadn't seen Herrera all day. I asked as we emerged what had happened.

"He broke," Bowen said simply.

I didn't say anything. It was a kind of shorthand talk among Consies. "Soandso broke." That meant: "Soandso toiled for years and years in the cause of the W.C.A. He gave up his nickels and dimes and the few pleasures they could buy him. He didn't marry and he didn't sleep with women because it would have imperiled security. He became possessed by doubts so secret that he didn't admit them to himself or us. The doubts and fears mounted. He was torn too many ways and he turned on himself and died."

"Herrera broke," I said stupidly.

"Don't brood about it," Bowen said sharply. "You're going North. You've got a job to do."

Indeed I had.

10

I WENT TO New York City almost respectably, in a cheap front-office suit, aboard a tourist rocket, steerage class. Above me the respectable Costa Rican consumers oohed and ahed at the view from the prism windows or anxiously counted their pennies, wondering how far they'd take them in the pleasures for sale by the colossus of the North.

Below decks we were a shabbier, tougher gang, but it was no labor freighter. We had no windows, but we had lights and vending machines and buckets. A plant protection man had made a little speech to us before we loaded: "You crumbs are going North, out of Costa Rican jurisdiction. You're going to better jobs. But don't forget that they are *jobs.* I want each and every one of you to remember that you're in hock to Chlorella and that Chlorella's claim on you is a prior lien. If any of you think you can break your contract, you're going to find out just how fast and slick extradition for a commercial offense can be. And if any of you think you can just disappear, try it. Chlorella pays Burns Detective Agency seven billion a year, and Burns delivers the goods. So if you crumbs want to give us a little easy exercise, go ahead; we'll be waiting for you. Is everything clear?" Everything was clear. "All right, crumbs. Get aboard and good luck. You have your assignment tickets. Give my regards to Broadway."

We slid into a landing at Montauk without incident. Down below, we sat and waited while the consumers on tourist deck filed out, carrying their baggage kits. Then we sat and waited while Food Customs inspectors, wearing the red-and-white A&P arm bands, argued vociferously with our stewards over the surplus rations—four of us had died on the trip, and the stewards, of course, had held out their Chicken Little cutlets to sell in the black market. Then we sat and waited.

Finally the order came to fall out in fifties. We lined up and had our wrists stamped with our entry permits; marched by squads to the subway; and entrained for the city. I had a bit of luck. My group drew a freight compartment.

At the Labor Exchange we were sorted out and tagged for our respective assignments. There was a bit of a scare when it came out that Chlorella had sold the contracts on twenty of us to I.G. Farben—nobody wants to work in the uranium mines—but I wasn't worried. The man next to me stared moodily as the guards cut out the unlucky twenty and herded them off. "Treat us like slaves," he said bitterly, plucking at my sleeve. "It's a crime. Don't you think so, Mac? It violates the essential dignity of labor."

I gave him an angry glare. The man was a Consie, pure and simple. Then I remembered that I was a Consie too, for the time being. I considered the use of the handclasp, and decided against it. He would be worth remembering if I needed help; but if I revealed myself prematurely he might call on *me*.

We moved on to the Chlorella depot in the Nyack suburbs.

Waste not, want not. Under New York, as under every city in the world, the sewage drains led to a series of settling basins and traps. I knew, as any citizen knows, how the organic waste of twenty-three million persons came water-borne through the venous tracery of the city's drains; how the salts were neutralized through ion-exchange, the residual liquid piped to the kelp farms in Long Island Sound, the sludge that remained pumped into tank barges for shipment to Chlorella. I knew about it, but I had never seen it.

My title was Procurement Expediter, Class 9. My job was coupling the flexible hoses that handled the sludge. After the first day, I shot a week's pay on soot-extractor plugs for my nostrils; they didn't filter out all the odor, but they made it possible to live in it.

On the third day I came off shift and hit the showers. I had figured it out in advance: after six hours at the tanks, where no vending machines were for the simple reason that no one could conceivably eat, drink, or smoke *anything* in the atmosphere, the pent-up cravings of the crew kept them on the Popsie-Crunchie-Starrs cycle for half an hour before the first man even thought of a shower. By sternly repressing the craving, weaker in me than in most because it had had less time to become established, I managed to have the showers almost alone. When the mob arrived, *I* hit the vending machines. It was a simple application of intelligence, and if that doesn't bear out the essential difference between consumer and copysmith mentality, what does? Of course, as I say, the habits weren't as strong in me.

There was one other man in the shower, but, with only two of us, we hardly touched. He handed me the soap as I came in; I lathered and let the water roar down over me under the full pressure of the recirculators. I was hardly aware he was there. But, as I passed the soap back to him, I felt his third finger touch my wrist, the index finger circle around the base of my thumb.

"Oh," I said stupidly, and returned the handclasp. "Are you my con—"

"Ssh!" he hissed. He gestured irritatedly to the Muzak spy-mike dangling from the ceiling. He turned his back on me and meticulously soaped himself again.

When he returned the soap a scrap of paper clung to it. In the locker room I squeezed it dry, spread it out. It read: "Tonight is pass night. Go to the Metropolitan Museum of Art, Classics Room. Be in front of the Maidenform exhibit at exactly five minutes before closing time."

I joined the queue at the supervisor's desk as soon as I was dressed. In less than half an hour I had a stamped pass authorizing me to skip bedcheck for the night. I returned to my bunk to pick up my belongings, warned the new occupant of the bed about the sleep-talking of the man in the tier above, turned in my bag to the supply room, and caught the shuttle down to Bronxville. I transferred to a north-bound local, rode one station, switched to the southbound side, and got out at Schocken Tower. No one appeared to be following me. I hadn't expected anyone to, but it never pays to take chances.

My Consie rendezvous at the Met was almost four hours off. I stood around in the lobby until a cop, contemptuously eyeing my cheap clothing, moved toward me. I had hoped Hester or perhaps even Fowler Schocken himself might come through; no such luck. I saw a good many faces I recognized, of course, but none I was sure I could trust. And, until I found out what lay behind the double cross on Starrzelius Glacier, I had no intention of telling just anybody that I was still alive.

The Pinkerton boomed, "You want to give the Schocken people your business, crumb? You got a big account for them, maybe?"

"Sorry," I said, and headed for the street door. It didn't figure that he would bother to follow me through the crowd in the lobby; he didn't. I dodged around the recreation room, where a group of consumers were watching a PregNot light love story on the screen and getting their samples of Coffiest, and ducked into the service elevators. "Eightieth," I said to the operator, and at once realized I had blundered. The operator's voice said sharply through the speaker grille:

"Service elevators go only to the seventieth floor, you in Car Five. What do you want?"

"Messenger," I lied miserably. "I got to make a pickup from Mr. Schocken's office. I *told* them I wouldn't be let in to Mr. Schocken's office, a fellow like me. I told them, 'Look, he's probably got twenty-five seckataries I got to go through before they let me see him.' I said—"

"The mail room is on forty-five," the operator said, a shade less sharply. "Stand in front of the door so I can see you."

I moved into range of the mike. I didn't want to, but I couldn't see any way out. I thought I heard a sound from the grille, but there was no way of being sure. I had never been in the elevator operators' room, a thousand feet below me, where they pushed the buttons that sent the cars up and down the toothed shafts; but I would have given a year's pay to have been able to look into it then.

I stood there for half a minute. Then the operator's voice said noncommittally, "All right, you. Back in the car. Forty-fifth floor, first slide to the left."

The others in the car stared at me through an incurious haze of Coffiest's alkaloids until I got out. I stepped on the left-bound slidewalk and went past the door marked "Mail Room," to the corridor juncture where my slidewalk dipped down around its roller. It took me a little while to find the stairway, but that was all right. I needed the time to catch up on my swearing. I didn't dare use the elevators again.

Have you ever climbed thirty-five flights of stairs?

Toward the end the going got pretty bad. It wasn't just that I was aching from toe to navel, or that I was wasting time, of which I had none too much anyway. It was getting on toward ten o'clock, and the consumers whose living quarters were on the stairs were beginning to drift there for the night. I was as careful as I could be, but it nearly came to a fist fight on the seventy-fourth, where the man on the third step had longer legs than I thought.

Fortunately, there were no sleepers above the seventy-eighth; I was in executive country.

I skulked along the corridors, very conscious of the fact that the first person who paid any attention to me would either recognize me or throw me out. Only clerks were in the corridors, and none I'd known at all well; my luck was running strong.

But not strong enough. Fowler Schocken's office was locked.

I ducked into the office of his secretary[3], which was deserted, and thought things over. Fowler usually played a few holes of golf at the country club after work. It was pretty late for him still to be there, but I thought I might as well take the chance—it was only four more flights to the club.

I made it standing up. The country club is a handsome layout, which is only fair because the dues are handsome too. Besides the golf links, the tennis court and the other sports facilities, the whole north end of the room is woods—more than a dozen beautifully simulated trees—and there are at least twenty recreation booths for reading, watching movies, or any other spectator pleasure.

A mixed foursome was playing golf. I moved close to their seats as unobtrusively as possible. They were intent on their dials and buttons, guiding their players along the twelfth hole fairway. I read their scores from the telltale with a sinking heart; all were in the high nineties. Duffers. Fowler Schocken averaged under eighty for the course. He couldn't be in a group like that, and as I came close I saw that both the men were strangers to me.

I hesitated before retreating, trying to decide what to do next. Schocken wasn't in sight anywhere in the club. Conceivably he was in one of the recreation booths, but I could scarcely open the doors of all of them to see; I'd be thrown out the first time I blundered into an occupied one, unless God smiled and the occupant was Fowler.

A babble of conversation from the golfers caught my ear.

One of the girls had just sunk a four-inch putt to finish the hole; smiling happily as the others complimented her, she leaned forward to pull the lever that brought the puppet players back to the tee and changed the layout to the dog-leg of the thirteenth hole, and I caught a glimpse of her face. It was Hester, my secretary.

That made it simple. I couldn't quite guess how Hester came to be in the country club, but I knew everything else there was to know about Hester. I retreated to an alcove near the entrance to the ladies' room; it was only about ten minutes' wait before she showed up.

She fainted, of course. I swore and carried her into the alcove. There was a couch; I put her on it. There was a door; I closed it.

She blinked up at me as consciousness came back. "Mitch," she said, in a tone between a whisper and a shriek.

"I am not dead," I told her. "Somebody else died, and they switched bodies. I don't know who 'they' are; but I'm not dead. Yes, it's really me. Mitch Courtenay, your boss. I can prove it. For instance, remember last year's Christmas party, when you were so worried about—"

"Never mind," she said hastily. "My God, Mitch—I mean, Mr. Courtenay—"

"Mitch is good enough," I said. I dropped the hand I had been massaging, and she pushed herself up to get a better look at me. "Listen," I said, "I'm alive, all right, but I'm in a kind of peculiar foul-up. I've got to get in touch with Fowler Schocken. Can you fix it—right away?"

"Uh." She swallowed and reached for a cigarette, recovering. I automatically took out a Starr. "Uh, no, Mitch. Mr. Schocken's on the Moon. It's a big secret, but I guess I can tell *you* about it. It's something to do with the Venus project. After you got killed—well, you know what I mean—after that, when he put Mr. Runstead on the project and it began to slip so, he decided to take matters into his own hands. I gave him all your notes. One of them said something about the Moon, I guess; anyway, he took off a couple of days ago."

"Hell," I said. "Well, who'd he leave in charge here? Harvey Bruner? Can you reach—"

Hester was shaking her head. "No, not Mr. Bruner, Mitch.

Mr. Runstead's in charge. Mr. Schocken switched in such a hurry, there wasn't anyone to spare to take over *his* job except Mr. Runstead. But I can call him right away."

"*No*," I said. I looked at my watch, and groaned. I would have just about time to make it to the Met. "Look," I said. "I've got to leave. Don't say anything to *anybody*, will you? I'll figure something out, and I'll call you. Let's see, when I call I'll say I'm—what's the name of that doctor of your mother's?—Dr. Gallant. And I'll arrange to meet you and tell you what we're going to do. I can count on you, Hester, can't I?"

"Sure, Mitch," she said breathlessly.

"Fine," I said. "Now you'll have to convoy me down in the elevator. I haven't got time to walk, and there'll be trouble if a guy like me gets caught on the club floor." I stopped and looked her over. "Speaking of which," I said, "what in the world are you doing here?"

Hester blushed. "Oh, you know how it is," she said unhappily. "After you were gone there weren't any other secretarial jobs; the rest of the executives had their girls, and I just couldn't be a consumer again, Mitch, not with the bills and all. And—well, there was this opening up here, you see. . . ."

"Oh," I said. I hope nothing showed on my face; God knows I tried. Damn you to hell, Runstead, I said to myself, thinking of Hester's mother and Hester's young man that she'd maybe been going to marry some day, and the absolute stinking injustice of a man like Runstead taking the law into his own hands and wrecking executive lives—mine—and staff lives—Hester's—and dragging them down to the level of consumers.

"Don't worry, Hester," I said gently. "I'll owe you something for this. And believe me, you won't have to remind me. I'll make everything up to you." And I knew how to do it, too. Quite a lot of the girls on the ZZ contract manage to avoid the automatic renewal and downgrading. It would cost a lot for me to buy out her contract before the year was up, so that was out of the question; but some of the girls do pretty well with single executives after their first year. And I was important enough so that if I made a suggestion to some branch head or bureau chief, he would not be likely to ignore it, or even to treat her badly.

I don't approve of sentiment in business matters, but as you see I'm an absolute sucker for it in any personal relationship.

Hester insisted on lending me some money, so I made it to the Met with time to spare by taking a cab. Even though I had paid the driver in advance, he could not refrain from making a nasty comment about high-living consumers as I got out; if I hadn't had more important things on my mind I would have taught him a lesson then and there.

I have always had a fondness for the Met. I don't go much for religion—partly, I suppose, because it's a Taunton account—but there is a grave, ennobling air about the grand old masterpieces in the Met that gives me a feeling of peace and reverence. I mentioned that I was a little ahead of time. I spent those minutes standing silently before the bust of G. Washington Hill, and I felt more relaxed than I had since that first afternoon at the South Pole.

At precisely five minutes before midnight I was standing before the big, late-period Maidenform—number thirty-five in the catalogue: "I Dreamed I Was Ice-Fishing in My Maidenform Bra"—when I became conscious of someone whistling in the corridor behind me. The notes were irrelevant; the cadence formed one of the recognition signals I'd learned in the hidey-hole under Chicken Little.

One of the guards was strolling away. She looked over her shoulder at me and smiled.

To all external appearances, it was a casual pickup. We linked arms, and I felt the coded pressure of her fingers on my wrist: "D-O-N-T T-A-L-K W-H-E-N I L-E-A-V-E Y-O-U G-O T-O T-H-E B-A-C-K O-F T-H-E R-O-O-M S-I-T D-O-W-N A-N-D W-A-I-T."

I nodded. She took me to a plastic-finished door, pushed it open, pointed inside. I went in alone.

There were ten or fifteen consumers sitting in straight-back chairs, facing an elderly consumer with a lectorial goatee. I found a seat in the back of the room and sat in it. No one paid any particular attention to me.

The lecturer was covering the high spots of some particularly boring precommercial period. I listened with half my mind, trying to catch some point of similarity in the varying types around me. All were Consies, I was reasonably sure—else why would I be here? But the basic stigmata, the surface mark of the lurking fanatic inside, that should have been apparent, escaped me. They were all consumers, with the pinched look that soyaburgers and Yeasties inevitably give; but I could have passed any of them in the street without a second glance. Yet—this was New York, and Bowen had spoken of it as though the Consies I'd meet here were pretty high up in the scale, the Trotskys and Tom Paines of the movement.

And that was a consideration too. When I got out of this mess—when I got through to Fowler Schocken and cleared up my status—I might be in a position to break up this whole filthy conspiracy, if I played my cards right. I looked over the persons in the room a little more attentively, memorizing their features. I didn't want to fail to recognize them, next time we came in contact.

There must have been some sort of signal, but I missed it. The lecturer stopped almost in mid-sentence, and a plump little man with a goatee stood up from the first row. "All right," he said in an ordinary tone, "we're all here and there's no sense wasting any more time. We're against waste; that's why we're here." He stepped on the little titter. "No noise," he warned, "and no names. For the purpose of this meeting we'll use numbers; you can call me 'One,' you 'Two'—" he pointed to the man in the next seat, "and so on by rows to the back of the room. All clear? Okay, now listen closely. We've got you together because you're all new here. You're in the big leagues now. This is world operational headquarters, right here in New York; you can't go any higher. Each of you was picked for some special quality—you know what they are. You'll all get assignments right here, tonight. But before you do, I want to point out one thing. You don't know me and I don't know you; every one of you got a big build-up from your last cells, but sometimes the men in the field get a little too enthusiastic. If they were wrong about you. . . . Well, you understand these things, eh?"

There was a general nod. I nodded too, but I paid particular attention to memorizing that plump little goatee. One by one numbers were called, and one by one the new-johns got up, conferred briefly with the goatee, and left, in couples and threes, for unannounced destinations. I was almost the last to be called; besides me, only a very young girl with orange hair and a cast in her eye was still in the room.

"Okay, you two," said the man with the goatee. "You two are going to be a team, so you might as well know names. Groby, meet Corwin. Groby's a kind of copysmith. Celia's an artist."

"Okay," she said, lighting a Starr from the butt of another in a flare of phosphorus. A perfect consumer type if only she hadn't been corrupted by these zealots; I noticed her jaws working on gum even while she chain-smoked.

"We'll get along fine," I said approvingly.

"You sure will," said the man in the goatee. "You have to. You understand these things, Groby. In order to give you a chance to show your stuff, we'll have to let you know a lot of stuff that we don't want to read in the morning paper. If you don't work out for us, Groby," he said pleasantly, "you see the fix we're in; we'll have to make some other arrangements for you." He tapped a little bottle of colorless fluid on the desk top. The tinny rattle of the aluminum top was no tinnier than my voice as I said, "Yes, sir," because I knew what little bottles of colorless fluid could reasonably be assumed to contain.

It turned out, though, that it wasn't much of a problem. I spent three difficult hours in that little room, then I pointed out that if I didn't get back to barracks I would miss the morning work call and there would be hell to pay. So they excused me.

But I missed work call anyhow. I came out of the Museum into a perfect spring dawn, feeling, all in all, pretty content with life. A figure loomed out of the smog and peered into my face. I recognized the sneering face of the taxi-runner who had brought me to the Museum. He said briskly, "Hel-lo, Mr. Courtenay," and then the obelisk from behind the Museum, or something very much like it, smacked me across the back of the neck.

11

"—AWAKE IN a few minutes," I heard somebody say.

"Is he ready for Hedy?"

"Good God, no!"

"I was only asking."

"You ought to know better. First you give them amphetamine, plasma, maybe a niacin megaunit. *Then* they're ready for Hedy. She doesn't like it if they keep blacking out. She sulks."

Nervous laugh with a chill in it.

I opened my eyes and said: "Thank God!" For what I could see was a cerebral-gray ceiling, the shade you find only in the brain room of an advertising agency. I was safe in the arms of Fowler Schocken Associates—or was I? I didn't recognize the face that leaned over me.

"Why so pleased, Courtenay?" the face inquired. "Don't you know where you are?"

After that it was easy to guess. "Taunton's," I croaked.

"That is correct."

I tried my arms and legs and found they didn't respond. I couldn't tell whether it was drugs or a plasticocoon. "Look," I said steadily. "I don't know what you people think you're doing, but I advise you to stop it. Apparently this is a kidnaping for business purposes. You people are either going to let me go or kill me. If you kill me without a Notification you'll get the *cerebrin*, so of course you won't kill me. You're going to let me go eventually, so I suggest that you do it now."

"Kill you, Courtenay?" asked the face with mocking wonder. "How would we do that? You're dead already. Everybody knows that. You died on Starrzelius Glacier; don't you remember?"

I struggled again, without results. "They'll brainburn you," I said. "Are you people crazy? Who wants to be brainburned?"

The face said nonchalantly: "You'd be surprised." And in an aside to somebody else: "Tell Hedy he'll be ready soon." Hands did something, there was a click, and I was helped to sit up. The skin-tight pulling at my joints told me it was a plasticocoon and that I might save my strength. There was no point to struggling.

A buzzer buzzed and I was told sharply: "Keep a respectful tongue in your head, Courtenay. Mr. Taunton's coming in."

B. J. Taunton lurched in, drunk. He looked just the way I had always seen him from afar at the speakers' table in hundreds of banquets: florid, gross, overdressed—and drunk.

He surveyed me, feet planted wide apart, hands on his hips, and swaying just a little. "Courtenay," he said. "Too bad. You might have turned out to be something if you hadn't cast your lot with that swindling son of a bitch Schocken. Too bad."

He was drunk, he was a disgrace to the profession, and he was responsible for crime after crime, but I couldn't keep my respect for an entrepreneur out of my voice. "Sir," I said evenly, "there must be some misunderstanding. There's been no provocation of Taunton Associates to commercial murder—has there?"

"Nope," he said, tight-lipped and swaying slightly. "Not as the law considers it provocation. All that bastard Schocken did was steal my groundwork, take over my Senators, suborn my committee witnesses, and *steal Venus from me!*" His voice had risen to an abrupt shriek. In a normal voice he continued: "No; no provocation. He's carefully refrained from killing any of my people. Shrewd Schocken; ethical Schocken; damned-fool Schocken!" he crooned.

His glassy eyes glared at me: "You bastard!" he said. "Of all the low-down, lousy, unethical, cheap-jack stunts ever pulled on me, yours was the rottenest. *I*—" he thumped his chest, briefly threatening his balance. "*I* figured out a way to commit a safe commercial murder, and you played possum like a scared yellow rat. You ran like a rabbit, you dog."

"Sir," I said desperately, "I'm sure I don't know what you're driving at." His years of boozing, I thought briefly, had finally caught up with him. The words he was uttering could only come from a wet brain.

He sat down unconcernedly; one of his men darted in and there was a chair seat to meet his broad rump in the nick of time. With an expansive gesture B. J. Taunton said to me: "Courtenay, I am essentially an artist."

The words popped out of me automatically: "Of course, Mr.—" I almost said "Schocken." It was a well-conditioned reflex. "Of course, Mr. Taunton," I said.

"Essentially," he brooded, "essentially an artist. A dreamer of dreams; a weaver of visions." It gave me an uncanny sense of double vision. I seemed to see Fowler Schocken sitting there instead of his rival, the man who stood against everything that Fowler Schocken stood for. "I wanted Venus, Courtenay, and I shall have it. Schocken stole it from me, and I am going to repossess it. Fowler Schocken's management of the Venus project will stink to high heaven. No rocket under Schocken's management is ever going to get off the ground, if I have to corrupt every one of his underlings and kill every one of his section heads. For I am essentially an artist."

"Mr. Taunton," I said steadily, "you can't kill section heads as casually as all that. You'll be brainburned. They'll give you *cerebrin*. You can't find anybody who'll take the risk for you. Nobody wants twenty years in hell."

He said dreamily: "I got a mechanic to drop that 'copter pod on you, didn't I? I got an unemployable bum to plug at you through your apartment window, didn't I? Unfortunately both missed. And then you crossed us up with that cowardly run-out on the glacier."

I didn't say anything. The run-out on the glacier had been no idea of mine. God only knew whose idea it had been to have Runstead club me, shanghai me, and leave a substitute corpse in my place.

"Almost you escaped," Taunton mused. "If it hadn't been for a few humble, loyal servants—a taxi-runner, a few others—we never would have had you back. But I have my tools, Courtenay.

"They might be better, they might be worse, but it's my destiny to dream dreams and weave visions. The greatness of an artist is in his simplicity, Courtenay. You say to me: 'Nobody wants to be brainburned.' That is because you are mediocre. *I* say: '*Find* somebody who wants to be brainburned and *use* him.' That is because I am great."

"Wants to be brainburned," I repeated stupidly. "Wants to be brainburned."

"Explain," said Taunton to one aide. "I want him thoroughly convinced that we are in earnest."

One of his men told me dryly: "It's a matter of population, Courtenay. Have you ever heard of Albert Fish?"

"No."

"He was a phenomenon of the dawn; the earliest days of the Age of Reason—1920 or thereabouts. Albert Fish stuck needles into himself, burned himself with alcohol-saturated wads of cotton, flogged himself—he *liked* it. He would have liked brainburning, I'll wager. It would have been twenty delightful subjective years of being flayed, suffocated, choked, and nauseated. It would have been Albert Fish's dream come true.

"There was only one Albert Fish in his day. Pressures and strains of a very high order are required to produce an Albert Fish. It would be unreasonable to expect more than one to be produced out of the small and scattered population of the period—less than three billion. With our vastly larger current population there are many Albert Fishes wandering around. You only have to find them. Our matchless research facilities here at Taunton have unearthed several. They turn up at hospitals, sometimes in very grotesque shape. They are eager would-be killers; they want the delights of punishment. A man like you says we can't hire killers because they'd be afraid of being punished. But Mr. Taunton, now, says we *can* hire a killer if we find one who *likes* being punished. And the best part of it all is, the ones who like to get hurt are the ones who just love hurting others. Hurting, for instance—you."

It had a bloodcurdlingly truthful ring to it. Our generation must be inured to wonder. The chronicles of fantastic heroism and abysmal wickedness that crowd our newscasts—I knew from research that they didn't have such courage or such depravity in the old days. The fact had puzzled me. We have such people as Malone, who quietly dug his tunnels for six years and then one Sunday morning blew up Red Bank, New Jersey. A Brink's traffic cop had got him sore. Conversely we have James Revere, hero of the *White Cloud* disaster. A shy, frail tourist-class steward, he had rescued on his own shoulders seventy-six passengers, returning again and again into the flames with his flesh charring from his bones, blind, groping his way along red-hot bulkheads with his hand-stumps. It was true. When there are *enough* people, you will always find somebody who can and will do any given thing. Taunton *was* an artist. He had grasped this broad and simple truth and used it. It meant that I was as good as dead. *Kathy*, I thought. *My Kathy.*

Taunton's thick voice broke in on my reflections. "You grasp the pattern?" he asked. "The big picture? The theme, the message, what I might call the essential juice of it is that I'm going to repossess Venus. Now, beginning at the beginning, tell us about the Schocken Agency. All its little secrets, its little weaknesses, its ins and outs, its corruptible employees, its appropriations, its Washington contacts—*you* know."

I was a dead man with nothing to lose—I thought. "No," I said.

One of Taunton's men said abruptly: "He's ready for Hedy," got up and went out.

Taunton said: "You've studied prehistory, Courtenay. You may recognize the name of Gilles de Rais." I did, and felt a tightness over my scalp, like a steel helmet slowly shrinking. "All the generations of prehistory added up to an estimated five billion population," Taunton rambled. "All the generations of prehistory produced only one Gilles de Rais, whom you perhaps think of as Bluebeard. Nowadays we have our pick of several. Out of all the people I might have picked to handle special work like that for me I picked Hedy. You'll see why."

The door opened and a pale, adenoidal girl with lank blond hair was standing in it. She had a silly grin on her face; her lips were thin and bloodless. In one hand she held a six-inch needle set in a plastic handle.

I looked into her eyes and began screaming. I couldn't stop screaming until they led her away and closed the door again. I was broken.

"Taunton," I whispered at last. "Please . . ."

He leaned back comfortably and said: "Give."

I tried, but I couldn't. My voice wouldn't work right and neither would my memory. I couldn't remember whether my firm was Fowler Schocken or Schocken Fowler, for instance.

Taunton got up at last and said: "We'll put you on ice for a while, Courtenay, so you can pull yourself together. I need a drink myself." He shuddered involuntarily, and then beamed again. "Sleep on it," he said, and left unsteadily.

Two of his men carted me from the brain room, down a corridor and into a bare cubbyhole with a very solid door. It seemed to be night in executives' country. Nothing was going on in any of the offices we passed, lights were low, and a single corridor guard was yawning at his desk.

I asked unsteadily: "Will you take the cocoon off me? I'm going to be a filthy mess if I don't get out of it."

"No orders about it," one of them said briefly, and they slammed the solid door and locked it. I flopped around the small floor trying to find something sharp enough to break the film and give me an even chance of bursting the plastic, but there was nothing. After incredible contortions and a dozen jarring falls I found that I could never get to my feet. The doorknob had offered a very, very faint ghost of hope, but it might as well have been a million miles away.

Mitchell Courtenay, copysmith. Mitchell Courtenay, key man of the Venus section. Mitchell Courtenay, destroyer-to-be of the Consies. Mitchell Courtenay flopping on the floor of a cell in the offices of the sleaziest, crookedest agency that ever blemished the profession, without any prospect except betrayal and—with luck—a merciful death. Kathy at least would never know. She would think I had died like a fool on the glacier, meddling with the power pack when I had no business to . . .

The lock of the door rattled and rattled. They were coming for me.

But when the door opened I saw from the floor not a forest of trousered legs but a single pair of matchstick ankles, nylon-clad.

"I love you," said the strange, dead voice of a woman. "They said I would have to wait, but I couldn't wait." It was Hedy. She had her needle.

I tried to cry for help, but my chest seemed paralyzed as she knelt beside me with shining eyes. The temperature of the room seemed to drop ten degrees. She clamped her bloodless lips on mine; they were like heated iron. And then I thought the left side of my face and head were being torn off. It lasted for seconds and blended into a red haze and unconsciousness.

"Wake up," the dead voice was saying. "I want you. Wake up." Lightning smashed at my right elbow, and I cried out and jerked my arm. My arm moved—

It moved.

The bloodless lips descended on mine again, and again her needle ran into my jaw, probing exactly for the great lump of the trigeminal facial nerve, and finding it. I fought the red haze that was trying to swallow me up. My arm had moved. She had perforated the membrane of the cocoon, and it could be burst. The needle searched again and somehow the pain was channeled to my right arm. In one convulsive jerk it was free.

I think I took the back of her neck in my hand and squeezed. I am not sure. I do not want to be sure. But after five minutes she and her love did not matter. I ripped and stripped the plastic from me and got to my feet an inch at a time, moaning from stiffness.

The corridor guard could not matter any more. If he had not come at my cries he would never come. I walked from the room and saw the guard apparently sleeping face-down on his desk. As I stood over him I saw a very little blood and serum puddled and coagulating in the small valley between the two cords of his shrunken old neck. One thrust transfixing the medulla had been enough for Hedy. I could testify that her knowledge of the nervous system's topography was complete.

The guard wore a gun that I hesitated over for a moment and then rejected. In his pockets were a few dollars that would be more useful. I hurried on to the ladders. His desk clock said 0605.

I knew already about climbing up stairs. I learned then about climbing down stairs. If your heart's in good shape there's little to choose between them. It took me an estimated thirty minutes in my condition to get down the ladders of executives' country and onto the populated stairs below. The first sullen stirrings of the work-bound consumers were well under way. I passed half a dozen bitter fist fights and one cutting scrape. The Taunton Building nightdwellers were a low, dirty lot who never would have been allowed stairspace in the Schocken Tower, but it was all to the good. I attracted no attention whatsoever in my filthy clothes and sporting a fresh stab wound in my face. Some of the bachelor girls even whistled, but that was all. The kind of people you have in the ancient, run-down slum buildings like R.C.A. and Empire State would have pulled me down if I'd taken their eye.

My timing was good. I left the building lobby in the very core of a cheek-by-jowl mob boiling out the door to the shuttle which would take them to their wretched jobs. I thought I saw hardguys in plain clothes searching the mob from second-floor windows, but I didn't look up and I got into the shuttle station.

At the change booth I broke all my bills and went into the washroom. "Split a shower, bud?" somebody asked me. I wanted a shower terribly, and by myself, but I didn't dare betray any white-collar traits. She and I pooled our coins for a five-minute salt, thirty-second fresh, with soap. I found that I was scrubbing my right hand over and over again. I found that when the cold water hit the left side of my face the pain was dizzying.

After the shower I wedged myself into the shuttle and spent two hours zigzagging under the city. My last stop was Times Square, in the heart of the market district. It was mostly a freight station. While cursing consumers hurled crates of protein ticketed for various parts of town onto the belts I tried to phone Kathy again. Again there was nobody home.

I got Hester at the Schocken Tower. I told her: "I want you to raise every cent you can, borrow, clean out your savings, buy a Starrzelius apparel outfit for me, and meet me with it soonest at the place where your mother broke her leg two years ago. The exact place, remember?"

"Mitch," she said. "Yes, I remember. But my contract—"

"Don't make me beg you, Hester," I pleaded. "Trust me. I'll see you through. For God's sake, hurry. And—if you get here and I'm in the hands of the guards, don't recognize me. Now, into action."

I hung up and slumped in the phone booth until the next party hammered indignantly on the door. I walked slowly around the station, had Coffiest and a cheese sandwich, and rented a morning paper at the newsstand. The story about me was a bored little item on page three out of a possible four: SOUGHT FOR CB & FEMICIDE. It said George Groby had failed to return from pass to his job with Chlorella and had used his free time to burglarize executives' country in the Taunton Building. He had killed a secretary who stumbled on him and made his escape.

Hester met me half an hour later hard by the loading chute from which a crate had once whizzed to break her mother's leg. She looked frantically worried; technically she was as guilty of contract breach as "George Groby."

I took the garment box from her and asked: "Do you have fifteen hundred dollars left?"

"Just about. My mother was frantic—"

"Get us reservations on the next Moon ship; today if possible. Meet me back here; I'll be wearing the new clothes."

"Us? The Moon?" she squeaked.

"Yes; us. I've got to get off the Earth before I'm killed. And this time it'll be for keeps."

12

MY LITTLE Hester squared her shoulders and proceeded to work miracles.

In ten hours we were grunting side by side under the take-off acceleration of the Moon ship *David Ricardo*. She had cold-bloodedly passed herself off as a Schocken employee on special detail to the Moon and me as Groby, a sales analyst 6. Naturally the dragnet for Groby, expediter 9, had not included the Astoria spaceport. Sewage workers on the lam from CB and femicide wouldn't have the money to hop a rocket, of course.

We rated a compartment and the max ration. The *David Ricardo* was so constructed that most passengers rated compartments and max rations. It wasn't a trip for the idly curious or the submerged fifteen sixteenths of the population. The Moon was strictly business—mining business—and some sight-seeing. Our fellow-passengers, what we saw of them at the ramp, were preoccupied engineers, a few laborers in the minute steerage, and silly-rich men and women who wanted to say they'd been there.

After take-off, Hester was hysterically gay for a while, and then snapped. She sobbed on my shoulder, frightened at the enormity of what she'd done. She'd been brought up in a deeply moral, sales-fearing home, and you couldn't expect her to commit the high commercial crime of breaking a labor contract without there being a terrific emotional lashback.

She wailed: "Mr. Courtenay—Mitch—if only I could be *sure* it was all right! I know you've always been good to me and I know you wouldn't do anything wrong, but I'm so scared and miserable!"

I dried her eyes and made a decision.

"I'll tell you what it's all about, Hester," I said. "You be the judge. Taunton has discovered something very terrible. He's found out that there are people who are not deterred by the threat of *cerebrin* as the punishment for an unprovoked commercial murder. He thinks Mr. Schocken grabbed the Venus project from him unethically, and he'll stop at nothing to get it back. He's tried twice at least to kill me. I thought Mr. Runstead was one of his agents, assigned to bitch up Schocken's handling of the Venus account. Now, I don't know. Mr. Runstead clubbed me when I went after him at the South Pole, spirited me away to a labor freighter under a faked identity, and left a substitute body for mine. And," I said cautiously, "there are Consies in it."

She uttered a small shriek.

"I don't know how they dovetail," I said. "But I was in a Consie cell—"

"Mis-ter *Courtenay!*"

"Strictly as a blind," I hastily explained. "I was stuck in Chlorella Costa Rica and the only way north seemed to be through the Consie network. They had a cell in the factory, I joined up, turned on the talent, and got transferred to New York. The rest you know."

She paused for a long time and asked: "Are you sure it's all right?"

Wishing desperately that it were, I firmly said: "Of course, Hester."

She gave me a game smile. "I'll get our rations," she said, unsnapping herself. "You'd better stay here."

*

Forty hours out I said to Hester: "The blasted black-marketing steward is going too far! Look at this!" I held up my bulb of water and my ration box. The seal had clearly been tampered with on both containers, and visibly there was water missing. "Max rations," I went on oratorically, "are supposed to be tamper-proof, but this is plain burglary. How do yours look?"

"Same thing," she said listlessly. "You can't do anything about it. Let's not eat just yet, Mr. Courtenay." She made a marked effort to be vivacious. "Tennis, anyone?"

"All right," I grumbled, and set up the field, borrowed from the ship recreation closet. She was better at tennis than I, but I took her in straight sets. Her co-ordination was way off. She'd stab for a right forecourt deep crosscourt return and like as not miss the button entirely—if she didn't send the ball into the net by failing to surge power with her left hand on the rheostat. A half hour of the exercise seemed to do both of us good. She cheered up and ate her rations and I had mine.

The tennis match before meals became a tradition. There was little enough to do in our cramped quarters. Every eight hours she would go for our tagged rations, I would grumble about the shortage and tampering, we'd have some tennis, and then eat. The rest of the time passed somehow, watching the ads come and go—all Schocken—on the walls. Well enough, I thought. Schocken's on the Moon and I won't be kept from him there. Things weren't so crowded. Moon to Schocken to Kathy—a twinge of feeling. I could have asked casually what Hester had heard about Jack O'Shea, but I didn't. I was afraid I might not like what she might have heard about the midget hero and his triumphal procession from city to city and woman to woman.

A drab service announcement at last interrupted the parade of ads: COOKS TO THE GALLEY (the *David Ricardo* was a British ship) FOR FINAL LIQUID FEEDING. THIS IS H-8 AND NO FURTHER SOLID OR LIQUID FOOD SHOULD BE CONSUMED UNTIL TOUCHDOWN.

Hester smiled and went out with our tray.

As usual it was ten minutes before she returned. We were getting some pull from the Moon by then: enough to unsettle my stomach. I burped miserably while waiting.

She came back with two Coffiest bulbs and reproached me gaily: "Why, Mitch, you haven't set up the tennis court!"

"Didn't feel like it. Let's eat." I put out my hand for my bulb. She didn't give it to me. "Well?"

"Just one set?" she coaxed.

"Hell, girl, you heard me," I snapped. "Let's not forget who's who around here." I wouldn't have said it if it hadn't been Coffiest, I suppose. The Starrzelius-red bulb kicked things off in me—nagging ghosts of withdrawal symptoms. I'd been off the stuff for a long time, but you never kick Coffiest.

She stiffened. "I'm sorry, Mr. Courtenay." And then she clutched violently at her middle, her face distorted. Astounded, I grabbed her. She was deathly pale and limp; she moaned with pain.

"Hester," I said, "what is it? What—?"

"Don't drink it," she croaked, her hand kneading her belly. "The Coffiest. Poison. Your rations. I've been tasting them." Her nails tore first the nylon of her midriff and then her skin as she clawed at the pain.

"Send a doctor!" I was yelling into the compartment mike. "Woman's dying here!"

The chief steward's voice answered me: "Right away, sir. Ship's doctor'll be there right away."

Hester's contorted face began to relax, frightening me terribly. She said softly: "Bitch Kathy. Running out on you. Mitch and bitch. Funny. You're too good for her. *She* wouldn't have. My life. Yours." There was another spasm across her face. "Wife versus secretary. A laugh. It always was. You never even kissed me—"

I didn't get a chance to. She was gone, and the ship's doctor was hauling himself briskly in along the handline. His face fell. We towed her to the lazarette and he put her in a cardiac-node exciter that started her heart going again. Her chest began to rise and fall and she opened her eyes.

"Where—are—you?" asked the doctor, loudly and clearly. She moved her head slightly, and a pulse of hope shot through me.

"Response?" I whispered to the doctor.

"Random," he said with professional coldness. He was right. There were more slight head movements and a nervous flutter of the eyelids, which were working independently. He kept trying with questions. "Who—are—you?" brought a wrinkle between her eyes and a tremor of the lip, but no more. Except for a minute, ambiguous residue, she was gone.

Gently enough, the doctor began to explain to me: "I'm going to turn it off. You mustn't think there's any hope left. Evidently irreversible clinical death has occurred. It's often hard for a person with emotional ties to believe—"

I watched her eyelids flutter, one with a two-four beat, the other with a three-four beat. "Turn it off," I said hoarsely. By "it" I meant Hester and not the machine. He cut the current and withdrew the needle.

"There was nausea?" he asked. I nodded. "Her first space flight?" I nodded. "Abdominal pain?" I nodded. "No previous distress?" I shook my head. "History of vertigo?" I nodded, though I didn't know. He was driving at something. He kept asking, and the answers he wanted were as obvious as a magician's forced card. Allergies, easy bleeding, headaches, painful menses, afternoon fatigue—at last he said decisively: "I believe it's Fleischman's Disease. We don't know much about it. It stems from some derangement of function in the adrenocorticotropic bodies under free flight, we think. It kicks off a chain reaction of tissue-incompatibilities which affects the cerebrospinal fluid—"

He looked at me and his tone changed. "I have some alcohol in the locker," he said. "Would you like—"

I reached for the bulb and then remembered. "Have one with me," I said.

He nodded and, with no stalling, drank from one of the nipples of a twin-valve social flask. I saw his Adam's apple work. "Not too much," he cautioned me. "Touchdown's soon."

I stalled with conversation for a few minutes, watching him, and then swallowed half a pint of hundred proof. I could hardly tow myself back to the compartment.

Hangover, grief, fear, and the maddening red tape of Moon debarkation. I must have acted pretty stupidly. A couple of times I heard crewmen say to port officials something like: "Take it easy on the guy. He lost his girl in flight."

The line I took in the cramped receiving room of the endless questionnaires was that I didn't know anything about the mission. I was Groby, a 6, and the best thing to do would be to send me to Fowler Schocken. I understood that we had been supposed to report to him. They pooh-poohed that possibility and set me to wait on a bench while queries were sent to the Schocken branch in Luna City.

I waited and watched and tried to think. It wasn't easy. The busy crowds in Receiving were made up of people going from one place to another place to do specified things. I didn't fit in the pattern; I was a sore thumb. They were going to get me . . .

A tube popped and blinked at the desk yards away. I read between half-closed eyes: S-C-H-O-C-K-E-N T-O R-E-C-E-I-V-I-N-G R-E Q-U-E-R-Y N-O M-I-S-S-I-O-N D-U-E T-H-I-S F-L-I-G-H-T N-O G-R-O-B-Y E-M-P-L-O-Y-E-D B-Y U-S F-O-W-L-E-R S-C-H-O-C-K-E-N U-N-Q-U-E-R-I-E-D B-U-T I-M-P-O-S-S-I-B-L-E A-N-Y U-N-D-E-R S-T-A-R-C-L-A-S-S P-E-R-S-O-N-N-E-L A-S-S-I-G-N-E-D R-E-P-O-R-T H-I-M A-C-T A-T D-I-S-C-R-E-T-I-O-N O-B-V-I-O-U-S-L-Y N-O-T O-U-R B-A-B-Y E-N-D

End indeed. They were glancing at me from the desk, and talking in low tones. In only a moment they would be beckoning the Burns Detective guards standing here and there.

I got up from the bench and sauntered into the crowd, with only one alternative left and that a frightening one. I made the casual gesture that, by their order and timing, constitute the Grand Hailing Sign of Distress of the Consies.

A Burns guard shouldered his way through the crowd and put the arm on me. "Are you going to make trouble?" he demanded.

"No," I said thickly. "Lead the way."

He waved confidently at the desk and they waved back, with grins. He marched me, with his nightstick in the small of my back, through the startled crowd. Numbly I let him take me from the receiving dome down a tunnel-like shopping street.

SOUVENIRS OF LUNA
CHEAPEST IN TOWN

YE TAYSTEE GOODIE SHOPPE ON YE MOONE

YOUR HOMETOWN PAPER

MOONSUITS RENTED
"50 Years Without a Blowout"

RELIABLE MOONSUIT RENTAL CO.
"73 Years Without a Blowout"

MOONMAID FASHIONS
Stunning Conversation Pieces
Prove You Were Here

Warren Astron, D.P.S.
Readings by Appointment Only

blinked and twinkled at me from the shopfronts as new arrivals sauntered up and down, gaping.

"Hold it," growled the guard. We stopped in front of the *Warren Astron* sign. He muttered: "Twist the nightstick away from me. Hit me a good lick over the head with it. Fire one charge at the streetlight. Duck into Astron's and give him the grip. Good luck—and try not to break my skull."

"You're—you're—" I stammered.

"Yeah," he said wryly. "I wish I hadn't seen the hailing sign. This is going to cost me two stripes and a raise. Get moving."

I did. He surrendered the nightstick, and I tried not to make it too easy or too hard when I clouted him. The buckshot charge boomed out of the stick's muzzle, shattered the light overhead, and brought forth shrieks of dismay from the strollers. It was thunderous in the vaulted street. I darted through the chaste white Adam door of Astron's in the sudden darkness and blinked at a tall, thin man with a goatee.

"What's the meaning of this?" he demanded. "I read by appointment—" I took his arm in the grip. "Refuge?" he asked, abruptly shedding a fussy professional manner.

"Yes. Fast."

He led me through his parlor into a small, high observatory with a transparent dome, a refracting telescope, Hindu star maps, clocks, and desks. One of these desks he heaved on mightily, and it turned back on hinges. There was a pit and handholds. "Down you go," he said.

Down I went, into darkness.

It was some six feet deep and six by four in area. It had a rough, unfinished feel to it. There was a pick and shovel leaned against one wall, and a couple of buckets filled with moonrock. Obviously a work in progress.

I inverted one of the buckets and sat on it in the dark. After five hundred and seventy-six counted pulse-beats I sat on the floor and stopped counting. After that got too rugged I tried to brush moonrock out of the way and lie down. After going through this cycle five times I heard voices directly overhead. One was the fussy, professional voice of Astron. The other was the globby, petulant voice of a fat woman. They seemed to be seated at the desk which sealed my hidey-hole.

"—really seems excessive, my dear doctor."

"As Madam wishes. If you will excuse me, I shall return to my ephemeris—"

"But Dr. Astron, I wasn't implying—"

"Madam will forgive me for jumping to the conclusion that she was unwilling to grant me my customary honorarium . . . that is correct. Now, please, the birth date and hour?"

She mumbled them, and I wondered briefly about the problem Astron must have with women who shaded their years.

"So . . . Venus in the house of Mars . . . Mercury ascendant in the trine . . ."

"What's that?" she asked with shrill suspicion. "I know quite a bit about the Great Art and I never heard that before."

Blandly: "Madam must realize that a Moon observatory makes possible many things of which she has never heard before. It is possible by lunar observations to refine the Great Art to a point unattainable in the days when observations were made perforce through the thick and muddled air of Earth."

"Oh—oh, of course. I've heard that, of course. Please go on, Dr. Astron. Will I be able to look through your telescope and see my planets?"

"Later, madam. So . . . Mercury ascendant in the trine, the planet of strife and chicanery, yet quartered with Jupiter, the giver of fortune, so . . ."

The "reading" lasted perhaps half an hour, and there were two more like it that followed, and then there was silence. I actually dozed off until a voice called me. The desk had been heaved back again and Astron's head was silhouetted against the rectangular opening. "Come on out," he said. "It's safe for twelve hours."

I climbed out stiffly and noted that the observatory dome had been opaqued.

"You're Groby," he stated.

"Yes," I said, dead-pan.

"We got a report on you by courier aboard the *Ricardo*. God knows what you're up to; it's too much for me." I noticed that his hand was in his pocket. "You turn up in Chlorella, you're a natural-born copysmith, you're transferred to New York, you get kidnaped in front of the Met—in earnest or by prearrangement—you kill a girl and disappear—and now you're on the Moon. God knows what you're up to. It's too much for me. A Central Committee member will be here shortly to try and figure you out. Is there anything you'd care to say? Like confessing that you're an *agent provocateur*? Or subject to manic-depressive psychosis?"

I said nothing

"Very well," he said. Somewhere a door opened and closed. "That will be she," he told me.

And my wife Kathy walked into the observatory.

13

"MITCH," SHE said dazedly. "My God, Mitch." She laughed, with a note of hysteria. "You wouldn't wait, would you? You wouldn't stay on ice."

The astrologer took the gun out of his pocket and asked her: "Is there—?"

"No, Warren. It's all right. I know him. You can leave us alone. Please."

He left us alone. Kathy dropped into a chair, trembling. I couldn't move. My wife was a king-pin Consie. I had thought I'd known her, and I'd been wrong. She had lied to me continuously and I had never known it.

"Aren't you going to say anything?" I asked flatly.

She visibly took hold of herself. "Shocked?" she asked. "You, a star-class copysmith consorting with a Consie? Afraid it'll get out and do you no good businesswise?" She forced a mocking smile that broke down as I looked at her. "Damn it," she flared, "all I ever asked from you after I came to my senses was for you to get out of my life and stay out. The biggest mistake I ever made was keeping Taunton from killing you."

"You had Runstead shanghai me?"

"Like a fool. What in God's name are you doing here? What are these wild-man stunts of yours? Why can't you leave me alone?" She was screaming by then.

Kathy a Consie. Runstead a Consie. Deciding what was best for poor Mitch and doing it. Taunton deciding what was best for poor Mitch and doing it. Moving me this way and that across the chessboard.

"Pawn queens," I said, and picked her up and slapped her. The staring intensity left her eyes and she looked merely surprised. "Get what's-his-name in here," I said.

"Mitch, what are you up to?" She sounded like herself.

"Get him in here."

"You can't order me—"

"You!" I yelled. "The witch-doctor!"

He came running, right into my fist. Kathy was on my back, a clawing wildcat, as I went through his pockets. I found the gun—a wicked .25 UHV machine pistol—and shoved her to the floor. She looked up at me in astonishment, mechanically rubbing a bruised hip. "You're a mean son of a bitch," she said wonderingly.

"All of a sudden," I agreed. "Does Fowler Schocken know you're on the Moon?"

"No," she said, rubbing her thumb and forefinger together.

"You're lying."

"My little lie-detector," she crooned jeeringly. "My little fire-eating copysmith—"

"Level with me," I said, "or you get this thing across the face."

"Good God," she said. "You mean it." She put her hand to her face slowly, looking at the gun.

"I'm glad that's settled. Does Fowler Schocken know you're on the Moon?"

"Not exactly," she said, still watching the gun. "He did advise me to make the trip—to help me get over my bereavement."

"Call him. Get him here."

She didn't say anything or move to the phone.

"Listen," I said. "This is Groby talking. Groby's been slugged, knifed, robbed, and kidnaped. He saw the only friend he had in the world poisoned a few hours ago. He's been played with by a lady sadist who knew her anatomy lessons. He killed her for it and he was glad of it. He's so deep in hock to Chlorella that he'll never get out. He's wanted for femicide and CB. The woman he thought he was in love with turned out to be a lying fanatic and a bitch. Groby has nothing to lose. I can put a burst through the dome up there and we'll all suck space. I can walk out into the street, give myself up, and tell exactly what I know. They won't believe me but they'll investigate to make sure, and sooner or later they'll get corroboration—after I've been brainburned, but that doesn't matter. I've nothing to lose."

"And," she asked flatly, "what have you got to gain?"

"Stop stalling. Call Schocken."

"Not without one more try, Mitch. One word hurt specially—'fanatic.' There were two reasons why I begged Runstead to shanghai you. I wanted you out of the way of Taunton's killers. And I wanted you to get a taste of the consumer's life. I thought—I don't know. I thought you'd see how fouled-up things have become. It's hard to see when you're star class. From the bottom it's easier to see. I thought I'd be able to talk sense to you after we brought you back to life, and we'd be able to work together on the only job worth doing. So it didn't work. That damned brain of yours—so good and so warped. All you want is to be star class again and eat and drink and sleep a little better than anybody else. It's too bad you're not a fanatic too. Same old Mitch. Well, I tried.

"Go ahead and do whatever you think you have to do. Don't fret about it hurting me. It's not going to hurt worse than the nights we used to spend screaming at each other. Or the times I was out on Consie business and couldn't tell you and had to watch you being jealous. Or shipping you to Chlorella to try and make you a whole sane man in spite of what copysmithing's done to you. Or never being able to love you all the way, never being able to give myself to you entirely, mind or body, because there was this secret. I've been hurt. Pistol-whipping's a joke compared to the way I've been hurt."

There was a pause that seemed to go on forever.

"Call Schocken," I said unsteadily. "Tell him to come here. Then get out and take the stargazer with you. I—I don't know what I'm going to tell him. But I'm going to give you and your friends a couple of days' grace. Time to change headquarters and hailing signs and the rest of your insane rigmarole. Call Schocken and get out of here. I don't ever want to see you again."

I couldn't read the look on her face as she picked up the phone and punched a number.

"Mr. Schocken's sec^3, please," she said. "This is Dr. Nevin—widow of Mr. Courtenay. You'll find me on the through list, I believe . . . thank you. Mr. Schocken's sec^2, please. This is Dr. Nevin, Mr. Courtenay's widow. May I speak to Mr. Schocken's secretary? I'm listed . . . thank you . . . Hello, Miss Grice; this is Dr. Nevin. May I speak to Mr. Schocken? . . . Certainly . . . thank you . . ." She turned to me and said: "I'll have to wait a few moments." They passed in silence, and then she said: "Hello, Mr. Schocken . . . Well, thank you. I wonder if you could come and see me about a matter of importance . . . business *and* personal . . . the sooner the better, I'm afraid . . . Shopping One, off Receiving—Dr. Astron's . . . no, nothing like that. It's just a convenient meeting place. Thank you very much, Mr. Schocken."

I wrenched the phone from her and heard Fowler Schocken's voice say: "Quite all right, my dear. The mystery is intriguing. Good-by." *Click.* She was quite clever enough to have faked a one-sided conversation, but had not. The voice was unmistakable. The memories it brought back of Board mornings with their brilliance of dialectic interplay, hard and satisfying hours of work climaxed with a "Well done!" and shrewd guidance through the intricacies of the calling overwhelmed me with nostalgia. I was almost home.

Silently and efficiently Kathy was shouldering the stargazer's limp body. Without a word she walked from the observatory. A door opened and closed.

The hell with her . . .

It was minutes before there was a jovial halloo in the voice of Fowler Schocken: "Kathy! Anybody home?"

"In here," I called.

Two of our Brink's men and Fowler Schocken came in. His

face went mottled purple. "Where's—" he began. And then: "You look like—*you are! Mitch!*" He grabbed me and waltzed me hilariously around the circular room while the guards dropped their jaws. "What kind of a trick was that to play on an old man? What's the story, boy? Where's Kathy?" He stopped, puffing even under moonweight.

"I've been doing some undercover work," I said. "I'm afraid I've got myself into some trouble. Would you call for more guards? We may have to stand off Luna City Inc.'s Burns men." Our Brink's men, who took an artisan's pride in their work, grinned happily at the thought.

"Sure, Mitch. Get it done," he said sidewise to the sergeant, who went happily to the phone. "Now what's all this about?"

"For the present," I said, "let's say it's been a field trip that went sour. Let's say I downgraded myself temporarily and voluntarily to assess Venus Section sentiment among the consumers—and I got stuck. Fowler, please let me beg off any more details. I'm in a bad way. Hungry, tired, scared, dirty."

"All right, Mitch. You know my policy. Find a good horse, give him his head, and back him to the limit. You've never let me down—and God knows I'm glad to see you around again. Venus Section can use you. Nothing's going right. The indices are down to 3.77 composite for North America when they should be 4.0 and rising. And turnover? God! I'm here recruiting, you know: a little raid on Luna City Inc., Moonmines, and the other outfits for some space-seasoned executives."

It was good to be home. "Who's heading it up?" I asked.

"I am. We rotated a few Board men through the spot and there wasn't any pickup. In spite of my other jobs I had to take over Venus Section direct. *Am* I glad to see you!"

"Runstead?"

"He's vice-ing for me, poor man. What's this jam you're in with the guards? Where's Kathy?"

"Please, later . . . I'm wanted for femicide and CB on Earth. Here I'm a suspicious character without clearance. Also I resisted arrest, clouted a guard, and damaged Luna City property."

He looked grave. "You know, I don't like the sound of CB," he said. "I assume there was a flaw in the contract?"

"Several," I assured him.

He brightened. "Then we'll pay off the fines on the rest of the stuff and fight the CB clear up to the Chamber of Commerce if we have to. What firm?"

"Chlorella Costa Rica."

"Hmm. Middling-sized, but solid. Excellent people, all of them. A pleasure to do business with."

Not from the bottom up, I thought, and said nothing.

"I'm sure they'll be reasonable. And if they aren't, I have a majority of the C of C in my pocket anyway. I ought to get something for my retainers, eh?" He dug me slyly in the ribs. His relief at getting Venus Section off his neck was overwhelming.

A dozen of our Brink's boys churned in. "That should do it," Fowler Schocken beamed. "Lieutenant, the Luna City Inc. Burns people may try to take Mr. Courtenay here away from us. We don't want that to happen, do we?"

"No, sir," said the lieutenant, dead-pan.

"Then let's go."

We strolled down Shopping One, amazing a few night-owl tourists. Shopping One gave way to Residential One, Two, and Three, and then to Commercial One.

"Hey, you!" a stray Burns patrolman called. We were in somewhat open order. Evidently he didn't realize that the Brink's men were my escort.

"Go play with your marbles, Punchy," a sergeant told him.

He went pale, but beeped his alarm, and went down in a tangle of fists and boots.

Burns patrolmen came bounding along the tunnel-like street in grotesque strides. Faces appeared in doorways. Our detail's weapons-squad leader said: "*Hup!*" and his boys began to produce barrels, legs, belts of ammo, and actions from their uniforms. Snap-snap-snap-snap-snap, and there were two machine guns mounted on the right tripod ready to rake both ends of the street. The Burns men braked grotesquely yards from us and stood unhappily, swinging their nightsticks.

Our lieutenant called out: "What seems to be the trouble, gentlemen?"

A Burns man called back: "Is that man George Groby?"

"Are you George Groby?" the lieutenant asked me.

"No. I'm Mitchell Courtenay."

"You hear him," the lieutenant called. The weapons men full-cocked their guns at a signal from the squad leader. The two clicks echoed from the vaulting, and the few last-ditch rubbernecks hanging from the doors vanished.

"Oh," said the Burns man weakly. "That's all right then. You can go ahead." He turned on the rest of the patrolmen. "Well? What are you dummies waiting for? Didn't you hear me?" They beat it, and we moved on down Commercial One, with the weapons men cradling their guns. The Fowler Schocken Associates Luna City Branch was 75 Commercial One, and we went in whistling. The weapons men mounted their guns in the lobby.

It was a fantastic performance. I had never seen its like. Fowler Schocken explained it as he led me down into the heart of the agency. "It's frontier stuff, Mitch. Something you've got to get into your copy. 'The Equalizer' is what they call it. A man's rank doesn't mean much up here. A well-drilled weapons squad is the law topside of the stratosphere. It's getting back to the elemental things of life, where a man's a man no matter how high his Social Security number."

We passed a door. "O'Shea's room," he said. "He isn't in yet, of course. The little man's out gathering rosebuds while he may—and the time isn't going to be long. The only Venus roundtripper. We'll lick that, won't we, Mitch?"

He showed me into a cubicle and lowered the bed with his own hands. "Cork off with these," he said, producing a sheaf of notes from his breast pocket. "Just some rough jottings for you to go over. I'll send in something to eat and some Coffiest. A good hour or two of work on them, and then the sound sleep of the just, eh?"

"Yes, Mr. Schocken."

He beamed at me and left, drawing the curtain. I stared glazedly at the rough jottings. "Six-color doubletrux. Downhold unsuccessful previous flights. Cite Learoyd 1959, Holden 1961, McGill 2002 et al heroic pioneers supreme sacrifice etc etc. *No* mention Myers-White flopperoo 2010 acct visibly exploded bfr passng moon orbit. Try get M-W taken out of newssheet files & history bks? Get cost estimate. Search archives for pix L H & McG. Shd be blond brunet & redhead.

Ships in backgrnd. Looming. Panting woman but heroic pioneers dedicated look in eye not interestd. Piquant bcs unavlbl . . ."

Thoughtfully, there was a pencil and copypaper in the cubicle. I began to write painfully: "We were ordinary guys. We liked the earth and the good things it gave us. The morning tang of Coffiest . . . the first drag on a Starr . . . the good feel of a sharp new Verily pinstripe suit . . . a warm smile from a girl in a bright spring dress—but they weren't enough. There were far places we had to see, things we had to know. The little guy's Learoyd. Nineteen fifty-nine. I'm Holden. Nineteen sixty-one. The redhead with the shoulders is McGill—twenty oh-two. Yes; we're dead. But we saw the far places and we learned what we had to learn before we died. Don't pity us; we did it for you. The long-hair astronomers could only guess about Venus. Poison gas, they said. Winds so hot they'd set your hair on fire and so strong they'd pick you up and throw you away. But they weren't sure. What do you do when you aren't sure? You go and see."

A guard came in with sandwiches and Coffiest. I munched and gulped with one hand and wrote with the other.

"We had good ships for those days. They packed us and enough fuel to get us there. What they didn't have was enough fuel to get us back. But don't pity us; we had to know. There was always the chance that the long-hairs were wrong, that we'd be able to get out, breathe clean air, swim in cool water—and then make fuel for the return trip with the good news. No; it didn't work out that way. It worked out that the long-hairs knew their stuff. Learoyd didn't wait to starve in his crate; he opened the hatch and breathed methane after writing up his log. My crate was lighter. The wind picked it up and broke it—and me with it. McGill had extra rations and a heavier ship. He sat and wrote for a week and then—well; it was pretty certain after two no-returns. He'd taken cyanide with him. But don't pity us. We went there and we saw it and in a way we sent back the news by not coming back ourselves. Now you folks know what to do and how to do it. You know the long-hairs weren't guessing. Venus is a mean lady and you've got to take the stuff and the know-how to tame her. She'll treat you right when you do. When you find us and our crates don't pity us. We did it for you. We knew you wouldn't let us down."

I was home again.

14

"PLEASE, Fowler," I said. "Tomorrow. Not today."

He gave me a steady look. "I'll go along, Mitch," he said. "I've never been a back-seat driver yet." He displayed one of the abilities that made him boss-man. He wiped clean out of his mind the burning curiosity about where I had been and what I had been doing. "That's good copy," he said, slapping my work of the previous night on his desk. "Clear it with O'Shea, won't you? He can give it some extra see-taste-smell-hear-feel if anybody can. And pack for return aboard the *Vilfredo Pareto*—I forgot. You haven't got anything to pack. Here's some scratch, and shop when you get a chance. Take a few of the boys with you, of course. The Equalizer—remember?" He twinkled at me.

I went to find O'Shea curled up like a cat in the middle of his full-sized bunk in the cubicle next to mine. The little man looked ravaged when he rolled over and stared blearily at me. "Mitch," he said thickly. " 'Nother goddam nightmare."

"Jack," I said persuasively. "Wake up, Jack."

He jerked bolt upright and glared at me. "What's the idea—? Hello, Mitch. I remember. Somebody said something when I got in 'smorning." He held his small head. "I'm dying," he said faintly. "Get me something, will you? My deathbed advice is this: don't ever be a hero. You're too nice a guy . . ."

The midget lapsed into torpor, swaying a little with each pulsebeat. I went to the kitchen and punched Coffiest, Thiamax, and a slice of Bredd. Halfway out, I returned, went to the bar, and punched two ounces of bourbon.

O'Shea looked at the tray and hiccuped. "What the hell's that stuff?" he said faintly, referring to the Coffiest, Thiamax, and Bredd. He shot down the bourbon and shuddered.

"Long time no see, Jack," I said.

"Ooh," he groaned. "Just what I needed. Why do clichés

add that extra something to a hang-over?" He tried to stand up to his full height of thirty-five inches and collapsed back onto the cot, his legs dangling. "My aching back," he said. "I think I'm going to enter a monastery. I'm living up to my reputation, and it's killing me by inches. Ooh, that tourist gal from Nova Scotia! It's springtime, isn't it? Do you think that explains anything? Maybe she has Eskimo blood."

"It's late fall," I said.

"Urp. Maybe she doesn't have a calendar . . . pass me that Coffiest." No "Please." And no "thank you." Just a cool, take-it-for-granted that the world was his for the asking. He had changed.

"Think you can do some work this morning?" I asked, a little stiffly.

"I might," he said indifferently. "This is Schocken's party after all. Say, what the hell ever became of you?"

"I've been investigating," I said.

"Seen Kathy?" he asked. "That's a wonderful girl you have there, Mitch." His smile might have been reminiscent. All I was sure of was that I didn't like it—not at all.

"Glad you enjoyed her," I said flatly. "Drop in any time." He sputtered into his Coffiest and said, carefully setting it down: "What's that work you mentioned?"

I showed him my copy. He gulped the Thiamax and began to steady on his course as he read.

"You got it all fouled up," he said at last, scornfully. "I don't know Learoyd, Holden, and McGill from so many holes in the ground, but like hell they were selfless explorers. You don't get *pulled* to Venus. You get *pushed*." He sat brooding, cross-legged.

"We're assuming they got pulled," I said. "If you like, we're trying to convince people that they got pulled. What we want from you is sense-impressions to sprinkle the copy with. Just talking off the front of your face, how do you resonate to it?"

"With nausea," he said, bored. "Would you reserve me a shower, Mitch? Ten minutes fresh, 100 degrees. Damn the cost. You too can be a celebrity. All you have to do is be lucky like me." He swung his short legs over the edge of the cot and contemplated his toes, six inches clear of the floor. "Well," he sighed, "I'm getting it while the getting's good."

"What about my copy?" I asked.

"See my reports," he said. "What about my shower?"

"See your valet," I said, and went out, boiling. In my own cubicle I sweated sense-impressions into the copy for a couple of hours and then picked up a guard squad to go shopping. There were no brushes with the patrolmen. I noticed that Warren Astron's shopfront now sported a chaste sign:

Dr. Astron Regrets That
Urgent Business
Has Recalled Him to Earth on
Short Notice

I asked one of our boys: "Has the *Ricardo* left?"

"Couple hours ago, Mr. Courtenay. Next departure's the *Pareto*, tomorrow."

So I could talk.

So I told Fowler Schocken the whole story.

And Fowler Schocken didn't believe a God-damned word of it.

He was nice enough and he tried not to hurt my feelings. "Nobody's blaming you, Mitch," he said kindly. "You've been through a great strain. It happens to us all, this struggle with reality. Don't feel you're alone, my boy. We'll see this thing through. There are times when anybody needs—help. My analyst—"

I'm afraid I yelled at him.

"Now, now," he said, still kind and understanding. "Just to pass the time—laymen shouldn't dabble in these things, but I think I know a thing or two about it and can discuss it objectively—let me try to explain—"

"Explain *this!*" I shouted at him, thrusting my altered Social Security tattoo under his nose.

"If you wish," he said calmly. "It's part of the whole pattern of your brief—call it a holiday from reality. You've been on a psychological bender. You got away from yourself. You assumed a new identity, and you chose one as far-removed from your normal, hard-working, immensely able self as possible. You chose the lazy, easy-going life of a scum-skimmer, drowsing in the tropic sun—"

I knew then who was out of touch with reality.

"Your horrible slanders against Taunton are crystal-clear to, ah, a person with some grasp of our unconscious drives. I was pleased to hear you voice them. They meant that you're halfway back to your real self. What is our central problem—the central problem of the real Mitchell Courtenay, copysmith? Lick the opposition! Crush the competing firms! Destroy them! Your fantasy about Taunton indicates to, ah, an informed person that you're struggling back to the real Mitchell Courtenay, copysmith. Veiled in symbols, obscured by ambivalent attitudes, the Taunton-fantasy is nevertheless clear. Your imagined encounter with the girl 'Hedy' might be a textbook example!"

"God damn it," I yelled, "look at my jaw! See that hole? It still hurts!"

He just smiled and said: "Let's be glad you did nothing worse to yourself, Mitch. The id, you see—"

"What about Kathy?" I asked hoarsely. "What about the complete data on the Consies I gave you? Grips, hailing signs, passwords, meeting places?"

"Mitch," he said earnestly, "as I say, I shouldn't be meddling, but they aren't real. Sexual hostility unleashed by the dissociation of your personality into 'Groby'-Courtenay identified your wife with a hate-and-fear object, the Consies. And 'Groby' carefully arranged things so that your Consie data is uncheckable and therefore unassailable. 'Groby' arranged for you—the *real* you—to withhold the imaginary 'data' until the Consies would have had a chance to change all that. 'Groby' was acting in self-defense. Courtenay was coming back and he knew it; 'Groby' felt himself being 'squeezed out.' Very well; he can bide his time. He arranged things so that he can make a comeback—"

"I'm not insane!"

"My analyst—"

"You've got to believe me!"

"These unconscious conflicts—"

"I tell you Taunton has killers!"

"Do you know what convinced me, Mitch?"

"What?" I asked bitterly.

"The fantasy of a Consie cell embedded in Chicken Little.

The symbolism—" he flushed a little, "well, it's quite unmistakable."

I gave up except on one point: "Do people still humor the insane, Mr. Schocken?"

"You're *not* insane, my boy. You need—help, like a lot of—"

"I'll be specific. Will you humor me in one respect?"

"Of course," he grinned, humoring me.

"Guard yourself and me too. Taunton has killers—all right; I think, or Groby thinks, or some damn body thinks that Taunton has killers. If you humor me to the extent of guarding yourself and me, I promise not to start swinging from the ceiling and gibbering. I'll even go to your analyst."

"All right," he smiled, humoring me.

Poor old Fowler. Who could blame him? His own dreamworld was under attack by every word I had to say. My story was blasphemy against the god of Sales. He couldn't believe it, and he couldn't believe that I—the real I—believed it. How could Mitchell Courtenay, copysmith, be sitting there and telling him such frightful things as:

> The interests of producers and consumers are not identical;
> Most of the world is unhappy;
> Workmen don't automatically find the job they do best;
> Entrepreneurs don't play a hard, fair game by the rules;
> The Consies are sane, intelligent, and well organized.

They were hammer-blows at him, but Fowler Schocken was nothing if not resilient. The hammer bounced right off and the dents it made were ephemeral. There was an explanation for everything and Sales could do no wrong. Therefore, Mitchell Courtenay, copysmith, was not sitting there telling him these things. It was Mitchell Courtenay's wicked, untamed id or the diabolic 'George Groby' or somebody—anybody but Courtenay.

In a dissociated fashion that would have delighted Fowler Schocken and his analyst I said to myself: "You know, Mitch, you're talking like a Consie."

I answered: "Why, so I am. That's terrible."

"Well," I replied, "I don't know about that. Maybe . . ."

"Yeah," I said thoughtfully. "Maybe . . ."

It's an axiom of my trade that things are invisible except against a contrasting background. Like, for instance, the opinions and attitudes of Fowler Schocken.

Humor me, Fowler, I thought. *Keep me guarded. I don't want to run into an ambivalent fantasy like Hedy again, ever. The symbolism may have been obvious, but she hurt me bad with her symbolic little needle.*

15

RUNSTEAD WASN'T there when our little procession arrived in executives' country of the Schocken Tower. There were Fowler, me, Jack O'Shea, secretaries—and the weapons squads I had demanded.

Runstead's secretary said he was down the hall, and we waited . . . and waited . . . and waited. After an hour I suggested that he wasn't coming back. After another hour word got to us that a body had been found smashed flat on the first setback of the Tower, hundreds of feet below. It was very, very difficult to identify.

The secretary wept hysterically and opened Runstead's desk and safe. Eventually we found a diary covering the past few months of Runstead's life. Interspersed with details of his work, his amours, memos for future campaigns, notes on good out-of-the-way restaurants, and the like were entries that said: "He was here again last night. He told me to hit harder on the shock-appeal. He scares me . . . He says the Starrzelius campaign needed guts. He scares *hell* out of me. Understand he used to scare everybody in the old days when he was alive . . . GWH again last night . . . *Saw him by daylight* first time. Jumped and yelled but nobody noticed. Wish he'd go away . . . GWH teeth seem bigger, pointier today. I ought to get help . . . He said I'm no good, disgrace to profession . . ."

After a while we realized that "he" was the ghost of George Washington Hill, father of our profession, founder of the singing commercial, shock-value, and God knows what else.

"Poor fellow," said Schocken, white-faced. "Poor, poor fellow. If only I'd known. If only he'd come to me in time."

The last entry said raggedly: "Told me I'm no good. I know I'm no good. Unworthy of the profession. They all know it. Can see it in their faces. Everybody knows it. He told them. Damn him. Damn him and his teeth. Damn—"

"Poor, poor fellow," said Schocken, almost sobbing. He turned to me and said: "You see? The strains of our profession . . ."

Sure I saw. A prefabricated diary and an unidentifiable splash of protoplasm. It might have been 180 pounds of Chicken Little down there on the first setback. But I would have been wasting my breath. I nodded soberly, humoring him.

I was restored to my job at the top of Venus Section. I saw Fowler's analyst daily. And I kept my armed guard. In tearful sessions the old man would say: "You must relinquish this symbol. It's all that stands between you and reality now, Mitch. Dr. Lawler tells me—"

Dr. Lawler told Fowler Schocken what I told Dr. Lawler. And that was the slow progress of my "integration." I hired a medical student to work out traumas for me backwards from the assumption that my time as a consumer had been a psychotic fugue, and he came up with some honeys. A few I had to veto as not quite consistent with my dignity, but there were enough left to make Dr. Lawler drop his pencil every once in a while. One by one we dug them up, and I have never been so bored in my life.

But one thing I would not surrender, and that was my insistence that my life and Fowler Schocken's life were in danger.

Fowler and I got closer and closer—a thing I've seen before. He thought he had made a convert. I was ashamed to string him along. He was being very good to me. But it was a matter of life or death. The rest was side show.

The day came when Fowler Schocken said gently: "Mitch, I'm afraid heroic measures are in order. I don't ask you to dispense with this fence of yours against reality. But *I* am going to dismiss *my* guards."

"They'll kill you, Fowler!" burst from me.

He shook his head gently. "You'll see. I'm not afraid." Argument was quite useless. After a bit of it, acting on sound psychological principles, he told the lieutenant of his office squad: "I won't be needing you any more. Please report with your men to Plant Security Pool for reassignment. Thank you very much for your loyalty and attention to detail during these weeks."

The lieutenant saluted, but he and his men looked sick. They were going from an easy job in executives' country to lobby patrol or night detail or mail guard or messenger service at ungodly hours. They filed out, and I knew Fowler Schocken's hours were numbered.

That night he was garroted on his way home by somebody who had slugged his chauffeur and substituted himself at the pedals of the Fowler Schocken Cadillac. The killer, apparently a near-moron, resisted arrest and was clubbed to death, giggling. His tattoo had been torn off; he was quite unidentifiable.

You can easily imagine how much work was done in the office the next day. There was a memorial Board meeting held and resolutions passed saying it was a dirty shame and a great profession never would forget and so on. Messages of condolence were sent by the other agencies, including Taunton's. I got some odd looks when I crumpled the Taunton message in my fist and used some very bad language. Commercial rivalry, after all, goes just so far. We're all gentlemen here, of course. A hard, clean fight and may the best agency win.

But no Board member paid it much mind. They all were thinking of just one thing: the Schocken block of voting shares.

Fowler Schocken Associates was capitalized at 7×10^{12} megabux, voting shares par at $M\$^2 0.1$, giving us 7×10^{13} shares. Of these, $3.5 \times 10^{13} + 1$ shares were purchasable only by employees holding AAAA labor contracts or better—roughly speaking, star class. The remaining shares by SEC order had been sold on the open market in order to clothe Fowler Schocken Associates with public interest. As customary, Fowler Schocken himself had through dummies snapped these up at the obscure stock exchanges where they had been put on sale.

In his own name he held a modest $.75 \times 10^{13}$ shares and distributed the rest with a lavish hand. I myself, relatively junior in spite of holding perhaps the number two job in the organization, had accumulated via bonuses and incentive pay only about $.857 \times 10^{12}$ shares. Top man around the Board table probably was Harvey Bruner. He was Schocken's oldest associate and had corralled $.83 \times 10^{13}$ shares over the years. (Nominally this gave him the bulge on Fowler—but he knew, of course, that in a challenge those other $3.5 \times 10^{13}+1$ shares would come rolling in on carloads of proxies, all backing Fowler with a mysterious unanimity. Besides, he was loyal.) He seemed to think he was heir-apparent, and some of the more naive Research and Development people were already sucking up to him, more fools they. He was an utterly uncreative, utterly honest wheel horse. Under his heavy hand the delicate thing that was Fowler Schocken Associates would disintegrate in a year.

If I were gambling, I would have given odds on Sillery, the Media chief, for copping the Schocken bloc and on down in descending order to myself, on whom I would have taken odds —long, long odds. That obviously was the way most of them felt, except the infatuated Bruner and a few dopes. You could tell. Sillery was surrounded by a respectful little court that doubtless remembered such remarks from Fowler as: "Media, gentlemen, is basic-basic!" and: "Media for brains, copysmiths for talent!" I was practically a leper at the end of the table, with my guards silently eyeing the goings-on. Sillery glanced at them once, and I could read him like a book: "*That's* been going on long enough; we'll knock off that eccentric first thing."

What we had been waiting for came about at last. "The gentlemen from the American Arbitration Association, Probate Section, are here, gentlemen."

They were of the funereal type, according to tradition. Through case-hardening or deficient senses of humor they refrained from giggling while Sillery gave them a measured little speech of welcome about their sad duty and how we wished we could meet them under happier circumstances and so on.

They read the will in a rapid mumble and passed copies around. The part I read first said: "To my dear friend and associate Mitchell Courtenay I bequeath and devise my ivory-inlaid oak finger-ring (inventory number 56,987) and my seventy-five shares of Sponsors' Stock in the Institute for the Diffusion of Psychoanalytic Knowledge, a New York Non-Profit Corporation, with the injunction that he devote his leisure hours to active participation in this organization and the furtherance of its noble aim." Well, Mitch, I told myself, you're through. I tossed the copy on the table and leaned back to take a swift rough inventory of my liquid assets.

"Hard lines, Mr. Courtenay," a brave and sympathetic research man I hardly knew told me. "Mr. Sillery seems pleased with himself."

I glanced at the bequest to Sillery—paragraph one. Sure enough, he got Fowler's personal shares and huge chunks of stock in Managerial Investment Syndicate, Underwriters Holding Corporation and a couple of others.

The research man studied my copy of the will. "If you don't mind my saying so, Mr. Courtenay," he told me, "the old man could have treated you better. I never heard of this outfit and I'm pretty familiar with the psychoanalytic field."

I seemed to hear Fowler chuckling nearby, and sat bolt upright. "Why the old so-and-so!" I gasped. It fitted like lock and key, with his bizarre sense of humor to oil the movement.

Sillery was clearing his throat and an instant silence descended on the Board room.

The great man spoke. "It's a trifle crowded here, gentlemen. I wish somebody would move that all persons other than Board members be asked to leave—"

I got up and said: "I'll save you the trouble, Sillery. Come on, boys. Sillery, I may be back." I and my guard left.

The Institute for the Diffusion of Psychoanalytic Knowledge, a New York Non-Profit Corporation, turned out to be a shabby three-room suite downtown in Yonkers. There was a weird old gal in the outer office pecking away at a typewriter. It was like something out of Dickens. A sagging rack held printed pamphlets with flyspecks on them.

"I'm from Fowler Schocken Associates," I told her.

She jumped. "Excuse me, sir! I didn't notice you. How is Mr. Schocken?"

I told her how he was, and she began to blubber. He was such a *good* man, giving so *generously* for the Cause. What on Earth would she and her poor brother ever do now? Poor Mr. Schocken! Poor her! Poor brother!

"All may not be lost," I told her. "Who's in charge here?" She sniffed that her brother was in the inner office. "Please break it to him gently, Mr. Courtenay. He's so delicate and sensitive—"

I said I would, and walked in. Brother was snoring-drunk, flopped over his desk. I joggled him awake, and he looked at me with a bleary and cynical eye. "Washawan?"

"I'm from Fowler Schocken Associates. I want to look at your books."

He shook his head emphatically. "Nossir. Only the old man himself gets to see the books."

"He's dead," I told him. "Here's the will." I showed him the paragraph and my identification.

"Well," he said. "The joy-ride's over. Or do you keep us going? You see what it says there, Mr. Courtenay? He enjoins you—"

"I see it," I told him. "The books, please."

He got them out of a surprising vault behind a plain door.

A mere three hours of backbreaking labor over them showed me that the Institute was in existence solely for holding and voting 56 per cent of the stock of an outfit called General Phosphate Reduction Corporation of Newark according to the whims of Fowler Schocken.

I went out into the corridor and said to my guards: "Come on, boys. Newark next."

I won't bore you with the details. It was single-tracked for three stages and then it split. One of the tracks ended two stages later in the Frankfort Used Machine Tool Brokerage Company, which voted 32 per cent of the Fowler Schocken Associates "public sale" stock. The other track forked again one stage later and wound up eventually in United Concessions Corp. and Waukegan College of Dentistry and Orthodontia, which voted the remainder.

Two weeks later on Board morning I walked into the Board room with my guards.

Sillery was presiding. He looked haggard and worn, as though he'd been up all night every night for the past couple of weeks looking for something.

"Courtenay!" he snarled. "I thought you understood that you were to leave your regiment outside!"

I nodded to honest, dumb old Harvey Bruner, whom I'd let

in on it. Loyal to Schocken, loyal to me, he bleated: "Mr. Chairman, I move that members be permitted to admit company plant-protection personnel assigned to them in such number as they think necessary for their bodily protection."

"Second the motion, Mr. Chairman," I said. "Bring them in, boys, will you?" My guards, grinning, began to lug in transfer cases full of proxies to me.

Eyes popped and jaws dropped as the pile mounted. It took a long time for them to be counted and authenticated. The final vote stood: For, 5.73×10^{13}; against, 1.27×10^{13}. All the Against votes were Sillery's and Sillery's alone. There were no abstentions. The others jumped to my side like cats on a griddle.

Loyal old Harve moved that chairmanship of the meeting be transferred to me, and it was carried unanimously. He then moved that Sillery be pensioned off, his shares of voting stock to be purchased at par by the firm and deposited in the bonus fund. Carried unanimously. Then—a slash of the whip just to remind them—he moved that one Thomas Heatherby, a junior Art man who had sucked up outrageously to Sillery, be downgraded from Board level and deprived without compensation of his minute block of voting shares. Carried unanimously. Heatherby didn't even dare scream about it. Half a loaf is better than none, he may have said to himself, choking down his anger.

It was done. I was master of Fowler Schocken Associates. And I had learned to despise everything for which it stood.

16

"FLASH-FLASH, Mr. Courtenay," said my secretary's voice. I hit the GA button.

"Consie arrested Albany on neighbor's denunciation. Shall I line it up?"

"God-damn it!" I exploded. "How many times do I have to give you standing orders? Of course you line it up. Why the hell not?"

She quavered: "I'm sorry, Mr. Courtenay—I thought it was kind of far out—"

"Stop thinking, then. Arrange the transportation." Maybe I shouldn't have been so rough on her—but I wanted to find Kathy, if I had to turn every Consie cell in the country upside down to do it. I had driven Kathy into hiding—out of fear that I would turn her in—now I wanted to get her back.

An hour later I was in the Upstate Mutual Protective Association's HQ. They were a local outfit that had a lot of contracts in the area, including Albany. Their board chairman himself met me and my guards at the elevator. "An honor," he burbled. "A great, great honor, Mr. Courtenay, and what may I do for you?"

"My secretary asked you not to get to work on your Consie suspect until I arrived. Did you?"

"Of course not, Mr. Courtenay! Some of the employees may have roughed him up a little, informally, but he's in quite good shape."

"I want to see him."

He led the way, anxiously. He was hoping to get in a word that might grow into a cliency with Fowler Schocken Associates, but was afraid to speak up.

The suspect was sitting on a stool under the usual dazzler. He was a white-collar consumer of thirty or so. He had a couple of bruises on his face.

"Turn that thing off," I said.

A square-faced foreman said: "But we always—" One of my guards, without wasting words, shoved him aside and switched off the dazzler.

"It's all right, Lombardo," the board chairman said hastily. "You're to co-operate with these gentlemen."

"Chair," I said, and sat down facing the suspect. I told him: "My name's Courtenay. What's yours?"

He looked at me with pupils that were beginning to expand again. "Fillmore," he said, precisely. "August Fillmore. Can you tell me what all this is about?"

"You're suspected of being a Consie."

There was a gasp from all the UMPA people in the room. I was violating the most elementary principle of jurisprudence by informing the accused of the nature of his crime. I knew all about that, and didn't give a damn.

"Completely ridiculous," Fillmore spat. "I'm a respectable

married man with eight children and another coming along. Who on earth told you people such nonsense?"

"Tell him who," I said to the board chairman.

He stared at me, goggle-eyed, unable to believe what he had heard. "Mr. Courtenay," he said at last, "with all respect, I can't take the responsibility for such a thing! It's quite unheard of. The entire body of law respecting the rights of informers—"

"I'll take the responsibility. Do you want me to put it in writing?"

"No, no, no, no, no! Nothing like that! Please, Mr. Courtenay—suppose I tell the informer's name to you, understanding that you know the law and are a responsible person—and then I leave the room?"

"Any way you want to do it is all right with me."

He grinned placatingly, and whispered in my ear: "A Mrs. Worley. The two families share a room. Please be careful, Mr. Courtenay—"

"Thanks," I said. He gathered eyes like a hostess and nervously retreated with his employees.

"Well, Fillmore," I told the suspect, "he says it's Mrs. Worley."

He began to swear, and I cut him off. "I'm a busy man," I said. "You know your goose is cooked, of course. You know what Vogt says on the subject of conservation?"

The name apparently meant nothing to him. "Who's that?" he asked distractedly.

"Never mind. Let's change subjects. I have a lot of money. I can set up a generous pension for your family while you're away if you co-operate and admit you're a Consie."

He thought hard for a few moments and then said: "Sure I'm a Consie. What of it? Guilty or innocent, I'm sunk so why not say so?"

"If you're such a red-hot Consie, suppose you quote me some passages from Osborne?"

He had never heard of Osborne, and slowly began to fake: "Well, there's the one that starts: 'A Consie's first duty, uh, is to, to prepare for a general uprising—' I don't remember the rest, but that's how it starts."

"Pretty close," I told him. "Now how about your cell meetings? Who-all's there?"

"I don't know them by name," he said more glibly. "We go by numbers. There's a dark-haired fellow, he's the boss, and, uh—"

It was a remarkable performance. It certainly, however, had nothing to do with the semi-mythical Conservationist heroes, Vogt and Osborne, whose books were required reading in all cells—when copies could be found.

We left.

I told the board chairman, hovering anxiously outside in the corridor: "I don't think he's a Consie."

I was president of Fowler Schocken Associates and he was only the board chairman of a jerkwater local police outfit, but *that* was too much. He drew himself up and said with dignity: "We administer justice, Mr. Courtenay. And an ancient, basic tenet of justice is: 'Better that one thousand innocents suffer unjustly than one guilty person be permitted to escape.'"

"I am aware of the maxim," I said. "Good day."

My instrument corporal went *boing* as the crash-crash priority signal sounded in his ear and handed me the phone. It was my secretary back in Schocken Tower, reporting another arrest, this one in Pile City Three, off Cape Cod.

We flew out to Pile City Three, which was rippling that day over a long, swelling sea. I hate the Pile Cities—as I've said, I suffer from motion sickness.

This Consie suspect turned out to be a professional criminal. He had tried a smash-and-grab raid on a jewelry store, intending to snatch a trayful of oak and mahogany pins, leaving behind a lurid note all about Consie vengeance and beware of the coming storm when the Consies take over and kill all the rich guys. It was intended to throw off suspicion.

He was very stupid.

It was a Burns-protected city, and I had a careful chat with their resident manager. He admitted first that most of their Consie arrests during the past month or so had been like that, and then admitted that *all* their Consie arrests for the past month or so had been like that. Formerly they had broken up authentic Consie cells at the rate of maybe one a week. He thought maybe it was a seasonal phenomenon.

From there we went back to New York, where another Consie had been picked up. I saw him and listened to him rant for a few minutes. He was posted on Consie theory and could quote you Vogt and Osborne by the page. He also asserted that God had chosen him to wipe the wastrels from the face of Mother Earth. He said of course he was in the regular Consie organization, but he would die before he gave up any of its secrets. And I knew he certainly would, because he didn't know any. The Consies wouldn't have accepted anybody that unstable if they were down to three members with one sinking fast.

We went back to Schocken Tower at sunset, and my guard changed. It had been a lousy day. It had been, as far as results were concerned, a carbon copy of all the days I had spent since I inherited the agency.

There was a meeting scheduled. I didn't want to go, but my conscience troubled me when I thought of the pride and confidence Fowler Schocken must have felt in me when he made me his heir. Before I dragged myself to the Board room I checked with a special detail I had set up in the Business Espionage section.

"Nothing, sir," my man said. "No leads whatsoever on your—on Dr. Nevin. The tracer we had on the Chlorella personnel man petered out. Uh, shall we keep trying—?"

"Keep trying," I said. "If you need a bigger appropriation or more investigators, don't hesitate. Do me a real job."

He swore loyalty and hung up, probably thinking that the boss was an old fool, mooning over a wife—not even permanently married to him—who had decided to slip out of the picture. What he made out of the others I had asked him to trace, I didn't know. All I knew was that they had vanished, all my few contacts with the Consies picked up in Costa Rica, the sewers of New York, and on the Moon. Kathy had never come back to her apartment or the hospital, Warren Astron had never returned to his sucker-trap on Shopping One, my Chlorella cellmates had vanished into the jungle—and so it went, all down the line.

Board meeting.

"Sorry to be late, gentlemen. I'll dispense with opening remarks. Charlie, how's Research and Development doing on the Venus question?"

He got up. "Mr. Courtenay, gentlemen, in my humble way I think I can say, informally, that R. and D. is in there punching and that my boys are a credit to Fowler Schocken Associates. Specifically, we've licked the greenhouse effect. *Quantitatively.* Experiments in vitro have confirmed the predictions of our able physical chemistry and thermodynamics section based on theory and math. A CO_2 blanket around Venus at forty thousand feet, approximately .05 feet thick, will be self-sustaining and self-regulating, and will moderate surface temperatures some five degrees a year, steadying at eighty to eighty-five degrees. We're exploring now the various ways this enormous volume of gas can be obtained and hurled at high velocity into the stratosphere of Venus. Considered broadly, we can find the CO_2, or manufacture it, or both. I say, find it. Volcanic activity is present, but your typical superficial Venus eruption would seem to be liquid NH_4 compressed by gravity in crevices until it seeps to a weaker formation through faults and porous rock and then blows its top. We are certain, however, that deep drilling would tap considerable reservoirs of liquid CO_2—"

"How certain?" I asked.

"Quite certain, Mr. Courtenay," he said, hardly able to suppress the you-couldn't-be-expected-to-understand smile that technical people give you. "Phase-rule analysis of the O'Shea reports—"

I interrupted again. "Would you go to Venus on the strength of that certainty, other things being equal?"

"Certainly," he said, a little offended. "Shall I go into the technical details?"

"No thanks, Charlie. Continue as before."

"Hrrmp. So—at present we are wrapping up the greenhouse-effect phase in two respects. We are preparing a maximum-probability map of drilling sites, and we are designing a standard machine for unattended deep drilling. My policy on the design is cheapness, self-power, and remote control. I trust this is satisfactory?"

"Very much so. Thank you, Charlie. One point, though. If the stuff is there and if it's abundant, we have a prospect of trouble. If it's *too* abundant and easy to get at, it might become feasible for Venus to export liquid CO_2 to Earth—which we definitely do not want. CO_2 is in good supply here, and no purpose would be served by underselling the earthside producers of it. Let's bear in mind always that Venus is going to pay its way with raw materials in short supply on Earth, and is not going to compete pricewise with the mother planet. Iron, yes. Nitrates, emphatically yes. We'll pay them a good enough price for such things to keep them buying earthside products and enable them to give earthside bankers, insurance companies, and carrying trade their business. But never forget that Venus is there for us to exploit, and don't ever get it turned around. I want you, Charlie, to get together with Auditing and determine whether tapping underground CO_2 pools will ever make it possible for Venus to deliver CO_2 F.O.B. New York at a competitive price. If it does, your present plans are *out*. You'll have to get your greenhouse-effect blanketing gas by manufacturing it in a more expensive way."

"Right, Mr. Courtenay," Charlie said, scribbling busily.

"Right. Does anybody else have anything special on the Venus program before we go on?"

Bernhard, our comptroller, stuck his hand up, and I nodded.

"Question about Mr. O'Shea," he rumbled. "We're carrying him as a consultant at a very healthy figure. I've been asking around—and I hope I haven't been going offside, Mr. Courtenay, but it's my job—I've been asking around and I find that we've been getting damn-all consultation from him. Also, I should mention that he's drawn heavily in recent weeks on retainers not yet due. If we canned—if we severed our connection with him at this time, he'd be owing us money. Also—well, this is trivial, but it gives you an idea. The girls in my department are complaining about his annoying them."

My eyebrows went up. "I think we should hang on to him for whatever prestige rubs off, Ben, though his vogue does seem to be passing. Give him an argument about further advances. And as for the girls—well, I'm surprised. I thought they didn't complain when he made passes at them."

"Seen him lately?" grunted Bernhard.

No; I realized I hadn't.

The rest of the meeting went fast.

Back in my office I asked my night-shift secretary whether O'Shea was in the building, and if so to send for him.

He came in smelling of liquor and complaining loudly. "Damn it, Mitch, enough is enough! I just stepped in to pick up one of the babes for the night and you grab me. Aren't you taking this consultation thing too seriously? You've got my name to use; what more do you want?"

He looked like hell. He looked like a miniature of the fat, petulant, shabby Napoleon I at Elba. But a moment after he had come in I suddenly couldn't think of anything but Kathy. It took me a moment to figure out.

"Well?" he demanded. "What are you staring at? Isn't my lipstick on straight?"

The liquor covered it up some, but a little came through: *Ménage à Deux*, the perfume I'd had created for Kathy and Kathy alone when we were in Paris, the stuff she loved and sometimes used too much of. I could hear her saying: "I can't help it, darling; it's *so* much nicer than formalin, and that's what I usually smell of after a day at the hospital . . ."

"Sorry, Jack," I said evenly. "I didn't know it was your howling-night. It'll keep. Have fun."

He grimaced and left, almost waddling on his short legs.

I grabbed my phone and slammed a connection through to my special detail in Business Espionage. "Put tails on Jack O'Shea," I snapped. "He's leaving the building soon. Tail him and tail everybody he contacts. Night and day. If I hit paydirt on this you and your men get upgraded and bonused. But God help you if you pull a butch."

17

I GOT SO nobody dared to come near me. I couldn't help myself. I was living for one thing only: the daily reports from the tails on O'Shea. Anything else I tried to handle bored and irritated me to distraction.

After a week there were twenty-four tails working at a time on O'Shea and people with whom he had talked. They were headwaiters, his lecture agent, girls, an old test-pilot friend of his stationed at Astoria, a cop he got into a drunken argument with one night—but was he really drunk and was it really an argument?—and other unsurprising folk.

One night, quietly added to the list was: "Consumer, female, about 30, 5'4", 102 lbs., redhead, eyes not seen, cheaply dressed.

Subject entered Hash Heaven (restaurant) 1837 after waiting 14 minutes outside and went immediately to table waited on by new contact, which table just vacated by party. Conjecture: subject primarily interested in waitress. Ordered hash, ate very lightly, exchanged few words with contact. Papers may have been passed but impossible to observe at tailing distance. Female operative has picked up contact."

About thirty, five-four, one-twenty. It could be. I phoned to say: "Bear down on that one. Rush me everything new that you get. How about finding out more from the restaurant?"

Business Espionage began to explain, with embarrassment, that they'd do it if I insisted, but that it wasn't good technique. Usually the news got to the person being tailed and—

"Okay," I said. "Do it your way."

"Hold it a minute, Mr. Courtenay, please. Our girl just checked in—the new contact went home to the Taunton Building. She has Stairs 17–18 on the Thirty-fifth floor."

"What's the thirty-fifth?" I asked, heavy-hearted.

"For couples."

"Is she—?"

"She's unattached, Mr. Courtenay. Our girl pretended to apply for the vacancy. They told her Mrs. 17 is holding 18 for the arrival of her husband. He's upstate harvesting."

"What time do the stairs close at Taunton's?" I demanded.

"2200, Mr. Courtenay."

I glanced at my desk clock. "Call your tail off her," I said. "That's all for now."

I got up and told my guards: "I'm going out without you, gentlemen. Please wait here. Lieutenant, can I borrow your gun?"

"Of course, Mr. Courtenay." He passed over a .25 UHV. I checked the magazine and went out on foot, alone.

As I left the lobby of Schocken Tower a shadowy young man detached himself from the wall and drifted after me. I crossed him up by walking in the deserted street, a dark, narrow slit between the mighty midtown buildings. Monoxide and smog hung heavily in the unconditioned air, but I had antisoot plugs. He did not. I heard him wheeze at a respectable distance behind me. An occasional closed cab whizzed past us, the driver puffing and drawn as he pumped the pedals.

Without looking back I turned the corner of Schocken Tower and instantly flattened against the wall. My shadow drifted past and stopped in consternation, peering into the gloom.

I slammed the long barrel of the pistol against the back of his neck in a murderous rabbit punch and walked on. He was probably one of my own men; but I didn't want anybody's men along.

I got to the Taunton Building's night-dweller entrance at 2159. Behind me the timelock slammed the door. There was an undersized pay elevator. I dropped in a quarter, punched 35, and read notices while it creaked upward. "NIGHT-DWELLERS ARE RESPONSIBLE FOR THEIR OWN POLICING. MANAGEMENT ASSUMES NO RESPONSIBILITY FOR THEFTS, ASSAULTS, OR RAPES." "NIGHT-DWELLERS WILL NOTE THAT BARRIERS ARE UPPED AT 2210 NIGHTLY AND ARRANGE THEIR CALLS OF NATURE ACCORDINGLY." "RENT IS DUE AND PAYABLE NIGHTLY IN ADVANCE AT THE AUTOCLERK." "MANAGEMENT RESERVES THE RIGHT TO REFUSE RENTAL TO PATRONS OF STARRZELIUS PRODUCTS."

The door opened on the stairwell of the thirty-fifth floor. It was like looking into a maggoty cheese. People, men and women, squirming uneasily, trying to find some comfort before the barriers upped. I looked at my watch and saw: 2208.

I picked my way carefully and very, very slowly in the dim light over and around limbs and torsos, with many apologies, counting . . . at the seventeenth step I stepped over a huddled figure as my watch said: 2210.

With a rusty clank, the barriers upped, cutting off steps seventeen and eighteen, containing me and—

She sat up, looking scared and angry, with a small pistol in her hand.

"Kathy," I said.

She dropped the pistol. "Mitch. You fool." Her voice was low and urgent. "What are you doing here? They haven't given up, they're still out to murder you—"

"I know all that," I said. "I'm grandstanding, Kathy. I'm putting my head into the lion's mouth to show you I mean it when I say that you're right and I was wrong."

"How did you find me?" she asked suspiciously.

"Some of your perfume came off on O'Shea. *Ménage à Deux.*"

She looked around at the cramped quarters and giggled. "It certainly is, isn't it?"

"The heat's off, Kathy," I told her. "I'm not just here to paw you, with or without your consent. I'm here to tell you that I'm on your side. Name it and you can have it."

She looked at me narrowly and asked: "Venus?"

"It's yours."

"Mitch," she said, "if you're lying—if you're lying—"

"You'll know by tomorrow if we get out of here alive. Until then there's nothing more to be said about it, is there? We're in for the night."

"Yes," she said. "We're in for the night." And then, suddenly, passionately: "God, how I've missed you!"

Wake-up whistles screamed at 0600. They were loaded with skull-rattling subsonics, just to make sure that no slugabeds would impede the morning evacuation.

Kathy began briskly to stow away the bedding in the stairs. "Barriers down in five minutes," she snapped. She lifted Stair seventeen's lid and fished around in it for a flat box that opened into a make-up kit. "Hold still."

I yelped as a razor raked across the top of my right eyebrow. "Hold—*still!*" R-R-R-R-ip! It cut a swathe across my left eyebrow. Briskly she touched my face here and there with mysterious brushes.

"Flup!" I said as she turned up my upper lip and tucked a pledget of plastic under it. Two gummy wads pasted my ears against my head and she said: "There," and showed me the mirror.

"Good," I told her. "I got out of here once in the morning rush. I think we can do it again."

"There go the barriers," she said tensely, hearing some preliminary noise that was lost on my inexperienced ear.

The barriers clanged down. We were the only night-dwellers left on the thirty-fifth floor. But we were not alone. B. J. Taunton and two of his boys stood there. Taunton was swaying a little on his feet, red-faced and grinning. Each of his boys had a machine pistol trained on me.

Taunton hiccuped and said: "This was a hell of an unfortunate place for you to go chippy-chasing, Courtenay, ol' man.

We have a photo-register for gate-crashers like you. Girlie, if you will kindly step aside—"

She didn't step aside. She stepped right into Taunton's arms, jamming her gun against his navel. His red face went the color of putty. "You know what to do," she said grimly.

"Boys," he said faintly, "drop the guns. For God's sake, drop them!"

They exchanged looks. "*Drop them!*" he begged.

They took an eternity to lay down their machine pistols, but they did. Taunton began to sob.

"Turn your backs," I told them, "and lie down." I had my borrowed UHV out. It felt wonderful.

The elevator could too easily have been flooded with gas. We walked down the stairs. It was a long, slow, careful business, though all night-dwellers had been cleared hours ago for B.J.'s coup. He sobbed and babbled all the way. At the tenth-floor landing he wailed: "I've got to have a drink, Courtenay. I'm dying. There's a bar right here, you can keep that gun on me—"

Kathy laughed humorlessly at the idea, and we continued our slow step-by-step progress.

At the night-dweller exit I draped my coat over Kathy's gun hand in spite of the winter outside. "It's all right!" B.J. called quaveringly to an astounded lobby guard who started our way. "These people are friends of mine. It's quite all right!"

We walked with him to the shuttlemouth and dived in, leaving him, gray-faced and sweating, in the street. It was safety in numbers. The only way he could get at us was by blowing up the entire shuttle, and he wasn't equipped for it. We zigzagged for an hour, and I called my office from a station phone. A plant protection detail rendezvoused with us at another station, and we were in the Schocken Tower fifteen minutes later.

A morning paper gave us our only laugh so far that day. It said, among other things, that a coolant leak had been detected at 0300 today in the stairwell of the Taunton Building. B. J. Taunton himself, at the risk of his life, had supervised the evacuation of the Taunton Building night-dwellers in record time and without casualties.

Over a tray breakfast on my desk I told Kathy: "Your hair looks like hell. Does that stuff wash out?"

"Enough of this lovemaking," she said. "You told me I could

have Venus. Mitch, I meant it. And Venus by-God belongs to us. We're the only people who know what to do with it and also we landed the first man there. O'Shea is one of us, Mitch."

"Since when?"

"Since his mother and father found he wasn't growing, that's since when. They knew the W.C.A. was going to need space-pilots soon—and the smaller the better. Earth didn't discover Venus. The W.C.A. did. And we demand the right to settle it. Can you deliver?"

"Sure," I said. "God, it's going to be a headache. We have our rosters filled now—eager suckers itching to get to Venus and be exploited by and for the Earth and Fowler Schocken. Well, I'll backtrack."

I punched the intercom to R. & D. "Charlie!" I said. "About the CO_2 competition with Earth producers. Forget about it. I've found that Taunton's bills most of the makers."

"Sure, Mr. Courtenay," Charlie said happily. "The preliminary work looks as if we'll give them a real kick in the groin."

I said to Kathy: "Can you bring Runstead back to life for me? I don't know where the W.C.A. has been holding him, but we need him here. This is going to be a job. A copysmith's highest art is to convince people without letting them know that they're being convinced. What I've got to do is make my copysmiths unconvince people without letting either the copysmiths or the people know what I'm doing to them. I can use some high-grade help that I can talk freely to."

"It can be arranged," she said, kissing me lightly. "That's for saying 'We.'"

"Huh?" I said. "Did I say 'we'?" Then I understood. "Oh. Look, darling, I've got a dandy executive's living suite, twelve by twelve, upstairs. You had a hard night. Suppose you head upstairs and cork off for a while. I've got a lot of work to do."

She kissed me again and said: "Don't work too hard, Mitch. I'll see you tonight."

18

I COULDN'T have done it without Runstead—not in time. He came whistling back from Chi, where he'd been holed up since he pretended suicide, in response to an underground message from Kathy. He arrived in the middle of a Board meeting; we shook hands and the Board cheerfully swallowed the story that he'd dropped out of sight to do some secret work. After all, they'd swallowed it once before. He knew what the job was; he sank his teeth in it.

Consie or no Consie, I still thought Runstead was a rat.

But I had to admit things were leaping.

On the surface level, Fowler Schocken Associates had launched a giant all-client slogan contest, with fifteen hundred first prizes—all of them a berth on the Venus rocket. There were eight hundred thousand prizes in all, but the others didn't matter. Judging was turned over to an impartial firm of contest analyzers, which turned out to be headed by the brother-in-law of a friend of Runstead's. Only fourteen hundred of the prize winners, Matt told me, were actually members of the Consie underground. The other hundred were dummy names entirely, to take care of last minute emergencies.

I took Kathy with me to Washington to spark the final clearance of the rocket for flight, while Runstead minded the baby back in New York. I'd been in Washington often enough for a luncheon or an afternoon, but this was going to be a two-day job; I looked forward to it like a kid. I parked Kathy at the hotel and made her promise not to do any solo sight-seeing, then caught a cab to the State Department. A morose little man in a bowler hat was waiting in the anteroom; when he heard my name he got up hastily and offered me his seat. Quite a change from the Chlorella days, Mitch, old boy, I told myself. Our attaché came flustering out to greet me; I calmed him and explained what I wanted.

"Easiest thing in the world, Mr. Courtenay," he promised. "I'll get the enabling bill put through committee this afternoon, and with any luck at all it'll clear both houses tonight."

I said expansively, "Fine. Need any backing?"

"Oh, I don't think so, Mr. Courtenay. Might be nice for you

to address the House in the morning, if you can find the time. They'd love to hear from you, and it would smooth things over a little for a quick passage."

"Glad to," I said, reaching down for my bag. The man in the bowler hat beat me to it and handed it to me with a little bow. "Just set your time, Abels," I told the legate. "I'll be there."

"Thank you very *much*, Mr. Courtenay!" He opened the door for me. The little man said tentatively:

"Mr. Abels?"

The legate shook his head. "You can see how busy I am," he said, not unkindly. "Come back tomorrow."

The little man smiled gratefully and followed me out the door. We both hailed a cab, and he opened the door for me. You know what cabs are like in Washington. "Can I drop you anywhere?" I asked.

"It's very good of you," he said, and followed me in. The driver leaned back on his pedals and looked in at us.

I told him: "The Park Starr for me. But drop this other gentleman off first."

"Sure." The driver nodded. "White House, Mr. President?"

"Yes, please," said the little man. "I can't tell you how pleased I am to meet you, Mr. Courtenay," he went on. "I overheard your conversation with Mr. Abels, you know. It was very interesting to hear that the Venus rocket is so near completion. Congress has pretty well got out of the habit of keeping me posted on what's going on. Of course, I know they're busy with their investigations and all. But—" He smiled. Mischievously, he said: "I entered your contest, Mr. Courtenay. My slogan was, 'I'm starry-eyed over Starrs, verily I am.' I don't suppose I could have gone along though, even if I'd won."

I said very sincerely: "I can't see how it would have been possible." And, a little less sincerely, "Besides, they must keep you pretty busy right here."

"Oh, not particularly. January's heavy; I convene Congress, you see, and they read me the State of the Union message. But the rest of the year passes slowly. Will you really address Congress tomorrow, Mr. Courtenay? It would mean a joint session, and they usually let me come for that."

"Be delighted to have you," I said cordially.

The little man had a warm smile, glinting through his glasses.

The cab stopped and the President shook my hand warmly and got out. He poked his head in the door. "Uh," he said, looking apprehensively at the driver, "you've been swell. I may be stepping out of line in saying this, but if I might make a suggestion—I understand something about astronomy, it's a kind of hobby, and I hope you won't delay the ship's take-off past the present conjunction."

I stared. Venus was within ten degrees of opposition and was getting farther away—not that it mattered, since most of the trip would be coasting anyhow.

He held a finger to his lips. "Good-by, sir," he said. I spent the rest of the trip staring at the backs of the driver's hairy ears, and wondering what the little man had been driving at.

We took the evening off, Kathy and I, to see the sights. I wasn't too much impressed. The famous cherry blossoms were beautiful, all right, but, with my new-found Conservationist sentiments, I found them objectionably ostentatious. "A dozen would have been plenty," I objected. "Scattering them around in vase after vase this way is a plain waste of the taxpayer's money. You know what they'd cost in Tiffany's?"

Kathy giggled. "Mitch, Mitch," she said. "Wait till we take over Venus. Did you ever think of what it's going to be like to have a whole *planet* to grow things in? Acres and acres of flowers—trees—everything?"

A plump schoolteacher-type leaning on the railing beside us straightened up, glared, sniffed, and walked away. "You're giving us a bad name," I told Kathy. "Before you get us in trouble, let's go to—let's go back to the hotel."

I woke up to an excited squeal from Kathy. "Mitch," she was saying from the bathroom, two round eyes peering wonderingly over the towel that was draped around her, "they've got a *tub* here! I opened the door to the shower stall, and it wasn't a stall at all! Can I, Mitch? Please?"

There are times when even an honest conservationist finds pleasure in being the acting head of Fowler Schocken Associates. I yawned and blew her a kiss and said, "Sure. And—make it all fresh water, hear?"

Kathy pretended to faint, but I noticed that she wasted no

time calling room service. While the tub was filling I dressed. We breakfasted comfortably and strolled to the Capitol hand in hand.

I found Kathy a seat in the pressbox and headed for the floor of the House. Our Washington lobby chief pushed through the crowd to me. He handed me a strip of facsimile paper. "It's all here, Mr. Courtenay," he said. "Uh—is everything all right?"

"Everything's just fine," I told him. I waved him off and looked at the facsimile. It was from Dicken, on the scene at the rocket:

> Passengers and crew alerted and on standby. First movement into ship begins at 1145 EST, loading completed by 1645 EST. Ship fully fueled, supplied, and provisioned since 0915. Security invoked but MIA, CIC, and Time-Life known to have filed coded dispatches through dummies. Chartroom asks please remind you: Take-off possible only in AM hours.

I rubbed the tape between my palms; it disintegrated into ash. As I climbed to the podium, someone tugged at my elbow. It was the President, leaning out of his ceremonial box. "Mr. Courtenay," he whispered, his smile masklike on his face, "I guess you understood what I was trying to tell you yesterday in the cab. I'm glad the rocket's ready. And—" he widened his grin and bobbed his head in the precise manner of a statesman exchanging inconsequentialities with a distinguished visitor, "you probably know this, but—he's here."

I had no chance to find out who "he" was. As the Speaker of the House came toward me hand outstretched and the applause started from the floor, I forced a smile to my face. But it was a trick of the rictus muscles entirely. I had little to smile about, if the news about the Venus rocket had trickled down to the President.

Fowler Schocken was a pious old hypocrite and Fowler Schocken was a grinning fraud, but if it hadn't been for Fowler Schocken I could never have got through that speech. I could hear his voice in my ears: "Sell 'em, Mitch; you can sell them if you'll keep in mind that they *want* to buy." And I sold the assembled legislators precisely what they wanted to own. I touched briefly on American enterprise and the home; I offered them a world to loot and a whole plunderable universe beyond it, once Fowler Schocken's brave pioneers had opened the way for it; I gave them a picture of assembly-line planets owned and operated by our very selves, the enterprising American businessmen who had made civilization great. They loved it. The applause was fantastic.

As the first waves died down, there were a dozen standing figures in the hall, clapping their hands and begging the chair for recognition. I hardly noticed; astonishingly, Kathy was gone from the pressbox. The Speaker selected white-haired old Colbee, lean and dignified with his four decades of service.

"The chair recognizes the gentleman from Yummy-Cola."

"Thank you very much, Mr. Speakuh." Colbee's face wore a courtly smile; but his eyes seemed to me the eyes of a snake. Yummy-Cola was nominally one of the few big independents; but I remembered that Fowler had commented once on their captive agency's surprising closeness to Taunton. "If I may ventuah to speak for the Upper Chamber, I should like to thank ouah distinguished guest for his very well-chosen remarks heah. I am certain that we all have enjoyed listening to a man of his calibeh and standing." Go back to the Berlitz school, you Westchester phony, I thought bitterly. I could feel the wienie coming as Colbee rumbled on. "With the permission of the chair, I should like to ask ouah guest a number of questions involving the legislation we have been asked to consider heah today." *Consider* indeed, you bastard, I thought. By now even the galleries had caught on to what was happening. I hardly needed to hear the rest:

"It may have escaped youah attention, but we are fortunate in having with us another guest. I refer of course to Mr. Taunton." He waved gracefully to the visitor's gallery, where B.J.'s red face appeared between two stolid figures that I should have recognized at the first moment as his bodyguards. "In a brief discussion before ouah meeting heah, Mr. Taunton was good enough to give me some information which I would like Mr. Co'tenay to comment upon. First—" the snake eyes were steel now, "I would ask Mr. Co'tenay if the name of George Groby, wanted for Contract Breach and Femicide, is familiar to him. Second, I would like to ask if Mr. Co'tenay *is* Mr. Groby. Third, I would like to ask Mr. Co'tenay if there is any truth to the repo't, given me in confidence by someone in whom Mr.

Taunton assures me I can repose absolute trust, that Mr. Co'tenay is a membeh in good standing of the World Conservation Association, known to most of us who are loyal Amurricans as—"

Even Colbee himself could not have heard the last words of his sentence. The uproar was like a physical blast.

19

SEEN IN retrospect, everything that happened in the next wild quarter of an hour blurs and disappears like the shapes in a spinning kaleidoscope. But I remember tableaux, frozen moments of time that seem almost to have no relation to each other:

The waves of contempt and hatred that flowed around me, the contorted face of the President below me, screaming something unheard to the sound engineer in his cubicle, the wrathful eyes of the Speaker as he reached out for me.

Then the wild motion halted as the President's voice roared through the chamber at maximum amplification: "I declare this meeting adjourned!"—and the stunned expressions of the legislators at his unbelievable temerity. There was greatness in that little man. Before anyone could move or think he clapped his hands—the magnified report was like atomic fission—and a smartly uniformed squad moved in on us. "Take him away," the President declaimed, with a magnificent gesture, and at double-time the squad surrounded me and hustled me off the podium. The President convoyed us as far as the door while the assembly gathered its wits. His face was white with fear, but he whispered: "I can't make it stick, but it'll take them all afternoon to get a ruling from the C of C. God bless you, Mr. Courtenay."

And he turned back to face them. I do not think Caligula's Christians walked more courageously into the arena.

The guards were the President's own, honor men from Brink's leadership academy. The lieutenant said never a word to me, but I could read the controlled disgust on his face as he read the slip of paper the President had handed him. I knew he didn't like what he was ordered to do, and I knew he would do it.

They got me to Anacostia and put me on the President's own transport; they stayed with me and fed me, and one of them played cards with me, as the jets flared outside the ports and we covered territory. All they would not do was talk to me.

It was a long flight in that clumsy old luxury liner that "tradition" gave the President. Time had been wasted at the airport, and below us I could see the fuzzy band of the terminator creeping past. As we came down for a landing, it was full dark. And the waiting was not yet over, nor the wondering if Kathy had got out all right too and when I would see her again. The lieutenant left the ship alone; he was gone for a long, long time.

I spent the time kicking questions around in my mind—questions that had occurred to me before, but which I had dismissed. Now, with all the time in the world, and a future full of ifs, I took them out and looked them over.

For instance:

Kathy and Matt Runstead and Jack O'Shea had plotted together to put me on ice literally. All right, that accounted for most of the things that puzzled me. But it didn't account for Hester. And, when you stopped to think of it, it didn't account for all of Runstead's work, either.

The Consies were in favor of space travel. But Runstead had sabotaged the Venus test in Cal-Mex. There was no doubt of that; I had as good as a confession from his fall-guy. Could it have been a double cross? Runstead posing as a Consie who was posing as a copysmith, and in reality what?

I began wishing for Kathy for a completely new reason.

When the lieutenant came back it was midnight. "All right," he said to me. "A cab's waiting for you outside. The runner knows where to go."

I climbed out and stretched. "Thanks," I said awkwardly.

The lieutenant spat neatly on the ground between my feet. The door slammed, and I scrambled out of the way of the take-off.

The cab-runner was Mexican. I tried him on a question; no English. I tried again in my Chlorella U. Spanish; he gaped at me. There were fifty good reasons why I didn't want to go along with him without a much better idea of what was up. But, when I stopped to think of it, I had damn-all choice. The lieutenant had followed his orders. Now the orders were complied with, and I could see his active little military mind framing the report that would tip someone off to where they could find the notorious Consie, Mitchell Courtenay.

I would be a sitting duck; it would depend on whether Taunton or the police got to me first. It was not a choice worth spending much time over.

I got in the cab.

You'd think the fact that the runner was a Mexican would have tipped me off. It didn't, though. It was not until I saw the glimmer of starlight on the massive projectile before me that I knew I was in Arizona, and knew what the President had done for me.

A mixed squad of Pinkertons and our own plant protection men closed in on me and hustled me past the sentry-boxes, across the cleared land, up to the rocket itself. The OIC showed me the crescent he could make with thumb and forefinger and said: "You're safe now, Mr. Courtenay."

"But I don't *want* to go to Venus!" I said.

He laughed out loud.

Hurry up and wait; hurry up and wait. The long, dreary flight had been a stasis; everything at both ends of it had been too frantic with motion over which I had no control to permit thought. They gave me no chance to think here, either; I felt someone grabbing the seat of my pants, and I was hoisted inside. There I was dragged more than led to an acceleration hammock, strapped in and left.

The hammock swung and jolted, and twelve titans brooded on my chest. Good-by, Kathy; good-by, Schocken Tower. Like it or not, I was on my way to Venus.

But it wasn't good-by to Kathy.

It was she herself who came to unstrap me when the first blast was over.

I got out of the hammock and tottered weightlessly, rubbing my back. I opened my mouth to make a casual greeting. What came out was a squeaky, "Kathy!"

It wasn't a brilliant speech, but I didn't have time for a brilliant speech. Kathy's lips and my lips were occupied.

When we stopped for breath I said, "What alkaloids do *you* put into the product?", but it was wasted. She wanted to be kissed again. I kissed her.

It was hard work, standing up. Every time she moved we lurched against the rail or drifted off the floor entirely; only a standby jet was operating and we were otherwise beyond the limit of weight.

We sat down.

After a while, we talked.

I stretched and looked around me. "Lovely place you have here," I said. "Now that that's taken care of, I have something else on my mind. Questions: two of them." I told her what the questions were.

I explained about Runstead's lousing up San Diego and Venus project. And about Hester's murder.

"Oh, Mitch," she said. "Where do I begin? How'd you ever get to be star class?"

"Went to night school," I said. "I'm still listening."

"Well, you should be able to figure it out. Sure, we Consies wanted space travel. The human race needs Venus. It needs an unspoiled, unwrecked, unexploited, unlooted, un—"

"Oh," I said.

"—unpirated, undevastated—well, you see. Sure we wanted a ship to go to Venus. But we didn't want Fowler Schocken on Venus. Or Mitchell Courtenay, either. Not as long as Mitchell Courtenay was the kind of guy who would gut Venus for an extra megabuck's billing. There aren't too many planets around that the race can expand into, Mitch. We couldn't have Fowler Schocken's Venus Project succeed."

"Um," I said, digesting. "And Hester?"

Kathy shook her head. "You figure that one out," she said.

"You don't know the answer?"

"I do know the answer. It isn't hard."

I coaxed, but she wouldn't play. So I kissed her for a while again, until some interfering character with a ship's-officer rosette on his shoulder came grinning in. "Care to look at the stars, folks?" he asked, in a tourist-guide way that I detested. It didn't pay to pull rank on him, of course; ships' officers always act a cut above their class, and it would have been ungraceful, at least, to brace him for it. Besides—

Besides.

The thought stopped me for a moment: I was used to being star class by now. It wasn't going to be fun, being one of the boys. I gave my Consie theory a quick mental run-through. No, there was nothing in it that indicated I would have a show-dog's chance of being sirred and catered to any more.

Hello, Kathy. Good-by, Schocken Tower.

Anyway, we went up to the forward observation port. All the faces were strange to me.

There isn't a window to be found on the Moon ships; radar-eyed, GCA-tentacled, they sacrifice the esthetic but useless spectacle of the stars for the greater strength of steel. I had never seen the stars in space before.

Outside the port was white night. Brilliant stars shining against a background of star particles scattered over a dust of stars. There wasn't a breadth of space the size of my thumbnail where there was blackness; it was all light, all fiery pastels. A rim of fire around the side of the port showed the direction of the sun.

We turned away from the port. "Where's Matt Runstead?" I asked.

Kathy giggled. "Back in Schocken Tower, living on wake-up pills, trying to untangle the mess. *Somebody* had to stay behind, Mitch. Fortunately, Matt can vote your proxies. We didn't have much time to talk in Washington; he's going to have a lot of questions to ask, and nobody around with the answers."

I stared. "What in the world was Runstead doing in Washington?"

"Getting you off the spot, Mitch! After Jack O'Shea broke—"

"After *what?*"

"Oh, good Lord. Look, let's take it in order. O'Shea broke. He got drunk one night too often, and he couldn't find a clear spot in his arm for the needle, and he picked out the wrong girl to break apart in front of. They had him sewed up tight.

All about you, and all about me, and the rocket, and everything."

"Who did?"

"Your great and good friend, B. J. Taunton." Kathy struck a match for her cigarette viciously. I could read her mind a little, too. Little Jack O'Shea, sixty pounds of jellied porcelain and melted wax, thirty-five inches of twisted guts and blubber. There had been times in the past weeks when I had not liked Jack. I canceled them all, paid in full, when I thought of that destructible tiny man in the hands of Taunton's anthropoids. "Taunton got it all, Mitch," Kathy said. "All that mattered, anyhow. If Runstead hadn't had a tap on Taunton's interrogation room we would have been had, right then. But Matt had time to get down to Washington and warn me and the President—oh, he's no Consie, the President, but he's a good man. He can't help being born into office. And—here we are."

The captain interrupted us. "Five minutes till we correct," he said. "Better get started back to your hammocks. The correction blasts may not be much—but you never know."

Kathy nodded and led me away. I plucked the cigarette from her lips, took a puff—and gave it back. "Why, Mitch!" she said.

"I'm reformed," I told her. "Uh—Kathy. One more question. It isn't a nice question."

She sighed. "The same as between you and Hester," she said.

I asked, "What was between Jack—uh?"

"You heard me. What was between Jack and me was the same as between you and Hester. All one way. Jack was in love with me, maybe. Something like that. I—wasn't." And torrentially: "Because I was too damn crazy mad in love with you!"

"Uh," I said. It seemed like the moment to reach out and kiss her again, but it must not have been because she pushed me away. I cracked my head against the corridor wall. "Ouch," I said.

"That's what you're so stupid about, curse you!" she was saying. "Jack wanted me, but I didn't want anyone but you, not ever. And you never troubled to figure it out—never knew how much I cared about you any more than you knew how much Hester cared about you. Poor Hester—who knew she could never have you. Good lord, Mitch, how blind can you be?"

"Hester in love with me?"

"Yes, damn it! Why else would she have committed suicide?" Kathy actually stamped her foot, and rose an inch above the floor as a result.

I rubbed my head. "Well," I said dazedly.

The sixty-second beeper went off. "Hammocks," said Kathy, and the tears in her eyes flooded out. I put my arm around her.

"This is a stinking undignified business," she said. "I have exactly one minute to kiss and make up, let you get over your question-and-answer period, intimate that I have a private cabin and there's two hammocks in it, and get us both fastened in."

I straightened up fast. "A minute is a long time, dear," I told her.

It didn't take that long.

MORE THAN HUMAN

Theodore Sturgeon

To His Gestaltitude

NICHOLAS SAMSTAG

Contents

1

THE FABULOUS IDIOT

2

BABY IS THREE

3

MORALITY

PART ONE

THE FABULOUS IDIOT

and without operable outgoing conduits. It took what it took and gave out nothing.

All around it, to its special senses, was a murmur, a sending. It soaked itself in the murmur, absorbed it as it came, all of it. Perhaps it matched and classified, or perhaps it simply fed, taking what it needed and discarding the rest in some intangible way. The idiot was unaware. The thing inside. . . .

Without words: *Warm when the wet comes for a little but not enough for long enough.* (Sadly): *Never dark again.* A feeling of pleasure. A sense of subtle crushing and *Take away the pink, the scratchy. Wait, wait, you can go back, yes, you can go back. Different, but almost as good.* (Sleep feelings): *Yes, that's it! That's the—oh!* (Alarm): *You've gone too far, come back, come back, come—* (A twisting, a sudden cessation; and one less "voice.") . . . *It all rushes up, faster, faster, carrying me.* (Answer): *No, no. Nothing rushes. It's still; something pulls you down on to it, that is all.* (Fury): *They don't hear us, stupid, stupid. . . . They do. . . . They don't, only crying, only noises.*

Without words, though. Impression, depression, dialogue. Radiations of fear, tense fields of awareness, discontent. Murmuring, sending, speaking, sharing, from hundreds, from thousands of voices. None, though, for the idiot. Nothing that related to him; nothing he could use. He was unaware of his inner ear because it was useless to him. He was a poor example of a man, but he was a man; and these were the voices of the children, the very young children, who had not yet learned to stop trying to be heard. *Only crying, only noises.*

Mr. Kew was a good father, the very best of fathers. He told his daughter Alicia so, on her nineteenth birthday. He had said as much to Alicia ever since she was four. She was four when little Evelyn had been born and their mother had died cursing him, her indignation at last awake and greater than her agony and her fear.

Only a good father, the very finest of fathers, could have delivered his second child with his own hands. No ordinary father could have nursed and nurtured the two, the baby and the infant, so tenderly and so well. No child was ever so protected from evil as Alicia; and when she joined forces with her father, a mighty structure of purity was created for Evelyn. "Purity triple-distilled," Mr. Kew said to Alicia on her nineteenth birthday. "I know good through the study of evil, and have taught you only the good. And that good teaching has become your good living, and your way of life is Evelyn's star. I know all the evil there is and you know all the evil which must be avoided; but Evelyn knows no evil at all."

At nineteen, of course, Alicia was mature enough to understand these abstracts, this "way of life" and "distillation" and the inclusive "good" and "evil." When she was sixteen he had explained to her how a man went mad if he was alone with a woman, and how the poison sweat appeared on his body, and how he would put it on her, and then it would cause the horror on her skin. He had pictures of skin like that in his books. When she was thirteen she had a trouble and told her father about it and he told her with tears in his eyes that this was because she had been thinking about her body, as indeed she had been. She confessed it and he punished her body until she wished she had never owned one. And she tried, she tried not to think like that again, but she did in spite of herself; and regularly, regretfully, her father helped her in her efforts to discipline her intrusive flesh. When she was eight he taught her how to bathe in darkness, so she would be spared the blindness of those white eyes of which he also had magnificent pictures. And when she was six he had hung in her bedroom the picture of a woman, called Angel, and the picture of a man, called Devil. The woman held her palms up and smiled and the man had his arms out to her, his hands like hooks, and protruding point-outward from his breastbone was a crooked knife blade with a wetness on it.

They lived alone in a heavy house on a wooded knoll. There was no driveway, but a path which turned and turned again, so that from the windows no one could see where it went. It went to a wall and in the wall was an iron gate which had not been opened in eighteen years and beside the gate was a steel panel. Once a day Alicia's father went down the path to the wall and with two keys opened the two locks in the panel. He would swing it up and take out food and letters, put money and mail in, and lock it again.

There was a narrow road outside which Alicia and Evelyn

had never seen. The woods concealed the wall and the wall concealed the road. The wall ran by the road for two hundred yards, east and west; it mounted the hill then until it bracketed the house. Here it met iron pickets, fifteen feet high and so close together a man could hardly press a fist between them. The tops of the pickets curved out and down, and between them was cement, and in the cement was broken glass. The pickets ran east and west, connecting the house to the wall; and where they joined, more pickets ran back and back into the woods in a circle. The wall and the house, then, were a rectangle and that was forbidden territory. And behind the house were the two square miles of fenced woodland, and that belonged to Evelyn, with Alicia to watch. There was a brook there; wild flowers and a little pond; friendly oaks and little hidden glades. The sky above was fresh and near and the pickets could not be seen for the shouldering masses of holly which grew next to them, all the way around, blocking the view, breaking the breeze. This closed circle was all the world to Evelyn, all the world she knew, and all in the world she loved lay in it.

On Alicia's nineteenth birthday Evelyn was alone by her pond. She could not see the house, she could not see the holly hedge nor the pickets, but the sky was there, up and up, and the water was there, by and by. Alicia was in the library with her father; on birthdays he always had special things planned for Alicia in the library. Evelyn had never been in the library. The library was a place where her father lived, and where Alicia went at special times. Evelyn never thought of going there, any more than she thought of breathing water like a speckled trout. She had not been taught to read, but only to listen and obey. She had never learned to seek, but only to accept. Knowledge was given to her when she was ready for it and only her father and sister knew just when that might be.

She sat on the bank, smoothing her long skirts. She saw her ankle and gasped and covered it as Alicia would do if she were here. She set her back against a willow-trunk and watched the water.

It was spring, the part of spring where the bursting is done, the held-in pressures of desiccated sap-veins and gum-sealed buds are gone, and all the world's in a rush to be beautiful.

The air was heavy and sweet; it lay upon lips until they parted, pressed them until they smiled, entered boldly to beat in the throat like a second heart. It was air with a puzzle to it, for it was still and full of the colors of dreams, all motionless; yet it had a hurry to it. The stillness and the hurry were alive and laced together, and how could that be? That was the puzzle.

A dazzle of bird notes stitched through the green. Evelyn's eyes stung and wonder misted the wood. Something tensed in her lap. She looked down in time to see her hands attack one another, and off came her long gloves. Her naked hands fled to the sides of her neck, not to hide something but to share something. She bent her head and the hands laughed at one another under the iron order of her hair. They found four hooks and scampered down them. Her high collar eased and the enchanted air rushed in with a soundless shout. Evelyn breathed as if she had been running. She put out her hand hesitantly, futilely, patted the grass beside her as if somehow the act might release the inexpressible confusion of delight within her. It would not, and she turned and flung herself face down in a bed of early mint and wept because the spring was too beautiful to be borne.

He was in the wood, numbly prying the bark from a dead oak, when it happened. His hands were still and his head came up hunting, harking. He was as aware of the pressures of spring as an animal, and slightly more than an animal could be. But abruptly the spring was more than heavy, hopeful air and the shifting of earth with life. A hard hand on his shoulder could have been no more tangible than this call.

He rose carefully, as if something around him might break if he were clumsy. His strange eyes glowed. He began to move —he who had never called nor been called, nor responded before. He moved toward the thing he sensed and it was a matter of will, not of external compulsion. Without analysis, he was aware of the bursting within him of an encysted need. It had been a part of him all his life but there was no hope in him that he might express it. And bursting so, it flung a thread across his internal gulf, linking his alive and independent core to the half-dead animal around it. It was a sending straight to what was human in him, received by an instrument which, up to now, had accepted only the incomprehensible radiations of the new-born, and so had been ignored. But now it spoke, as it were, in his own tongue.

He was careful and swift, careful and silent. He turned his wide shoulders to one side and the other as he moved, slipping through the alders, passing the pines closely as if it were intolerable to leave the direct line between himself and his call. The sun was high; the woods were homogeneously the woods, front, right, left; yet he followed his course without swerving, not from knowledge, not by any compass, but purely in conscious response.

He arrived suddenly, for the clearing was, in the forest, a sudden thing. For fifty feet outward the earth around the close-set pickets had been leached and all trees felled years ago, so that none might overhang the fence. The idiot slipped out of the wood and trotted across the bare ground to the serried iron. He put out his arms as he ran, slid his hands between the pickets and when they caught on his starved bony forearms, his legs kept moving, his feet sliding, as if his need empowered him to walk through the fence and the impenetrable holly beyond it.

The fact that the barrier would not yield came to him slowly. It was as if his feet understood it first and stopped trying and then his hands, which withdrew. His eyes, however, would not give up at all. From his dead face they yearned through the iron, through the holly, ready to burst with answering. His mouth opened and a scratching sound emerged. He had never tried to speak before and could not now; the gesture was an end, not a means, like the starting of tears at a crescendo of music.

He began to move along the fence walking sidewise, finding it unbearable to turn away from the call.

It rained for a day and a night and for half the next day, and when the sun came out it rained again, upward; it rained light from the heavy jewels which lay on the rich new green. Some jewels shrank and some fell and then the earth in a voice of softness, and leaves in a voice of texture, and flowers speaking in color, were grateful.

Evelyn crouched on the window seat, elbows on the sill, her

hands cupped to the curve of her cheeks, their pressure making it easy to smile. Softly, she sang. It was strange to hear for she did not know music; she did not read and had never been told of music. But there were birds, there was the bassoon of wind in the eaves sometimes; there were the calls and cooings of small creatures in that part of the wood which was hers and, distantly, from the part which was not. Her singing was made of these things, with strange and effortless fluctuations in pitch from an instrument unbound by the diatonic scale, freely phrased.

But I never touch the gladness
May not touch the gladness
Beauty, oh beauty of touchness
Spread like a leaf, nothing between me and the sky but light,
Rain touches me
Wind touches me
Leaves, other leaves, touch and touch me. . . .

She made music without words for a long moment and was silent, making music without sound, watching the raindrops fall in the glowing noon.

Harshly, "What are you doing?"

Evelyn started and turned. Alicia stood behind her, her face strangely tight. "What are you doing?" she repeated.

Evelyn made a vague gesture toward the window, tried to speak.

"Well?"

Evelyn made the gesture again. "Out there," she said. "I—I—" She slipped off the window seat and stood. She stood as tall as she could. Her face was hot.

"Button up your collar," said Alicia. "What is it, Evelyn? Tell me!"

"I'm trying to," said Evelyn, soft and urgent. She buttoned her collar and her hands fell to her waist. She pressed herself, hard. Alicia stepped near and pushed the hands away. "Don't do that. What was that . . . what you were doing? Were you talking?"

"Talking, yes. Not you, though. Not Father."

"There isn't anyone else."

"There is," said Evelyn. Suddenly breathless, she said, "Touch me, Alicia."

"*Touch* you?"

"Yes, I . . . want you to. Just . . ." She held out her arms. Alicia backed away.

"We don't touch one another," she said, as gently as she could through her shock. "What is it, Evelyn? Aren't you well?"

"Yes," said Evelyn. "No. I don't know." She turned to the window. "It isn't raining. It's dark here. There's so much sun, so much—I want the sun on me, like a bath, warm all over."

"Silly. Then it would be all light in your bath. . . . We don't talk about bathing, dear."

Evelyn picked up a cushion from the window seat. She put her arms around it and with all her strength hugged it to her breast.

"Evelyn! Stop that!"

Evelyn whirled and looked at her sister in a way she had never used before. Her mouth twisted. She squeezed her eyes tight closed and when she opened them, tears fell. "I want to," she cried, "I want to!"

"Evelyn!" Alicia whispered. Wide-eyed, she backed away to the door. "I shall have to tell Father."

Evelyn nodded, and drew her arms even tighter around the cushion.

When he came to the brook, the idiot squatted down beside it and stared. A leaf danced past, stopped and curtsied, then made its way through the pickets and disappeared in the low gap the holly had made for it.

He had never thought deductively before and perhaps his effort to follow the leaf was not thought-born. Yet he did, only to find that the pickets were set in a concrete channel here. They combed the water from one side to the other; nothing larger than a twig or a leaf could slip through. He wallowed in the water, pressing against the iron, beating at the submerged cement. He swallowed water and choked and kept trying, blindly, insistently. He put both his hands on one of the pickets and shook it. It tore his palm. He tried another and another and suddenly one rattled against the lower cross-member.

It was a different result from that of any other attack. It is doubtful whether he realized that this difference meant that the iron here had rusted and was therefore weaker; it simply gave hope because it was different.

He sat down on the bottom of the brook and in water up to his armpits, he placed a foot on each side of the picket which had rattled. He got his hands on it again, took a deep breath and pulled with all his strength. A stain of red rose in the water and whirled downstream. He leaned forward, then back with a tremendous jerk. The rusted underwater segment snapped. He hurtled backward, striking his head stingingly on the edge of the channel. He went limp for a moment and his body half rolled, half floated back to the pickets. He inhaled water, coughed painfully, and raised his head. When the spinning world righted itself, he fumbled under the water. He found an opening a foot high but only about seven inches wide. He put his arm in it, right up to the shoulder, his head submerged. He sat up again and put a leg into it.

Again he was dimly aware of the inexorable fact that will alone was not enough; that pressure alone upon the barrier would not make it yield. He moved to the next picket and tried to break it as he had the one before. It would not move, nor would the one on the other side.

At last he rested. He looked up hopelessly at the fifteen-foot top of the fence with its close-set, outcurving fangs and its hungry rows of broken glass. Something hurt him; he moved and fumbled and found himself with the eleven-inch piece of iron he had broken away. He sat with it in his hands, staring stupidly at the fence.

Touch me, touch me. It was that, and a great swelling of emotion behind it; it was a hunger, a demand, a flood of sweetness and of need. The call had never ceased, but this was something different. It was as if the call were a carrier and this a signal suddenly impressed upon it.

When it happened that thread within him, bridging his two selves, trembled and swelled. Falteringly, it began to conduct. Fragments and flickerings of inner power shot across, were laden with awareness and information, shot back. The strange eyes fell to the piece of iron, the hands turned it. His reason itself ached with disuse as it stirred; then for the first time came into play on such a problem.

He sat in the water, close by the fence, and with the piece of iron he began to rub against the picket just under the cross-member.

It began to rain. It rained all day and all night and half the next day.

"She *was* here," said Alicia. Her face was flushed.

Mr. Kew circled the room, his deepset eyes alight. He ran his whip through his fingers. There were four lashes. Alicia said, remembering, "And she wanted me to touch her. She asked me to."

"She'll be touched," he said. "Evil, evil," he muttered. "Evil can't be filtered out," he chanted, "I thought it could, I thought it could. You're evil, Alicia, as you know, because a woman touched you, for years she handled you. But not Evelyn . . . it's in the blood and the blood must be let. Where is she, do you think?"

"Perhaps outdoors . . . the pool, that will be it. She likes the pool. I'll go with you."

He looked at her, her hot face, bright eyes. "This is for me to do. Stay here!"

"Please . . ."

He whirled the heavy-handled whip. "You too, Alicia?"

She half turned from him, biting into a huge excitement. "Later," he growled. He ran out.

Alicia stood a moment trembling, then plunged to the window. She saw her father outside, striding purposefully away. Her hands spread and curled against the sash. Her lips writhed apart and she uttered a strange wordless bleat.

When Evelyn reached the pool, she was out of breath. Something—an invisible smoke, a magic—lay over the water. She took it in hungrily, and was filled with a sense of nearness. Whether it was a thing which was near or an event, she did not know; but it was near and she welcomed it. Her nostrils arched and trembled. She ran to the water's edge and reached out toward it.

There was a boiling in the upstream end and up from under the holly stems he came. He thrashed to the bank and lay there gasping, looking up at her. He was wide and flat, covered with scratches. His hands were puffy and water-wrinkled; he was gaunt and worn. Shreds of clothing clung to him here and there, covering him not at all.

She leaned over him, spellbound, and from her came the call—floods of it, loneliness and expectancy and hunger, gladness and sympathy. There was a great amazement in her but no shock and no surprise. She had been aware of him for days and he of her, and now their silent radiations reached out to each other, mixed and mingled and meshed. Silently they lived in each other and then she bent and touched him, touched his face and shaggy hair.

He trembled violently, and kicked his way up out of the water. She sank down beside him. They sat close together, and at last she met those eyes. The eyes seemed to swell up and fill the air; she wept for joy and sank forward into them, wanting to live there, perhaps to die there, but at very least to be a part of them.

She had never spoken to a man and he had never spoken to anyone. She did not know what a kiss was and any he might have seen had no significance to him. But they had a better thing. They stayed close, one of her hands on his bare shoulder, and the currents of their inner selves surged between them. They did not hear her father's resolute footsteps, nor his gasp, nor his terrible bellow of outrage. They were aware of nothing but each other until he leapt on them, caught her up, lifted her high, threw her behind him. He did not look to see where or how she struck the ground. He stood over the idiot, his lips white, his eyes staring. His lips parted and again he made the terrible sound. And then he lifted the whip.

So dazed was the idiot that the first multiple blow, and the second, seemed not to affect him at all, though his flesh, already soaked and cut and beaten, split and spouted. He lay staring dully at that midair point which had contained Evelyn's eyes and did not move.

Then the lashes whistled and clacked and buried their braided tips in his back again and the old reflex returned to him. He pressed himself backward trying to slide feet-first into the water.

The man dropped his whip and caught the idiot's bony wrist in both his hands. He literally ran a dozen steps up the bank, the idiot's long tattered body flailing along behind him. He kicked the creature's head, ran back for his whip. When he returned with it the idiot had managed to rear up on his elbows. The man kicked him again, rolled him over on his back. He put one foot on the idiot's shoulder and pinned him down and slashed at the naked belly with the whip.

There was a devil's shriek behind him and it was as if a bullock with tiger's claws had attacked him. He fell heavily and twisted, to look up into the crazed face of his younger daughter. She had bitten her lips and she drooled and bled. She clawed at his face; one of her fingers slipped into his left eye. He screamed in agony, sat up, twined his fingers in the complexity of lace at her throat, and clubbed her twice with the loaded whip-handle.

Blubbering, whining, he turned to the idiot again. But now the implacable demands of escape had risen, flushing away everything else. And perhaps another thing was broken as the whip-handle crushed the consciousness from the girl. In any case there was nothing left but escape, and there could be nothing else until it was achieved. The long body flexed like a snap-beetle, flung itself up and over in a half-somersault. The idiot struck the bank on all fours and sprang as he struck. The lash caught him in midair; his flying body curled around it, for a brief instant capturing the lashes between the lower ribs and the hipbone. The handle slipped from the man's grasp. He screamed and dove after the idiot, who plunged into the arch at the holly roots. The man's face buried itself in the leaves and tore; he sank and surged forward again in the water. With one hand he caught a naked foot. It kicked him on the ear as he pulled it toward him. And then the man's head struck the iron pickets.

The idiot was under and through already and lay half out of the brook, twitching feebly in an exhausted effort to bring his broken body to its feet. He turned to look back and saw the man clinging to the bars, raging, not understanding about the underwater gap in the fence.

The idiot clung to the earth, pink bloody water swirling away from him and down on his pursuer. Slowly the escape reflex left him. There was a period of blankness and then a strange new feeling came to him. It was as new an experience as the call which had brought him here and very nearly as strong. It was a feeling like fear but where fear was a fog to him, clammy and blinding, this was something with a thirsty edge to it, hard and purposeful.

He relaxed his grasp on the poisoned weeds which grew sickly in the leached ground by the brook. He let the water help him and drifted down again to the bars, where the insane father mouthed and yammered at him. He brought his dead face close to the fence and widened his eyes. The screaming stopped.

For the first time he used the eyes consciously, purposely, for something other than a crust of bread.

When the man was gone he dragged himself out of the brook and, faltering, crawled toward the woods.

When Alicia saw her father returning, she put the heel of her hand in her mouth and bit down until her teeth met. It was not his clothes, wet and torn, nor even his ruined eye. It was something else, something which—"*Father!*"

He did not answer, but strode up to her. At the last possible instant before being walked down like a wheat stalk, she numbly stepped aside. He stamped past her and through the library doors, leaving them open. "Father!"

No answer. She ran to the library. He was across the room, at the cabinets which she had never seen open. One was open now. From it he took a long-barreled target revolver and a small box of cartridges. This he opened, spilling the cartridges across his desk. Methodically he began to load.

Alicia ran to him. "What is it? What is it? You're hurt, let me help you, what are you . . ."

His one good eye was fixed and glassy. He breathed slowly, too deeply, the air rushing in for too long, being held for too long, whistling out and out. He snapped the cylinder into place, clicked off the safety, looked at her and raised the gun.

She was never to forget that look. Terrible things happened then and later, but time softened the focus, elided the details. But that look was to be with her forever.

He fixed the one eye on her, caught and held her with it; she squirmed on it like an impaled insect. She knew with a horrifying certainty that he did not see her at all, but looked at some unknowable horror of his own. Still looking through her, he put the muzzle of the gun in his mouth and pulled the trigger.

There was not much noise. His hair fluffed upward on top. The eye still stared, she was still pierced by it. She screamed his name. He was no less reachable dead than he had been a moment before. He bent forward as if to show her the ruin which had replaced his hair and the thing that held her broke, and she ran.

Two hours, two whole hours passed before she found Evelyn. One of the hours was simply lost; it was a blackness and a pain. The other was too quiet, a time of wandering about the house followed by a soft little whimpering that she made herself: "What?" she whimpered, "what's that you say?" trying to understand, asking and asking the quiet house for the second hour.

She found Evelyn by the pool, lying on her back with her eyes wide open. On the side of Evelyn's head was a puffiness, and in the center of the puffiness was a hollow into which she could have laid three fingers.

"Don't," said Evelyn softly when Alicia tried to lift her head. Alicia set it back gently and knelt and took her hands and squeezed them together. "Evelyn, oh, what happened?"

"Father hit me," Evelyn said calmly. "I'm going to go to sleep."

Alicia whimpered.

Evelyn said, "What is it called when a person needs a . . . person . . . when you want to be touched and the . . . two are like one thing and there isn't anything else at all anywhere?"

Alicia, who had read books, thought about it. "Love," she said at length. She swallowed. "It's a madness. It's bad."

Evelyn's quiet face was suffused with a kind of wisdom. "It isn't bad," she said. "I had it."

"You have to get back to the house."

"I'll sleep here," said Evelyn. She looked up at her sister and smiled. "It's all right . . . Alicia?"

"Yes."

"I won't ever wake up," she said with that strange wisdom. "I wanted to do something and now I can't. Will you do it for me?"

"I'll do it," Alicia whispered.

"For me," Evelyn insisted. "You won't want to."

"I'll do it."

"When the sun is bright," Evelyn said, "take a bath in it. There's more, wait." She closed her eyes. A little furrow came and went on her brow. "Be in the sun like that. Move, run. Run and . . . jump high. Make a wind with running and moving. I so wanted that. I didn't know until now that I wanted it and now I . . . oh, *Alicia!*"

"What is it, what is it?"

"There it is, there it is, can't you see? The love, with the sun on its body!"

The soft wise eyes were wide, looking at the darkling sky. Alicia looked up and saw nothing. When she looked down again, she knew that Evelyn was also seeing nothing. Not any more.

Far off, in the woods beyond the fence, there was a rush of weeping.

Alicia stayed there listening to it and at last put out her hand and closed Evelyn's eyes. She rose and went toward the house and the weeping followed her and followed her, almost until she reached the door. And even then it seemed to go on inside her.

When Mrs. Prodd heard the hoof thuds in the yard, she muttered under her breath and peered out between the dimity kitchen curtains. By a combination of starlight and deep familiarity with the yard itself, she discerned the horse and stoneboat, with her husband plodding beside it, coming through the gate. He'll get what for, she mumbled, off to the woods so long and letting her burn dinner.

He didn't get what for, though. One look at his broad face precluded it. "What is it, Prodd?" she asked, alarmed.

"Gimme a blanket."

"Why on earth—"

"Hurry now. Feller bad hurt. Picked him up in the woods. Looks like a bear chewed him. Got the clo'es ripped off him."

She brought the blanket, running, and he snatched it and went out. In a moment he was back, carrying a man. "Here," said Mrs. Prodd. She flung open the door to Jack's room. When Prodd hesitated, the long limp body dangling in his arms, she said, "Go on, go on, never mind the spread. It'll wash."

"Get a rag, hot water," he grunted. She went out and he gently lifted off the blanket. "Oh my God."

He stopped her at the door. "He won't last the night. Maybe we shouldn't plague him with that." He indicated the steaming basin she carried.

"We got to try." She went in. She stopped and he deftly took the basin from her as she stood, white-faced, her eyes closed. "Ma—"

"Come," she said softly. She went to the bed and began to clean the tattered body.

He lasted the night. He lasted the week too and it was only then that the Prodds began to have hope for him. He lay motionless in the room called Jack's room, interested in nothing, aware of nothing except perhaps the light as it came and went at the window. He would stare out as he lay, perhaps seeing, perhaps watching, perhaps not. There was little to be seen out there. A distant mountain, a few of Prodd's sparse acres; occasionally Prodd himself, a doll in the distance, scratching the stubborn soil with a broken harrow, stooping for weed-shoots. His inner self was encysted and silent in sorrow. His outer self seemed shrunken, unreachable also. When Mrs. Prodd brought food—eggs and warm sweet milk, home-cured ham and johnnycake—he would eat if she urged him, ignore both her and the food if she did not.

In the evenings, "He say anything yet?" Prodd would ask, and his wife would shake her head. After ten days he had a thought; after two weeks he voiced it. "You don't suppose he's tetched, do you, Ma?"

She was unaccountably angry. "How do you mean tetched?"

He gestured. "You know. Like feeble-minded. I mean, maybe he don't talk because he can't."

"No!" she said positively. She looked up to see the question in Prodd's face. She said, "You ever look in his eyes? He's no idiot."

He had noticed the eyes. They disturbed him; that was all he could say of them. “Well, I wish he’d say something.”

She touched a thick coffee cup. “You know Grace.”

“Well, you told me. Your cousin that lost her little ones.”

“Yes. Well, after the fire, Grace was almost like that, lying quiet all day. Talk to her, it was like she didn’t hear. Show her something, she might’ve been blind. Had to spoon-feed her, wash her face.”

“Maybe it’s that then,” he allowed. “That feller, he sure walked into something worth forgetting, up there . . . Grace, she got better, didn’t she?”

“Well, she was never the same,” said his wife. “But she got over it. I guess sometimes the world’s too much to live with and a body sort of has to turn away from it to rest.”

The weeks went by and broken tissues knit and the wide flat body soaked up nourishment like a cactus absorbing moisture. Never in his life had he had rest and food and . . .

She sat with him, talked to him. She sang songs, “Flow Gently, Sweet Afton” and “Home on the Range.” She was a little brown woman with colorless hair and bleached eyes, and there was about her a hunger very like one he had felt. She told the moveless, silent face all about the folks back East and second grade and the time Prodd had come courting in his boss’s Model T and him not even knowing how to drive it yet. She told him all the little things that would never be altogether in the past for her: the dress she wore to her confirmation, with a bow here and little gores here and here, and the time Grace’s husband came home drunk with his Sunday pants all tore and a live pig under his arm, squealing to wake the dead. She read to him from the prayer book and told him Bible stories. She chattered out everything that was in her mind, except about Jack.

He never smiled nor answered and the only difference it made in him was that he kept his eyes on her face when she was in the room and patiently on the door when she was not. What a profound difference this was, she could not know; but the flat starved body tissues were not all that were slowly filling out.

A day came at last when the Prodds were at lunch—“dinner,”

they called it—and there was a fumbling at the inside of the door of Jack's room. Prodd exchanged a glance with his wife, then rose and opened it.

"Here, now, you can't come out like that." He called, "Ma, throw in my other overalls."

He was weak and very uncertain, but he was on his feet. They helped him to the table and he slumped there, his eyes cloaked and stupid, ignoring the food until Mrs. Prodd tantalized his nostrils with a spoonful. Then he took the spoon in his broad fist and got his mouth on it and looked past his hand at her. She patted his shoulder and told him it was just wonderful, how well he did.

"Well, Ma, you don't have to treat him like a two-year-old," said Prodd. Perhaps it was the eyes, but he was troubled again.

She pressed his hand warningly; he understood and said no more about it just then. But later in the night when he thought she was asleep, she said suddenly, "I do so have to treat him like a two-year-old, Prodd. Maybe even younger."

"How's that?"

"With Grace," she said, "it was like that. Not so bad, though. She was like six, when she started to get better. Dolls. When she didn't get apple pie with the rest of us one time, she cried her heart out. It was like growing up all over again. Faster, I mean, but like traveling the same road again."

"You think he's going to be like that?"

"Isn't he like a two-year-old?"

"First I ever saw six foot tall."

She snorted in half-pretended annoyance. "We'll raise him up just like a child."

He was quiet for a time. Then, "What'll we call him?"

"Not Jack," she said before she could stop herself.

He grunted an agreement. He didn't know quite what to say then.

She said, "We'll bide our time about that. He's got his own name. It wouldn't be right to put another to him. You just wait. He'll get back to where he remembers it."

He thought about it for a long time. He said, "Ma, I hope we're doing the right thing." But by then she was asleep.

*

There were miracles.

The Prodds thought of them as achievements, as successes, but they were miracles. There was the time when Prodd found two strong hands at the other end of a piece of 12x12 he was snaking out of the barn. There was the time Mrs. Prodd found her patient holding a ball of yarn, holding it and looking at it only because it was red. There was the time he found a full bucket by the pump and brought it inside. It was a long while, however, before he learned to work the handle.

When he had been there a year, Mrs. Prodd remembered and baked him a cake. Impulsively she put four candles on it. The Prodds beamed at him as he stared at the little flames, fascinated. His strange eyes caught and held hers, then Prodd's. "Blow it out, son."

Perhaps he visualized the act. Perhaps it was the result of the warmth outflowing from the couple, the wishing for him, the warmth of caring. He bent his head and blew. They laughed together and rose and came to him, and Prodd thumped his shoulder and Mrs. Prodd kissed his cheek.

Something twisted inside him. His eyes rolled up until, for a moment, only the whites showed. The frozen grief he carried slumped and flooded him. This wasn't the call, the contact, the exchange he had experienced with Evelyn. It was not even like it, except in degree. But because he could now feel to such a degree, he was aware of his loss, and he did just what he had done when first he lost it. He cried.

It was the same shrill tortured weeping that had led Prodd to him in the darkening wood a year ago. This room was too small to contain it. Mrs. Prodd had never heard him make a sound before. Prodd had, that first night. It would be hard to say whether it was worse to listen to such a sound or to listen to it again.

Mrs. Prodd put her arms around his head and cooed small syllables to him. Prodd balanced himself awkwardly nearby, put out a hand, changed his mind, and finally retreated into a futile reiteration: "Aw. Aw. . . . Aw, now."

In its own time, the weeping stopped. Sniffling, he looked at them each in turn. Something new was in his face; it was as if the bronze mask over which his facial skin was stretched had disappeared. "I'm sorry," Prodd said. "Reckon we did something wrong."

"It wasn't wrong," said his wife. "You'll see."

He got a name.

The night he cried, he discovered consciously that if he wished, he could absorb a message, a meaning, from those about him. It had happened before, but it happened as the wind happened to blow on him, as reflexively as a sneeze or a shiver. He began to hold and turn this ability, as once he had held and turned the ball of yarn. The sounds called speech still meant little to him, but he began to detect the difference between speech directed to him and that which did not concern him. He never really learned to hear speech; instead, ideas were transmitted to him directly. Ideas in themselves are formless and it is hardly surprising that he learned very slowly to give ideas the form of speech.

"What's your name?" Prodd asked him suddenly one day. They were filling the horse trough from the cistern and there was that about water running and running in the sun which tugged deeply at the idiot. Utterly absorbed, he was jolted by the question. He looked up and found his gaze locked with Prodd's.

Name. He made a reaching, a flash of demand, and it returned to him carrying what might be called a definition. It came, though, as pure concept. *"Name" is the single thing which is me and what I have done and been and learned.*

It was all there, waiting for that single symbol, a name. All the wandering, the hunger, the loss, the thing which is worse than loss, called lack. There was a dim and subtle awareness that even here, with the Prodds, he was not a something, but a substitute for something.

All alone.

He tried to say it. Directly from Prodd he took the concept and its verbal coding and the way it ought to sound. But understanding and expressing were one thing; the physical act of enunciation was something else again. His tongue might have been a shoe sole and his larynx a rusty whistle. His lips writhed. He said, "Ul . . . ul . . ."

"What is it, son?"

All alone. It was transmitted clear and clean, complete, but as a thought only and he sensed instantly that a thought sent this way had no impact whatever on Prodd, though the farmer strained to receive what he was trying to convey. "Ul-ul . . . lone," he gasped.

"Lone?" said Prodd.

It could be seen that the syllable meant something to Prodd, something like the codification he offered, though far less.

But it would do.

He tried to repeat the sound, but his unaccustomed tongue became spastic. Saliva spurted annoyingly and ran from his lips. He sent a desperate demand for help, for some other way to express it, found it, used it. He nodded.

"Lone," repeated Prodd.

And again he nodded; and this was his first word and his first conversation; another miracle.

It took him five years to learn to talk and always he preferred not to. He never did learn to read. He was simply not equipped.

There were two boys for whom the smell of disinfectant on tile was the smell of hate.

For Gerry Thompson it was the smell of hunger, too, and of loneliness. All food was spiced with it, all sleep permeated with disinfectant, hunger, cold, fear . . . all components of hatred. Hatred was the only warmth in the world, the only certainty. A man clings to certainties, especially when he has only one; most especially when he is six years old. And at six Gerry was very largely a man—at least, he had a grown man's appreciation of that gray pleasure which comes merely with the absence of pain; he had an implacable patience, found usually only in men of purpose who must appear broken until their time of decision arrives. One does not realize that for a six-year-old the path of memory stretches back for just as long a lifetime as it does for anyone, and is as full of detail and incident. Gerry had had trouble enough, loss enough, illness enough, to make a man of anyone. At six he looked it, too; it was then that he began to accept, to be obedient, and to wait. His small, seamed face became just another face, and his voice no longer protested. He lived like this for two years, until his day of decision.

Then he ran away from the state orphanage, to live by him-

self, to be the color of gutters and garbage so he would not be picked up; to kill if cornered; to hate.

For Hip there was no hunger, no cold, and no precocious maturity. There was the smell of hate, though. It surrounded his father the doctor, the deft and merciless hands, the somber clothes. Even Hip's memory of Doctor Barrows' voice was the memory of chlorine and carbolic.

Little Hip Barrows was a brilliant and beautiful child, to whom the world refused to be a straight, hard path of disinfected tile. Everything came easily to him, except control of his curiosity—and "everything" included the cold injections of rectitude administered by his father the doctor, who was a successful man, a moral man, a man who had made a career of being sure and of being right.

Hip rose through childhood like a rocket, burnished, swift, afire. His gifts brought him anything a young man might want, and his conditioning constantly chanted to him that he was a kind of thief, not entitled to that which he had not earned; for such was the philosophy of his father the doctor, who had worked hard for everything. So Hip's talents brought him friends and honors, and friendships and honors brought him uneasiness and a sick humility of which he was quite unaware.

He was eight when he built his first radio, a crystal set for which he even wound the coils. He suspended it from the bedsprings so it could not be seen except by lifting the bed itself and buried an earphone inside the mattress so he could lie awake at night and hear it. His father the doctor discovered it and forbade his ever touching so much as a piece of wire in the house again. He was nine when his father the doctor located his cache of radio and electronics texts and magazines and piled them all up in front of the fireplace and made him burn them, one by one; they were up all night. He was twelve when he won a Science Search engineering scholarship for his secretly designed tubeless oscilloscope, and his father the doctor dictated his letter of refusal. He was a brilliant fifteen when he was expelled from premedical school for playfully cross-wiring the relays in the staff elevators and adding some sequence switches, so that every touch of a control button was an unappreciated adventure. At sixteen, happily disowned, he was making his

own living in a research laboratory and attending engineering school.

He was big and bright and very popular. He needed to be very popular and this, like all his other needs, he accomplished with ease. He played the piano with a surprisingly delicate touch and played swift and subtle chess. He learned to lose skilfully and never too often at chess and at tennis and once at the harassing game of being "first in the Class, first in the School." He always had time—time to talk and to read, time to wonder quietly, time to listen to those who valued his listening, time to rephrase pedantries for those who found them arduous in the original. He even had time for ROTC and it was through this that he got his commission.

He found the Air Force a rather different institution from any school he had ever attended and it took him a while to learn that the Colonel could not be softened by humility or won by a witticism like the Dean of Men. It took him even longer to learn that in Service it is the majority, not the minority, who tend to regard physical perfection, conversational brilliance and easy achievement as defects rather than assets. He found himself alone more than he liked and avoided more than he could bear.

It was on the anti-aircraft range that he found an answer, a dream, and a disaster. . . .

Alicia Kew stood in the deepest shade by the edge of the meadow. "Father, Father, forgive me!" she cried. She sank down on the grass, blind with grief and terror, torn, shaken with conflict.

"Forgive me," she whispered with passion. "Forgive me," she whispered with scorn.

She thought, Devil, why won't you be dead? Five years ago you killed yourself, you killed my sister, and still it's "Father, forgive me." Sadist, pervert, murderer, devil . . . *man*, dirty poisonous *man!*

I've come a long way, she thought, I've come no way at all. How I ran from Jacobs, gentle Lawyer Jacobs, when he came to help with the bodies; oh, how I ran, to keep from being alone with him, so that he might not go mad and poison me. And when he brought his wife, how I fled from her too, think-

ing women were evil and must not touch me. They had a time with me, indeed they did; it was so long before I could understand that I was mad, not they . . . it was so long before I knew how very good, how very patient, Mother Jacobs was with me; how much she had to do with me, for me. "But child, no one's worn clothes like those for forty years!" And in the cab, when I screamed and couldn't stop, for the people, the hurry, the *bodies*, so many bodies, all touching and so achingly visible; bodies on the streets, the stairs, great pictures of bodies in the magazines, men holding women who laughed and were brazenly unfrightened . . . Dr. Rothstein who explained and explained and went back and explained again; there is no poison sweat, and there must be men and women else there would be no people at all. . . . I had to learn this, Father, dear devil Father, because of you; because of you I had never seen an automobile or a breast or a newspaper or a railroad train or a sanitary napkin or a kiss or a restaurant or an elevator or a bathing suit or the hair on—oh forgive me, Father.

I'm not afraid of a whip, I'm afraid of hands and eyes, thank you Father. One day, one day, you'll see, Father, I shall live with people all around me, I shall ride on their trains and drive my own motorcar; I shall go among thousands on a beach at the edge of a sea which goes out and out without walls, I shall step in and out among them with a tiny strip of cloth here and here and let them see my navel, I shall meet a man with white teeth, Father, and round strong arms, Father, and I shall oh what will become of me, what have I become now, Father forgive me.

I live in a house you never saw, one with windows overlooking a road, where the bright gentle cars whisper past and children play outside the hedge. The hedge is not a wall and, twice for the drive and once for the walk, it is open to anyone. I look through the curtains whenever I choose, and see strangers. There is no way to make the bathroom black dark and in the bathroom is a mirror as tall as I am; and one day, Father, I shall leave the towel off.

But all that will come later, the moving about among strangers, the touchings without fear. Now I must live alone, and think; I must read and read of the world and its works, yes, and of madmen like you, Father, and what twists them so terribly;

Dr. Rothstein insists that you were not the only one, that you were so rare, really, only because you were so rich.

Evelyn . . .

Evelyn never knew her father was mad. Evelyn never saw the pictures of the poisoned flesh. I lived in a world different from this one, but her world was just as different, the world Father and I made for her, to keep her pure. . . .

I wonder, I wonder how it happened that you had the decency to blow your rotten brains out. . . .

The picture of her father, dead, calmed her strangely. She rose and looked back into the woods, looked carefully around the meadow, shadow by shadow, tree by tree. "All right, Evelyn, I will, I will. . . ."

She took a deep breath and held it. She shut her eyes so tight there was red in the blackness of it. Her hands flickered over the buttons on her dress. It fell away. She slid out of underwear and stockings with a single movement. The air stirred and its touch on her body was indescribable; it seemed to blow through her. She stepped forward into the sun and with tears of terror pressing through her closed lids, she danced naked, for Evelyn, and begged and begged her dead father's pardon.

When Janie was four, she hurled a paperweight at a Lieutenant because of an unanalyzed but accurate feeling that he had no business around the house while her father was overseas. The Lieutenant's skull was fractured and, as is often the case in concussion, he was forever unable to recall the fact that Janie stood ten feet away from the object when she threw it. Janie's mother whaled the tar out of her for it, an episode which Janie accepted with her usual composure. She added it, however, to the proofs given her by similar occasions that power without control has its demerits.

"She gives me the creeps," her mother told her other Lieutenant later. "I can't stand her. You think there's something wrong with me for talking like that, don't you?"

"No I don't," said the other Lieutenant, who did. So she invited him in for the following afternoon, quite sure that once he had seen the child, he would understand.

He saw her and he did understand. Not the child, nobody understood her; it was the mother's feelings he understood.

Janie stood straight up, with her shoulders back and her face lifted, legs apart as if they wore jackboots, and she swung a doll by one of its feet as if it were a swagger-stick. There was a rightness about the child which, in a child, was wrong. She was, if anything, a little smaller than average. She was sharp featured and narrow eyed; her eyebrows were heavy. Her proportions were not quite those of most four-year-olds, who can bend forward from the waist and touch their foreheads to the floor. Janie's torso was a little too short or her legs a little too long for that. She spoke with a sweet clarity and a devastating lack of tact. When the other Lieutenant squatted clumsily and said, "*Hel*-lo, Janie. Are we going to be friends?" she said, "No. You smell like Major Grenfell." Major Grenfell had immediately preceded the injured Lieutenant.

"Janie!" her mother shouted, too late. More quietly, she said, "You know perfectly well the Major was only in for cocktails." Janie accepted this without comment, which left an appalling gap in the dialogue. The other Lieutenant seemed to realize all in a rush that it was foolish to squat there on the parquet and sprang to his feet so abruptly he knocked over the coffee table. Janie achieved a wolfish smile and watched his scarlet ears while he picked up the pieces. He left early and never came back.

Nor, for Janie's mother, was there safety in numbers. Against the strictest orders, Janie strode into the midst of the fourth round of Gibsons one evening and stood at one end of the living room, flicking an insultingly sober gray-green gaze across the flushed faces. A round yellow-haired man who had his hand on her mother's neck extended his glass and bellowed, "You're Wima's little girl!"

Every head in the room swung at once like a bank of servo-switches, turning off the noise, and into the silence Janie said, "You're the one with the—"

"*Janie!*" her mother shouted. Someone laughed. Janie waited for it to finish. "—big, fat—" she enunciated. The man took his hand off Wima's neck. Someone whooped, "Big fat what, Janie?"

Topically, for it was wartime, Janie said, "—meat market."

Wima bared her teeth. "Run along back to your room, darling. I'll come and tuck you in in a minute." Someone looked straight at the blond man and laughed. Someone said in an echoing whisper, "There goes the Sunday sirloin." A drawstring could not have pulled the fat man's mouth so round and tight and from it his lower lip bloomed like strawberry jam from a squeezed sandwich.

Janie walked quietly toward the door and stopped as soon as she was out of her mother's line of sight. A sallow young man with brilliant black eyes leaned forward suddenly. Janie met his gaze. An expression of bewilderment crossed the young man's face. His hand faltered out and upward and came to rest on his forehead. It slid down and covered the black eyes.

Janie said, just loud enough for him to hear, "Don't you ever do that again." She left the room.

"Wima," said the young man hoarsely, "that child is telepathic."

"Nonsense," said Wima absently, concentrating on the fat man's pout. "She gets her vitamins every single day."

The young man started to rise, looking after the child, then sank back again. "God," he said, and began to brood.

When Janie was five she began playing with some other little girls. It was quite a while before they were aware of it. They were toddlers, perhaps two and a half years old, and they looked like twins. They conversed, if conversation it was, in high-pitched squeaks, and tumbled about on the concrete courtyard as if it were a haymow. At first Janie hung over her windowsill, four and a half stories above, and contemplatively squirted saliva in and out between her tongue and her hard palate until she had a satisfactory charge. Then she would crane her neck and, cheeks bulging, let it go. The twins ignored the bombardment when it merely smacked the concrete, but yielded up a most satisfying foofaraw of chitterings and squeals when she scored a hit. They never looked up but would race around in wild excitement, squealing.

Then there was another game. On warm days the twins could skin out of their rompers faster than the eye could follow. One moment they were as decent as a deacon and in the next one or both would be fifteen feet away from the little scrap of cloth. They would squeak and scramble and claw back into them, casting deliciously frightened glances at the basement door. Janie discovered that with a little concentration she could move the rompers—that is, when they were unoccupied. She practiced diligently, lying across the windowsill, her chest and chin on a cushion, her eyes puckered with effort. At first the garment would simply lie there and flutter weakly, as if a small dust-devil had crossed it. But soon she had the rompers scuttling across the concrete like little flat crabs. It was a marvel to watch those two little girls move when that happened, and the noise was a pleasure. They became a little more cautious about taking them off and sometimes Janie would lie in wait for forty minutes before she had a chance. And sometimes, even then, she held off and the twins, one clothed, one bare, would circle around the romper, and stalk it like two kittens after a beetle. Then she would strike, the romper would fly, the twins would pounce; and sometimes they caught it immediately, and sometimes they had to chase it until their little lungs were going like a toy steam engine.

Janie learned the reason for their preoccupation with the basement door when one afternoon she had mastered the knack of lifting the rompers instead of just pushing them around. She held off until the twins were lulled into carelessness and were shucking out of their clothes, wandering away, ambling back again, as if to challenge her. And still she waited, until at last both rompers were lying together in a little pink-and-white mound. Then she struck. The rompers rose from the ground in a steep climbing turn and fluttered to the sill of a first-floor window. Since the courtyard was slightly below street level, this put the garments six feet high and well out of reach. There she left them.

One of the twins ran to the center of the courtyard and jumped up and down in agitation, stretching and craning to see the rompers. The other ran to the building under the first-floor window and reached her little hands up as high as she could get them, patting at the bricks fully twenty-eight inches under her goal. Then they ran to each other and twittered anxiously. After a time they tried reaching up the wall again, side by side. More and more they threw those terrified glances at the basement door; less and less was there any pleasure mixed with the terror.

At last they hunkered down as far as possible away from the

door, put their arms about one another and stared numbly. They slowly quieted down, from chatters to twitters to coo-ings, and at last were silent, two tiny tuffets of terror.

It seemed hours—weeks—of fascinated anticipation before Janie heard a thump and saw the door move. Out came the janitor, as usual a little bottle-weary. She could see the red crescents under his sagging yellow-whited eyes. "Bonnie!" he bellowed, "Beanie! Wha y'all?" He lurched out into the open and peered around. "Come out yeah! Look at *yew*! I gwine snatch yew bald-headed! Wheah's yo' clo'es?" He swooped down on them and caught them, each huge hand on a tiny biceps. He held them high, so that each had one toe barely touching the concrete and their little captured elbows pointed skyward. He turned around, once, twice, seeking, and at last his eye caught the glimmer of the rompers on the sill. "How you do dat?" he demanded. "You trine th'ow away yo' 'spensive clo'es? Oh, I gwine whop you."

He dropped to one knee and hung the two little bodies across the other thigh. It is probable that he had the knack of cupping his hand so that he produced more sound than fury, but however he did it, the noise was impressive. Janie giggled.

The janitor administered four equal swats to each twin and set them on their feet. They stood silently side by side with their hands pressed to their bottoms and watched him stride to the windowsill and snatch the rompers off. He threw them down at their feet and waggled his right forefinger at them. "Cotch you do dat once mo', I'll git Mr. Milton the conductah come punch yo' ears fulla holes. *Heah?*" he roared. They shrank together, their eyes round. He lurched back to the door and slammed it shut behind him.

The twins slowly climbed into their rompers. Then they went back to the shadows by the wall and hunkered down, supporting themselves with their backs and their feet. They whispered to one another. There was no more fun for Janie that day.

Across the street from Janie's apartment house was a park. It had a bandstand, a brook, a moulting peacock in a wire enclo-sure and a thick little copse of dwarf oak. In the copse was a hidden patch of bare earth, known only to Janie and several thousand people who were wont to use it in pairs at night. Since Janie was never there at night she felt herself its discoverer and its proprietor.

Some four days after the spanking episode, she thought of the place. She was bored with the twins; they never did anything interesting any more. Her mother had gone to lunch somewhere after locking her in her room. (One of her admirers, when she did this, had once asked, "What about the kid? Suppose there's a fire or something?" "Fat chance!" Wima had said with regret.)

The door of her room was fastened with a hook-and-eye on the outside. She walked to the door and looked up at the corresponding spot inside. She heard the hook rise and fall. She opened the door and walked down the hall and out to the elevators. When the self-service car arrived, she got in and pressed the third-, second- and first-floor buttons. One floor at a time the elevator descended, stopped, opened its gate, closed its gate, descended, stopped, opened its gate . . . it amused her, it was so stupid. At the bottom she pushed all of the buttons and slid out. Up the stupid elevator started. Janie clucked pityingly and went outdoors.

She crossed the street carefully, looking both ways. But when she got to the copse she was a little less ladylike. She climbed into the lower branches of the oak and across the multiple crotches to a branch she knew which overhung the hidden sanctuary. She thought she saw a movement in the bushes, but she was not sure. She hung from the branch, went hand over hand until it started to bend, waited until she had stopped swinging, and then let go.

It was an eight-inch drop to the earthen floor—usually. This time . . .

The very instant her fingers left the branch, her feet were caught and snatched violently backward. She struck the ground flat on her stomach. Her hands happened to be together, at her midriff; the impact turned them inward and drove her own fist into her solar plexus. For an unbearably long time she was nothing but one tangled knot of pain. She fought and fought and at long last sucked a tearing breath into her lungs. It would come out through her nostrils but she could get no more in. She fought again in a series of sucking sobs and blowing hisses, until the pain started to leave her.

She managed to get up on her elbows. She spat out dirt, part dusty, part muddy. She got her eyes open just enough to see one of the twins squatting before her, inches away. "Ho-ho," said the twin, grabbed her wrists, and pulled hard. Down she went on her face again. Reflexively she drew up her knees. She received a stinging blow on the rump. She looked down past her shoulder as she flung herself sideways and saw the other twin just in the midst of the follow-through with the stave from a nail keg which she held in her little hands. "He-hee," said the twin.

Janie did what she had done to the sallow, black-eyed man at the cocktail party. "Eeep," said the twin and disappeared, flickered out the way a squeezed appleseed disappears from between the fingers. The little cask stave clattered to the packed earth. Janie caught it up, whirled, and brought it down on the head of the twin who had pulled her arms. But the stave whooshed down to strike the ground; there was no one there.

Janie whimpered and got slowly to her feet. She was alone in the shadowed sanctuary. She turned and turned back. Nothing. No one.

Something plurped just on the center part of her hair. She clapped her hand to it. Wet. She looked up and the other twin spit too. It hit her on the forehead. "Ho-ho," said one. "He-hee," said the other.

Janie's upper lip curled away from her teeth, exactly the way her mother's did. She still held the cask stave. She slung it upward with all her might. One twin did not even attempt to move. The other disappeared.

"Ho-ho." There she was, on another branch. Both were grinning widely.

She hurled a bolt of hatred at them the like of which she had never even imagined before.

"Ooop," said one. The other said "Eeep." Then they were both gone.

Clenching her teeth, she leapt for the branch and swarmed up into the tree.

"Ho-ho."

It was very distant. She looked up and around and down and back; and something made her look across the street.

Two little figures sat like gargoyles on top of the courtyard wall. They waved to her and were gone.

For a long time Janie clung to the tree and stared at the wall. Then she let herself slide down into the crotch, where she could put her back against the trunk and straddle a limb. She unbuttoned her pocket and got her handkerchief. She licked a fold of it good and wet and began wiping the dirt off her face with little feline dabs.

They're only three years old, she told herself from the astonished altitude of her seniority. Then, *They knew who it was all along, that moved those rompers.*

She said aloud, in admiration, "Ho-ho . . ." There was no anger left in her. Four days ago the twins couldn't even reach a six-foot sill. They couldn't even get away from a spanking. And now look.

She got down on the street side of the tree and stepped daintily across the street. In the vestibule, she stretched up and pressed the shiny brass button marked JANITOR. While waiting she stepped off the pattern of tiles in the floor, heel and toe.

"Who push dat? You push dat?" His voice filled the whole world.

She went and stood in front of him and pushed up her lips the way her mother did when she made her voice all croony, like sometimes on the telephone. "Mister Widdecombe, my mother says can I play with your little girls."

"She say dat? *Well!*" The janitor took off his round hat and whacked it against his palm and put it on again. "Well. Dat's mighty nice . . . little gal," he said sternly, "is yo' mother to home?"

"Oh *yes*," said Janie, fairly radiating candor.

"You wait raht cheer," he said, and pounded away down the cellar steps.

She had to wait more than ten minutes this time. When he came back with the twins he was fairly out of breath. They looked very solemn.

"Now don't you let 'em get in any mischief. And see ef you cain't keep them clo'es on 'em. They ain't got no more use for clo'es than a jungle monkey. Gwan, now, hole hands, chillun, an' mine you don't leave go tel you git there."

The twins approached guardedly. She took their hands. They watched her face. She began to move toward the elevators, and they followed. The janitor beamed after them.

Janie's whole life shaped itself from that afternoon. It was a time of belonging, of thinking alike, of transcendent sharing. For her age, Janie had what was probably a unique vocabulary, yet she spoke hardly a word. The twins had not yet learned to talk. Their private vocabulary of squeaks and whispers was incidental to another kind of communion. Janie got a sign of it, a touch of it, a sudden opening, growing rush of it. Her mother hated her and feared her; her father was a remote and angry entity, always away or shouting at mother or closed sulkily about himself. She was talked to, never spoken to.

But here was converse, detailed, fluent, fascinating, with no sound but laughter. They would be silent; they would all squat suddenly and paw through Janie's beautiful books; then suddenly it was the dolls. Janie showed them how she could get chocolates from the box in the other room without going in there and how she could throw a pillow clear up to the ceiling without touching it. They liked that, though the paintbox and easel impressed them more.

It was a thing together, binding, immortal; it would always be new for them and it would never be repeated.

The afternoon slid by, as smooth and soft and lovely as a passing gull, and as swift. When the hall door banged open and Wima's voice clanged out, the twins were still there.

"All righty, all righty, come in for a drink then, who wants to stand out there all night." She pawed her hat off and her hair swung raggedly over her face. The man caught her roughly and pulled her close and bit her face. She howled. "You're crazy, you old crazy you." Then she saw them, all three of them peering out. "Dear old Jesus be to God," she said, "she's got the place filled with niggers."

"They're going home," said Janie resolutely. "I'll take 'em home right now."

"Honest to God, Pete," she said to the man, "this is the God's honest first time this ever happened. You got to believe that, Pete. What kind of a place you must think I run here, I hate to think how it looks to you. Well get them the hell out!" she screamed at Janie. "Honest to God, Pete, so help me, never before—"

Janie walked down the hall to the elevators. She looked at Bonnie and at Beanie. Their eyes were round. Janie's mouth was as dry as a carpet and she was so embarrassed her legs cramped. She put the twins into an elevator and pressed the bottom button. She did not say goodbye, though she felt nothing else.

She walked slowly back to the apartment and went in and closed the door. Her mother got up from the man's lap and clattered across the room. Her teeth shone and her chin was wet. She raised claws—not a hand, not a fist, but red, pointed claws.

Something happened inside Janie like the grinding of teeth, but deeper inside her than that. She was walking and she did not stop. She put her hands behind her and tilted her chin up so she could meet her mother's eyes.

Wima's voice ceased, snatched away. She loomed over the five-year-old, her claws out and forward, hanging, curving over, a blood-tipped wave about to break.

Janie walked past her and into her room, and quietly closed the door.

Wima's arms drew back, strangely, as if they must follow the exact trajectory of their going. She repossessed them and the dissolving balance of her body and finally her voice. Behind her the man's teeth clattered swiftly against a glass.

Wima turned and crossed the room to him, using the furniture like a series of canes and crutches. "Oh God," she murmured, "but she gives me the creeps. . . ."

He said, "You got lots going on around here."

Janie lay in bed as stiff and smooth and contained as a round toothpick. Nothing would get in, nothing could get out; somewhere she had found this surface that went all the way through, and as long as she had it, nothing was going to happen.

But if anything happens, came a whisper, *you'll break.*

But if I don't break, nothing will happen, she answered.

But if anything . . .

The dark hours came and grew black and the black hours labored by.

Her door crashed open and the light blazed. "He's gone and baby, I've got business with you. Get out here!" Wima's bathrobe swirled against the doorpost as she turned and went away.

Janie pushed back the covers and thumped her feet down. Without understanding quite why, she began to get dressed. She got her good plaid dress and the shoes with two buckles, and the knit pants and the slip with the lace rabbits. There were little rabbits on her socks too, and on the sweater, the buttons were rabbits' fuzzy nubbin tails.

Wima was on the couch, pounding and pounding with her fist. "You wrecked my cel," she said, and drank from a square-stemmed glass, "ebration, so you ought to know what I'm celebrating. You don't know it but I've had a big trouble and I didn't know how to hannel it, and now it's all done for me. And I'll tell you all about it right now, little baby Miss Big Ears. Big Mouth. Smarty. Because your father, I can hannel him any time, but what was I going to do with your big mouth going day and night? That was my trouble, what was I going to do about your big mouth when he got back. Well it's all fixed, he won't be back, the Heinies fixed it up for me." She waved a yellow sheet. "Smart girls know that's a telegram, and the telegram says, says here, 'Regret to inform you that your husband.' They shot your father, that's what they regret to say, and now this is the way it's going to be from now on between you and me. Whatever I want to do I do, an' whatever you want to nose into, nose away. Now isn't that fair?"

She turned to be answered but there was no answer. Janie was gone.

Wima knew before she started that there wasn't any use looking, but something made her run to the hall closet and look in the top shelf. There wasn't anything up there but Christmas tree ornaments and they hadn't been touched in three years.

She stood in the middle of the living room, not knowing which way to go. She whispered, "Janie?"

She put her hands on the sides of her face and lifted her hair away from it. She turned around and around, and asked, "What's the matter with me?"

Prodd used to say, "There's this about a farm: when the market's good there's money, and when it's bad there's food." Actually the principle hardly operated here, for his contact with markets was slight. It was a long haul to town and what if there's a tooth off the hayrake? "We've still got a workin' majority." Two off, eight, twelve? "Then make another pass. No road will go by here, not ever. Place will never get too big, get out of hand." Even the war passed them by, Prodd being over age and Lone—well, the sheriff was by once and had a look at the halfwit working on Prodd's, and one look was enough.

When Prodd was young the little farmhouse was there, and when he married they built on to it—a little, not a lot, just a room. If the room had ever been used the land wouldn't have been enough. Lone slept in the room of course but that wasn't quite the same thing. That's not what the room was for.

Lone sensed the change before anyone else, even before Mrs. Prodd. It was a difference in the nature of one of her silences. It was a treasure-proud silence, and Lone felt it change as a man's kind of pride might change when he turned from a jewel he treasured to a green shoot he treasured. He said nothing and concluded nothing; he just knew.

He went on with his work as before. He worked well; Prodd used to say that whatever anyone might think, that boy was a farmer before his accident. He said it not knowing that his own style of farming was as available to Lone as water from his pump. So was anything else Lone wanted to take.

So the day Prodd came down to the south meadow, where Lone was stepping and turning tirelessly, a very part of his whispering scythe, Lone knew what it was that he wanted to say. He caught Prodd's gaze for half a breath in those disturbing eyes and knew as well that saying it would pain Prodd more than a little.

Understanding was hardly one of his troubles any more, but niceties of expression were. He stopped mowing and went to the forest margin nearby and let the scythe-point drop into a rotten stump. It gave him time to rehearse his tongue, still thick and unwieldy after eight years here.

Prodd followed slowly. He was rehearsing too.

Suddenly, Lone found it. "Been thinking," he said.

Prodd waited, glad to wait. Lone said, "I should go." That wasn't quite it. "Move along," he said, watching. That was better.

"Ah, Lone. Why?"

Lone looked at him. *Because you want me to go.*

"Don't you like it here?" said Prodd, not wanting to say that at all.

"Sure." From Prodd's mind, he caught, *Does he know?* and his own answered, *Of course I know!* But Prodd couldn't hear that. Lone said slowly, "Just time to be moving along."

"Well." Prodd kicked a stone. He turned to look at the house and that turned him away from Lone, and that made it easier. "When we came here, we built Jack's, *your* room, the room you're using. We call it Jack's room. You know why, you know who Jack is?"

Yes, Lone thought. He said nothing.

"Long as you're . . . long as you want to leave anyway, it won't make no difference to you. Jack's our son." He squeezed his hands together. "I guess it sounds funny. Jack was the little guy we were so sure about, we built that room with seed money. Jack, he—"

He looked up at the house, at its stub of a built-on wing, and around at the rock-toothed forest rim. "—never got born," he finished.

"Ah," said Lone. He'd picked that up from Prodd. It was useful.

"He's coming now, though," said Prodd in a rush. His face was alight. "We're a bit old for it, but there's a daddy or two quite a bit older, and mothers too." Again he looked up at the barn, the house. "Makes sense in a sort of way, you know, Lone. Now, if he'd been along when we planned it, the place would've been too small when he was growed enough to work it with me, and me with no place else to go. But now, why, I reckon when he's growed we just naturally won't be here any more, and he'll take him a nice little wife and start out just about like we did. So you see it does make a kind of sense?" He seemed to be pleading. Lone made no attempt to understand this.

"Lone, listen to me, I don't want you to feel we're turning you out."

"Said I was going." Searching, he found something and amended, "'Fore you told me." *That*, he thought, *was very right.*

"Look, I got to say something," said Prodd. "I heard tell of folk who want kids and can't have 'em, sometimes they just give up trying and take in somebody else's. And sometimes, with a kid in the house, they turn right round and have one of their own after all."

"Ah," said Lone.

"So what I mean is, we taken you in, didn't we, and now look."

Lone did not know what to say. "Ah" seemed wrong.

"We got a lot to thank you for, is what I mean, so we don't want you to feel we're turning you out."

"I already said."

"Good then." Prodd smiled. He had a lot of wrinkles on his face, mostly from smiling.

"Good," said Lone. "About Jack." He nodded vehemently. "Good." He picked up the scythe. When he reached his windrow, he looked after Prodd. *Walks slower than he used to*, he thought.

Lone's next conscious thought was, Well, that's finished.

What's finished? he asked himself.

He looked around. "Mowing," he said. Only then he realized that he had been working for more than three hours since Prodd spoke to him, and it was as if some other person had done it. He himself had been—*gone* in some way.

Absently he took his whetstone and began to dress the scythe. It made a sound like a pot boiling over when he moved it slowly, and like a shrew dying when he moved it fast.

Where had he known this feeling of time passing, as it were, behind his back?

He moved the stone slowly. Cooking and warmth and work. A birthday cake. A clean bed. A sense of . . . "Membership" was not a word he possessed but that was his thought.

No, obliterated time didn't exist in those memories. He moved the stone faster.

Death-cries in the wood. Lonely hunter and its solitary prey. The sap falls and the bear sleeps and the birds fly south, all doing it together, not because they are all members of the same thing, but only because they are all solitary things hurt by the same thing.

That was where time had passed without his awareness of it. Almost always, before he came here. That was how he had lived.

Why should it come back to him now, then?

He swept his gaze around the land, as Prodd had done, taking in the house and its imbalancing bulge, and the land, and the woods which held the farm like water in a basin. When I was alone, he thought, time passed me like that. Time passes like that now, so it must be that I am alone again.

And then he knew that he had been alone the whole time. Mrs. Prodd hadn't raised him up, not really. She had been raising up her Jack the whole time.

Once in the wood, in water and agony, he had been a part of something, and in wetness and pain it had been torn from him. And if, for eight years now, he had thought he had found something else to belong to, then for eight years he had been wrong.

Anger was foreign to him; he had only felt it once before. But now it came, a wash of it that made him swell, that drained and left him weak. And he himself was the object of it. For hadn't he known? Hadn't he taken a name for himself, knowing that the name was a crystallization of all he had ever been and done? All he had ever been and done was *alone*. Why should he have let himself feel any other way?

Wrong. Wrong as a squirrel with feathers, or a wolf with wooden teeth; not injustice, not unfairness—just a wrongness that, under the sky, could not exist . . . the idea that such as he could belong to anything.

Hear that, *son*? Hear, that, *man*?

Hear that, Lone?

He picked up three long fresh stalks of timothy and braided them together. He upended the scythe and thrust the handle deep enough into the soft earth so it would stand upright. He tied the braided grass to one of the grips and slipped the whetstone into the loops so it would stay. Then he walked off into the woods.

*

It was too late even for the copse's nocturnal habitants. It was cold at the hidden foot of the dwarf oak and as dark as the chambers of a dead man's heart.

She sat on the bare earth. As time went on, she had slid down a little and her plaid skirt had moved up. Her legs were icy, especially when the night air moved on them. But she didn't pull the skirt down because it didn't matter. Her hand lay on one of the fuzzy buttons of her sweater because, two hours ago, she had been fingering it and wondering what it was like to be a bunny. Now she didn't care whether or not the button was a bunny's tail or where her hand happened to be.

She had learned all she could from being there. She had learned that if you leave your eyes open until you have to blink and you don't blink, they start to hurt. Then if you leave them open even longer, they hurt worse and worse. And if you still leave them open, they suddenly stop hurting.

It was too dark there to know whether they could still see after that.

And she had learned that if you sit absolutely still for long enough it hurts too, and then stops. But then you mustn't move, not the tiniest little bit, because if you do it will hurt worse than anything.

When a top spins it stands up straight and walks around. When it slows a little it stands in one place and wobbles. When it slows a lot it waggles around like Major Grenfell after a cocktail party. Then it almost stops and lies down and bumps and thumps and thrashes around. After that it won't move any more.

When she had the happy time with the twins she had been spinning like that. When Mother came home the top inside didn't walk any more, it stood still and waggled. When Mother called her out of her bed she was waving and weaving. When she hid here her spinner inside bumped and kicked. Well, it wasn't doing it any more and it wouldn't.

She started to see how long she could hold her breath. Not with a big deep lungful first, but just breathing quieter and quieter and missing an *in* and quieter and quieter still, and missing an *out*. She got to where the misses took longer than the breathings.

The wind stirred her skirt. All she could feel was the movement and that too was remote, as if she had a thin pillow between it and her legs.

Her spinner, with the lift gone out of it, went round and round with its rim on the floor and went slower and slower and at last

stopped

. . . and began to roll back the other way, but not very far, not fast and

stopped

and a little way back, it was too dark for anything to roll, and even if it did you wouldn't be able to see it, you couldn't even hear it, it was so dark.

But anyway, she rolled. She rolled over on her stomach and on her back and pain squeezed her nostrils together and filled up her stomach like too much soda water. She gasped with the pain and gasping was breathing and when she breathed she remembered who she was. She rolled over again without wanting to, and something like little animals ran on her face. She fought them weakly. They weren't pretend-things, she discovered; they were real as real. They whispered and cooed. She tried to sit up and the little animals ran behind her and helped. She dangled her head down and felt the warmth of her breath falling into the front of her dress. One of the little animals stroked her cheek and she put up a hand and caught it.

"Ho-ho," it said.

On the other side, something soft and small and strong wriggled and snuggled tight up against her. She felt it, smooth and alive. It said "He-hee."

She put one arm around Bonnie and one arm around Beanie and began to cry.

Lone came back to borrow an ax. You can do just so much with your bare hands.

When he broke out of the woods he saw the difference in the farm. It was as if every day it existed had been a gray day, and now the sun was on it. All the colors were brighter by an immensurable amount; the barn-smells, growth-smells, stove-smoke smells were clearer and purer. The corn stretched skyward with such intensity in its lines that it seemed to be threatening its roots.

Prodd's venerable stake-bed pick-up truck was grunting and howling somewhere down the slope. Following the margins, Lone went downhill until he could see the truck. It was in the fallow field which, apparently, Prodd had decided to turn. The truck was hitched to a gang plow with all the shares but one removed. The right rear wheel had run too close to the furrow, dropped in, and buried, so that the truck rested on its rear axle and the wheel spun almost free. Prodd was pounding stones under it with the end of a pick-handle. When he saw Lone he dropped it and ran toward him, his face beaming like firelight. He took Lone's upper arms in his hands and read his face like the page of a book, slowly, a line at a time, moving his lips. "Man, I thought I wouldn't see you again, going off like you did."

"You want help," said Lone, meaning the truck.

Prodd misunderstood. "Now wouldn't you know," he said happily. "Come all the way back just to see if you could lend a hand. Oh, I been doing fine by myself, Lone, believe me. Not that I don't appreciate it. But I feel like it these days. Working, I mean."

Lone went and picked up the pick-handle. He prodded at the stones under the wheel. "Drive," he said.

"Wait'll Ma sees you," said Prodd. "Like old times." He got in and started the truck. Lone put the small of his back against the rear edge of the truck-bed, clamped his hands on it, and as the clutch engaged, he heaved. The body came up as high as the rear springs would let it, and still higher. He leaned back. The wheel found purchase and the truck jolted up and forward onto firm ground.

Prodd climbed out and came back to look into the hole, the irresistible and useless act of a man who picks up broken china and puts its edges together. "I used to say, I bet you were a farmer once," he grinned. "But now I know. You were a hydraulic jack."

Lone did not smile. He never smiled. Prodd went to the plow and Lone helped him wrestle the hitch back to the truck. "Horse dropped dead," Prodd explained. "Truck's all right but sometimes I wish there was some way to keep this from happening. Spend half my time diggin' it out. I'd get another horse, but you know—hold everything till after Jack gets here. You'd think that would bother me, losing the horse." He looked up at the house and smiled. "Nothing bothers me now. Had breakfast?"

"Yes."

"Well come have some more. You know Ma. Wouldn't forgive either of us if she wasn't to feed you."

They went back to the house, and when Ma saw Lone she hugged him hard. Something stirred uncomfortably in Lone. He wanted an ax. He thought all these other things were settled. "You sit right down there and I'll get you some breakfast."

"Told you," said Prodd, watching her, smiling. Lone watched her too. She was heavier and happy as a kitten in a cowshed. "What you doing now, Lone?"

Lone looked into his eyes to find some sort of an answer. "Working," he said. He moved his hand. "Up there."

"In the woods?"

"Yes."

"What you doing?" When Lone waited, Prodd asked, "You hired out? No? Then what—trapping?"

"Trapping," said Lone, knowing that this would be sufficient.

He ate. From where he sat he could see Jack's room. The bed was gone. There was a new one in there, not much longer than his forearm, all draped with pale-blue cotton and cheesecloth with dozens of little tucks sewn into it.

When he was finished they all sat around the table and for a time nobody said anything. Lone looked into Prodd's eyes and found *He's a good boy but not the kind to set around and visit.* He couldn't understand the *visit* image, a vague and happy blur of conversation-sounds and laughter. He recognized this as one of the many lacks he was aware of in himself—lacks, rather than inadequacies; things he could not do and would never be able to do. So he just asked Prodd for the ax and went out.

"You don't s'pose he's mad at us?" asked Mrs. Prodd, looking anxiously after Lone.

"Him?" said Prodd. "He wouldn't have come back here if

he was. I was afraid of that myself until today." He went to the door. "Don't you lift nothing heavy, hear?"

Janie read as slowly and carefully as she could. She didn't have to read aloud, but only carefully enough so the twins could understand. She had reached the part where the woman tied the man to the pillar and then let the other man, the "my rival, her laughing lover" one, out of the closet where he had been hidden and gave him the whip. Janie looked up at that point and found Bonnie gone and Beanie in the cold fireplace, pretending there was a mouse hiding in the ashes. "Oh, you're not listening," she said.

Want the one with the pictures, the silent message came.

"I'm getting so tired of that one," said Janie petulantly. But she closed *Venus in Furs* by von Sacher-Masoch and put it on the table. "This's anyway got a story to it," she complained, going to the shelves. She found the wanted volume between *My Gun Is Quick* and *The Illustrated Ivan Bloch*, and hefted it back to the armchair. Beanie disappeared from the fireplace and reappeared by the chair. Bonnie stood on the other side; wherever she had been, she had been aware of what was happening. If anything, she liked this book even better than Beanie.

Janie opened the book at random. The twins leaned forward breathless, their eyes bugging.

Read it.

"Oh, all right," said Janie. " 'D34556. Tieback. Double shirred. 90 inches long. Maize, burgundy, hunter green and white. $24.68. D34557. Cottage style. Stuart or Argyll plaid, see illus. $4.92 pair. D34—' "

And they were happy again.

They had been happy ever since they got here and much of the hectic time before that. They had learned how to open the back of a trailer-truck and how to lie without moving under hay, and Janie could pull clothespins off a line and the twins could appear inside a room, like a store at night, and unlock the door from the inside when it was fastened with some kind of lock that Janie couldn't move, the way she could a hook-and-eye or a tower bolt which was shot but not turned. The best thing they had learned, though, was the way the twins could attract attention when somebody was chasing Janie.

They'd found out for sure that to have two little girls throwing rocks from second-floor windows and appearing under their feet to trip them and suddenly sitting on their shoulders and wetting into their collars, made it impossible to catch Janie, who was just ordinarily running. Ho-ho.

And this house was just the happiest thing of all. It was miles and miles away from anything or anybody and no one ever came here. It was a big house on a hill, in forest so thick you hardly knew it was there. It had a big high wall around it on the road side, and a big high fence on the woods side and a brook ran through. Bonnie had found it one day when they had gotten tired and gone to sleep by the road. Bonnie woke up and went exploring by herself and found the fence and went along it until she saw the house. They'd had a terrible time finding some way to get Janie in, though, until Beanie fell into the brook where it went through the fence, and came up on the inside.

There were zillions of books in the biggest room and plenty of old sheets they could wrap around themselves when it was cold. Down in the cold dark cellar rooms they had found a half-dozen cases of canned vegetables and some bottles of wine, which later they smashed all over because, although it tasted bad, it smelled just wonderful. There was a pool out back to swim in that was more fun than the bathrooms, which had no windows. There were plenty of places for hide-and-seek. There was even a little room with chains on the walls, and bars.

It went much faster with the ax.

He never would have found the place at all if he had not hurt himself. In all the years he had wandered the forests, often blindly and uncaring, he had never fallen into such a trap. One moment he was stepping over the crest of an outcropping, and next he was twenty feet down, in a bramble-choked, humus-floored pitfall. He hurt one of his eyes and his left arm hurt unbearably at the elbow.

Once he had thrashed his way out, he surveyed the place. Perhaps it had once been a pool in the slope, with the lower side thin and erosible. It was gone, however, and what was left was a depression in the hillside, thickly grown inside, ever more thickly screened on both sides and at the front. The rock over which he had stepped rose out of the hill and overhung the depression.

At one time it had not mattered in the least to Lone whether he was near men or not. Now, he wanted only to be able to be what he knew he was—alone. But eight years at the farm had changed his way of life. He needed shelter. And the more he looked at this hidden place, with its overhanging rock wall-ceiling and the two earthen wings which flanked it, the more shelterlike it seemed.

At first his work on it was primitive. He cleared out enough brush so that he might lie down comfortably and pulled up a bush or two so that the brambles would not flay him as he went in and out. Then it rained and he had to channel the inside so that water would not stand inside, and he made a rough thatch at the crest.

But as time went on he became increasingly absorbed in the place. He pulled up more bush and pounded the earth until he had a level floor. He removed all the rock he could find loose on the rear wall, and discovered that some of the wall had ready-made shelves and nooks for the few things he might want to store. He began raiding the farms that skirted the foot of the mountain, operating at night, taking only a very little at each place, never coming back to any one place if he could help it. He got carrots and potatoes and tenpenny spikes and haywire, a broken hammer and a cast-iron pot. Once he found a side of bacon that had fallen from an abattoir truck. He stored it and when he came back he found that a lynx had been at it. That determined him to make walls, which was why he went back for the ax.

He felled trees, the biggest he could handle after trimming, and snaked them up to the hillside. He buried the first three so that they bounded the floor, and the side ones butted against the rock. He found a red clay which, when mixed with peat moss, made a mortar that was vermin-proof and would not wash away. He built up his walls and a door. He did not bother with a window, but simply left out a yard of mortar between six of the wall logs, on each side, and trimmed long side-tapered sticks to wedge in them when he wanted them closed.

His first fireplace was Indian-style, out near the center of the enclosure, with a hole at the top to let the smoke out. High up were hooks embedded in rock fissures, for hanging meat where the smoke could get to it, if he were ever fortunate enough to get some.

He was out hunting for flagstones for the fireplace when an invisible something began to tug at him. He recoiled as if he had been burned and shrank back against a tree and cast about him like a cornered elk.

It had been a long time since he had been aware of his inner sensitivity to the useless (to him) communication of infants. He was losing it; he had begun to be insensitive to it when he began to gain speech.

But someone had called to him this way—someone who "sent" like a child, but who was not a child. And though what he felt now was faint, it was in substance unbearably similar. It was sweet and needful, yes; but it was also the restimulation of a stinging lash and a terror of crushing kicks and obscene shouting, and the greatest loss he had ever known.

There was nothing to be seen. Slowly he left the tree and went back to the slab of stone he had been pawing at to free it from the earth. For perhaps half an hour he worked doggedly, trying to ignore the call. And he failed.

He rose, shaken, and began to walk to the call in a world turned dreamlike. The longer he walked, the more irresistible the call became and the deeper his enchantment. He walked for an hour, never going around anything if he could possibly go over it or through it, and by the time he reached the leached clearing he was nearly somnambulant. To permit himself any more consciousness would have been to kindle such an inferno of conflict that he could not have gone on. Stumbling blindly, he walked right up to and into the rusting fence which struck him cruelly over his hurt eye. He clung to it until his vision cleared, looked around to see where he was, and began to tremble.

He had one moment of clear, conscious determination: to get out of this terrible place and stay out of it And even as he felt this touch of reason, he heard the brook and was turning toward it.

Where brook and fence met, he lowered himself in the water

and made his way to the foot of the pickets. Yes, the opening was still here.

He peered in through the fence, but the ancient holly was thicker than ever. There was nothing to be heard, either—aurally. But the call . . .

Like the one he had heard before, it was a hunger, an aloneness, a wanting. The difference was in what it wanted. It said without words that it was a little afraid, and burdened, and was solicitous of the burden. It said in effect *who will take care of me now?*

Perhaps the cold water helped. Lone's mind suddenly became as clear as it ever could. He took a deep breath and submerged. Immediately on the other side he stopped and raised his head. He listened carefully, then lay on his stomach with only his nostrils above the water. With exquisite care, he inched forward on his elbows, until his head was inside the arch and he could see through.

There was a little girl on the bank, dressed in a torn plaid dress. She was about six. Her sharp-planed, unchildlike face was down-drawn and worried. And if he thought his caution was effective, he was quite wrong. She was looking directly at him.

"Bonnie!" she called sharply.

Nothing happened.

He stayed where he was. She continued to watch him, but she continued to worry. He realized two things: that it was this worriment of hers which was the essence of the call; and that although she was on her guard, she did not consider him important enough to divert her from her thoughts.

For the first time in his life he felt that edged and spicy mixture of anger and amusement called pique. This was followed by a great surge of relief, much like what one would feel on setting down a forty-pound pack after forty years. He had not known . . . he had not *known* the size of his burden!

And away went the restimulation. Back into the past went the whip and the bellowing, the magic and the loss—remembered still, but back where they belonged, with their raw-nerve tendrils severed so that never again could they reach into his present. The call was no maelstrom of blood and emotion, but the aimless chunterings of a hungry brat.

He sank and shot backward like a great lean crawfish, under the fence. He slogged up out of the brook, turned his back on the call and went back to his work.

When he got back to his shelter, streaming with perspiration, an eighteen-inch flagstone on his shoulder, he was weary enough to forget his usual caution. He crashed in through the underbrush to the tiny clearing before his door, and stopped dead.

There was a small naked infant about four years old squatting in front of his door.

She looked up at him and her eyes—her whole dark face—seemed to twinkle. "He-hee!" she said happily.

He tipped the stone off his shoulder and let it fall. He loomed over her, shadowed her; sky-high and full of the threats of thunder.

She seemed completely unafraid. She turned her eyes away from him and busily began nibbling at a carrot, turning it squirrel-wise, around and around as she ate.

A high movement caught his eye. Another carrot was emerging from the ventilation chinks in the log wall. It fell to the ground and was followed by still another.

"Ho-ho." He looked down, and there were *two* little girls.

The only advantage which Lone possessed under these circumstances was a valuable one: he had no impulse whatever to question his sanity and start a confusing debate with himself on the matter. He bent down and scooped one of the children up. But when he straightened she wasn't there any more.

The other was. She grinned enchantingly and started on one of the new carrots.

Lone said, "What you doing?" His voice was harsh and ill-toned, like that of a deaf-mute. It startled the child. She stopped eating and looked up at him open-mouthed. The open mouth was filled with carrot chips and gave her rather the appearance of a pot-bellied stove with the door open.

He sank down on his knees. Her eyes were fixed on his and his were eyes which had once commanded a man to kill himself and which, many times, violated the instincts of others who had not wanted to feed him. Without knowing why he was careful. There was no anger in him or fear; he simply wanted her to stay still.

When he was done, he reached for her. She exhaled noisily, blowing tiny wet chips of raw carrot into his eyes and nostrils, and vanished.

He was filled with astonishment—a strange thing in itself, for he had seldom been interested enough in anything to be astonished. Stranger still, it was a respectful astonishment.

He rose and put his back against the log wall, and looked for them. They stood side by side, hand in hand, looking up at him out of little wooden wondering faces, waiting for him to do something else.

Once, years ago, he had run to catch a deer. Once he had reached up from the ground to catch a bird in a treetop. Once he had plunged into a stream after a trout.

Once.

Lone was simply not constituted to chase something he knew empirically that he could not catch. He bent and picked up his flagstone, reached up and slid aside the outside bar which fastened his door and shouldered into the house.

He bedded his flagstone by the fire and swept the guttering embers over part of it. He threw on more wood and blew it up brightly, set up his green-stick crane and swung the iron pot on it. All the while there were two little white-eyed knobs silhouetted in the doorway, watching him. He ignored them.

The skinned rabbit swung on the high hook by the smoke hole. He got it down, tore off the quarters, broke the back and dropped it all into the pot. From a niche he took potatoes and a few grains of rock salt. The salt went into the pot and so did the potatoes after he had split them in two on his ax-blade. He reached for his carrots. Somebody had been at his carrots.

He wheeled and frowned at the doorway. The two heads whipped back out of sight. From outdoors came small soprano giggles.

Lone let the pot boil for an hour while he honed the ax and tied up a witch's broom like Mrs. Prodd's. And slowly, a fraction of an inch at a time, his visitors edged into the room. Their eyes were fixed on the seething pot. They fairly drooled.

He went about his business without looking at them. When

he came close they retreated and when he crossed the room they entered again—that little fraction more each time. Soon their retreats were smaller and their advances larger until at last Lone had a chance to slam the door shut—which he did.

In the sudden darkness, the simmer of the pot and the small hiss of the flames sounded very loud. There was no other sound. Lone stood with his back against the door and closed his eyes very tight to adjust them more quickly to the darkness. When he opened them, the bars of waning daylight at the vents and the fireglow were quite sufficient for him to see everything in the room.

The little girls were gone.

He put on the inner bar and slowly circled the room. Nothing.

He opened the door cautiously, then flung it wide. They were not outside either.

He shrugged. He pulled on his lower lip and wished he had more carrots. Then he set the pot aside to cool enough so that he could eat and finished honing the ax.

At length he ate. He had reached the point of licking his fingers by way of having dessert, when a sharp knock on the door caused him to leap eighteen inches higher than upright, so utterly unexpected was it.

In the doorway stood the little girl in the plaid dress. Her hair was combed, her face scrubbed. She carried with a superb air an object which seemed to be a handbag but which at second glance revealed itself as a teakwood cigarette box with a piece of binder-twine fastened to it with four-inch nails. "Good evening," she said concisely. "I was passing by and thought I would come to call. You *are* at home?"

This parroting of a penurious beldame who once was in the habit of cadging meals by this means was completely incomprehensible to Lone. He resumed licking his fingers but he kept his eyes on the child's face. Behind the girl, suddenly, appeared the heads of his two previous visitors peeping around the doorpost.

The child's nostrils, then her eyes, found the stew pot. She wooed it with her gaze, yearned. She yawned, too, suddenly. "I beg your pardon," she said demurely. She pried open the lid of the cigarette box, drew out a white object and folded it quickly but not quickly enough to conceal the fact that it was a large man's sock, and patted her lips with it.

Lone rose and got a piece of wood and placed it carefully on the fire and sat down again. The girl took another step. The other two scuttled in and stood, one on each side of the doorway like toy soldiers. Their faces were little knots of apprehension. And they were clothed this time. One wore a pair of lady's linen bloomers, the like of which has not been seen since cars had tillers. It came up to her armpits, and was supported by two short lengths of the same hairy binder-twine, poked through holes torn in the waistband and acting as shoulder straps. The other one wore a heavy cotton slip, or at least the top third of it. It fell to her ankles where it showed a fringe of torn and unhemmed material.

With the exact air of a lady crossing a drawing room toward the bonbons, the white child approached the stewpot, flashed Lone a small smile, lowered her eyelids and reached down with a thumb and forefinger, murmuring, "May I?"

Lone stretched out one long leg and hooked the pot away from her and into his grasp. He set it on the floor on the side away from her and looked at her woodenly.

"You're a real cheap stingy son of a bitch," the child quoted.

This also missed Lone completely. Before he had learned to be aware of what men said, such remarks had been meaningless. Since, he had not been exposed to them. He stared at her blankly and pulled the pot protectively closer.

The child's eyes narrowed and her color rose. Suddenly she began to cry. "Please," she said. "I'm hungry. *We're* hungry. The stuff in the cans, it's all gone." Her voice failed her but she could still whisper. "Please," she whispered, "please."

Lone regarded her stonily. At length she took a timid step toward him. He lifted the pot into his lap and hugged it defiantly. She said, "Well, I didn't want any of your old . . ." but then her voice broke. She turned away and went to the door. The others watched her face as she came. They radiated silent disappointment; their eloquent expressions took the white girl to task far more than they did him. She had the status of provider and she had failed them, and they were merciless in their expression of it.

He sat with the warm pot in his lap and looked out the open

door into the thickening night. Unbidden, an image appeared to him—Mrs. Prodd, a steaming platter of baked ham flanked by the orange gaze of perfect eggs, saying, "Now you set right down and have some breakfast." An emotion he was unequipped to define reached up from his solar plexus and tugged at his throat.

He snorted, reached into the pot, scooped out half a potato and opened his mouth to receive it. His hand would not deliver. He bent his head slowly and looked at the potato as if he could not quite recognize it or its function.

He snorted again, flung the potato back into the pot, thumped the pot back on the floor and leapt to his feet. He put one hand on each side of the door and sent his flat harsh voice hurtling out: "*Wait!*"

The corn should have been husked long since. Most of it still stood but here and there the stalks lay broken and yellowing, and soldier-ants were prospecting them and scurrying off with rumors. Out in the fallow field the truck lay forlornly, bogged, with the seeder behind it, tipped forward over its hitch and the winter wheat spilling out. No smoke came from the chimney up at the house and the half-door into the barn, askew and perverted amid the misery, hollowly applauded.

Lone approached the house, mounted the stoop. Prodd sat on the porch glider which now would not glide, for one set of end-chains was broken. His eyes were not closed but they were more closed than open.

"Hi," said Lone.

Prodd stirred, looked full into Lone's face. There was no sign of recognition. He dropped his gaze, pushed back to sit upright, felt aimlessly around his chest, found a suspender strap, pulled it forward and let it snap back. A troubled expression passed through his features and left it. He looked up again at Lone, who could sense self-awareness returning to the farmer like coffee soaking upward into a lump of sugar.

"Well, Lone, boy!" said Prodd. The old words were there but the tone behind them behaved like his broken hay rake. He rose, beaming, came to Lone, raised his fist to thump Lone's arm but then apparently forgot it. The fist hovered there for a moment and then gravitated downward.

"Corn's for husking," said Lone.

"Yeah, yeah, I know," Prodd half said, half sighed. "I'll get to it. I can handle it all right. One way or 'tother, always get done by the first frost. Ain't missed milkin' once," he added with wan pride.

Lone glanced through the door pane and saw, for the very first time, crusted dishes, heavy flies in the kitchen. "The baby come," he said, remembering.

"Oh, yes. Fine little feller, just like we . . ." Again he seemed to forget. The words slowed and were left suspended as his fist had been. "Ma!" he shrieked suddenly, "fix a bite for the boy, here!" He turned to Lone, embarrassedly. "She's yonder," he said pointing. "Yell loud enough, I reckon she'd hear. Maybe."

Lone looked where Prodd pointed, but saw nothing. He caught Prodd's gaze and for a split second started to probe. He recoiled violently at the very nature of what was there before he got close enough to identify it. He turned away quickly. "Brought your ax."

"Oh, that's all right. You could've kept it."

"Got my own. Want to get that corn in?"

Prodd gazed mistily at the corn patch. "Never missed a milking," he said.

Lone left him and went to the barn for a corn hook. He found one. He also discovered that the cow was dead. He went up to the corn patch and got to work. After a time he saw Prodd down the line, working too, working hard.

Well past midday and just before they had the corn all cut, Prodd disappeared into the house. Twenty minutes later he emerged with a pitcher and a platter of sandwiches. The bread was dry and the sandwiches were corned beef from, as Lone recalled, Mrs. Prodd's practically untouched "rainy day" shelf. The pitcher contained warm lemonade and dead flies. Lone asked no questions. They perched on the edge of the horse trough and ate.

Afterward Lone went down to the fallow field and got the truck dug out. Prodd followed him down in time to drive it out. The rest of the day was devoted to the seeding with Lone loading the seeder and helping four different times to free the truck from the traps it insisted upon digging for itself. When that was finished, Lone waved Prodd up to the barn where he got a rope around the dead cow's neck and hauled it as near as the truck would go to the edge of the wood. When at last they ran the truck into the barn for the night, Prodd said, "Sure miss that horse."

"You said you didn't miss it a-tall," Lone recalled tactlessly.

"Did I now." Prodd turned inward and smiled, remembering. "Yeah, nothing bothered me none, because of, you know." Still smiling, he turned to Lone and said, "Come back to the house." He smiled all the way back.

They went through the kitchen. It was even worse than it had looked from outside and the clock was stopped, too. Prodd, smiling, threw open the door of Jack's room. Smiling, he said, "Have a look, boy. Go right on in, have a look."

Lone went in and looked into the bassinet. The cheesecloth was torn and the blue cotton was moist and reeking. The baby had eyes like upholstery tacks and skin the color of mustard. Short blue-black horsehair covered its skull, and it breathed noisily.

Lone did not change expression. He turned away and stood in the kitchen looking at one of the dimity curtains, the one which lay on the floor.

Smiling, Prodd came out of Jack's room and closed the door. "See, he's not Jack, that's the one blessing," he smiled. "Ma, she had to go off looking for Jack, I reckon, yes; that would be it. She wouldn't be happy with anything less; well, you know that your own self." He smiled twice. "What that in there is, that's what the doctor calls a mongoloid. Just leave it be, it'll grow up to maybe size three and stay so for thirty year. Get him to a big city specialist for treatments and he'll grow up to maybe size ten." He smiled as he talked. "That's what the doctor said anyway. Can't shovel him into the ground now, can you? That was all right for Ma, way she loved flowers and all."

Too many words, some hard to hear through the wide, tight smiling. Lone brought his eyes to bear on Prodd's.

He found out exactly what Prodd wanted—things that Prodd himself did not know. He did the things.

When he was finished he and Prodd cleaned up the kitchen and took the bassinet and burned it, along with the carefully sewn diapers made out of old sheets and piled in the linen closet and the new oval enamel bath pan and the celluloid rattle and the blue felt booties with the white puffballs in their clear cellophane box.

Prodd waved cheerfully to him from the porch. "Just you wait'll Ma gets back; she'll stuff you full o' johnny-cake till we got to scrape you off the wall."

"Mind you fix that barn door," Lone rasped. "I'll come back."

With his burden he plodded up the hill and into the forest. He struggled numbly with thoughts that would not be words or pictures. About those kids, now; about the Prodds. The Prodds were one thing and when they took him in they became something else; he knew it now. And then when he was by himself he was one thing; but taking those kids in he was something else. He had no business going back to Prodd's today. But now, the way he was, he *had* to do it. He'd go back again too.

Alone. Lone Lone alone. Prodd was alone now and Janie was alone and the twins, well they had each other but they were like one split person who was alone. He himself, Lone, was still alone, it didn't make any difference about the kids being there.

Maybe Prodd and his wife had not been alone. He wouldn't have any way of knowing about that. But there was nothing like Lone anywhere in the world except right here inside him. The whole world threw Lone away, you know that? Even the Prodds did, when they got around to it. Janie got thrown out, the twins too, so Janie said.

Well, in a funny way it helps to know you're alone, thought Lone.

The night was sun-stained by the time he got home. He kneed the door open and came in. Janie was making pictures on an old china plate with spit and mud. The twins as usual were sitting on one of the high rock niches, whispering to one another.

Janie jumped up. "What's that? What'd you bring?"

Lone put it down carefully on the floor. The twins appeared, one on each side of it. "It's a baby," said Janie. She looked up at Lone. "Is it a baby?"

Lone nodded. Janie looked again. "Nastiest one I ever saw."

Lone said, "Well never mind that. Give him something to eat."

"What?"

"I don't know," said Lone. "You're a baby, almost. You should know."

"Where'd you get him?"

"A farm yonder."

"You're a kidnapper," said Janie. "Know that?"

"What's a kidnapper?"

"Man that steals babies, that's what. When they find out about it the policeman will come and shoot you dead and put you in the electric chair."

"Well," said Lone, relieved, "ain't nobody going to find out. Only man knows about it, I fixed it so he's forgotten. That's the daddy. The ma, she's dead, but he don't know that either. He thinks she's back East. He'll hang on waiting for her. Anyway, feed him."

He pulled off his jacket. The kids kept it too hot in here. The baby lay still with its dull button eyes open, breathing too loudly. Janie stood before the fire, staring thoughtfully at the stewpot. Finally she dipped into it with a ladle and dribbled the juice into a tin can. "Milk," she said while she worked. "You got to start swiping milk for him, Lone. Babies, they eat more milk'n a cat."

"All right," said Lone.

The twins watched, wall-eyed, as Janie slopped the broth on the baby's disinterested mouth.

"He's getting some," said Janie optimistically.

Without humor and only from visible evidence, Lone said, "Maybe through his ears."

Janie pulled at the baby's shirt and half sat him up. This favored the neck rather than the ears but still left the mouth intake in doubt.

"Oh, maybe I can!" said Janie suddenly, as if answering a comment. The twins giggled and jumped up and down. Janie drew the tin can a few inches away from the baby's face and narrowed her eyes. The baby immediately started to choke and spewed up what was unequivocally broth.

"That's not right yet but I'll get it," said Janie. She spent half an hour trying. At last the baby went to sleep.

One afternoon Lone watched for a while and then prodded Janie with his toe. "What's going on there?"

She looked. "He's talking to them."

Lone pondered. "I used to could do that. Hear babies."

"Bonnie says all babies can do it, and you were a baby, weren't you? I forget if I ever did," she added. "Except the twins."

"What I mean," said Lone laboriously, "When I was growed I could hear babies."

"You must've been an idiot, then," said Janie positively. "Idiots can't understand people but can understand babies. Mr. Widdecombe, he's the man the twins lived with, he had a girl friend once who was an idiot and Bonnie told me."

"Baby's s'posed to be some kind of a idiot," Lone said.

"Yes, Beanie, she says he's sort of different. He's like a adding machine."

"What's a adding machine?"

Janie exaggerated the supreme patience that her nursery school teacher had affected. "It's a thing you push buttons and it gives you the right answer."

Lone shook his head.

Janie essayed, "Well, if you have three cents and four cents and five cents and seven cents and eight cents—how many you got altogether?"

Lone shrugged hopelessly.

"Well if you have a adding machine, you push a button for *two* and a button for *three* and a button for all the other ones and then you pull a handle, the machine tells you how many you got altogether. And it's always right."

Lone sorted all this out slowly and finally nodded. Then he waved toward the orange crate that was now Baby's bassinet, and the twins hanging spellbound over him. "He got no buttons you push."

"That was just a finger of speech," Janie said loftily. "Look, you tell Baby something, and then you tell him something else. He will put the somethings together and tell you what they come out to, just like the adding machine does with one and two and—"

"All right, but what kind of somethings?"

"Anything." She eyed him. "You're sort of stoopid, you know that, Lone. I got to tell you every little thing four times. Now listen, if you want to know something you tell me and I'll tell Baby and he'll get the answer and tell the twins and they'll tell me and I'll tell you, now what do you want to know?"

Lone stared at the fire. "I don't know anything I want to know."

"Well, you sure think up a lot of silly things to ask me."

Lone, not offended, sat and thought. Janie went to work on a scab on her knee, picking it gently round and round with fingernails the color and shape of parentheses.

"Suppose I got a truck," Lone said a half hour later, "it gets stuck in a field all the time, the ground's too tore up. Suppose I want to fix it so it won't stick no more. Baby tell me a thing like that?"

"Anything, I told you," said Janie sharply. She turned and looked at Baby. Baby lay as always, staring dully upward. In a moment she looked at the twins.

"He don't know what is a truck. If you're going to ask him anything you have to explain all the pieces before he can put 'em together."

"Well you know what a truck is," said Lone, "and soft ground and what stickin' is. You tell him."

"Oh all right," said Janie.

She went through the routine again, sending to Baby, receiving from the twins. Then she laughed. "He says stop driving on the field and you won't get stuck. You could of thought of that yourself, you dumbhead."

Lone said, "Well suppose you got to use it there, then what?"

"You 'spect me to go on askin' him silly questions all *night?*"

"All right, he can't answer like you said."

"He can too!" Her facts impugned, Janie went to the task with a will. The next answer was, "Put great big wide wheels on it."

"Suppose you ain't got money nor time nor tools for that?"

This time it was, "Make it real heavy where the ground is hard and real light where the ground is soft and anything in between."

Janie very nearly went on strike when Lone demanded to know how this could be accomplished and reached something of a peak of impatience when Lone rejected the suggestion of loading and unloading rocks. She complained that not only was this silly, but that Baby was matching every fact she fed him with every other fact he had been fed previously and was giving correct but unsolicited answers to situational sums of tires plus weight plus soup plus bird's nests, and babies plus soft dirt plus wheel diameters plus straw. Lone doggedly clung to his basic question and the day's impasse was reached when it was determined that there was such a way but it could not be expressed except by facts not in Lone's or Janie's possession. Janie said it sounded to her like radio tubes and with only that to go on, Lone proceeded by entering the next night a radio service shop and stealing a heavy armload of literature. He bulled along unswerving, unstoppable, until at last Janie relinquished her opposition because she had not energy for it and for the research as well. For days she scanned elementary electricity and radio texts which meant nothing to her but which apparently Baby could absorb faster than she scanned.

And at last the specifications were met: something which Lone could make himself, which would involve only a small knob you pushed to make the truck heavier and pulled to make it lighter, as well as an equally simple attachment to add power to the front wheels—according to Baby a *sine qua non*.

In the half-cave, half-cabin, with the fire smoking in the center of the room and the meat turning slowly in the updraft, with the help of two tongue-tied infants, a mongoloid baby and a sharp-tongued child who seemed to despise him but never failed him, Lone built the device. He did it, not because he was particularly interested in the thing for itself, nor because he wished to understand its principles (which were and would always be beyond him), but only because an old man who had taught him something he could not name was mad with bereavement and needed to work and could not afford a horse.

He walked most of the night with it and installed it in the dim early hours of the morning. The idea of "pleasant surprise" was far too whimsical a thing for Lone but it amounted to the same thing. He wanted it ready for the day's work, without any time lost by the old man prancing around asking questions that he couldn't answer.

The truck stood bogged in the field. Lone unwound the device from around his neck and shoulders and began to attach it according to the exact instructions he had winnowed out of Baby. There wasn't much to do. A slender wire wrapped twice around the clutch housing outside and led to clamps on the front spring shackles, the little brushes touching the insides of the front wheels; and that was the front-wheel drive. Then the little box with its four silvery cables, box clamped to steering post, each cable leading to a corner of the frame.

He got in and pulled the knob toward him. The frame creaked as the truck seemed to raise itself on tiptoe. He pushed the knob forward. The truck settled its front axle and differential housing on solid ground with a bump that made his head rock. He looked at the little box and its lever admiringly, then returned the lever to a neutral position. He scanned the other controls there, the ones which came with the truck: pedals and knobs and sticks and buttons. He sighed.

He wished he had wit enough to drive a truck.

He got out and climbed the hill to the house to wake Prodd. Prodd wasn't there. The kitchen door swung in the breeze, the glass gone out of it and lying on the stoop. Mud wasps were building under the sink. There was a smell of dirty dry floorboards, mildew, and ancient sweat. Otherwise it was fairly neat, about the way it was when he and Prodd had cleaned up last time he was here. The only new thing there aside from the mud wasps' nest was a paper nailed to the wall by all four corners. It had writing all over it. Lone detached it as carefully as he could, and smoothed it out on the kitchen table, and turned it over twice. Then he folded it, put it in his pocket. Again he sighed.

He wished he had sense enough to learn to read.

He left the house without looking back and plunged into the forest. He never returned. The truck stood out in the sun, slowly deteriorating, slowly weakening its already low resistance to rust, slowly falling to pieces around the bright, strong, strange silver cables. Powered inexhaustibly by the slow release of atomic binding energy, the device was the practical solution of flight without wings, the simple key to a new era in transportation, in materials handling, and in interplanetary travel. Made by an idiot, harnessed idiotically to replace a spavined horse, stupidly left, numbly forgotten . . . Earth's first antigravity generator.

The *idiot*!

> *Dear loan Ill nale this up wher you cant hep see it I am cleering ot of here I dont no why I stade as long as I did. Ma is back east Wmsport pennsilvana and she been gone a long time and I am tied of wating. And I was goin to sell the truck to hep me on the way but it is stuck so bad now I cant get it to town to sell it. So now I am jest goin to go whatever and Ill make it some way long as I no Ma is at the othr end. Dont take no trouble about the place I guess I had enuf of it Anyway. And borrow any thing you want if you should want any Thing. You are a good boy you been a good frend well goodbeye until I see you if I ever do god Bless you your old frend E. Prodd.*

Lone made Janie read him the letter four times in a three-week period, and each reading seemed to add a fresh element to the yeasty seething inside him. Much of this happened silently; for some of it he asked help.

He had believed that Prodd was his only contact with anything outside himself and that the children were merely fellow occupants of a slag dump at the edge of mankind. The loss of Prodd—and he knew with unshakeable certainty that he would never see the old man again—was the loss of life itself. At the very least, it was the loss of everything conscious, directed, cooperative; everything above and beyond what a vegetable could do by way of living.

"Ask Baby what is a friend."

"He says it's somebody who goes on loving you whether he likes you or not."

But then, Prodd and his wife had shucked him off when he was in the way, after all those years, and that meant they were ready to do it the first year and the second and the fifth—all the time, any time. You can't say you're a part of anything, anybody, that feels free to do that to you. But friends . . . maybe they just didn't like him for a while, maybe they loved him all the way through.

"Ask Baby can you be truly part of someone you love."

"He says only if you love yourself."

His bench-mark, his goal-point, had for years been that thing which happened to him on the bank of the pool. He had to understand that. If he could understand that, he was sure he could understand everything. Because for a second there was this *other*, and himself, and a flow between them without guards or screens or barriers—no language to stumble over, no ideas to misunderstand, nothing at all but a merging.

What had he been then? What was it Janie had said?

Idiot. An idiot.

An idiot, she had said, was a grown person who could hear only babies' silent speech. Then—what was the creature with whom he had merged on that terrible day?

"Ask Baby what is a grown person who can *talk* like the babies."

"He says, an innocent."

He had been an idiot who could hear the soundless murmur. She had been an innocent who, as an adult, could speak it.

"Ask Baby what if an idiot and an innocent are close together."

"He says when they so much as touched, the innocent would stop being an innocent and the idiot would stop being an idiot."

He thought, An innocent is the most beautiful thing there can be. Immediately he demanded of himself, What's so beautiful about an innocent? And the answer, for once almost as swift as Baby's: It's the waiting that's beautiful.

Waiting for the end of innocence. And an idiot is waiting for the end of idiocy too, but he's ugly doing it. So each ends himself in the meeting, in exchange for a merging.

Lone was suddenly deep-down glad. For if this was true, he had made something, rather than destroyed something . . . and when he had lost it, the pain of the loss was justified. When he had lost the Prodds the pain wasn't worth it.

What am I doing? What am I doing? he thought wildly. Trying and trying like this to find out what I am and what I belong to. . . . Is this another aspect of being outcast, monstrous, *different*?

"Ask Baby what kind of people are all the time trying to find out what they are and what they belong to."

"He says, *every* kind."

"What kind," Lone whispered, "am I, then?"

A full minute later he yelled, "*What kind?*"

"Shut up a while. He doesn't have a way to say it . . . uh . . . Here. He says he is a figure-outer brain and I am a body and the twins are arms and legs and you are the head. He says the 'I' is all of us."

"I belong. I belong. Part of you, part of you and you too."

"The head, silly."

Lone thought his heart was going to burst. He looked at them all, every one: arms to flex and reach, a body to care and repair, a brainless but faultless computer and—the head to direct it.

"And we'll grow, Baby. We just got born!"

"He says not on your life. He says not with a head like that. We can do practically *anything* but we most likely won't. He says we're a thing, all right, but the thing is an idiot."

So it was that Lone came to know himself; and like the handful of people who have done so before him he found, at this pinnacle, the rugged foot of a mountain.

PART TWO

BABY IS THREE

I FINALLY got in to see this Stern. He wasn't an old man at all. He looked up from his desk, flicked his eyes over me once, and picked up a pencil. "Sit over there, Sonny."

I stood where I was until he looked up again. Then I said, "Look, if a midget walks in here, what do you say—sit over there, Shorty?"

He put the pencil down again and stood up. He smiled. His smile was as quick and sharp as his eyes. "I was wrong," he said, "but how am I supposed to know you don't want to be called Sonny?"

That was better, but I was still mad. "I'm fifteen and I don't have to like it. Don't rub my nose in it."

He smiled again and said okay, and I went and sat down.

"What's your name?"

"Gerard."

"First or last?"

"Both," I said.

"Is that the truth?"

I said, "No. And don't ask me where I live either."

He put down his pencil. "We're not going to get very far this way."

"That's up to you. What are you worried about? I got feelings of hostility? Well, sure I have. I got lots more things than that wrong with me or I wouldn't be here. Are you going to let that stop you?"

"Well, no, but—"

"So what else is bothering you? How you're going to get paid?" I took out a thousand-dollar bill and laid it on the desk. "That's so you won't have to bill me. *You* keep track of it. Tell me when it's used up and I'll give you more. So you don't need my address. Wait," I said, when he reached toward the money. "Let it lay there. I want to be sure you and I are going to get along."

He folded his hands. "I don't do business this way, Son—I mean, Gerard."

"Gerry," I told him. "You do, if you do business with me."

"You make things difficult, don't you? Where did you get a thousand dollars?"

"I won a contest. Twenty-five words or less about how much fun it is to do my daintier underthings with Sudso." I leaned forward. "This time it's the truth."

"All right," he said.

I was surprised. I think he knew it, but he didn't say anything more. Just waited for me to go ahead.

"Before we start—*if* we start," I said, "I got to know something. The things I say to you—what comes out while you're working on me—is that just between us, like a priest or a lawyer?"

"Absolutely," he said.

"No matter what?"

"No matter what."

I watched him when he said it. I believed him.

"Pick up your money," I said. "You're on."

He didn't do it. He said, "As you remarked a minute ago, that is up to me. You can't buy these treatments like a candy bar. We have to work together. If either one of us can't do that, it's useless. You can't walk in on the first psychotherapist you find in the phone book and make any demand that occurs to you just because you can pay for it."

I said tiredly, "I didn't get you out of the phone book and I'm not just guessing that you can help me. I winnowed through a dozen or more head-shrinkers before I decided on you."

"Thanks," he said, and it looked as if he was going to laugh at me, which I never like. "Winnowed, did you say? Just how?"

"Things you hear, things you read. You know. I'm not saying, so just file that with my street address."

He looked at me for a long time. It was the first time he'd used his eyes on me for anything but a flash glance. Then he picked up the bill.

"What do I do first?" I demanded.

"What do you mean?"

"How do we start?"

"We started when you walked in here."

So then I had to laugh. "All right, you got me. All I had was an opening. I didn't know where you would go from there, so I couldn't be there ahead of you."

"That's very interesting," Stern said. "Do you usually figure everything out in advance?"

"Always."

"How often are you right?"

"All the time. Except—but I don't have to tell you about no exceptions."

He really grinned this time. "I see. One of my patients has been talking."

"One of your ex-patients. Your patients don't talk."

"I ask them not to. That applies to you, too. What did you hear?"

"That you know from what people say and do what they're about to say and do, and that sometimes you let'm do it and sometimes you don't. How did you learn to do that?"

He thought a minute. "I guess I was born with an eye for details, and then let myself make enough mistakes with enough people until I learned not to make too many more. How did you learn to do it?"

I said, "You answer that and I won't have to come back here."

"You really don't know?"

"I wish I did. Look, this isn't getting us anywhere, is it?"

He shrugged. "Depends on where you want to go." He paused, and I got the eyes full strength again. "Which thumbnail description of psychiatry do you believe at the moment?"

"I don't get you."

Stern slid open a desk drawer and took out a blackened pipe. He smelled it, turned it over while looking at me. "Psychiatry attacks the onion of the self, removing layer after layer until it gets down to the little sliver of unsullied ego. Or: psychiatry drills like an oil well, down and sidewise and down again, through all the muck and rock until it strikes a layer that yields. Or: psychiatry grabs a handful of sexual motivations and throws them on the pinball machine of your life, so they bounce on down against episodes. Want more?"

I had to laugh. "That last one was pretty good."

"That last one was pretty bad. They are all bad. They all try to simplify something which is complex by its very nature. The only thumbnail you'll get from me is this: no one knows what's really wrong with you but you; no one can find a cure for it but you; no one but you can identify it as a cure; and once you find it, no one but you can do anything about it."

"What are *you* here for?"

"To listen."

"I don't have to pay somebody no day's wage every hour just to listen."

"True. But you're convinced that I listen selectively."

"Am I?" I wondered about it. "I guess I am. Well, don't you?"

"No, but you'll never believe that."

I laughed. He asked me what that was for. I said, "You're not calling me Sonny."

"Not you." He shook his head slowly. He was watching me while he did it, so his eyes slid in their sockets as his head moved. "What is it you want to know about yourself, that made you worried I might tell people?"

"I want to find out why I killed somebody," I said right away.

It didn't faze him a bit. "Lie down over there."

I got up. "On that couch?"

He nodded.

As I stretched out self-consciously, I said, "I feel like I'm in some damn cartoon."

"What cartoon?"

"Guy's built like a bunch of grapes," I said, looking at the ceiling. It was pale gray.

"What's the caption?"

" 'I got trunks full of 'em.' "

"Very good," he said quietly. I looked at him carefully. I knew then he was the kind of guy who laughs way down deep when he laughs at all.

He said, "I'll use that in a book of case histories some time. But it won't include yours. What made you throw that in?" When I didn't answer, he got up and moved to a chair behind me where I couldn't see him. "You can quit testing, Sonny. I'm good enough for your purposes."

I clenched my jaw so hard, my back teeth hurt. Then I relaxed. I relaxed all over. It was wonderful. "All right," I said, "I'm sorry." He didn't say anything, but I had that feeling again that he was laughing. Not at me, though.

"How old are you?" he asked me suddenly.

"Uh—fifteen."

"Uh—fifteen," he repeated. "What does the 'uh' mean?"

"Nothing. I'm fifteen."

"When I asked your age, you hesitated because some other number popped up. You discarded that and substituted 'fifteen.'"

"The hell I did! I am fifteen!"

"I didn't say you weren't." His voice came patiently. "Now what was the other number?"

I got mad again. "There wasn't any other number! What do you want to go pryin' my grunts apart for, trying to plant this and that and make it mean what you think it ought to mean?"

He was silent.

"I'm fifteen," I said defiantly, and then, "I don't like being only fifteen. You know that. I'm not trying to insist I'm fifteen."

He just waited, still not saying anything.

I felt defeated. "The number was eight."

"So you're eight. And your name?"

"Gerry." I got up on one elbow, twisting my neck around so I could see him. He had his pipe apart and was sighting through the stem at the desk lamp. "Gerry, without no 'uh!'"

"All right," he said mildly, making me feel real foolish.

I leaned back and closed my eyes.

Eight, I thought. Eight.

"It's cold in here," I complained.

Eight. Eight, plate, state, hate. I ate from the plate of the state and I hate. I didn't like any of that and I snapped my eyes open. The ceiling was still gray. It was all right. Stern was somewhere behind me with his pipe, and he was all right. I took two deep breaths, three, and then let my eyes close. Eight. Eight years old. Eight, hate. Years, fears. Old, cold. *Damn* it! I twisted and twitched on the couch, trying to find a way to keep the cold out. I ate from the plate of the—

I grunted and with my mind I took all the eights and all the rhymes and everything they stood for, and made it all black.

But it wouldn't stay black. I had to put something there, so I made a great big luminous figure eight and just let it hang there. But it turned on its side and inside the loops it began to shimmer. It was like one of those movie shots through binoculars. I was going to have to look through whether I liked it or not.

Suddenly I quit fighting it and let it wash over me. The binoculars came close, closer, and then I was there.

Eight. Eight years old, cold. Cold as a bitch in the ditch. The ditch was by a railroad. Last year's weeds were scratchy straw. The ground was red, and when it wasn't slippery, clingy mud, it was frozen hard like a flowerpot. It was hard like that now, dusted with hoar-frost, cold as the winter light that pushed up over the hills. At night the lights were warm, and they were all in other people's houses. In the daytime the sun was in somebody else's house too, for all the good it did me.

I was dying in that ditch. Last night it was as good a place as any to sleep and this morning it was as good a place as any to die. Just as well. Eight years old, the sick-sweet taste of pork fat and wet bread from somebody's garbage, the thrill of terror when you're stealing a gunny-sack and you hear a footstep.

And I heard a footstep.

I'd been curled up on my side. I whipped over on my stomach because sometimes they kick your belly. I covered my head with my arms and that was as far as I could get.

After a while I rolled my eyes up and looked without moving. There was a big shoe there. There was an ankle in the shoe, and another shoe close by. I lay there waiting to get tromped. Not that I cared much any more, but it was such a damn shame. All these months on my own, and they'd never caught up with me, never even come close, and now this. It was such a shame I started to cry.

The shoe took me under the armpit, but it was not a kick. It rolled me over. I was so stiff from the cold, I went over like a plank. I just kept my arms over my face and head and lay there with my eyes closed. For some reason I stopped crying. I think people only cry when there's a chance of getting help from somewhere.

When nothing happened, I opened my eyes and shifted my

forearms a little so I could see up. There was a man standing over me and he was a mile high. He had on faded dungarees and an old Eisenhower jacket with deep sweat-stains under the arms. His face was shaggy, like the guys who can't grow what you could call a beard, but still don't shave.

He said, "Get up."

I looked down at his shoe, but he wasn't going to kick me. I pushed up a little and almost fell down again, except he put his big hand where my back would hit it. I lay against it for a second because I had to, and then got up to where I had one knee on the ground.

"Come on," he said. "Let's go."

I swear I felt my bones creak, but I made it. I brought a round white stone up with me as I stood. I hefted the stone. I had to look at it to see if I was really holding it, my fingers were that cold. I told him, "Stay away from me or I'll bust you in the teeth with this rock."

His hand came out and down so fast I never saw the way he got one finger between my palm and the rock and flicked it out of my grasp. I started to cuss at him, but he just turned his back and walked up the embankment toward the tracks. He put his chin on his shoulder and said, "Come on, will you?"

He didn't chase me, so I didn't run. He didn't talk to me so I didn't argue. He didn't hit me, so I didn't get mad. I went along after him. He waited for me. He put out his hand to me and I spit at it. So he went on, up to the tracks, out of my sight. I clawed my way up. The blood was beginning to move in my hands and feet and they felt like four point-down porcupines. When I got up to the roadbed, the man was standing there waiting for me.

The track was level just there, but as I turned my head to look along it, it seemed to be a hill that was steeper and steeper and turned over above me. And next thing you know, I was lying flat on my back looking up at the cold sky.

The man came over and sat down on the rail near me. He didn't try to touch me. I gasped for breath a couple of times and suddenly felt I'd be all right if I could sleep for a minute—just a little minute. I closed my eyes. The man stuck his finger in my ribs, hard. It hurt.

"Don't sleep," he said.

I looked at him.

He said, "You're frozen stiff and weak with hunger. I want to take you home and get you warmed up and fed. But it's a long haul up that way, and you won't make it by yourself. If I carry you, will that be the same to you as if you walked it?"

"What are you going to do when you get me home?"

"I told you."

"All right," I said.

He picked me up and carried me down the track. If he'd said anything else in the world, I'd of laid right down where I was until I froze to death. Anyway, what did he want to ask me for, one way or the other? I couldn't of done anything.

I stopped thinking about it and dozed off.

I woke up once when he turned off the right of way. He dove into the woods. There was no path, but he seemed to know where he was going. The next time I woke from a crickling noise. He was carrying me over a frozen pond and the ice was giving under his feet. He didn't hurry. I looked down and saw the white cracks raying out under his feet, and it didn't seem to matter a bit. I bleared off again.

He put me down at last. We were there. "There" was inside a room. It was very warm. He put me on my feet and I snapped out of it in a hurry. The first thing I looked for was the door. I saw it and jumped over there and put my back against the wall beside it, in case I wanted to leave. Then I looked around.

It was a big room. One wall was rough rock and the rest was logs with stuff shoved between them. There was a big fire going in the rock wall, not in a fireplace, exactly; it was a sort of hollow place. There was an old auto battery on a shelf opposite, with two yellowing electric light bulbs dangling by wires from it. There was a table, some boxes and a couple of three-legged stools. The air had a haze of smoke and such a wonderful, heartbreaking, candy-and-crackling smell of food that a little hose squirted inside my mouth.

The man said, "What have I got here, Baby?"

And the room was full of kids. Well, three of them, but somehow they seemed to be more than three kids. There was a girl about my age—eight, I mean—with blue paint on the side of her face. She had an easel and a palette with lots of paints and a fistful of brushes, but she wasn't using the brushes. She was smearing the paint on with her hands. Then there was a little Negro girl about five with great big eyes who stood gaping at me. And in a wooden crate, set up on two sawhorses to make a kind of bassinet, was a baby. I guess about three or four months old. It did what babies do, drooling some, making small bubbles, waving its hands around very aimless, and kicking.

When the man spoke, the girl at the easel looked at me and then at the baby. The baby just kicked and drooled.

The girl said, "His name's Gerry. He's mad."

"What's he mad at?" the man asked. He was looking at the baby.

"Everything," said the girl. "Everything and everybody."

"Where'd he come from?"

I said, "Hey, what is this?" but nobody paid any attention. The man kept asking questions at the baby and the girl kept answering. Craziest thing I ever saw.

"He ran away from a state school," the girl said. "They fed him enough, but no one bleshed with him."

That's what she said—"bleshed."

I opened the door then and cold air hooted in. "You louse," I said to the man, "you're from the school."

"Close the door, Janie," said the man. The girl at the easel didn't move, but the door banged shut behind me. I tried to open it and it wouldn't move. I let out a howl, yanking at it.

"I think you ought to stand in the corner," said the man. "Stand him in the corner, Janie."

Janie looked at me. One of the three-legged stools sailed across to me. It hung in midair and turned on its side. It nudged me with its flat seat. I jumped back and it came after me. I dodged to the side, and that was the corner. The stool came on. I tried to bat it down and just hurt my hand. I ducked and it went lower than I did. I put one hand on it and tried to vault over it, but it just fell and so did I. I got up again and stood in the corner, trembling. The stool turned right side up and sank to the floor in front of me.

The man said, "Thank you, Janie." He turned to me. "Stand there and be quiet, you. I'll get to you later. You shouldn'ta kicked up all that fuss." And then, to the baby, he said, "He got anything we need?"

And again it was the little girl who answered. She said, "Sure. He's the one."

"Well," said the man. "What do you know!" He came over. "Gerry, you can live here. I don't come from no school. I'll never turn you in."

"Yeah, huh?"

"He hates you," said Janie.

"What am I supposed to do about that?" he wanted to know.

Janie turned her head to look into the bassinet. "Feed him." The man nodded and began fiddling around the fire.

Meanwhile, the little Negro girl had been standing in the one spot with her big eyes right out on her cheekbones, looking at me. Janie went back to her painting and the baby just lay there same as always, so I stared right back at the little Negro girl. I snapped, "What the hell are you gawking at?"

She grinned at me. "Gerry ho-ho," she said, and disappeared. I mean she really disappeared, went out like a light, leaving her clothes where she had been. Her little dress billowed in the air and fell in a heap where she had been, and that was that. She was gone.

"Gerry hee-hee," I heard. I looked up, and there she was, stark naked, wedged in a space where a little outcropping on the rock wall stuck out just below the ceiling. The second I saw her she disappeared again.

"Gerry ho-ho," she said. Now she was on top of the row of boxes they used as storage shelves, over on the other side of the room.

"Gerry hee-hee!" Now she was under the table. "Gerry ho-ho!" This time she was right in the corner with me, crowding me.

I yelped and tried to get out of the way and bumped the stool. I was afraid of it, so I shrank back again and the little girl was gone.

The man glanced over his shoulder from where he was working at the fire. "Cut it out, you kids," he said.

There was a silence, and then the girl came slowly out from the bottom row of shelves. She walked across to her dress and put it on.

"How did you do that?" I wanted to know.

"Ho-ho," she said.

Janie said, "It's easy. She's really twins."

"Oh," I said. Then another girl, exactly the same, came from somewhere in the shadows and stood beside the first. They were identical. They stood side by side and stared at me. This time I let them stare.

"That's Bonnie and Beanie," said the painter. "This is Baby and that—" she indicated the man— "that's Lone. And I'm Janie."

I couldn't think of what to say, so I said, "Yeah."

Lone said, "Water, Janie." He held up a pot. I heard water trickling, but didn't see anything. "That's enough," he said, and hung the pot on a crane. He picked up a cracked china plate and brought it over to me. It was full of stew with great big lumps of meat in it and thick gravy and dumplings and carrots. "Here, Gerry. Sit down."

I looked at the stool. "On that?"

"Sure."

"Not me," I said. I took the plate and hunkered down against the wall.

"Hey," he said after a time. "Take it easy. We've all had chow. No one's going to snatch it away from you. Slow down!"

I ate even faster than before. I was almost finished when I threw it all up. Then for some reason my head hit the edge of the stool. I dropped the plate and spoon and slumped there. I felt real bad.

Lone came over and looked at me. "Sorry, kid," he said. "Clean up, will you, Janie?"

Right in front of my eyes, the mess on the floor disappeared. I didn't care about that or anything else just then. I felt the man's hand on the side of my neck. Then he tousled my hair.

"Beanie, get him a blanket. Let's all go to sleep. He ought to rest a while."

I felt the blanket go around me, and I think I was asleep before he put me down.

I don't know how much later it was when I woke up. I didn't know where I was and that scared me. I raised my head and saw the dull glow of the embers in the fireplace. Lone was stretched out on it in his clothes. Janie's easel stood in the reddish blackness like some great preying insect. I saw the baby's head pop up out of the bassinet, but I couldn't tell whether he was looking straight at me or away. Janie was lying on the floor near the door and the twins were on the old table. Nothing moved except the baby's head, bobbing a little.

I got to my feet and looked around the room. Just a room, only the one door. I tiptoed toward it. When I passed Janie, she opened her eyes.

"What's the matter?" she whispered.

"None of your business," I told her. I went to the door as if I didn't care, but I watched her. She didn't do anything. The door was as solid tight closed as when I'd tried it before.

I went back to Janie. She just looked up at me. She wasn't scared. I told her, "I got to go to the john."

"Oh," she said. "Why'n't you say so?"

Suddenly I grunted and grabbed my guts. The feeling I had I can't begin to talk about. I acted as if it was a pain, but it wasn't. It was like nothing else that ever happened to me before. Something went *splop* on the snow outside.

"Okay," Janie said. "Go on back to bed."

"But I got to—"

"You got to what?"

"Nothing." It was true. I didn't have to go no place.

"Next time tell me right away. I don't mind."

I didn't say anything. I went back to my blanket.

"That's all?" said Stern. I lay on the couch and looked up at the gray ceiling. He asked, "How old are you?"

"Fifteen," I said dreamily. He waited until, for me, the gray ceiling acquired walls on a floor, a rug and lamps and a desk and a chair with Stern in it. I sat up and held my head a second, and then I looked at him. He was fooling with his pipe and looking at me. "What did you do to me?"

"I told you. I don't do anything here. You do it."

"You hypnotized me."

"I did not." His voice was quiet, but he really meant it.

"What was all that, then? It was . . . it was like it was happening for real all over again."

"Feel anything?"

"Everything." I shuddered. "*Every* damn thing. What was it?"

"Anyone doing it feels better afterward. You can go over it

all again now any time you want to, and every time you do, the hurt in it will be less. You'll see."

It was the first thing to amaze me in years. I chewed on it and then asked, "If I did it by myself, how come it never happened before?"

"It needs someone to listen."

"Listen? Was I talking?"

"A blue streak."

"Everything that happened?"

"How can I know? I wasn't there. You were."

"You don't believe it happened, do you? Those disappearing kids and the footstool and all?"

He shrugged. "I'm not in the business of believing or not believing. Was it real to you?"

"Oh, hell, yes!"

"Well, then, that's all that matters. Is that where you live, with those people?"

I bit off a fingernail that had been bothering me. "Not for a long time. Not since Baby was three." I looked at him. "You remind me of Lone."

"Why?"

"I don't know. No, you don't." I added suddenly. "I don't know what made me say that." I lay down abruptly.

The ceiling was gray and the lamps were dim. I heard the pipestem click against his teeth. I lay there for a long time.

"Nothing happens," I told him.

"What did you expect to happen?"

"Like before."

"There's something there that wants out. Just let it come."

It was as if there was a revolving drum in my head, and on it were photographed the places and things and people I was after. And it was as if the drum was spinning very fast, so fast I couldn't tell one picture from another. I made it stop, and it stopped at a blank segment. I spun it again, and stopped it again.

"Nothing happens," I said.

"Baby is three," he repeated.

"Oh," I said. "That." I closed my eyes.

That might be it. Might, sight, night, light. I might have the sight of a light in the night. Maybe the baby. Maybe the sight of the baby at night because of the light . . .

There was night after night when I lay on that blanket, and a lot of nights I didn't. Something was going on all the time in Lone's house. Sometimes I slept in the daytime. I guess the only time everybody slept at once was when someone was sick, like me the first time I arrived there. It was always sort of dark in the room, the same night and day, the fire going, the two old bulbs hanging yellow by their wires from the battery. When they got too dim, Janie fixed the battery and they got bright again.

Janie did everything that needed doing, whatever no one else felt like doing. Everybody else did things, too. Lone was out a lot. Sometimes he used the twins to help him, but you never missed them, because they'd be here and gone and back again *bing!* like that. And Baby, he just stayed in his bassinet.

I did things myself. I cut wood for the fire and I put up more shelves, and then I'd go swimming with Janie and the twins sometimes. And I talked to Lone. I didn't do a thing that the others couldn't do, but they all did things I couldn't do. I was mad, mad all the time about that. But I wouldn't of known what to do with myself if I wasn't mad all the time about something or other. It didn't keep us from bleshing. Bleshing, that was Janie's word. She said Baby told it to her. She said it meant everyone all together being something, even if they all did different things. Two arms, two legs, one body, one head, all working together, although a head can't walk and arms can't think. Lone said maybe it was a mixture of "blending" and "meshing," but I don't think he believed that himself. It was a lot more than that.

Baby talked all the time. He was like a broadcasting station that runs twenty-four hours a day, and you can get what it's sending any time you tune in, but it'll keep sending whether you tune in or not. When I say he talked, I don't mean exactly that. He semaphored mostly. You'd think those wandering vague movements of his hands and arms and legs and head were meaningless, but they weren't. It was semaphore, only instead of a symbol for a sound, or such like, the movements were whole thoughts.

I mean spread the left hand and shake the right high up, and thump with the left heel, and it means, "Anyone who thinks a starling is a pest just don't know anything about how a starling thinks" or something like that. Janie said she made Baby invent the semaphore business. She said she used to be able to hear the twins thinking—that's what she said; hear them thinking—and they could hear Baby. So she would ask the twins whatever she wanted to know, and they'd ask Baby, and then tell her what he said. But then as they grew up they began to lose the knack of it. Every young kid does. So Baby learned to understand when someone talked, and he'd answer with this semaphore stuff.

Lone couldn't read the stuff and neither could I. The twins didn't give a damn. Janie used to watch him all the time. He always knew what you meant if you wanted to ask him something, and he'd tell Janie and she'd say what it was. Part of it, anyway. Nobody could get it all, not even Janie.

All I know is Janie would sit there and paint her pictures and watch Baby, and sometimes she'd bust out laughing.

Baby never grew any. Janie did, and the twins, and so did I, but not Baby. He just lay there. Janie kept his stomach full and cleaned him up every two or three days. He didn't cry and he didn't make any trouble. No one ever went near him.

Janie showed every picture she painted to Baby, before she cleaned the boards and painted new ones. She had to clean them because she only had three of them. It was a good thing, too, because I'd hate to think what that place would of been like if she'd kept them all; she did four or five a day. Lone and the twins were kept hopping getting turpentine for her. She could shift the paints back into the little pots on her easel without any trouble, just by looking at the picture one color at a time, but turps was something else again. She told me that Baby remembered all her pictures and that's why she didn't have to keep them. They were all pictures of machines and gear-trains and mechanical linkages and what looked like electric circuits and things like that. I never thought too much about them.

I went out with Lone to get some turpentine and a couple of picnic hams one time. We went through the woods to the railroad track and down a couple of miles to where we could see the glow of a town. Then the woods again, and some alleys, and a back street.

Lone was like always, walking along, thinking, thinking.

We came to a hardware store and he went up and looked at the lock and came back to where I was waiting, shaking his head. Then we found a general store. Lone grunted and we went and stood in the shadows by the door. I looked in.

All of a sudden Beanie was in there, naked like she always was when she traveled like that. She came and opened the door from the inside. We went in and Lone closed it and locked it.

"Get along home, Beanie," he said, "before you catch your death."

She grinned at me and said, "Ho-ho," and disappeared.

We found a pair of fine hams and a two-gallon can of turpentine. I took a bright yellow ballpoint pen and Lone cuffed me and made me put it back.

"We only take what we need," he told me.

After we left, Beanie came back and locked the door and went home again. I only went with Lone a few times, when he had more to get than he could carry easily.

I was there about three years. That's all I can remember about it. Lone was there or he was out, and you could hardly tell the difference. The twins were with each other most of the time. I got to like Janie a lot, but we never talked much. Baby talked all the time, only I don't know what about.

We were all busy and we bleshed.

I sat up on the couch suddenly.

Stern said, "What's the matter?"

"Nothing's the matter. This isn't getting me any place."

"You said that when you'd barely started. Do you think you've accomplished anything since then?"

"Oh, yeah, but—"

"Then how can you be sure you're right this time?" When I didn't say anything, he asked me, "Didn't you like this last stretch?"

I said angrily, "I didn't like or not like. It didn't mean nothing. It was just—just talk."

"So what was the difference between this last session and what happened before?"

"My gosh, plenty! The first one, I felt everything. It was all really happening to me. But this time—nothing."

"Why do you suppose that was?"

"I don't know. You tell me."

"Suppose," he said thoughtfully, "that there was some episode so unpleasant to you that you wouldn't dare relive it."

"Unpleasant? You think freezing to death isn't unpleasant?"

"There are all kinds of unpleasantness. Sometimes the very thing you're looking for—the thing that'll clear up your trouble—is so revolting to you that you won't go near it. Or you try to hide it. Wait," he said suddenly, "maybe 'revolting' and 'unpleasant' are inaccurate words to use. It might be something very desirable to you. It's just that you don't want to get straightened out."

"I *want* to get straightened out."

He waited as if he had to clear something up in his mind, and then said, "There's something in that 'Baby is three' phrase that bounces you away. Why is that?"

"Damn if I know."

"Who said it?"

"I dunno . . . uh . . ."

He grinned. "Uh?"

I grinned back at him. "I said it."

"Okay. When?"

I quit grinning. He leaned forward, then got up.

"What's the matter?" I asked.

He said, "I didn't think anyone could be that mad." I didn't say anything. He went over to his desk. "You don't want to go on any more, do you?"

"No."

"Suppose I told you you want to quit because you're right on the very edge of finding out what you want to know?"

"Why don't you tell me and see what I do?"

He just shook his head. "I'm not telling you anything. Go on, leave if you want to. I'll give you back your change."

"How many people quit just when they're on top of the answer?"

"Quite a few."

"Well, I ain't going to." I lay down.

He didn't laugh and he didn't say, "Good," and he didn't

make any fuss about it. He just picked up his phone and said, "Cancel everything for this afternoon," and went back to his chair, up there out of my sight.

It was very quiet in there. He had the place sound-proofed.

I said, "Why do you suppose Lone let me live there so long when I couldn't do any of the things that the other kids could?"

"Maybe you could."

"Oh, no," I said positively. "I used to try. I was strong for a kid my age and I knew how to keep my mouth shut, but aside from those two things I don't think I was any different from any kid. I don't think I'm any different right now, except what difference there might be from living with Lone and his bunch."

"Has this anything to do with 'Baby is three'?"

I looked up at the gray ceiling. "Baby is three. Baby is three. I went up to a big house with a winding drive that ran under a sort of theater-marquee thing. Baby is three. Baby . . ."

"How old are you?"

"Thirty-three," I said, and the next thing you know I was up off that couch like it was hot and heading for the door.

Stern grabbed me. "Don't be foolish. Want me to waste a whole afternoon?"

"What's that to me? I'm paying for it."

"All right, it's up to you."

I went back. "I don't like any part of this," I said.

"Good. We're getting warm then."

"What made me say 'Thirty-three'? I ain't thirty-three. I'm fifteen. And another thing . . ."

"Yes?"

"It's about that 'Baby is three.' It's me saying it, all right. But when I think about it—it's not my voice."

"Like thirty-three's not your age?"

"Yeah," I whispered.

"Gerry," he said warmly, "there's nothing to be afraid of."

I realized I was breathing too hard. I pulled myself together. I said, "I don't like remembering saying things in somebody else's voice."

"Look," he told me. "This head-shrinking business, as you

called it a while back, isn't what most people think. When I go with you into the world of your mind—or when you go yourself, for that matter—what we find isn't so very different from the so-called real world. It seems so at first, because the patient comes out with all sorts of fantasies and irrationalities and weird experiences. But everyone lives in that kind of world. When one of the ancients coined the phrase 'truth is stranger than fiction,' he was talking about that.

"Everywhere we go, everything we do, we're surrounded by symbols, by things so familiar we don't ever look at them or don't see them if we do look. If anyone ever could report to you exactly what he saw and thought while walking ten feet down the street, you'd get the most twisted, clouded, partial picture you ever ran across. And nobody ever looks at what's around him with any kind of attention until he gets into a place like this. The fact that he's looking at past events doesn't matter; what counts is that he's seeing clearer than he ever could before, just because, for once, he's trying.

"Now—about this 'thirty-three' business. I don't think a man could get a nastier shock than to find he has someone else's memories. The ego is too important to let slide that way. But consider: all your thinking is done in code and you have the key to only about a tenth of it. So you run into a stretch of code which is abhorrent to you. Can't you see that the only way you'll find the key to it is to stop avoiding it?"

"You mean I'd started to remember with . . . with somebody else's mind?"

"It looked like that to you for a while, which means something. Let's try to find out what."

"All right." I felt sick. I felt tired. And I suddenly realized that being sick and being tired was a way of trying to get out of it.

"Baby is three," he said.

Baby is maybe. Me, three, thirty-three, me, you Kew you.

"Kew!" I yelled. Stern didn't say anything. "Look, I don't know why, but I think I know how to get to this, and this isn't the way. Do you mind if I try something else?"

"You're the doctor," he said.

I had to laugh. Then I closed my eyes.

*

There, through the edges of the hedges, the ledges and wedges of windows were shouldering up to the sky. The lawns were sprayed-on green, neat and clean, and all the flowers looked as if they were afraid to let their petals break and be untidy.

I walked up the drive in my shoes. I'd had to wear shoes and my feet couldn't breathe. I didn't want to go to the house, but I had to.

I went up the steps between the big white columns and looked at the door. I wished I could see through it, but it was too white and thick. There was a window the shape of a fan over it, too high up though, and a window on each side of it, but they were all crudded up with colored glass. I hit on the door with my hand and left dirt on it.

Nothing happened so I hit it again. It got snatched open and a tall, thin colored woman stood there. "What you want?"

I said I had to see Miss Kew.

"Well, Miss Kew don't want to see the likes of you," she said. She talked too loud. "You got a dirty face."

I started to get mad then. I was already pretty sore about having to come here, walking around near people in the daytime and all. I said, "My face ain't got nothin' to do with it. Where's Miss Kew? Go on, find her for me."

She gasped. "You can't speak to me like that!"

I said, "I didn't want to speak to you like any way. Let me in." I started wishing for Janie. Janie could of moved her. But I had to handle it by myself. I wasn't doing so hot, either. She slammed the door before I could so much as curse at her.

So I started kicking on the door. For that, shoes are great. After a while, she snatched the door open again so sudden I almost went on my can. She had a broom with her. She screamed at me, "You get away from here, you trash, or I'll call the police!" She pushed me and I fell.

I got up off the porch floor and went for her. She stepped back and whupped me one with the broom as I went past, but anyhow I was inside now. The woman was making little shrieking noises and coming for me. I took the broom away from her and then somebody said, "Miriam!" in a voice like a grown goose.

I froze and the woman went into hysterics. "Oh, Miss Alicia, look out! He'll kill us all. Get the police. Get the—"

"Miriam!" came the honk, and Miriam dried up.

There at the top of the stairs was this prune-faced woman with a dress on that had lace on it. She looked a lot older than she was, maybe because she held her mouth so tight. I guess she was about thirty-three—*thirty-three.* She had mean eyes and a small nose.

I asked, "Are you Miss Kew?"

"I am. What is the meaning of this invasion?"

"I got to talk to you, Miss Kew."

"Don't say 'got to.' Stand up straight and speak out."

The maid said, "I'll get the police."

Miss Kew turned on her. "There's time enough for that, Miriam. Now, you dirty little boy, what do you want?"

"I got to speak to you by yourself," I told her.

"Don't you let him do it, Miss Alicia," cried the maid.

"Be quiet, Miriam. Little boy, I told you not to say 'got to.' You may say whatever you have to say in front of Miriam."

"Like hell." They both gasped. I said, "Lone told me not to."

"Miss Alicia, are you goin' to let him—"

"Be quiet, Miriam! Young man, you will keep a civil—" Then her eyes popped up real round. "*Who* did you say . . ."

"Lone said so."

"Lone." She stood there on the stairs looking at her hands. Then she said, "Miriam, that will be all." And you wouldn't know it was the same woman, the way she said it.

The maid opened her mouth, but Miss Kew stuck out a finger that might as well of had a rifle-sight on the end of it. The maid beat it.

"Hey," I said, "here's your broom." I was just going to throw it, but Miss Kew got to me and took it out of my hand.

"In there," she said.

She made me go ahead of her into a room as big as our swimming hole. It had books all over and leather on top of the tables, with gold flowers drawn into the corners.

She pointed to a chair. "Sit there. No, wait a moment." She went to the fireplace and got a newspaper out of a box and brought it over and unfolded it on the seat of the chair. "Now sit down."

I sat on the paper and she dragged up another chair, but didn't put no paper on it.

"What is it? Where is Lone?"

"He died," I said.

She pulled in her breath and went white. She stared at me until her eyes started to water.

"You sick?" I asked her. "Go ahead, throw up. It'll make you feel better."

"Dead? Lone is dead?"

"Yeah. There was a flash flood last week and when he went out the next night in that big wind, he walked under a old oak tree that got gullied under by the flood. The tree come down on him."

"*Came* down on him," she whispered. "Oh, no . . . it's not true."

"It's true, all right. We planted him this morning. We couldn't keep him around no more. He was beginning to st—"

"Stop!" She covered her face with her hands.

"What's the matter?"

"I'll be all right in a moment," she said in a low voice. She went and stood in front of the fireplace with her back to me. I took off one of my shoes while I was waiting for her to come back. But instead she talked from where she was. "Are you Lone's little boy?"

"Yeah. He told me to come to you."

"Oh, my dear child!" She came running back and I thought for a second she was going to pick me up or something, but she stopped short and wrinkled up her nose a little bit. "Wh-what's your name?"

"Gerry," I told her.

"Well, Gerry, how would you like to live with me in this nice big house and—and have new clean clothes—and everything?"

"Well, that's the whole idea. Lone told me to come to you. He said you got more dough than you know what to do with, and he said you owed him a favor."

"A favor?" That seemed to bother her.

"Well," I tried to tell her, "he said he done something for you once and you said some day you'd pay him back for it if you ever could. This is it."

"What did he tell you about that?" She'd got her honk back by then.

"Not a damn thing."

"Please don't use that word," she said, with her eyes closed. Then she opened them and nodded her head. "I promised and I'll do it. You can live here from now on. If—if you want to."

"That's got nothin' to do with it. Lone *told* me to."

"You'll be happy here," she said. She gave me an up-and-down. "I'll see to that."

"Okay. Shall I go get the other kids?"

"*Other* kids—children?"

"Yeah. This ain't for just me. For all of us—the whole gang."

"Don't say 'ain't.'" She leaned back in her chair, took out a silly little handkerchief and dabbed her lips with it, looking at me the whole time. "Now tell me about these—these other children."

"Well, there's Janie, she's eleven like me. And Bonnie and Beanie are eight, they're twins, and Baby. Baby is three."

I screamed. Stern was kneeling beside the couch in a flash, holding his palms against my cheeks to hold my head still; I'd been whipping it back and forth.

"Good boy," he said. "You found it. You haven't found out *what* it is, but now you know *where* it is."

"But for sure," I said hoarsely. "Got water?"

He poured me some water out of a thermos flask. It was so cold it hurt. I lay back and rested, like I'd climbed a cliff. I said, "I can't take anything like that again."

"You want to call it quits for today?"

"What about you?"

"I'll go on as long as you want me to."

I thought about it. "I'd like to go on, but I don't want no thumping around. Not for a while yet."

"If you want another of those inaccurate analogies," Stern said, "psychiatry is like a road map. There are always a lot of different ways to get from one place to another place."

"I'll go around by the long way," I told him. "The eight-lane highway. Not that track over the hill. My clutch is slipping. Where do I turn off?"

He chuckled. I liked the sound of it. "Just past that gravel driveway."

"I been there. There's a bridge washed out."

"You've been on this whole road before," he told me. "Start at the other side of the bridge."

"I never thought of that. I figured I had to do the whole thing, every inch."

"Maybe you won't have to, maybe you will, but the bridge will be easy to cross when you've covered everything else. Maybe there's nothing of value on the bridge and maybe there is, but you can't get near it till you've looked everywhere else."

"Let's go." I was real eager, somehow.

"Mind a suggestion?"

"No."

"Just talk," he said. "Don't try to get too far into what you're saying. That first stretch, when you were eight—you really lived it. The second one, all about the kids, you just talked about. Then, the visit when you were eleven, you felt that. Now just talk again."

"All right."

He waited, then said quietly, "In the library. You told her about the other kids."

I told her about . . . and then she said . . . and something happened, and I screamed. She comforted me and I cussed at her.

But we're not thinking about that now. We're going on.

In the library. The leather, the table, and whether I'm able to do with Miss Kew what Lone said.

What Lone said was, "There's a woman lives up on the top of the hill in the Heights section, name of Kew. She'll have to take care of you. You got to get her to do that. Do everything she tells you, only stay together. Don't you ever let any one of you get away from the others, hear? Aside from that, just you keep Miss Kew happy and she'll keep you happy. Now you do what I say." That's what Lone said. Between every word there was a link like steel cable, and the whole thing made something that couldn't be broken. Not by me it couldn't.

Miss Kew said, "Where are your sisters and the baby?"

"I'll bring 'em."

"Is it near here?"

"Near enough." She didn't say anything to that, so I got up. "I'll be back soon."

"Wait," she said. "I—really, I haven't had time to think. I mean—I've got to get things ready, you know."

I said, "You don't need to think and you are ready. So long."

From the door I heard her saying, louder and louder as I walked away, "Young man, if you're to live in this house, you'll learn to be a good deal better-mannered—" and a lot more of the same.

I yelled back at her, "Okay, *okay!*" and went out.

The sun was warm and the sky was good, and pretty soon I got back to Lone's house. The fire was out and Baby stunk. Janie had knocked over her easel and was sitting on the floor by the door with her head in her hands. Bonnie and Beanie were on a stool with their arms around each other, pulled up together as close as they could get, as if it was cold in there, although it wasn't.

I hit Janie in the arm to snap her out of it. She raised her head. She had gray eyes—or maybe it was more a kind of green—but now they had a funny look about them, like water in a glass that had some milk left in the bottom of it.

I said, "What's the matter around here?"

"What's the matter with what?" she wanted to know.

"All of yez," I said.

She said, "We don't give a damn, that's all."

"Well, all right," I said, "but we got to do what Lone said. Come on."

"No." I looked at the twins. They turned their backs on me. Janie said, "They're hungry."

"Well, why not give 'em something?"

She just shrugged. I sat down. What did Lone have to go get himself squashed for?

"We can't blesh no more," said Janie. It seemed to explain everything.

"Look," I said, "I've got to be Lone now."

Janie thought about that and Baby kicked his feet. Janie looked at him. "You can't," she said.

"I know where to get the heavy food and the turpentine," I

said. "I can find that springy moss to stuff in the logs, and cut wood, and all."

But I couldn't call Bonnie and Beanie from miles away to unlock doors. I couldn't just say a word to Janie and make her get water and blow up the fire and fix the battery. I couldn't make us blesh.

We all stayed like that for a long time. Then I heard the bassinet creak. I looked up. Janie was staring into it.

"All right," she said. "Let's go."

"Who says so?"

"Baby."

"Who's running things now?" I said, mad. "Me or Baby?"

"Baby," Janie said.

I got up and went over to bust her one in the mouth, and then I stopped. If Baby could make them do what Lone wanted, then it would get done. If I started pushing them all around, it wouldn't. So I didn't say anything. Janie got up and walked out the door. The twins watched her go. Then Bonnie disappeared. Beanie picked up Bonnie's clothes and walked out. I got Baby out of the bassinet and draped him over my shoulders.

It was better when we were all outside. It was getting late in the day and the air was warm. The twins flitted in and out of the trees like a couple of flying squirrels, and Janie and I walked along like we were going swimming or something. Baby started to kick, and Janie looked at him a while and got him fed, and he was quiet again.

When we came close to town, I wanted to get everybody close together, but I was afraid to say anything. Baby must of said it instead. The twins came back to us and Janie gave them their clothes and they walked ahead of us, good as you please. I don't know how Baby did it. They sure hated to travel that way.

We didn't have no trouble except one guy we met on the street near Miss Kew's place. He stopped in his tracks and gaped at us, and Janie looked at him and made his hat go so far down over his eyes that he like to pull his neck apart getting it back up again.

What do you know, when we got to the house somebody had washed off all the dirt I'd put on the door. I had one hand on Baby's arm and one on his ankle and him draped over my neck, so I kicked the door and left some more dirt.

"There's a woman here name of Miriam," I told Janie. "She says anything, tell her to go to hell."

The door opened and there was Miriam. She took one look and jumped back six feet. We all trailed inside. Miriam got her wind and screamed, "Miss Kew! Miss Kew!"

"Go to hell," said Janie, and looked at me. I didn't know what to do. It was the first time Janie ever did anything I told her to.

Miss Kew came down the stairs. She was wearing a different dress, but it was just as stupid and had just as much lace. She opened her mouth and nothing came out, so she just left it open until something happened. Finally she said, "Dear gentle Lord preserve us!"

The twins lined up and gawked at her. Miriam sidled over to the wall and sort of slid along it, keeping away from us, until she could get to the door and close it. She said, "Miss Kew, if those are the children you said were going to live here, I quit."

Janie said, "Go to hell."

Just then Bonnie squatted down on the rug. Miriam squawked and jumped at her. She grabbed hold of Bonnie's arm and went to snatch her up. Bonnie disappeared, leaving Miriam with one small dress and the damnedest expression on her face. Beanie grinned enough to split her head in two and started to wave like mad. I looked where she was waving, and there was Bonnie, naked as a jaybird, up on the banister at the top of the stairs.

Miss Kew turned around and saw her and sat down plump on the steps. Miriam went down, too, like she'd been slugged. Beanie picked up Bonnie's dress and walked up the steps past Miss Kew and handed it over. Bonnie put it on. Miss Kew sort of lolled around and looked up. Bonnie and Beanie came back down the stairs hand in hand to where I was. Then they lined up and gaped at Miss Kew.

"What's the matter with her?" Janie asked me.

"She gets sick every once in a while."

"Let's go back home."

"No," I told her.

Miss Kew grabbed the banister and pulled herself up. She

stood there hanging on to it for a while with her eyes closed. All of a sudden she stiffened herself. She looked about four inches taller. She came marching over to us.

"Gerard," she honked.

I think she was going to say something different. But she sort of checked herself and pointed. "What in heaven's name is *that?*" And she aimed her finger at me.

I didn't get it right away, so I turned around to look behind me. "What?"

"That! That!"

"Oh!" I said. "That's Baby."

I slung him down off my back and held him up for her to look at. She made a sort of moaning noise and jumped over and took him away from me. She held him out in front of her and moaned again and called him a poor little thing, and ran and put him down on a long bench, with cushions under the colored-glass window. She bent over him and put her knuckle in her mouth and bit on it and moaned some more. Then she turned to me.

"How long has he been like this?"

I looked at Janie and she looked at me. I said, "He's always been like he is."

She made a sort of cough and ran to where Miriam was lying flaked out on the floor. She slapped Miriam's face a couple of times back and forth. Miriam sat up and looked us over. She closed her eyes and shivered and sort of climbed up Miss Kew hand over hand until she was on her feet.

"Pull yourself together," said Miss Kew between her teeth. "Get a basin with some hot water and soap. Washcloth. Towels. Hurry!" She gave Miriam a big push. Miriam staggered and grabbed at the wall, and then ran out.

Miss Kew went back to Baby and hung over him, titch-titching with her lips all tight.

"Don't mess with him," I said. "There's nothin' wrong with him. We're hungry."

She gave me a look like I'd punched her. "Don't speak to me!"

"Look," I said, "we don't like this any more'n you do. If Lone hadn't told us to, we wouldn't never have come. We were doing all right where we were."

"Don't say 'wouldn't never,' " said Miss Kew. She looked at all of us, one by one. Then she took that silly little hunk of handkerchief and pushed it against her mouth.

"See?" I said to Janie. "All the time gettin' sick."

"Ho-ho," said Bonnie.

Miss Kew gave her a long look. "Gerard," she said in a choked sort of voice, "I understood you to say that these children were your sisters."

"Well?"

She looked at me as if I was real stupid. "We don't have little colored girls for sisters, Gerard."

Janie said, "*We* do."

Miss Kew walked up and back, real fast. "We have a great deal to do," she said, talking to herself.

Miriam came in with a big oval pan and towels and stuff on her arm. She put it down on the bench thing and Miss Kew stuck the back of her hand in the water, then picked up Baby and dunked him right in it. Baby started to kick.

I stepped forward and said, "Wait a minute. Hold on now. What do you think you're doing?"

Janie said, "Shut up, Gerry. He says it's all right."

"All right? She'll drown him."

"No, she won't. Just shut up."

Working up a froth with the soap, Miss Kew smeared it on Baby and turned him over a couple of times and scrubbed at his head and like to smothered him in a big white towel. Miriam stood gawking while Miss Kew lashed up a dishcloth around him so it come out pants. When she was done, you wouldn't of known it was the same baby. And by the time Miss Kew finished with the job, she seemed to have a better hold on herself. She was breathing hard and her mouth was even tighter. She held out the baby to Miriam.

"Take this poor thing," she said, "and put him—"

But Miriam backed away. "I'm sorry, Miss Kew, but I am leaving here and I don't care."

Miss Kew got her honk out. "You can't leave me in a predicament like this! These children need help. Can't you see that for yourself?"

Miriam looked me and Janie over. She was trembling. "You ain't safe, Miss Alicia. They ain't just dirty. They're crazy!"

"They're victims of neglect, and probably no worse than you or I would be if we'd been neglected. And don't say 'ain't.' Gerard!"

"What?"

"Don't say—oh, dear, we have so much to do. Gerard, if you and your—these other children are going to live here, you shall have to make a great many changes. You cannot live under this roof and behave as you have so far. Do you understand that?"

"Oh, sure. Lone said we was to do whatever you say and keep you happy."

"Will you do whatever I say?"

"That's what I just said, isn't it?"

"Gerard, you shall have to learn not to speak to me in that tone. Now, young man, if I told you to do what Miriam says, too, would you do it?"

I said to Janie, "What about that?"

"I'll ask Baby." Janie looked at Baby and Baby wobbled his hands and drooled some. She said, "It's okay."

Miss Kew said, "Gerard, I asked you a question."

"Keep your pants on," I said. "I got to find out, don't I? Yes, if that's what you want, we'll listen to Miriam too."

Miss Kew turned to Miriam. "You hear that, Miriam?"

Miriam looked at Miss Kew and at us and shook her head. Then she held out her hands a bit to Bonnie and Beanie.

They went right to her. Each one took hold of a hand. They looked up at her and grinned. They were probably planning some sort of hellishness, but I guess they looked sort of cute. Miriam's mouth twitched and I thought for a second she was going to look human. She said, "All right, Miss Alicia."

Miss Kew walked over and handed her the baby and she started upstairs with him. Miss Kew herded us along after Miriam. We all went upstairs.

They went to work on us then and for three years they never stopped.

"That was hell," I said to Stern.

"They had their work cut out."

"Yeah, I s'pose they did. So did we. Look, we were going to do exactly what Lone said. Nothing on earth could of stopped us from doing it. We were tied and bound to doing every last little thing Miss Kew said to do. But she and Miriam never seemed to understand that. I guess they felt they had to push every inch of the way. All they had to do was make us understand what they wanted, and we'd of done it. That's okay when it's something like telling me not to climb into bed with Janie. Miss Kew raised holy hell over that. You'd of thought I'd robbed the Crown Jewels, the way she acted.

"But when it's something like, 'You must behave like little ladies and gentlemen,' it just doesn't mean a thing. And two out of three orders she gave us were like that. 'Ah-ah!' she'd say. 'Language, language!' For the longest time I didn't dig that at all. I finally asked her what the hell she meant, and then she finally came out with it. But you see what I mean."

"I certainly do," Stern said. "Did it get easier as time went on?"

"We only had real trouble twice, once about the twins and once about Baby. That one was real bad."

"What happened?"

"About the twins? Well, when we'd been there about a week or so we began to notice something that sort of stunk. Janie and me, I mean. We began to notice that we almost never got to see Bonnie and Beanie. It was like that house was two houses, one part for Miss Kew and Janie and me, and the other part for Miriam and the twins. I guess we'd have noticed it sooner if things hadn't been such a hassle at first, getting us into new clothes and making us sleep all the time at night, and all that. But here was the thing: We'd all get turned out in the side yard to play, and then along comes lunch, and the twins got herded off to eat with Miriam while we ate with Miss Kew. So Janie said, 'Why don't the twins eat with us?'

" 'Miriam's taking care of them, dear,' Miss Kew says.

"Janie looked at her with those eyes. 'I know that. Let 'em eat here and I'll take care of 'em.'

"Miss Kew's mouth got all tight again and she said, 'They're little colored girls, Jane. Now eat your lunch.'

"But that didn't explain anything to Janie or me, either. I said, 'I want 'em to eat with us. Lone said we should stay together.'

" 'But you *are* together,' she says. 'We all live in the same house. We all eat the same food. Now let us not discuss the matter.'

"I looked at Janie and she looked at me and she said, 'So why can't we all do this livin' and eatin' right here?'

"Miss Kew put down her fork and looked hard. 'I have explained it to you and I have said that there will be no further discussion.'

"Well, I thought that was real nowhere. So I just rocked back my head and bellowed, 'Bonnie! Beanie!' And *bing*, there they were.

"So all hell broke loose. Miss Kew ordered them out and they wouldn't go, and Miriam come steaming in with their clothes, and she couldn't catch them, and Miss Kew got to honking at them and finally at me. She said this was too much. Well, maybe she'd had a hard week, but so had we. So Miss Kew ordered us to leave.

"I went and got Baby and started out, and along came Janie and the twins. Miss Kew waited till we were all out the door and next thing you know she ran out after us. She passed us and got in front of me and made me stop. So we all stopped.

" 'Is this how you follow Lone's wishes?' she asked.

"I told her yes. She said she understood Lone wanted us to stay with her. And I said, 'Yeah, but he wanted us to stay together more.'

"She said come back in, we'd have a talk. Janie asked Baby and Baby said okay, so we went back. We had a compromise. We didn't eat in the dining room no more. There was a side porch, a sort of verandah thing with glass windows, with a door to the dining room and a door to the kitchen, and we all ate out there after that. Miss Kew ate by herself.

"But something funny happened because of that whole cockeyed hassle."

"What was that?" Stern asked me.

I laughed. "Miriam. She looked and sounded like always but she started slipping us cookies between meals. You know, it took me years to figure out what all that was about. I mean it. From what I've learned about people, there seems to be two armies fightin' about race. One's fightin' to keep 'em apart, and one's fightin' to get 'em together. But I don't see why both sides are so *worried* about it! Why don't they just forget it?"

"They can't. You see, Gerry, it's necessary for people to believe they are superior in some fashion. You and Lone and the kids—you were a pretty tight unit. Didn't you feel you were a little better than all of the rest of the world?"

"Better? How could we be better?"

"Different, then."

"Well, I suppose so, but we didn't think about it. Different, yes. Better, no."

"You're a unique case," Stern said. "Now go on and tell me about the other trouble you had. About Baby."

"Baby. Yeah. Well, that was a couple of months after we moved to Miss Kew's. Things were already getting real smooth, even then. We'd learned all the 'yes, ma'am, no, ma'am' routines by then and she'd got us catching up with school—regular periods morning and afternoon, five days a week. Janie had long ago quit taking care of Baby, and the twins walked to wherever they went. That was funny. They could pop from one place to another right in front of Miss Kew's eyes and she wouldn't believe what she saw. She was too upset about them suddenly showing up bare. They quit doing it and she was happy about it. She was happy about a lot of things. It had been years since she'd seen anybody—years. She'd even had the meters put outside the house so no one would ever have to come in. But with us there, she began to liven up. She quit wearing those old-lady dresses and began to look halfway human. She ate with us sometimes, even.

"But one fine day I woke up feeling real weird. It was like somebody had stolen something from me when I was asleep, only I didn't know what. I crawled out of my window and along the ledge into Janie's room, which I wasn't supposed to do. She was in bed. I went and woke her up. I can still see her eyes, the way they opened a little slit, still asleep, and then popped up wide. I didn't have to tell her something was wrong. She knew, and she knew what it was.

" 'Baby's gone!' she said.

"We didn't care then who woke up. We pounded out of her room and down the hall and into the little room at the end where Baby slept. You wouldn't believe it. The fancy crib he had and the white chest of drawers and all that mess of rattles and so on, they were gone, and there was just a writing desk there. I mean it was as if Baby had never been there at all.

"We didn't say anything. We just spun around and busted into Miss Kew's bedroom. I'd never been in there but once and Janie only a few times. But forbidden or not, this was different. Miss Kew was in bed, with her hair braided. She was wide awake before we could get across the room. She pushed herself back and up until she was sitting against the headboard. She gave the two of us the cold eye.

" 'What is the meaning of this?' she wanted to know.

" 'Where's Baby?' I yelled at her.

" 'Gerard,' she says, 'there is no need to shout.'

"Janie was a real quiet kid, but she said, 'You better tell us where he is, Miss Kew,' and it would of scared you to look at her when she said it.

"So all of a sudden Miss Kew took off the stone face and held out her hands to us. 'Children,' she said, 'I'm sorry. I really am sorry. But I've just done what is best. I've sent Baby away. He's gone to live with some children like him. We could never make him really happy here. You know that.'

"Janie said, 'He never told us he wasn't happy.'

"Miss Kew brought out a hollow kind of laugh. 'As if he could talk, the poor little thing!'

" 'You better get him back here,' I said. 'You don't know what you're fooling with. I told you we wasn't ever to break up.'

"She was getting mad, but she held on to herself. 'I'll try to explain it to you, dear,' she said. 'You and Jane here and even the twins are all normal, healthy children and you'll grow up to be fine men and women. But poor Baby's—different. He's not going to grow very much more, and he'll never walk and play like other children.'

" 'That doesn't matter,' Janie said. 'You had no call to send him away.'

"And I said, 'Yeah. You better bring him back, but quick.'

"Then she started to jump salty. 'Among the many things I have taught you is, I am sure, not to dictate to your elders. Now then, you run along and get dressed for breakfast, and we'll say no more about this.'

"I told her, nice as I could, 'Miss Kew, you're going to wish you brought him back right now. But you're going to bring him back soon. Or else.'

"So then she got up out of her bed and ran us out of the room."

I was quiet a while, and Stern asked, "What happened?"

"Oh," I said, "she brought him back." I laughed suddenly. "I guess it's funny now, when you come to think of it. Nearly three months of us getting bossed around, and her ruling the roost, and then all of a sudden we lay down the law. We'd tried our best to be good according to her ideas, but, by God, that time she went too far. She got the treatment from the second she slammed her door on us. She had a big china pot under her bed, and it rose up in the air and smashed through her dresser mirror. Then one of the drawers in the dresser slid open and a glove come out of it and smacked her face.

"She went to jump back on the bed and a whole section of plaster fell off the ceiling onto the bed. The water turned on in her little bathroom and the plug went in, and just about the time it began to overflow, all her clothes fell off their hooks. She went to run out of the room, but the door was stuck, and when she yanked on the handle it opened real quick and she spread out on the floor. The door slammed shut again and more plaster come down on her. Then we went back in and stood looking at her. She was crying. I hadn't known till then that she could.

" 'You going to get Baby back here?' I asked her.

"She just lay there and cried. After a while she looked up at us. It was real pathetic. We helped her up and got her to a chair. She just looked at us for a while, and at the mirror, and at the busted ceiling, and then she whispered, 'What happened? What happened?'

" 'You took Baby away,' I said. 'That's what.'

"So she jumped up and said real low, real scared, but real strong: 'Something struck the house. An airplane. Perhaps there was an earthquake. We'll talk about Baby after breakfast.'

"I said, 'Give her more, Janie.'

"A big gob of water hit her on the face and chest and made her nightgown stick to her, which was the kind of thing that upset her most. Her braids stood straight up in the air, more and more, till they dragged her standing straight up. She opened her mouth to yell and the powder puff off the dresser rammed into it. She clawed it out.

"'What are you doing? What are you doing?' she says, crying again.

"Janie just looked at her and put her hands behind her, real smug. 'We haven't done anything,' she said.

"And I said, 'Not yet we haven't. You going to get Baby back?'

"And she screamed at us, 'Stop it! Stop it! Stop talking about that mongoloid idiot! It's no good to anyone, not even itself! How could I ever make believe it's mine?'

"I said, 'Get rats, Janie.'

"There was a scuttling sound along the baseboard. Miss Kew covered her face with her hands and sank down on the chair. 'Not rats,' she said. 'There are no rats here.' Then something squeaked and she went all to pieces. Did you ever see anyone really go to pieces?"

"Yes," Stern said.

"I was about as mad as I could get," I said, "but that was almost too much for me. Still, she shouldn't have sent Baby away. It took a couple of hours for her to get straightened out enough so she could use the phone, but we had Baby back before lunch time." I laughed.

"What's funny?"

"She never seemed able to rightly remember what had happened to her. About three weeks later I heard her talking to Miriam about it. She said it was the house settling suddenly. She said it was a good thing she'd sent Baby out for that medical checkup—the poor little thing might have been hurt. She really believed it, I think."

"She probably did. That's fairly common. We don't believe anything we don't want to believe."

"How much of this do you believe?" I asked him suddenly.

"I told you before—it doesn't matter. I don't want to believe or disbelieve it."

"You haven't asked me how much of it I believe."

"I don't have to. You'll make up your own mind about that."

"Are you a *good* psychotherapist?"

"I think so," he said. "Whom did you kill?"

The question caught me absolutely off guard. "Miss Kew," I said. Then I started to cuss and swear. "I didn't mean to tell you that."

"Don't worry about it," he said. "What did you do it for?"

"That's what I came here to find out."

"You must have really hated her."

I started to cry. Fifteen years old and crying like that!

He gave me time to get it all out. The first part of it came out in noises, grunts and squeaks that hurt my throat. Much more than you'd think came out when my nose started to run. And finally—words.

"Do you know where I came from? The earliest thing I can remember is a punch in the mouth. I can still see it coming, a fist as big as my head. Because I was crying. I been afraid to cry ever since. I was crying because I was hungry. Cold, maybe. Both. After that, big dormitories, and whoever could steal the most got the most. Get the hell kicked out of you if you're bad, get a big reward if you're good. Big reward: they let you alone. Try to live like that. Try to live so the biggest, most wonderful thing in the whole damn world is just to have 'em let you alone!

"So a spell with Lone and the kids. Something wonderful: you belong. It never happened before. Two yellow bulbs and a fireplace and they light up the world. It's all there is and all there ever has to be.

"Then the big change: clean clothes, cooked food, five hours a day school; Columbus and King Arthur and a 1925 book on Civics that explains about septic tanks. Over it all a great big square-cut lump of ice, and you watch it melting and the corners curve, and you know it's because of you, Miss Kew . . . hell, she had too much control over herself ever to slobber over us, but it was there, that feeling. Lone took care of us because it was part of the way he lived. Miss Kew took care of us and none of it was the way she lived. It was something she wanted to do.

"She had a weird idea of 'right' and a wrong idea of 'wrong,' but she stuck to them, tried to make her ideas do us good. When she couldn't understand, she figured it was her own failure . . . and there was an almighty lot she didn't understand and never could. What went right was our success. What went wrong was her mistake. That last year, that was . . . oh, good."

"So?"

"So I killed her. Listen," I said. I felt I had to talk fast. I wasn't short of time, but I had to get rid of it. "I'll tell you all I know about it. The one day before I killed her. I woke up in the morning and the sheets crackly clean under me, the sunlight coming in through white curtains and bright red-and-blue drapes. There's a closet full of my clothes—mine, you see; I never had anything that was really mine before—and downstairs Miriam clinking around with breakfast and the twins laughing. Laughing with *her*, mind you, not just with each other like they always did before.

"In the next room, Janie moving around, singing, and when I see her, I know her face will shine inside and out. I get up. There's *hot* hot water and the toothpaste bites my tongue. The clothes fit me and I go downstairs and they're all there and I'm glad to see them and they're glad to see me, and we no sooner get set around the table when Miss Kew comes down and everyone calls out to her at once.

"And the morning goes by like that, school with a recess, there in the big long living room. The twins with the ends of their tongues stuck out, drawing the alphabet instead of writing it, and then Janie, when it's time, painting a picture, a real picture of a cow with trees and a yellow fence that goes off into the distance. Here I am lost between the two parts of a quadratic equation, and Miss Kew bending close to help me, and I smell the sachet she has on her clothes. I hold up my head to smell it better, and far away I hear the shuffle and klunk of filled pots going on the stove back in the kitchen.

"And the afternoon goes by like that, more school and some study and boiling out into the yard, laughing. The twins chasing each other, running on their two feet to get where they want to go; Janie dappling the leaves in her picture, trying to get it just the way Miss Kew says it ought to be. And Baby, he's got a big play-pen. He don't move around much any more, he just watches and dribbles some, and gets packed full of food and kept as clean as a new sheet of tinfoil.

"And supper, and the evening, and Miss Kew reading to us, changing her voice every time someone else talks in the story, reading fast and whispery when it embarrasses her, but reading every word all the same.

"And I had to go and kill her. And that's all."

"You haven't said why," Stern said.

"What are you—stupid?" I yelled.

Stern didn't say anything. I turned on my belly on the couch and propped up my chin in my hands and looked at him. You never could tell what was going on with him, but I got the idea that he was puzzled.

"I said why," I told him.

"Not to me."

I suddenly understood that I was asking too much of him. I said slowly, "We all woke up at the same time. We all did what somebody else wanted. We lived through a day someone else's way, thinking someone else's thoughts, saying other people's words. Jane painted someone else's pictures, Baby didn't talk to anyone, and we were all happy with it. Now do you see?"

"Not yet."

"God!" I said. I thought for a while. "We didn't blesh."

"Blesh? Oh. But you didn't after Lone died, either."

"That was different. That was like a car running out of gas, but the car's there—there's nothing wrong with it. It's just waiting. But after Miss Kew got done with us, the car was taken all to pieces, see?"

It was his turn to think a while. Finally he said, "The mind makes us do funny things. Some of them seem completely reasonless, wrong, insane. But the cornerstone of the work we're doing is this: there's a chain of solid, unassailable logic in the things we do. Dig deep enough and you find cause and effect as clearly in this field as you do in any other. I said *logic*, mind; I didn't say 'correctness' or 'rightness' or 'justice' or anything of the sort. Logic and truth are two very different things, but they often look the same to the mind that's performing the logic.

"When that mind is submerged, working at cross-purposes with the surface mind, then you're all confused. Now in your case, I can see the thing you're pointing at—that in order to preserve or to rebuild that peculiar bond between you kids, you had to get rid of Miss Kew. But I don't see the logic. I don't see that regaining that 'bleshing' was worth destroying this new-found security which you admit was enjoyable."

I said desperately, "Maybe it wasn't worth destroying it."

Stern leaned forward and pointed his pipe at me. "It *was* because it made you do what you did. After the fact, maybe things look different. But when you were moved to do it, the important thing was to destroy Miss Kew and regain this thing you'd had before. I don't see why and neither do you."

"How are we going to find out?"

"Well, let's get to the most unpleasant part, if you're up to it."

I lay down. "I'm ready."

"All right. Tell me everything that happened just before you killed her."

I fumbled through that last day, trying to taste the food, hear the voices. A thing came and went and came again: it was the crisp feeling of the sheets. I thrust it away because it was at the beginning of that day, but it came back again, and I realized it was at the end, instead.

I said, "What I just told you, all that about the children doing things other people's way instead of their own, and Baby not talking, and everyone happy about it, and finally that I had to kill Miss Kew. It took a long time to get to that, and a long time to start doing it. I guess I lay in bed and thought for four hours before I got up again. It was dark and quiet. I went out of the room and down the hall and into Miss Kew's bedroom and killed her."

"How?"

"That's all there is!" I shouted, as loud as I could. Then I quieted down. "It was awful dark . . . it still is. I don't know. I don't want to know. She did love us. I know she did. But I had to kill her."

"All right, all right," Stern said. "I guess there's no need to get too gruesome about this. You're—"

"What?"

"You're quite strong for your age, aren't you, Gerard?"

"I guess so. Strong enough, anyway."

"Yes," he said.

"I still don't see that logic you were talking about." I began to hammer on the couch with my fist, hard, once for each word: "Why — did — I — have — to — go — and — do — that?"

"Cut that out," he said. "You'll hurt yourself."

"I ought to get hurt," I said.

"Ah?" said Stern.

I got up and went to the desk and got some water. "What am I going to do?"

"Tell me what you did after you killed her, right up until the time you came here."

"Not much," I said. "It was only last night. I took her check-book. I went back to my room, sort of numb. I put all my clothes on except my shoes. I carried them. I went out. Walked a long time, trying to think, went to the bank when it opened. Cashed a check for eleven hundred bucks. Got the idea of getting some help from a psychiatrist, spent most of the day looking for one, came here. That's all."

"Didn't you have any trouble cashing the check?"

"I never have any trouble making people do what I want them to do."

He gave a surprised grunt.

"I know what you're thinking—I couldn't make Miss Kew do what I wanted."

"That's part of it," he admitted.

"If I had of done that," I told him, "she wouldn't of been Miss Kew any more. Now the banker—all I made him do was be a banker."

I looked at him and suddenly realized why he fooled with the pipe all the time. It was so he could look down at it and you wouldn't be able to see his eyes.

"You killed her," he said—and I knew he was changing the subject—"and destroyed something that was valuable to you. It must have been less valuable to you than the chance to rebuild this thing you used to have with the other kids. And you're not sure of the value of that." He looked up. "Does that describe your main trouble?"

"Just about."

"You know the single thing that makes people kill?" When I didn't answer, he said, "Survival. To save the self or something which identifies with the self. And in this case that doesn't apply, because your setup with Miss Kew had far more survival value for you, singly and as a group, than the other."

"So maybe I just didn't have a good enough reason to kill her."

"You had, because you did it. We just haven't located it yet. I mean we have the reason, but we don't know why it was important enough. The answer is somewhere in you."

"Where?"

He got up and walked some. "We have a pretty consecutive life-story here. There's fantasy mixed with the fact, of course, and there are areas in which we have no detailed information, but we have a beginning and a middle and an end. Now I can't say for sure, but the answer may be in that bridge you refused to cross a while back. Remember?"

I remembered all right. I said, "Why that? Why can't we try something else?"

He quietly pointed out, "Because you just said it. Why are you shying away from it?"

"Don't go making big ones out of little ones," I said. Sometimes the guy annoyed me. "That bothers me. I don't know why, but it does."

"Something's lying hidden in there and you're bothering *it* so it's fighting back. Anything that fights to stay concealed is very possibly the thing we're after. Your trouble is concealed, isn't it?"

"Well, yes," I said, and I felt that sickness and faintness again, and again I pushed it away. Suddenly I wasn't going to be stopped any more. "Let's go get it." I lay down.

He let me watch the ceiling and listen to silence for a while, and then he said, "You're in the library. You've just met Miss Kew. She's talking to you; you're telling her about the children."

I lay very still. Nothing happened. Yes, it did; I got tense inside all over, from the bones out, more and more. When it got as bad as it could, still nothing happened.

I heard him get up and cross the room to the desk. He fumbled there for a while; things clicked and hummed. Suddenly I heard my own voice:

"Well, there's Janie, she's eleven like me. And Bonnie and Beanie are eight, they're twins, and Baby. Baby is three."

And the sound of my own scream—
And nothingness.

Sputtering out of the darkness, I came up flailing with my fists. Strong hands caught my wrists. They didn't check my arms; they just grabbed and rode. I opened my eyes. I was soaking wet. The thermos lay on its side on the rug. Stern was crouched beside me, holding my wrists. I quit struggling.

"What happened?"

He let me go and stood back watchfully. "Lord," he said, "what a charge!"

I held my head and moaned. He threw me a hand-towel and I used it. "What hit me?"

"I've had you on tape the whole time," he explained. "When you wouldn't get into the recollection, I tried to nudge you into it by using your own voice as you recounted it before. It works wonders sometimes."

"It worked wonders this time," I growled. "I think I blew a fuse."

"In effect, you did. You were on the trembling verge of going into the thing you don't want to remember, and you let yourself go unconscious rather than do it."

"What are you so pleased about?"

"Last-ditch defense," he said tersely. "We've got it now. Just one more try."

"Now hold on. The last-ditch defense is that I drop dead."

"You won't. You've contained this episode in your subconscious mind for a long time and it hasn't hurt you."

"Hasn't it?"

"Not in terms of killing you."

"How do you know it won't when we drag it out?"

"You'll see."

I looked up at him sideways. Somehow he struck me as knowing what he was doing.

"You know a lot more about yourself now than you did at the time," he explained softly. "You can apply insight. You can evaluate it as it comes up. Maybe not completely, but enough to protect yourself. Don't worry. Trust me. I can stop it if it gets too bad. Now just relax. Look at the ceiling. Be aware of your toes. Don't look at your toes. Look straight up. Your toes, your big toes. Don't move your toes, but feel them. Count outward from your big toes, one count for each toe. One, two, three. Feel that third toe. Feel the toe, feel it, feel it go limp, go limp, go limp. The toe next to it on both sides gets limp. So limp because your toes are limp, all of your toes are limp—"

"What are you doing?" I shouted at him.

He said in the same silky voice, "You trust me and so do your toes trust me. They're all limp because you trust me. You—"

"You're trying to hypnotize me. I'm not going to let you do that."

"You're going to hypnotize yourself. You do everything yourself. I just point the way. I point your toes to the path. Just point your toes. No one can make you go anywhere you don't want to go, but you want to go where your toes are pointed where your toes are limp where your . . ."

On and on and on. And where was the dangling gold ornament, the light in the eyes, the mystic passes? He wasn't even sitting where I could see him. Where was the talk about how sleepy I was supposed to be? Well, he knew I wasn't sleepy and didn't want to be sleepy. I just wanted to be toes. I just wanted to be limp, just a limp toe. No brains in a toe, a toe to go, go, go eleven times, eleven, I'm eleven . . .

I split in two, and it was all right, the part that watched the part that went back to the library, and Miss Kew leaning toward me, but not too near, me with the newspaper crackling under me on the library chair, me with one shoe off and my limp toes dangling . . . and I felt a mild surprise at this. For this was hypnosis, but I was quite conscious, quite altogether there on the couch with Stern droning away at me, quite able to roll over and sit up and talk to him and walk out if I wanted to, but I just didn't want to. Oh, if this was what hypnosis was like, I was all for it. I'd work at this. This was all right.

There on the table I'm able to see that the gold will unfold on the leather, and whether I'm able to stay by the table with you, with Miss Kew, with Miss Kew . . .

". . . and Bonnie and Beanie are eight, they're twins, and Baby. Baby is three."

"Baby is three," she said.

There was a pressure, a stretching apart, and a . . . a breakage. And with a tearing agony and a burst of triumph that drowned the pain, it was done.

And this is what was inside. All in one flash, but all this.

Baby is three? My baby would be three if there were a baby, which there never was . . .

Lone, I'm open to you. Open, is this open enough?

His irises like wheels. I'm sure they spin, but I never catch them at it. The probe that passes invisibly from his brain, through his eyes, into mine. Does he know what it means to me? Does he care? He doesn't care, he doesn't know; he empties me and I fill as he directs me to; he drinks and waits and drinks again and never looks at the cup.

When I saw him first, I was dancing in the wind, in the wood, in the wild, and I spun about and he stood there in the leafy shadows, watching me. I hated him for it. It was not my wood, not my gold-spangled fern-tangled glen. But it was my dancing that he took, freezing it forever by being there. I hated him for it, hated the way he looked, the way he stood, ankle-deep in the kind wet ferns, looking like a tree with roots for feet and clothes the color of earth. As I stopped he moved, and then he was just a man, a great ape-shouldered, dirty animal of a man, and all my hate was fear suddenly and I was just as frozen.

He knew what he had done and he didn't care. Dancing . . . never to dance again, because never would I know the woods were free of eyes, free of tall, uncaring, dirty animal-men. Summer days with the clothes choking me, winter nights with the precious decencies round and about me like a shroud, and never to dance again, never to remember dancing without remembering the shock of knowing he had seen me. How I hated him! Oh, how I hated him!

To dance alone where no one knew, that was the single thing I hid to myself when I was known as Miss Kew, that Victorian, older than her years, later than her time; correct and starched, lace and linen and lonely. Now indeed I would be all they said, through and through, forever and ever, because he had robbed me of the one thing I dared to keep secret.

He came out into the sun and walked to me, holding his great head a little on one side. I stood where I was, frozen inwardly and outwardly and altogether by the core of anger and the layer of fear. My arm was still out, my waist still bent from my dance, and when he stopped, I breathed again because by then I had to.

He said, "You read books?"

I couldn't bear to have him near me, but I couldn't move. He put out his hard hand and touched my jaw, turned my head up until I had to look into his face. I cringed away from him, but my face would not leave his hand, though he was not holding it, just lifting it. "You got to read some books for me. I got no time to find them."

I asked him, "Who are you?"

"Lone," he said. "You going to read books for me?"

"No. Let me go, let me go!" He wasn't holding me.

"What books?" I cried.

He thumped my face, not very hard. It made me look up a bit more. He dropped his hand away. His eyes, the irises were going to spin. . . .

"Open up in there," he said. "Open way up and let me see."

There were books in my head, and he was looking at the titles . . . he was not looking at the titles, for he couldn't read. He was looking at what I knew of the books. I suddenly felt terribly useless, because I had only a fraction of what he wanted.

"What's that?" he barked.

I knew what he meant. He'd gotten it from inside my head. I didn't know it was in there, even, but he found it.

"Telekinesis," I said.

"How is it done?"

"Nobody knows if it can be done. Moving physical objects with the mind!"

"It can be done," he said. "This one?"

"Teleportation. That's the same thing—well, almost. Moving your own body with mind power."

"Yeah, yeah, I see it," he said gruffly.

"Molecular interpenetration. Telepathy and clairvoyance. I don't know anything about them. I think they're silly."

"Read about 'em. It don't matter if you understand or not. What's this?"

It was there in my brain, on my lips. "*Gestalt.*"

"What's that?"

"Group. Like a cure for a lot of diseases with one kind of treatment. Like a lot of thoughts expressed in one phrase. The whole is greater than the sum of the parts."

"Read about that, too. Read a whole lot about that. That's the *most* you got to read about. That's important."

He turned away, and when his eyes came away from mine it was like something breaking, so that I staggered and fell to one knee. He went off into the woods without looking back. I got my things and ran home. There was anger, and it struck me like a storm. There was fear, and it struck me like a wind. I knew I would read the books, I knew I would come back, I knew I would never dance again.

So I read the books and I came back. Sometimes it was every day for three or four days, and sometimes, because I couldn't find a certain book, I might not come back for ten. He was always there in the little glen, waiting, standing in the shadows, and he took what he wanted of the books and nothing of me. He never mentioned the next meeting. If he came there every day to wait for me, or if he only came when I did, I have no way of knowing.

He made me read books that contained nothing for me, books on evolution, on social and cultural organization, on mythology, and ever so much on symbiosis. What I had with him were not conversations; sometimes nothing audible would pass between us but his grunt of surprise or small, short hum of interest.

He tore the books out of me the way he would tear berries from a bush, all at once; he smelled of sweat and earth and the green juices his heavy body crushed when he moved through the wood.

If he learned anything from the books, it made no difference in him.

There came a day when he sat by me and puzzled something out.

He said, "What book has something like this?" Then he waited for a long time, thinking. "The way a termite can't digest wood, you know, and microbes in the termite's belly can, and what the termite eats is what the microbe leaves behind. What's that?"

"Symbiosis," I remembered. I remembered the words. Lone

tore the content from words and threw the words away. "Two kinds of life depending upon one another for existence."

"Yeah. Well, is there a book about four-five kinds doing that?"

"I don't know."

Then he asked, "What about this? You got a radio station, you got four-five receivers, each receiver is fixed up to make something different happen, like one digs and one flies and one makes noise, but each one takes orders from the one place. And each one has its own power and its own thing to do, but they are all apart. Now: is there life like that, instead of radio?"

"Where each organism is a part of the whole, but separated? I don't think so . . . unless you mean social organizations, like a team, or perhaps a gang of men working, all taking orders from the same boss."

"No," he said immediately, "not like that. Like one single animal." He made a gesture with his cupped hand which I understood.

I asked, "You mean a *gestalt* life-form? It's fantastic."

"No book has about that, huh?"

"None I ever heard of."

"I got to know about that," he said heavily. "There is such a thing. I want to know if it ever happened before."

"I can't see how anything of the sort could exist."

"It does. A part that fetches, a part that figures, a part that finds out, and a part that talks."

"Talks? Only humans talk."

"I know," he said, and got up and went away.

I looked and looked for such a book but found nothing remotely like it. I came back and told him so. He was still a very long time, looking off to the blue-on-blue line of the hilly horizon. Then he drove those about-to-spin irises at me and searched.

"You learn, but you don't think," he said, and looked again at the hills.

"This all happens with humans," he said eventually. "It happens piece by piece right under folks' noses, and they don't see it. You got mind-readers. You got people can move things with their mind. You got people can move themselves with their mind. You got people can figure anything out if you just think to ask them. What you ain't got is the one kind of person who can pull 'em all together, like a brain pulls together the parts that press and pull and feel heat and walk and think and all the other things.

"I'm one," he finished suddenly. Then he sat still for so long I thought he had forgotten me.

"Lone," I said, "what do you do here in the woods?"

"I wait," he said. "I ain't finished yet." He looked at my eyes and snorted in irritation. "I don't mean 'finished' like you're thinking. I mean I ain't—completed yet. You know about a worm when it's cut, growin' whole again? Well, forget about the cut. Suppose it just grew that way, for the first time, see? I'm getting parts. I ain't finished. I want a book about that kind of animal that is me when I'm finished."

"I don't know of such a book. Can you tell me more? Maybe if you could, I'd think of the right book or a place to find it."

He broke a stick between his huge hands, put the two pieces side by side and broke them together with one strong twist.

"All I know is I got to do what I'm doing like a bird's got to nest when it's time. And I know that when I'm done I won't be anything to brag about. I'll be like a body stronger and faster than anything there ever was, without the right kind of head on it. But maybe that's because I'm one of the first. That picture you had, the caveman . . ."

"Neanderthal."

"Yeah. Come to think of it, he was no great shakes. An early try at something new. That's what I'm going to be. But maybe the right kind of head'll come along after I'm all organized. Then it'll be something."

He grunted with satisfaction and went away.

I tried, for days I tried, but I couldn't find what he wanted. I found a magazine which stated that the next important evolutionary step in man would be in a psychic rather than a physical direction, but it said nothing about a—shall I call it a *gestalt* organism? There was something about slime molds, but they seem to be more a hive activity of amoebae than even a symbiosis.

To my own unscientific, personally uninterested mind, there was nothing like what he wanted except possibly a band marching together, everyone playing different instruments with different techniques and different notes, to make a single thing move along together. But he hadn't meant anything like that.

So I went back to him in the cool of an early fall evening, and he took what little I had in my eyes, and turned from me angrily with a gross word I shall not permit myself to remember.

"You can't find it," he told me. "Don't come back."

He got up and went to a tattered birch and leaned against it, looking out and down into the wind-tossed crackling shadows. I think he had forgotten me already. I know he leaped like a frightened animal when I spoke to him from so near. He must have been completely immersed in whatever strange thoughts he was having, for I'm sure he didn't hear me coming.

I said, "Lone, don't blame me for not finding it. I tried."

He controlled his startlement and brought those eyes down to me. "Blame? Who's blamin' anybody?"

"I failed you," I told him, "and you're angry."

He looked at me so long I became uncomfortable.

"I don't know what you're talkin' about," he said.

I wouldn't let him turn away from me. He would have. He would have left me forever with not another thought; he didn't *care!* It wasn't cruelty or thoughtlessness as I have been taught to know those things. He was as uncaring as a cat is of the bursting of a tulip bud.

I took him by the upper arms and shook him, it was like trying to shake the front of my house. "You *can* know!" I screamed at him. "You know what I read. You must know what I think!"

He shook his head.

"I'm a person, a woman," I raved at him. "You've used me and used me and you've given me nothing. You've made me break a lifetime of habits—reading until all hours, coming to you in the rain and on Sunday—you don't talk to me, you don't look at me, you don't know anything about me and you don't care. You put some sort of a spell on me that I couldn't break. And when you're finished, you say, 'Don't come back.' "

"Do I have to give something back because I took something?"

"People do."

He gave that short, interested hum. "What do you want me to give you? I ain't got anything."

I moved away from him. I felt . . . I don't know what I felt. After a time I said, "I don't know."

He shrugged and turned. I fairly leaped at him, dragging him back. "I want you to—"

"Well, damn it, what?"

I couldn't look at him; I could hardly speak. "I don't know. There's something, but I don't know what it is. It's something that—I couldn't say if I knew it." When he began to shake his head, I took his arms again. "You've read the books out of me; can't you read the . . . the *me* out of me?"

"I ain't never tried." He held my face up and stepped close. "Here," he said.

His eyes projected their strange probe at me and I screamed. I tried to twist away. I hadn't wanted this, I was sure I hadn't. I struggled terribly. I think he lifted me right off the ground with his big hands. He held me until he was finished, and then let me drop. I huddled to the ground, sobbing. He sat down beside me. He didn't try to touch me. He didn't try to go away. I quieted at last and crouched there, waiting.

He said, "I ain't going to do much of that no more."

I sat up and tucked my skirt close around me and laid my cheek on my updrawn knees so I could see his face. "What happened?"

He cursed. "Damn mishmash inside you. Thirty-three years old—what you want to live like that for?"

"I live very comfortably," I said with some pique.

"Yeah," he said. "All by yourself for ten years now 'cept for someone to do your work. Nobody else."

"Men are animals, and women . . ."

"You really hate women. They all know something you don't."

"I don't want to know. I'm quite happy the way I am."

"Hell you are."

I said nothing to that. I despise that kind of language.

"Two things you want from me. Neither makes no sense." He looked at me with the first real expression I have ever seen in his face: a profound wonderment. "You want to know all about me, where I came from, how I got to be what I am."

"Yes, I do want that. What's the other thing I want that you know and I don't?"

"I was born some place and growed like a weed somehow," he said, ignoring me. "Folks who didn't give even enough of a damn to try the orphanage routine. So I just ran loose, sort of in training to be the village idiot. I'da made it, but I took to the woods instead."

"Why?"

He wondered why, and finally said, "I guess because the way people lived didn't make no sense to me. Out here I can grow like I want."

"How is that?" I asked over one of those vast distances that built and receded between him and me so constantly.

"What I wanted to get from your books."

"You never told me."

For the second time he said, "You learn, but you don't think. There's a kind of—well, *person.* It's all made of separate parts, but it's all one person. It has like hands, it has like legs, it has like a talking mouth, and it has like a brain. That's me, a brain for that person. Damn feeble, too, but the best I know of."

"You're mad."

"No, I ain't," he said, unoffended and completely certain. "I already got the part that's like hands. I can move 'em anywhere and they do what I want, though they're too young yet to do much good. I got the part that talks. That one's real good."

"I don't think you talk very well at all," I said. I cannot stand incorrect English.

He was surprised. "I'm not talking about me! She's back yonder with the others."

"She?"

"The one that talks. Now I need one that thinks, one that can take anything and add it to anything else and come up with a right answer. And once they're all together, and all the parts get used together often enough, I'll be that new kind of thing I told you about. See? Only—I wish it had a better head on it than me."

My own head was swimming. "What made you start doing this?"

He considered me gravely. "What made you start growing hair in your armpits?" he asked me. "You don't figure a thing like that. It just happens."

"What is that . . . that thing you do when you look in my eyes?"

"You want a name for it? I ain't got one. I don't know how I do it. I know I can get anyone I want to do anything. Like you're going to forget about me."

I said in a choked voice, "I don't want to forget about you."

"You will." I didn't know then whether he meant I'd forget, or I'd *want* to forget. "You'll hate me, and then after a long time you'll be grateful. Maybe you'll be able to do something for me some time. You'll be that grateful that you'll be glad to do it. But you'll forget, all right, everything but a sort of . . . feeling. And my name, maybe."

I don't know what moved me to ask him, but I did, forlornly. "And no one will ever know about you and me?"

"Can't," he said. "Unless . . . well, unless it was the head of the animal, like me, or a better one." He heaved himself up.

"Oh, wait, wait!" I cried. He mustn't go yet, he mustn't. He was a tall, dirty beast of a man, yet he had enthralled me in some dreadful way. "You haven't given me the other . . . whatever it was."

"Oh," he said. "Yeah, that."

He moved like a flash. There was a pressure, a stretching apart, and a . . . a breakage. And with a tearing agony and a burst of triumph that drowned the pain, it was done.

I came up out of it, through two distinct levels:

I am eleven, breathless from shock from a transferred agony of that incredible entrance into the ego of another. And:

I am fifteen, lying on the couch while Stern drones on, ". . . quietly, quietly limp, your ankles and legs as limp as your toes, your belly goes soft, the back of your neck is as limp as your belly, it's quiet and easy and all gone soft and limper than limp. . . ."

I sat up and swung my legs to the floor. "Okay," I said.

Stern looked a little annoyed. "This is going to work," he said, "but it can only work if you cooperate. Just lie—"

"It did work," I said.

"What?"

"The whole thing. A to Z." I snapped my fingers. "Like that."

He looked at me piercingly. "What do you mean?"

"It was right there, where you said. In the library. When I was eleven. When she said, 'Baby is three.' It knocked loose something that had been boiling around in her for three years, and it all came blasting out. I got it, full force; just a kid, no warning, no defenses. It had such a—a pain in it, like I never knew could be."

"Go on," said Stern.

"That's really all. I mean that's not what was in it; it's what it did to me. What it was, a sort of hunk of her own self. A whole lot of things that happened over about four months, every bit of it. She knew Lone."

"You mean a whole *series* of episodes?"

"That's it."

"You got a series all at once? In a split second?"

"That's right. Look, for that split second I *was* her, don't you see? I was her, everything she'd ever done, everything she'd ever thought and heard and felt. Everything, everything, all in the right order if I wanted to bring it out like that. Any part of it if I wanted it by itself. If I'm going to tell you about what I had for lunch, do I have to tell you everything else I've ever done since I was born? No. I tell you I *was* her, and then and forever after I can remember anything she could remember up to that point. In just that one flash."

"A *gestalt*," he murmured.

"Aha!" I said, and thought about that. I thought about a whole lot of things. I put them aside for a moment and said, "Why didn't I know all this before?"

"You had a powerful block against recalling it."

I got up excitedly. "I don't see why. I don't see that at all."

"Just natural revulsion," he guessed. "How about this? You had a distaste for assuming a female ego, even for a second."

"You told me yourself, right at the beginning, that I didn't have that kind of a problem."

"Well, how does this sound to you? You say you felt pain in that episode. So—you wouldn't go back into it for fear of re-experiencing the pain."

"Let me think, let me think. Yeah, yeah, that's part of it—that thing of going into someone's mind. She opened up to me because I reminded her of Lone. I went in. I wasn't ready; I'd never done it before, except maybe a little, against resistance. I went all the way in and it was too much; it frightened me away from trying it for years. And there it lay, wrapped up, locked away. But as I grew older, the power to do that with my mind got stronger and stronger, and still I was afraid to use it. And the more I grew, the more I felt, down deep, that Miss Kew had to be killed before she killed the . . . what I am. My God!" I shouted. "Do you know what I am?"

"No," he said. "Like to tell me about it?"

"I'd like to," I said. "Oh, yes, I'd like that."

He had that professional open-minded expression on his face, not believing or disbelieving, just taking it all in. I had to tell him, and I suddenly realized that I didn't have enough words. I knew the things, but not the names for them.

Lone took the meanings and threw the words away.

Further back: *"You read books. Read books for me."*

The look of his eyes. That—"opening up" thing.

I went over to Stern. He looked up at me, I bent close. First he was startled, then he controlled it, then he came even closer to me.

"My God," he murmured. "I didn't look at those eyes before. I could have sworn those irises spun like wheels. . . ."

Stern read books. He'd read more books than I ever imagined had been written. I slipped in there, looking for what I wanted.

I can't say exactly what it was like. It was like walking in a tunnel, and in this tunnel, all over the roof and walls, wooden arms stuck out at you, like the thing at the carnival, the merry-go-round, the thing you snatch the brass rings from. There's a brass ring on the end of each of these arms, and you can take any one of them you want to.

Now imagine you make up your mind which rings you want, and the arms hold only those. Now picture yourself with a thousand hands to grab the rings off with. Now just suppose the tunnel is a zillion miles long, and you can go from one end of it to the other, grabbing rings, in just the time it takes you to blink once. Well, it was like that, only easier.

It was easier for me to do than it had been for Lone.

Straightening up, I got away from Stern. He looked sick and frightened.

"It's all right," I said.

"What did you do to me?"

"I needed some words. Come on, come on. Get professional."

I had to admire him. He put his pipe in his pocket and gouged the tips of his fingers hard against his forehead and cheeks. Then he sat up and he was okay again.

"I know," I said. "That's how Miss Kew felt when Lone did it to her."

"What *are* you?"

"I'll tell you. I'm the central ganglion of a complex organism which is composed of Baby, a computer; Bonnie and Beanie, teleports; Janie, telekineticist; and myself, telepath and central control. There isn't a single thing about any of us that hasn't been documented: the teleportation of the Yogi, the telekinetics of some gamblers, the idio-savant mathematicians, and most of all, the so-called poltergeist, the moving about of household goods through the instrumentation of a young girl. Only in this case every one of my parts delivers at peak performance.

"Lone organized it, or it formed around him; it doesn't matter which. I replaced Lone, but I was too underdeveloped when he died, and on top of that I got an occlusion from that blast from Miss Kew. To that extent you were right when you said the blast made me subconsciously afraid to discover what was in it. But there was another good reason for my not being able to get in under that 'Baby is three' barrier.

"We ran into the problem of what it was I valued more than the security Miss Kew gave us. Can't you see now what it was? My *gestalt* organism was at the point of death from that security. I figured she had to be killed or it—*I*—would be. Oh, the parts would live on: two little colored girls with a speech impediment, one introspective girl with an artistic bent, one mongoloid idiot, and me—ninety per cent short-circuited potentials and ten per cent juvenile delinquent." I laughed. "Sure, she had to be killed. It was self-preservation for the *gestalt*."

Stern bobbled around with his mouth and finally got out: "I don't—"

"You don't need to," I laughed. "This is wonderful. You're good—real good. Now I want to tell you this, because you can appreciate a fine point in your specialty. You talk about occlusions! I couldn't get past the 'Baby is three' thing because in it lay the clues to what I really am. I couldn't find that out because I was afraid to remember that I was two things—Miss Kew's little boy, and something a hell of a lot bigger. I couldn't be both, and I wouldn't release either one."

He said, with his eyes on his pipe, "Now you can?"

"I have."

"And what now?"

"What do you mean?"

Stern leaned back against the corner of his desk. "Did it occur to you that maybe this—*gestalt* organism of yours is already dead?"

"It isn't."

"How do you know?"

"How does your head know your arm works?"

He touched his face. "So . . . now what?"

I shrugged. "Did the Pekin man look at Homo Sap walking erect and say, 'Now what?' We'll live, that's all, like a man, like a tree, like anything else that lives. We'll feed and grow and experiment and breed. We'll defend ourselves." I spread my hands. "We'll just do what comes naturally."

"But what can you do?"

"What can an electric motor do? It depends on where we apply ourselves."

Stern was very pale. "Just what do you—*want* to do?"

I thought about that. He waited until I was quite finished thinking and didn't say anything. "Know what?" I said at last. "Ever since I was born, people been kicking me around, right up until Miss Kew took over. And what happened with her? She damn near killed me."

I thought some more, and said, "Everybody's had fun but me. The kind of fun everybody has is kicking someone around, someone small who can't fight back. Or they do you favors until they own you, or kill you." I looked at him and grinned. "I'm just going to have fun, that's all."

He turned his back. I think he was going to pace the floor,

but right away he turned again. I knew then he would keep an eye on me. He said, "You've come a long way since you walked in here."

I nodded. "You're a *good* head-shrinker."

"Thanks," he said bitterly. "And you figure you're all cured now, all adjusted and ready to roll."

"Well sure. Don't you?"

He shook his head. "All you've found out is what you are. You have a lot more to learn."

I was willing to be patient. "Like?"

"Like finding out what happens to people who have to live with guilt like yours. You're different, Gerry, but you're not that different."

"I should feel guilty about saving my life?"

He ignored that. "One other thing: You said a while back that you'd been mad at everybody all your life—that's the way you lived. Have you ever wondered why?"

"Can't say I have."

"One reason is that you were so alone. That's why being with the other kids, and then with Miss Kew, came to mean so much."

"So? I've still got the kids."

He shook his head slowly. "You *and* the kids are a single creature. Unique. Unprecedented." He pointed the pipestem at me. "*Alone.*"

The blood started to pound in my ears.

"Shut up," I said.

"Just think about it," he said softly. "You can do practically anything. You can have practically everything. And none of it will keep you from being alone."

"Shut up, shut up . . . Everybody's alone."

He nodded. "But some people learn how to live with it."

"How?"

He said, after a time, "Because of something you don't know anything about. It wouldn't mean anything to you if I told you."

"Tell me and see."

He gave me the strangest look. "It's sometimes called morality."

"I guess you're right. I don't know what you're talking

about." I pulled myself together. I didn't have to listen to this. "You're afraid," I said. "You're afraid of *Homo Gestalt*."

He made a wonderful effort and smiled. "That's bastard terminology."

"We're a bastard breed," I said. I pointed. "Sit down over there."

He crossed the quiet room and sat at the desk. I leaned close to him and he went to sleep with his eyes open. I straightened up and looked around the room. Then I got the thermos flask and filled it and put it on the desk. I fixed the corner of the rug and put a clean towel at the head of the couch. I went to the side of the desk and opened it and looked at the tape recorder.

Like reaching out a hand, I got Beanie. She stood by the desk, wide-eyed.

"Look here," I told her. "Look good, now. What I want to do is erase all this tape. Go ask Baby how."

She blinked at me and sort of shook herself, and then leaned over the recorder. She was there—and gone—and back, just like that. She pushed past me and turned two knobs, moved a pointer until it clicked twice. The tape raced backward past the head swiftly, whining.

"All right," I said, "beat it."

She vanished.

I got my jacket and went to the door. Stern was still sitting at the desk, staring.

"A *good* head-shrinker," I murmured. I felt fine.

Outside I waited, then turned and went back in again.

Stern looked up at me. "Sit over there, Sonny."

"Gee," I said. "Sorry, sir. I got in the wrong office."

"That's all right," he said.

I went out and closed the door. All the way down to the police station I grinned. They'd take my report on Miss Kew and like it. And sometimes I laughed, thinking about this Stern, how he'd figure the loss of an afternoon and the gain of a thousand bucks. Much funnier than thinking about him being dead.

What the hell *is* morality, anyway?

PART THREE

MORALITY

"WHAT'S HE to you, Miss Gerald?" demanded the sheriff.

"Gerard," she corrected. She had gray-green eyes and a strange mouth. "He's my cousin."

"All Adam's chillun are cousins, one way or the other. You'll have to tell me a little more than that."

"He was in the Air Force seven years ago," she said. "There was some—trouble. He was discharged. Medical."

The sheriff thumbed through the file on the desk before him. "Remember the doctor's name?"

"Thompson first, then Bromfield. Dr. Bromfield signed the discharge."

"Guess you do know something about him at that. What was he before he did his hitch in the Air Force?"

"An engineer. I mean, he would have been if he'd finished school."

"Why didn't he?"

She shrugged. "He just disappeared."

"So how do you know he's here?"

"I'd recognize him anywhere," she said. "I saw . . . I saw it happen."

"Did you now." The sheriff grunted, lifted the file, let it drop. "Look, Miss Gerald, it's not my business to go advising people. But you seem like a nice respectable girl. Why don't you just forget him?"

"I'd like to see him, if I may," she said quietly.

"He's crazy. Did you know that?"

"I don't think so."

"Slammin' his fist through a plate glass window. For nothing."

She waited. He tried again. "He's dirty. He don't know his own name, hardly."

"May I see him?"

The sheriff uttered a wordless growl and stood up. "Them Air Force psychos had any sense, they'd've put him where he would never even get near a jail. This way."

The walls were steel plates like a ship's bulkhead, studded with rivets, painted a faded cream above and mustard color below. Their footsteps echoed. The sheriff unlocked a heavy door with one small high grating and slid it aside. They stepped through and he closed and locked it. He motioned her ahead of him and they came into a barnlike area, concrete on walls and ceiling. Built around it was a sort of balcony; under and over this were the cells, steel walled, fronted by close-set bars. There were perhaps twenty cells. Only a half dozen were occupied. It was a cold, unhappy place.

"Well, what did you expect?" demanded the sheriff, reading her expression. "The Waldorf Plaza or something?"

"Where is he?" she asked.

They walked to a cell on the lower tier. "Snap out of it, Barrows. Lady to see you."

"Hip! Oh, Hip!"

The prisoner did not move. He lay half on, half off a padded steel bunk, one foot on the mattress, one on the floor. His left arm was in a dirty sling.

"See? Nary a word out of him. Satisfied, Miss?"

"Let me in," she breathed. "Let me talk to him."

He shrugged and reluctantly unlocked the door. She stepped in, turned. "May I speak to him alone?"

"Liable to get hurt," he warned.

She gazed at him. Her mouth was extraordinarily expressive. "Well," he said at length, "I'll stay in the area here. You yell if you need help. S'help me I'll put a slug through your neck, Barrows, if you try anything." He locked the barred door behind the girl.

She waited until he stepped away and then went to the prisoner. "Hip," she murmured. "Hip Barrows."

His dull eyes slid in their sockets until they approximated her direction. The eyes closed and opened in a slow, numb blink.

She knelt beside him. "Mr. Barrows," she whispered, "you don't know me. I told them I was your cousin. I want to help you."

He was silent.

She said, "I'm going to get you out of here. Don't you want to get out?"

For a long moment he watched her face. Then his eyes went to the locked door and back to her face again.

She touched his forehead, his cheek. She pointed at the dirty sling. "Does it hurt much?"

His eyes lingered, withdrew from her face, found the bandage. With effort, they came up again. She asked, "Aren't you going to say anything? Don't you want me to help?"

He was silent for so long that she rose. "I'd better go. Don't forget me. I'll help you." She turned to the door.

He said, "Why?"

She returned to him. "Because you're dirty and beaten and don't care—and because none of that can hide what you are."

"You're crazy," he muttered tiredly.

She smiled. "That's what they say about you. So we have something in common."

He swore, foully.

Unperturbed, she said, "You can't hide behind that either. Now listen to me. Two men will come to see you this afternoon. One is a doctor. The other is a lawyer. We'll have you out of here this evening."

He raised his head and for the first time something came into his lethargic face. Whatever it was was not pretty. His voice came from deep in his chest. He growled, "What type doctor?"

"For your arm," she said evenly. "Not a psychiatrist. You'll never have to go through that again."

He let his head drop back. His features slowly lost their expression. She waited and when he had nothing else to offer, she turned and called the sheriff.

It was not too difficult. The sentence was sixty days for malicious mischief. There had been no alternative fine offered. The lawyer rapidly proved that there should have been, and the fine was paid. In his clean new bandages and his filthy clothes, Barrows was led out past the glowering sheriff, ignoring him and his threat as to what the dirty bum could expect if he ever showed up in town again.

The girl was waiting outside. He stood stupidly at the top of the jailhouse steps while she spoke to the lawyer. Then the lawyer was gone and she touched his elbow. "Come on, Hip."

He followed like a wound-up toy, walking whither his feet had been pointed. They turned two corners and walked five blocks and then up the stone steps of a clean, dried spinster of a house with a bay window and colored glass set into the main door. The girl opened the main door with one key and a door in the hallway with another. He found himself in the room with the bay window. It was high ceilinged, airy, clean.

For the first time he moved of his own volition. He turned around, slowly, looking at one wall after another. He put out his hand and lifted the corner of a dresser scarf, and let it fall. "Your room?"

"Yours," she said. She came to him and put two keys on the dresser. "Your keys." She opened the top drawer. "Your socks and handkerchiefs." With her knuckles she rapped on each drawer in turn. "Shirts. Underclothes." She pointed to a door. "Two suits in there; I think they'll fit. A robe. Slippers, shoes." She pointed to another door. "Bathroom. Lots of towels, lots of soap. A razor."

"Razor?"

"Anyone who can have keys can have a razor," she said gently. "Get presentable, will you? I'll be back in fifteen minutes. Do you know how long it is since you've eaten anything?"

He shook his head.

"Four days. 'Bye now."

She slipped through the door and was gone, even as he fumbled for something to say to her. He looked at the door for a long time. Then he swore and fell limply back on the bed.

He scratched his nose and his hand slid down to his jaw. It was ragged, itchy. He half rose, muttered, "Damn if I will," and lay back. And then, somehow, he was in the bathroom, peering at himself in the mirror. He wet his hands, splashed water on his face, wiped the dirt off onto a towel and peered again. He grunted and reached for the soap.

He found the razor, he found the underclothes, the slacks, socks, slippers, shirt, jacket. When he looked into the mirror he wished he had a comb. When she elbowed the door open she put her packages on the top of the dresser and then she was smiling up at him, her hand out, the comb in it. He took it wordlessly and went and wet his head and combed it.

"Come on, it's all ready," she called from the other room. He emerged. She had taken the lamp off the night table and had spread out a thick oval platter on which was a lean, rare steak, a bottle of ale, a smaller bottle of stout, a split Idaho potato with butter melting in it, hot rolls in a napkin, a tossed salad in a small wooden bowl.

"I don't want nothing," he said, and abruptly fell to. There was nothing in the world then but the good food filling his mouth and throat, the tingle of ale and the indescribable magic of the charcoal crust.

When the plate was empty, it and the table suddenly wanted to fly upward at his head. He toppled forward, caught the sides of the table and held it away from him. He trembled violently. She spoke from behind him, "All right. It's all right," and put her hands on his shoulders, pressed him back into his chair. He tried to raise his hand and failed. She wiped his clammy forehead and upper lip with the napkin.

In time, his eyes opened. He looked round for her, found her sitting on the edge of the bed, watching him silently. He grinned sheepishly. "*Whew!*"

She rose. "You'll be all right now. You'd better turn in. Good night!"

She was in the room, she was out of it. She had been with him, he was alone. It made a change which was too important to tolerate and too large to understand. He looked from the door to the bed and said "Good night," only because they were the last words she had said, and they hung shimmering in the silence.

He put his hands on the chair arms and forced his legs to cooperate. He could stand but that was all. He fell forward and sidewise, curling up to miss the table as he went down. He lay across the counterpane and blackness came.

"Good morning."

He lay still. His knees were drawn up and the heels of his hands were tight on his cheekbones. He closed his eyes tighter than sleep to shut out the light. He closed his kinesthetic sense to shut out the slight tilting of the mattress which indicated where she sat on the bed. He disconnected his hearing lest she speak again. His nostrils betrayed him; he had not expected there to be coffee in the room and he was wanting it, wanting it badly, before he thought to shut it out.

Fuzzily he lay thinking, thinking something about her. If

she spoke again, he thought, he'd show her. He'd lie there till she spoke again and when she spoke he'd ignore her and lie still some more.

He waited.

Well, if she wasn't going to speak again, he couldn't ignore her, could he?

He opened his eyes. They blazed, round and angry. She sat near the foot of the bed. Her body was still, her face was still, her mouth and her eyes were alive.

He coughed suddenly, violently. It closed his eyes and when he opened them he was no longer looking at her. He fumbled vaguely at his chest, then looked down at himself.

"Slep' in my clothes all night," he said.

"Drink your coffee."

He looked at her. She still had not moved, and did not. She was wearing a burgundy jacket with a gray-green scarf. She had long, level, gray-green eyes, the kind which in profile are deep clear triangles. He looked away from her, farther and farther away, until he saw the coffee. A big pot, a thick hot cup, already poured. Black and strong and good. "Whoo," he said, holding it, smelling it. He drank. "Whoo."

He looked at the sunlight now. Good. The turn and fall and turn again of the breeze-lifted marquisette at the window, in and out of a sunbeam. Good. The luminous oval, a shadow of the sunlight itself, where the sun glanced off the round mirror on one wall to the clean paint on the adjoining one. Good. He drank more good coffee.

He set the cup down and fumbled at his shirt buttons. He was wrinkled and sweaty. "Shower," he said.

"Go ahead," said the girl. She rose and went to the dresser where there was a cardboard box and some paper sacks. She opened the box and took out an electric hot plate. He got three buttons undone and somehow the fourth and fifth came off with little explosive tearing sounds. He got the rest of his clothes off somehow. The girl paid him no attention, neither looking at him nor away, just calmly doing things with the hot plate. He went into the bathroom and fussed for a long time with the shower handles, getting the water just right. He got in and let the water run on the nape of his neck. He found soap in the dish, so he let the water run on his head and then rubbed it furiously with the cake of soap until he was mantled in warm, kind, crawling lather. *God*, the thought came from somewhere, *I'm thin as a xylophone. Got to put some beef back on or I'll get sick and . . .* The same thought looped back on him, interrupting itself: *Not supposed to get well. Get good and sick, stay sick. Get sicker.* Angrily he demanded, "Who says I got to get sick?" but there was no answer except a quick echo off the tiles.

He shut off the water and stepped out and took an oversized towel from the rack. He started one end of it on his scalp, worked it on his hair from one end to the other. He threw it on the floor, in the corner, and took another towel and rubbed himself pink. He threw that one down too and came out into the room. The robe lay over the arm of an easy chair by the door so he put it on.

The girl was spooning fragrant bacon grease over and over three perfect eggs in a pan. When he sat down on the edge of the bed she slid the eggs deftly onto a plate, leaving all the grease behind in the pan. They were perfect, the whites completely firm, the yolks unbroken, liquid, faintly filmed over. There was bacon, four brief seconds less than crisp, paper dried and aromatic. There was toast, golden outside, soft and white inside, with butter melting quickly, running to find and fill the welcoming caves and crevices; two slices with butter, one with marmalade. And these lay in some sunlight, giving off a color possible only to marmalade and to stained glass.

He ate and drank coffee; ate more and drank coffee and coffee. All the while she sat in the easy chair with his shirt in her lap and her hands like dancers, while the buttons grew back onto the material under their swift and delicate paces.

He watched her and when she was finished he came to her and put out his hand for the shirt, but she shook her head and pointed. "A clean one."

He found a knitted pullover polo shirt. While he dressed she washed his dishes and the frying pan and straightened out the bed. He lay back in the easy chair and she knelt before him and worked the soggy dressing off his left hand, inspected the cuts and bound them up again. The bandage was firm and comforting. "You can do without the sling now," she said, pleased. She got up and went to the bed. She sat there facing him, still again except for her eyes, except for her mouth.

Outside an oriole made a long slender note, broke it, and let the fragments fall through the shining air. A stake-bed truck idled past, busily shaking the string of cowbells on its back, while one hoarse man and one with a viola voice flanked it afoot, chanting. In one window came a spherical sound with a fly at its heart and at the other appeared a white kitten. Out by the kitten went the fly and the kitten reared up and batted at it, twisted and sprang down out of sight as if it had meant all along to leave; only a fool would have thought it had lost its balance.

And in the room was quiet and a watchfulness which was without demand, except perhaps a guarding against leaving anything unwatched. The girl sat with her hands aslumber and her eyes awake, while a pipe-cleaner man called Healing was born in all his cores, all his marrow, taking the pose of his relaxed body, resting and growing a little and resting again and growing.

Later, she rose. Without consultation, but merely because it seemed time to do so, she picked up a small handbag and went to the door where she waited. He stirred, rose, went to her. They went out.

They walked slowly to a place where there was smooth rolling land, mowed and tended. Down in the hollow some boys played softball. They stood for a while, watching. She studied his face and when she saw reflected in it only the moving figures and not the consecutive interest of the game itself, she touched his elbow and moved on. They found a pond where there were ducks and straight cinder paths with flower beds. She picked a primrose and put it in his lapel. They found a bench. A man pushed a bright clean wagon up to them. She bought a frankfurter and a bottle of soda and handed them to him. He ate and drank silently.

It was a quiet time they had together.

When it began to grow dark, she brought him back to the room. She left him alone for half an hour and returned to find him sitting just where she had left him. She opened packages and cooked chops and mixed a salad, and while he was eating, made more coffee. After dinner he yawned. She was on her feet immediately. "Good night," she said, and was gone.

He turned slowly and looked at the closed door. After a time he said, "Good night." He undressed and got into bed and turned out the light.

The next day was the day they rode on a bus and lunched in a restaurant.

The day after that was the one they stayed out a little later to see a band concert.

Then there was the afternoon when it rained and they went to a movie which he watched wordlessly, not smiling, not frowning, not stirring to the musical parts.

"Your coffee." "Let's get these to the laundry." "Come." "Good night." These were the things she said to him. Otherwise she watched his face and, undemandingly, she waited.

He awoke, and it was too dark. He did not know where he was. The face was there, wide-browed, sallow, with its thick lenses and its pointed chin. Wordlessly, he roared at it and it smiled at him. When he realized that the face was in his mind and not in the room, it disappeared . . . no; it was simply that he knew it was not there. He was filled with fury that it was not there; his brain was fairly melting with rage. *Yes, but who is he?* he asked, and answered, "I don't know, I don't know, I don't know . . ." and his voice became a moan, softer and softer and softer until it was gone. He inhaled deeply and then something inside him slipped and fell apart and he began to cry. Someone took his hand, took his other hand, held them together; it was the girl; she'd heard him, she'd come. He was not alone.

Not alone . . . it made him cry harder, bitterly. He held her wrists as she bent over him, looked up through darkness at her face and her hair and he wept.

She stayed with him until he was finished and for as long afterward as he held her hand. When he released it he was asleep, and she drew the blanket up to his chin and tiptoed out.

In the morning he sat on the edge of the bed, watching the steam from his coffee spread and fade in the sunlight, and when she put the eggs before him he looked up at her. His mouth quivered. She stood before him, waiting.

At last he said, "Have you had your breakfast yet?"

Something was kindled in her eyes. She shook her head.

He looked down at the plate, puzzling something out. Finally he pushed it away from him a fraction of an inch and stood up. "You have this," he said. "I'll fix some more."

He had seen her smile but he had not noticed it before. Now, it was as if the warmth of all of them was put together for this one. She sat down and ate. He fried his eggs, not as well as she had done, and they were cooked before he thought of toast and the toast burned while he was eating the eggs. She did not attempt to help him in any way, even when he stared blankly at the little table, frowned and scratched his jaw. In his own time he found what he was looking for—the other cup on top of the dresser. He poured fresh coffee for her and took the other which she had not touched, for himself, and she smiled again.

"What's your name?" he asked her, for the very first time.

"Janie Gerard."

"Oh."

She considered him carefully, then stretched down to the footpost of the bed where her handbag hung by its strap. She drew it toward her, opened it, and took out a short piece of metal. At first glance, it was a piece of aluminum tubing, perhaps eight inches long and oval in cross-section. But it was flexible—woven of tiny strands rather than extruded. She turned his right hand palm up, where it lay beside his coffee cup, and put the tubing into it.

He must have seen it for he was staring down into the cup. He did not close his fingers on it. His expression did not change. At length he took a slice of toast. The piece of tubing fell, rolled over, hung on the edge of the table and dropped to the floor. He buttered his toast.

After that first shared meal there was a difference. There were many differences. Never again did he undress before her or ignore the fact that she was not eating. He began to pay for little things—bus fares, lunches, and, later, to let her precede him through doorways, to take her elbow when they crossed streets. He went to the market with her and carried the packages.

He remembered his name; he even remembered that the "Hip" was for "Hippocrates." He was, however, unable to remember how he came by the name, or where he had been born, or anything else about himself. She did not urge him, ask him. She simply spent her days with him, waiting. And she kept the piece of aluminum webbing in sight.

It was beside his breakfast plate almost every morning. It would be in the bathroom, with the handle of his toothbrush thrust into it. Once he found it in his side jacket pocket where the small roll of bills appeared regularly; this one time the bills were tucked into the tubing. He pulled them out and absently let the tubing fall and Janie had to pick it up. She put it in his shoe once and when he tried to put the shoe on and could not, he tipped it out onto the floor and let it lie there. It was as if it were transparent or even invisible to him; when, as in the case of finding his money in it, he had to handle it, he did so clumsily, with inattention, rid himself of it and apparently forgot it. Janie never mentioned it. She just quietly put it in his path, time and time again, patient as a pendulum.

His afternoons began to possess a morning and his days, a yesterday. He began to remember a bench they had used, a theater they had attended, and he would lead the way back. She relinquished her guidance as fast as he would take it up until it was he who planned their days.

Since he had no memory to draw on except his time with her, they were days of discovery. They had picnics and rode learningly on buses. They found another theater and a place with swans as well as ducks.

There was another kind of discovery too. One day he stood in the middle of the room and turned, looking at one wall after another, at the windows and the bed. "I was sick, wasn't I?"

And one day he stopped on the street, stared at the grim building on the other side. "I was in there."

And it was several days after that when he slowed, frowned, and stood gazing into a men's furnishing shop. No—not into it. At it. At the window.

Beside him Janie waited, watching his face.

He raised his left hand slowly, flexed it, looked down at the curled scar on the back of his hand, the two straight ones, one long, one short, on his wrist.

"Here," she said. She pressed the piece of tubing into his hand.

Without looking at it he closed his fingers, made a fist. Surprise flickered across his features and then a flash of sheer terror and something like anger. He swayed on his feet.

"It's all right," said Janie softly.

He grunted questioningly, looked at her as if she were a stranger and seemed slowly to recognize her. He opened his hand and looked carefully at the piece of metal. He tossed it, caught it. "That's mine," he said.

She nodded.

He said, "I broke that window." He looked at it, tossed the piece of metal again, and put it in his pocket and began to walk again. He was quiet for a long time and just as they mounted the steps of their house he said, "I broke the window and they put me in that jail. And you got me out and I was sick and you brought me here till I was well again."

He took out his keys and opened the door, stood back to let her pass in. "What did you want to do that for?"

"Just wanted to," she said.

He was restless. He went to the closet and turned out the pockets of his two suit jackets and his sport coat. He crossed the room and pawed aimlessly at the dresser scarf and opened and shut drawers.

"What is it?"

"That thing," he said vaguely. He wandered into and out of the bathroom. "You know, that piece of pipe, like."

"Oh," she said.

"I had it," he muttered unhappily. He took another turn around the room and then shouldered past Janie where she sat on the bed, and reached to the night table. "Here it is!"

He looked at it, flexed it, and sat down in the easy chair. "Hate to lose that," he said relievedly. "Had it a long time."

"It was in the envelope they were holding for you while you were in jail," Janie told him.

"Yuh. Yuh." He twisted it between his hands, then raised it

and shook it at her like some bright, thick, admonishing forefinger. "This thing—"

She waited.

He shook his head. "Had it a long time," he said again. He rose, paced, sat down again. "I was looking for a guy who . . . *Ah!*" he growled, "I can't remember."

"It's all right," she said gently.

He put his head in his hands. "Damn near almost found him too," he said in a muffled voice. "Been looking for him a long time. I've *always* been looking for him."

"Always?"

"Well, ever since . . . Janie, I can't remember again."

"All right."

"All right, all right, it isn't all right!" He straightened and looked at her. "I'm sorry, Janie. I didn't mean to yell at you."

She smiled at him. He said, "Where was that cave?"

"Cave?" she echoed.

He waved his arms up, around. "Sort of a cave. Half cave, half log house. In the woods. Where was it?"

"Was I there with you?"

"No," he said immediately. "That was before, I guess. I don't remember."

"Don't worry about it."

"I *do* worry about it!" he said excitedly. "I can worry about it, can't I?" As soon as the words were out, he looked to her for forgiveness and found it. "You got to understand," he said more quietly, "this is something I—I got to—Look," he said, returning to exasperation, "can something be more important than anything else in the world, and you can't even remember what it is?"

"It happens."

"It's happened to me," he said glumly. "I don't like it either."

"You're getting yourself all worked up," said Janie.

"Well, sure!" he exploded. He looked around him, shook his head violently. "What is this? What am I doing here? Who are you, anyway, Janie? What are you getting out of this?"

"I like seeing you get well."

"Yeah, get well," he growled. "I should get well! I ought to be sick. Be sick and get sicker."

"Who told you that?" she rapped.

"Thompson," he barked and then slumped back, looking at her with stupid amazement on his face. In the high, cracking voice of an adolescent he whimpered, "Thompson? Who's Thompson?"

She shrugged and said, matter-of-factly, "The one who told you you ought to be sick, I suppose."

"Yeah," he whispered, and again, in a soft-focused flood of enlightenment, "yeah-h-h-h . . ." He wagged the piece of mesh tubing at her. "I saw him. Thompson." The tubing caught his eye then and he held it still, staring at it. He shook his head, closed his eyes. "I was looking for . . ." His voice trailed off.

"Thompson?"

"Nah!" he grunted. "I never wanted to see *him*! Yes I did," he amended. "I wanted to beat his brains out."

"You did?"

"Yeah. You see, he—he was—aw, what's the matter with my *head?*" he cried.

"Sh-h-h," she soothed.

"I can't remember, I can't," he said brokenly. "It's like . . . you see something rising up off the ground, you got to grab it, you jump so hard you can feel your knee-bones crack, you stretch up and get your fingers on it, just the tips of your fingers. . . ." His chest swelled and sank. "Hang there, like forever, your fingers on it, knowing you'll never make it, never get a grip. And then you fall, and you watch it going up and up away from you, getting smaller and smaller, and you'll never—" He leaned back and closed his eyes. He was panting. He breathed, barely audible, "And you'll never . . ."

He clenched his fists. One of them still held the tubing and again he went through the discovery, the wonder, the puzzlement. "Had this a long time," he said, looking at it. "Crazy. This must sound crazy to you, Janie."

"Oh, no."

"You think I'm crazy?"

"*No.*"

"I'm sick," he whimpered.

Startlingly, she laughed. She came to him and pulled him to his feet. She drew him to the bathroom and reached in and switched on the light. She pushed him inside, against the washbasin, and rapped the mirror with her knuckles. "Who's sick?"

He looked at the firm-fleshed, well-boned face that stared out at him, at its glossy hair and clear eyes. He turned to Janie, genuinely astonished. "I haven't looked this good in years! Not since I was in the . . . Janie, was I in the Army?"

"Were you?"

He looked into the mirror again. "Sure don't *look* sick," he said, as if to himself. He touched his cheek. "Who keeps telling me I'm sick?"

He heard Janie's footsteps receding. He switched off the light and joined her. "I'd like to break that Thompson's back," he said. "Throw him right through a—"

"What is it?"

"Funny thing," he said, "was going to say, through a brick wall. I was thinking it so hard I could see it, me throwing him."

"Perhaps you did."

He shook his head. "It wasn't a wall. It was a plate glass window. I know!" he shouted. "I saw him and I was going to hit him. I saw him standing right there on the street looking at me and I yelled and jumped him and . . . and . . ." He looked down at his scarred hand. He said, amazed, "I turned right around and hauled off and hit the window instead. God."

He sat down weakly. "That's what the jail was for and it was all over. Just lie there in that rotten jail, sick. Don't eat, don't move, get sick and sicker and it's all over."

"Well, it isn't all over, is it?"

He looked at her. "No. No, it isn't. Thanks to you." He looked at her eyes, her mouth. "What about you, Janie? What are you after, anyway?"

She dropped her eyes.

"Oh, I'm sorry, I'm sorry. That must've sounded . . ." He put out a hand to her, dropped it without touching her. "I don't know what's gotten into me today. It's just that . . . I don't figure you, Janie. What did I ever do for you?"

She smiled quickly. "Got better."

"It's not enough," he said devoutly. "Where do you live?"

She pointed. "Right across the hall."

"Oh," he said. He remembered the night he had cried, and

pushed the picture away in embarrassment. He turned away, hunting for a change of subject, any change. "Let's go out."

"All right." Was that relief he detected in her voice?

They rode on a roller coaster and ate cotton candy and danced in an outdoor pavilion. He wondered aloud where he had ever learned to dance, but that was the only mention he made of the things which were troubling him until late in the evening. It was the first time he had consciously enjoyed being with Janie; it was an Occasion, rather than a way of life. He had never known her to laugh so easily, to be so eager to ride this and taste that and go yonder to see what was there. At dusk they stood side by side, leaning on a railing which overlooked the lake, watching the bathers. There were lovers on the beach, here and there. Hip smiled at the sight, turned to speak to Janie about it and was arrested by the strange wistfulness which softened her taut features. A surge of emotion, indefinable and delicate, made him turn away quickly. It was in part a recognition of the rarity of her introspection and an unwillingness to interrupt it for her; and partly a flash of understanding that her complete preoccupation with him was not necessarily all she wanted of life. Life had begun for him, to all intents and purposes, on the day she came to his cell. It had never occurred to him before that her quarter of a century without him was not the clean slate that his was.

Why had she rescued him? Why him, if she must rescue someone? And—why?

What could she want from him? Was there something in his lost life that he might give her? If there was, he vowed silently, it was hers, whatever it might be; it was inconceivable that anything, anything at all she might gain from him would be of greater value than his own discovery of the life which produced it.

But what could it be?

He found his gaze on the beach and its small galaxy of lovers, each couple its own world, self-contained but in harmony with all the others adrift in the luminous dusk. Lovers . . . he had felt the tuggings of love . . . back somewhere in the mists, he couldn't quite remember where, with whom . . . but it was there, and with it his old, old reflex, *not until I've hunted him down and—* But again he lost the thought. Whatever it was, it had been more important to him than love or marriage or a job or a colonelcy. (Colonelcy? Had he ever wanted to be a colonel?)

Well, then maybe it was a conquest. Janie loved him. She'd seen him and the lightning had struck and she wanted him, so she was going about it in her own way. Well, then! If that's what she wanted . . .

He closed his eyes, seeing her face, the tilt of her head in that waiting, attentive silence; her slim strong arms and lithe body, her magic hungry mouth. He saw a quick sequence of pictures taken by the camera of his good male mind, but filed under "inactive" in his troubled, partial one: Janie's legs silhouetted against the window, seen through the polychrome cloud of her liberty silk skirt. Janie in a peasant blouse, with a straight spear of morning sunlight bent and molded to her bare shoulder and the soft upper curve of her breast. Janie dancing, bending away and cleaving to him as if he and she were the gold leaves of an electroscope. (*Where had he seen . . . worked with . . . an electroscope? Oh, of course! In the . . .* But it was gone.) Janie barely visible in the deep churning dark, palely glowing through a mist of nylon and the flickering acid of his tears, strongly holding his hands until he quieted.

But this was no seduction, this close intimacy of meals and walks and long shared silences, with never a touch, never a wooing word. Lovemaking, even the suppressed and silent kind, is a demanding thing, a thirsty and yearning thing. Janie demanded nothing. She only . . . she only waited. If her interest lay in his obscured history she was taking a completely passive attitude, merely placing herself to receive what he might unearth. If something he had been, something he had done, was what she was after, wouldn't she question and goad, probe and pry the way Thompson and Bromfield had done? *(Bromfield? Who's he?)* But she never had, never.

No, it must be this other, this thing which made her look at lovers with such contained sadness, with an expression on her face like that of an armless man spellbound by violin music. . . .

Picture of Janie's mouth, bright, still, waiting. Picture of Janie's clever hands. Picture of Janie's body, surely as smooth as her shoulder, as firm as her forearm, warm and wild and willing—

They turned to each other, he the driving, she the driven gear. Their breath left them, hung as a symbol and a promise between them, alive and merged. For two heavy heartbeats they had their single planet in the lovers' spangled cosmos; and then Janie's face twisted in a spasm of concentration, bent not toward a ponderous control, but rather to some exquisite accuracy of adjustment.

A thing happened to him, as if a small sphere of the hardest vacuum had appeared deep within him. He breathed again and the magic about them gathered itself and whipped in with the breath to fill the vacuum which swallowed and killed it, all of it, in a tick of time. Except for the brief spastic change in her face, neither had moved; they still stood in the sunset, close together, her face turned up to his, here gloried, here tinted, there self-shining in its own shadow. But the magic was gone, the melding; they were two, not one, and this was Janie quiet, Janie patient, Janie not damped, but unkindled. But no—the real difference was in him. His hands were lifted to go round her and no longer cared to and his lips lost their grip on the unborn kiss and let it fall away and be lost. He stepped back. "Shall we go?"

A swift ripple of regret came and went across Janie's face. It was a thing like many other things coming now to plague him: smooth and textured things forever presenting themselves to his fingertips and never to his grasp. He almost understood her regret, it was there for him, it was there—and gone, altogether gone, dwindling high away from him.

They walked silently back to the midway and the lights, their pitiable thousands of candlepower; and to the amusement rides, their balky pretense at motion. Behind them in the growing dark they left all real radiance, all significant movement. All of it; there was not enough left for any particular reaction. With the compressed air guns which fired tennis balls at wooden battleships; the cranks they turned to make the toy greyhounds race up a slope; the darts they threw at balloons—with these they buried something now so negligible it left no mound.

At an elaborate stand were a couple of war surplus servomechanisms rigged to simulate radar gun directors. There was a miniature anti-aircraft gun to be aimed by hand, its slightest movement followed briskly by the huge servo-powered gun at the back. Aircraft silhouettes were flashed across the domed half ceiling. All in all, it was a fine conglomeration of gadgetry and dazzle, a truly high-level catchpenny.

Hip went first, amused, then intrigued, then enthralled as his small movements were so obediently duplicated by the whip and weave of the massive gun twenty feet away. He missed the first "plane" and the second; after that he had the fixed error of the gun calculated precisely and he banged away at every target as fast as they could throw them and knocked out every one. Janie clapped her hands like a child and the attendant awarded them a blurred and glittering clay statue of a police dog worth all of a fifth of the admission price. Hip took it proudly, and waved Janie up to the trigger. She worked the aiming mechanism diffidently and laughed as the big gun nodded and shook itself. His cheeks flushed, his eyes expertly anticipating the appearance-point of each target, Hip said out of the corner of his mouth, "Up forty or better on your right quadrant, corp'r'l, or the pixies'll degauss your fuses."

Janie's eyes narrowed a trifle and perhaps that was to help her aiming. She did not answer him. She knocked out the first target that appeared before it showed fully over the artificial horizon, and the second, and the third. Hip swatted his hands together and called her name joyfully. She seemed for a moment to be pulling herself together, the odd, effortful gesture of a preoccupied man forcing himself back into a conversation. She then let one go by and missed four in a row. She hit two, one low, one high, and missed the last by half a mile. "Not very good," she said tremulously.

"Good enough," he said gallantly. "You don't have to hit 'em these days, you know."

"You don't?"

"Nah. Just get near. Your fuses take over from there. This is the world's most diabetic dog."

She looked down from his face to the statuette and giggled. "I'll keep it always," she said. "Hip, you're getting that nasty sparkle stuff all over your jacket. Let's give it away."

They marched up and across and down and around the tinsel stands in search of a suitable beneficiary, and found him at last—a solemn urchin of seven or so, who methodically sucked the memory of butter and juice from a well-worn corncob. "This is for *you*," caroled Janie. The child ignored the extended gift and kept his frighteningly adult eyes on her face.

Hip laughed. "No sale!" He squatted beside the boy. "I'll make a deal with you. Will you haul it away for a dollar?"

No response. The boy sucked his corncob and kept watching Janie.

"Tough customer," grinned Hip.

Suddenly Janie shuddered. "Oh, let's leave him alone," she said, her merriment gone.

"He can't outbid *me*," said Hip cheerfully. He set the statue down by the boy's scuffed shoes and pushed a dollar bill into the rip which looked most like a pocket. "Pleasure to do business with you, sir," he said and followed Janie, who had already moved off.

"Regular chatterbox," laughed Hip as he caught up with her. He looked back. Half a block away, the child still stared at Janie. "Looks like you've made a lifelong impress— *Janie!*"

Janie had stopped dead, eyes wide and straight ahead, mouth a triangle of shocked astonishment. "The little *devil!*" she breathed. "At his age!" She whirled and looked back.

Hip's eyes obviously deceived him for he saw the corncob leave the grubby little hands, turn ninety degrees and thump the urchin smartly on the cheekbone. It dropped to the ground; the child backed away four paces, shrilled an unchivalrous presumption and an unprintable suggestion at them and disappeared into an alley.

"Whew!" said Hip, awed. "You're so right!" He looked at her admiringly. "What clever ears you have, grandma," he said, not very successfully covering an almost prissy embarrassment with badinage. "I didn't hear a thing until the second broadside he threw."

"Didn't you?" she said. For the first time he detected annoyance in her voice. At the same time he sensed that he was not the subject of it. He took her arm. "Don't let it bother you. Come on, let's eat some food."

She smiled and everything was all right again.

Succulent pizza and cold beer in a booth painted a too-bright, edge-worn green. A happy-weary walk through the darkening booths to the late bus which waited, breathing. A sense of membership because of the fitting of the spine to the calculated average of the bus seats. A shared doze, a shared smile, at sixty miles an hour through the flickering night, and at last the familiar depot on the familiar street, echoing and empty but *my* street in *my* town.

They woke a taxi driver and gave him their address. "Can I be more alive than this?" he murmured from his corner and then realized she had heard him. "I mean," he amended, "it's as if my whole world, everywhere I lived, was once in a little place inside my head, so deep I couldn't see out. And then you made it as big as a room and then as big as a town and tonight as big as . . . well, a lot bigger," he finished weakly.

A lonely passing streetlight passed her answering smile over to him. He said, "So I was wondering how much bigger it can get."

"Much bigger," she said.

He pressed back sleepily into the cushions. "I feel fine," he murmured. "I feel . . . Janie," he said in a strange voice, "I feel sick."

"You know what that is," she said calmly.

A tension came and went within him and he laughed softly. "Him again. He's wrong. He's wrong. He'll never make me sick again. *Driver!*"

His voice was like soft wood tearing. Startled, the driver slammed on his brakes. Hip surged forward out of his seat and caught the back of the driver under his armpit. "Go back," he said excitedly.

"Goddlemighty," the driver muttered. He began to turn the cab around. Hip turned to Janie, an answer, some sort of answer, half formed, but she had no question. She sat quietly and waited. To the driver Hip said, "Just the next block. Yeah, here. Left. Turn left."

He sank back then, his cheek to the window glass, his eyes raking the shadowed houses and black lawns. After a time he said, "There. The house with the driveway, there where the big hedge is."

"Want I should drive in?"

"No," Hip said. "Pull over. A little further . . . there, where I can see in."

When the cab stopped, the driver turned around and peered back. "Gettin' out here? That's a dollar 'n —"

"*Shh!*" The sound came so explosively that the driver sat stunned. Then he shook his head wearily and turned to face forward. He shrugged and waited.

Hip stared through the driveway's gap in the hedge at the faintly gleaming white house, its stately porch and porte-cochère, its neat shutters and fanlit door.

"Take us home," he said after a time.

Nothing was said until they got there. Hip sat with one hand pressing his temples, covering his eyes. Janie's corner of the cab was dark and silent.

When the machine stopped Hip slid out and absently handed Janie to the walk. He gave the driver a bill, accepting the change, pawed out a tip and handed it back. The cab drove off.

Hip stood looking down at the money in his hand, sliding it around on his palm with his fingers. "Janie?"

"Yes, Hip."

He looked at her. He could hardly see her in the darkness. "Let's go inside."

They went in. He switched on the lights. She took off her hat and hung her bag on the bedpost and sat down on the bed, her hands on her lap. Waiting.

He seemed blind, so deep was his introspection. He came awake slowly, his gaze fixed on the money in his hand. For a moment it seemed without meaning to him; then slowly, visibly, he recognized it and brought it into his thoughts, into his expression. He closed his hand on it, shook it, brought it to her and spread it out on the night table—three crumpled bills, some silver. "It isn't mine," he said.

"Of course it is!"

He shook his head tiredly. "No it isn't. None of it's been mine. Not the roller coaster money or the shopping money or coffee in the mornings or . . . I suppose there's rent here."

She was silent.

"That house," he said detachedly. "The instant I saw it I knew I'd been there before. I was there just before I got arrested. I didn't have any money then. I remember. I knocked on the door and I was dirty and crazy and they told me to go around the back if I wanted something to eat. I didn't have any money; I remember that *so* well. All I had was . . ."

Out of his pocket came the woven metal tube. He caught lamplight on its side, flicked it off again, squeezed it, then pointed with it at the night table. "Now, ever since I came here, I have money. In my left jacket pocket every day. I never wondered about it. It's your money, isn't it, Janie?"

"It's yours. Forget about it, Hip. It's not important."

"What do you mean it's mine?" he barked. "Mine because you give it to me?" He probed her silence with a bright beam of anger and nodded. "Thought so."

"Hip!"

He shook his head, suddenly, violently, the only expression he could find at the moment for the great tearing wind which swept through him. It was anger, it was humiliation, it was a deep futility and a raging attack on the curtains which shrouded his self-knowledge. He slumped down into the easy chair and put his hands over his face.

He sensed her nearness, then her hand was on his shoulder. "Hip . . ." she whispered. He shrugged the shoulder and the hand was gone. He heard the faint sound of springs as she sat down again on the bed.

He brought his hands down slowly. His face was twisted, hurt. "You've got to understand, I'm not mad at you, I haven't forgotten what you've done, it isn't that," he blurted. "I'm all mixed up again," he said hoarsely. "Doing things, don't know why. Things I *got* to do, I don't know what. Like . . ." He stopped to think, to sort the thousand scraps that whirled and danced in the wind which blew through him. "Like knowing this is wrong, I shouldn't be here, getting fed, spending money, but I don't know who ever said I shouldn't, where I learned it. And . . . and like what I told you, this thing about finding somebody and I don't know who it is and I don't know why. I said tonight . . ." He paused and for a long moment filled the room with the hiss of breath between his teeth, his tense-curled lips. "I said tonight, my world . . . the place I live, it's getting bigger all the time. It just now got big enough to take in that house where we stopped. We passed that corner and I knew the house was there and I had to look at it. I knew I'd been there before, dirty and all excited . . . knocked . . . they told me to go around back . . . I yelled at them . . . somebody else came. I asked them, I wanted to know about some—"

The silence, again the hissing breath.

"—children who lived there, and no children lived there. And I shouted again, everybody was afraid, I straightened out a little. I told them just tell me what I wanted to know, I'd go away, I didn't want to frighten anybody. I said all right, no children, then tell me where is Alicia Kew, just let me talk to Alicia Kew."

He straightened up, his eyes alight, and pointed the piece of tubing at Janie. "You see? I remember, I remember her name, Alicia Kew!" He sank back. "And they said, 'Alicia Kew is dead.' And then they said, oh *her* children! And they told me where to go to find them. They wrote it down someplace, I've got it here somewhere. . . ." He began to fumble through his pockets, stopped suddenly and glared at Janie. "It was the old clothes, *you* have it, *you've* hidden it!"

If she had explained, if she had answered, it would have been all right but she only watched him.

"All right," he gritted. "I remembered one thing, I can remember another. Or I can go back there and ask again. I don't need you."

Her expression did not change but, watching it, he knew suddenly that she was holding it still and that it was a terrible effort for her.

He said gently, "I did need you. I'd've died without you. You've been . . ." He had no word for what she had been to him so he stopped searching for one and went on, "It's just that I've got so I don't need you that way any more. I have some things to find out but I have to do it myself."

At last she spoke: "You have done it yourself, Hip. Every bit of it. All I've done is to put you where you could do it. I—want to go on with that."

"You don't need to," he reassured her. "I'm a big boy now. I've come a long way; I've come alive. There can't be much more to find out."

"There's a lot more," she said sadly.

He shook his head positively. "I tell you, I *know!* Finding out about those children, about this Alicia Kew, and then the address where they'd moved—that was right at the end; that was the place where I got my fingertips on the—whatever it was I was trying to grab. Just that one more place, that address where the children are; that's all I need. That's where he'll be."

"He?"

"The one, you know, the one I've been looking for. His name is—" He leapt to his feet. "His name's—"

He brought his fist into his palm, a murderous blow. "I forgot," he whispered.

He put his stinging hand to the short hair at the back of his head, screwed up his eyes in concentration. Then he relaxed. "It's all right," he said. "I'll find out, now."

"Sit down," she said. "Go on, Hip. Sit down and listen to me."

Reluctantly he did; resentfully he looked at her. His head was full of almost-understood pictures and phrases. He thought, *Can't she let me alone? Can't she let me think a while?* But because she . . . Because she was Janie, he waited.

"You're right, you can do it," she said. She spoke slowly and with extreme care. "You can go to the house tomorrow, if you like, and get the address and find what you've been looking for. And it will mean absolutely—*nothing*—to you. Hip, I *know!*"

He glared at her.

"Believe me, Hip; believe me!"

He charged across the room, grabbed her wrists, pulled her up, thrust his face to hers. "You know!" he shouted. "I *bet* you know. You know every damn thing, don't you? You have all along. Here I am going half out of my head wanting to know and you sit there and watch me squirm!"

"Hip! Hip, my arms—"

He squeezed them tighter, shook her. "You *do* know, don't you? All about me?"

"Let me go. Please let me go. Oh, Hip, you don't know what you're doing!"

He flung her back on the bed. She drew up her legs, turned on her side, propped up on one elbow and, through tears, incredible tears, tears which didn't belong to any Janie he had yet seen, she looked up at him. She held her bruised forearm, flexed her free hand. “You don’t know,” she choked, “what you’re . . .” And then she was quiet, panting, sending, through those impossible tears, some great, tortured, thwarted message which he could not read.

Slowly he knelt beside the bed. “Ah, Janie. Janie.”

Her lips twitched. It could hardly have been a smile but it wanted to be. She touched his hair. “It’s all right,” she breathed.

She let her head fall to the pillow and closed her eyes. He curled his legs under him, sat on the floor, put his arms on the bed and rested his cheek on them.

She said, with her eyes closed, “I understand, Hip; I do understand. I want to help, I want to go on helping.”

“No you don’t,” he said, not bitterly, but from the depths of an emotion something like grief.

He could tell—perhaps it was her breath—that he had started the tears again. He said, “You know about me. You know everything I’m looking for.” It sounded like an accusation and he was sorry. He meant it only to express his reasoning. But there wasn’t any other way to say it. “Don’t you?”

Still keeping her eyes closed, she nodded.

“Well then.”

He got up heavily and went back to his chair. *When she wants something out of me*, he thought viciously, *she just sits and waits for it.* He slumped into the chair and looked at her. She had not moved. He made a conscious effort and wrung the bitterness from his thought, leaving only the content, the advice. He waited.

She sighed then and sat up. At sight of her rumpled hair and flushed cheeks, he felt a surge of tenderness. Sternly he put it down.

She said, “You have to take my word. You’ll have to trust me, Hip.”

Slowly he shook his head. She dropped her eyes, put her hands together. She raised one, touched her eye with the back of her wrist.

She said, “That piece of cable.”

The tubing lay on the floor where he had dropped it. He picked it up. “What about it?”

"When was the first time you remembered you had it—remembered it was yours?"

He thought. "The house. When I went to the house, asking."

"No," she said, "I don't mean that. I mean, after you were sick."

"Oh." He closed his eyes briefly, frowned. "The window. The time I remembered the window, breaking it. I remembered that and then it . . . oh!" he said abruptly. "You put it in my hand."

"That's right. And for eight days I'd been putting it in your hand. I put it in your shoe, once. On your plate. In the soap dish. Once I stuck your toothbrush inside it. Every day, half a dozen times a day—eight days, Hip!"

"I don't—"

"You don't understand! Oh, I can't blame you."

"I wasn't going to say that. I was going to say, I don't believe you."

At last she looked at him; when she did he realized how rare it was for him to be with her without her eyes on his face. "Truly," she said intensely. "Truly, Hip. That's the way it was."

He nodded reluctantly. "All right. So that's the way it was. What has that to do with—"

"Wait," she begged. "You'll see . . . now, every time you touched the bit of cable, you refused to admit it existed. You'd let it roll right out of your hand and you wouldn't see it fall to the floor. You'd step on it with your bare feet and not even feel it. Once it was in your food, Hip; you picked it up with a forkful of lima beans, you put the end of it in your mouth, and then just let it slip away; you didn't know it was there!"

"Oc—" he said with an effort, then, "occlusion. That's what Bromfield called it." *Who was Bromfield?* But it escaped him; Janie was talking.

"That's right. Now listen carefully. When the time came for the occlusion to vanish, it did; and there you stood with the cable in your hand, knowing it was real. But nothing I could do beforehand could make that happen until it was ready to happen!"

He thought about it. "So—what made it ready to happen?"

"You went back."

"To the store, the plate glass window?"

"Yes," she said and immediately, "No. What I mean is this: You came alive in this room, and you—well, you said it yourself: the world got bigger for you, big enough to let there be a room, then big enough for a street, then a town. But the same thing was happening with your memory. Your memory got big enough to include yesterday, and last week, and then the jail, and then the thing that got you into jail. Now look: At that moment, the cable meant something to you, something terribly important. But when it happened, for all the time after it happened, the cable meant nothing. It didn't mean anything until the second your memory could go back that far. Then it was real again."

"Oh," he said.

She dropped her eyes. "I knew about the cable. I could have explained it to you. I tried and tried to bring it to your attention but you couldn't see it until you were ready. All right—I know a lot more about you. But don't you see that if I told you, *you wouldn't be able to hear me?*"

He shook his head, not in denial but dazedly. He said, "But I'm not—sick any more!"

He read the response in her expressive face. He said faintly, "Am I?" and then anger curled and kicked inside him. "Come on now," he growled, "you don't mean to tell me I'd suddenly get deaf if you told me where I went to high school."

"Of course not," she said impatiently. "It's just that it wouldn't mean anything to you. It wouldn't relate." She bit her lip in concentration. "Here's one: You've mentioned Bromfield a half dozen times."

"Who? Bromfield? I have not."

She looked at him narrowly. "Hip—you have. You mentioned him not ten minutes ago."

"Did I?" He thought. He thought hard. Then he opened his eyes wide. "By God, I did!"

"All right. Who is he? What was he to you?"

"Who?"

"Hip!" she said sharply.

"I'm sorry," he said. "I guess I'm a little mixed up." He thought again, hard, trying to recall the entire sequence, every word. At last, "B-bromfield," he said with difficulty.

"It will hardly stay with you. Well, it's a flash from a long way back. It won't mean anything to you until you go back that far and get it."

"Go back? Go back how?"

"Haven't you been going back and back—from being sick here to being in jail to getting arrested, and just before that, to your visit to that house? Think about that, Hip. Think about why you went to the house."

He made an impatient gesture. "I don't need to. Can't you see? I went to that house because I was searching for something—what was it? Oh, children; some children who could tell me where the halfwit was." He leapt up, laughed. "You see? The halfwit—I remembered. I'll remember it all, you'll see. The halfwit . . . I'd been looking for him for years, forever. I . . . forget why, but," he said, his voice strengthening, "that doesn't matter any more now. What I'm trying to tell you is that I don't have to go all the way back; I've done all I need to do. I'm back on the path. Tomorrow I'm going to that house and get that address and then I'll go to wherever that is and finish what I started out to do in the first place when I lost the—"

He faltered, looked around bemusedly, spied the tubing lying on the chair arm, snatched it up. "This," he said triumphantly. "It's part of the—the—oh, *damn* it!"

She waited until he had calmed down enough to hear her. She said, "You see?"

"See what?" he asked brokenly, uncaring, miserable.

"If you go out there tomorrow, you'll walk into a situation you don't understand, for reasons you can't remember, asking for someone you can't place, in order to go find out something you can't conceive of. But," she admitted, "you are right, Hip—you *can* do it."

"If I did," he said, "it would all come back."

She shook her head. He said harshly, "You know everything, don't you?"

"Yes, Hip."

"Well, I don't care. I'm going to do it anyway."

She took one deep breath. "You'll be killed."

"*What?*"

"If you go out there you will be killed," she said distinctly.

"Oh, Hip, haven't I been right so far? Haven't I? Haven't you gotten back a lot already—really gotten it back, so it doesn't slip away from you?"

Agonized, he said, "You tell me I can walk out of here tomorrow and find whatever it is I've been looking—Looking? *Living* for . . . and you tell me it'll kill me if I do. What do you want from me? What are you trying to tell me to do?"

"Just keep on," she pleaded. "Just keep on with what you've been doing."

"For what?" he raged. "Go back and back, go farther away from the thing I want? What good will—"

"Stop it!" she said sharply. To his own astonishment he stopped. "You'll be biting holes in the rug in a minute," she said gently and with a gleam of amusement. "That won't help."

He fought against her amusement but it was irresistible. He let it touch him and thrust it away; but it had touched him. He spoke more quietly: "You're telling me I mustn't *ever* find the —the halfwit and the . . . whatever it is?"

"Oh," she said, her whole heart in her inflection, "oh, *no!* Hip, you'll find it, truly you will. But you have to know what it is; you have to know why."

"How long will it take?"

She shook her head soberly. "I don't know."

"I can't wait. Tomorrow—" He jabbed a finger at the window. The dark was silvering, the sun was near, pressing it away. "*Today*, you see? *Today* I could go there . . . I've got to; you understand how much it means, how long I've been . . ." His voice trailed off; then he whirled on her. "You say I'll be killed; I'd rather be killed, there with it in my hands; it's what I've been living for anyway!"

She looked up at him tragically. "Hip—"

"No!" he snapped. "You can't talk me out of it."

She started to speak, stopped, bent her head. Down she bent, to hide her face on the bed.

He strode furiously up and down the room, then stood over her. His face softened. "Janie," he said, "help me. . . ."

She lay very still. He knew she was listening. He said, "If there's danger . . . if something is going to try to kill me . . . tell me what. At least let me know what to look for."

She turned her head, faced the wall, so he could hear her but not see her. In a labored voice she said, "I didn't say anything will try to kill you. I said you *would* be killed."

He stood over her for a long time. Then he growled, "All right. I will. Thanks for everything, Janie. You better go home."

She crawled off the bed slowly, weakly, as if she had been flogged. She turned to him with such a look of pity and sorrow in her face that his heart was squeezed. But he set his jaw, looked toward the door, moved his head toward it.

She went, not looking back, dragging her feet. It was more than he could bear. But he let her go.

The bedspread was lightly rumpled. He crossed the room slowly and looked down at it. He put out his hand, then fell forward and plunged his face into it. It was still warm from her body and for an instant so brief as to be indefinable, he felt a thing about mingled breaths, two spellbound souls turning one to the other and about to be one. But then it was gone, everything was gone and he lay exhausted.

Go on, get sick. Curl up and die. "All right," he whispered.

Might as well. What's the difference anyway? Die or get killed, who cares?

Not Janie.

He closed his eyes and saw a mouth. He thought it was Janie's, but the chin was too pointed. The mouth said, "*Just lie down and die, that's all,*" and smiled. The smile made light glance off the thick glasses which must mean he was seeing the whole face. And then there was a pain so sharp and swift that he threw up his head and grunted. His hand, his hand was cut. He looked down at it, saw the scars which had made the sudden, restimulative pain. "Thompson, I'm gonna kill that Thompson."

Who was Thompson who was Bromfield who was the halfwit in the cave . . . cave, where is the cave where the children . . . children . . . no, it was *children's* . . . where the children's . . . *clothes*, that's it! Clothes, old, torn, rags; but that's how he . . .

Janie. . . . You will be killed. *Just lie down and die.*

His eyeballs rolled up, his tensions left him in a creeping lethargy. It was not a good thing but it was more welcome than feeling. Someone said, "Up forty or better on your right quadrant, corp'r'l, or the pixies'll degauss your fuses." Who said that?

He, Hip Barrows. He said it.

Who'd he say it to?

Janie with her clever hand on the ack-ack prototype.

He snorted faintly. Janie wasn't a corporal. "Reality isn't the most pleasant of atmospheres, Lieutenant. But we like to think we're engineered for it. It's a pretty fine piece of engineering, the kind an engineer can respect. Drag in an obsession and reality can't tolerate it. Something has to give; if reality goes, your fine piece of engineering is left with nothing to operate on. Nothing it was designed to operate on. So it operates badly. So kick the obsession out; start functioning the way you were designed to function."

Who said that? Oh—Bromfield. The jerk! He should know better than to try to talk engineering to an engineer. "Cap'n Bromfield" (tiredly, the twenty damn thousandth time), "if I wasn't an engineer I wouldn't've found it, I wouldn't've recognized it and I wouldn't give a damn now." Ah, it doesn't matter.

It doesn't matter. Just curl up and as long as Thompson don't show his face. *Just curl up and* . . . "No, by God," roared Hip Barrows. He sprang off the bed, stood quaking in the middle of the room. He clapped his hands over his eyes and rocked like a storm-blown sapling. He might be all mixed up, Bromfield's voice, Thompson's face, a cave full of children's clothes, Janie who wanted him killed; but there was one thing he was sure of, one thing he *knew*: Thompson wasn't going to make him curl up and die. Janie had rid him of *that* one!

He whimpered as he rocked, "Janie . . . ?"

Janie didn't want him to die.

Janie didn't want him killed; what's the matter here? Janie just wants . . . go back. Take time.

He looked at the brightening window.

Take time? Why, maybe today he could get that address and see those children and find the halfwit and . . . well, find him anyway; that's what he wanted, wasn't it? *Today.* Then by God he'd show Bromfield who had an obsession!

If he lived, he'd show Bromfield.

But no; what Janie wanted was to go the other way, go back. For how long? More hungry years, nobody believes you, no one helps, you hunt and hunt, starve and freeze, for a little clue and another to fit it: the address that came from the house with the porte-cochère which came from the piece of paper in the children's clothes which were . . . in the . . .

"Cave," he said aloud. He stopped rocking, straightened.

He had found the cave. And in the cave were children's clothes, and among them was the dirty little scrawled-up piece of paper and that had led him to the porte-cochère house, right here in town.

Another step backward, a big one too; he was deeply certain of that. Because it was the discovery in the cave that had really proved he had seen what Bromfield claimed he had not seen; he had a piece of it! He snatched it up and bent it and squeezed it: silvery, light, curiously woven—the piece of tubing. Of course, of *course!* The piece of tubing had come from the cave too. Now he had it.

A deep excitement began to grow within him. She'd said "Go back," and he had said no, it takes too long. How long for this step, this rediscovery of the cave and its treasures?

He glanced at the window. It couldn't have been more than thirty minutes—forty at the outside. Yes, and while he was all messed up, exhausted, angry, guilty, hurt. Suppose he tried this going-back business head-on, rested, fed, with all his wits about him, with—with Janie to help?

He ran to the door, threw it open, bounded across the hall, shoved the opposite door open. "Janie, listen," he said, wildly excited. "Oh, Janie—" and his voice was cut off in a sharp gasp. He skidded to a stop six feet into the room, his feet scurrying and slipping, trying to get him back out into the hall again, shut the door. "I beg your—excuse *me*," he bleated out of the shock which filled him. His back struck the door, slammed it; he turned hysterically, pawed it open, and dove outside. God, he thought, I wish she'd *told* me! He stumbled across the hall to his own room, feeling like a gong which had just been struck. He closed and locked his door and leaned against it. Somewhere he found a creaky burst of embarrassed laughter which helped. He half turned to look at the panels of his locked door, drawn to them against his will. He tried to prevent his mind's eye from going back across the hall and through the other door; he failed; he saw the picture of it again, vividly, and again he laughed, hot-faced and uncomfortable. "She should've told me," he muttered.

His bit of tubing caught his eye and he picked it up and sat down in the big chair. It drove the embarrassing moment away; brought back the greater urgency. He had to see Janie. Talk with her. Maybe it was crazy but she'd know: maybe they could do the going-back thing fast, really fast, so fast that he could go find that halfwit today after all. Ah . . . it was probably hopeless; but Janie, Janie'd know. Wait then. She'd come when she was ready; she had to.

He lay back, shoved his feet as far out as they would go, tilted his head back until the back of the chair snugged into the nape of his neck. Fatigue drifted and grew within him like a fragrant smoke, clouding his eyes and filling his nostrils.

His hands went limp, his eyes closed. Once he laughed, a small foolish snicker; but the picture didn't come clear enough or stay long enough to divert him from his deep healthy plunge into sleep.

Bup-bup-bup-bup-bup-bup-bup-bup.

(Fifties, he thought, way off in the hills. Lifelong ambition of every red-blooded boy: get a machine gun and make like a garden hose with it.)

Wham-wham-wham-wham!

(Oerlikons! Where'd they dredge those things up from? Is this an ack-ack station or is it a museum?)

"Hip! Hip Barrows!"

(For Pete's sake, when is that corporal going to learn to say "Lieutenant"? Not that I give a whistle, one way or another, but one of these days he'll do it in front of some teen-age Air Force Colonel and get us both bounced for it.)

Wham! Wham! "Oh . . . Hip!"

He sat up palming his eyes, and the guns were knuckles on a door and the corporal was Janie, calling somewhere, and the anti-aircraft base shattered and misted and blew away to the dream factory.

"Hip!"

"Come on," he croaked. "Come on in."

"It's locked."

He grunted and got numbly to his feet. Sunlight poured in through the curtains. He reeled to the door and opened it. His eyes wouldn't track and his teeth felt like a row of cigar butts.

"Oh, Hip!"

Over her shoulder he saw the other door and he remembered. He drew her inside and shut his door. "Listen, I'm awful sorry about what happened. I feel like a damn fool."

"Hip—don't," she said softly. "It doesn't matter, you know that. Are you all right?"

"A little churned up," he admitted and was annoyed by the reappearance of his embarrassed laugh. "Wait till I put some cold water on my face and wake up some." From the bathroom he called, "Where you been?"

"Walking. I had to think. Then . . . I waited outside. I was afraid you might—you know. I wanted to follow you, be with you. I thought I might help. . . . You really are all right?"

"Oh sure. And I'm not going anywhere without talking to you first. But about the other thing—I hope *she's* all right."

"What?"

"I guess she got a worse shock than I did. I wish you'd told me you had somebody in there with you. I wouldn't've barged—"

"Hip, what are you talking about? What happened?"

"Oh!" he said. "Omigosh. You came straight here—you haven't been in your room yet."

"No. What on *earth* are you—"

He said, actually blushing, "I wish she'd told you about it rather than me. Well, I suddenly had to see you, but *bad*. So I steamed across the hall and charged in, never dreaming there would be anyone but you there, and here I am halfway across the room before I could even stop, and there stood this friend of yours."

"Who? Hip, for heaven's sake—"

"The woman. Had to be someone you know, Janie. Burglars aren't likely to prance around naked."

Janie put a slow hand up to her mouth.

"A colored woman. Girl. Young."

"Did she . . . what did she . . ."

"I don't know what she did. I didn't get but a flash glimpse of her—if that's any comfort to her. I hightailed right out of there. Aw, Janie, I'm sorry. I know it's sort of embarrassing, but it can't be *that* bad. Janie!" he cried in alarm.

"He's found us . . . We've got to get out of here," she whispered. Her lips were nearly white; she was shaking. "Come on, oh, come *on!*"

"Now wait! Janie, I got to talk to you. I—"

She whirled on him like a fighting animal. She spoke with such intensity that her words blurred. "Don't talk! Don't ask me. I can't tell you; you wouldn't understand. Just get out of here, get away." With astonishing power her hand closed on his arm and pulled. He took two running steps or he would have been flat on the floor. She was at the door, opening it, as he took the second step, and she took the slack of his shirt in her free hand, pulled him through, pushed him down the hall toward the outer exit. He caught himself against the doorpost; surprise and anger exploded together within him and built an instant of mighty stubbornness. No single word she might have uttered could have moved him; braced and on guard as he was, not even her unexpected strength could have done anything but cause him to strike back. But she said nothing nor did she touch him; she ran past, white and whimpering in terror, and bounded down the steps outside.

He did the only thing his body would do, without analysis or conscious decision. He found himself outside, running a little behind her. "Janie . . ."

"Taxi!" she screamed.

The cab had barely begun to slow down when she had the door open. Hip fell in after her. "Go on," said Janie to the driver and knelt on the seat to peer through the rear window.

"Go where?" gasped the driver.

"Just go. Hurry."

Hip joined her at the window. All he could see was the dwindling house front, one or two gaping pedestrians. "What was it? What happened?"

She simply shook her head.

"What was it?" he insisted. "The place going to explode or something?"

Again she shook her head. She turned away from the window and cowered into the corner. Her white teeth scraped and

The installation itself, for that matter, was obsolete in that it had been superseded years ago by larger and more efficient defense nets and was now part of no system. But it had a function in training gunners and their officers, radar men and technicians.

The Lieutenant, in one of his detested idle moments, went rummaging into some files and came up with some years-old research figures on the efficiency of proximity fuses, and some others on the minimum elevations at which these ingenious missiles, with their fist-sized radar transmitters, receivers and timing gear, might be fired. It would seem that ack-ack officers would much rather knock out a low-flying plane than have their sensitive shells pre-detonated by an intervening treetop or power pole.

Lieutenant Barrows' eye, however, was one of those which pick up mathematical discrepancies, however slight, with the accuracy of the Toscanini ear for pitch. A certain quadrant in a certain sector in the range contained a tiny area over which passed more dud shells than the law of averages should respectably allow. A high-dud barrage or two or three perhaps, over a year, might indicate bad quality control in the shells themselves; but when every flight of low-elevation "prox" shells over a certain point either exploded on contact or not at all, the revered law was being broken. The scientific mind recoils at law-breaking of this sort, and will pursue a guilty phenomenon as grimly as ever society hunted its delinquents.

What pleased the Lieutenant most was that he had here an exclusive. There had been little reason for anyone to throw great numbers of shells at low elevations anywhere. There had been less reason to do so over the area in question. Therefore it was not until Lieutenant Barrows hunted down and compared a hundred reports spread over a dozen years that anyone had had evidence enough to justify an investigation.

But it was going to be *his* investigation. If nothing came of it, nothing need be said. If on the other hand it turned out to be important, he could with immense modesty and impressive clarity bring the matter to the attention of the Colonel; and perhaps then the Colonel might be persuaded to revise his opinion of ROTC Lieutenants. So he made a field trip on his own time and discovered an area wherein to varying degrees his pocket voltmeter would not work properly. And it dawned on him that what he had found was something which inhibited magnetism. The rugged but sensitive coils and relays in the proximity fuses, to all intents and purposes, ceased to exist when they passed this particular hillside lower than forty yards. Permanent magnets were damped just as electromagnets.

Nothing in Barrows' brief but brilliant career had even approached this incredible phenomenon in potential. His accurate and imaginative mind drank and drank of it and he saw visions: the identification and analysis of the phenomenon (Barrows Effect, perhaps?) and then a laboratory effort—successful of course—to duplicate it. Then, application. A field generator which would throw up an invisible wall of the force; aircraft and their communications—even their intercoms—failing with the failure of their many magnets. Seeking gear on guided missiles, arming and blasting devices, and of course the disarming of proximity fuses . . . the perfect defensive weapon for the electromagnetic age . . . and how much else? No limit to it. Then there would be the demonstrations of course, the Colonel introducing him to renowned scientists and military men: *"This, gentlemen, is your ROTC man!"*

But first he had to find what was doing it, now that he knew where it was being done; and so he designed and built a detector. It was simple and ingenious and very carefully calibrated. While engaged in the work, his irrepressible mind wrought and twisted and admired and reworked the whole concept of "contramagnetism." He extrapolated a series of laws and derived effects just as a mathematical pastime and fired them off to the Institute of Electrical Engineers, who could appreciate them and did; for they were later published in the Journal. He even amused himself in gunnery practice by warning his men against low-elevation shelling over his area, because "the pixies would degauss (demagnetize) their proximity fuses." And this gave him a high delight, for he pictured himself telling them later that his fanciful remark had been nothing but the truth and that had they the wit God gave a goose they could have gone out and dug up the thing, whatever it was, for themselves.

At last he finished his detector. It involved a mercury switch and a solenoid and a variable power supply and would detect the very slightest changes in the field of its own magnet. It weighed about forty pounds but this mattered not at all since he did not intend to carry it. He got the best ordnance maps of the area that he could find, appointed as a volunteer the stupidest-looking Pfc he could find, and spent a long day of his furlough time out on the range, carefully zig-zagging the slope and checking the readings off on his map until he located the center of the degaussing effect.

It was in a field on an old abandoned farm. In the middle of the field was an ancient truck in the last stages of oxidation. Drought and drift, rain and thaw had all but buried the machine and the Lieutenant flogged himself and his patient soldier into a frenzy of explosive excavation. After sweaty hours, they had dug and scraped and brushed until what was left of the truck stood free and clear; and under it they found the source of the incredible field.

From each corner of the frame ran a gleaming silvery cable. They came together at the steering column and joined and thence a single cable ran upward to a small box. From the box protruded a lever. There was no apparent power source but the thing was operating.

When Barrows pushed the lever forward, the twisted wreck groaned and sank noticeably into the soft ground. When he pulled the lever back, it crackled and creaked and lifted up to the limits of its broken springs and wanted to lift even more.

He returned the lever to neutral and stepped back.

This was everything he had hoped to find certainly and made practical the wildest of his dreams. It was the degaussing generator, awaiting only his dissection and analysis. But it was all these things as a by-product.

Lever forward, this device made the truck *heavier*. Lever back, *lighter*.

It was antigravity!

Antigravity: a fantasy, a dream. Antigravity, which would change the face of the earth in ways which would make the effects of steam, electricity, even nuclear power, mere sproutings of technology in the orchard this device would grow. Here was skyward architecture no artist had yet dared to paint; here was wingless flight and escape to the planets, to the stars, perhaps. Here was a new era in transportation, logistics, even the dance, even medicine. And oh, the research . . . and it was all his.

The soldier, the dull-witted Pfc, stepped forward and yanked the lever full back. He smiled and threw himself at Barrows' legs. Barrows kicked free, stood, sprang so his knees crackled. He stretched, reached, and the tips of his fingers touched the cool bright underside of one of the cables. The contact could not have lasted longer than a tenth of a second; but for years afterward, for all the years Barrows was to live, part of him seemed to stay there in the frozen instant, his fingertips on a miracle, his body adrift and free of earth.

He fell.

Nightmare.

First the breast-bursting time of pounding heart and forgotten breathing, the madness of an ancient ruin rising out of its element, faster and faster, smaller and smaller into the darkening sky, a patch, a spot, a speck, a hint of light where the high sunlight touched it. And then a numbness and pain when the breath came again.

From somewhere the pressure of laughter; from somewhere else, a fury to hate it and force it down.

A time of mad shouting arguments, words slurred into screams, the widening crescents of laughing eyes, and a scuttling shape escaping him, chuckling. *He did it . . . and he tripped me besides.*

Kill . . .

And nothing to kill; racing into the growing dark and nothing there; pound-pound of feet and fire in the guts and flame in the mind. Falling, hammering the uncaring sod.

The lonely return to the empty, so empty, so very empty hole in the ground. Stand in it and yearn upward for the silver cables you will never see again.

A yellow-red eye staring. Bellow and kick; the detector rising too, but only so high, turning over and over, smashed, the eye blind.

The long way back to barracks, dragging an invisible man called Agony whose heavy hands were clamped upon a broken foot.

Fall down. Rest and rise. Splash through, wallow, rise and rest and then the camp.

HQ. Wooden steps, the door dark; hollow hammering; blood and mud and hammering. Footsteps, voices: astonishment, concern, annoyance, anger.

The white helmets and the brassards: MP. Tell them, bring the Colonel. No one else, only the Colonel.

Shut up, you'll wake the Colonel.

Colonel, it's anti-magnetron, to the satellite, and freight; no more jets!

Shut up, ROTC boy.

Fight them then and someone screamed when someone stepped on the broken foot.

The nightmare lifted and he was on a white cot in a white room with black bars on the windows and a big MP at the door.

"Where am I?"

"Hospital, prison ward, Lieutenant."

"God, what happened?"

"Search me, Sir. Mostly you seemed to want to kill some GI. Kept telling everybody what he looks like."

He put a forearm over his eyes. "The Pfc. Did you find him?"

"Lieutenant, there ain't such a man on the roster. Honest. Security's been through every file we got. You better take it easy, Sir."

A knock. The MP opened the door. Voices.

"Lieutenant, Major Thompson wants to talk to you. How you feel?"

"Lousy, Sergeant. Lousy. . . . I'll talk to him, if he wants."

"He's quiet now, Sir."

A new voice—*that* voice! Barrows pressed down on the forearm he held over his eyes until sparks shone. *Don't look; because if you're right, you'll kill him.*

The door. Footsteps. "Evening, Lieutenant. Ever talk to a psychiatrist before?"

Slowly, in terror of the explosion he knew must come, Barrows lowered his arm and opened his eyes. The clean, well-cut jacket with a Major's leaves and the Medical Corps insignia did not matter. The man's professionally solicitous manner, the words he spoke—these meant nothing. The only thing in the universe was the fact that the last time he had seen this face, it belonged to a Pfc, who had uncomplainingly and disinterestedly hauled his heavy detector around for a whole, hot day; who had shared his discovery; and who had suddenly smiled at him, pulled the lever, let a wrecked truck and a lifetime dream fall away upward into the sky.

Barrows growled and leapt.

The nightmare closed down again.

They did everything they could to help him. They let him check the files himself and prove that there was no such Pfc. The "degaussing" effect? No observations of it. Of course, the Lieutenant himself admitted that he had taken all pertinent records to his quarters. No, they are not in the quarters. Yes, there was a hole in the ground out there and they'd found what he called his "detector," though it made no sense to anyone; it merely tested the field of its own magnet. As to Major Thompson, we have witnesses who can prove he was in the air on his way here when it happened. If the Lieutenant would only rid himself of the idea that Major Thompson is the missing Pfc, we'd get along much better; he isn't, you know; he couldn't be. But of course, Captain Bromfield might be better for you at that. . . .

I know what I did, I know what I saw. I'll find that device or whoever made it. And I'll kill that Thompson!

Bromfield was a good man and heaven knows he tried. But the combination in the patient of high observational talent and years of observational training would not accept the denial of its own data. When the demands for proof had been exhausted and the hysterical period was passed and the melancholia and finally the guarded, superficial equilibrium was reached, they tried facing him with the Major. He charged and it took five men to protect the Major.

These brilliant boys, you know. They crack.

So they kept him a while longer, satisfying themselves that Major Thompson was the only target. Then they wrote the Major a word of warning and they kicked the Lieutenant out. Too bad, they said.

The first six months was a bad dream. He was still full of

Captain Bromfield's fatherly advice and he tried to get a job and stay with it until this "adjustment" the Captain talked about should arrive. It didn't.

He'd saved a little and he had his separation pay. He'd take a few months off and clear this thing out of his mind.

First, the farm. The device was on the truck and the truck obviously belonged to the farmer. Find him and there's your answer.

It took six months to find the town records (for the village had been preempted when the ack-ack range was added to the base) and to learn the names of the only two men who might tell him about the truck. A. Prodd, farmer. A halfwitted hired hand, name unknown, whereabouts unknown.

But he found Prodd, nearly a year later. Rumor took him to Pennsylvania and a hunch took him to the asylum. From Prodd, all but speechless in the last gasp of his latest dotage, he learned that the old man was waiting for his wife, that his son Jack had never been born, that old Lone maybe was an idiot, but nobody ever was a better hand at getting the truck out of the mud; that Lone was a good boy, that Lone lived in the woods with the animals, and that he, Prodd, had never missed a milking.

He was the happiest human being Hip had ever seen.

Barrows went into the woods with the animals. For three and a half years he combed those woods. He ate nuts and berries and trapped what he could; he got his pension check until he forgot about picking it up. He forgot engineering; he very nearly forgot his name. The only thing he cared to know was that to put such a device on such a truck was the act of an idiot, and that this Lone was a halfwit.

He found the cave, some children's clothes and a scrap of the silvery cable. An address.

He found the address. He learned where to find the children. But then he ran into Thompson—and Janie found him.

Seven years.

It was cool where he lay and under his head was a warm pillow and through his hair strayed a gentling touch. He was asleep, or he had been asleep. He was so completely exhausted, used, drained that sleeping and waking were synonymous anyway and it didn't matter. Nothing mattered. He knew who he was, who he had been. He knew what he wanted and where to find it; and find it he would when he had slept.

He stirred happily and the touch in his hair ceased and moved to his cheek where it patted him. In the morning, he thought comfortably, I'll go see my halfwit. But you know what, I think I'll take an hour off just remembering things. I won the sack race at the Sunday school picnic and they awarded me a khaki handkerchief. I caught three pike before breakfast at the Scout camp, trolling, paddling the canoe and holding the fishing line in my teeth; the biggest of the fish cut my mouth when he struck. I hate rice pudding. I love Bach and liverwurst and the last two weeks in May and deep clear eyes like . . . "Janie?"

"I'm here."

He smiled and snuggled his head into the pillow and realized it was Janie's lap. He opened his eyes. Janie's head was a black cloud in a cloud of stars; a darker night in nighttime. "Nighttime?"

"Yes," she whispered. "Sleep well?"

He lay still, smiling, thinking of how well he had slept. "I didn't dream because I knew I could."

"I'm glad."

He sat up. She moved cautiously. He said, "You must be cramped up in knots."

"It's all right," she said. "I liked to see you sleep like that."

"Let's go back to town."

"Not yet. It's my turn, Hip. I have a lot to tell you."

He touched her. "You're cold. Won't it wait?"

"No—oh, no! You've got to know everything before he . . . before we're found."

"*He*? Who's he?"

She was quiet a long time. Hip almost spoke and then thought better of it. And when she did talk, she seemed so far from answering his question that he almost interrupted; but again he quelled it, letting her lead matters in her own way, in her own time.

She said, "You found something in a field; you had your hands on it just long enough to know what it was, what it could mean to you and to the world. And then the man who was with you, the soldier, made you lose it. Why do you suppose he did that?"

"He was a clumsy, brainless bastard."

She made no immediate comment but went on, "The medical officer then sent in to you, a Major, looked exactly like that Pfc to you."

"They proved otherwise."

He was close enough to her to feel the slight movement in the dark as she nodded. "Proof: the men who said they were with him in a plane all afternoon. Now, you had a sheaf of files which showed a perturbation of some sort which affected proximity fuses over a certain area. What happened to them?"

"I don't know. My room was locked, as far as I know, from the time I left that day until they went to search it."

"Did it ever occur to you that those three things—the missing Pfc, the missing files, and the resemblance of the Major to the Pfc—were the things which discredited you?"

"That goes without saying. I think if I could've straightened out any one or any two of those three things, I wouldn't have wound up with that obsession."

"All right. Now think about this. You stumbled and grubbed through seven years, working your way closer and closer to regaining what you had lost. You traced the man who built it and you were just about to find him. But something happened."

"My fault. I bumped into Thompson and went crazy."

She put her hand on his shoulder. "Suppose it wasn't carelessness that made that Pfc pull the lever. Suppose it was done on purpose."

He could not have been more shocked if she had fired a flashbulb in his face. The light was as sudden, as blinding, as that. When he could, he said, "Why didn't I ever think of that?"

"You weren't allowed to think of it," she said bitterly.

"What do you mean, I wasn't—"

"Please. Not yet," she said. "Now, just suppose for a moment that someone did this to you. Can you reason out who it was—why he did it—*how* he did it?"

"No," he said immediately. "Eliminating the world's first and only antigravity generator makes no sense at all. Picking on me to persecute and doing it through such an elaborate method means even less. And as to method, why, he'd have to be able to reach into locked rooms, hypnotize witnesses and read minds!"

"He did," said Janie. "He can."

"Janie—*who*?"

"Who made the generator?"

He leaped to his feet and released a shout that went rolling down and across the dark field.

"Hip!"

"Don't mind me," he said, shaken. "I just realized that the only one who would dare to destroy that machine is someone who could make another if he wanted it. Which means that—oh, my *God!*—the soldier and the halfwit, and maybe Thompson—yes, Thompson: he's the one made me get jailed when I was just about to find him again—they're all the same!— Why didn't I ever think of that before?"

"I told you. You weren't allowed."

He sank down again. In the east, dawn hung over the hills like the loom of a hidden city. He looked at it, recognizing it as the day he had chosen to end his long, obsessive search and he thought of Janie's terror when he had determined to go headlong into the presence of this—this monster—without his sanity, without his memory, without arms or information.

"You'll have to tell me, Janie. All of it."

She told him—all of it. She told him of Lone, of Bonnie and Beanie and of herself; Miss Kew and Miriam, both dead now, and Gerry. She told how they had moved, after Miss Kew was killed, back into the woods, where the old Kew mansion hid and brooded, and how for a time they were very close. And then . . .

"Gerry got ambitious for awhile and decided to go through college, which he did. It was easy. Everything was easy. He's pretty unremarkable looking when he hides those eyes of his behind glasses, you know; people don't notice. He went through medical school too, and psych."

"You mean he really is a psychiatrist?" asked Hip.

"He is not. He just qualifies by the book. There's quite a difference. He hid in crowds; he falsified all sorts of records to get into school. He was never caught at it because all he had to do with anyone who was investigating him was to give them a small charge of that eye of his and they'd forget. He never failed any exam as long as there was a men's room he could go to."

"A what? Men's room?"

"That's right." She laughed. "There was hell to pay one time. See, he'd go in and lock himself in a booth and call Bonnie or Beanie. He'd tell them where he was stumped and they'd whip home and tell me and I'd get the answer from Baby and they'd flash back with the information, all in a few seconds. So one fine day another student heard Gerry talking and stood up in the next booth and peeked over. You can imagine! Bonnie and Beanie can't carry so much as a toothpick with them when they teleport, let alone clothes."

Hip clapped a hand to his forehead. "What happened?"

"Oh, Gerry caught up with the kid. He'd charged right out of there yelling that there was a naked girl in the john. Half of the student body dove in there; of course she was gone. And when Gerry caught up with the kid, he just naturally forgot all about it and wondered what all the yelling was about. They gave him a pretty bad time over it.

"Those were good times," she sighed. "Gerry was so interested in everything. He read all the time. He was at Baby all the time for information. He was interested in people and books and machines and history and art—everything. I got a lot from it. As I say, all the information cleared through me.

"But then Gerry began to . . . I was going to say, get sick, but that's not the way to say it." She bit her lip thoughtfully. "I'd say from what I know of people that only two kinds are really progressive—really dig down and learn and then use what they learn. A few are genuinely interested; they're just built that way. But the great majority want to prove something. They want to be better, richer. They want to be famous or powerful or respected. With Gerry the second operated for a while. He'd never had any real schooling and he'd always been a little afraid to compete. He had it pretty rough when he was a kid; ran away from an orphanage when he was seven and lived like a sewer rat until Lone picked him up. So it felt good to get honors in his classes and make money with a twist of his wrist any time he wanted it. And I think he was genuinely interested in some things for a little while: music and biology and one or two other things.

"But he soon came to realize that he didn't need to prove anything to anyone. He was smarter and stronger and more powerful than anybody. Proving it was just dull. He could have anything he wanted.

"He quit studying. He quit playing the oboe. He gradually quit everything. Finally he slowed down and practically stopped for a year. Who knows what went on in his head? He'd spend weeks lying around, not talking.

"Our *Gestalt*, as we call it, was once an idiot, Hip, when it had Lone for a 'head.' Well, when Gerry took over it was a new, strong, growing thing. But when this happened to him, it was in retreat like what used to be called a manic-depressive."

"Uh!" Hip grunted. "A manic-depressive with enough power to run the world."

"He didn't want to run the world. He knew he could if he wanted to. He didn't see any reason why he should.

"Well, just like in his psych texts he retreated and soon he regressed. He got childish. And his kind of childishness was pretty vicious.

"I started to move around a little; I couldn't stand it around the house. I used to hunt around for things that might snap him out of it. One night in New York I dated a fellow I know who was one of the officers of the I.R.E."

"Institute of Radio Engineers," said Hip. "Swell outfit. I used to be a member."

"I know. This fellow told me about you."

"About *me*?"

"About what you called a 'mathematical recreation,' anyway. An extrapolation of the probable operating laws and attendant phenomena of magnetic flux in a gravity generator."

"God!"

She made a short and painful laugh. "Yes, Hip. I did it to you. I didn't know then of course. I just wanted to interest Gerry in something.

"He was interested all right. He asked Baby about it and got the answer pronto. You see, Lone built that thing before Gerry came to live with us. We'd forgotten about it pretty much."

"Forgotten! A thing like *that*?"

"Look, we don't think like other people."

"You don't," he said thoughtfully and, "Why should you?"

"Lone built it for the old farmer, Prodd. That was just like Lone. A gravity generator, to increase and decrease the weight of Prodd's old truck so he could use it as a tractor. All because Prodd's horse died and he couldn't afford another."

"No!"

"Yes. He was an idiot all right. Well, he asked Baby what effect it would have if this invention got out and Baby said plenty. He said it would turn the whole world upside down, worse than the industrial revolution. Worse than anything that ever happened. He said if things went one way we'd have such a war, you wouldn't believe it. If they went the other way, science would go too far, too fast. Seems that gravitics is the key to everything. It would lead to the addition of one more item to the Unified Field—what we now call psychic energy, or 'psionics.'"

"Matter, energy, space, time and psyche," he breathed, awed.

"Yup," Janie said casually, "all the same thing and this would lead to proof. There just wouldn't *be* any more secrets."

"That's the—the biggest thing I ever heard. So—Gerry decided us poor half-developed apes weren't worthy?"

"Not Gerry! He doesn't care what happens to you apes! One thing he found out from Baby, though, was that whichever way it went the device would be traced to us. You should know. You did it by yourself. But Central Intelligence would've taken seven weeks instead of seven years.

"And that's what bothered Gerry. He was in retreat. He wanted to stew in his own juice in his hideout in the woods. He didn't want the Armed Forces of the United Nations hammering at him to come out and be patriotic. Oh sure, he could have taken care of 'em all in time, but only if he worked full time at it. Working full time was out of his field. He got mad. He got mad at Lone who was dead and he especially got mad at you."

"Whew. He could have killed me. Why didn't he?"

"Same reason he didn't just go out and confiscate the device before you saw it. I tell you, he was vicious and vengeful—childish. You'd bothered him. He was going to fix you for it.

"Now I must confess I didn't care much one way or the other, it did me so much good to see him moving around again. I went with him to the base.

"Now, here's something you just wouldn't remember. He walked right into your lab while you were calibrating your detector. He looked you once in the eye and walked out again with all the information you had, plus the fact that you meant to take it out and locate the device, and that you intended to—what was your phrase?—'appoint a volunteer.' "

"I was a hotshot in those days," said Hip ruefully.

She laughed. "You don't know. You just don't know. Well, out you came with that big heavy instrument on a strap. I saw you, Hip; I can still see you, your pretty tailored uniform, the sun on your hair . . . I was seventeen.

"Gerry told me to lift a Pfc shirt quick. I did, out of the barracks."

"I didn't know a seventeen-year-old could get in and out of a barracks with a whole skin. Not a female type seventeen-year-old."

"I didn't go in!" she said. Hip shouted in sheer surprise as his own shirt was wrenched and twisted. The tails flew up from under his belt and flapped wildly in the windless dawn. "Don't *do* that!" he gasped.

"Just making a point," she said, twinkling. "Gerry put on the shirt and leaned against the fence and waited for you. You marched right up to him and handed him the detector. 'Come on, soldier,' you said. 'You just volunteered for a picnic. You carry the lunch.' "

"What a little stinker I was!"

"I didn't think so. I was peeping out from behind the MP shack. I thought you were sort of wonderful. I did, Hip."

He half laughed. "Go on. Tell me the rest."

"You know the rest. Gerry flashed Bonnie to get the files out of your quarters. She found them and threw them down to me. I burned them. I'm sorry, Hip. I didn't know what Gerry was planning."

"Go on."

"Well, that's it. Gerry saw to it that you were discredited. Psychologically, it had to be that way. You claimed the existence of a Pfc no one had ever seen. You claimed he was the psychiatrist—a real danger sign, as any graduate medic knows. You claimed files, facts and figures to back you up and they couldn't be traced. You could prove that you'd dug something up, but there was nothing to show what it might have been. But most of all, you had a trained scientist's mind, in full possession of facts which the whole world could prove weren't so—and did. Something had to give."

"Cute," murmured Hip from deep in his chest.

"And just for good measure," said Janie with some difficulty, "he handed you a post-hypnotic command which made it impossible for you to relate him either as Major Thompson, psychiatrist, or as the Pfc, to the device.

"When I found out what he'd done I tried to make him help you. Just a little. He—he just laughed at me. I asked Baby what could be done. He said nothing. He said only that the command might be removed by a reverse abreaction."

"What in time is that?"

"Moving backward, mentally, to the incident itself. Abreaction is the process of reliving, in detail, an event. But you were blocked from doing that because you'd have to start from the administration of the command; that's where the incident started. And the only way would be to immobilize you completely, not tell you why, and unpeel all subsequent events one by one until you reached the command. It was a 'from now on' command like all such. It couldn't stop you when you were traveling in reverse.

"And how was I ever going to find you and immobilize you without letting you know why?"

"Holy smoke," Hip said boyishly. "This makes me feel kind of important. A guy like that taking all that trouble."

"Don't flatter yourself!" she said acidly, then: "I'm sorry, Hip. I didn't mean that the way it sounded. . . . It was no trouble for him. He swatted you like a beetle. He gave you a push and forgot all about you."

Hip grunted. "Thank *you*."

"He did it again!" she said furiously. "There you were, seven good youthful years shot, your good engineer's mind gone, with nothing left but a starved, dirty frame and a numb obsession that you were incapable of understanding or relieving. Yet, by heaven, you had enough of—whatever it is that makes you what you are—to drag through those seven years picking up the pieces until you were right at his doorstep. When he saw you coming—it was an accident, he happened to be in town—he knew immediately who you were and what you were after. When you charged him he diverted you into that plate glass window with just a blink of those . . . rotten . . . poison . . . eyes of his . . ."

"Hey," he said gently. "Hey, Janie, take it easy!"

"Makes me mad," she whispered, dashing her hand across her eyes. She tossed her hair back, squared her shoulders. "He sent you flying into the window and at the same time gave you that 'curl up and die' command. I saw it, I saw him do it. . . . S-so rotten. . . ."

She said, in a more controlled tone, "Maybe if it was the only one I could have forgotten it. I never could have approved it but I once had faith in him . . . you've got to understand, we're a part of something together, Gerry and I and the kids; something real and alive. Hating him is like hating your legs or your lungs."

"It says in the Good Book, 'If thine eye offend thee, pluck it out and cast it from thee. If thy right hand—' "

"Yes, your eye, your hand!" she cried. "Not your *head!*" She went on, "But yours wasn't the only case. Did you ever hear that rumor about the fusion of Element 83?"

"A fairy tale. Bismuth won't play those games. I remember vaguely . . . some crazy guy called Klackenhorst."

"A crazy guy called Klackenheimer," she corrected. "Gerry got into one of his bragging phases and let go with a differential he shouldn't have mentioned. Klack picked it up. He fusioned bismuth all right. And Gerry got worried; a thing like that would make too much of a splash and he was afraid he'd be bothered by a mob of people who might trace him. So he got rid of poor old Klack."

"Klackenheimer died of cancer!" snorted Hip.

She gave him a strange look. "I know," she said softly.

Hip beat his temples softly with his fists. Janie said, "There've been more. Not all big things like that. I dared him into wooing a girl once, strictly on his own, without using his talents. He lost out to someone else, an awfully sweet kid who sold washing machines door-to-door and was doing pretty well. The kid wound up with *acne rosacea.*"

"The nose like a beet. I've seen it."

"Like an extra-boiled, extra-swollen beet," she amended. "No job."

"No girl," he guessed.

She smiled and said, "She stuck by him. They have a little ceramics business now. He stays in the back."

He had a vague idea of where the business had come from. "Janie, I'll take your word for it. There were lots of 'em. But—why me? You went all out for me."

"Two good reasons. First, I saw him do that to you in town, make you charge his image in the glass, thinking it was him. It was the last piece of casual viciousness I ever wanted to see. Second, it was—well, it was *you*."

"I don't get you."

"Listen," she said passionately, "we're not a group of freaks. We're *Homo Gestalt*, you understand? We're a single entity, a new kind of human being. We weren't invented. We evolved. We're the next step up. We're alone; there are no more like us. We don't live in the kind of world you do, with systems of morals and codes of ethics to guide us. We're living on a desert island with a herd of goats!"

"I'm the goat."

"Yes, yes, you *are*, can't you see? But we were born on this island with no one like us to teach us, tell us how to behave. We can learn from the goats all the things that make a goat a good goat, but that will never change the fact that we're *not* a goat! You can't apply the same set of rules to us as you do to ordinary humans; we're just not the same thing!"

She waved him down as he was about to speak. "But listen, did you ever see one of those museum exhibits of skeletons of, say horses, starting with the little Eohippus and coming right up the line, nineteen or twenty of them, to the skeleton of a Percheron? There's an awful lot of difference between number one and number nineteen. But what real difference is there between number fifteen and number sixteen? *Damn* little!" She stopped and panted.

"I hear you. But what's that to do with—"

"With you? Can't you see? *Homo Gestalt* is something new, something different, something superior. But the parts—the arms, the guts of it, the memory banks, just like the bones in those skeletons—they're the same as the step lower, or very little different. I'm *me*, I'm *Janie.* I saw him slap you down like that; you were like a squashed rabbit, you were mangy and not as young as you should be. But I recognized you. I saw you and then I saw you seven years ago, coming out into the yard with your detector and the sun on your hair. You were wide and tall and pressed and you walked like a big glossy stallion. You were the reason for the colors on a bantam rooster, you were a part of the thing that shakes the forest when the bull moose challenges; you were shining armor and a dipping pennant and my lady's girdle on your brow, you were, you were . . . I was *seventeen*, damn it, Barrows, whatever else I was. I was seventeen years old and all full of late spring and dreams that scared me."

Profoundly shaken, he whispered, "Janie . . . Janie . . ."

"Get away from me!" she spat. "Not what you think, not love at first sight. That's childish; love's a different sort of thing, hot enough to make you flow into something, interflow, cool and anneal and be a weld stronger than what you started with. I'm not talking about love. I'm talking about being seventeen and feeling . . . all . . ." She covered her face. He waited. Finally she put her hands down. Her eyes were closed and she was very still. ". . . all . . . *human*," she finished.

Then she said, matter-of-factly, "So that's why I helped you instead of anyone else."

He got up and walked into the fresh morning, bright now, new as the fright in a young girl's frightening dream. Again he recalled her total panic when he had reported Bonnie's first appearance; through her eyes he saw what it would be like if he, blind, numb, lacking weapons and insight, had walked again under that cruel careless heel.

He remembered the day he had emerged from the lab, stepped down into the compound, looking about for a slave. Arrogant, self-assured, shallow, looking for the dumbest Pfc in the place.

He thought more then about himself as he had been that day; not about what had happened with Gerry, for that was on the record, accomplished; susceptible to cure but not in fact to change. And the more he thought of himself as he had been the more he was suffused with a deep and choking humility.

He walked almost into Janie as she sat watching her hands sleeping in her lap as he had slept and he thought, surely they too must be full of pains and secrets and small magics too, to smile at.

He knelt beside her. "Janie," he said, and his voice was cracked, "you have to know what was inside that day you saw me. I don't want to spoil you-being-seventeen . . . I just want to tell you about the part of it that was me, some things that—weren't what you thought." He drew a deep breath. "I can remember it better than you because for you it's been seven years and for me it's only just before I went to sleep and dreamed that I went hunting for the halfwit. I'm awake again and the dream is gone, so I remember it all very well. . . .

"Janie, I had trouble when I was a child and the first thing I learned was that I was useless and the things I wanted were by definition worthless. I hardly questioned that until I broke away and found out that my new world had different values from my old one and in the new I was valuable. I was wanted, I belonged.

"And then I got into the Air Force and suddenly I wasn't a football hero and captain of the Debating Society. I was a bright fish with drying scales, and the mud-puppies had it all their way. I nearly died there, Janie.

"Yes, I found the degaussing field all by myself. But what I want you to know is that when I stepped out of the lab that day and you saw me, I wasn't the cockerel and the bull moose and those other things. I was going to discover something and bring it to humanity, not for humanity's sake, but so that they would . . ." he swallowed painfully, ". . . ask me to play the piano at the officers' club and slap me on the back and . . . look at me when I came in. That's all I wanted. When I found out that it was more than magnetic damping (which would make me famous) but antigravity (which would change the face of Earth) I felt only that it would be the President who asked me to play and generals who would slap my back; the things I wanted were the same."

He sank back on his haunches and they were quiet together for a long time. Finally she said, "What do you want now?"

"Not that any more," he whispered. He took her hands.

"Not any more. Something different." Suddenly he laughed. "And you know what, Janie? *I don't know what it is!*"

She squeezed his hands and released them. "Perhaps you'll find out. Hip, we'd better go."

"All right. Where?"

She stood beside him, tall. "Home. *My* home."

"Thompson's?"

She nodded.

"Why, Janie?"

"He's got to learn something that a computer can't teach him. He's got to learn to be ashamed."

"Ashamed?"

"I don't know," she said, looking away from him, "how moral systems operate. I don't know how you get one started. All I know about morals is that if they're violated, you feel ashamed. I'll start him with that."

"What can I do?"

"Just come," she flashed. "I want him to see you—what you are, the way you think. I want him to remember what you were before, how much brilliance, how much promise you had, so he'll know how much he has cost you."

"Do you think any of that will really make a difference?"

She smiled; one could be afraid of someone who could smile like that. "It will," she said grimly. "He will have to face the fact that he is not omnipotent and that he can't kill something better than he is just because he's stronger."

"You want him to try to kill me?"

She smiled again and this time it was the smile of deep achievement. "He won't." She laughed, then turned to him quickly. "Don't worry about it, Hip. *I am his only link with Baby.* Do you think he'd perform a prefrontal lobotomy on himself? Do you think he'd risk cutting himself off from his memory? It isn't the kind of memory a man has, Hip. It's *Homo Gestalt's.* It's all the information it has ever absorbed, plus the computation of each fact against every other fact in every possible combination. He can get along without Bonnie and Beanie, he can get things done at a distance in other ways. He can get along without any of the other things I do for him. But he can't get along without Baby. He's had to ever since I began working with you. By this time he's frantic. He can touch Baby, lift him, talk to him. But he can't get a thing out of him unless he does it through me!"

"I'll come," he said quietly. Then he said, "You won't have to kill yourself."

They went first to their own house and Janie laughed and opened both locks without touching them. "I've wanted so to do that but I didn't dare," she laughed. She pirouetted into his room. "Look!" she sang. The lamp on the night table rose, sailed slowly through the air, settled to the floor by the bathroom. Its cord curled like a snake, sank into a baseboard outlet and the switch clicked. It lit. "Look!" she cried. The percolator hopped forward on the dresser-top, stopped. He heard water trickling and slowly condensed moisture formed on the outside as the pot filled up with ice water. "Look," she called, "look, look!" and the carpet grew a bulge which scuttled across and became nothing at the other side, the knives and forks and his razor and toothbrush and two neckties and a belt came showering around and down and lay on the floor in the shape of a heart with an arrow through it. He shouted with laughter and hugged her and spun her around. He said, "Why haven't I ever kissed you, Janie?"

Her face and body went quite still and in her eyes was an indescribable expression—tenderness, amusement and something else. She said, "I'm not going to tell you because you're wonderful and brave and clever and strong, but you're also just a little bit prissy." She spun away from him and the air was full of knives and forks and neckties, the lamp and the coffeepot, all going back to their places. At the door she said, "Hurry," and was gone.

He plunged after her and caught her in the hall. She was laughing.

He said, "I know why I never kissed you."

She kept her eyes down, but could not do the same with the corners of her mouth. "You do?"

"You can add water to a closed container. Or take it away." It was not a question.

"I can?"

"When we poor males start pawing the ground and horning the low branches off trees, it might be spring and it might be concreted idealism and it might be love. But it's always triggered by hydrostatic pressures in a little tiny series of reservoirs smaller than my little fingernail."

"It is?"

"So when the moisture content of these reservoirs is suddenly lowered, I—we—uh . . . well, breathing becomes easier and the moon has no significance."

"It hasn't?"

"And that's what you've been doing to me."

"I have?"

She pulled away from him, gave him her eyes and a swift, rich arpeggio of laughter. "You can't say it was an immoral thing to do," she said.

He gave her laughter back to her. "No *nice* girl would do a thing like that."

She wrinkled her nose at him and slipped into her room. He looked at her closed door and probably through it, and then turned away.

Smiling and shaking his head in delight and wonderment, encasing a small cold ball of terror inside him with a new kind of calm he had found; puzzled, enchanted, terrified and thoughtful, he turned the shower on and began to undress.

They stood in the road until after the taxi had gone and then Janie led the way into the woods. If they had ever been cut, one could not know it now. The path was faint and wandering but easy to follow, for the growth overhead was so thick that there was little underbrush.

They made their way toward a mossy cliff; and then Hip saw that it was not a cliff but a wall, stretching perhaps a hundred yards in each direction. In it was a massive iron door. It clicked as they approached and something heavy slid. He looked at Janie and knew that she was doing it.

The gate opened and closed behind them. Here the woods were just the same, the trees as large and as thick, but the path was of brick and took only two turns. The first made the wall invisible and the second, a quarter of a mile further, revealed the house.

It was too low and much too wide. Its roof was mounded rather than peaked or gabled. When they drew closer to it, he could see at each flank the heavy, gray-green wall, and he knew that this whole area was in prison.

"I don't, either," said Janie. He was glad she watched his face.

Gooble.

Someone stood behind a great twisted oak near the house, peeping at them. "Wait, Hip." Janie walked quickly to the tree and spoke to someone. He heard her say, "You've *got* to. Do you want me dead?"

That seemed to settle the argument. As Janie returned he peered at the tree, but now there seemed to be no one there.

"It was Beanie," said Janie. "You'll meet her later. Come."

The door was ironbound, of heavy oak planks. It fitted with curious concealed hinges into the massive archway from which it took its shape. The only windows to be seen were high up in the moundlike gables and they were mere barred slits.

By itself—or at least, without a physical touch—the door swung back. It should have creaked, but it did not; it was silent as a cloud. They went in, and when the door closed there was a reverberation deep in the subsonic; he could feel it pounding on his belly.

On the floor was a reiteration of tiles, darkest yellow and a brownish gray, in hypnotic diamond shapes they were repeated in the wainscoting and in the upholstery of furniture either built-in or so heavy it had never been moved. The air was cool but too humid and the ceiling was too close. I am walking, he thought, in a great sick mouth.

From the entrance room they started down a corridor which seemed immensely long and was not at all, for the walls came in and the ceiling drew even lower while the floor rose slightly, giving a completely disturbing false perspective.

"It's all right," said Janie softly. He curled his lips at her, meaning to smile but quite unable to, and wiped cold water from his upper lip.

She stopped near the end door and touched the wall. A section of it swung back, revealing an anteroom with one other door in it. "Wait here, will you, Hip?" She was completely composed. He wished there were more light.

He hesitated. He pointed to the door at the end of the hall. "Is he in there?"

"Yes." She touched his shoulder. It was partly a salutation, partly an urging toward the little room. "I have to see him first," she said. "Trust me, Hip."

"I trust you all right. But are you—is he—"

"He won't do anything to me. Go on, Hip."

He stepped through. He had no chance to look back, for the door swung swiftly shut. It gave no more sign of its existence on this side than it had on the other. He touched it, pushed it. It might as well have been that great wall outside. There was no knob, no visible hinge or catch. The edges were hidden in the paneling; it simply had ceased to exist as a door.

He had one blinding moment of panic and then it receded. He went and sat down across from the other door which led, apparently, into the same room to which the corridor led.

There was not a sound.

He picked up an ottoman and placed it against the wall. He sat with his back tight against the paneling, watching the door with wide eyes.

Try that door, see if it's locked too.

He didn't dare, he realized. Not yet. He sensed vaguely what he would feel if he found it locked; he wanted no more just now than that chilling guess.

"Listen," he hissed to himself, furiously, "you'd better do something. Build something. Or maybe just *think*. But don't sit here like this."

Think. Think about that mystery in there, the pointed face with its thick lenses, which smiled and said, Go on, die.

Think about something else! Quick!

Janie. By herself, facing the pointed face with the—

Homo Gestalt, a girl, two tongue-tied Negroes, a mongoloid idiot and a man with a pointed face and—

Try that one again. *Homo Gestalt*, the next step upward. Well, sure, why not a psychic evolution instead of the physical? *Homo sapiens* stood suddenly naked and unarmed but for the wrinkled jelly in his king-sized skull; he was as different as he could be from the beasts which bore him.

Yet he was the same, the same; to this day he was hungry to breed, hungry to own; he killed without compunction; if he was strong he took, if he was weak he ran; if he was weak and could not run, he died.

Homo sapiens was going to die.

The fear in him was a good fear. Fear is a survival instinct; fear in its way is a comfort for it means that somewhere hope is alive.

He began to think about survival.

Janie wanted *Homo Gestalt* to acquire a moral system so that such as Hip Barrows would not get crushed. But she wanted her *Gestalt* to thrive as well; she was a part of it. My hand wants me to survive, my tongue, my belly wants me to survive.

Morals: they're nothing but a coded survival instinct!

Aren't they? What about the societies in which it is immoral not to eat human flesh? What kind of survival is that?

Well, but those who adhere to morality survive within the group. If the group eats human flesh, you do too.

There must be a name for the code, the set of rules, by which an individual lives in such a way as to help his species—something over and above morals.

Let's define that as the ethos.

That's what *Homo Gestalt* needs: not morality, but an ethos. And shall I sit here, with my brains bubbling with fear, and devise a set of ethics for a superman?

I'll try. It's all I can do.

Define:

Morals: Society's code for individual survival. (That takes care of our righteous cannibal and the correctness of a naked man in a nudist group.)

Ethics: An individual's code for society's survival. (And that's your ethical reformer: he frees his slaves, he won't eat humans, he "turns the rascals out.")

Too pat, too slick; but let's work with 'em.

As a group, *Homo Gestalt* can solve his own problems. But as an entity:

He can't have a morality, because he is alone.

An ethic then. "An individual's code for society's survival." He has no society; yet he has. He has no species; he is his own species.

Could he—should he choose a code which would serve all of humanity?

With the thought, Hip Barrows had a sudden flash of insight, completely intrusive in terms of his immediate problem; yet with it, a load of hostility and blind madness lifted away from him and left him light and confident. It was this:

Who am I to make positive conclusions about morality, and codes to serve all of humanity?

Why—I am the son of a doctor, a man who chose to serve mankind, and who was positive that this was right. And he tried to make me serve in the same way, because it was the only rightness he was sure of. And for this I have hated him all my life . . . I see now, Dad. I see!

He laughed as the weight of old fury left him forever, laughed in purest pleasure. And it was as if the focus was sharper, the light brighter, in all the world, and as his mind turned back to his immediate problem, his thought seemed to place its fingers better on the rising undersurface, slide upward toward the beginnings of a grip.

The door opened. Janie said, "Hip—"

He rose slowly. His thought reeled on and on, close to something. If he could get a grip, get his fingers curled over it . . . "Coming."

He stepped through the door and gasped. It was like a giant greenhouse, fifty yards wide, forty deep; the huge panes overhead curved down and down and met the open lawn—it was more a park—at the side away from the house. After the closeness and darkness of what he had already seen it was shocking but it built in him a great exhilaration. It rose up and up and up rose his thought with it, pressing its fingertips just a bit higher. . . .

He saw the man coming. He stepped quickly forward, not so much to meet him as to be away from Janie if there should be an explosion. There was going to be an explosion; he knew that.

"Well, Lieutenant. I've been warned, but I can still say—this *is* a surprise."

"Not to me," said Hip. He quelled a surprise of a different nature; he had been convinced that his voice would fail him and it had not. "I've known for seven years that I'd find you."

"By God," said Thompson in amazement and delight. It was not a good delight. Over Hip's shoulder he said, "I apologize, Janie. I really didn't believe you until now." To Hip he said, "You show remarkable powers of recovery."

"Homo sap's a hardy beast," said Hip.

Thompson took off his glasses. He had wide round eyes, just the color and luminescence of a black-and-white television screen. The irises showed the whites all the way around; they were perfectly round and they looked as if they were just about to spin.

Once, someone had said, *Keep away from the eyes and you'll be all right.*

Behind him Janie said sharply, "Gerry!"

Hip turned. Janie put up her hand and left a small glass cylinder, smaller than a cigarette, hanging between her lips. She said, "I warned you, Gerry. You know what this is. Touch him and I bite down on it—and then you can live out the rest of your life with Baby and the twins like a monkey in a cage of squirrels."

The thought, the thought—"I'd like to meet Baby."

Thompson thawed; he had been standing, absolutely motionless, staring at Janie. Nov he swung his glasses around in a single bright circle. "You wouldn't like him."

"I want to ask him a question."

"Nobody asks him questions but me. I suppose you expect an answer too?"

"Yes."

Thompson laughed. "Nobody gets answers these days."

Janie said quietly, "This way, Hip."

Hip turned toward her. He distinctly felt a crawling tension behind him, in the air, close to his flesh. He wondered if the Gorgon's head had affected men that way, even the ones who did not look at her.

He followed her down to a niche in the house wall, the one which was not curved glass. In it was a crib the size of a bathtub.

He had not known that Baby was so fat.

"Go ahead," said Janie. The cylinder bobbed once for each of her syllables.

"Yes, go ahead." Thompson's voice was so close behind him that he started. He had not heard the man following him at all and he felt boyish and foolish. He swallowed and said to Janie, "What do I do?"

"Just think your question. He'll probably catch it. Far as I know he receives everybody."

Hip leaned over the crib. Eyes gleaming dully like the uppers of dusty black shoes caught and held him. He thought, *Once this Gestalt had another head. It can get other telekines, teleports. Baby: Can you be replaced?*

"He says yes," said Janie. "That nasty little telepath with the corncob—remember?"

Thompson said bitterly, "I didn't think you'd commit such an enormity, Janie. I could kill you for that."

"You know how," said Janie pleasantly.

Hip turned slowly to Janie. The thought came closer, or he went high and faster than it was going. It was as if his fingers actually rounded a curve, got a barest of purchases.

If Baby, the heart and core, the ego, the repository of all this new being had ever been or done or thought—if Baby could be replaced, then *Homo Gestalt* was *immortal*!

And with a rush, he had it. He had it all.

He said evenly, "I asked Baby if he could be replaced; if his memory banks and computing ability could be transferred."

"Don't tell him that!" Janie screamed.

Thompson had slipped into his complete, unnatural stillness. At last he said, "Baby said yes. I already know that. Janie, you knew that all along, didn't you?"

She made a sound like a gasp or a small cough.

Thompson said, "And you never told me. But of course, you wouldn't. Baby can't talk to me; the next one might. I can get the whole thing from the Lieutenant, right now. So go ahead with the dramatics. I don't need you, Janie."

"Hip! Run! Run!"

Thompson's eyes fixed on Hip's. "No," he said mildly. "Don't run."

They were going to spin; they were going to spin like wheels, like fans, like . . . like . . .

Hip heard Janie scream and scream again and there was a crunching sound. Then the eyes were gone.

He staggered back, his hand over his eyes. There was a gabbling shriek in the room, it went on and on, split and spun around itself. He peeped through his fingers.

Thompson was reeling, his head drawn back and down almost to his shoulderblades. He kicked and elbowed backward.

Holding him, her hands over his eyes, her knee in the small of his back, was Bonnie, and it was from her the gabbling came.

Hip came forward running, starting with such a furious leap that his toes barely touched the floor in the first three paces. His fist was clenched until pain ran up his forearm and in his arm and shoulders was the residual fury of seven obsessive years. His fist sank into the taut solar plexus and Thompson went down soundlessly. So did the Negro but she rolled clear and bounced lithely to her feet. She ran to him, grinning like the moon, squeezed his biceps affectionately, patted his cheek and gabbled.

"And I thank *you*!" he panted. He turned. Another dark girl, just as sinewy and just as naked, supported Janie who was sagging weakly. "Janie!" he roared. "Bonnie, Beanie, whoever you are—did she . . ."

The girl holding her gabbled. Janie raised her eyes. They were deeply puzzled as she watched him come. They strayed from his face to Gerry Thompson's still figure. And suddenly she smiled.

The girl with her, still gabbling, reached and caught his sleeve. She pointed to the floor. The cylinder lay smashed under their feet. A slight stain of moisture disappeared as he watched. "Did I?" repeated Janie. "I never had a chance, once this butterfly landed on me." She sobered, stood up, came into his arms. "Gerry . . . is he . . ."

"I don't think I killed him," said Hip and added, "yet."

"I can't tell you to kill him," Janie whispered.

"Yes," he said. "Yes, I know."

She said, "It's the first time the twins ever touched him. It was very brave. He could have burned out their brains in a second."

"They're wonderful. Bonnie!"

"Ho."

"Get me a knife. A sharp one with a blade at least so long. And a strip of black cloth, so-by-so."

Bonnie looked at Janie. Janie said, "What—"

He put his hand on her mouth. Her mouth was very soft. "Sh."

Janie said, panicked, "Bonnie, don't—"

Bonnie disappeared. Hip said, "Leave me alone with him for a while."

Janie opened her mouth to speak then turned and fled through the door. Beanie vanished.

Hip walked over to the prone figure and stood looking down at it. He did not think. He had his thought; all he had to do was hold it there.

Bonnie came through the door. She held a length of black velvet and a dagger with an eleven-inch blade. Her eyes were very big and her mouth was very small.

"Thanks, Bonnie." He took them. The knife was beautiful. Finnish, with an edge he could have shaved with, and a point drawn down almost to invisibility. "Beat it, Bonnie!"

She left—blip!—like a squirted appleseed. Hip put the knife and the cloth down on a table and dragged Thompson to a chair. He gazed about him, found a bell-pull and tore it down. He did not mind if a bell rang somewhere; he was rather sure he would not be interrupted. He tied Thompson's elbows and ankles to the chair, tipped the head back and made the blindfold.

He drew up another chair and sat close. He moved his knife hand gently, not quite tossing it, just feeling the scend of its superb balance in his palm. He waited.

And while he was waiting he took his thought, all of it, and placed it like a patterned drape across the entrance to his mind. He hung it fairly, attended to its folds and saw with meticulous care that it reached quite to the bottom, quite to the top and that there were no gaps at the sides.

The pattern read:

Listen to me, orphan boy, I am a hated boy too. You were persecuted; so was I.

Listen to me, cave boy. You found a place to belong and you learned to be happy in it. So did I.

Listen to me, Miss Kew's boy. You lost yourself for years until you went back and learned again. So did I.

Listen to me, *Gestalt* boy. You found power within you beyond your wildest dreams and you used it and loved it. So did I.

Listen to me, Gerry. You discovered that no matter how great your power, nobody wanted it. So did I.

You want to be wanted. You want to be needed. So do I.

Janie says you need morals. Do you know what morals are? Morals are an obedience to rules that people laid down to help you live among them.

You don't need morals. No set of morals can apply to you. You can obey no rules set down by your kind because there are no more of your kind. And you are not an ordinary man, so the morals of ordinary men would do you no better than the morals of an anthill would do me.

So nobody wants you and you are a monster.

Nobody wanted me when I was a monster.

But Gerry, there is another kind of code for you. It is a code which requires belief rather than obedience. It is called ethos.

The ethos will give you a code for survival too. But it is a greater survival than your own, or my species, or yours. What it is really is a reverence for your sources and your posterity. It is a study of the main current which created you, and in which you will create still a greater thing when the time comes.

Help humanity, Gerry, for it is your mother and your father now; you never had them before. And humanity will help you for it will produce more like you and then you will no longer be alone. Help them as they grow; help them to help humanity and gain still more of your own kind. For you are immortal, Gerry. You are immortal now.

And when there are enough of your kind, your ethics will be their morals. And when their morals no longer suit their species, you or another ethical being will create new ones that vault still farther up the main stream, reverencing you, reverencing those who bore you and the ones who bore them, back and back to the first wild creature who was different because his heart leapt when he saw a star.

I was a monster and I found this ethos. You are a monster. It's up to you.

Gerry stirred.

Hip Barrows stopped tossing the knife and held it still.

Gerry moaned and coughed weakly. Hip pulled the limp head back, cupped it in the palm of his left hand. He set the point of the knife exactly on the center of Gerry's larynx.

Gerry mumbled inaudibly. Hip said, "Sit quite still, Gerry."

He pressed gently on the knife. It went in deeper than he wanted it to. It was a beautiful knife. He said, "That's a knife at your throat. This is Hip Barrows. Now sit still and think about that for a while."

Gerry's lips smiled but it was because of the tension at the sides of his neck. His breath whistled through the not-smile.

"What are you going to do?"

"What would you do?"

"Take this thing off my eyes. I can't see."

"You see all you need to."

"Barrows. Turn me loose. I won't do anything to you. I promise. I can do a lot for you, Barrows. I can do anything you want."

"It is a moral act to kill a monster," said Hip. "Tell me something, Gerry. Is it true you can snatch out the whole of a man's thought just by meeting his eyes?"

"Let me go. Let me go," Gerry whispered.

With the knife at the monster's throat, with this great house which could be his, with a girl waiting, a girl whose anguish for him he could breathe like ozoned air, Hip Barrows prepared his ethical act.

When the blindfold fell away there was amazement in the strange round eyes, enough and more than enough to drive away hate. Hip dangled the knife. He arranged his thought, side to side, top to bottom. He threw the knife behind him. It clattered on the tiles. The startled eyes followed it, whipped back. The irises were about to spin. . . .

Hip bent close. "Go ahead," he said softly.

After a long time, Gerry raised his head and met Hip's eyes again.

Hip said, "Hi."

Gerry looked at him weakly. "Get the hell out of here," he croaked.

Hip sat still.

"I could've killed you," said Gerry. He opened his eyes a little wider. "I still could."

"You won't though." Hip rose, walked to the knife and picked it up. He returned to Gerry and deftly sliced the knots of the cord which bound him. He sat down again.

Gerry said, "No one ever . . . I never . . ." He shook himself and drew a deep breath. "I feel ashamed," he whispered. "No one ever made me feel ashamed." He looked at Hip, and the amazement was back again. "I know a lot. I can find out anything about anything. But I never . . . how did *you* ever find out all that?"

"Fell into it," said Hip. "An ethic isn't a fact you can look up. It's a way of thinking."

"God," said Gerry into his hands. "What I've done . . . the things I could have. . . ."

"The things you *can* do," Hip reminded him gently. "You've paid quite a price for the things you've done."

Gerry looked around at the huge glass room and everything in it that was massive, expensive, rich. "I have?"

Hip said, from the scarred depths of memory, "People all around you, you by yourself." He made a wry smile. "Does a superman have super-hunger, Gerry? Super-loneliness?"

Gerry nodded, slowly. "I did better when I was a kid." He shuddered. "Cold. . . ."

Hip did not know what kind of cold he meant, and did not ask. He rose. "I'd better go see Janie. She thinks maybe I killed you."

Gerry sat silently until Hip reached the door. Then he said, "Maybe you did."

Hip went out.

Janie was in the little anteroom with the twins. When Hip entered, Janie moved her head slightly and the twins disappeared.

Hip said, "I could tell them too."

"Tell me," Janie said. "They'll know."

He sat down next to her. She said, "You didn't kill him."

"No."

She nodded slowly, "I wonder what it would be like if he died. I—don't want to find out."

"He'll be all right now," Hip said. He met her eyes. "He was ashamed."

She huddled, cloaking herself, her thoughts. It was a waiting, but a different one from that he had known, for she was watching herself in her waiting, not him.

"That's all I can do. I'll clear out." He breathed once, deeply. "Lots to do. Track down my pension checks. Get a job."

"Hip—"

Only in so small a room, in such quiet, could he have heard her. "Yes, Janie."

"Don't go away."

"I can't stay."

"Why?"

He took his time and thought it out, and then he said, "You're a part of something. I wouldn't want to be part of someone who was . . . part of something."

She raised her face to him and he saw that she was smiling. He could not believe this, so he stared at her until he had to believe it.

She said, "The *Gestalt* has a head and hands, organs and a mind. But the most *human* thing about anyone is a thing he learns and . . . and earns. It's a thing he can't have when he's very young; if he gets it at all, he gets it after a long search and a deep conviction. After that it's truly part of him as long as he lives."

"I don't know what you mean. I—you mean I'm . . . I could be part of the . . . No, Janie, no." He could not escape from that sure smile. "What part?" he demanded.

"The prissy one who can't forget the rules. The one with the insight called ethics who can change it to the habit called morals."

"The still small voice!" He snorted. "I'll be damned!"

She touched him. "I don't think so."

He looked at the closed door to the great glass room. Then he sat down beside her. They waited.

It was quiet in the glass room.

For a long time the only sound was Gerry's difficult breathing. Suddenly even this stopped, as something happened, something—*spoke.*

It came again.

Welcome.

The voice was a silent one. And here, another, silent too, but another for all that. *It's the new one. Welcome, child!*

Still another: *Well, well, well! We thought you'd never make it.*

He had to. There hasn't been a new one for so long . . .

Gerry clapped his hands to his mouth. His eyes bulged. Through his mind came a hush of welcoming music. There was warmth and laughter and wisdom. There were introductions; for each voice there was a discrete personality, a comprehensible sense of something like stature or rank, and an accurate locus, a sense of physical position. Yet, in terms of amplitude, there was no difference in the voices. They were all here, or, at least, all equally near.

There was happy and fearless communion, fearlessly shared with Gerry—cross-currents of humor, of pleasure, of reciprocal thought and mutual achievement. And through and through, *welcome, welcome.*

They were young, they were new, all of them, though not as new and as young as Gerry. Their youth was in the drive and resilience of their thinking. Although some gave memories old in human terms, each entity had lived briefly in terms of immortality and they were all immortal.

Here was one who had whistled a phrase to Papa Haydn, and here one who had introduced William Morris to the Rossettis. Almost as if it were his own memory, Gerry saw Fermi being shown the streak of fission on a sensitive plate, a child Landowska listening to a harpsichord, a drowsy Ford with his mind suddenly lit by the picture of a line of men facing a line of machines.

To form a question was to have an answer.

Who are you?

Homo Gestalt.

I'm one; part of; belonging . . .

Welcome.

Why didn't you tell me?

You weren't ready. You weren't finished. What was Gerry before he met Lone?

And now . . . is it the ethic? Is that what completed me?

Ethic is too simple a term. But yes, yes . . . multiplicity is our first characteristic; unity our second. As your parts know they are parts of you, so must you know that we are parts of humanity.

Gerry understood then that the things which shamed him

were, each and all, things which humans might do to humans, but which humanity could not do. He said, "I was punished."

You were quarantined.

And—are you . . . we . . . responsible for all humanity's accomplishments?

No! We share. We are humanity!

Humanity's trying to kill itself.

(A wave of amusement, and a superb confidence, like joy.) *Today, this week, it might seem so. But in terms of the history of a race . . . O new one, atomic war is a ripple on the broad face of the Amazon!*

Their memories, their projections and computations flooded in to Gerry, until at last he knew their nature and their function; and he knew why the ethos he had learned was too small a concept. For here at last was power which could not corrupt; for such an insight could not be used for its own sake, or against itself. Here was why and how humanity existed, troubled and dynamic, sainted by the touch of its own great destiny. Here was the withheld hand as thousands died, when by their death millions might live. And here, too, was the guide, the beacon, for such times as humanity might be in danger; here was the Guardian of Whom all humans knew—not an exterior force nor an awesome Watcher in the sky, but a laughing thing with a human heart and a reverence for its human origins, smelling of sweat and new-turned earth rather than suffused with the pale odor of sanctity.

He saw himself as an atom and his *Gestalt* as a molecule. He saw these others as a cell among cells, and he saw in the whole the design of what, with joy, humanity would become.

He felt a rising, choking sense of worship, and recognized it for what it has always been for mankind—self-respect.

He stretched out his arms, and the tears streamed from his strange eyes. *Thank you*, he answered them. *Thank you, thank you . . .*

And humbly, he joined their company.

THE LONG TOMORROW

Leigh Brackett

"No city, no town, no community of more than one thousand people or two hundred buildings to the square mile shall be built or permitted to exist anywhere in the United States of America."

CONSTITUTION OF THE UNITED STATES
Thirtieth Amendment

Book One

1

LEN COLTER sat in the shade under the wall of the horse barn, eating pone and sweet butter and contemplating a sin. He was fourteen years old, and he had lived all of them on the farm at Piper's Run, where opportunities for real sinning were comfortably few. But now Piper's Run was more than thirty miles away, and he was having a look at the world, bright with distractions and gaudy with possibilities. He was at the Canfield Fair. And for the first time in his life Len Colter was faced with a major decision.

He was finding it difficult.

"Pa will beat the daylights out of me," he said, "if he finds out."

Cousin Esau said, "You scared?" He had turned fifteen just three weeks ago, which meant that he would not have to go to school any more with the children. He was still a long way from being counted among the men, but it was a big step and Len was impressed by it. Esau was taller than Len, and he had dark eyes that glittered and shone all the time like the eyes of an unbroken colt, looking everywhere for something and never quite finding it, perhaps because he did not know yet what it was. His hands were restless and very clever.

"Well?" demanded Esau. "Are you?"

Len would have liked to lie, but he knew that Esau would not be fooled for a minute. He squirmed a little, ate the last bite of pone, sucked the butter off his fingers, and said, "Yes."

"Huh," said Esau. "I thought you were getting grown-up. You should have still stayed home with the babies this year. Afraid of a licking!"

"I've had lickings before," said Len, "and if you think Pa can't lay 'em on, you try it some time. And I ain't even cried the last two years now. Well, not much, anyway." He brooded, his knees hunched up and his hands crossed on top of them, and his chin on his hands. He was a thin, healthy, rather solemn-faced boy. He wore homespun trousers and sturdy hand-pegged boots, covered thick in dust, and a shirt of coarse-loomed cotton with a narrow neckband and no collar. His hair was a light brown, cut off square above the shoulders and again above the eyes, and on his head he wore a brown flat-crowned hat with a wide brim.

Len's people were New Mennonites, and they wore brown hats to distinguish themselves from the original Old Mennonites, who wore black ones. Back in the Twentieth Century, only two generations before, there had been just the Old Mennonites and Amish, and only a few tens of thousands of them, and they had been regarded as quaint and queer because they held to the old simple handcraft ways and would have no part of cities or machines. But when the cities ended, and men found that in the changed world these of all folk were best fitted to survive, the Mennonites had swiftly multiplied into the millions they now counted.

"No," said Len slowly, "it's not the licking I'm scared of. It's Pa. You know how he feels about these preachin's. He forbid me. And Uncle David forbid you. You know how they feel. I don't think I want Pa mad at me, not that mad."

"He can't do no more than lick you," Esau said.

Len shook his head. "I don't know."

"Well, all right. Don't go, then."

"You going, for sure?"

"For sure. But I don't need you."

Esau leaned back against the wall and appeared to have forgotten Len, who moved the toes of his boots back and forth to make two stubby fans in the dust and continued to brood. The warm air was heavy with the smell of feed and animals, laced through with wood smoke and the fragrances of cooking. There were voices in the air, too, many voices, all blended together into a humming noise. You could think it was like a swarm of bees, or a wind rising and falling in the jack pines, but it was more than that. It was the world talking.

Esau said, "They fall down on the ground and scream and roll."

Len breathed deep, and his insides quivered. The fairgrounds stretched away into immensity on all sides, crammed with wagons and carts and sheds and stock and people, and this was the last day. One more night lying under the wagon, wrapped up tight against the September chill, watching the fires burn red and mysterious and wondering about the strangers who slept around them. Tomorrow the wagon would rattle away, back to Piper's Run, and he would not see such a thing again for another year. Perhaps never. In the midst of life we are in death. Or he might break a leg next year, or Pa might make him stay home like Brother James had had to this time, to see to Granma and the stock.

"Women, too," said Esau.

Len hugged his knees tighter. "How do you know? You never been."

"I heard."

"Women," whispered Len. He shut his eyes, and behind the lids there were pictures of wild preachings such as a New Mennonite never heard, of great smoking fires and vague frenzies and a figure, much resembling Ma in her bonnet and voluminous homespun skirts, lying on the ground and kicking like Baby Esther having a tantrum. Temptation came upon him, and he was lost.

He stood up, looking down at Esau. He said, "I'll go."

"Ah," said Esau. He got up too. He held out his hand, and Len shook it. They nodded at each other and grinned. Len's heart was pounding and he had a guilty feeling as though Pa stood right behind him listening to every word, but there was an exhilaration in this, too. There was a denial of authority, an assertion of self, a sense of being. He felt suddenly that he had grown several inches and broadened out, and that Esau's eyes showed a new respect.

"When do we go?" he asked.

"After dark, late. You be ready. I'll let you know."

The wagons of the Colter brothers were drawn up side by side, so that would not be hard. Len nodded.

"I'll pretend like I'm asleep, but I won't be."

"Better not," said Esau. His grip tightened, enough to squeeze Len's knuckles together so he'd remember. "Just don't let on about this, Lennie."

"Ow," said Len, and stuck his lip out angrily. "What do you think I am, a baby?"

Esau grinned, lapsing into the easy comradeship that is becoming between men. " 'Course not. That's settled, then. Let's go look over the horses again. I might want to give my dad some advice about that black mare he's thinking of trading for."

They walked together along the side of the horse barn. It

was the biggest barn Len had ever seen, four or five times as long as the one at home. The old siding had been patched a good bit, and it was all weathered now to an even gray, but here and there where the original wood was protected you could still see a smudge of red paint. Len looked at it, and then he paused and looked around the fairground, screwing up his eyes so that everything danced and quivered.

"What you doing now?" demanded Esau impatiently.

"Trying to see."

"Well, you can't see with your eyes shut. Anyway, what do you mean, trying to see?"

"How the buildings looked when they were all painted like Gran said. Remember? When she was a little girl."

"Yeah," said Esau. "Some red, some white. They must have been something." He squinted his eyes up too. The sheds and the buildings blurred, but remained unpainted.

"Anyway," said Len stoutly, giving up, "I bet they never had a fair as big as this one before, ever."

"What are you talking about?" Esau said. "Why, Gran said there was a million people here, and a million of those automobiles or cars or whatever you called them, all lined up in rows as far as you could see, with the sun just blazing on the shiny parts. A million of 'em!"

"Aw," said Len, "there couldn't be. Where'd they all have room to camp?"

"Dummy, they didn't have to camp. Gran said they came here from Piper's Run in less than an hour, and they went back the same day."

"I know that's what Gran said," Len remarked thoughtfully. "But do you really believe it?"

"Sure I believe it!" Esau's dark eyes snapped. "I wish I'd lived in those days. I'd have done things."

"Like what?"

"Like driving one of those cars, *fast*. Like even flying, maybe."

"Esau!" said Len, deeply shocked. "Better not let your pa hear you say that."

Esau flushed a little and muttered that he was not afraid, but he glanced around uneasily. They turned the corner of the barn. On the gable end, up above the door, there were four numbers made out of pieces of wood and nailed on. Len looked up at them. A one, a nine with a chunk gone out of the tail, a five, with the little front part missing, and a two. Esau said that was the year the barn was built, and that would be before even Gran was born. It made Len think of the meetinghouse in Piper's Run—Gran still called it a church—that had a date on it too, hidden way down behind the lilac bushes. That one said 1842—before, Len thought, almost anybody was born. He shook his head, overcome with a sense of the ancientness of the world.

They went in and looked at the horses, talking wisely of withers and cannon bones but keeping out of the way of the men who stood in small groups in front of this stall and that, with slow words and very quick eyes. They were almost all New Mennonites, differing from Len and Esau only in size and in the splendid beards that fanned across their chests, though their upper lips were clean shaven. A few, however, wore full whiskers and slouch hats of various sorts, and their clothes were cut to no particular pattern. Len stared at these furtively, with an intense curiosity. These men, or others like them—perhaps even still other kinds of men that he had not seen yet—were the ones who met secretly in fields and woods and preached and yelled and rolled on the ground. He could hear Pa's voice saying, "A man's religion, his sect, is his own affair. But those people have no religion or sect. They're a mob, with a mob's fear and cruelty, and with half-crazy, cunning men stirring them up against others." And then getting close-lipped and grim when Len questioned further and saying, "You're forbidden to go, that's all. No God-fearing person takes part in such wickedness." He understood now, and no wonder Pa hadn't wanted to talk about those women rolling on the ground and probably showing their drawers and everything. Len shivered with excitement and wished it would come night.

Esau decided that although the black mare in question was a trifle ewe-necked she looked as though she would handle well in harness, though his own choice would have been the fine bay stallion at the top of the row. And wouldn't *he* just take a cart flying! But you had to think of the women, who needed something safe and gentle. Len agreed, and they wandered out again, and Esau said, "Let's see what they're doing about those cows."

They meant Pa and Uncle David, and Len discovered that he would rather not see Pa just now. So he suggested going down to the traders' wagons instead. Cows you could and did see all the time. But traders' wagons were another matter. Three, four times in a summer, maybe, you saw one in Piper's Run, and here there were nineteen of them all together in one place at the same time.

"Besides," said Len with pure and simple greed, "you never can tell. Mr. Hostetter might give us some more of those sugar nuts."

"Fat chance," said Esau. But he went.

The traders' wagons were all drawn up in a line, their tongues outward and their backs in against a long shed. They were enormous wagons, with canvas tilts and all sorts of things hung to their ribs inside, so they were like dim, odorous caves on wheels.

Len looked at them, wide-eyed. To him they were not wagons, they were adventurous ships that had voyaged here from afar. He had listened to the traders' casual talk, and it had given him a vague vision of the whole wide and cityless land, the green, slow, comfortable agrarian land in which only a very few old folk could remember the awesome cities that had dominated the world before the Destruction. His mind held a blurred jumble of the faraway places of which the traders spoke: the little shipping settlements and fishing hamlets along the Atlantic, the lumber camps of the Appalachians, these endless New Mennonite farm lands of the Midwest, the Southern hunters and hill farmers, the great rivers westward with their barges and boats, the plains beyond and the horsemen and ranches and herds of wild cattle, the lofty mountains and the land and sea still farther west. A land as wide now as it had been centuries before, and through its dusty roads and sleepy villages these great trader wagons rolled, and rested, and rolled again.

Mr. Hostetter's wagon was the fifth one down, and Len knew it very well, because Mr. Hostetter brought it to Piper's Run every spring on his way north, and again every fall on his way south, and he had been doing that for more years than Len could personally remember. Other traders dropped through haphazardly, but Mr. Hostetter seemed like one of their own, though he had come from somewhere in Pennsylvania. He wore the same flat brown hat and the same beard, and went to meeting when he happened to be there on the Sabbath, and he had rather disappointed Len by telling him that where he came from was no different from where Len came from except that there were mountains around it, which did not seem right for a place with a magical name like Pennsylvania.

"If," said Len, harking back to the sugar nuts, "we offered to feed and water his team——" One could not beg, but the laborer is worthy of his hire.

Esau shrugged. "We can try."

The long shed, open on its front but closed in back to afford protection from rain, was partitioned off into stalls, one for each wagon. There wasn't much left in them now, after two and a half days, but women were still bargaining over copper kettles, and knives from the village forges of the East, or bolts of cotton cloth brought up from the South, or clocks from New England. The bulk cane sugar, Len knew, had gone early, but he was hoping that Mr. Hostetter had held onto a few small treasures for the sake of old friends.

"Huh," said Esau. "Look at that."

Mr. Hostetter's stall was empty and deserted.

"Sold out."

Len stared at the stall, frowning. Then he said, "His team still have to eat, don't they? And maybe we can help load stuff in the wagon. Let's go out back."

They went through the doorway at the rear of the stall, ducking around under the tailboard of the wagon and on past its side. The great wheels with the six-inch iron tires stood higher than Len did, and the canvas tilt loomed up like a cloud overhead, with EDW. HOSTETTER, GENERAL MERCHANDISE painted on it in neat letters, faded to gray by the sun and rain.

"He's here," said Len. "I can hear him talking."

Esau nodded. They went past the front wheel. Mr. Hostetter was just opposite, on the other side of the wagon.

"You're crazy," said Mr. Hostetter. "I'm telling you——"

The voice of another man interrupted. "Don't worry so much, Ed. It's all right. I've got to——"

The man broke off short as Len and Esau came around the front of the wagon. He was facing them across Mr. Hostetter's shoulder, a tall lean young fellow with long ginger hair and a full beard, dressed in plain leather. He was a trader from somewhere down South, and Len had seen him before in the shed. The name on his wagon tilt was William Soames.

"Company," he said to Mr. Hostetter. He did not seem to mind, but Mr. Hostetter turned around. He was a big man, large-jointed and awkward, very brown in the skin and blue in the eyes, and with two wide streaks of gray in his sandy beard, one on each side of his mouth. His movements were always slow and his smile was always friendly. But now he turned around fast, and he was not smiling at all, and Len stopped as though something had hit him. He stared at Mr. Hostetter as at a stranger, and Mr. Hostetter looked at him with a queer kind of a hot, blank glare. And Esau muttered, "I guess they're busy, Len. We better go."

"What do you want?" said Hostetter.

"Nothing," said Len. "We just thought maybe . . ." He let his voice trail off.

"Maybe what?"

"We could feed your horses," said Len, feebly.

Esau caught him by the arm. "He wanted more of those sugar nuts," he said to Hostetter. "You know how kids are. Come on, Len."

Soames laughed. "Don't reckon he's got any more. But how would some pecans do? Mighty fine!"

He reached into his pocket and pulled out four or five nuts. He put them in Len's hand. Len said, "Thank you," looking from him to Mr. Hostetter, who said quietly, "My team's all taken care of. Run along now, boys."

"Yes, sir," said Len, and ran. Esau loped at his heels. When they were around the corner of the shed they stopped and shared out the pecans.

"What was the matter with *him*?" he asked, meaning Hostetter. He was as astonished as though old Shep back at the farm had turned and snarled at him.

"Aw," said Esau, cracking the thin brown shells, "he and the foreigner were rowing over some trading deal, that's all." He was mad at Hostetter, so he gave Len a good hard shove. "You and your sugar nuts! Come on, it's almost time for supper. Or have you forgotten we're going somewhere tonight?"

"No," said Len, and something pricked with a delightful pain inside his belly. "I ain't forgotten."

2

THAT NERVOUS pricking in his middle was all that kept Len awake at first, after he had rolled up for the night under the family wagon. The outside air was chilly, the blanket was warm, he was comfortably full of supper, and it had been a long day. His eyelids would droop and things would get dim and far away, all washed over with a pleasant darkness. Then *pung!* would go that particular nerve, warning him, and he would tense up again, remembering Esau and the preaching.

After a while he began to hear things. Ma and Pa snored in the wagon overhead, and the fairgrounds were dark except for burned-out coals of the fires. They should have been quiet. But they were not. Horses moved and harness jingled. He heard a light cart go with a creak and a rattle, and way off somewhere a heavy wagon groaned on its way, the team snorting as they pulled. The strange people, the non-Mennonites like the gingery trader in his buckskin clothes, had all left just after sundown, heading for the preaching place. But these were other people going, people who did not want to be seen. Len stopped being sleepy. He listened to the unseen hoofs and the stealthy wheels, and he began to wish that he had not agreed to go.

He sat up cross-legged under the wagon bed, the blanket pulled around his shoulders. Esau had not come yet. Len stared across at Uncle David's wagon, hoping maybe Esau had gone to sleep himself. It was a long way, and cold and dark, and they would get caught sure. Besides that, he had felt guilty all through supper, not wanting to look straight at Pa. It was the first time he had, deliberately and of choice, disobeyed his father, and he knew the guilt must show all over his face. But Pa hadn't noticed it, and somehow that made Len feel worse instead of better. It meant Pa trusted him so much that he never bothered to look for it.

There was a stir in the shadows under Uncle David's wagon, and it was Esau, coming quietly on all fours.

I'll tell him, thought Len. I'll say I won't go.

Esau crept closer. He grinned, and his eyes shone bright in the glow of the banked-up fire. He put his head close to Len's and whispered, "They're all asleep. Roll your blanket up like you were still in it, just in case."

I won't go, thought Len. But the words never came out of his mouth. He rolled up his blanket and slid away after Esau, into the night. And right away, as soon as he was out of sight of the wagon, he was glad. The darkness was full of motion, of a going and a secret excitement, and he was going too. The taste of wickedness was sweet in his mouth, and the stars had never looked so bright.

They went carefully until they came to an open lane, and then they began to run. A high-wheeled cart raced by them, the horse stepping high and fast, and Esau panted, "Come on, come on!" He laughed, and Len laughed, running. In a few minutes they were out of the fairgrounds and on the main road, deep in dust from three rainless weeks. Dust hung in the air, roiled up by the passing wheels and roiled again before it could settle. A team of horses loomed up in it, huge and ghostly, shaking foam off their bits. They were pulling a wagon with an open tilt, and the man who drove them looked like a blacksmith, with thick arms and a short blond beard. There was a stout red-cheeked woman beside him. She had a rag tied over her head instead of a bonnet and her skirts blew out on the wind. From under the tied-up edge of the tilt there looked a row of little heads, all yellow as corn silk. Esau ran fast beside the wagon, shouting, with Len pounding along behind him. The man pulled down his horses and squinted at them. The woman looked too, and they both laughed.

"Lookit 'em," the man said. "Little flat-hats. Where you goin' without your mama, little flat-hats?"

"We're going to the preaching," Esau said, mad about the flat-hat and madder still about the little, but not mad enough to lose the chance of a lift. "May we ride with you?"

"Why not?" said the man, and laughed again. He said some stuff about Gentiles and Samaritans that Len did not quite understand, and some more about listening to a Word, and then he told them to get in, that they were late already. The horses had not stopped all this time, and Len and Esau were floundering in the roadside briers, keeping up. They scrambled in over the tailboard and lay gasping on the straw that was there, and the man yelled to the horses and they were off again, banging and bumping and the dust flying up through the cracks in the floor boards. The straw was dusty. There was a big dog in it, and seven kids, all staring at Len and Esau with round-eyed hostility. They stared back, and then the oldest boy pointed and said, "Looka the funny hats." They all laughed. Esau asked, "What's it to you?" and the boy said, "This's our wagon, that's what's it to me, and if you don't like it you can get out." They went on making fun of their clothes, and Len glowered, thinking that they didn't have much room to talk. They were all seven barefoot and had no hats at all, though they looked thrifty enough, and clean. He didn't say anything back, though, and neither did Esau. Three or four miles was a long way to walk at night.

The dog was friendly. He licked their faces all over and sat on them impartially, all the way to the preaching ground. And Len wondered if the woman on the wagon seat would get down on the ground and roll, and if the man would roll with her. He thought how silly they would look, and giggled, and suddenly he was not mad at the yellow-haired kids any more.

The wagon came in finally among many others in a very large open field that sloped down toward a little river, running maybe twenty feet wide now with the dry weather, and low between its banks. Len thought there must be as many people as there had been at the fair, only they were all crowded together, the rigs jammed in a rough circle at the back and everybody gathered in the center, sitting on the ground. One flat-bed wagon, with the horses unhitched, was pulled close to the riverbank. Everybody was facing it, and a man was standing on it, in the light of a huge bonfire. He was a young man, tall and big-chested. His black beard came down almost to his waist, shiny as a crow's breast in the spring, and he kept shaking it as he moved around, tossing his head and shouting. His voice was high and piercing, and it did not come in a continuous flow of words. It came in short sharp pieces that stabbed the air, each one, clear to the farthest rows before the next one was flung out. It was a minute before Len realized the man was preaching. He was used to a different way of it in Sabbath meeting, when Pa or Uncle David or anybody could get up and speak to God, or about Him. They always did it quietly, with their hands folded.

He had been staring out over the side of the wagon. Now, before the wheels had fairly stopped turning, Esau punched him and said, "Come on." He jumped out over the tailboard. Len followed him. The man called something after them about the Word, and all seven of the kids made faces. Len said politely, "Thank you for the ride." Then he ran after Esau.

From here the preaching man looked small and far away, and Len couldn't hear much of what he said. Esau whispered, "I think we can get right up close, but don't make any noise." Len nodded. They scuttled around behind the parked rigs, and Len noticed that there were others who seemed to want to remain out of sight. They hung back on the edges of the crowd, in among the wagons, and Len could see them only as dark shapes silhouetted against the firelight. Some of them had taken their hats off, but the cut of their clothes and hair still gave them away. They were of Len's own people. He knew how they felt. He had a shyness himself about being seen.

As he and Esau worked their way down toward the river, the voice of the preaching man grew louder. There was something strident about it, and stirring, like the scream of an angry stallion. His words came clearer.

"—went a-whoring after strange gods. You know that, my friends. Your own parents have told you, your own old grannies and your aged grandpas have confessed it, how that the hearts of the people were full of wickedness, and blasphemies, and lust——"

Len's skin prickled with excitement. He followed Esau in and out through a confusion of wheels and horses' legs, holding his breath. And finally they were where they could see out from the shelter of a good black shadow between the wheels of a cart, and the preacher was only a few yards away.

"They lusted, my brethren. They lusted after everything strange, and new, and unnatural. And Satan saw that they did and he blinded their eyes, the heavenly eyes of the soul, so that they were like foolish children, crying after the luxuries and the soul-rotting pleasures. And they forgot God."

A moaning and a rocking swept over the people who sat on

the ground. Len caught hold of a wheel spoke in each hand and thrust his face between them.

The preaching man sprang to the very edge of the wagon. The night wind shook out his beard and his long black hair, and behind him the fire burned and shot up smoke and sparks, and the preaching man's eyes burned too, huge and black. He flung his arm out straight, pointing at the people, and said in a curious harsh whisper that carried like a cry, "*They forgot God!*"

Again the rocking and the moaning. It was louder this time. Len's heart had begun to pound.

"Yes, my brethren. They forgot. But did God forget? No, I tell you, He did not forget! He watched them. He saw their iniquities. He saw how the Devil had hold on them, and He saw that they liked it—yes, my friends, they liked old Satan the Betrayer, and they would not leave his ways for the ways of God. And why? Because Satan's ways were easy and smooth, and there was always some new luxury just around the next bend in the downward path."

Len became conscious of Esau, crouched beside him in the dust. He was staring at the preaching man, and his eyes glittered. His mouth was open wide. Len's pulses hammered. The voice of the preaching man seemed to flick him like a whip on nerves he had never known he had before. He forgot about Esau. He hung to his wheelspokes and thought hungrily, Go on, go on!

"And so what did God do, when He saw that His children had turned from Him? You know what He did, my brethren! You know!"

Moan and rock, and the moaning became a low strange howl.

"He said, 'They have sinned! They have sinned against My laws, and against My prophets, who warned them even in old Jerusalem against the luxuries of Egypt and of Babylon! And they have exalted themselves in their pride. They have climbed up into the heavens which are My throne, and they have rent open the earth which is My footstool, and they have loosed the sacred fire which lies at the very heart of things, and which only I, the Lord Jehovah, should dare to touch.' And God said, 'Even so, I am merciful. Let them be cleansed of their sin.' "

The howling rose louder, and all across the open field there was a tossing of arms and a writhing of heads.

"Let them be cleansed!" cried the preaching man. His body was strained up, quivering, and the sparks shot up past him. "God said it, and they were cleansed, my brethren! With their own sins they were chastised. They were burned with the fires of their own making, yea, and the proud towers vanished in the blazing of the wrath of God! And with fire and famine and thirst and fear they were driven from their cities, from the places of iniquity and lust, even our own fathers and our fathers' fathers, who had sinned, and the places of iniquity were made not, even as Sodom and Gomorrah."

Somewhere across the crowd a woman screamed and fell backward, beating her head against the earth. Len never noticed.

The voice of the preaching man sank down again to that harsh far-carrying whisper.

"And so we were spared of God's mercy, to find His way and follow it."

"Hallelujah," screamed the crowd. "Hallelujah!"

The preaching man held up his hands. The crowd quieted. Len held his breath, waiting. His eyes were fixed on the black burning eyes of the man on the wagon. He saw them narrow down, until they looked like the eyes of a cat just ready to spring, only they were the wrong color.

"But," said the preaching man, "Satan is still with us."

The rows of people jerked forward with a feral yelp, held down and under by the hands of the preacher.

"He wants us back. He remembers what it was like, the Devil does, when he had all those soft fair women to serve him, and all the rich men, and the cities all shining with lights to be his shrines! He remembers, and he wants them back! So he sends his emissaries among us—oh, you wouldn't know them from your own God-fearing folk, my brethren, with their meek ways and sober garments! But they go about secretly proselyting, tempting our boys and young men, dangling the forbidden serpent's fruit in front of them, and on the brow of every one of them is the mark of the beast—the mark of Bartorstown!"

Len pricked his ears up higher at that. He had heard the name of Bartorstown just once before, from Granma, and he remembered it because of the way Pa had shut her up. The crowd yowled, and some of them got up on their feet. Esau pressed up closer against Len, and he was quivering all over. "Ain't this something?" he whispered. "Ain't this something!"

The preaching man looked all around. He didn't quiet the people this time, he let them quiet down of themselves, out of their eagerness to hear what he had to say next. And Len sensed something new in the air. He did not know what it was, but it excited him so he wanted to scream and leap up and down, and at the same time it made him uneasy. It was something these people understood, they and the preaching man together.

"Now," said the man on the wagon, quietly, "there are some sects, all God-fearing folk, I'm not saying they don't try, that think it's enough to say to one of these emissaries of Satan, Go, leave our community, and don't come back. Now maybe they just don't understand that what they're really saying is, Go and corrupt somebody else, we'll keep our own house clean!" A sharp downward wave of his hands stifled a cry from the people as though he had shoved a cork in their mouths. "No, my friends. That is not our way. We think of our neighbor as ourself. We honor the government law that says there shall be no more cities. And we honor the Word of God, who saith that if our right eye offend us we must pluck it out, and if our right hand offend us we must cut it off, and that the righteous can have no part with evil men, no, not if they be our own brothers or fathers or sons!"

A noise went up from the people now that turned Len hot all over and closed up his throat and made his eyeballs prick. Somebody threw wood on the bonfire. It roared up a torrent of sparks and a yellow glaring of flame, and there were people rolling on the ground now, men and women both, clawing up the dirt with their fingers and screaming. Their eyes were all white, and it was not funny. And over the crowd and the firelight went the voice of the preaching man, howling shrill and mighty like a great animal in the night.

"If there be evil among you, cast it forth!"

A lank boy with the beard just sprouting on his chin leaped up. He pointed. He cried out, "I accuse him!" and the froth ran wet in the corners of his mouth.

There was a sudden violent surge in one place. A man had sprung up and tried to run, and others caught him. Their shoulders heaved and their legs danced, and the people around them hunkered out of the way, pushing and tugging at them. They dragged the man back finally, and Len got a clear look at him. It was the ginger-haired trader William Soames. But his face was different now, pale and still and awful.

The preaching man yelled something about root and branch. He was crouched on the edge of the wagon now, his hands high in the air. They began to strip the trader. They tore the stout leather shirt off his back and they ripped the buckskin breeches from his legs, exposing him white and stark. He wore soft boots on his feet and one of these came off, and the other they forgot and left on him. Then they drew back away from him, so that he was all alone in the middle of an open space. Somebody threw a stone.

It hit Soames on the mouth. He reeled over a little and put up his arms, but another stone came, and another, and sticks and clods of earth, and his white skin was all blotched and streaked. He turned this way and that, falling, stumbling, doubling up, trying to find a way out, trying to ward off the blows. His mouth was open and his teeth showed with the blood running over them and down into his beard, but Len couldn't hear whether he cried out or not because of the noise the crowd was making, a gasping screeching greedy obscene gabble, and the stones kept hitting him. Then the whole mob began to move toward the river, driving him. He came close past the cart, past the shadow where Len was watching through the spokes, and Len saw clearly into his eyes. The men came after him, their boots striking heavy on the dusty ground, and the women came too, with their hair flying and the stones in their hands. Soames fell down the bank into the shallow river. The men and women went after him and covered him the way flies cover a piece of offal after a butchering, and their hands rose and fell.

Len turned his head and looked at Esau. He was crying, and his face was white. Esau had his arms folded tight across his middle, and his body was bent over them. His eyes were huge and staring. Suddenly he turned and rushed away on all fours under the cart. Len bolted after him, scrambling, crabwise, with the air dark and whirling around him. All he could think about was the pecans Soames had given him. He turned sick and stopped to vomit, with a terrible icy coldness on him. The crowd still screamed by the riverbank. When he straightened up, Esau was gone in the shadows.

In a panic he fled between the carts and the wagons. He kept saying, "Esau! Esau!" but there was no answer, or if there was he couldn't hear it for the voice of murder in his ears. He shot out blindly into an open space, and there was a tall looming figure there that stretched out long arms and caught him.

"Len," it said. "Len Colter."

It was Mr. Hostetter. Len felt his knees give. It got very black and quiet, and he heard Esau's voice, and then Mr. Hostetter's, but far and tiny, like voices carried by the wind on a heavy day. Then he was in a wagon, huge and full of unfamiliar smells, and Mr. Hostetter was boosting Esau in after him. Esau looked like a ghost. Len said, "You said it would be fun." And Esau said, "I didn't know they ever——" He hiccuped and sat down beside Len, his head on his knees.

"Stay put," said Mr. Hostetter. "I have to get something."

He went away. Len raised up and watched, his eyes drawn toward the fire glare and the wailing, sobbing, shrieking mob that wavered to and fro crying that they were saved. Glory glory, hallelujah, the wages of sin are death, hallelujah!

Mr. Hostetter ran across the open space to another trader's wagon, parked beside a clump of trees. Len couldn't see the name on the canvas, but he was sure it was Soames's wagon. Esau watched too. The preaching man was going at it again, waving his arms high in the air.

Mr. Hostetter jumped out of the other wagon and ran back. He was carrying a small chest, maybe a foot long, under one arm. He climbed up onto the seat, and Len scuttled forward inside the wagon. "Please," he said. "Can I sit beside you?"

Hostetter handed him the box. "Stow this inside. All right, climb up. Where's Esau?"

Len looked back. Esau was curled up on the floor, lying with his face down on a bundle of homespun. He called him, but

Esau did not answer. "Passed out," said Hostetter. He uncurled his whip with a crack and shouted to the horses. The six great bays leaned like one horse into the breastbands and the wagon rolled. It rolled faster and faster, and the firelight was left behind, and the voice of the crowd. There was the dark road and the dark tree beside it, the smell of dust, and the peaceful fields. The horses slowed to an easier gait. Mr. Hostetter put his arm around Len, and Len clung to him.

"Why did they do it?" he asked.

"Because they're afraid."

"Of what?"

"Of yesterday," said Mr. Hostetter. "Of tomorrow." Suddenly, with astounding fury, he cursed them. Len stared at him, open-mouthed. Hostetter shut his jaws tight in the middle of a word and shook his head. Len could feel him tremble all over. When he spoke again his voice was normal, or almost.

"Stick with your own people, Len. You won't find any better."

Len murmured, "Yes, sir." Nobody spoke after that. The wagon rocked along and the motion made Len drowsy, not a good drowsiness of sleep, but the sickish kind that comes with exhaustion. Esau was very quiet in the back. Finally the team slowed to a walk, and Len saw that they were back in the fairgrounds.

"Where's your wagon?" asked Hostetter, and Len told him. When they came in sight of it, the fire was built up again and Pa and Uncle David were standing beside it. They looked grim and angry, and when the boys got down they did not say a word, except to thank Hostetter for bringing them back. Len looked at Pa. He wanted to get down on his knees and say, "Father, I have sinned." But all he could do was to stand there and begin to sob and shake again.

"What happened?" asked Pa.

Hostetter told him, in four words. "There was a stoning."

Pa looked at Esau and Uncle David, and then he looked at Len and sighed. "Only once in a long time do they really do such a thing, but this had to be the time. The boys were forbidden, but they would go, and so they had to see it." He said to Len, "Hush, boy. Hush now, it's all over." He pushed him, not ungently, toward the wagon. "Go on, Lennie, you get into your blanket and go to sleep."

Len crept under the wagon and rolled the blanket around him and lay there. A weak, dark feeling came over him, and the world began to slip away, carrying with it the memory of Soames's dying face. Through the canvas he heard Mr. Hostetter saying, "I tried to warn the man this afternoon that the fanatics were whispering about him. I followed him there tonight, to get him to come away. But I was too late, there was nothing I could do."

Uncle David asked, "Was he guilty?"

"Of proselyting? You know better than that. The men of Bartorstown don't proselyte."

"Then he was from Bartorstown?"

"Soames came from Virginia. I knew him as a trader, and a fellow man."

"Guilty or not," Pa said heavily, "it's an unchristian thing. And blasphemous. But as long as there are crazed or crafty leaders to play on old fears, a mob like that will turn cruel."

"All of us," answered Hostetter, "have our old fears."

He climbed up on the seat again and drove away. But Len never heard the end of his going.

3

THREE WEEKS had gone by, lacking a day or two, and in Piper's Run it was October, and a Sabbath afternoon. Len sat alone on the side stoop.

After a while the door behind him opened, and he knew from the scuffling footsteps and the thump of the cane that it was Gran coming out. She clamped one bony, amazingly strong hand on his wrist and clambered down two steps and then sat, folding up stiffly like a dry twig when you bend it.

"Thank you, thank you," said Gran, and began arranging her several layers of skirts around her ankles.

"Do you want a rug for under you?" asked Len. "Or do you want your shawl?"

"No, it's warm in the sun."

Len sat down again, beside her. With his brows pulled together and his mouth pulled down, he looked nearly as old as

Gran and much more solemn. She peered at him closely, and he began to feel uncomfortable, knowing that he had been sought out.

"You're mighty broody these days, Lennie."

"I guess so."

"You ain't sulking, are you? I hate a sulker."

"No, Gran. I'm not sulking."

"Your pa was right to punish you. You disobeyed him, and you know now he forbid you for your own good."

Len nodded. "I know."

Pa had not delivered the expected beating. In fact, he had been gentler than Len would have dreamed possible. He had spoken very seriously about what Len had done and what he had seen, and he had finished with the statement that Len was not to go to the fair next year at all, and perhaps not the year after, unless he had been able to prove by then that he could be trusted. Len considered that Pa had been mighty decent. Uncle David had licked Esau to the last inch of his skin. And since at this moment Len did not feel that he ever wanted to see the fair again, being denied it was no hardship.

He said so, and Gran smiled her toothless ancient smile and patted his knee. "You'll feel different a year from now. That's when it'll hurt."

"Maybe."

"Well, if you're not sulking, there's something else the matter with you. What is it?"

"Nothing."

"Lennie, I've had a lot to do with boys, and I know no natural healthy boy should mope around like you do. And on a day like this, even if it is the Sabbath." She looked up at the deep blue sky and sniffed the golden air, and then she looked at the woods that encircled the farmstead, seeing them not as groups of individual trees but as a glorious blur of colors she had almost forgotten the names for. She sighed, half in pleasure, half in regret.

"Seems like this is the only time you see real colors any more, when the trees turn in the fall. The world used to be full of colors. You wouldn't believe it, Lennie, but I had a dress once, as red as that tree."

"It must have been pretty." He tried to picture Gran as a

little girl in a red dress and failed, partly because he could not imagine her as anything but an old woman, and partly because he had never seen anybody dressed in red.

"It was beautiful," said Gran slowly, and sighed again.

They sat together on the step, and did not speak, and looked at nothing. And all at once Gran said, "I know what ails you. You're still thinking about the stoning."

Len began to shake a little. He did not want to, but he couldn't make it stop. He blurted out, "Oh, Gran, it was—— He still had one boot on. He was all naked except for this one boot, and he looked so funny. And they kept on throwing stones——"

If he shut his eyes, he could see again how the blood and the dirt ran together on the man's white skin, and how the hands of the people rose and fell.

"Why did they do it, Gran? Why?"

"Better ask your pa."

"He said they were afraid, and that fear makes stupid people do wicked things, and that I should pray for them." Len ran the back of his hand violently across his nose. "I wouldn't pray a word for them, except that somebody would throw stones at them."

"You've only seen one bad thing," said Gran, shaking her head with the close white cap slowly from side to side, her eyes half shut and looking inward. "If you'd seen the things I saw, you'd know what fear can do. And I was younger than you, Lennie."

"It was awful bad, wasn't it, Gran?"

"I'm an old woman, an old old woman, and I still dream—— There were fires in the sky, red fires, there and there and there." Her gaunt hand pointed out three places in a semicircle westward, and from south to north. "They were cities burning. The cities I used to go to with my mother. And the people from them came, and the soldiers came, and there were shelters in every field, and people crowded into the barns and the houses anywhere they could, and all our stock was butchered to feed them, forty head of fine dairy cows. Those were bad, bad times. It's a mercy anybody lived through them."

"Is that why they killed the man?" asked Len. "Because they're afraid he might bring all that back again—the cities, and all?"

"Isn't that what they said at the preaching?" said Gran, knowing full well, since she had been to preachings herself many decades ago when the terror brought the great boiling up of faith that birthed new sects and strengthened the old ones.

"Yes. They said he tempted the boys with some kind of fruit, I guess they meant from the Tree of Knowledge like it says in the Bible. And they said he came from a place called Bartorstown. What is Bartorstown, Gran?"

"You ask your pa," she said, and began to fuss with her apron. "Where'd I put that handkerchief? I know I had it——"

"I did ask him. He said there wasn't any such place."

"Hmph," said Gran.

"He said only children and fanatics believed in it."

"Well, I ain't going to tell you any different, so don't try to make me."

"I won't, Gran. But was there ever, maybe a long time ago?"

Gran found her handkerchief. She wiped her face and her eyes with it, and snuffled, and put it away, and Len waited.

"When I was a little girl," said Gran, "we had this war."

Len nodded. Mr. Nordholt, the schoolmaster, had told them a good bit about it, and it had got connected in his mind with the Book of Revelations, grand and frightening.

"It came on for a long time, I guess," Gran continued. "I remember on the teevee they talked about it a lot, and they showed pictures of the bombs that made clouds just like a tremendous mushroom, and each one could wipe out a city, all by itself. Oh yes, Lennie, there was a rain of fire from heaven and many were consumed in it! The Lord gave it to the enemy for a day to be His flail."

"But we won."

"Oh yes, in the end we won."

"Did they build Bartorstown then?"

"Before the war. The gover'ment built it. That was when the gover'ment was still in Washington, and it was a lot different than it is now. Bigger, somehow. I don't know, a little girl doesn't care much about those things. But they built a lot of secret places, and Bartorstown was the most secret of all, way out West somewhere."

"If it was so secret, how did you know about it?"

"They told about it on the teevee. Oh, they didn't tell where it was or what it was for, and they said it might be only a rumor. But I remember the name."

"Then," said Len softly, "it was real!"

"But that's not saying it is now. That was a long time ago. It's maybe just the memory of it hung on, like your pa said, with children and fanatics." She added tartly under her breath that she wasn't either one of those, herself. Then she said, "You leave it alone, Lennie. Don't have any truck with the Devil, and he won't have any with you. You don't want happening to you what happened to that man at the preaching."

Lennie turned hot and cold all over again. But curiosity made him ask in spite of that, "Is Bartorstown such a terrible place?"

"It is," said Gran with sour wisdom, "if everybody thinks it is. Oh, I know! All my life I've had to watch my tongue. I can remember the world the way it was before. I was only a little girl, but I was old enough for that, almost as old as you. And I can remember very well how we got to be Mennonites, that never were Mennonites before. Sometimes I wish——" She broke off, and looked again at the flaming trees. "I did love that red dress."

Another silence.

"Gran."

"Well, what is it?"

"What were the cities like, really?"

"Better ask your pa."

"You know what he always says. Besides, he never saw them. You did, Gran. You can remember."

"The Lord in His infinite wisdom destroyed them. It's not up to you to question. Nor me."

"I'm not questioning—I'm only asking. What were they like?"

"They were big. A hundred Piper's Runs wouldn't have made up a half of even a small city. They had all hard pavements, with walks at the side for the people, and big wide roads in the middle for the cars, and there were great big buildings that went way up in the air. They were noisy, and the air smelled different, and there were always a lot of people hurrying back and forth. I always liked to go to the city. Nobody thought they were wicked then."

Len's eyes were large and round.

"They had big movie theaters, huge, with plush seats, and supermarkets twice as big as that barn, with every kind of food in them, all in bright shiny packages—the things you could buy any day in the week that you've never even heard of, Lennie! White sugar, we thought nothing of it. And spices, and fresh vegetables all winter, frozen into little bricks. And the things there were in the stores! Oh, so many things, I couldn't begin to tell you, clothes and toys and 'lectric washers and books and radios and teevee sets——"

She rocked back and forth a little, and her old eyes flashed.

"Christmas time," she said. "Oh, at Christmas time with the windows all decorated and the lights and the carols! All colors and brightness and people laughing. It wasn't wicked. It was wonderful."

Len's jaw dropped. He sat that way, with his mouth open, and a heavy step vibrated along the floor from inside, and he tried to tell Gran to hush, but she had forgotten he was there.

"Cowboys on the teevee," she mumbled, reaching far back across the troubled decades. "Music, and ladies in beautiful dresses that left their shoulders all bare. I thought I would look like that when I got big. Picture books, and Mr. Bloomer's drugstore with the ice cream and the chocolate rabbits at Easter——"

Pa came out the door. Len got up and went down to the bottom of the steps. Pa looked at him, and Len crumbled inside, thinking that life had been nothing but trouble for the last three weeks.

"Water," said Gran, "that ran out of shiny faucets when you turned them. And a bathroom right in the house, and 'lectric light——"

Pa said to Len, "Did you get her talking?"

"No, honest," said Len. "She started off herself, about a red dress."

"Easy," said Gran. "All easy, and bright, and comfortable. That was the world. And then it was gone. So fast."

Pa said, "Mother."

She glanced up at him, sidelong, and her eyes were like two faded sparks, snapping and flaring. She said, "Flat-hat."

"Now, Mother——"

"I wish I had it back," said Gran. "I wish I had a red dress, and a teevee, and a nice white porcelain toilet, and all the other things. It was a good world! I wish it hadn't ended."

"But it did end," said Pa. "And you are a foolish old woman to question the goodness of God." He was talking less to her than to Len, and he was very angry. "Did any of those things help you to survive? Did they help the people of the cities? Did they?"

Gran turned her face away and would not answer.

Pa came down and stood in front of her. "You understand me, Mother. Answer me. Did they?"

Tears came into Gran's eyes, and the fire died out of them. "I'm an old woman," she said. "It isn't right for you to yell at me that way."

"Mother. Did those things help one single person to survive?"

She let her head fall forward and moved it slowly from side to side.

"No," said Pa, "and I know because you told me how no food came in any more to the markets, and nothing would work on the farms because there was no power any more, and no fuel. And only those who had always lived without all the luxuries, and done for themselves with their own hands, and had no truck with the cities, came through without hurt and led us all in the path of peace and plenty and humility before God. And you dare to scoff at the Mennonites! Chocolate rabbits," said Pa, and stamped his boots on the earth. "Chocolate rabbits! No wonder the world fell."

He swung around to include Len in the circle of his wrath. "Haven't you got any thankfulness in your hearts, either of you? Can't you be grateful for a good harvest, and good health, and a warm house, and plenty to eat? What more does God have to give you to make you happy?"

The door opened again. Ma Colter's face appeared, round and pink and full of reproof, framed in a tight white cap. "Elijah! Are you raising your voice to your mother, and on the Sabbath day?"

"I had provocation," said Pa, and stood breathing hard through his nose for a minute or two. Then, more quietly, he said to Len, "Go to the barn."

Len's heart sank down into his knees. He began to shuffle away across the yard. Ma came clear out the door, onto the stoop.

"Elijah, the Sabbath day is no time——"

"It's for the good of the boy's soul," said Pa, in the voice that meant no more argument. "Just leave this to me, please."

Ma shook her head, but she went back inside. Pa walked behind Len toward the open barn doors. Gran sat where she was on the steps.

"I don't care," she whispered. "Those things were good." After a minute she repeated fiercely, "Good, good, *good!*" Tears ran slowly down her cheeks and dropped onto the bosom of her drab homespun dress.

Inside the barn, warm and shadowy and sweet with the stored hay, Pa took the length of harness strap down from its nail on the wall, and Len took off his jacket. He waited, but Pa stood there looking at him and frowning, drawing the supple leather through his fingers. Finally he said, "No, that's not the way," and hung the strap back on the wall.

"Aren't you going to lick me?" Len whispered.

"Not for your grandmother's foolishness. She's very old, Len, and the very old are like children. Also, she lived through terrible years and worked hard and uncomplainingly for a long lifetime—perhaps I shouldn't blame her too much for thinking of the easeful things she had in her childhood. And I suppose it's not in the nature of a human boy not to listen to it."

He turned away, walking up and down by the stanchions, and when he stopped he kept his face turned from Len.

He said, "You saw a man die. That's your trouble, isn't it, and the cause of all these questions?"

"Yes, Pa. I just can't forget it."

"Don't forget it," said Pa with sudden forcefulness. "Since you saw it, remember it always. That man chose a certain path, and it led him to a certain end. The way of the transgressor has always been hard, Len. It'll never be easy."

"I know," said Len. "But just because he came from a place called Bartorstown——"

"Bartorstown is more than a place. I don't know whether it exists or not, in the way that Piper's Run exists, and if it does, I don't know whether any of the things they say about it are true. Whether they are or not doesn't matter. Men believe them. Bartorstown is a way of thought, Len. The trader was stoned to death because he chose that way."

"The preaching man said he wanted to bring the cities back. Is Bartorstown a city, Pa? Do they have things there like Gran had when she was little?"

Pa turned and put his hands on Len's shoulders. "Many and many is the time, Len, that my father beat me, here in this very place, for asking questions like that. He was a good man, but he was like your uncle David, quicker with the strap than he was with his tongue. I heard all the stories, from Mother and from all the people of the generation before her who were still alive then and remembered even better than she did. And I used to think how fine all the luxuries must have been, and I wondered why they were so sinful. And Father told me I was headed straight for hell and strapped me until I could hardly stand. He'd lived through the Destruction himself, and the fear of God was stronger in his heart than it was in mine. That was bitter medicine, Len, but I'm not sure it didn't save me. And if I must, I'll treat you the same way, though I'd rather you didn't make me."

"I won't, Pa," Len said hastily.

"I hope not. Because you see, Len, it's all so useless. Forget for a moment about whether it's sinful or not, and just think about the solid facts. All those things that Gran talks about, the teevees, the cars, the railroads, and the airplanes, depended on the cities." He frowned and made motions with his hands, trying to explain. "Concentration, Len. Organization. Like the works of a clock, every little piece depending on every other little piece to make it go. One man didn't make an automobile, the way a good wainwright makes a wagon. It took thousands of men, all working together, and depending on thousands of other men in other places to make the fuel and the rubber so the automobiles could run when they did build them. It was the cities that made those things possible, Len, and when the cities went they were not possible any more. So we don't have them. We never will have them."

"Not ever, as long as the world?" asked Len, with a wistful sense of loss.

"That's in the hands of the Lord," said Pa. "But we won't

live as long as the world. Len, you'd as well hanker after the Pharaohs of Egypt as after the things that were lost in the Destruction."

Len nodded, deep in thought. "I still don't see, though, Pa—why did they have to *kill* the man?"

Pa sighed. "Men do what they believe to be right, or what they think is necessary to protect themselves. A terrible scourge came onto this world. Those of us who survived it have labored and fought and sweat for two generations to recover from it. Now we're prosperous and at peace, and nobody wants that scourge to come back. When we find men who seem to carry the seeds of it, we take steps against them, according to our different ways. And some ways are violent."

He handed Len his jacket. "Here, put it on. And then I want you to go into the fields and look around you, and think about what you see, and I want you to ask God for the greatest gift He has in His power to give, a contented heart. And I want you to think of the dead man as a sign that was given you to remind you of the wages of folly, which are just as bad as the wages of sin."

Len pulled his jacket on. He nodded and smiled at Pa, loving him.

Pa said, "Just one more thing. Esau got you to go to that preaching."

"I didn't say——"

"You don't have to, I know you and I know Esau. Now I'm going to tell you something, and you needn't repeat it. Esau's headstrong, and he makes it a point of pride to be off-ox and ornery about everything just to show he's smart. He was born for trouble as the sparks fly upward, and I don't want you tagging in after him like a pup at his heels. If it happens again, you'll get such a thrashing as you never dreamed of. Understand?"

"Yes, *sir*!"

"Then get."

Len did not make Pa tell him again. He went away across the dooryard. He passed the gate and the cart road and went out over the west field, moving sedately, with his head bowed and the thoughts going round and round in it until it ached.

Yesterday the men had cut corn here, the long sickle-shaped knives going *whick-whick!* against the rustling stalks, and the boys had shocked it. Len liked the harvest. Everybody got together and helped everybody else, and there was a certain excitement to it, a sense of final victory in the battle you had fought since planting time, a feeling of tucking in for the winter that was right and natural as the falling of the leaves and the preparations of the squirrels. Len scuffed along slowly between the stubble rows and the tall shocks, and he got to smelling the sun on the dry corn, and hearing the crows cawing somewhere in the edge of the woods, and then the colors of the trees began to get to him. Suddenly he realized that the whole countryside was ablaze and burning with beauty, and he walked on toward the woods, with his head up to see the crests of red and gold against the sky. There was a clump of sumacs at the edge of the field, so triumphantly scarlet that they made him blink. He stopped beside them and looked back.

From here he could see almost the whole farm, the neat pattern of the fields, the snake fences in good repair, the buildings tight and well-roofed with split shakes, weathered to a silver gray that glistened in the sun. Sheep grazed in the upper pasture, and in the lower one were the cows, the harness mare, and the great thick-muscled draft team, all sleek and fat. The barn and the granary were full. The root cellar was full. The spring house was full, and in the home cellar there were crocks and jars, and flitches of bacon, and hams new from the smokehouse, and they had taken every bit of it from the earth with their own hands. A sense of warmth began to spread all through Len, and with it came a passionate, wordless love for this place that he was looking at, the fields and the house, the barn, the rough woods, the sky. He understood what Pa meant. It was good, and God was good. He understood what Pa meant about a contented heart. He prayed. When he was finished praying he turned and went in between the trees.

He had been this way so often that there had come to be a narrow path beaten through the brush. Len's step was light now, and his head was high. His broad-brimmed hat caught in the low branches, and he took it off. Pretty soon he took off his jacket, too. The path joined a deer trail. Several times he bent to look at fresh signs, and when he crossed a clearing with long grass in it he could see the round crushed places where the deer had bedded.

In a few minutes he came into a long glade. The brush thinned, shaded out by the mighty maples that grew here. Len sat down and rolled up his jacket, and then he lay down on his back with the jacket under his head and looked up at the trees. The branches made a twisty pattern of black, holding a cloud of golden leaves, and above them the sky was so blue and deep and still that you felt you could drown in it. From time to time a little shower of leaves shook down, drifting slow and bright on the quiet air. Len meditated, but his thoughts had no shape to them any more. For the first time since the preaching, they were merely happy. After a while, with a feeling of absolute peacefulness, he dozed off. And then all at once he started bolt upright, his heart thumping and the sweat springing out on his skin.

There was a sound in the woods.

It was not a right sound. It was not made by any animal or bird or wind or tree branch. It was a crackling and hissing and squealing all mixed together, and out of the middle of it came a sudden roar. It was not loud, it sounded small and distant, and yet at the same time it seemed to come from not too far away. Suddenly it was gone, as though cut off sharp with a knife.

Len stood still and listened.

It came again, but very faintly now, very stealthily, blending with the rustle of the breeze in the high branches. Len sat down and took off his shoes. Then he padded barefoot over the moss and grass to the end of the glade, and then as quietly as he could along the bed of a little stream until the brush thinned out again in a grove of butternuts. He passed through these, ducked into a clump of thorn apples, and went on his hands and knees until he could look out the other side. The sound had not grown any louder, but it was closer. Much closer.

Beyond the thorn apples was a bank of grass, where the violets grew thick in the springtime. It was a wedge-shaped bank, made where the run that gave the village its name slid into the slow brown Pymatuning. It had a big tree leaning over at its tip, with half its roots exposed by the cutting out of the earth in time of flood. It was as private a place as you could find on a Sabbath afternoon in October, in the very heart and center of the woods and at the farthest point away from the farms on either side of the river.

Esau was there. He was sitting hunched over a fallen log, and the noise came from something he held between his hands.

4

LEN CAME out of the thorn apples. Esau leaped up in a guilty panic. He tried to run away, and hide the object behind his back, and ward off an expected blow, all at the same time, and when he saw that it was only Len he fell back down on the log as though his knees had given under him.

"What did you want to do that for?" he said between his teeth. "I thought it was Dad."

His hands were shaking. They were still trying to cover up and conceal what they held. Len stopped where he was, startled at Esau's fright.

"What you got there?" he asked.

"Nothing. Just an old box."

It was a poor lie. Len ignored it. He went closer to Esau and looked. The thing was box-shaped. It was small, only a few inches across, and flat. It was made of wood, but there was a different look about it from any wooden object Len had ever seen before. He could not tell quite what the difference was, but it was there. It had curious openings in it, and several knobs sticking out from it, and in one place was a spool of thread fitted into a recess, only this thread was metal. It hummed and whispered softly to itself.

Awed and more than a little scared, Len asked, "What is it?"

"You know the thing Gran talks about sometimes? Where the voices come out of the air?"

"Teevee? But that was big, and it had pictures."

"No," said Esau. "I mean the other thing that just had voices."

Len drew in a long unsteady breath and let it go again in a quivering "Oh-h!" He reached out a finger and touched the humming box, very lightly, just to be sure it was really there. He said,

"A radio?"

Esau rested it on his knees and held it firm with one hand. The other shot out and caught Len by the front of his shirt. His face had such a fierceness in it that Len did not try to break away or fight back. Anyway, he was afraid to struggle, lest the radio get broken.

"If you tell anybody," said Esau, "I'll kill you. I swear I'll kill you."

He looked as though he meant it, and Len did not blame him. He said, "I won't, Esau. Honest, swear-on-the-Book." His eyes were drawn back to the wonderful, terrifying, magical thing in Esau's lap. "Where'd you get it? Does it work? Can you really hear voices from it?" He hunkered down until his chin was almost resting on Esau's thigh.

Esau's hand withdrew from Len's shirt and went back to stroke the smooth wooden surface of the box. At this close range Len could see that it had worn places on it around the knobs, made by the rubbing of fingers, and that one corner was chipped. These intimate things made it suddenly real. Someone had owned it and used it for a long time.

"I stole it," Esau said. "It belonged to Soames, the trader."

The familiar nerve tightened and twanged in Len's middle. He drew back a little and looked up at Esau and then all around, as though he expected stones to come flying at them out of the thorn-apple clump.

"How did *you* get it?" he asked, unconsciously dropping his voice.

"You remember when Mr. Hostetter put us in the wagon, he went to get something?"

"Yes, he got a box out of Soames's wagon—oh!"

"It was in the box. There was some other stuff, too, books I think, and little things, but it was dark and I didn't dare make any noise. I could *feel* that this was something different, like the old things Gran talks about. I hid it in my shirt."

Len shook his head, more in amazement than reproach. "And all the time we thought you were fainted. What made you do it, Esau? I mean, how did you know there was anything in the box?"

"Well, Soames was from Bartorstown, wasn't he?"

"That's what they said at the preaching. But——" Len broke off short as a corollary truth dawned on him, shining with a great light. He looked at the radio. "He was from Bartorstown. And there is a Bartorstown. It's real."

"When I saw Hostetter coming back with that box, I just had to look inside it. Coins or anything like that I wouldn't touch, but this——" Esau caressed the radio, turning it gently in his hands. "Look at those knobs, and the way this part here is done. You couldn't do that by hand in any village smithy, Len. It must have been machined. The way it's all put together, and inside——" He squinted in through the grilled openings, trying to catch the light so it would reflect on what was beyond them. "Inside there's the strangest things." He put it down again. "I didn't know what it was at first. I only felt what it was like. I had to have it."

Len got up slowly. He walked over to the edge of the bank and looked down at the clear brown water, low and slack and half covered over with red and gold leaves. Esau said nervously, "What's the matter? If you think you're going to tell, I'll say you stole it with me. I'll say——"

"I ain't going to tell," said Len angrily. "You've had the thing all this time and never told me, and I can keep a secret as good as you."

Esau said, "I was afraid to. You're young, Lennie, and used to minding your pa." He added with some truth, "Anyway, we've hardly seen each other since the preaching."

"It don't matter," Len said. It did matter, of course, and he felt hurt and indignant that Esau had not trusted him, but he was not going to let Esau know that. "I was just thinking."

"What?"

"Well, Mr. Hostetter knew Soames. He went to the preaching to try and help him, and then he took the box out of Soames's wagon. Maybe——"

"Yes," said Esau. "I thought of that. Maybe Mr. Hostetter is from Bartorstown, too, and not from Pennsylvania at all."

Great vistas of terrifying and wonderful possibility were opened up in Len's mind. He stood there on the bank of the Pymatuning, while the gold and scarlet leaves came down and the crows laughed their harsh derisive laughter, and the horizons widened and shone around him until he was dizzy with them. Then he remembered why he was here, or rather why it was that Pa had sent him into the fields and woods to meditate, and how he had made peace with God and the world just such a little time before, and how good it had felt. And now it was all gone again.

He turned around. "Can you hear voices with it?"

"I haven't yet," said Esau. "But I'm going to keep on till I do."

They tried that afternoon, cautiously turning one knob and then another. Esau had turned one too far, or Len would never have heard it. They had not the remotest idea how a radio worked or what the knobs and openings and the spool of thin wire were for. They could only experiment, and all they got was the now-familiar crackle and hiss and squeal. But even that was a thing of wonder. It was a sound never heard before, full of mystery and a sense of great unseen spaces, and it was made by a machine. They did not leave it until the sun was so low that they were afraid to stay any longer. Then Esau hid the radio carefully in a hollow tree, wrapping it first in a bit of canvas and making sure that the main knob was turned clear around till it clicked and there was no more sound, lest the hum and crackle should attract the attention of some chance hunter or fisherman.

That hollow tree became the pivot of Len's days, and it was the most exciting and wildly frustrating thing imaginable. Now that he had a reason for going, it seemed almost impossible to find time and excuses for going to the woods. The weather turned cold and nasty, with rain and sleet and then snow. The stock had to be put in the barn, and after that there was not much time to do anything but feed, water, and clean up after a great houseful of animals. There was milking, and the henhouse to see to, and then there was helping Ma with the churning and carrying stovewood, and such, around the house.

After morning chores, when it was still hardly light, he tramped the mile and a half to the village over roads that were one day deep in mud and frozen hard as iron the next, with yesterday's ruts immortalized in ice. On the west side of the village square, beyond the smithy but not so far as the cobblers' shop, was the house of Mr. Nordholt, the schoolmaster, and there, with the other young of Piper's Run, Len struggled with his sums and his letters, his reading and his Bible history until noon, when he was turned loose to walk home again. After that there were other things. Len often felt that he had more to do than Pa and brother James put together.

Brother James was nineteen and arranging to marry the oldest daughter of Mr. Spofford, the miller. He was a lot like Pa, square and strong and quiet, proud of his fine new beard in spite of the fact that it was nearly pink. When the weather was right, Len went with him and Pa to the wood lot, or around to mend fence or clear hedgerows, and sometimes they would go hunting, both for meat and for skins, because nothing was ever wasted or thrown away. There were deer, and coon, and possum, and woodchuck at the right time of the year, and squirrel, and rumors of bear in the wilder parts of the Pennsylvania hills that might be expected to drift west into Ohio, and sometimes if the winter was very bad they would hear rumors of wolves up north beyond the lakes. There were foxes to keep out of the henroost, and rats to keep out of the corn, and rabbits out of the young orchard. And every evening there was milking again, and the windup chores, and then dinner and bed. It did not leave much time for the radio.

And yet waking or sleeping it was never out of his mind. Two things were linked with it, a memory and a dream. The memory was the death of Soames. Time had transfigured him until he was taller and more noble and splendid than any ginger-haired trader had ever been, and the firelight on him had merged into the glory of martyrdom. The dream was of Bartorstown. It was pieced together out of Gran's stories, and bits of sermons, and descriptions of heaven. It had big white buildings that went high up in the air, and it was full of colors and sounds, and people strangely dressed, and it blazed with light, and in it there was every kind of thing that Gran had told about, machines and luxuries and pleasures.

The most agonizing part of the little radio was that both he and Esau knew that it was a link with Bartorstown and if they only understood how to use it they could actually hear people talking from it and about it. They might even learn where it was and how a person might get there if he decided to go. But it was as hard for Esau to come to the woods as it was for Len, and in their few stolen moments they got nothing from the radio but meaningless noises.

The temptation to ask Gran questions about radios was almost more than Len could hold in. But he did not dare, and anyway he was sure she wouldn't know any more about it than he did.

"We need a book," said Esau. "That's what we need. A book that tells all about these things."

"Yes," said Len. "Sure. But where are you going to get one?"

Esau didn't answer.

The great cold waves rolled down from the north and northwest, one after the other. Snows fell and then melted in a warmer blow from the south, and then the slush they left behind them froze again as the temperature plunged down. Sometimes it rained, very cold and dreary, and the bare woods dripped. The manure pile behind the barn grew into a brown and strawy alp. And Len thought.

Whether it was the stimulus of the radio, or simply that he was growing up, or both, he saw everything about him in a new way, as though he had managed to get a little distance off so that his sight wasn't blurred by being too close. He did not do this all the time, of course. He was too busy and too tired. But now and then he would see Gran sitting by the fire, knitting with her old, old unsteady hands, and he would think how long she had been alive and all she had seen, and he would feel sorry for her because she was old and Baby Esther, a minute copy of Ma in her tiny cap and apron and full skirts, was young and just beginning.

He would see Ma, always working at something, washing, sewing, spinning, weaving, quilting, making sure the table was loaded with food for hungry men, a thick, solid woman, very kind and quiet. He would see the house he lived in, the familiar whitewashed rooms of which he knew every crack and knothole in the wooden walls. It was an old house. Gran said it had been built only a year or two after the church. The floors ran up and down every which way and the walls leaned, but it was still sound as a mountain, put together out of great timbers by the first Colter who had come here, many generations before the Destruction. Yet it was not too different from the new houses that were built now. The ones that had been built in Gran's childhood or just before were the ones that really looked queer, little flat-roofed things that had mostly to be re-sided with wood, and their great gaping windows boarded in. He would stretch up and try to touch the ceiling, figuring that by next year he could do it. And a great wave of love would come over him, and he would think, I'll never leave here, never! And his conscience would hurt him with a physical pain because he knew he was doing wrong to fool with the forbidden radio and the forbidden dream of Bartorstown.

For the first time he really saw Brother James and envied him. His face was as smooth and placid as Ma's, without a glimmer of curiosity in it. He would not care if there were twenty Bartorstowns just across the Pymatuning. All he wanted was to marry Ruth Spofford and stay right where he was. Len felt dimly that Brother James was one of the happy ones who had never had to pray for a contented heart.

Pa was different. Pa had had to fight. The fighting had left lines in his face, but they were good lines, strong ones. And his contentment was different from Brother James's. It hadn't just happened. Pa had had to sweat for it, like getting a good crop from a poor field. You could feel it when you were around him, if you thought about it, and it was a fine thing, a thing you would like to get hold of for yourself.

But could you? Could you give up all the mystery and wonder of the world? Could you never see it, and never want to see it? Could you stop the waiting, hoping eagerness to hear a voice from nowhere, out of a little square box?

In January, just after the turn of the year, there was an ice storm on a Sabbath evening. On Monday morning Len walked to school just as the sun came up, and every tree and twig and stiff dead weed glittered with a cold glory. He lagged on the way, looking at the familiar woods turned strange and shining like a forest of glass—a sight rarer and lovelier than the clinging snows that made them all a still, hushed white—and he was late when he crossed the village square, past the chunky granite monument that said it was in memory of the veterans of all wars, erected by the citizens of Piper's Run. It had had a bronze eagle on it once, but there was nothing left of that now but a lump of corroded metal in the shape of two claws. It too was all sheathed in ice, and the ground underfoot was slippery. Ashes had been thrown on the steps of Mr. Nordholt's house. Len clambered up onto the porch and went inside.

The room was still chilly in spite of a roaring fire in the grate. It had a tremendously high ceiling and very tall double doors and very long windows, so that more cold leaked in than a fire could handily take care of. The walls were of whitewashed plaster, with a lot of ornamental woodwork polished down to the original dark grain of the native black walnut. The students sat on rough benches, without backs, but with long trestle tables in front of them. They were graded in size, from the littlest ones in front to the biggest in the back, girls on one side, boys on the other. There were twenty-three in all. Each one had a small slab of smooth slate, a squeaky pencil, and a rag, and they were taught everything but their sums from the Bible.

This morning they were all sitting very still with their hands in their laps, each one trying to blend into the room like a rabbit into a hedgerow so as not to be noticed. Mr. Nordholt was standing facing them. He was a tall, thin man, with a white beard and an expression of gentle sternness that frightened only the very young. But this morning he was angry. He was angry clear through with a towering and indignant wrath, and his eyes shot such a glare at Len that he quailed before it. Mr. Nordholt was not alone. Mr. Glasser was there, and Mr. Harkness, and Mr. Clute, and Mr. Fenway. They were the law and council of Piper's Run, and they sat stiffly in a row looking thunder and lightning at the students.

"If," said Mr. Nordholt, "you will be good enough to take your seat, *Mister* Colter——"

Len slid into his place on the back bench without stopping to take off his thick outer jacket or the scarf around his neck. He sat there trying to look small and innocent, wondering what on earth the trouble was and thinking guiltily of the radio.

Mr. Nordholt said, "For three days over the New Year I was in Andover, visiting my sister. I did not lock my door when I went away, because it has never been necessary in Piper's Run to lock our doors against thieves."

Mr. Nordholt's voice was choked with some very strong emotion, and Len knew that something bad had happened. He went rapidly over his own actions on those three days but found nothing that could be brought up against him.

"Someone," said Mr. Nordholt, "entered this house during my absence and stole from it three books."

Len stiffened in his seat. He remembered Esau saying, "We need a book——"

"Those books," said Mr. Nordholt, "are the property of the township of Piper's Run. They are pre-Destruction books, and therefore irreplaceable. And they are not for idle or indiscriminate use. I want them back."

He stood aside, and Mr. Harkness rose. Mr. Harkness was short and thick, and bandy-legged from walking all his life after a plow, and his voice had a rusty creak in it. He always prayed the longest prayers in meeting. Now he looked along the rows of benches with two little steely eyes that were usually as friendly as a beagle's.

"Now then," said Mr. Harkness, "I'm going to ask each one of you in turn, did you take them or do you know who did. And I don't want any lies or any bearing of false witness."

He stumped over to the left-hand corner and began, walking down the benches and back again. Len listened to the monotonous *No Mr. Harkness* coming closer and closer, and he sweated profusely and tried to loosen his tongue. After all, he did not know that it was Esau. Thou shalt not bear false witness, Mr. Harkness just said so, and to look guilty when you're not is a sort of false-witnessing. Besides, if they get to looking around too close they might find out about the——

Harkness' eye and finger were pointed straight at him.

"No," said Len, "Mr. Harkness."

It seemed to him that all the guilt and fear in the world were loud and quivering in those three words, but Mr. Harkness passed on. When he came to the end of the last row he said,

"Very well. Perhaps you're all telling the truth, perhaps not. We'll find out. Now I'll say this. If you see a book that you know does not belong to the person who has it, you are to come to me, or to Mr. Nordholt or to Mr. Glasser or Mr. Clute or Mr. Fenway. You are to ask your parents to do the same. Do you understand that?"

Yes, Mr. Harkness.

"Let us pray. Oh God, Who knowest all things, forgive the erring child, or man, as it may be, who has broken Thy commandment against theft. Turn his soul toward righteousness, that he may return that which is not his, and make him patient of chastisement——"

Len took a chance on his way home and made a circle down through the woods, running most of the way to make up for the extra distance. The sun had melted some of the icy armor on the trees, but it was still bright enough to hurt the eyes, and the footing was treacherous. He was blown and weary by the time he got to the hollow tree.

There were three books in it, wrapped up in canvas beside the radio, dry and safe. The covers and the paper inside fascinated him with faded colors for the eye and unfamiliar textures for the touch. They had an indefinable something in common with the radio.

One was a dark green book called *Elementary Physics.* One was thin and brownish, with a long title: *Radioactivity and Nucleonics: An Introduction.* The third was fat and gray, and its name was *History of the United States.* The words of the first two meant nothing to Len, except that he recognized the *Radio* part. He turned the pages, hastily, with shaking fingers, trying to take it all in at one glance and seeing nothing but a blur of print and pictures and curious line drawings. Here and there on the pages someone had marked and written in the margins, "Monday, test," or "To here," or "Write paper on La. Purchase."

Len felt a hunger and a craving he had not known before, because nothing had ever aroused them. They were up in his head, and they were so strong they made it ache. He wanted to read. He wanted to take the books and wrap himself around them and absorb them to the last word and picture. He knew perfectly well what his duty was. He did not do it. He folded the canvas around the books again and replaced them carefully in the hollow tree. Then he ran back on the circuitous route home, and his mind was spinning all the way with stratagems to deceive Pa and make guilty trips to the woods appear innocent. His conscience made a single peep, no louder than a day-old chick, and then was still.

5

ESAU WAS almost in tears. He flung down the book he was holding and said furiously, "I don't know what the words mean, so what good does it do me? I just took a big risk for nothing!"

He had been over and over the book on physics and the one on radioactivity, and Len had been over and over them with him. The one on radioactivity they had laid aside because it didn't seem to have anything to do with radios, and anyway they could not make head or tail of what it was about. But the book on physics—another puzzling misuse of a word that had almost caused Esau to pass it by in his search through Mr. Nordholt's library—did have a part in it about radio. They had scowled and mumbled over it until the queer-shaped and unpronounceable words were stamped on their brains and they could have drawn diagrams of waves and circuits, triodes and oscillators in their sleep, without in the least understanding what they were.

Len picked the book up from between his feet, where it had landed, and brushed the dirt from its cover. Then he looked inside it and shook his head. He said sadly,

"It doesn't tell you how to make voices come out."

"No. It doesn't tell what the knobs and the spool are for, either." Esau turned the radio gloomily between his hands. One of the knobs they knew made it noisy or quiet—alive or dead, Len thought of it unconsciously. But the others remained a mystery. By making the noise very soft and holding the radio against their ears they had learned that the sound came out of one of the openings. What the other two were for was also a mystery. No one of the three looked like its mates, so it was logical to guess that they were for three different purposes. Len was pretty sure that one of them was to let heat out, like the ventilators in the hayloft, because you could feel it get warm if you held your hand over it for a while. But that still left one, and the enigmatic spool of metal thread. He reached out and took the radio from Esau, just liking the feel of it between his hands, a kind of humming quiver it had like a blade of swamp grass in the wind.

"Mr. Hostetter must know how it works," he said.

They were sure in their hearts that Mr. Hostetter, like Mr. Soames, was from Bartorstown.

Esau nodded. "But we don't dare ask him."

"No."

Len turned the radio over and over, fingering the knobs, the spool, the openings. A chill wind rattled the bare branches overhead. There was ice in the Pymatuning, and the fallen log he sat on was bitter underneath him.

"I just wonder," he said slowly.

"Wonder what?"

"Well, if they talk back and forth with these radios, they wouldn't do it much in the daytime, would they? I mean, people might hear them. If it was me, I'd wait until night, when everybody would be asleep."

"Well, it ain't you," said Esau crossly. But he thought about it, and gradually he got excited. "I'll bet that's right. I'll bet that's just exactly right! We only fooled with it in the daytime, and naturally they wouldn't talk then. Can you see Mr. Hostetter doing it up in the town square, with everybody swarming around and a dozen kids hanging on every wheel?"

He got up and began to pace up and down, blowing on his cold fingers. "We'll have to make plans, Len. We'll have to get away at night."

"Yes," said Len eagerly, and then was sorry he had spoken. That was not going to be so easy.

"Coon hunt," said Esau.

"No. My brother'd want to go. Maybe Pa, too."

Possum hunt was the same thing, and jacklighting deer was no better.

"Well, keep thinking." Esau began to put the books and the radio away. "I got to get back."

"Me, too." Len looked regretfully at the fat gray history, wishing he could take it with them. Esau had picked it up on impulse because it had pictures of machines in it. It was hard going and full of strange names and a lot he did not understand, but it tormented him all the time he was reading it, wondering what was coming on the next page. "Maybe it'd be best just to watch a chance and slip away alone, whichever one of us can, and not try to come together."

"No, sir! I stole it, and I stole the books, and nobody's going to hear a voice without me there!"

He looked so savage that Len said all right.

Esau made sure everything was safe and stepped back. He looked at the hollow tree, scowling. "Not much use to come back here any more till then. And we'll be sugarin' off 'fore long, and there's lambing, and then——"

With a mature depth of bitterness that startled Len, Esau said, "Always something, always some reason why you can't know or learn or do! I'm sick of it. And I'm damned if I'm going to spend my whole life that way, shoveling dung and pulling cow tits!"

Len walked home alone, pondering deeply on those words. He could feel something growing in him, and he knew it was growing in Esau, too. It frightened him. He didn't want it to grow. But he knew that if it stopped growing he would be partly dead, not physically, but like cows or sheep, who eat the grass but do not care what makes it grow.

That was the end of January. In February there was a warm spell, and all over the countryside men and boys went with taps and spiles and buckets to the maple trees. The smoke from the sugarbush blew out on the wind, the first banner of oncoming spring. The last deep snow came and melted off again. There was a period of alternating freeze and thaw that made Pa worry about the winter wheat heaving out of the ground. The wind blew chill from the northwest, and it seemed as though it would never get warm again. The first lamb came bleating into the world. And as Esau had said, there was no spare time for anything.

The willows turned yellow, and then a pale, feathery green. There were some warm days that made you feel all lazy and slithering like a winter snake thawing in the sun. New calves bawled and staggered after their mothers, with more yet to come. The cows were nervous and troublesome, and Len began to get an idea. It was so simple he wondered why he had not thought of it before. After evening chores, when Brother James had closed the barn, Len sneaked back and opened the lower door. An hour later they were all out in the cold dark rounding up cows, and when they got them back inside and counted, two were missing. Pa muttered angrily about the stupid obstinacy of beasts that preferred to run away and calve under a bush, where if anything went wrong there was no help. He gave Len a lantern and told him to run the half mile down the road to Uncle David's house and ask him and Esau to help. It was as easy as that.

Len covered the half mile at a fast lope, his mind busy foreseeing possibilities and preparing for them with a deceitful ease that rather horrified him. He had been given much to laziness, but never to lying, and it was awful how fast he was learning. He tried to excuse himself by thinking that he hadn't told anybody a direct falsehood. But it didn't do any good. He was like one of those whited sepulchers they told about in the Bible, fair without and full of wickedness within. And off to his right as he ran the woods showed in the starlight, very black and strange.

Uncle David's kitchen was warm. It smelled of cabbage and steam and drying boots, and it was so clean that Len hesitated to step into it even after he had scraped his feet outside. There was a scrap of rag rug just inside the door and he stood on that, getting his message out between gasping for breath and trying to catch Esau's eye without looking too transparently guilty. Uncle David grumbled and muttered, but he began to pull on his boots, and Aunt Mariah got his jacket and a lantern. Len took a deep gulp of air.

"I think I saw something white moving down in the west field," he said. "Come on, Esau, let's look!"

And Esau came, with his hat on crooked and one arm still out of his jacket. They ran away together before Uncle David could think to stop them, stumbling and leaping over rough pasture where every hollow was full from recent rain, and then into the west field, angling all the time toward the woods. Len muffled the lantern under his coat so that Uncle David could not see from the road when they actually entered the woods, and he kept it hidden for some time afterward, knowing the way pretty well even in the dark, once he found his trail.

"We can say later that the lantern went out," he told Esau.

"Sure," said Esau, in a strange, tight voice. "Let's hurry."

They hurried. Esau grabbed the lantern and ran recklessly on ahead. When they got to the place where the waters met he set the light down and got out the radio with hands that could hardly hold it for shaking. Len sat down on the log, his mouth wide open, his arms pressed to his aching sides. Piper's Run was roaring like a real river, bankfull. It made a riffle and a swirl where it swept into the Pymatuning. The water rushed by foaming, very high now, almost level with the land where they were, dim and disturbed in the starlight, and the night was filled with the sound of it.

Esau dropped the radio.

Len jumped forward with a cry. Esau made a grab, fast and frantic. He caught the radio by the protruding spool. The spool came loose and the radio continued to fall, but slower now, swinging on the end of the wire that unreeled from Esau's hand. It fell with a soft thump into the last year's grass. Esau stood staring at it, and at the spool, and the wire between.

"It's broken," he said. "It's broken."

Len went down on his knees. "No it isn't. Look here." He moved the radio close to the lantern and pointed. "See those two little springs? The spool is meant to come out, and the wire unwinds——"

Enormously excited, he turned the knob. This was something they had not known or tried before. He waited until the humming began. It sounded stronger than it had. He motioned Esau to move back, and he did, reeling out the wire, and the noise got stronger and stronger, and suddenly without warning a man's voice was saying, very scratchy and far away, "—back out to civilization myself next fall, I hope. Anyway, the stuff's on the river ready to load as soon as the——"

The voice faded with a roar and a swoop. Like one half stunned, Esau reeled the wire out to the very end. And a faint, faint voice said, "Sherman wants to know if you've heard from Byers. He hasn't con——"

And that was all. The roaring and whistling and humming went on, so loud that they were afraid it might be heard all the way to where the others were out hunting cows. Once or twice they thought they could hear voices again behind it, but they could not make any more words come clear. Len turned the knob and Esau rolled the wire on the spool and clipped it back in place. They put the radio in the hollow tree, and picked up the lantern, and went away through the woods. They did not speak. They did not even look at each other. And in the dim light of the lantern their eyes were wide and brightly shining.

6

THE CLOUD of dust showed first, far down the road. Then the top of the canvas tilt glinted white where the sun fell on it, shining strongly through the green trees. The tilt got higher and rounder, and the wagon began to show underneath it, and the team in front lengthened out from a confused dark blob of motion to six great bay horses stepping along as proud as emperors, their harness gleaming and the trace chains all ajingle.

High up on the wagon seat, handling the long reins lightly, was Mr. Hostetter, his beard rippling in the wind and his hat and shoulders and the trouser legs over his shins all powdered brown from the road.

Len said, "I'm scared."

"What have you got to be scared about?" said Esau. "You ain't going."

"And maybe you're not, either," muttered Len, looking up at the log bridge as the wagon rocked and rattled over it. "I don't think it's that easy."

It was June, in full bright leaf. Len and Esau stood beside Piper's Run just at the edge of the village, where the mill wheel hung slack in the water and kingfishers dropped like bolts of blue flame. The town square was less than a hundred yards away, and the whole township was in it, everybody who was not too young, too old, or too sick to be moved. There were friends and relatives up from Vernon and down from Williamsfield, and from Andover and Farmdale and Burghill and the lonely farmsteads across the Pennsylvania line that were nearer to Piper's Run than to any village of their own. It was the strawberry festival, the first big social event of the summer, where people who had perhaps not seen each other since the first snow could get together and talk and pleasantly stuff themselves, sitting in the dappled sunshine under the elms.

A crowd of boys had run out along the road to meet the

wagon. They were running beside it now, shouting up to Mr. Hostetter. The girls, and the boys still too little to run, stood along the edges of the square and waved and called out, the girls in their bonnets and their long skirts blowing in the warm wind, the tiny boys exactly like their fathers in homespun and broad brown hats. Then everybody began to move, flowing across the square toward the wagon, which went slower and slower and finally stopped, the six great horses tossing their heads and snorting as though they had done a mighty thing to get that wagon there and were proud of it. Mr. Hostetter waved and smiled and a boy climbed up and put a dish of strawberries in his hand.

Len and Esau stayed where they were, looking at Mr. Hostetter from a distance. Len felt a curious thrill go through him, partly of sheer guiltiness because of the stolen radio and partly of intimacy, almost of comradeship, because he knew a secret about Mr. Hostetter and was in a sense set apart himself. Somehow, though, he did not want to meet Mr. Hostetter's eyes.

"How are you going to do it?" he asked Esau.

"I'll find a way."

He was staring at the wagon with a fanatic intensity. Ever since that night when they had heard voices Esau had turned somehow strange and wild, not outside but inside, so that sometimes Len hardly knew him any more. *I'm going there*, he had said, meaning Bartorstown, and he had been like one possessed, waiting for Mr. Hostetter.

Esau reached out and took Len by the arm, his grip painfully tight. "Won't you come with me?"

Len hung his head. He stood for a moment, quite still, and then he said, "No, I can't." He moved away from Esau. "Not now."

"Maybe next year. I'll tell him about you."

"Maybe."

Esau started to say something more, but he could not seem to find any words for it. Len moved farther away. He started up the bank, slowly at first and then faster and faster until he was running, with the tears hot in his eyes and his own mind shouting at him, Coward, coward, he's going to Bartorstown and you don't dare!

He did not look back again.

Mr. Hostetter stayed three days in Piper's Run. They were the longest, hardest days Len had ever lived through. Temptation kept telling him, You can still go. And then Conscience would point out Ma and Pa and home and duty and the wickedness of running away without a word. Esau had not given Uncle David and Aunt Mariah a second thought, but Len could not feel that way about Pa and Ma. He knew how Ma would cry, and how Pa would take the blame on himself that he hadn't trained Len right somehow, and that was the biggest part of his cowardice. He didn't want to be responsible for making them unhappy.

There was a third voice in him, too. It lived way back of the others and it had no name. It was a voice he had never heard before, and it only said *No—danger!* whenever he thought of going with Esau to Mr. Hostetter. It spoke so loud and so firm without ever being asked that Len could not ignore it, and in fact when he tried to it became a physical restraint on him just like the reins on a horse, pulling him this way and that past a word or an action that might have been irretrievable. It was Len's first active encounter with his own subconscious. He never forgot it.

He moped and sulked and brooded around the farm, burdened with his secret, bobbling his chores and making excuses not to go into town when the family did, until Ma worried and dosed him heavily with physics and sassafras tea. And all the time his ears were stretched and quivering, waiting to hear hoofbeats on the road, waiting to hear Uncle David rush in saying that Esau was gone.

On the evening of the third day he heard the hoofbeats, coming fast. He was just helping Ma clear off the supper dishes, and the light was still in the sky, reddening toward the west. His nerves jerked taut with a painful snap. The dishes became slippery and enormous in his hands. The horse turned in to the dooryard with the cart rattling behind him, and after that a second horse and cart, and after that a third. Pa went to the door, and Len followed him, with a sickness settling in all his bones. One horse and cart for Uncle David he had expected. But three——

Uncle David was there, all right. He sat in his own cart, and Esau was beside him, sitting still and as white as a sheet, and Mr. Harkness was on the other side of him. Mr. Hostetter was in the second cart with Mr. Nordholt, the schoolmaster, and Mr. Clute was driving. Mr. Fenway and Mr. Glasser were in the third.

Uncle David got down. He motioned to Pa, who had gone out toward the carts. Mr. Hostetter joined them, and Mr. Nordholt, and Mr. Glasser. Esau sat where he was. His head was bent forward and he did not lift it. Mr. Harkness stared at Len, who had stayed in the doorway. His look was outraged, accusing, and sad. Len met it for a fractional second and then dropped his own eyes. He felt very sick now and quite cold. He wanted to run away, but he knew it would not be any use.

The men moved all together to Uncle David's cart, and Uncle David said something to Esau. Esau continued to stare at his hands. He did not speak or nod, and Mr. Nordholt said, "He didn't mean to tell, it just slipped out of him. But he did say it."

Pa turned and looked at Len and said, "Come here."

Len walked out, quite slowly. He would not lift his head to look at Pa, not because of the anger in Pa's face, but because of the sorrow that was there.

"Len."

"Yes, sir."

"Is it true that you have a radio?"

"I—yes, sir."

"Is it true that you tried to use it to get in touch with Bartorstown?"

"Yes, sir."

"Did you read certain books that were stolen? Did you know where they were, and didn't tell Mr. Nordholt? Did you know what Esau was planning to do, and didn't tell me or Uncle David?"

Len sighed. With a gesture curiously like that of an old and tired man, he raised his head and threw his shoulders back. "Yes," he said. "I did all those things."

Pa's face, in the deepening dusk, had become like something cut from a gray rock.

"Very well," he said. "Very well."

"You can ride with us," said Mr. Glasser. "Save harnessing up, just for that little distance."

"All right," said Pa. And he gave Len a cold and blazing glance that meant Come with me.

Len followed him. He passed close to Mr. Hostetter, who was standing with his head half turned away, and under his hatbrim Len thought he saw an expression of pity and regret. But they passed without speaking, and Esau never stirred. Pa climbed up into the cart with Mr. Fenway, and Mr. Glasser climbed in after him.

"Up behind," said Pa.

Len climbed slowly onto the shelf, and every movement was an effort. He clung there, and the carts jolted off in line, out of the dooryard and across the road and out around the margin of the west field, toward the woods.

They stopped about where the sumacs grew. They all got out and the men spoke together. And then Pa turned and said, "Len." He pointed at the woods. "Show us."

Len did not move.

Esau spoke for the first time. "You might as well," he said, in a voice heavy with hate. "They'll get it anyway if they have to burn the whole woods."

Uncle David cuffed him backhanded across the mouth and called him something angry and Biblical.

Pa said again, "Len."

Len yielded. He led the way into the woods. And the path looked just the same, and so did the trees, and the tiny stream, and the familiar clumps of thorn apple. But something was changed. Something was gone. They were only trees now, and thorn apples, and the rocky bed of a trickle of water. They no longer belonged to him. They were withdrawn and unwelcoming, and their outlines were harsh, and the big boots of the men crushed down the ferns.

They came out on the point at the meeting of the waters. Len stopped beside the hollow tree.

"Here," he said. His voice sounded unfamiliar in his ears. The bright glow of the west fell clearly here along the open stream, painting the leaves and grass a lurid green, tinting the brown Pymatuning with copper. Crows flapped homeward overhead, dropping their jeering laughter as they went. It seemed to Len that the laughter was meant for him.

Uncle David gave Esau a rough, hard shove. "Get it out."

Esau stood for a minute beside the tree. Len watched him, and the look that was on him in the sunset light. The crows went away, and it was very still.

Esau reached into the hollow of the tree. He brought out the books, wrapped in canvas, and handed them to Mr. Nordholt.

"They're not hurt," he said.

Mr. Nordholt unwrapped them, moving out from under the tree so he could see better. "No," he said. "No, they're not hurt." He wrapped them again and held them against his chest.

Esau lifted out the radio.

He stood holding it, and the tears came up into his eyes and glittered there but did not fall. A hesitancy had come over the men. Mr. Hostetter said, as though he had said it before but was afraid it might not have been understood, "Soames had asked me if anything happened to take his personal belongings and give them to his wife. He had shown me the chest they were in. The people at the preaching were about to loot his wagon. I did not stop to see what was in the chest."

Uncle David stepped forward. He knocked the radio from Esau's hands, driving his fist downward like a hammer. It lay on the turf, and he stamped on it, over and over with his heavy boot. Then he picked up what was left of it and flung it out into the Pymatuning.

Esau said, "I hate you." He looked at them all. "You can't stop me. Someday I'll go to Bartorstown."

Uncle David hit him again, and spun him around, and started to march him back through the woods. Over his shoulder he said, "I'll see to him."

The rest followed in a straggling line, after Mr. Harkness poked his hand around in the hollow of the tree to make sure nothing more was in there. And Mr. Hostetter said,

"I wish my wagon to be searched."

Mr. Harkness said, "We've known you a long time, Ed. I don't think that'll be necessary."

"No, I demand it," said Hostetter, speaking so that everyone could hear. "This boy has made an accusation that I can't let pass. I want my wagon searched from top to bottom, so that there can be no doubt as to whether I possess anything I should not have. Suspicion once started is hard to kill, and news travels. I wouldn't want *other* people to think of me what they thought of Soames."

A shiver ran through Len. He realized suddenly that Hostetter was making an explanation and an apology.

He also understood that Esau had made a fatal mistake.

It seemed a long way back across the west field. This time the carts did not enter the farmyard. They stopped in the road and Len and Pa got down, and the others shifted around so that Esau and Uncle David were alone in their own cart. Then Mr. Harkness said, "We will want to see the boys tomorrow." His voice was ominously quiet. He drove away toward the village, with the second cart behind him. Uncle David started the other way, toward home.

Esau leaned out of the cart and shouted hysterically at Len. "Don't give up. They can't make you stop thinking. No matter what they do to you they can't——"

Uncle David turned the cart sharp around and brought it into the farmyard.

"We'll see about that," he said. "Elijah, I'm going to use your barn."

Pa frowned, but he did not say anything. Uncle David went across to the barn, shoving Esau roughly in front of him. Ma came running out of the house. Uncle David called out, "You bring Len. I want him here." Pa frowned again and then said, "All right." He put out his hands to Ma and drew her aside and said a few words to her, very low, shaking his head. Ma looked at Len. "Oh no," she said. "Oh, Lennie, how could you!" Then she went back to the house with her apron up over her face, and Len knew that she was crying. Pa pointed to the barn. His lips were set tight together. Len thought that Pa did not like what Uncle David was going to do, but that he did not feel he could question it.

Len did not like it either. He would rather have had this just between himself and Pa. But that was like Uncle David. He always figured if you were a kid you had no more rights or feelings than any other possession around the farm. Len shrank from going into the barn.

Pa pointed again, and he went.

It was dark now, but there was a lantern burning inside. Uncle David had taken the harness leather down off the wall. Esau was facing him, in the wide space between the rows of empty stanchions.

"Get down on your knees," said Uncle David.

"No."

"Get down!" And the harness strap cracked.

Esau made a noise between a whimper and a curse. He went down on his knees.

"Thou shalt not steal," said Uncle David. "You've made me the father of a thief. Thou shalt not bear false witness. You've made me the father of a liar." His arm was rising and falling in cadence with his words, so that every pause was punctuated by a sharp *whuk!* of flat leather against Esau's shoulders. "You know what it says in the Book, Esau. He who loveth his child chasteneth him, but he who hateth his son withholdeth the rod. I'm not going to withhold it."

Esau was not able to keep silent any longer. Len turned his back.

After a while Uncle David stopped, breathing hard. "You defied me a bit ago. You said I couldn't make you change your mind. Do you still feel that way?"

Crouched on the floor, Esau screamed at his father. "Yes!"

"You still think you'll go to Bartorstown?"

"Yes!"

"Well," said Uncle David. "We'll see."

Len tried not to listen. It seemed to go on and on. Once Pa stepped forward and said, "David——" But Uncle David only said, "Tend to your own whelp, Elijah. I always told you you were too soft with him." He turned again to Esau. "Have you changed your mind yet?"

Esau's answer was unintelligible but abject in surrender.

"You," said Uncle David suddenly to Len, and jerked him around. "Look at that, and see what boasting and insolence come to in the end."

Esau was groveling on the barn floor, in the dust and straw. Uncle David stirred him with his foot.

"Do you still think you'll go to Bartorstown?"

Esau muttered and moaned, hiding his face in his arms. Len

tried to pull away but Uncle David held him, with a hot heavy hand. He smelled of sweat and anger. "There's your hero," he said to Len. "Remember him when your turn comes."

"Let me go," Len whispered. Uncle David laughed. He pushed Len away and handed Pa the harness strap. Then he reached down and got Esau by the neckband of his shirt and pulled him up onto his feet.

"Say it, Esau. Say it out."

Esau sobbed like a little child. "I repent," he said. "I repent."

"Bartorstown," said Uncle David, in the same tone in which Nahum must have pronounced the bloody city. "Get out. Get home and meditate on your sins. Good night, Elijah, and remember—your boy is as guilty as mine."

They went out into the darkness. A minute later Len heard the cart drive off.

Pa sighed. His face looked tired and sad, and deeply angry in a way that was much more frightening than Uncle David's raging. He said slowly, "I trusted you, Len. You betrayed me."

"I didn't mean to."

"But you did."

"Yes."

"Why, Len? You knew those things were wrong. Why did you do them?"

Len cried, "Because I couldn't help it. I want to learn, I want to *know!*"

Pa took off his hat and rolled up his sleeve. "I could preach a long sermon on that text," he said. "But I've already done that, and it was breath wasted. You remember what I told you, Len."

"Yes, Pa." And he set his jaw and curled his two hands up tight.

"I'm sorry," said Pa. "I didn't ever want to have to do this. But I'm going to purge you of your pride, Len, just as Esau was purged."

Inside himself Len said fiercely, No, you won't, you won't make me get down and crawl. I'm not going to give them up, Bartorstown and books and knowing and all the things there are in the world outside of Piper's Run!

But he did. In the dust and straw of the barn he gave them

up, and his pride with them. And that was the end of his childhood.

7

HE HAD slept for a while, a black heavy sleep, and then he had waked again to stare at the darkness, and feel, and think. His body hurt, not with the mere familiar smart of a licking but in a serious way that he would not forget in a hurry. It did not hurt anything like as much as the intangible parts of him, and he lay and wrestled with the agony in the little lopsided room under the eaves that was still stifling from the day's sun. It was almost dawn before anything stood clear from the blind fury of grief and rage and resentment and utter shame that shook around in him like big winds in a small place. Then, perhaps because he was too exhausted to be violent any more, he began to see a thing or two, and understand.

He knew that when he had groveled in Esau's tracks in the dust and forsworn himself, he had lied. He was not going to give up Bartorstown. He could not give it up without giving up the most important part of himself. He did not know quite what that most important part was, but he knew it was there, and he knew that nobody, not even Pa, had the right to lay hands on it. Good or bad, righteous or sinful, it lay beyond whim or attitude or passing play. It was himself, Len Colter, the individual, unique. He could not forswear it and live.

When he understood that, he slept again, quietly, and woke with a salt taste of tears in his mouth to see the window clear and bright and the sun just coming up. The air was full of sound, the screaming of jays and the harsh call of a pheasant in the hedgerow, the piping and chirping of innumerable birds. Len looked out, past the lightning-blasted stub of a giant maple with one indomitable spray of green still sprouting from its side, over the henhouse roof and the home field with the winter wheat ripening on it, to the rough hill slope and the upper wood rising to a crest on which were three dark pines. And a dull sadness came over him, because he was looking at it for the last time. He did not arrive at that decision by any conscious line of reasoning. He only knew it, immediately he waked.

He rose and went stiffly about his chores, white and remote, speaking only when he was spoken to, avoiding people's eyes. With rough kindness, Brother James told him, out of Pa's earshot, to buck up. "It's for your own good, Lennie, and someday you'll look back and be thankful you were caught in time. After all, it's not the end of the world."

Oh yes it is, thought Len. And that's all people know.

After the midday meal he was sent upstairs to wash himself and put on the suit that ordinarily he wore only on the Sabbath. And pretty soon Ma came up with a clean shirt still warm from the iron and made a pretense of looking sternly behind his ears and under his back hair. All the while the tears stole out of her eyes, and suddenly she caught him to her and said rapidly in a whisper, "How could you have done it, Lennie, how could you have been so wicked, to offend the good God and disobey your father?"

Len felt himself beginning to crumble. In a minute or two he would be crying in Ma's arms and all his resolve gone for the time being. So he pushed away from her and said, "Please, Ma, that hurts."

"Your poor back," she murmured. "I forgot." She took his hands. "Lennie, be humble, be patient, and this will all pass away. God will forgive you, you're so young. Too young to realize——"

Pa hollered up the stairs, and that ended it. Ten minutes later the cart was rattling out of the yard, with Len sitting very stiffly beside his father, and neither of them speaking. And Len was thinking about God, and Satan, and the town elders and the preaching man, and Soames and Hostetter and Bartorstown, and it was all confused, but he knew one thing. God was not going to forgive him. He had chosen the way of the transgressor, and he was beyond all hope damned. But he would have all of Bartorstown to keep him company.

Uncle David's cart caught up with them and they went into town together, with Esau huddled in the corner and looking small and fallen-in, as though the bones had all been taken out of him. When they came to the house of Mr. Harkness, Pa and Uncle David got out and stood talking together, leaving Len and Esau to hitch the horses. Esau did not look at Len. He avoided even turning toward him. Len did not look at him, either. But they were side by side at the hitching rack, and Len said fiercely under his breath, "I'll wait for you on the point till moonrise. Then I'm going on."

He could feel Esau start and stiffen. Before he could open his mouth Len said, "Shut up." Then he turned and walked away, to stand respectfully behind his father.

There was a very long, very unhappy session in the parlor of Mr. Harkness' house. Mr. Fenway, Mr. Glasser, and Mr. Clute were there too, and Mr. Nordholt. When they were through, Len felt as though he had been skinned and drawn, like a rabbit with its inmost parts exposed. It made him angry. It made him hate all these slow-spoken bearded men who tore and picked and peeled at him.

Twice he felt that Esau was on the point of betraying him, and he was all ready to make his cousin out a liar. But Esau held his tongue, and after a while Len thought he saw a little stiffening come back into Esau's backbone.

The examination was finished at last. The men conferred. At last Mr. Harkness said to Pa and Uncle David, "I'm sorry that such a disgrace should be brought upon you, for you're both good men and old friends. But perhaps it will serve as a reminder to everybody that youth is not to be trusted, and that constant watchfulness is the price of a Christian soul."

He swung about very grimly on the boys. "A public birching for both of you, on Saturday morning. And after that, if you should be found guilty a second time, you know what the punishment will be."

He waited. Esau looked at his boots. Len stared steadily past Mr. Harkness' shoulder.

"Well," said Mr. Harkness sharply. "Do you know?"

"Yes," said Len. "You'll make us go away and never come back." He looked Mr. Harkness in the eye and added, "There won't be a second time."

"I sincerely hope not," said Mr. Harkness. "And I recommend that both of you read your Bibles, and meditate, and pray, that God may give you wisdom as well as forgiveness."

There was some more talk among the elders, and then the Colters went out and got into their carts and started home again. They passed Mr. Hostetter's wagon in the town square, but Mr. Hostetter was not in sight.

Pa was silent most of the way, except that all at once he said, "I hold myself to blame in this as much as you, Len."

Len said, "I did it. It wasn't any fault of yours, Pa. It couldn't be."

"Somewhere I failed. I didn't teach you right, didn't make you understand. Somewhere you got away from me." Pa shook his head. "I guess David was right. I spared the rod too much."

"Esau was in it more than me," said Len. "He stole the radio in the first place, and all Uncle David's lickings didn't stop him. It wasn't any way your fault, Pa. It was all mine." He felt bad. Somehow he knew this was the real guilt, and it couldn't be helped.

"James was never like this," said Pa to himself, wondering. "Never a moment's worry. How can the same seed produce two such different fruits?"

They did not speak again. When they got home Ma and Gran and Brother James were waiting. Len was sent to his room, and as he climbed the narrow stairs he could hear Pa telling briefly what had happened, and Ma letting out a little whimpering sob. And suddenly he heard Gran's voice lifted high and shrill in mighty anger.

"You're a fool and a coward, Elijah. That's what you all are, fools and cowards, and the boy is worth the lot of you! Go ahead and break his spirit if you can, but I hope you never do it. I hope you never teach him to be afraid of knowing the truth."

Len smiled and a little quiver went through him, because he knew that was meant for his ears as much as Pa's. All right, Gran, he thought. I'll remember.

That night, when the house was stone-dead quiet, he tied his boots around his neck and crept out the window to the summer-kitchen roof, and from there to the limb of a pear tree, and from there to the ground. He stole out of the farmyard and across the road, and there he put his boots on. Then he walked on, skirting the west field where this season's young oats were growing. The woods loomed very dark ahead. He did not once look back.

It was black and still and lonely in among the trees. Len

thought, It's going to be like this a lot from now on, you might as well get used to it. When he reached the point he sat down on the same log where he had sat so often before, and listened to the night music of the frogs and the quiet slipping of the Pymatuning between its banks. The world felt huge, and there was a coldness at his back as though some protective covering had been sheared away. He wondered if Esau would come.

It began to get light down in the southeast, a smudgy grayness brightening slowly to silver. Len waited. He won't come, he thought, he's scared, and I'll have to do this alone. He got up, listening, watching the first thin edge of the moon come up. And a voice inside him said, You can still run home and climb in the window again, and nobody will ever know. He hung on hard to the limb of a tree to keep himself from doing it.

There was a rustle and a thrashing in the dark woods, and Esau came.

They peered at each other for a moment, like owls, and then they caught each other's hands and laughed.

"Public birching," Esau said, panting. "Public birching, hell. The hell with them."

"We'll walk downstream," Len said, "until we find a boat."

"But after that, what?"

"We keep on going. Rivers run into other rivers. I saw the map in the history book. If you keep going long enough you come to the Ohio, and that's the biggest river there is hereabouts."

Esau said stubbornly, "But why the Ohio? It's way south, and everybody knows Bartorstown is west."

"But where west? West is an awful big place. Listen, don't you remember the voice we heard? The stuff is on the river ready to load as soon as the something. They were Bartorstown men talking, about stuff that was going to Bartorstown. And the Ohio runs west. It's the main highway. After that, there's other rivers. And boats must go there. And that's where we're going."

Esau thought about it a minute. Then he said, "Well, all right. It's a place to start from, anyway. Besides, who knows? I still think we were right about Hostetter, even if he did lie about it. Maybe he'll tell the others, maybe they'll talk about us over their radios, how we ran away to find them. Maybe they'll help us, even, when they find a safe time. Who knows?"

"Yes," said Len. "Who knows?"

They walked off along the bank of the Pymatuning, going south. The moon climbed up to give them light. The water rippled and the frogs sang, and in Len Colter's mind the name of Bartorstown rang with the sound of a great bell.

Book Two

8

THE NARROW brown waters of the Pymatuning fatten the Shenango. The Shenango flows down to meet the Mahoning, and the two of them together make the Beaver. The Beaver fattens the Ohio, and the Ohio runs grandly westward to help make mighty the Father of Waters.

Time flows, too. Little units grow into big ones, minutes into months and months into years. Boys become men, and the milestones of a long search multiply and are left behind. But the legend remains a legend, and the dream a dream, glimmering, fading, ever somewhere farther on toward the sunset.

There was a town called Refuge, and a yellow-haired girl, and they were real.

Refuge was not at all like Piper's Run. It was bigger, so much bigger that its boundaries were already straining against the lawful limits, but size was not the chief difference. It was a matter of feeling. Len and Esau had noticed that same feeling in a number of places as they worked their way along the river valleys, particularly where, as in Refuge, highway and waterway conjoined. Piper's Run lived and breathed with the slow calm rhythm of the seasons, and the thoughts of the folk who lived there were calm too. Refuge bustled. The people moved faster, and thought faster, and talked louder, and the streets were noisier at night, with a passing of drays and wagons and the voices of stevedores along the wharves.

Refuge stood on the north bank of the Ohio. It had come by its name, Len understood, because people from a city farther along the river had taken refuge there during the Destruction. It was the terminus now for two main trading routes stretching as far as the Great Lakes, and the wagons rolled day and night while the roads were passable, bringing down baled furs and iron and woolen cloth, flour and cheeses. From east and west along the river came other traffic, bearing other things, copper and hides and tallow and salt beef from the plains, coal and scrap metal from Pennsylvania, salt fish from the Atlantic, kegs of nails, fine guns, paper. The river traffic moved around the clock, too, from spring to early winter, flatboats and launches and tugs towing long strings of loaded barges, going with a fine brave smoke and clatter from their steam engines. These were the first engines Len and Esau had ever seen, and at first they were frightened out of their wits by the noise, but they soon got used to them. They had, one winter, worked in a little foundry near the mouth of the Beaver, making boilers and feeling as though they were already helping to mechanize the world. The New Mennonites frowned on the use of any artificial power, but the river-boat men belonged to different sects and had different problems. They had to get cargoes upriver against the current, and if they could harness steam in a simple and easily handmade engine to help them, they were going to do it, cutting the ethic to fit the need.

On the Kentucky side of the river, just opposite, there was a place called Shadwell. Shadwell was much smaller than Refuge and much newer, but it was swelling out so fast that even Len and Esau could see the difference in the year or so they had been there. The people of Refuge did not care much for Shadwell, which had only happened because traders had begun to come up out of the South with sugar and blackstrap and cotton and tobacco, drawn by the commerce of the Refuge markets. A couple of temporary sheds had gone up, and a ferry dock, and a cabin or two, and before anybody realized it there was a village, with wharves and warehouses of its own, and a name, and a growing population. And Refuge, already as large as a town was permitted by law to be, sat sourly by and watched the overplus of trade it could not handle flow into Shadwell.

There were few Amish or Mennonites in Refuge. The people mostly belonged to the Church of Holy Thankfulness, and were called Kellerites after the James P. Keller who founded the sect. Len and Esau had found that there were few Mennonites anywhere in the settlements that lived by commerce rather than by agriculture. And since they were excommunicate themselves, with no wish to be traced back to Piper's Run, they had long ago discarded the distinctive dress of their childhood faith for the nondescript homespuns of the river towns. They wore their hair short and their chins naked, because it was the custom among the Kellerites for a man to remain clean-shaven until he married, when he was expected to grow the beard that distinguished him more plainly than any removable ring. They went every Sunday to the Church of Holy

Thankfulness, and joined in the regular daily devotions of the family they boarded with, and sometimes they forgot that they had ever been anything but Kellerites.

Sometimes, Len thought, they even forgot why they were here and what they were looking for. And he would make himself remember the night when he had waited for Esau on the point above the Pymatuning, and everything that had gone before to bring him there, and it was easy enough to remember the physical things, the chill air and the smell of leaves, the beating, and the way Pa's face had looked as he lifted the strap and brought it whistling down. But the other part of it, the way he had felt inside, was harder to call to mind. Sometimes he could do it only with a real effort. Other times he could not do it at all. And at still other times—and these were the worst—the way he had felt about leaving home and finding Bartorstown seemed to him childish and absurd. He would see home and family so clearly that it was a physical pain in him, and he would think, I threw them all away for a name, a voice in the air, and here I am, a wanderer, and where is Bartorstown? He had found out that time can be a traitor and that thoughts are like mountaintops, a different shape on every side, changing as you move away.

Time had played him another trick, too. It had made him grow up and given him a lot of brand-new things to worry about.

Including the yellow-haired girl.

It was an evening in mid-June, hot and sultry, with the sunset swallowed up in the blackness of an oncoming storm. The two candles on the table burned straight up, with no quiver of air from the open windows to trouble them. Len sat with his hands folded and his head bent, looking down into the remains of a milk pudding. Esau sat on his right, in the same attitude. The yellow-haired girl sat across from them. Her name was Amity Taylor. Her father was saying grace after meat, sitting at the head of the table, and at the foot, her mother listened reverently.

"—didst stretch out the garment of Thy mercy to shelter us in the day of Destruction——"

Amity glanced up from under the shadows of her brows in the candlelight, looking first at Len and then at Esau.

"—our thanks for the limitless abundance of Thy blessing——"

Len felt the girl's eyes on him. His skin was thin and sensitive to that touch, so that without even looking up he knew what she was doing. His heart began to thump. He felt hot. Esau's hands were in his line of vision, folded between Esau's knees. He saw them move and tighten, and he knew that Amity had looked at Esau too, and he got even hotter, thinking about the garden and the shadowy place under the rose arbor.

Wouldn't Judge Taylor ever shut up?

The Amen came at last, muffled in the louder voice of thunder. Hurry, thought Len. Hurry with the dishes or there won't be any walking in the garden. Not for anybody. He jumped up, scraping his chair back over the bare floor. Esau jumped up too, and he and Len went to picking up plates off the table so fast they jostled each other. On the other side of the candlelight, Amity slowly stacked the cups, and smiled.

Mrs. Taylor went out, carrying two serving dishes into the kitchen. At the hall door, the judge seemed on the point of going to his study, as he always did immediately after the final grace. Esau turned suddenly and gave Len a covert glare of anger, and whispered, "Stay out of this."

Amity walked toward the kitchen door, balancing the stack of cups in her two hands. Her yellow hair hung down her back in a thick braid. She wore a dress of gray cotton, high in the neck and long in the skirt, but it did not look on her at all the way a similar dress did on her mother. She had a wonderful way of walking. It made Len's heart come up in his throat every time he saw it. He glared back at Esau and started after her with his own load of plates, making long strides to get ahead. And Judge Taylor said quietly from the hall door, "Len—come into the study when you've put those down. They can get along without you for one washing."

Len stopped. He gave Taylor a startled and apprehensive look, and said, "Yes, sir." Taylor nodded and left the room. Len glanced briefly at Esau, who was openly upset.

"What does he want?" asked Esau.

"How should I know?"

"Listen. Listen, have you been up to anything?"

Amity went slowly through the swinging door, with her skirt moving gracefully around her ankles. Len flushed.

"No more'n you have, Esau," he said angrily. He went after Amity and put his pile of dishes down on the sink board. Amity began to roll her sleeves up. She said to her mother, "Len can't help tonight. Daddy wants him."

Reba Taylor turned from the stove, where a pot of wash water simmered over the coals. She had a mild, pleasant, rather vacuous face, and Len had marked her long ago as one of the incurious ones. Life had passed over her so easily.

"Dear, dear," she said. "Surely you haven't done anything wrong, Len?"

"I hope not, ma'am."

"I'll bet you," said Amity, "that it's about Mike Dulinsky and his warehouse."

"*Mr.* Dulinsky," said Reba Taylor sharply, "and get about your dishes, young lady. They're your concern. Run along, Len. Very likely the judge only wants to give you some advice, and you could do worse than listen to it."

"Yes, ma'am," said Len, and went out, across the dining room and into the hall and along that to the study, wondering all the way whether he had been seen kissing Amity in the garden, or whether it was about the Dulinsky business, or what. He had often gone to the judge's study, and he had often talked with him, about books and the past and the future and sometimes even the present, but he had never been called in before.

The study door was open. Taylor said, "Come in, Len." He was sitting behind his big desk in the angle of the windows. They faced the west, and the sky beyond them was a dull black as though it had been wiped all over with soot. The trees looked sickly and colorless, and the river lay at one side like a strip of lead. Taylor had been sitting there looking out, with an unlighted candle and an unopened book beside him. He was rather a small man, with smooth cheeks and a high forehead. His hair and beard were always neatly trimmed, his linen was fresh every day, and his dark plain suit was cut from the finest cloth that came into the Refuge market. Len liked him. He had books and read them and encouraged other people to read them, and he was not afraid of knowledge, though he never made a parade of having any more than he needed in his profession. "Don't call undue attention to yourself," he often told Len, "and you will avoid a great deal of trouble."

Now he told Len to come in and shut the door. "I'm afraid we're going to have a really serious talk, and I wanted you here alone because I want you to be free to think and make your decisions without any—well, any other influences."

"You don't think much of Esau, do you?" asked Len, sitting down where the judge had set a chair for him.

"No," said Taylor, "but that is neither here nor there. Except that I'll say further that I do think a great deal of you. And now we'll leave personalities alone. Len, you work for Mike Dulinsky."

"Yes, sir," said Len, and began to bristle up a bit, defensively. So that was it.

"Are you going to continue working for him?"

Len hesitated only a short second before he said again, "Yes, sir."

Taylor thought, looking out at the black sky and the ugly dusk. A beautiful forked blaze ran down the clouds. Len counted slowly, and when he reached seven there was a roll of thunder. "It's still quite a ways off," he said.

"Yes, but we'll catch it. When they come from that direction, we always do. You've done a lot of reading this last year, Len. Have you learned anything from it?"

Len ran his eye lovingly over the shelves. It was too dark to see titles, but he knew the books by their size and place and he had read an awful lot of them.

"I hope so," he said.

"Then apply what you've learned. It isn't any good to you shut up inside your head in a separate cupboard. Do you remember Socrates?"

"Yes."

"He was a greater and a wiser man than you or I will ever be, but that didn't save him when he ran too hard against the whole body of law and public belief."

Lightning flashed again, and this time the interval was shorter. The wind began to blow, tossing the branches of the trees around and riffling the blank surface of the river. Distant figures labored on the wharves to make fast the moorings of the barges, or to hustle bales and sacks under cover. Landward, between the trees, the whitewashed or weathered-silver houses of Refuge glimmered in the last wan light from overhead.

"Why do you want to hasten the day?" asked Taylor quietly. "You'll never live to see it, and neither will your children, nor your grandchildren. Why, Len?"

"Why what?" asked Len, now blankly confused, and then he gasped as Taylor answered him, "Why do you want to bring back the cities?"

Len was silent, peering into the gloom that had suddenly deepened until Taylor was no more than a shadow four feet away.

"They were dying even before the Destruction," said Taylor. "Megalopolis, drowned in its own sewage, choked with its own waste gases, smothered and crushed by its own population. 'City' sounds like a musical word to your ear, but what do you really know about them?"

They had been over this ground before. "Gran used to say——"

"That she was a little girl then, and little girls would hardly see the dirt, the ugliness, the crowded poverty, the vice. The cities were sucking all the life of the country into themselves and destroying it. Men were no longer individuals, but units in a vast machine, all cut to one pattern, with the same tastes and ideas, the same mass-produced education that did not educate but only pasted a veneer of catchwords over ignorance. Why do you want to bring that back?"

An old argument, but applied in a totally unexpected way. Len stammered, "I haven't been thinking about cities one way or the other. And I don't see what Mr. Dulinsky's new warehouse has to do with them."

"Len, if you're not honest with yourself, life will never be honest with you. A stupid man could say that he didn't see and be honest, but not you. Unless you're still too much of a child to think beyond the immediate fact."

"I'm old enough to get married," said Len hotly, "and that ought to be old enough for anything."

"Quite," said Taylor. "Quite. Here comes the rain, Len. Help me with the windows." They shut them, and Taylor lit the candle. The room was now unbearably close and hot. "What a pity," he said, "that the windows always have to be closed just when the cool wind starts to blow. Yes, you're old enough to get married, and I think Amity has a thought or two in that direction herself. It's a possibility I want you to consider."

Len's heart began to pound, the way it always did when Amity was involved. He felt wildly excited, and at the same time it was as though a trap had been set before his feet. He sat down again, and the rain thrashed on the windows like hail.

Taylor said slowly, "Refuge is a good town just the way it stands. You could have a good life here. I can take you off the docks and make a lawyer out of you, and in time you'd be an important man. You would have leisure for study, and all the wisdom of the world is there in those books. And there's Amity. Those are the things I can give you. What does Dulinsky offer?"

Len shook his head. "I do my work, and he pays me. That's all."

"You know he's breaking the law."

"It's a silly law. One warehouse more or less——"

"One warehouse more, in this case, violates the Thirtieth Amendment, which is the most basic law of this land. It won't be overlooked."

"But it isn't fair. Nobody here in Refuge wants to see Shadwell spring up and take a lot of business away because there aren't enough warehouses and wharves and shelters on this side to take care of all the trade."

"One more warehouse," said Taylor, pointedly repeating Len's words, "and then more wharves to serve it, and more housing for the traders, and pretty soon you'll need another warehouse still, and that is the way in which cities are born. Len, has Dulinsky ever mentioned Bartorstown to you?"

Len's heart, which had been beating so hard for Amity, now stopped in sudden fear. He shivered and said, with perfect truthfulness, "No, sir. Never."

"I just wondered. It seems the kind of a thing a Bartorstown man might do. But then I've known Mike since we were boys together, and I can't remember any possible influence—no, I suppose not. But that may not save him, Len, and it may not save you."

Len said carefully, "I don't think I understand."

"You and Esau are strangers. People will accept you as long as you don't run counter to their ways, but if you do, look out." He leaned his elbows on the desk and looked at Len. "You haven't been altogether truthful about yourself."

"I haven't told any lies."

"That isn't always necessary. Anyway, I can pretty well guess. You're a country boy. I would lay odds that you were New Mennonite. And you ran away from home. Why?"

"I guess," said Len, choosing his words as a man on the edge of a pitfall chooses his steps, "that it was because Pa and me couldn't agree on how much was right for me to know."

"Thus far," said Taylor thoughtfully, "and no farther. That has always been a difficult line to draw. Each sect must decide for itself, and to a certain degree, so must every man. Have you found your limit, Len?"

"Not yet."

"Find it," Taylor said, "before you go too far."

They sat for a moment in silence. The rain poured and a lightning bolt came down so close that it made an audible hissing before it hit. The resultant thunder shook the house like an explosion.

"Do you understand," asked Taylor, "why the Thirtieth Amendment was passed?"

"So there wouldn't be any more cities."

"Yes, but do you comprehend the reasoning behind that interdiction? I was brought up in a certain body of belief, and in public I wouldn't dream of contradicting any part of it, but here in private I can say that I do not believe that God directed the cities to be destroyed because they were sinful. I've read too much history. The enemy bombed the big key cities because they were excellent targets, centers of population, centers of manufacture and distribution, without which the country would be like a man with his head cut off. And it worked out just that way. The enormously complex system of supply broke down, the cities that were not bombed had to be abandoned because they were not only dangerous but useless, and everyone was thrown back on the simple basics of survival, chiefly the search for food.

"The men who framed the new laws were determined that that should not happen again. They had the people dispersed now, and they were going to keep them that way, close to their source of supply and offering no more easy targets to a potential enemy. So they passed the Thirtieth Amendment. It was a wise law. It suited the people. They had just had a fearful object lesson in what kind of deathtraps the cities could be. They didn't want any more of them, and gradually that became an article of faith. The country has been healthy and prosperous under the Thirtieth Amendment, Len. Leave it alone."

"Maybe you're right," said Len, scowling at the candle flame. "But when Mr. Dulinsky says how the country has really started to grow again and shouldn't be stopped by outgrown laws, I think he's right, too."

"Don't let him fool you. He's not worried about the country. He's a man who owns four warehouses and wants to own five and is sore because the law says he can't do it."

The judge stood up.

"You'll have to decide what's right in your own mind. But I want to make one thing clear to you. I have my wife and my daughter and myself to think about. If you go on with Dulinsky you'll have to leave my house. No more walks with Amity. No more books. And I warn you, if I am called upon to judge you, judge you I will."

Len stood up too. "Yes, sir."

Taylor dropped a hand on his shoulder. "Don't be a fool, Len. Think it over."

"I will." He went out, feeling sullen and resentful and at the same time convinced that the judge was talking sense. Amity, marriage, a place in the community, a future, roots, no more Dulinsky, no more doubt. No more Bartorstown. No more dreaming. No more seeking and never finding.

He thought about being married to Amity, and what it would be like. It frightened him so that he sweated like a colt seeing harness for the first time. No more dreaming for fair. He thought of Brother James, who by now must be the father of several small Mennonites, and he wondered whether, on the whole, Refuge was very different from Piper's Run, and if

Amity was worth having come all this way for. Amity, or Plato. He had not read Plato in Piper's Run, and he had read him in Refuge, but Plato did not seem like the whole answer, either.

No more Bartorstown. But would he ever find it, anyway? Was he crazy to think of exchanging a girl for a phantom?

The hall was dark, except for the intermittent flashes of lightning. There was one of these as he passed the foot of the stairs, and in its brief glare he saw Esau and Amity in the triangular alcove under the treads. They were pressed close together and Esau was kissing her hard, and Amity was not protesting.

9

IT WAS the Sabbath afternoon. They were standing in the shadow of the rose arbor, and Amity was glaring at him.

"You did not see me doing any such thing, and if you tell anybody you did I'll say you're lying!"

"I know what I saw," said Len, "and so do you."

She made her thick braid switch back and forth, in a way she had of tossing her head. "I'm not promised to you."

"Would you like to be, Amity?"

"Maybe. I don't know."

"Then why were you kissing Esau?"

"Well, because," she said very reasonably, "how would I know which one of you I like the best, if I didn't?"

"All right," said Len. "All right, then." He reached out and pulled her to him, and because he was thinking of how Esau had done it he was rather rough about it. For the first time he held her really tight and felt how soft and firm she was and how her body curved amazingly. Her eyes were close to his, so close that they became only a blue color without any shape, and he felt dizzy and shut his own, and found her mouth just by touch alone.

After a while he pushed her away a little and said, "Now which is it?" He was shaking all over, but there was only the faintest flush in Amity's cheeks and the look she gave him was quite cool. She smiled.

"I don't know," she said. "You'll have to try again."

"Is that what you told Esau?"

"What do you care what I told Esau?" Again the yellow braid went swish-swish across the back of her dress. "You mind your own business, Len Colter."

"I could make it my business."

"Who said?"

"Your father said, that's who."

"Oh," said Amity. "He did." Suddenly it was as though a curtain had dropped between them. She drew away, and the line of her mouth got hard.

"Amity," he said. "Listen, Amity, I——"

"You leave me alone. You hear, Len?"

"What's so different now? You were anxious enough a minute ago."

"Anxious! That's all you know. And if you think because you've been sneaking around to my father behind my back——"

"I didn't sneak. Amity, listen." He caught her again and pulled her toward him, and she hissed at him between her teeth. "Let me go, I don't belong to you, I don't belong to anybody! Let me go——"

He held her, struggling. It excited him, and he laughed and bent his head to kiss her again.

"Aw, come on, Amity, I love you——"

She squalled like a cat and clawed his cheek. He let her go, and she was not pretty any more, her face was all twisted and ugly and her eyes were mean. She ran away from him down the path. The air was warm and the smell of roses was heavy around him. For a while he stood looking after her, and then he walked slowly to the house and up to the room he shared with Esau.

Esau was lying on the bed, half asleep. He only grunted and rolled over when Len came in. Len opened the door of the shallow cupboard. He took out a small sack made of tough canvas and began to pack his belongings into it, methodically, ramming each article down into place with unnecessary force. His face was flushed and his brows pulled down into a heavy scowl.

Esau rolled back again. He blinked at Len and said, "What do you think you're doing?"

"Packing."

"Packing!" Esau sat up. "What for?"

"What do people usually do it for? I'm leaving."

Esau's feet hit the floor. "Are you crazy? What do you mean, you're leaving, just like that. Don't I have anything to say about it?"

"Not about me leaving, you don't. You can do what you want to. Look out, I want those boots."

"All right! But you can't—— Wait a minute. What's that on your cheek?"

"What?" Len swiped at his cheek with the back of his hand. It came away with a little red smear on it. Amity had dug deep.

Esau began to laugh.

Len straightened up. "What's funny?"

"She finally told you off, did she? Oh, don't give me any story about how the cat scratched you, I know claw marks when I see them. Good. I told you to keep away from her, but you wouldn't listen. I——"

"Do you figure," asked Len quietly, "that she belongs to you?"

Esau smiled. "I could have told you that, too."

Len hit him. It was the first time in his life that he had hit anybody in genuine anger. He watched Esau fall backward onto the bed, his eyes bulging with surprise and a thin red trickle springing out of the corner of his mouth, and it all seemed to happen very slowly, giving him plenty of time to feel guilty and regretful and confused. It was almost as though he had struck his own brother. But he was still angry. He grabbed up his bag and started out the door, and Esau sprang off the bed and caught him by the shoulder of his jacket, spinning him around. "Hit me, will you?" he panted. "Hit me, you dirty——" He called Len a name he had picked up along the river docks and swung his fist, hard.

Len ducked. Esau's knuckles slid along the side of his jaw and on into the solid jamb of the door. Esau howled and danced away, holding his hand under his other arm and cursing. Len started to say something like "I'm sorry," but changed his mind and turned again to go. And Judge Taylor was in the hall.

"Stop that," he said to Esau, and Esau stopped, standing still in the middle of the room. Taylor looked from one to the other and to the bag in Len's hand. "I've just spoken to Amity," he said, and Len could see that underneath his judicial manner Taylor was in a seething rage. "I'm sorry, Len. I seem to have made an error of judgment."

"Yes, sir," said Len. "I was just going."

Taylor nodded. "All the same," he said, "what I told you is true. Remember it." He looked keenly at Esau.

"Let him go," Esau said. "I'm staying right here."

"I think not," said Taylor.

Esau said, "But he——"

"I hit him first," said Len.

"That is neither here nor there," said the judge. "Get your things together, Esau."

"But why? I make enough to pay the rent. I haven't done any——"

"I'm not sure yet exactly what you have done, but much or little, that's an end to it. The room is no longer for rent. And if I catch you around my daughter again I'll have you run out of town. Is that clear?"

Esau glowered at him, but he did not say anything. He started to throw his things into a pile on the bed. Len went out past the judge, along the hall and down the stairs. He went out the back way, and as he passed the kitchen he caught a glimpse through the half-open door of Amity bent over the kitchen table, sobbing like a wildcat, and Mrs. Taylor watching her with an expression of blank dismay, one hand raised as though for a comforting pat on the shoulder but stopped in midair and forgotten.

Len let himself out by the back gate, avoiding the rose arbor.

Sabbath lay quiet and heavy on the town. Len stuck to the alleys, walking steadily along in the dust. He did not have any idea where he was going, but habit and the general configuration of Refuge took him down to the river and onto the docks where Dulinsky's four big warehouses stood in line. He stopped there, uncertain and sullen, only just beginning to realize that things had changed very radically for him in the last few minutes.

The river ran green as bottle glass, and among the trees of its farther bank the roofs of Shadwell glimmered in the hot sun. There was a string of river craft tied up along the dock. The men who belonged to them were either in the town or asleep below deck. Nothing moved but the river, and the clouds, and a half-grown cat playing a game with itself on the foredeck of one of the barges. Off to his right, further down, was the big bare rectangle of the new warehouse site. The foundation stones were already laid. Timbers and planks were set by in neat piles, and there was a sawmill with a heap of pale yellow dust below it. Two men, widely separated, lounged inconspicuously in the shade. Len frowned. They looked to him almost as though they were on guard.

Perhaps they were. It was a stupid world, full of stupid people. Fearful people, thinking that if the least little thing was changed the whole sky would fall on them. Stupid world. He hated it. Amity lived in it, and somewhere in it Bartorstown was hidden so it could never be found, and life was dark and full of frustrations.

He was still brooding when Esau came onto the dock after him.

Esau was carrying his own belongings in a hasty bundle, and his face looked red and ugly. His lip was swollen on one side. He threw the bundle down and stood in front of Len and said, "I've got a couple of things to settle with you."

Len breathed hard through his nose. He was not afraid of Esau, and he felt low and mean enough now that a fight would be a pleasant thing. He was not quite as tall as Esau but his shoulders were wider and thicker. He hunched them up and waited.

"What did you want to go and get us thrown out of there for?" Esau said.

"*I* left. It was you that got thrown out."

"Fine cousin you are. What did you say to old man Taylor to make him do that?"

"Nothing. Didn't have to."

"What do you mean by that?"

"He doesn't like you, that's what I mean. Don't come picking a fight with me unless you mean it, Esau."

"Sore, aren't you? Well go ahead and be sore, and I'll tell you something. And you can tell the judge. Nobody can keep me away from Amity. I'll see her anytime I want to, and do anything I want to with her, because *she* likes me whether her father does or not."

"Big mouth," said Len. "That's all you got, a great big windy mouth."

"I wouldn't talk," said Esau bitterly. "If it hadn't been for you I'd never left home. I'd be there now, probably with the whole farm by now, and a wife and kids if I wanted them, instead of roaming to hell and gone around the country looking for——"

"Shut up," said Len fiercely.

"All right, but you know what I mean, and not even knowing where I'm going to sleep tonight. Trouble, Len. That's all you ever made for me, and now you made it with my girl."

In utter indignation, Len said, "Esau, you're a yellow-bellied liar." And Esau hit him.

Len had got so mad that he had forgotten to be on guard, and the blow took him by surprise. It knocked his hat off and stung most painfully on his cheekbone. He sucked in a sharp breath and went for Esau. They scuffled and banged each other around on the dock for a minute or two and then suddenly Esau said, "Hold it, hold off, somebody's coming and you know what you get for fighting on the Sabbath."

They drew apart, breathing hard. Len picked up his hat, trying to look as though he had not been doing anything. Out of the corner of his eye he saw Mike Dulinsky and two other men coming onto the dock.

"We'll finish this later," he whispered to Esau.

"Sure."

They stood to one side. Dulinsky recognized them and smiled. He was a big powerful man, run slightly to fat around the middle. He had very bright eyes that seemed to see everything, including a lot that was out of sight, but they were cold eyes that never really warmed up even when they smiled. Len admired Mike Dulinsky. He respected him. But he did not particularly like him. The two men with him were Ames and Whinnery, both warehouse owners.

"Well," said Dulinsky. "Down looking over the project?"

"Not exactly," said Len. "We—uh—could we have permission to sleep in the office tonight? We—aren't rooming at the Taylors' any more."

"Oh?" said Dulinsky, raising his eyebrows. Ames made a sardonic sound that was not quite a snicker.

Len ignored that. "Is it all right, sir?"

"Of course. Make yourselves at home. You have the key with you? Good. Come along, gentlemen."

He went off with Whinnery and Ames. Len got his bag and Esau his bundle and they walked back a way up the dock to the office, a long two-story shed where the paper work of the warehouses was done. Len had the key to it because it was part of his job to open the office every morning. While he was fiddling with the lock, Esau looked back and said, "He's got 'em down there showing 'em the foundations. They don't look too happy."

Len glanced back too. Dulinsky was waving his arms and talking animatedly, but Ames and Whinnery looked worried and shook their heads.

"He'll have to do more than talk to convince them," said Esau.

Len grunted and went inside. In a few minutes, after they had gone up into the loft to stow their belongings, they heard somebody come in. It was Dulinsky, and he was alone. He gave them a direct, hard stare and said, "Are you scared too? Are you going to run out on me?"

He did not give them time to answer, jerking his head toward the outside.

"*They're* scared. They want more warehouses, too. They want Refuge to grow and make them rich, but they don't want to take any of the risk. They want to see what happens to me first. The bastards. I've been trying to convince them that if we all work together—— Why did the judge make you leave his house? Was it on account of me?"

"Well," said Len. "Yes."

Esau looked surprised, but he did not say anything.

"I need you," said Dulinsky. "I need all the men I can get. I hope you'll stick with me, but I won't try to hold you. If you're worried, you better go now."

"I don't know about Len," said Esau, grinning, "but I'm going to stay." He was not thinking about warehouses.

Dulinsky looked at Len. Len flushed and looked at the floor. "I don't know," he said. "It isn't that I'm afraid to stay, it's just that maybe I want to leave Refuge and go on down-river."

"I'll get along," said Dulinsky.

"I'm sure you will," said Len, stubbornly, "but I want to think about it."

"Stick with me," said Dulinsky, "and get rich. My great-great-grandfather came here from Poland, and he never got rich because things were already built. But now they're ready to be built again, and I'm going to get in on the ground floor. I know what the judge has been telling you. He's a negativist. He's afraid of believing in anything. I'm not. I believe in the greatness of this country, and I know that these outmoded shackles have got to be broken off if it's ever to grow again. They won't break themselves. Somebody, men like you and me, will have to get in there and do it."

"Yes, sir," said Len. "But I still want to think it over."

Dulinsky studied him keenly, and then he smiled. "You don't push easily, do you? Not a bad trait—— All right, go ahead and think."

He left them. Len looked at Esau, but the mood was gone and he did not feel like fighting any more. He said, "I'm going for a walk."

Esau shrugged, making no attempt to join him. Len walked slowly along the dock, thinking of the westbound boats, wondering if any of them were secretly bound for Bartorstown, wondering if it was any use to go blindly from place to place, wondering what to do. He reached the end of the dock and stepped off it, going on past the warehouse site. The two men watched him closely until he turned away.

He was perhaps not consciously thinking of going there, but a few minutes more of wandering about brought him to the edge of the traders' compound, an area of hard-packed earth where the wagons were drawn up between long ranks of stable sheds and auction sheds and permanent shelter houses for the men. Len hung around here a good bit. Partly his work for Dulinsky required him to, but there was more to it than that. There was all the gossip and excitement of the roads, and sometimes there was even news of Piper's Run, and there was the never-ending hope that someday he would hear the word he had been waiting all these years to hear. He never had. He had never even seen a familiar face, Hostetter's face in particular, and that was odd because he knew that Hostetter went South in the winter season and therefore would have to cross the river somewhere. Len had been at all the ferry points, but Hostetter had not appeared. He had often wondered if Hostetter had gone back to Bartorstown, or if something had happened to him and he was dead.

The area was quiet now, for no business was done on the Sabbath, and the men were sitting and talking in the shade, or off somewhere to afternoon prayer meeting. Len knew most of them at least by sight, and they knew him. He joined them, glad of some talk to get his mind off his problems for a while. Some of them were New Mennonites. Len always felt shy around them, and a little unhappy, because they brought back to him many things he would just as soon not think about. He had never let on that he had once been one of them.

They talked awhile. The shadows got longer and a cool breeze came up off the river. There began to be a smell of wood smoke and cooking food, and it occurred to Len that he did not have any place to eat supper. He asked if he could stay.

"Of course, and welcome," said a New Mennonite named Fisher. "Tell you what, Len, if you was to go and get some more wood off the big pile it would help."

Len took the barrow and trundled off across to the edge of the compound where the great wood stack was. He had to pass along beside the stable sheds to do this. He filled the barrow with firewood and turned back again. When he reached a certain point beside the stables, the lines of wagons hid him from the shelter houses and the men, who were now all getting busy around the fires. It was dark inside the stables. A sweet warm smell of horse came out of them, and a sound of munching.

A voice came out of them, too. It said his name.

"Len Colter."

Len stopped. It was a hushed and hurried voice, very sharp, insistent. He looked around, but he could not see anything.

"Don't look for me unless you want to get us both in trouble," said the voice. "Just listen. I have a message for you, from a friend. He says to tell you that you'll never find what you're looking for. He says go home to Piper's Run and make your peace. He says——"

"Hostetter," Len whispered. "Are you Hostetter?"

"—get out of Refuge. There will be a bath of fire, and you'll get burned in it. Get out, Len. Go home. Now walk on, as though nothing had happened."

Len started to walk. But he said, into the dark of the stables, in a whispered cry of wild triumph, "You know there's only one place I want to go! If you want me to leave Refuge, you'll have to take me there."

And the voice answered, on a fading sigh, "Remember the night of the preaching. You may not always be saved."

10

TWO WEEKS later, the frame of the new warehouse had taken shape and men were starting to work on the roof. Len worked where he was told to, now on the construction gang and now in the office when the papers got stacked too high. He did this in a state of tense excitement, going through a lot of the motions automatically while his mind was on other things. He was like a man waiting for an explosion to happen.

He had moved his sleeping quarters to a hut in the traders' section, leaving Esau in full possession of Dulinsky's loft. He spent every spare minute there, quite forgetting Amity, forgetting everything but the hope that now, any minute, after all these years, things would break for him the way he wanted them to. He went over and over in his mind every word the voice had said. He heard them in his light uneasy sleep. And he would not have left Refuge and Dulinsky now for any reason under the sun.

He knew there was danger. He was beginning to feel it in the air and see it in the faces of some of the men who dropped by to watch as the timbers of the warehouse went up. There were too many strangers among them. The countryside around Refuge was populous and prosperous farm land, and only partly New Mennonite. On market days there were always farmers in town, and the country preachers and the storekeepers and the traders came and went, and it was obvious that the word was spreading around. Len knew he was taking a chance, and he knew that it was perhaps not fair to Hostetter or whoever it was that had risked giving him that warning. But he was fiercely determined not to go.

He was angry with Hostetter and the men of Bartorstown.

It was perfectly apparent now that they must have known where he and Esau were ever since they left Piper's Run. He could think of half a dozen times when a trader had happened along providentially to help them out of a bad spot, and he was sure now that these were not accidents. He was sure that the reason he had never met Hostetter was not accidental either. Hostetter had avoided them, and probably the men of Bartorstown had avoided using the facilities of whatever town the Colter boys happened to be in. That was why there had never been a clue. Hostetter knew perfectly well why they had run away, and he had spread the warning, and for all these years the men of Bartorstown had been deliberately keeping them from all hope of finding what they were after. And at the same time, the men of Bartorstown could easily, at any moment, have simply picked them up and taken them where they wanted to go. Len felt like a child deceived by its elders. He wanted to get his hands on Hostetter.

He had not said anything about this to Esau. He did not like Esau very well any more, and he was not sure of him. He figured there was plenty of time for talking later on, and in the meantime everybody, including Esau, was safer if he didn't know.

Len hung around the traders, not asking any questions or saying anything, just there with his eyes and his ears wide open. But he did not see anybody he knew, and no secret voice spoke to him again. If it was Hostetter, he was still keeping out of sight.

He would hardly be able to do that in Refuge. Len decided that if it was Hostetter, he was staying across the river in Shadwell. And immediately Len felt a compulsion to go there. Perhaps, away from people who knew him too well, another contact might be made.

He didn't have any excuse to go to Shadwell, but it did not take him long to think one up. One evening as he was helping Dulinsky close the office he said, "I've just been thinking it wouldn't be a bad idea if I was to go over to Shadwell and see what they think about what you're doing. After all, if you're successful, it'll mean the bread out of their mouths."

"I know what they think," said Dulinsky. He slammed a desk drawer shut and looked out the window at the dark framework of the building rising against the blue west. After a minute he said, "I saw Judge Taylor today."

Len waited. He was fidgety and nervous all the time these days. It seemed hours before Dulinsky spoke again.

"He told me if I didn't stop building that he and the town authorities would arrest me and everyone connected with me."

"Do you think they will?"

"I reminded him that I hadn't violated any local law. The Thirtieth Amendment is a Federal law, and he has no jurisdiction over that."

"What did he say?"

Dulinsky shrugged. "Just what I expected. He'll send immediately to the federal court in Maryland, asking for authority or a federal officer."

"Oh well," said Len, "that'll take a while. And public opinion——"

"Yes," said Dulinsky. "Public opinion is the only hope I have. Taylor knows it. The elders know it. Old man Shadwell knows it. This thing isn't going to wait for any federal judge to jog trot all the way from Maryland."

"You'll carry the rally tomorrow night," said Len confidently. "Refuge is pretty sore about Shadwell taking business away from them. The people are behind you, most of them."

Dulinsky grunted. "Maybe it wouldn't be amiss if you did go to Shadwell. This rally is important. I'll stand or fall by the way it goes, and if old man Shadwell is fixing to come over and make me some trouble, I want to know it. I'll give you some business to do, so it won't look too much as though you're spying. Don't ask any questions, just see what you can pick up. Oh, and don't take Esau."

Len hadn't been intending to, but he asked, "Why not?"

"You've got wit enough to stay out of trouble. He hasn't. Do you know where he spends his nights?"

"Why," said Len, surprised, "right here, I suppose."

"Maybe. I hope so. You take the morning ferry, Len, and

come back on the afternoon. I want you here for the rally. I need every voice I can get shouting Hooray for Mike."

"All right," said Len. "Good night."

He walked past the new warehouse on his way. It smelled fragrantly of new wood and had a satisfying hugeness. Len felt that it was good to build. For the moment he agreed passionately with Dulinsky.

A voice challenged him from the shadow of a pile of planks, and he said, "Hello, Harry, it's me." He walked on. There were four men on guard now. They carried big billets of wood in their hands, and fires burned all night to light the area. He understood that Mike Dulinsky came down there every so often to look around, as though he was too uneasy to sleep.

Len did not sleep well himself. He sat around talking for a while after supper and then rolled in, but he was thinking about tomorrow, thinking how he would walk through Shadwell to the traders' compound and Hostetter would be there, and he would say something to him, something quiet but significant, and Hostetter would nod and say, "All right, it's no use fighting you any longer, I'll take you where you want to go." He played that scene over and over in his mind, and all the time he knew it was only one of those things you dream up when you're a child and haven't learned yet about reality. Then he got to thinking about Dulinsky asking where Esau spent his nights, and sleep was out of the question. Len wanted to know too.

He thought he did know. And it was amazing, considering that he didn't care at all about Amity, how much the idea upset him.

He rose and went out into the warm night. The compound was dark and silent, except for an occasional thump from the stables where the big horses moved in their stalls. He crossed it and went up through the sleeping streets of the town, deliberately taking the long way round so as not to pass the new warehouse. He didn't want to talk to the guards.

The long way round was long enough to take him past Judge Taylor's house. Nothing was stirring there, and no light showed. He picked out Amity's window, and then he felt ashamed and moved on, down to the docks.

The door of Dulinsky's office was locked, but Esau had a key now, so that didn't mean anything. Len hesitated. The wet smell of the river was strong in the air, a presage of rain, and the sky was clouded. The watch fires burned, farther down the bank. It was quiet, and somehow the office shed had the feel of an empty building. Len unlocked the door and went in.

Esau was not there.

Len stood still for quite a while, in a black fury at first, but calming down gradually into a sort of disgusted contempt for Esau's stupidity. As for Amity, if that was what she wanted she was welcome to it. He wasn't angry. Not much.

Esau's cot had not been touched. Len turned back the quilt, folding it carefully. He set Esau's spare boots straight under the edge of the cot, picked up a soiled shirt and hung it neatly on a peg. Then he lit the lamp beside Esau's bed, turned it low, and left it burning. He went out, locking the office door behind him.

It was very late when he got back to the compound. Even so, he sat for a long time on the doorstep, looking at the night and thinking. Lonely thoughts.

In the morning he stopped by to pick up the letter Dulinsky had for him to take to Shadwell, and Esau was there, looking so gray and old about the face that Len almost felt sorry for him.

"What's the matter with you?" he demanded.

Esau snarled at him.

"You look scared to death," said Len deliberately. "Is somebody making you threats about the warehouse?"

"Mind your own damn business," said Esau, and Len smiled inwardly. Let him sweat. Let him wonder who was here last night, when he was where he had no business to be. Let him wonder who knows, and wait.

He went down and got on board the ferry, a great lumbering flat thing with a shack to shelter the boiler and the wood stack. A light, steady rain had begun to fall, and the far shore was obscured in mist. A southbound trader with a load of woolens and leather was crossing too. Len helped him with his team and then sat with him in the wagon, remembering what magic things these wagons had been to him when he was a boy. The Canfield Fair seemed like something that happened a million years ago. The trader was a thin man with a gingery beard that reminded him of Soames. He shuddered and looked away, down-river, where the slow strong current ran forever to the west. A launch was beating its way up against it. The launch made a mournful hooting at the ferry, and the ferry answered, and then from the east a third voice spoke and a string of barges went down well in front of them, loaded with coal that glistened bright and black in the rain.

Shadwell was little and new and raw, and growing so fast that there were half-built buildings wherever Len looked. The waterfront hummed, and up on a rise behind it the big Shadwell house sat watching with all its glassy eyes.

Len walked up to the warehouse office where he had to go to deliver his letter. A lot of the men who would have been building were not working today on account of the rain. There was a little gang of them bunched up on the porch of the general store. It seemed to Len as though they watched him pretty close, but then that was probably only because he was a stranger off the ferry. He went in and gave the letter to a small elderly man named Gerrit, who read it hurriedly and then eyed Len as though he had crept out of the mud at low water.

"You tell Mike Dulinsky," he said, "that I follow the words of the Good Book that forbid me to have any dealings with unrighteous men. And as for you, I'd advise you to do the same. But you're a young man, and the young are always sinful, so I won't waste my breath. Git."

He flung the letter in a box of wastepaper and turned away. Len shrugged and went out. He headed off across the muddy square toward the traders' compound. One of the men on the porch of the general store came down the steps and ambled across to Gerrit's office. It was raining harder, and little streams of yellow water ran everywhere along the naked ground.

There were a lot of wagons in the compound, but none of them bore Hostetter's name. Most of the men were under cover. He did not see anyone he knew, and no one spoke to him. After a while he turned around and went back.

The square was full of men. They stood in the rain, and the yellow water splashed around their boots, but they did not seem to mind. They were all facing one way, toward Len.

One of them said, "You're from Refuge."

Len nodded.

"You work for Dulinsky."

Len shrugged and started to push by him.

Two other men came up on either side of him and caught his arms. He tried to get free, but they held him tight, one on each side, and when he tried to kick they stomped his ankles.

The first man said, "We got a message for Refuge. You tell them. We ain't going to let them take away what is rightfully ours. If they don't stop Dulinsky, we will. Can you remember that?"

Len glared at him. He was scared. He did not say anything.

"Make him remember it, boys," said the first man.

The two men holding him were joined by two more. They threw Len face down in the mud. He got up, and when he was halfway to his feet they kicked him flat again and grabbed his arms and rolled him. Then somebody else grabbed him and then another and another, roughing him around the square between them, perfectly quiet except for the little grunts of effort, not really hurting him too badly but never giving him a chance to fight back. When they were through they went away and left him, dizzy and gasping for breath, spitting out mud and water. He scrambled to his feet and looked around, but the square was deserted. He went down to the ferry and got aboard, although it was a long time before it was due to go back again. He was wet to the skin and shivering, although he was not conscious of being cold.

The ferry captain was a native of Refuge. He helped Len clean up and gave him a blanket out of his own locker. Then Len looked up along the streets of Shadwell.

"I'll kill 'em," said Len. "I'll kill 'em."

"Sure," said the ferry captain. "And I'll tell you one thing. They better not come over to Refuge and start trouble, or they'll find out what trouble is."

Toward midafternoon the rain stopped, and by five o'clock, when the ferry docked again at Refuge, the sky was clearing. Len reported to Dulinsky, who looked grave and shook his head.

"I'm sorry, Len," he said. "I should have known better."

"Well," said Len, "they didn't do me any damage, and now you know. They'll likely come over to the rally."

Dulinsky nodded. His eyes began to shine and he rubbed his hands together. "Maybe that's just what we want," he said. "Go change your clothes and get some supper. I'll see you later."

Len started home, but Dulinsky was already ahead of him, posting men to watch along the docks and doubling the warehouse guard.

At the compound Fisher spotted Len and asked him, "What happened to you?"

"I had a little trouble with the Shads," said Len, still too sore to want to talk about it. He went into his cabin and shut the door, and began to strip off his clothes, dried stiff with the yellow mud. And he wondered.

He wondered if Hostetter had abandoned him. And he wondered if Hostetter or anyone else would really be able to do much, when the time came. He remembered the voice saying, You may not always be saved.

When it was dark, he walked over to the town square, and the rally.

11

THE MAIN square of Refuge was wide and grassy, with trees to make shade there in the summer. The church, austere and gaunt and authoritative, dominated the square from its northern side. On the east and west were lesser buildings, stores, houses, a school, but on the southern side the town hall stood, not as tall as the church but broader, spreading out into wings that housed the courtrooms, the archives, the various offices necessary to the orderly running of a township. The shops and the public buildings were now closed and dark, and Len noticed that some of the shopkeepers had put up their storm shutters.

The square was full. It seemed as though all the men and half the women of Refuge were there, standing around on the wet grass or moving back and forth to talk, and there were others there, farmers in from the country, a handful of New Mennonites. A sort of pulpit stood in the middle of the square.

It was a permanent structure, and it was used chiefly by visiting preachers at open-air prayer meetings, but political speakers used it too at the time of a local or national election. Mike Dulinsky was going to use it tonight. Len remembered what Gran had told him about the old days, when a speaker could talk to everybody in the country at once through the teevee boxes, and he wondered with a quivering thrill of excitement if tonight was the start of the long road back to that kind of a world—Mike Dulinsky talking to a handful of people in a village named Refuge on the dark Ohio. He had read enough of Judge Taylor's history books to know that that was the way things happened sometimes. His heart began to beat faster, and he walked nervously back and forth, vaguely determined that Dulinsky should talk, no matter who tried to stop him.

The preacher, Brother Meyerhoff, came out of the side door of the church. Four of the deacons were with him, and a fifth man Len did not recognize until they came into the light of one of the bonfires that burned there. It was Judge Taylor. They passed on and Len lost them in the crowd, but he was sure they were heading for the speaker's stand. He followed them, slowly. He was about halfway across the grassy open when Mike Dulinsky came from the other side and there was a general motion toward the center, and the crowd suddenly clotted up so he couldn't get through it without pushing. There were half a dozen men with Dulinsky, carrying lanterns on long poles. They put these in brackets around the speaker's pulpit, so that it stood up like a bright column in the darkness. Dulinsky climbed up and began to speak.

"Tonight," he said, "we stand at a crossroads."

Somebody pulled at Len's sleeve, and he turned around. It was Esau, nodding to him to come away from the crowd.

"There's boats on the river," Esau said, when they were out of earshot. "Coming this way. You warn him, Len, I got to get back to the docks." He looked furtively around. "Is Amity here?"

"I don't know. The judge is."

"Oh Lord," said Esau. "Listen, I got to go. If you see Amity, tell her I won't be around for a while. She'll understand."

"Will she? Anyway, I thought you were bragging how nobody could——"

"Oh, shut up. You tell Dulinsky they're coming. Watch yourself, Len. Don't get in any more trouble than you can help."

"It looks to me," said Len, "as though you're the one in trouble. If I don't see Amity, I'll give the message to her father."

Esau swore and disappeared into the dark. Len began to edge his way through the crowd. They were standing quiet, listening, very grave and intent. Dulinsky was talking to them with a passionate sincerity. This was his one time, and he was giving everything he had to it.

"—that was eighty years ago. No danger menaces us now. Why should we continue to live in the shadow of a fear for which there is no longer any cause?"

A ripple of sound, half choked, half eager, ran across the crowd. Dulinsky gave it no time to die.

"I'll tell you why!" he shouted. "It's because the New Mennonites climbed into the saddle and have hung onto the government ever since. They don't like growth, they don't like change. Their creed rejects them both, and so does their greed. Yes, I said greed! They're farmers. They don't want to see the trading centers like Refuge get rich and fat. They don't want a competitive market, and above all they don't want people like us pushing them out of their nice seats in Congress where they can make all the laws. So they forbid us to build a new warehouse when we need it. Now do you think that's fair or right or godly? You there, Brother Meyerhoff, do you say the New Mennonites should tell us all how to live, or should our own Church of Holy Thankfulness have something to say about it too?"

Brother Meyerhoff answered, "It hasn't to do with them or with us. It has to do with you, Dulinsky, and you're talking blasphemy!"

A cry of voices, mostly female, seconded him. Len pushed himself to the foot of the stand. Dulinsky was leaning over, looking at Meyerhoff. There were beads of sweat on his forehead.

"Blaspheming, am I?" he demanded. "You tell me where."

"You've been to church. You've read the Book and listened to the sermons. You know how the Almighty cleansed the land of cities, and bade His children that He saved to walk henceforth in the path of righteousness, to love the things of the spirit and not the things of the flesh! In the words of the prophet Nahum——"

"I don't want to build a city," said Dulinsky. "I want to build a warehouse."

There was a nervous tittering, quickly hushed. Meyerhoff's face was crimson above his beard. Len mounted the steps and spoke to Dulinsky, who nodded. Len climbed down again. He wanted to tell Dulinsky to lay off the New Mennonites, but he did not quite dare for fear of giving himself away.

"Who," asked Dulinsky of Meyerhoff, "has been telling you about cities?" He paused, and then he pointed and said, "Is it you, Judge Taylor?"

In the glare of the lanterns, Len saw that Taylor's face was oddly pale and strained. His voice, when he spoke, was quiet but it rang all over the square.

"There is an amendment to the Constitution of the United States that forbids you to do this. No amount of talk will change that, Dulinsky."

"Ah," said Dulinsky, in a satisfied voice as though he had made Judge Taylor fall into some trap, "that's where you're wrong. Talk is exactly what *will* change it. If enough people talk, and talk loud enough and long enough, that amendment will be changed so that a man can build a warehouse if he needs it to shelter flour or hides, or a house if he needs it to shelter his family." He raised his voice in a sudden shout. "You think about that, you people! Your own kids have had to leave Refuge, and more and more of them will have to go, because they can't build any more houses here when they get married. Am I right?"

He got a response on that. Dulinsky grinned. Out on the dark edges of the crowd a man appeared, and then another and another, coming softly from the direction of the river. And Meyerhoff said, in a voice shaking with anger, "Always, in every age, the unbeliever has prepared the way for evil."

"Maybe," said Dulinsky. He was looking out over Meyerhoff's head, to the edges of the crowd. "And I'll admit that I'm an unbeliever." He glanced down at Len, giving him the warning, while the crowd gasped over that. Then he went on, fast and smooth.

"I'm an unbeliever in poverty, in hunger, in misery. I don't know anybody who does believe in those things, except the New Ishmaelites, but I can't recall we ever thought much of them. In fact, we drove 'em out. I'm an unbeliever in taking a healthy growing child and strapping it down with bands so it won't get any taller than somebody thinks it should. I——"

Judge Taylor brushed past Len and mounted the steps. Dulinsky looked surprised and stopped in midsentence. Taylor gave him one burning glance and said, "A man can make anything he wants to out of words." He turned to the crowd. "I'm going to give you a fact, and then we'll see if Dulinsky can talk it away. If you break the township law it won't affect Refuge alone. It will affect all the country around it. Now, the New Mennonites are peaceful folk and their creed forbids them from violence. They will proceed by due process of law, no matter how long it takes. But there are other sects in the countryside, and their beliefs are different. They look on it as their duty to take up the cudgel for the Lord."

He paused, and in the stillness Len could hear the breathing of the people.

"You'd better think twice," said Taylor, "before you provoke them into taking it up against you."

There was a burst of applause from the outer edge of the crowd. Dulinsky asked scornfully, "Who are you afraid of, Judge—the farmers or the Shadwell men?" He leaned out over the rail and beckoned. "Come on up here, you Shads, up where we can see you. You don't have to be afraid, you're brave men. I got a lad here who knows how brave you are. Len, climb up here a minute."

Len did as he was told, avoiding Judge Taylor's eyes. Dulinsky pushed him to the rail.

"Some of you know Len Colter. I sent him to Shadwell this morning on business. Tell us what kind of a welcome you gave him, you Shads, or are you ashamed?"

The crowd began to mutter and turn around.

"What's the matter?" cried a deep, rough voice from the background. "Didn't he like the taste of Shadwell mud?" The Shadwell men all laughed, and then another voice, one that Len remembered only too well, called to him, "Did you give them our message?"

"Yes," said Dulinsky. "Give the people that message, Len. Say it real loud, so they can all hear."

Judge Taylor said suddenly, under his breath, "You'll regret this night." He ran down the steps.

Len glared out into the shadows. "They're going to stop you," he told the people of Refuge. "The Shads won't let you grow. That's why they're here tonight." His voice went up a notch until it cracked. "I don't care who's afraid of them," he said. "I'm not." He jumped over the rail onto the ground and charged into the crowd. All the helpless rage of the morning was back on him a hundredfold, and he did not care what anybody else did, or what happened to him. He butted his way through until a path was suddenly opened for him and the Shadwell men were standing in a bunch in front of him. Dulinsky's voice was shouting something in which the names of Shadwell and Refuge were coupled together with the word fear. The crowd was beginning to move. A woman was screaming. The Shadwell men were pulling clubs out from under their coats. Len sprang like a panther. A great roar went up from the crowd, and the riot was on.

Len bore his man down and pounded him. Legs churned around them and people fell over them. There was a lot of screaming now, and women were running away out of the square. Clubs, fists, and boots flailed wildly. Somebody hit Len on the back of the head. The world turned upside down for a minute, and when it steadied again he was staggering along in the midst of a little boiling whirlpool of hard-breathing men, hanging onto somebody's coat and punching blindly with his free hand. The whirlpool spun and heaved and threw him up against a shuttered window and passed on. He stayed there, confused and shaking his head, blowing blood out of his nose. The crowd had broken up. The lanterns still burned around the pulpit in the middle of the square, but there was nobody in it now, and nothing left on the grassy space around it but some hats and some gouged-out places in the turf. The fighting had moved off. He could hear it streaming away down the streets and alleys that led to the docks. He grunted and began to run after it. He was glad Pa could not see him now. He felt hot and queer inside, and he liked it. He wanted to fight some more.

By the time he reached the docks the Shadwell men were

piling into their boats as fast as they could, shaking their fists and cursing. The Refuge men were all lined up at the water's edge, helping them. Three or four Shads were in the river and being hauled up into the boats. The air rang with hoots and catcalls. Mike Dulinsky was right in the middle of it, his good dark coat torn and his hair on end, and a splatter of blood down his shirt from a cut mouth. "You going to stop us, are you?" he was yelling at the Shadwell men. "You going to tell Refuge what to do?"

The men on either side of Dulinsky caught him suddenly and hoisted him up onto their shoulders and cheered him. The Shadwell men pulled slowly and sullenly out into the dark river. When they were out of sight the crowd turned, still carrying Dulinsky and cheering, to where the fires burned around the framework of the warehouse. They marched round and round, and the guards cheered too. Len watched them, feeling dizzy but triumphant. Then, looking around, he saw a blaze of light in the direction of the traders' compound. He stared at it, frowning, and in the intervals of the noise behind him he could hear the distant voices of men and the whickering of horses. He began to walk toward the compound.

Lanterns and torches burned all around to give light. The men were bringing their teams out of the stables and harnessing them, and going over their gear, and getting the wagons ready to go. Len watched a minute or two, and all the feeling of triumph and excitement left him. He felt tired, and his nose hurt.

He saw Fisher and went up to him, standing by the head of the team while Fisher worked.

"Why is everybody going?" he asked.

Fisher gave him a long, stern look from under the brim of his broad hat.

"The farmers went out of here primed for trouble," he said. "They'll bring it, and we don't aim to wait."

He made sure his reins were clear and climbed up onto the seat. Len stood aside, and Fisher looked down at him, in something the same way Pa had looked so long ago.

"I thought better of you, Len Colter," Fisher said. "But them that picks up a burning brand will get burned by it. The Lord have mercy on you!"

He shook the reins and shouted, and his wagon creaked and moved, and the other wagons rolled, and Len stood looking after them.

12

TWO O'CLOCK of a hot, still day. The men were laying up sheeting boards on the north and east sides of the warehouse, working in the shade. Refuge was quiet, so quiet that the sound of the hammers rang out like bells on a Sabbath morning. Most of the shipping was gone from the docks, and the wharves were empty.

Esau said, "Do you think they'll come?"

"I don't know." Len looked searchingly at the distant roofs of Shadwell across the river, and up and down the wide stretch of water. He didn't know exactly what he was looking for, Hostetter, a friendly face, anything to break the emptiness and the sense of waiting. All morning since before sunup, cartloads of women and children had been leaving the town, and there were some men with them too, and bundles of household goods.

"They won't do anything," said Esau. "They wouldn't dare."

His voice carried no conviction. Len glanced at him and saw that his face was drawn and nervous. They were standing at the door of the office, not doing anything, just feeling the heat and the quietness. Dulinsky had gone up into the town, and Len said, "I wish he'd come back."

"He's got men out on the roads. If there's any news, we'll be the first to know it."

"Yes," said Len. "I reckon."

The hammers rang sharp on the new yellow wood. Along the edges of the warehouse site, well back in the trees, men loitered and watched. There were more of them on the docks, restless, uneasy, gathering in little groups to talk and then breaking up again, moving back and forth. They kept looking sidelong at the office, and at Len and Esau standing in the doorway, and at the men working on the warehouse, but they did not come close or speak to them. Len did not like that. It made him feel alone and conspicuous, and it worried him because he could feel the doubt and uncertainty and apprehension of these men who were up against something new and did not quite know what to do about it. From time to time a jug of corn was pulled out of a hiding place behind a stump or a stack of barrels, passed around, and put away again, but only one or two of them were drunk.

On impulse, Len stepped to the end of the dock and shouted to a group standing under a tree and talking. "What's the news from town?"

One of them shook his head. "Nothing yet." He was one who had shouted the loudest for Dulinsky last night, but today his face showed no enthusiasm. Suddenly he stooped and picked up a stone and threw it at a little gang of boys who were skulking in the background watching hopefully for trouble. "Get out of here!" he yelled at them. "This ain't no game for your amusement. Go on, git!"

They went, but not far. Len returned to the doorway. It was very hot, very still. Esau shuffled, kicking his heel against the doorpost.

"Len."

"What?"

"What'll we do if they do come?"

"How do I know? Fight, I guess. See what happens. How do I know?"

"Well, I know one thing," said Esau defiantly. "I ain't going to get my neck broke for Dulinsky. The hell with that."

"All right, you figure something." There was an anger in Len now, a vague thing as yet, and undirected, but enough to make him irritable and impatient. Perhaps it was because he was afraid, and that made him angry. But he knew the way Esau's thoughts were running, and he didn't want to have to go through every step of it out loud.

"You bet I'll figure something," said Esau. "You bet I will. It's his warehouse, not mine. Let him fight for it. He sure wouldn't risk his skin for anything of mine. I——"

"Shut up," said Len. "Look."

Judge Taylor was coming along the dock. Esau swore nervously and slid back through the door, out of sight. Len waited, conscious that the men were watching, as though what happened might have great significance.

Taylor came up to the door and stopped. "Tell Mike I want to see him," he said.

Len answered, "He isn't here."

The judge looked at him, deciding whether or not he was lying. There was a pinched grayness about the corners of his mouth, and his eyes were curiously hard and bright.

"I've come," he said, "to offer Mike his last chance."

"He's somewhere up in the town," said Len. "Maybe you can find him there."

Taylor shook his head. "It's the Lord's will," he said, and turned and walked away. At the corner of the office he stopped and spoke again. "I warned you, Len. But none are so blind as those who will not see."

"Wait," said Len. He went up to the judge and looked into his eyes, and shivered. "You know something. What is it?"

"The Lord's will," said the judge, "will be made clear to you when it is time."

Len reached out and caught him by the collar of his fine cloth coat and shook him. "Speak for yourself," he said angrily. "The Lord must be sick to death of everybody hiding behind Him. Nothing happens in this town that you don't have a finger in. What is it?"

Some of the fey light went out of Taylor's eyes. He looked down with a kind of shocked surprise at Len's hands laid roughly upon him, and Len let him go.

"I'm sorry," he said. "But I want to know."

"Yes," said Judge Taylor quietly, "you want to know. That was always your trouble. Didn't I tell you to find your limit before it was too late?"

His face softened, became compassionate and full of a genuine sorrow. "It's too bad, Len. I could have loved you like my own son."

"What have you done?" asked Len, moving a step closer, and the judge answered, "There will be no more cities. There is a law, and the law must be obeyed."

"You're scared," said Len, in a slow, astonished voice. "I

understand now, you're scared. You think if a city grows up here the bombs will come again, and you'll be under them. Did you tell the farmers you wouldn't try to stop them if——"

"Hush," said the judge, and held up his hand.

Len turned to listen. So did the men under the trees and along the docks. Esau came out from the doorway. And at the warehouse, one by one the hammers stopped.

There was a sound of singing.

It was faint, but that was only because it was still a long way off. It was deep, and sonorous, a masculine sound, martial and somehow terrifying, coming with the solemn inevitability of a storm that does not stop or swerve. Len could not make out any words, but after he had listened for a minute he knew what they were. Mine eyes have seen the glory of the coming of the Lord. "Good-by, Len," said the judge, and was gone, walking with his head up high and his face white and stern in the heat of the July sun.

"We've got to go," whispered Esau. "We've got to get out of here."

He bolted back into the office, and Len could hear his feet clattering up the wooden stairs to the loft. Len hesitated a minute. Then he began to run, up toward the town, toward the distant, oncoming hymn. I have read a fiery gospel writ in burnished rows of steel . . . Glory! glory! Hallelujah, His truth is marching on. A tight, cold knot of fear cramped up in Len's belly, and the air turned icy against his skin. The men along the docks and under the trees began to move too, straggling up by other ways, uncertainly at first and then faster, until they were running too. People had come out of their houses. Women, old men, children, listening, shouting at each other and at the men passing in the street, asking what it was, what was going to happen. Len came into the square, and a cart rushed past him so close that the foam from the horse's bit spattered him. There was a whole family in it, the man whipping up the horse and yelling, the women screaming, the kids all clinging together and crying. There was a scattering of people in the square, some heading toward the main north road, some running around aimlessly, women asking if anybody had seen their husbands or their boys, asking, always asking, what is it, what's happening? Len dodged through them and ran out on the north road.

Dulinsky was out on the edge of town, where the wide road ran between fields of wheat almost ripe for the cutting. There were perhaps two hundred men with him, armed with clubs and iron bars, with rifles and duck guns, with picks and frows. They looked grim and anxious. Dulinsky's face, burned brick red by the sun, was only ruddy on the surface. Underneath it was white. He kept wiping his hands on his trousers, one after the other, shifting his grip on the heavy club he held. Len came up beside him. Dulinsky glanced at him but did not speak. His attention was northward, where a solid yellow-brown wall of dust advanced, spreading across the road and into the wheat on either side. The sound of the hymn came out of it, and a rhythmic thud and trample of feet, and across its leading edge there was a pricking here and there of brilliance, as though some bright thing of metal caught the sun.

"It's our town," said Len. "They've got no right in it. We can beat 'em."

Dulinsky wiped his face on his shirt sleeve. He grunted. It might have been a question or a laugh. Len looked around at the Refuge men.

"They'll fight," he said.

"Will they?" said Dulinsky.

"They were all for you last night."

"That was last night. This is now."

The wall of dust rolled up, and it was full of men. It stopped, and the dust blew away or settled, but the men remained, standing in a great heavy solid blot across the road and in the trampled wheat. The spots of brilliance became scythe blades, and corn knives, and here and there a gun barrel. "Some of them must have walked all night," said Dulinsky. "Look at 'em. Every goddamned dung-head farmer in three counties." He wiped his face again and spoke to the men behind him. "Stand steady, boys. They're not going to do anything." He stepped forward, his expression lofty and impassive, his eyes darting hard little glances this way and that.

A man with white hair and a stern leathery face came forward to meet him. He carried a shotgun in the crook of his arm, and his walk was a farmer's walk, heavy and rolling. But he stretched up his head and yelled out at the Refuge men waiting in the road, and there was something about his harsh strident voice that made Len remember the preaching man.

"Stand aside!" he shouted. "We don't want killing, but we can if we have to, so stand aside, in the name of the Lord!"

"Wait a minute," said Dulinsky. "Just a minute, now. This is our town. May I ask what business you think you have in it?"

The man looked at him and said, "We will have no cities in our midst."

"Cities," said Dulinsky. "Cities!" He laughed. "Now look here, sir. You're Noah Burdette, aren't you? I know you well by sight and reputation. You have quite a name as a preacher in the section around Twin Lakes."

He stepped a little closer, speaking in an easier tone, as a man talks when he knows he is going to turn the argument his way.

"You're a sincere and honest man, Mr. Burdette, and I realize that you're acting on what you believe to be truthful information. So I know you're going to be thankful to learn that your information is wrong, and there's no need for any violence at all. I——"

"Violence," said Burdette, "I don't seek. But I don't run from it, neither, when it's in a good cause." He looked Dulinsky up and down, slowly, deliberately, with a face as hard as flint. "I know you, too, by sight and reputation, and you can save your wind. Are you going to stand aside?"

"Listen," said Dulinsky, with a note of desperation coming into his voice. "You've been told that I'm trying to build a city here, and that's crazy. I'm only trying to build a warehouse, and I've got as good a right to it as you've got to a new barn. You can't come here and order me around any more than I could go to your farm and do it!"

"I'm here," said Burdette.

Dulinsky glanced back over his shoulder. Len moved toward him, as though to say, I'm with you. And then Judge Taylor came up through the loose ranks of the Refuge men, saying, "Disperse, go to your homes, and stay there. No harm will come to you. Lay down your weapons and go home."

They hesitated, looking at one another, looking at Dulinsky

and the solid mass of the farmers. And Dulinsky said to the judge in weary scorn, "You sheepfaced coward. You were in on this."

"You've done enough harm, Mike," said the judge, very white and standing very stiff and straight. "No need to make everybody in Refuge suffer for it. Stand aside."

Dulinsky glared at him and then at Burdette. "What are you going to do?"

"Cleanse the evil," said Burdette slowly, "as the Book instructs us to, by burning it with fire."

"In plain English," said Dulinsky, "you're going to burn my warehouses, and anything else that happens to take your fancy. The hell you are." He turned around and shouted to the Refuge men. "Listen, you fools, do you think they're going to stop at my warehouses? They'll have the whole town flaming around your ears. Don't you see this is the time, the act that's going to decide how you live for decades yet to come? Are you going to be free men or a gang of belly-crawling slaves?"

His voice rose up to a howl. "Come on and fight, God damn you, fight!"

He spun around and rushed at Burdette, raising his club high in the air.

Without haste and without pity, Burdette swung the shotgun over and fired.

It made a very loud noise. Dulinsky stopped as though he had struck against a solid wall. He stood for a second or two, and then the club dropped out of his hands and he lowered his arms and folded them over his belly. His knees bent and he sank down onto them in the dust.

Len ran forward.

Dulinsky looked up at him with an expression of stunned surprise. His mouth opened. He seemed to be trying to say something, but only blood came out between his lips. Then suddenly his face became blank and remote, like a window when somebody blows out the candle. He fell forward and was still.

"Mike," said Judge Taylor. "Mike?" He looked at Burdette, his eyes widening. "What have you done?"

"Murderer," said Len, and the word encompassed both Burdette and the judge. His voice broke, rising to a harsh scream. "God-damned yellow-bellied murderer!" He put up his fists and ran toward Burdette, but the line of farmers had begun to move, as though the death of Dulinsky was a signal they had waited for, and Len was caught up in it as in the forefront of a wave. Burdette was gone, and facing him instead was a burly young farmer with a long neck and sloping shoulders and the kind of a mouth that had cried out the accusation against Soames. He carried a length of peeled wood like those used for fence posts, and he brought it down on Len's head, laughing with a sort of cackling haste, his eyes gleaming with immense excitement. Len fell down. Boots clumped and kicked and stumbled over him and he curled up instinctively with his arms over his head and neck. It had become very dark and the Refuge men were far off behind a wavering veil, but he could see them going, melting away until the road was empty in front of the farmers and there was nothing between them and the town any more. They went on into Refuge in the hot afternoon, raising up the dust again as they moved, and when that settled there was only Len, and Dulinsky's body lying three or four feet away from him, and Judge Taylor standing still in the middle of the road, just standing and looking at Dulinsky.

13

LEN GOT slowly to his feet. His head hurt and he felt sick, but his compulsion to get away from there was so great that he forced himself to walk in spite of it. He went carefully around Dulinsky, avoiding the dark stains that were in the dust there, and he passed Judge Taylor. They did not speak, nor look at each other. Len went on toward Refuge until just a little bit before the square, where there was an apple orchard beside the road. He turned off among the trees, and when he felt that he was out of sight he sat down in the long grass and put his head between his knees and vomited. An icy coldness came over him, and a shaking. He waited until they passed, and then he got up again and went on, circling west through the trees.

There was a confused noise in the distance, toward the river. A puff of smoke rose in the clear air, and then another, and suddenly there was a dull booming roar and the whole river front seemed to burst into flame and the smoke poured up black and greasy and very thick, lighted on its underside by the kind of flames that come from stored-up barrels of pitch and lamp oil. The streets of the town were choked now with carts and horses and people running. Here and there somebody was helping carry a hurt man. Len avoided them, sticking to the back alleys and the peripheral fields. The smoke came blacker and heavier, rolling over the sky and blotting the sun to an ugly copper color. There were sparks in it now, and bits of flaming stuff tossed up. When he came to a high place, Len could see men on some of the roofs of the houses, and on the church and the town hall, making up bucket lines to wet the buildings down. He could see the waterfront, too. The new warehouse was burning, and the four others that had belonged to Dulinsky, but things had not stopped there. There was a scurrying, a tossing of weapons and a swaying back and forth of little knots of men, and all along the line of docks and warehouses new fires were springing up.

Across the river Shadwell watched but did not stir.

The stables of the traders' compound were blazing when Len came by them. Sparks had fallen in the straw and the hay piles, and other sparks were smoldering on the roofs of the shelters. Len ran into the one he had been occupying and grabbed up his canvas bag and his blanket. When he came out the door he heard men coming and he fled hastily in among the trees at one side. The green leaves were already crisping, and the boughs were shaken by a strange unhealthy wind. A gang of farmers came up from the river. They paused at the edge of the compound, panting, staring about with bright hard eyes. The auction sheds were untouched. One of them, a huge red-bearded man with inflamed cheeks and a roaring voice, pointed to the sheds and bellowed something about money-changers. They made a hungry breathless sound like a pack of dogs after a coon and ran to the long line of sheds, smashing everything they could smash and piling it together and setting fire to it with a torch that one of them was carrying. Then they passed on, kicking over and trampling and breaking down anything in their path. Len thought of Judge Taylor, standing alone in the middle of the road, looking at Dulinsky's body. He would have a lot of things to look at when this day was over.

He went on cautiously between the trees, edging down to the river through a weird sulphurous twilight. The air was choked with the smells of burning, of pitch and wood and oil and hides. Ash fell like a gray and scorching snow. He could hear the fire bell ringing desperately up in the town, but he could not see much that way because of the smoke and the trees. He came out on the riverbank well below the site of the new warehouse and began to work his way back, looking for Esau.

The whole riverbank as far as he could see ahead of him was a solid mass of flame. The heat had driven everybody away and some of them had come downstream past the wreck of the new warehouse, men with their eyes white and staring in blackened faces, men with burned hands and torn clothing and a look of desperation. Three or four were bent over one who lay on the ground moaning and twisting, and there were others sitting down here and there, as though they had come that far and then quit. Most of them were just standing and watching. One man still carried a bucket half full of water.

Len did not see Esau, and he began to be afraid. He went up to several of the men and asked, but they only shook their heads or did not seem to hear him at all. Finally one of them, a clerk named Watts, who had come to the office frequently on business, said bitterly, "Don't worry about him. He's safe if anybody is."

"What do you mean?"

"I mean nobody's seen *him* since the trouble began. He took off, him and the girl both."

"Girl?" asked Len, startled out of his resentment at Watts's tone.

"Judge Taylor's girl, who else? And where were you, hiding in a hole somewhere? And where's Dulinsky? I thought that son of a bitch was such a mighty fighter, to hear him tell it."

"I was up on the north road," said Len. "And Dulinsky's dead. So I guess he fought harder than you did."

A man standing nearby had turned around at the sound of Dulinsky's name. Under the grime and the soot, the singed hair and the clothing burned partly off him, it was a minute before Len recognized Ames, the warehouse owner who had come down with Dulinsky and the other man that morning to look at the new warehouse and shake his head at Dulinsky's plea for unity.

"Dead," said Ames. "Dead, is he?"

"They shot him. A farmer named Burdette."

"Dead," said Ames. "I'm sorry. He should have lived. He should have lived long enough for a hanging." He lifted his hands and shook them at the blaze and smoke. "Look what he's done to us!"

"He wasn't alone," said Watts. "The Colter boys were in with him, from the beginning."

"If you'd stuck by him this wouldn't have happened," Len said. "He asked you, Mr. Ames. You and Whinnery and the others. He asked the whole town. And what happened? You all danced around and cheered last night—yes, you too, Watts, I saw you!—and then you all ran like rabbits at the first smell of trouble. There wasn't a man of 'em up in the north road that lifted a hand. They left it up to Mike to get killed."

Len's voice had got loud and harsh without his realizing it. The men within earshot had closed in to listen.

"It seems to me," said Ames, "that for a stranger, you take an almighty interest in what we do. Why? What makes you think it's up to you to try and change things? I worked all my life to build up what I had, and then you come, and Dulinsky——"

He stopped. Tears were running out of his eyes and his mouth trembled like a child's.

"Yeah," said Watts. "Why? Where did you come from? Who sent you to call us cowards because we don't want to break the law?"

Len looked around. There were men on all sides of him now. Their faces were grotesque masks of burns and fury. The smoke rolled in a sooty cloud and the flames roared softly with a purring sound as they ate the wealth of Refuge. Up in the town the fire bell had stopped ringing.

Somebody spoke the name of Bartorstown, and Len began to laugh.

Watts reached out and cuffed him. "Funny, is it? All right, where did you come from?"

"Piper's Run, born and raised."

"Why'd you leave it? Why'd you come here to make trouble?"

"He's lying," said another man. "Sure he comes from Bartorstown. They want the cities back."

"It doesn't matter," said Ames, in a low, still voice. "He was in on it. He helped." He turned around, his hands moving as though they groped for something. "There ought to be one piece of rope left unburned in Refuge."

Instantly an eagerness came over the men. "Rope," said somebody. "Yeah. We'll find some." And somebody else said, "Look for the other bastard. We'll hang them both." Some of them ran off down the riverbank, and others began to beat the bushes looking for Esau. Watts and two others tackled Len and bore him down, savaging him with their fists and knees. Ames stood by and watched, looking alternately from Len to the fire.

The men came back. They had not found Esau, but they had found a rope, the mooring line of a skiff tied to the bank farther down. Watts and the others hauled Len to his feet. One of the men tied a clumsy slipknot in the rope and made a noose and put it over Len's head. The rope was damp. It was old and soft and frayed, and it smelled of fish. Len kicked out violently and tore his arms free. They caught him again and hustled him toward the trees, a close-bunched confusion of men lurching along in short erratic bursts of motion with Len struggling in the center, kicking, clawing, banging them with his knees and elbows. And even so, he sensed dimly that it was not men he was fighting at all, but the whole vast soggy smothering continent from sea to sea and from north to south, millions of houses and people and fields and villages all sleeping comfortably and not wanting to be disturbed. The rope was cold and scratchy around his neck, and he was afraid, and he knew he couldn't fight off the idea, the belief and way of life of which these men were only a tiny, tiny part.

He was very dizzy, from the pounding and the blow on the head he had already had up on the north road, so that he was not sure what happened except that suddenly there seemed to be more men, more bodies around him, more upheaval. He was thrown sharply aside. The hands seemed to have let go of him. He hit a tree trunk and slid down it to the ground. There was a face above him. It had blue eyes and a sandy beard with two wide streaks of gray in it, one at each corner of the mouth. He said to the face, "If there weren't so many of you I could kill you all." And it answered him, "You don't want to kill me, Len. Come on, boy, get up."

Tears came suddenly into Len's eyes. "Mr. Hostetter," he said. "Mr. Hostetter." He put up his hands and caught hold of him, and it seemed like a long time ago, in another hour of darkness and fear. Hostetter gave him a strong pull up to his feet and jerked the rope from around his neck.

"Run," he said. "Run like the devil."

Len ran. There were several other men with Hostetter, and they must have charged in hard with the poles and boat hooks they had, because the Refuge men were pretty well scattered. But they were not going to give Len up without a fight, and the intrusion of Hostetter and his party had convinced them that they were right about Bartorstown. They were determined now to get Hostetter too, shouting and cursing, gathering together again and searching for anything they could use as weapons, stones, fallen branches, clods. Len staggered and stumbled as he went, and Hostetter put a hand under his arm and rushed him along.

"Boat waiting," he said. "Farther down."

Things began to fly through the air around them. A stone bounced off Hostetter's back and he hunched his head down until his broad-brimmed hat seemed to sit flat on his shoulders. They ran in among a grove of trees and out on the other side, and Len stopped suddenly.

"Esau," he said. "Can't go without Esau."

"He's already aboard," said Hostetter. "Come on!"

They ran again, across a pasture sloping down to the water's edge, and the cows went bucketing away with their tails in the air. At the lower end of the pasture was another clump of trees, growing right on the bank, and in their partial concealment a big steam barge was tied up, with a couple of men standing on the deck holding axes, ready to chop the lines free. Smoke began to puff up suddenly from the single low stack, as though a banked fire had been stirred swiftly to life. Len saw Esau hanging over the rail, and there was someone beside him, someone with yellow hair and a long skirt.

There was a board laid from the bank to the rail. They scrambled up over it onto the deck and Hostetter shouted at the men with the axes. Stones were flying again, and Esau caught Amity and hurried her around to the other side of the deckhouse. The axes flashed. There was more shouting, and the Refuge men, with Watts in the lead, rushed right down to the bank and Watts and two others ran out onto the plank. Len did not see Ames among them. The lines parted and went snaking into the water. Hostetter and Len and some others grabbed up long poles and pushed off hard. The plank fell into the water with Watts and the other men that were on it. There was a roar and a clatter from below, the deck shook and sparks burst up through the stack. The barge began to move out into the current. Watts stood waist-deep in the muddy water by the bank and shook his fists at them.

"We know you now!" he shouted, his voice coming thin across the widening gap. "You won't get away!"

The men on the bank behind him shouted too. Their voices grew fainter but the note of hatred remained in them, and the ugliness in the gestures of their hands. Len looked back at Refuge. They were well out in the river now and he could see past the waterfront. Smoke obscured much of the town, but he could see enough. What Burdette's farmers had left untouched the spreading fire was taking for its own.

Len sat down on the deck with his back against the house. He put his arms across his knees and laid his head on them and felt an overwhelming desire to cry like a little boy, but he was too tired even to do that. He just sat and tried to make his mind as blank as the rest of him felt. But he could not do it, and over and over he saw Dulinsky stop and fall down slowly into the hot dust of the north road, and he smelled the smell of a great burning, and Burdette's harsh voice sounded in his ears, saying, "We will have no cities in our midst."

After a while he became aware that somebody was standing over him. He looked up, and it was Hostetter, holding his hat in his hand and wiping his forehead wearily on his coat sleeve.

"Well, boy," he said, "you've got your wish. You're on your way to Bartorstown."

14

IT WAS NIGHT, warm and tranquil. There was a moon, lighting the surface of the river and turning the two banks into masses of black shadow. The barge slipped along, chuffing gently as it added a bit to the thrust of the current. There was a lot of cargo on the deck, tied down securely and covered with canvas against the rain. Len had found a place in it. He had slept for a while, and he was sitting now with his back against a bale, watching the river go by.

Hostetter came by, walking slowly along the narrow space left clear on the foredeck, trailing a fragrance of tobacco smoke from an old pipe. He saw Len sitting up, and stopped. "Feel better?"

"I feel sick," Len said, so viciously that Hostetter knew what he meant. He nodded.

"You know now how I felt the night they killed Bill Soames."

"Murderers," said Len. "Cowards. Bastards." He cursed them until the words choked in his throat. "You should have seen them standing there across the road. And then Burdette shot him. He shot him just the way you'd shoot some vermin you found in the corn."

"Yes," said Hostetter slowly, "we'd have had you out of there sooner if you hadn't gone up after Dulinsky. Poor devil. But I'm not surprised."

"Couldn't you have helped him?"

"Us? You mean Bartorstown?"

"He wanted the same things you want. Growth, progress, intelligence, a future. Couldn't you have helped?"

There was an edge to Len's voice, but Hostetter only took the pipe out of his mouth and asked quietly, "How?"

Len thought about that. After a while he said, "I suppose you couldn't."

"Not without an army. We don't have an army, and if we did have we wouldn't use it. It takes an almighty force to make people change their whole way of thinking and living. We had a force like that just yesterday as time goes for a nation, and we don't want any more of them."

"That's what the judge was afraid of. Change. And he just stood there and watched Dulinsky die." Len shook his head. "He died for nothing. That's what he died for, *nothing*."

"No," said Hostetter, "I wouldn't say that. But it takes more than one Dulinsky. It takes a lot of them, one after the other, in different places——"

"And more Burdettes, and more burnings."

"Yes. And someday one will come along at the right time, and the change will be made."

"That's a lot to look forward to."

"That's the way it is. And then all the Dulinskys will become martyrs to a great ideal. In the meantime, you're disturbers of the peace. And damn it, Len, you know in a way they're right. They're comfortable and happy. Who are you—or any of us—to tell them it's all got to be torn up and changed?"

Len turned and looked at Hostetter in the moonlight. "Is that why you just stand by and watch?"

Hostetter said, with just the faintest note of impatience in his voice, "I don't think you understand about us yet. We're not supermen. We've got all we can do just to stay alive, without trying to remake a country that doesn't want to be remade."

"But how can you say they're right? Ignorant butchers like Burdette, hypocrites like the judge——"

"Honest men, Len, both of them. Yes, they are. Both of them got up this morning all fired up with nobility and good purpose and went and did the right as they saw it. There's never been an act done since the beginning, from a kid stealing candy to a dictator committing genocide, that the person doing it didn't think he was fully justified. That's a mental trick called rationalizing, and it's done the human race more harm than anything else you can name."

"Burdette, maybe," said Len. "He's another one like the man at the preaching that night. But not the judge. He knew better."

"Not at the time. That's the hell of it. The doubts always come later, and they're usually too late. Take yourself, Len. When you ran away from home, did you have any doubts about it? Did you say to yourself, I am now going to do an evil thing and make my parents very unhappy?"

Len looked down at the gleaming water for a long time without answering. Finally he said, in an oddly quiet voice, "How are they? Are they all right?"

"The last I heard they were fine. I didn't go up this spring myself."

"And Gran?"

"She died, a year ago last December."

"Yes," said Len. "She was terrible old." It was strange how sad he felt about Gran, as though a part of his life had gone. Suddenly, with painful clarity, he saw her again sitting on the stoop in the sunlight, looking at the flaming October trees and talking about the red dress she had had so long ago, when the world was a different place.

He said, "Pa couldn't ever quite make her shut up."

Hostetter nodded. "My own grandmother was much the same way."

Silence again. Len sat and watched the river, and the past lay heavy on him, and he did not want to go to Bartorstown. He wanted to go home.

"Your brother's doing fine," said Hostetter. "Has two boys of his own now."

"That's good."

"Piper's Run hasn't changed much."

"No," said Len. "I reckon not." And then he added, "Oh, shut up!"

Hostetter smiled.

"That's the advantage I have over you. I'm going home. It's been a long time."

"Then you didn't come from Pennsylvania at all."

"My people did, originally. I was born in Bartorstown."

An old anger rose and pricked at Len. "Listen," he said, "you knew why we ran away. You must have known all along where we were and what we were doing."

"I felt sort of responsible," Hostetter admitted. "I kept tabs."

"All right," said Len, "why did you make us wait so long? You knew where we wanted to go."

Hostetter said, "Do you remember Soames?"

"I'll never forget him."

"He trusted a boy."

"But," said Len, "I wouldn't——" Then he remembered how Esau had put Hostetter in a bad place. "I guess I see what you mean."

"We've got one unbreakable law in Bartorstown. That law is Hands Off, and because of it we've been able to keep going all these years when the very name of Bartorstown is enough to hang you. Soames broke it. I'm breaking it now, but I got permission. And believe me, that was the feat of the century. For one solid week I talked myself hoarse to Sherman——"

"Sherman," said Len, straightening up. "Yes, Sherman. Sherman wants to know if you've heard from Byers——"

"What the hell are you talking about?" asked Hostetter, staring.

"Over the radio," said Len, and the old excitement came back on him like a stroke of summer lightning. "The voices talking that night I let the cows out of the barn and we went after them down to the creek, and Esau dropped the radio. The spool thing reeled out, and the voices came—Sherman wants to know. And something about the river. That's why we went down to the Ohio."

"Oh yes," said Hostetter. "The radio. That was the start of the whole thing, wasn't it? I owed Esau something for stealing it. I owed him for the blood I sweated when I found it was gone." Hostetter shivered. "Christ. When I think how close he came to exposing me—— I'd never have made it back alive, you know. Your own people would have told me to go and never show my face again, but the word would have spread. I had to throw Esau to the wolves, and I won't say I was sorry. But it was too bad you got dragged into it."

"I never blamed you. I told Esau it wasn't going to be that easy."

"Well, you can thank the farmers, because if it hadn't been for them I'd never have talked Sherman into letting me pick you up. I told him you were sure to get it from one side or the other, and I didn't want your blood on my conscience. He finally gave in, but I'll tell you, Len, the next time somebody gives you a piece of good advice, you take it."

Len rubbed his neck where the rope had scratched it. "Yes, sir. And thanks. I won't forget what you did."

Quite sternly, speaking as Pa had used to speak sometimes, Hostetter said, "Don't. Not for me particularly, or for Sherman, but because of a lot of people and ideas that might just depend on your not forgetting."

Len said slowly, "Are you afraid you can't trust me?"

"It isn't exactly a question of trust."

"What is it, then?"

"You're going to Bartorstown."

Len frowned, trying to understand what he was getting at. "But that's where I want to go. That's why—all this happened."

Hostetter pushed the flat-brimmed hat back from his forehead so that his face showed clear in the moonlight. His eyes rested shrewdly and steadily on Len.

"You're going to Bartorstown," he repeated. "You have a place all dreamed up inside your head, and you call it by that name, but that isn't where you're going. You're going to the real Bartorstown, and it's probably not going to be very much like the place in your head at all. You may not like it. You may come to have pretty strong feelings about it. And that's why I say, don't forget you owe us something."

"Listen," said Len. "Can you learn in Bartorstown? Can you read books and talk about things, and use machines, and really *think*?"

Hostetter nodded.

"Then I'll like it there." Len looked out at the dark still country slipping by in the night, the sleeping, murderous, hateful country. "I never want to see any of this again. Ever."

"For my sake," said Hostetter, "I hope you'll fit in. I'm going to have trouble enough as it is, explaining the girl to Sherman. She wasn't included. But I couldn't see what else to do."

"I was wondering about her," Len said.

"Well, she'd come down there to Esau, to try and help him get away. She said she couldn't go back to her parents. She said she was going to stay with Esau. And it seemed like she pretty well had to."

"Why?" asked Len.

"Don't you know?"

"No."

"Best reason in the world," said Hostetter. "She's got his child."

Len sat staring with his mouth open. Hostetter got up. And a man came out of the deckhouse and said to him, "Sam's talking to Collins on the radio. Maybe you'd better come down, Ed."

"Trouble?"

"Well, it seems like our friend we dumped in the water back there meant what he said. Collins says two towboats went by together just after moonrise. They didn't have any tow, and they were chock full of men. One was from Refuge, the other from Shadwell."

Hostetter scowled, knocking the ashes out of his pipe and crushing them carefully under his boots. He said to Len, "We asked Collins to keep watch, just in case. He's got a shanty-boat and acts as a mobile post. Well, come on. This is all part of being a Bartorstown man. You might as well get used to it."

15

LEN FOLLOWED Hostetter and the other man, whose name was Kovacs, into the deckhouse. This was about two thirds the length of the boat, and it was built more as a roof over the cargo hold than it was to provide any elegance for the crew. There were some narrow bunks built in around the walls, and Amity was lying in one of them, her hair all tumbled around her head and her face pale and swollen with tears. Esau was sitting on the edge of the bunk, holding her hand. He looked as though he had been sitting there a long time, and he had an expression Len could not remember seeing on him before, haggard and careworn and concerned.

Len looked at Amity. She spoke to him, not meeting his eyes, and he said hello, and it was like speaking to a stranger. He thought, with an already fading pang, of the yellow-haired girl he had kissed in the rose arbor and wondered where she had gone so swiftly. This was a woman here, somebody else's woman, already marked by the cares and troubles of living, and he did not know her.

"Did you see my father, Len?" she asked. "Is he all right?"

"He was, the last I saw of him," Len told her. "The farmers weren't after him. They never touched him."

Esau got up. "You get some sleep now. That's what you need." He patted her hand and then pulled down a thin blanket that had been nailed overhead by way of a curtain. She whimpered a little, protestingly, and told Esau not to go too far away. "Don't worry about that," said Esau, with just the faintest trace of despair. "There isn't any place to go." He glanced quickly at Len, and then at Hostetter, and Len said, "Congratulations, Esau."

A slow red flush crept up over Esau's cheekbones. He straightened his shoulders and said almost defiantly, "I think it's great. And you know how it was, Len. I mean, why we couldn't get married before, on account of the judge."

"Sure," said Len. "I know."

"And I'll tell you one thing," said Esau. "I'll be a better father to it than my dad ever was to me."

"I don't know," said Len. "My father was the best in the world, and I didn't turn out so good either."

He followed Hostetter and Kovacs down a steep hatch ladder into the cargo hold.

The barge did not draw much water, but she was sixty feet long and eighteen wide, and every foot of space in her was crammed with chests and bales and sacks. She smelled strongly of wood and river water, flour and cloth, old tallow and pitch, and a lot of things Len could not identify. From beyond the after bulkhead, sounding muffled and thunderous, came the thumping rhythm of the engine. Just under the hatch a sort of well had been left so that a man could come down the ladder and see that nothing had broached or shifted, and the ladder looked like a solid piece of construction butting onto a solid deck. But a square section of the planking had been swung aside and there was a little pit there, and in the pit was a thing that Len recognized as a radio, although it was larger than the one he and Esau had had, and different in other ways. A man was sitting beside it, talking, with a single lantern hung overhead to give him light.

"Here they are now," he said. "Wait a minute." He turned and spoke to Hostetter. "Collins reckons the best thing would be to contact Rosen at the falls. The river's fairly low now, and he figures with a little help we could slip them there."

"Worth trying," said Hostetter. "What do you think, Joe?"

Kovacs said he thought Collins was right. "We sure don't want any fights, and they're bound to catch up to us, running light."

Esau had come down the ladder, too. He was standing by Len, listening.

"Watts?" he asked.

"I guess so. He must have gone scurrying around clear over to Shadwell to get men."

"They're crazy mad," said Kovacs. "They can't very well get back at the farmers, so they'll take it out on us. Besides, we're fair game whenever you find us." He was a big burly young man, very brown from the sun. He looked as though it would take a great deal to frighten him, and he did not seem frightened now, but Len was impressed by his great determination not to be caught by the boats from Refuge.

Hostetter nodded to the man at the radio. "All right, Sam. Let's talk to Rosen."

Sam said good-by to Collins and began to fiddle with the knobs. "God," said Esau, almost sobbing, "do you remember how we worked with that thing and couldn't raise a whisper, and I stole those books——" He shook his head.

"If you hadn't happened to listen in at night," said Hostetter, "you never would have heard anything." He was crouched down beside the pit now, hanging over Sam's shoulder.

"That was Len's idea," said Esau. "He figured you'd run too much risk of being seen or overheard in the daytime."

"Like now," said Kovacs. "We've got the aerial up—pretty obvious, if you had light enough to see it."

"Shut up," said Sam, bending over the radio. "How do you expect me to—— Hey, will you guys give me a clear channel for a minute? This is an emergency." A jumble of voices coming in tinny confusion from the speaker clarified into a single voice which said, "This is Petto at Indian Ferry. Do you want me to relay?"

"No," said Sam. "I want Rosen. He's within range. Lay low, will you? We've got bandits on our tail."

"Oh," said the voice of Petto. "Sing out if you want help."

"Thanks." Sam fiddled with the knobs some more and continued to call for Rosen. Len stood by the ladder and watched and listened, and it seemed in retrospect that he had spent nearly all of his life in Piper's Run down by the Pymatuning trying to make voices come out of an obstinate little box. Now, in a daze of wonder and weariness, he heard, and saw, and could not realize yet that he was actually a part of it.

"This is so much bigger than the one we had," said Esau, moving forward. His eyes shone, the way they had before, so that his handsome, willful face looked like a boy's face again, and the subtle weakness of the mouth was lost in eagerness. "How does it work? What's an aerial? How——"

Kovacs began to explain rather vaguely about batteries and transistors. His mind was not on it. Len's gaze was drawn to Hostetter's face, half shaded by the brim of his hat—the familiar brown Amish hat, the familiar square cut of the hair and the shape of the beard—and he thought of Pa, and he thought of Brother James and his two boys, and of Gran who would not regret the old world any more, and of Baby Esther who must be grown tall by now, and he turned his head away so that he could not see Hostetter but only the impersonal dark beyond the lantern's circle, full of dim and meaningless cargo shapes. The engine thumped, slow and steady, with a short sighing like the breathing of someone asleep. He could hear the paddle blades strike the water, and now he could hear other sounds too, the woody creaking of the barge itself and the sloughing and bubbling of the river sliding underneath the hull. One of those moments of disorientation came to him, a wild interval of wondering what he was doing in this place, ending in a realization that a lot had happened in the last twenty-four hours and he was tired out.

Sam was talking to Rosen.

"We're going to crack on some speed now. It should be right after daybreak, if we don't run onto a sand bar."

"Well, watch it," said the scratchy voice of Rosen from the speaker. "The channel's tricky now."

"Is anything getting down the rapids?"

"Nothing but driftwood. It's all locking through, and I've got them piled up at both ends of the canal. I don't want to tamper with the gates unless I'm forced to it. I've spent years building myself up here, but the slightest breath of suspicion——"

"Yeah," said Sam. "It would look a little coincidental, I guess. Of course, we could just ram through——"

"Not with my barge," said Kovacs. "We've got a long way to go in her yet, and I like her bottom in one piece. There must be another way."

"Let me think," said Rosen.

There was a long pause while he thought. The men waited around the radio, breathing heavily.

Rather timidly, a voice spoke, saying, "This is Petto again, at Indian Ferry."

"Okay. What?"

"Well, I was just thinking. The river's low now, and the channel's narrow. It ought to be easy to block."

"Do you have anything in mind?" asked Hostetter.

"There's a dredge working right off the end of the point," said Petto. "The men come in at night to the village, so we don't have to worry about anyone drowning. Now, if you could pass here while it's still dark, and I could be out by the dredge ready to turn her loose, the river makes a bend right here and the current would swing her on broadside, and I'll bet nothing but a canoe would get by her till she was towed off again."

"Petto," said Sam, "I love you. Did you hear that, Rosen?"

"I heard. Sounds like a solution."

"It does," said Kovacs, "but when we get there, lock us through fast, just in case."

"I'll be watching," said Rosen. "So long."

"All right," said Sam. "Petto?" They began to talk, arranging signals and timing, discussing the condition of the channel between their present position and Indian Ferry. Kovacs turned and looked at Len and Esau.

"Come on," he said. "I've got a job for you. Know anything about steam engines?"

"A little," said Len.

"Well, all you have to know about this one is to keep the fire up. We're in a hurry."

"Sure," said Len, glad of something to do. He was tired, but he could stand to be more tired if it would stop his mind from whirling around over old memories and unhappy thoughts, and the picture of Dulinsky's dying face, which was already becoming confused with the face of Soames. He scrambled up the ladder after Kovacs. In the deckhouse, Amity had apparently fallen asleep, for she made no move when they passed, Esau going on his tiptoes and looking nervously at the blanket curtaining her bunk. For a minute the night air touched them, clean and cool, and then they went down again into the pit where the boiler was. Here there was a smell of hot iron and coal dust, and a very sweaty-looking man with a broad shovel moving between the bin and the fire door. Kovacs said, "Here's some help, Charlie. We're going to move."

Charlie nodded. "Extra shovels over there." He kicked open the door and began to pile in the coal. Len took his shirt off. Esau started to, but stopped with it half unbuttoned and said, looking at the boiler, "I thought it would be different."

"What?" said Kovacs.

"Well, the engine. I mean, coming from Bartorstown, you could have any kind of an engine you want, and I thought——"

Kovacs shook his head. "Wood and coal are all the fuel there is. We have to use 'em. Besides, you stop a lot of places along the river, and a lot of people come aboard, and the first thing they want to see is your engine. They'd know in a minute if it was different. And suppose you have a breakdown? What would you do then, send all the way back to Bartorstown for parts?"

"Yeah," said Esau. "I suppose so." He was obviously disappointed. Kovacs went away. Esau finished taking his shirt off, got a shovel, and fell in beside Len at the coalbin. They fed the fire while Charlie worked the draft and watched the safety valve. The thump of the piston came faster and faster, churning the paddle wheel, and the barge picked up speed, going away with the current. Finally Charlie motioned them to hold it for a while, and they stopped, leaning on their shovels and wiping the sweat off their faces. And Esau said, "I don't think Bartorstown is going to turn out much like we thought it would."

"Nothing," said Len, "ever seems to."

It seemed like an awfully long time before another man came with word that the race was over and told Len and Esau they could quit. They stumbled up on deck, and Len felt the barge jerk and quiver as the paddles were reversed. It was not the first time that night, and Len thought that Kovacs must either have, or be himself, the devil and all of a pilot.

He leaned against the deckhouse, shivering in the cool air. It was that slack, dark time when the moon has left the sky and the sun hasn't come yet. The bank was a low black smudge with an edge of mist along it. Ahead it seemed to curve in like a solid wall, as though the river ended there, and in a minute the barge would run head on into it. Len yawned and listened to the frogs. The barge swung, and there was a bend in the river. In the hollow of the bend there was a village, the square shapes of the houses sensed rather than seen. Close by the end of the point a couple of red lights burned, hung apparently in midair.

Up on the foredeck, a lantern was shown and then covered three times in quick succession. From very low down on the water came an answering series of blinks. Because he knew it was there, Len was able to make out a dim canoe with a man in it, and then all at once the huge spectral shape of the dredger seemed to spring at him out of the gloom. It slid by, a skeletal thing like a partly dismantled house set on a flat platform, very massive and weighted with the heavy iron scoop. Then it was behind them, and Len watched the red lights. For a long time they did not seem to move, and then they seemed to shift a little, and then a little more, and then with a ponderous and mighty slowness they swung in a long arc toward the opposite shore and stopped, and the noise came down the river a moment later.

Esau said, "They'll be lucky if they have her out of there by this time tomorrow."

Len nodded. He could feel the tension lifting, or perhaps it was only because for the first time in weeks he felt safe himself. The Refuge men could not follow now, and whatever word they might send ahead would be too late to stop them.

"I'm going to turn in," he said, and went into the deckhouse. Amity still slept behind her curtain. Len picked a bunk as far away from hers as he could get, and fell almost instantly asleep. The last thought he had was of Esau being a father, and it didn't seem right at all, somehow. Then the face of Watts intruded, and a horrible smell of damp rope. Len choked and whimpered, and then the darkness flowed over him, still and deep.

16

THEY WENT through the canal next morning, one of a long line of craft, towboats, steam barges, flatboats, going down with the current all the way to the gulf, traders' floating stores that were like the shoregoing wagons, going to lonely little towns where the river was the only road. It was a slow process, even though Kovacs said that Rosen was locking them through faster than usual, and there was a lot of time just to sit and watch. The sun had come up in a welter of mist. That was gone now, but the quality of the heat had changed from the dry burning clarity of the day before. The air was thick and heavy, and the slightest movement brought a wash of sweat over the skin. Kovacs sniffed and said it smelled of storm.

"About midafternoon," said Hostetter, squinting at the sky.

"Yup," said Kovacs. "Better start figuring a place to tie up."

He went away, busy nursing his barge. Hostetter was sitting on the deck in what shade he could find under the edge of the house, and Len sat beside him. Amity had gone back to her bunk, and Esau was with her. From time to time Len could hear the murmur of their voices through the small slit windows, but not any of the words they said.

Hostetter glanced enviously after Kovacs and then looked at his own big hands with the thick pads of callus on them from the long handling of reins. "I miss 'em," he said.

"What?" said Len, who had been thinking his own thoughts.

"My horses. The wagon. Seems funny, after all these years, just to sit. I wonder if I'm going to like it."

"I thought you were happy, going home."

"I am. And high time, too, while most of my old friends are still around. But this business of leading two lives has its drawbacks. I've been away from Bartorstown for close onto thirty years and only been back once in all that time. Places like Piper's Run seem more like home to me now. When I told them last fall I was quitting the road, they asked me to settle there—and you know something? I could have done it."

He brooded, watching the men at work on the lock without really seeing them.

"I suppose it'll all come back to me," he said. "After all, the place you were born and grew up in—— But it'll seem funny to shave again. And I've worn these clothes so long——"

Water sucked and purled out of the lock and the barge sank slowly until you had to look up to see the top of the bank. The sun beat down, and no breeze stirred in that sunken pocket. Len half shut his eyes and drew his feet in under him because they were in the sun and burning.

"What are you?" he asked.

Hostetter turned his head and looked at him. "A trader."

"I mean really. What are you in Bartorstown?"

"A trader."

Len frowned. "I guess I don't understand. I thought all the Bartorstown men were something—scientists, or machine makers—something."

"I'm a trader," repeated Hostetter. "Kovacs, he's a river-boat man. Rosen is a good administrator and keeps the canal in repair and running smoothly because it's vital to us. Petto, back there at Indian Ferry—I used to know Petto's father, and he was a pretty good man in electronics, but the boy is a trader like me, except that he stays more in one place. There are only so many potential scientists and technicians in Bartorstown, like any community. And they need the rest of us to keep them going."

"You mean," said Len slowly, revising some deep-rooted ideas, "that all these years you've really been——"

"Trading," said Hostetter. "Yes. There are over four hundred people in Bartorstown, not counting us outside. They all have to eat and wear clothes. Then there's other things too, iron and alloys and chemicals and drugs, and so on. It all has to be brought in from outside."

"I see," said Len. There was a long pause. Then he said sadly, "Four hundred people. That isn't even half as many as there were in Refuge."

"It's about ninety per cent more than there were ever supposed to be. Originally there were thirty-five or forty men, all specialists, working on this hush-hush project for the government. Then when the reaction came after the war and things began to get nasty, they brought in a lot of other men and their families, scientists, teachers, people who weren't very popular on the outside any more. We've been lucky. There were a lot of other secret installations in the country, but Bartorstown is the only one that wasn't discovered or betrayed, or didn't have to be abandoned."

Len's hands tightened on his knees, and his eyes were bright. "What were they doing there—the forty men, the specialists?"

A kind of a peculiar look came into Hostetter's face. But he only said, "They were trying to find an answer to something. I can't tell you what it was, Len. All I can tell you is, they didn't find it."

"Are they still trying?" asked Len. "Or can't you tell me that, either?"

"You wait till you get there. Then you can ask all the questions you want to, from the men who are authorized to answer them. I'm not."

"When I get there," Len murmured. "It sure sounds strange. When I get to Bartorstown—I've said it a million times in my mind, but now it's real. When I get to Bartorstown."

"Be careful how you throw that name around."

"Don't worry. But—what's it like there?"

"Physically," said Hostetter, "it's a hole. Piper's Run, Refuge, Louisville over there, they've all got it beat a mile."

Len looked at the pleasant village strung out along the canal, and at the wide green plain beyond it, dotted with farmsteads and grazing cattle, and he said, remembering a dream, "No lights? No towers?"

"Lights? Well, yes and no. Towers—I'm afraid not."

"Oh," said Len, and was silent. The barge glided on. Pitch bubbled gently in the deck seams and it was an effort to breathe. After a while Hostetter took off his broad hat and wiped his forehead and said, "Oh no, it's too hot. This can't last."

Len glanced up at the sky. It was cloudless and intensely blue, but he said, "It's going to break. We'll get a good one." He turned his attention back to the village. "That used to be a city, didn't it?"

"A big one."

"I remember now, it was named after the king of France. Mr. Hostetter——"

"Hm?"

"Whatever happened to those countries—I mean, like France?"

"They're just about like us—the ones on the winning side. Lord knows what happened to the ones that lost. The whole world has jogged back to pretty much what it was when Louisville was this size before, and this canal was first dug. With a difference, though. Then they were anxious to grow and change."

"Will it always stay like this?"

"Nothing," said Hostetter, "ever stays always like anything."

"But not in my time," Len murmured, echoing Judge Taylor's words, "nor in my children's." And in his mind was the far, sad sound of the falling down of high buildings built on clouds.

"In the meantime," said Hostetter, "it's a good world. Enjoy it."

"Good," said Len bitterly. "When it's full of men like Burdette, and Watts, and the people who killed Soames?"

"Len, the world has always been full of men like that, and it always will be. Don't ask the impossible." He looked at Len's face, and then he smiled. "I shouldn't ask the impossible either."

"What do you mean?"

"It's a matter of age," said Hostetter. "Don't worry. Time will take care of it."

They passed through the lower locks and out onto the river again below the great falls. By midafternoon the whole northern sky had turned a purplish black, and a silence had fallen over the land. "Line squalls," said Kovacs, and sent Len and Esau down to stoke again. The barge went boiling downstream, her paddles lashing up the spray. It got stiller yet, and hotter, until it seemed the world would have to burst with it, and then the first crackings and rumblings of that bursting made themselves heard over the scrape of the shovels and the clang of the fire door. Finally Sam put his head down the ladder and shouted to Charlie to let off and bank up. Drenched and reeling, Len and Esau emerged into a portentous twilight, with the sky drawn down over the country like a black cowl.

They were tied up now in midstream in the lee of an island, and the north bank rose up in a protecting bluff.

"Here she comes," said Hostetter.

They ducked for the shelter of the house. The wind hit first, laying the trees over and turning up the lighter sides of their leaves. Then the rain came, riding the wind in a white smother that blotted everything from sight, and it was mixed with leaves and twigs and flying branches. After that was the lightning, and the thunder, and the cracking of trees, and then after a long time only the rain was left, pouring down straight and heavy as though it was tipped out of a bucket. They went out on deck and made sure everything was fast, shivering in the new chill, and then took turns sleeping. The rain slacked and almost stopped, and then came on again with a new storm, and during his watch Len could see lightning flaring all along the horizon as the squalls danced on the forward edge of the cool air mass moving down from the north. About midnight, through diminished rain and distant thunder, Len heard a new sound, and knew that it was the river rising.

They started on again in a clear bright dawn, with a fine breeze blowing and a sky like scoured porcelain dotted with white clouds, and only the torn branches of the trees and the river water roiled with mud and debris were left to show the wildness of the night. Half a mile below where Kovacs had tied up they passed a towboat and a string of barges, tossed up all along the south bank, and below that again a mile or two was a trader's boat sunk in the shallows where she had run onto a snag.

That was the beginning of a long journey, and a long strange period for Len that had the quality of a dream. They followed the Ohio to its mouth and turned north into the Mississippi. They were breasting the current now, beating a slow and careful way up a channel that switched constantly back and forth between the banks, so that the barge seemed always to be about to run onto the land beside some whitewashed marker. They used up the coal, and took on wood at a station on the Illinois side, and beat on again to the mouth of the Missouri, and after that for days they wallowed their way up the chutes of the Big Muddy. Mostly it was hot. There were storms, and rain, and around the middle of August there came a few nights cold enough to hint of fall. Sometimes the wind blew so hard against them they had to tie up and wait, and watch the down-river traffic go past them flying. Sometimes after a rain the water would rise and run so fast that they could make no head-way, and then it would fall just as quickly and show them too late how the treacherous channel had shifted, and they would have to work the barge painfully and with much labor and swearing off the sand bar where she had stuck fast. The muddy water fouled the boiler, and they had to stop and clean it, and other times they had to stop for more wood. And Esau grumbled, "This is a hell of a way for Bartorstown men to travel."

"Esau," said Hostetter, "I'll tell you. If we had planes we'd be glad to fly them. But we don't have planes, and this is better than walking—as you will find out."

"Do we have much farther to go?" asked Len.

Hostetter made a pushing movement with his head against the west. "Clear to the Rockies."

"How much longer?"

"Another month. Maybe more if we run into trouble. Maybe less if we don't."

"And you won't tell us what it's like?" asked Esau. "What it's really like, the way it looks, how it is to live there."

But Hostetter only said curtly, "You'll find out when you get there."

He refused to talk to them about Bartorstown. He made that one statement about Piper's Run being a pleasanter place, and then he would not say any more. Neither would the other men. No matter how the question was phrased, how subtly the conversation was twisted around to trap them, they would not talk about Bartorstown. And Len realized that it was because they were afraid to.

"You're afraid we might give it away," he said to Hostetter. And then, not in any spirit of reproach but merely as a statement of fact, "I guess you don't trust us yet."

"It isn't a question of trust. It's just that no Bartorstown man ever talks about it, and you ought to know better than to ask."

"I'm sorry," said Len. "It's just that we've thought about it so long. I guess we've got a lot to learn."

"Quite a lot," said Hostetter thoughtfully. "It won't be easy, either. So many things will jar against every belief you've grown up with, and I don't care how you scoff at it, some of it sticks to you."

"That won't bother me," said Esau.

"No," said Hostetter, "I doubt if it will. But Len's different."

"How different?" demanded Len, bristling a bit.

"Esau plays it all by ear," said Hostetter. "You worry." Later, when Esau was gone, he put his hand on Len's shoulder and smiled, giving him a close, deep look at the same time, and Len smiled back and said, "There's times when you make me think an awful lot of Pa."

"I don't mind," said Hostetter. "I don't mind at all."

17

THE CHARACTER of the country changed. The green rolling forest land flattened out and thinned away, and the sky became an enormous thing, stretched incredibly across a gray-green plain that seemed to go on and on over the rim of the world, drawing a man's gaze into its emptiness until his eyes ached with it, and until he searched hungrily for a tree or even a high bush to break the blank horizon. There were prosperous villages along the river, and Hostetter said it was good farming country in spite of how it looked, but Len hated the flat monotony of it, after the lush valleys he was used to. At night, though, there was a grandeur to it, a feeling of windy vastness all ablaze with more stars than Len had ever seen before.

"It takes a while to get used to it," Hostetter said. "But it has its own beauty. Most places do, if you don't shut your eyes and your mind against it. That's why I'm sorry I made that crack about Bartorstown."

"You meant it, though," said Len. "You know what I think? I think you're sorry you're going back."

"Change is always a sorry thing," said Hostetter. "You get used to doing things in a certain way, and it's always a wrench to break it up."

A thought came to Len which had curiously enough never

come to him before. He asked, "Do you have a family in Bartorstown?"

Hostetter shook his head. "I've always had too much of a roving foot. Never wanted any ties to it."

They both, unconsciously, looked forward along the deck to where Esau sat with Amity.

"And they're so easy to get," said Hostetter.

There was something possessive in Amity's posture, in the way her head was bent toward Esau and the way her hand rested on his. She was getting plump, and her mouth was petulant, and she was taking her approaching, if still distant, motherhood very seriously. Len shivered, remembering the rose arbor.

"Yes," said Hostetter, chuckling. "I agree. But you've got to admit they sort of deserve each other."

"I just can't figure Esau as a father, somehow."

"You might be surprised," said Hostetter. "And besides, she'll keep him in line. Don't be too toplofty, boy. Your time will come."

"Not if I know it first," said Len.

Hostetter chuckled again.

The barge thrashed its way on toward the mouth of the Platte. Len worked and ate and slept, and between times he thought. Something had been taken away from him, and after a while he realized what it was and why its going made him unhappy. It was the picture of Bartorstown he had carried with him, the vision he had followed all the long way from home. That was gone now, and in its place was only a little collection of facts and a blank waiting to be filled in. Bartorstown—a pre-war, top-secret military installation for some kind of research, named for Henry Waltham Bartor, the Secretary of Defense who had it built—was undergoing a painful translation from dream to reality. The reality was yet to come, and in the meantime there was nothing, and Len felt vaguely as though somebody had died. Which, of course, Gran had, and the two things were so closely connected in his mind that he couldn't think about Bartorstown without thinking about Gran too, and remembering the defiant things she had said that made Pa so mad. He wondered if she knew he was going there. He hoped so. He thought she would be pleased.

They tied up one night by a low bank in the middle of nowhere, with nothing in sight but the prairie grass and the endless sky, and no sound but the wind that never got tired of blowing, and the ceaseless running of the river. In the morning they started to unload the barge, and around noon Len paused a moment to catch his breath and wipe the sweat out of his eyes. And he saw a pillar of dust moving far off on the prairie, coming toward the river.

Hostetter nodded. "It's our men, bringing the wagons. We'll angle up from here to the valley of the Platte, and pick up the rest of our party at a point on the South Fork."

"And then?" asked Len, with a stir of the old excitement making his heart beat faster.

"Then we're on the last stretch."

A few hours later the wagons came in, eight of them, great lumbering things made for the hauling of freight and drawn by mules. The men who drove them were brown and leathery, with the tops of their foreheads all white when they took their hats off, and a network of pale lines around their eyes where the sun hadn't got to the bottom of the squinted-up wrinkles. They greeted Kovacs and the bargemen as old friends, and shook Hostetter's hand warmly as a sort of welcome-home. Then one of them, an old fellow with a piercing glance and a pair of shoulders that looked as though they could carry a wagon alone if the mules gave out, peered closely at Len and Esau and said to Hostetter, "So these are your boys."

"Well," said Hostetter, coloring slightly.

The old man walked around them slowly, his head on one side. "My son was in the Ohio country couple-three years ago. He said all you heard about was Hostetter's boys. Where were they, what were they doing, let him know when they moved on."

"It wasn't that bad," said Hostetter. His face was now brick red. "Anyway, a couple of kids—— And I'd known them since they were born."

The old man finished his circuit and stood in front of Len and Esau. He put out a hand like a slab of oak and shook with them gravely in turn. "Hostetter's boys," he said, "I'm glad you got here before my old friend Ed had a total breakdown."

He went away laughing. Hostetter snorted and began to

throw boxes and barrels around. Len grinned, and Kovacs burst out laughing.

"He isn't just joking, either," said Kovacs, jerking his head toward the old man. "Ed kept every radio in that part of the country hot."

"Well, damn it," grumbled Hostetter, "a couple of kids. What would you have done?"

They camped that night beside the river, and next day they loaded the wagons, taking great care with the stowage of each piece in the beds, and leaving a place in one where Amity could ride and sleep. Kovacs was going on into the Upper Missouri, and shortly after noon they got up steam on the barge and chuffed away. The mules were rounded up by two or three of the men, riding small wiry horses of a type Len had not seen before. He helped them to harness up and then took his seat in one of the wagons. The long whips cracked and the drivers shouted. The mules leaned their necks into the collars and the wagons rolled slowly over the prairie grass, with a heavy creaking and complaint of axles. At nightfall, across the flat land, Len could still see the barge on the river. In the morning it was still there, but farther off, and sometime during the day he lost it. And the prairie became immensely large and lonely.

The Platte runs wide and shallow between hills of sand. The sun beats down and the wind blows, and the land goes on forever. Len remembered the Ohio with an infinite longing. But after a while, when he got used to it, he became aware of a whole new world here, a way of living that didn't seem half bad, once you shucked off a habit of thought that called for green woods and green grass, rain and plowing. The dusty cottonwoods that grew by the water became as beautiful as oaks, and the ranch houses that clung close to the river were more welcome than the villages of his own country because they were so much more infrequent. They were rough and sun-bitten, but they were comfortable enough, and Len liked the people, the brown hardy women and the men who seemed to have lost some of themselves when they came apart from their horses. Beyond the sand hills was the prairie, and on the prairie were the great wild herds of cattle and the roving horse bands that made the living of these hunters and traders. Hostetter said that the wild herds were the descendants of the pre-war range stock, turned loose in the great upheaval that followed the abandonment of the cities and the consequent breakdown of the system of supply and demand.

"Their range runs clear down to the Mexican border," he said, "and there isn't a fence on it now. The dry-farmers all quit long ago. For generations there hasn't been a single plow to scratch up the plains, and the grass is coming back even in the worst of the man-made deserts, like the good Lord meant it to be." He took a deep breath, looking all around the horizon. "There's something about it, isn't there, Len? I mean, in some ways the East is closed in, with hills and woods and the other side of a river valley."

"You ain't going to get me to say I don't like the East," said Len. "But I'm getting to like this too. It's just so big and empty I keep feeling like I'm going to fall in."

It was dry, too. The wind beat and picked at him, sucking the moisture out of him like a great leech. He drank and drank, and there was always sand in the bottom of the cup, and he was always thirsty. The mules rolled the miles back under the wagon wheels, but so gradually and through such a sameness of country that Len got a feeling they hadn't moved. Through deep ravines in the sand hills the wild cattle came down to drink, and at night the coyotes yapped and howled and then fell into respectful silence before the deeper and more blood-chilling voice of some wayfaring wolf. Sometimes they would go for days without seeing a ranch house or any sign of human life, and then they would pass a camp where the hunters had made a great kill and were busy jerking or salting down the beef and rough-curing the hides. And time passed. And like the time on the river, it was timeless.

They reached the rendezvous on the South Fork, in a meadow faded and sun-scorched, but still greener than the glaring sandy desolation that spread around it as far as the eye could reach, broken only by the shallow rushing of the river. When they went on again there were thirty-one wagons in the party, and some seventy men. Some of them had come directly across the Great Plains, others had come from the north and west, and they were loaded with everything from wool and iron pigs to gunpowder. Hostetter said that other freight trains like this came up from Arkansas and the wide country to the south and west, and that others still followed the old trail through the South Pass from the country west of the mountains. All the supplies had to be fetched before winter, because the Plains were a cruel place when the northers blew and the single pass into Bartorstown was blocked with snow.

From time to time, at particular points, they would find groups of men encamped and waiting for them, and they would stop to trade, and at one place, where another stream trickled into the South Fork and there was a village of four houses, they picked up two more wagons loaded with hides and dried beef. And Len asked, when he was sure he was alone with Hostetter, "Don't these people ever get suspicious? I mean, about where we're going."

Hostetter shook his head.

"But I should think they'd guess."

"They don't have to. They know."

"They *know* we're going to Bartorstown?" said Len incredulously.

"Yes," said Hostetter, "but they don't know they know it. You'll see what I mean when you get there."

Len did not ask any more, but he thought about it, and it didn't seem to make any kind of sense.

The wagons lumbered on through the heat and the glare. And on a late afternoon when the Rockies hung blue and misty like a curtain across the west, there came a sudden shout from up ahead. It was flung back all along the line, from driver to driver, and the wagons jolted to a stop. Hostetter reached back for a gun, and Len asked, "What is it?"

Hostetter said, "I suppose you've heard of the New Ishmaelites."

"Yes."

"Well, now you're going to see them."

Len followed Hostetter's gesture, squinting against the reddening light. And on top of a low and barren bluff he saw a gathering of people, perhaps half a hundred of them, looking down.

18

He jumped to the ground with Hostetter. The driver stayed put, so he could move the wagon into a defensive line if the order came. Esau joined them, and some other men, and the old chap with the bright eyes and the mighty shoulders, whose name was Wepplo. Most of them had guns.

"What do we do?" asked Len, and the old man answered, "Wait."

They waited. Two men and a woman came slowly down from the bluff, and the leader of the train went just as slowly out to meet them, with half a dozen armed men behind to cover him. And Len stared.

The people gathered on the bluff were like an awkward frieze of scarecrows put together out of old bones and strips of blackened leather. There was something horrible about seeing that there were children among them, peering with a normal childlike wonder and excitement at the strange men and the wagons. They wore goatskins, very much like old Bible pictures of John the Baptist, or else long wrappings of dirty white cloth like winding sheets. Their hair hung long and matted down their backs, and the men had beards to their waists. They were gaunt, and even the children had a wild and starveling look. Their eyes were sunken, and perhaps it was only a trick of the lowering sun, but it seemed to Len that they burned and smoldered with an actual glow, like the eyes he had seen once on a dog that had the mad sickness.

"Will they fight us?" he asked.

"Can't tell yet," said Wepplo. "Sometimes yes, other times no. Depends."

"What do you mean," demanded Esau, "it depends?"

"On whether they've been 'struck' or not. Mostly they just wander and pray and do a lot of real holy starving. But then all of a sudden one of 'em'll start screaming and frothing and fall down kicking, and that's a sign they've been struck by the Lord's special favor. So the rest of 'em whoop and screech and beat themselves with thorny branches or maybe whips—whips, you see, is the only personal article their religion allows them to own—and when they're worked up enough they all pile down and butcher some rancher that's affronted the Lord by pampering his flesh with a sod roof and a full belly. They can do a real nice job of butchering, too."

Len shivered. The faces of the Ishmaelites frightened him. He remembered the faces of the farmers when they marched into Refuge, and how their stony dedication had frightened him then. But they were different. Their fanaticism roused up only when it was prodded. These people lived by it, lived for it, and served it without rhyme, reason, or thought.

He hoped they would not fight.

They did not. The two wild-looking men and the woman—a wiry creature with sharp shin bones showing under her shroud when she walked, and a tangle of black hair blowing over her shoulders—were too far away for any of their talk to be heard, but after a few minutes the leader of the train turned and spoke to the men behind him, and two of them turned and came back to the train. They sought out a particular wagon, and Wepplo grunted.

"Not this time. They only want some powder."

"Gunpowder?" asked Len incredulously.

"Their religion don't seem to call for them starving quite to death, and every gang of them—this is only one band, you understand—does own a couple of guns. I hear they never shoot a young cow, though, but only the old bulls, which are tough enough to mortify anybody's flesh."

"But powder," said Len. "Don't they use it on the ranchers, too?"

The old man shook his head. "They're knife-and-claw killers, when they kill. I guess they can get closer to their work that way. Besides, they only get enough powder to barely keep them going." He nodded toward the two men, who were going back again carrying a small keg. A thin sound, half wailing and half waspish, penetrated from the second wagon down, and Esau said, "Oh Lord, there's Amity calling me. She's probably scared to death." He turned and went immediately. Len watched the New Ishmaelites.

"Where did they come from?" he asked, trying to remember what he had heard about them. They were one of the very earliest extreme sects, but he didn't know much more than that.

"Some of them were here to begin with," Hostetter said. "Under other names, of course, and not nearly so crazy because the pressure of society sort of held them down, but a fertile seed bed. Others came here of their own accord when the New Ishmaelite movement took shape and really got going. A lot more were driven here out of the East, being natural-born troublemakers that other people wanted to be rid of."

The small keg of powder changed hands. Len said, "What do they trade you for it?"

"Nothing. Buying and selling are no part of holiness, and anyway, they don't have anything. When you come right down to it, I don't know why we do give it to them. I guess," said Wepplo, "probably it's on account of the kids. You know, once in a while you find one of 'em like a coyote pup, lost in the sagebrush. If they're young enough, and brought up right, they turn out just as smart and nice as anyone."

The woman lifted her arms up high, whether for a curse or a blessing Len couldn't tell. The wind tossed the lank hair back from her face, and he saw with a shock that she was young, and might have been handsome if her cheeks were full and her eyes less hunger-bright and staring. Then she and the two men climbed back to the top of the bluff, and in five minutes they were all gone, hidden by the cut-up hills. But that night the Bartorstown men doubled the watch.

Two days later they filled every cask, bottle, and bucket with water and left the river, striking south and west into a waste and very empty land, sun-scorched, wind-scourged, and dry as an old skull. They were climbing now, toward distant bastions of red rock with tumbled masses of peaks rising blue and far away behind them. The mules and the men labored together, toiling slowly, and Len learned to hate the sun. And he looked up at the blank, cruel peaks, and wondered. Then, when the water was almost gone, a red scarp swung away to the west and showed an opening about as wide as two wagons, and Hostetter said, "This is the first gate."

They filed into it. It was smooth like a made road, but it was steep, and everybody was walking now to ease the mules, except Amity. After a little while, without any order that Len could hear, or for any reason that he could see, they stopped.

He asked why.

"Routine," Hostetter said. "We're not exactly overrun with people, as you might guess from the country, but not even a rabbit can get through here without being seen, and it's customary to stop and be looked over. If somebody doesn't, we know right away it's a stranger."

Len craned his neck, but he could not see anything but red rock. Esau was walking with them, and Wepplo. Wepplo laughed and said, "Boy, they're looking at you right now in Bartorstown. Yes, they are. Studying you real close, and if they don't like your looks, all they have to do is push one little button and *boom!*" He made a sweeping gesture with his hand, and Len and Esau both ducked. Wepplo laughed again.

"What do you mean, *boom*?" said Esau angrily, glaring around. "You mean somebody in Bartorstown could kill us here? That's crazy."

"It's true," said Hostetter. "But I wouldn't get excited. They know we're coming."

Len felt the skin between his shoulders turn cold and crawl. "How can they see us?"

"Scanners," said Hostetter, pointing vaguely at the rock. "Hidden in the cracks, where you can't see 'em. A scanner is kind of like an eye, way off from the body. Whoever comes through here, they know it in Bartorstown, and it's still a day's journey away."

"And all they have to do is push something?" said Esau, wetting his lips.

Wepplo swung his hand again, and repeated, "*Boom!*"

"They must have really had something almighty secret here," said Esau, "to go to all that trouble."

Wepplo opened his mouth, and Hostetter said, "Give a hand with the wagon here, will you?" Wepplo shut his mouth again and leaned onto the tail gate of a wagon that seemed already to be rolling smoothly. Len looked sharply at Hostetter, but his head was bent and his whole attention appeared to be on the pushing. Len smiled. He did not say anything.

Beyond the cut was a road. It was a good, wide road, and Hostetter said it had been made a long time ago before the Destruction. He called it a switchback. It zigzagged right up the side of a mountain, and Len could still see the marks on the rock where huge iron teeth had bitten it away. They moved up slowly, the teams grunting and puffing, and the men helping them, and Hostetter pointed to a ragged notch very high up against the sky. He said, "Tomorrow."

Len's heart began to beat fast and the nerves pricked all through his stomach. But he shook his head, and Hostetter asked, "What's the matter?"

"I never thought there'd be a road to it. I mean, just a road."

"How did you think we'd get in and out?"

"I don't know," said Len, "but I thought there'd be at least walls or guards or something. Of course they can stop people in the cut back there——"

"They *could*. They never have."

"You mean people walk right through there? And up this road? And through that pass into Bartorstown?"

"They do," said Hostetter, "and they don't. Didn't you ever hear that the best way to hide something is to leave it right out in the open?"

"I don't understand," said Len. "Not at all."

"You will."

"I guess so." Len's eyes were shining again in that particular way, and he said softly, "Tomorrow," as though it was a beautiful word.

"It's been a long way, hasn't it?" said Hostetter. "You really wanted to come, to stick to it like that." He was silent a minute, looking up at the pass. Then he said, "Give it time, Len. It won't be all that you've dreamed about, but give it time. Don't make any snap decisions."

Len turned and studied him gravely. "You keep sounding all the time like you're trying to warn me about something."

"I'm just trying to tell you to—not be impatient. Give yourself a chance to get adjusted." Suddenly, almost angrily, he said, "This is a hard life, that's what I'm trying to tell you. It's hard for everybody, even in Bartorstown, and it doesn't get any easier, and don't expect a shiny tinsel heaven and then break your heart because it isn't there."

He looked hard at Len, very briefly, and then looked away, breathing hard and doing the mechanical things with his hands that a man does when he's upset and trying not to show it. And Len said slowly, "You hate the place."

He could not believe it. But when Hostetter said sharply, "That's ridiculous, of course I don't," he knew that it was true.

"Why did you come back? You could have stayed in Piper's Run."

"So could you."

"But that's different."

"No, it isn't. You had a reason. So have I." He walked on for a minute with his head bent down. Then he said, "Just don't ever plan on going back."

He went ahead fast, leaving Len behind, and Len did not see him alone again the rest of that day and night. But he felt as shocked as he would have if, in the old days, Pa had suddenly told him that there was no God.

He did not say anything to Esau. But he kept glancing up at the pass, and wondering. Toward late afternoon they were high enough up on the mountain that he could see back the other way, over the ridge of the scarp, to where the desert lay all lonely and burning. A terrible feeling of doubt came over him. The red and yellow rock, the sharp peaks that hung against the sky, the gray desert and the dust and the dryness, the pitiless light that was never softened by a cloud or gentled by rain, the vast ringing silences where nothing lived but the wind, all seemed to mock him with their cheerlessness and lack of hope. He wished he was back—no, not home, because he would have to face Pa there, and not in Refuge, either. Just somewhere where there was life and water and green grass. Somewhere where the ugly rock did not stand up every way you looked, like——

Like what?

Like the truth, when all the dreams are torn away from it?

It wasn't a happy thought. He tried to ignore it, but every time he saw Hostetter it came to him again. Hostetter seemed broody and withdrawn, and after they camped and had supper he disappeared. Len started to look for him and then had sense enough to stop.

They were camped in the mouth of the pass, where there was a wide space on both sides of the road. The wind blew and it was bitterly cold. Just before dark Len noticed some letters cut in the side of a cliff above the road. They were crumbling and weatherworn, but they were big, and he could make them out. They said FALL CREEK 13 mi.

Hostetter was gone, so Len hunted up Wepplo and asked him what they meant.

"Can't you read, boy? They mean just what they say. Fall Creek, thirteen miles. That's from here to there."

"Thirteen miles," said Len, "from here to Fall Creek. All right. But what's Fall Creek?"

"Town," said Wepplo.

"Where?"

"In Fall Creek Canyon." He pointed. "Thirteen miles."

He was grinning. Len began to hate the old man's sense of humor. "What about Fall Creek?" he asked. "What does it have to do with us?"

"Why," said Wepplo, "it's got damn near everything to do with us. Didn't you know, boy? That's where we're going."

Then he laughed. Len walked away fast. He was mad at Wepplo, mad at Hostetter, mad at Fall Creek. He was mad at the world. He rolled up in his blanket and lay shivering and cursing. He was dog-tired. But it was a long time before he fell asleep, and then he dreamed. He dreamed that he was trying to find Bartorstown. He knew he was almost there, but there was fog and darkness and the road kept shifting its direction. He kept asking an old man how to get there, but the old man had never heard of Bartorstown and would only say over and over that it was thirteen miles to Fall Creek.

They went through the pass the next day. Both Len and Hostetter were now morose and did not talk much. They crossed the saddleback before noon, and after that they went much faster, going down. The mules stepped out smartly as though they knew they were almost home. The men got cheerful and eager. Esau kept running up as often as he could get away from Amity and asking, "Are we almost there?" And Hostetter would nod and say, "Almost."

They came out of the pass with the afternoon sun in their eyes. The road pitched down in another switchback along the side of a cliff, and way at the bottom of the cliff there was a canyon, with the blue shadow of the opposite wall already sliding across it. Hostetter pointed. His voice was neither excited, nor happy, nor sad. It was just a voice, saying, "There it is."

Book Three

19

THE WAGONS went down the wide steep road with the brake shoes screeching and the mules braced back on their haunches. Len looked over the edge, into the canyon. He looked a long time without speaking. Esau came and walked beside him, and they both looked. And it was Esau who turned around with his face all white and angry and shouted at Mr. Hostetter, "What do you think this is, a joke? Do you think this is real funny, bringing us all this way——"

"Oh, shut up," said Hostetter. He sounded tired now, all of a sudden, and impatient, and he spoke to Esau the way a man speaks to an annoying child. Esau shut up. Hostetter glanced at Len. Len did not turn or lift his head. He was still staring down into the bottom of the canyon.

There was a town there. Seen from this height and angle it was mostly a collection of roofs, clustered along the sides of a stream bed where some cottonwoods grew. They were ordinary roofs of ordinary little houses such as Len had been used to seeing all his life, and he thought that many of the houses were made of logs, or slab. At the north end of the canyon was a small dam with a patch of blue water behind it. Beside the dam, straggling up a slope, there were a couple of high, queer-looking buildings. Close by them rails ran up and down the slope, leading from a hole in the cliff to a dump of broken rock. There were tiny cars on the rails. At the foot of the slope were several more buildings, low and flat ones this time, with a curving top. They were a rusty color. From the other side of the dam a short road led to another hole in the cliff, but there were no rails or cars or anything connected with this one, and rocks had rolled down across the road.

Len could see people moving around. Smoke came from some of the chimneys. A team of tiny mules brought a string of tiny cars down the rails on the slope, and the carts were dumped. After a minute or two the sound drifted up to him, faint and thin like an echo.

He turned and looked at Hostetter.

"Fall Creek," said Hostetter. "It's a mining town. Silver. Not very high-grade ore, but good enough and a lot of it. We still take it out. There's no secret about Fall Creek, never has been." He swept his hand out in a brief, curt gesture. "We live here."

Len said slowly, "But it isn't Bartorstown."

"No. That's kind of a wrong name, anyway. It isn't really a town at all."

Even more slowly, Len said, "Pa told me there was no such place. He told me it was only a state of mind."

"Your Pa was wrong. There is such a place, and it's real. Real enough to keep hundreds of people working for it all their lives."

"But where?" said Esau furiously. "Where?"

"You've waited this long. You can wait a few hours longer."

They went on, down the steep road. The shadow of the mountain widened and filled the canyon, and began to flow up the eastern wall to meet them. Farther down, on the breast of an old fall, a stand of pines caught the light and turned a harsh green, too bright against the red and ochers of the rock.

Len said, "Fall Creek is just another town."

"You can't get clear out of the world," Hostetter said. "You can't now and you couldn't then. The houses are built of logs and slab because we had to build them out of what there was. Originally Fall Creek had electricity because it was the fashion then. Now it isn't the fashion, so we don't have it. Main thing is to look like everybody else, and then they don't notice you."

"But a real secret place," said Len. "A place nobody knew about." He frowned, trying to puzzle it out. "A place you don't dare let anybody know about now—and yet you just live openly in a town, with a road to it, and strangers come and go."

"When you start barring people out they know you have something to hide. Fall Creek was built first. It was built quite openly. What few people there were in this Godforsaken part of the country got used to it, got used to the trucks and a particular kind of plane going to and from it. It was only a mining town. Bartorstown was built later, behind the cover of Fall Creek, and nobody ever suspected it."

Len thought that over. Then he asked, "Didn't they even guess it when all the new people started coming in?"

"The world was full of refugees, and thousands of them headed for places just like this, as far back in the hills as they could get."

The shadow reached up and they went into it, and it was twilight. Lamps were being lit in the town. They were just lamps, such as were lit in Piper's Run, or Refuge, or a thousand other towns. The road flattened out. The mules were tired, but they pricked their long ears forward and swung along fast, and the drivers yelled and made their whips crack like rifle shots. There was quite a crowd waiting for them under the cottonwoods, lanterns burning, women calling out to their men on the wagons, children running up and down and shouting. They did not look any different from any other people Len had seen in this part of the country. They wore the same kinds of clothes, and their manners were the same. Hostetter said again, as though he knew what Len was thinking, "You have to live in the world. You can't get away from it."

Len said with a quiet bitterness, "There isn't even as much here as we had in Piper's Run. No farms, no food, nothing but rocks all around. Why do people stay here?"

"They have a reason."

"It must be a mighty damn big one," retorted Len, in a tone that said he did not believe in anything any more.

Hostetter did not answer.

The wagons stopped. The drivers got down and everybody that was riding got out, Esau lifting down a pale and rumpled Amity, who stared about her distrustfully. Boys and young men ran up and took the mules and led them away with the wagons. There were a terrible lot of strange faces, and after a while Len realized that they were nearly all staring at him and Esau. They hung together instinctively, close to Hostetter. Hostetter was craning his head around, yelling for Wepplo, and the old man came up grinning, with his arm around a girl. She was kind of a small girl, with dark hair and snapping dark eyes like Wepplo's, and a face that was perhaps a little too sharp and determined. She wore a shirt with the neck open and the sleeves rolled up, and a skirt that came down just over the tops of a pair of soft high boots. She looked first at Amity, and then at Esau, and then at Len. She looked the longest at Len, and her eyes were not at all shy about meeting his.

"My granddaughter," said Wepplo, as though she was made of pure gold. "Joan. Mrs. Esau Colter, Mr. Esau Colter, Mr. Len Colter."

"Joan," said Hostetter, "will you take Mrs. Colter with you for a while?"

"Sure," said Joan, rather sulkily. Amity hung onto Esau and started a protest, but Hostetter shut her up.

"Nobody's going to bite you. Go along, and Esau will come as soon as he can."

Amity went, reluctantly, leaning on the dark girl's shoulder. She looked as big as a house, and not from the baby, either, which was still a long way off. The dark girl gave Len a sly laughing glance and then disappeared in the crowd. Hostetter nodded to Wepplo and hitched up his pants and said to Len and Esau, "All right, come on."

They followed him, and all along the way people stared at them and talked, not in an unfriendly way, but as though Len and Esau were of tremendous interest to them. Len said, "They don't seem to be very used to strangers."

"Not strangers coming to live with them. Anyway, they've been hearing about you two for a long time. They're curious."

"Hostetter's boys," said Len, and grinned for the first time in two days.

Hostetter grinned too. He led them down a dark lane between scattered houses to where a fairly large frame house with a porch across its front was set on a slope, higher than the others and facing the mine. The clapboards were old and weathered, and the porch had been shored up underneath with logs.

"This was built for the mine superintendent," said Hostetter. "Sherman lives in it now."

"Sherman is the boss?" asked Esau.

"Of a lot of things, yes. There's Gutierrez and Erdmann, too. They have the say about other things."

"But Sherman let us come," said Len.

"He had to talk to the others. They all had to agree to that."

There was lamplight in the house. They went up the steps onto the porch, and the door opened before Hostetter could knock on it. A tall thin gray-haired woman with a pleasant face stood in the doorway, smiling and holding out her arms to Hostetter. He said, "Hello, Mary," and she said, "Ed! Welcome home!" and kissed him on the cheek. "Well," said Hostetter. "It's been a long time." "Eleven, no, twelve years," said Mary. "It's good to have you back."

She looked at Len and Esau.

"This is Mary Sherman," said Hostetter, as though he felt he had to explain, "an old friend. She used to play with my sister when we were all young—my sister's dead now. Mary, these are the boys."

He introduced them. Mary Sherman smiled at them, half sadly, as though she had much she could say. But all she did say was, "Yes, they're waiting for you. Come inside."

They stepped into the living room. The floor was bare and clean, the pine boards worn down to the grain. The furniture was old, most of it, and plain, of a kind Len had seen before that was made before the Destruction. There was a big table with a lamp on it, and three men were sitting around it. Two of them were about Hostetter's age, and one was younger, perhaps forty or so. One of the older ones, a big square blocky man with a clean-shaven chin and light eyes, got up and shook hands with Hostetter. Then Hostetter shook hands with the others, and there was some talk. Len looked around uncomfortably and saw that Mary Sherman was already gone.

"Come here," said the big blocky man, and Len realized that he was being spoken to. He stepped into the circle of lamplight, close to the table. Esau came with him. The big man studied them. His eyes were the color of a winter sky just before snow, very keen and penetrating. The younger man sat beside him, leaning forward on the table. He had reddish hair and he wore spectacles and his face looked tired, not as though he needed to rest right now but as though it always looked tired. Behind him, in the shadows between the table and the big iron stove, was the third man, small, swarthy and bitter, with a neat pointed beard as white as linen. Len stared back at them, not knowing whether to be angry or awed or what, and beginning to sweat from sheer nervousness.

The big man said abruptly, "I'm Sherman. This is Mr. Erdmann"—the younger man nodded—"and Mr. Gutierrez." The small bitter man grunted. "I know you're both Colters. But which is which?"

They named themselves. Hostetter had withdrawn into the shadows, and Len heard him filling his pipe.

Sherman said to Esau, "Then you're the one with the—ah—expectant mother."

Esau started to explain, and Sherman stopped him. "I know all about it, and I've already given Hostetter his tongue-lashing for exceeding authority, so we can forget it, except for one thing. I want you to bring her here at exactly ten o'clock tomorrow morning. The minister will be here. Nobody needs to know about it. Is that understood?"

"Yes, sir," said Esau. Sherman was not threatening or unpleasant. He was just used to giving orders, and the answer was automatic.

He looked from Esau to Len, and asked, "Why did you want to come here?"

Len bent his head and did not say anything.

"Go ahead," said Hostetter. "Tell him."

"How can I?" said Len. "All right. We thought it would be a place where people were different, where they could think about things and talk about them without getting into trouble. Where there were machines and—oh, all the things there used to be."

Sherman smiled. It made him no longer a cold-eyed blocky man used to giving orders, but a human being who had lived a long time and learned not to fight it. Like Hostetter. Like Pa. Len recognized him, and suddenly he felt that he was not entirely among strangers.

"You thought," said Sherman, "that we'd have a city, just like the old ones, with everything in it."

"I guess so," said Len, and he was not angry now, only regretful.

"No," said Sherman. "All we have is the first part of what you wanted."

Erdmann said, "And we're looking for the second."

"Oh yes," said Gutierrez. His voice was thin and bitter like the rest of him. "We have a cause. You'll understand about that—you young men have had a cause yourselves. Do you want me to tell them, Harry?"

"Later," Sherman said. He leaned forward and spoke to Len and Esau, and his eyes were hard again, and cold. "You have Hostetter to thank——"

"Not entirely," said Hostetter, breaking in. "You had your reason."

"A man can always find a reason to justify himself," said

Sherman cynically. "But all right, I admit I had one. However, most of it was Hostetter. Otherwise you would both be dead now, at the hands of the mob in that town—what's the name——?"

"Refuge," said Len. "Yes, we know that."

"I'm not rubbing it in, merely getting the facts straight. We've done you a favor, and I won't try to impress upon you what a very big favor it is because you won't be able to understand until you've been here awhile. Then I won't have to tell you. In the meantime, I'm going to ask you to repay it by doing as you're told and not asking too many questions."

He paused. Erdmann cleared his throat nervously in the silence, and Gutierrez muttered, "Give them the shaft, Harry. Swift and clean."

Sherman turned around. "Have you been drinking, Julio?"

"No. But I will."

Sherman grunted. "Well, anyway, what he means is this. You're not to leave Fall Creek. Don't do anything that even looks like leaving. We have a great deal at stake here, more than you can possibly imagine as yet, and we can't risk it."

He finished simply with three words. "You'll be shot."

20

THERE WAS another silence. Then Esau said, just a little too loudly, "We worked hard enough to get here, we're not likely to run away."

"People change their minds. It was only fair to tell you."

Esau put his hands on the table and said, "Can I ask just one question?"

"Go ahead."

"Where the hell *is* Bartorstown?"

Sherman leaned back in his chair and looked hard at Esau, frowning. "You know something, Colter? I wouldn't answer that, now or later, if there was any way to keep it from you. You boys have made us quite a problem. When strangers come in here we keep our mouths shut and are careful, and that isn't much of a worry because there are very few strangers and they don't stay long. But you two are going to live here. Sooner or later, inevitably, you're going to find out all about us. And yet you don't really belong here. Your whole life, your training, your background, your conditioning, are totally at odds with everything we believe in."

He glanced at Len, harshly amused. "No use getting red around the ears, young fellow. I know you're sincere. I know you've gone through hell to get here, which is more than a lot of us would do. But—tomorrow is another day. How are you going to feel then, or the day after?"

"I should think you're pretty safe," said Len, "as long as you have plenty of bullets."

"Oh," said Sherman. "That. Yes. Well, I suppose so. Anyway, we decided to take a chance on you, and so we haven't any choice. So you'll be told about Bartorstown. But not tonight." He got up and shoved his hand unexpectedly at Len. "Bear with me."

Len shook hands with him and smiled.

Hostetter said, "I'll see you, Harry." He nodded to Len and Esau, and they went out again, into full dark and air that had a crisp edge of chill on it, and a lot of unfamiliar smells. They walked back through the town. Lamps were going on in every house, people were talking loud and laughing, and going from place to place in little groups. "There's always a celebration," said Hostetter. "Some of the men have been away a long time."

They wound up in a neat, solid log house that belonged to the Wepplos, the old man and his son and daughter-in-law, and the girl Joan. They ate dinner and a lot of people drifted in and out, saying hello to Hostetter and nipping out of a big jug that got to passing around. The girl Joan watched Len all evening, but she didn't say much. Quite late, Gutierrez came in. He was dead drunk, and he stood looking down at Len so solemnly and for such a long time that Len asked him what he wanted.

Gutierrez said, "I just wanted to see a man who wanted to come here when he didn't have to."

He sighed and went away. Pretty soon Hostetter tapped him on the shoulder. "Come on, Lennie," he said, "unless you want to sleep on Wepplo's floor."

He seemed in a jovial frame of mind, as though coming

home had not after all been as bad as he thought it would be. Len walked along beside him through the cold night. Fall Creek was quieter now, and the lamps were going out. He told Hostetter about Gutierrez.

Hostetter said, "Poor Julio. He's in a bad frame of mind."

"What's wrong with him?"

"He's been working on this thing for three years. Actually, he's been working on it most of his life, but this particular point of attack, I mean. Three years. And he's just found out it's no good. Clear the slate, try again. Only Julio's beginning to think he isn't going to live long enough."

"Long enough for what?"

But Hostetter only said, "We'll have to bunk in the bachelor's shack. But that isn't bad. Lots of company."

The bachelor's shack turned out to be a long two-story frame building, part of the original construction of Fall Creek, with some later additions running out from it in clumsy wings. The room Hostetter led him into was at the back of one of these wings, with its own door and some stubby pine trees close by to scent the air and whisper when the breeze blew. They had brought their blanket rolls from Wepplo's. Hostetter pitched his into one of the two bunks and sat down and began to take off his boots.

"How do you like her?" he said.

"Like who?" asked Len, spreading his blankets.

"Joan Wepplo."

"How should I know? I hardly saw her."

Hostetter laughed. "You hardly took your eyes off her all evening."

"I've got better things to think about," said Len angrily, "than some girl."

He rolled into the bunk. Hostetter blew out the candle, and a few minutes later he was snoring. Len lay wide awake, every surface of him exposed and sensitive and quivering, feeling and hearing. The bunk was a new shape. Everything was strange: the smells of earth and dust and pine needles and pine resin and walls and floor and cooking, the dim sounds of movement and of voices in the night, everything. And yet it was not strange, either. It was just another part of the world, another town, and no matter what Bartorstown turned out to be now it would not be anything at all that he had hoped for. He felt awful. He felt so awful, and he was so angry with everything for being as it was that he kicked the wall, and then he felt so childish that he began to laugh. And in the middle of his laughing, the face of Joan Wepplo floated by, watching him with bright speculative eyes.

When he woke up it was morning, and Hostetter had already been out somewhere because he was just coming back.

"Got a clean shirt?"

"I think so."

"Well, get busy and put it on. Esau wants you to stand up with him."

Len muttered something under his breath about it being late in the day for formalities like that, but he washed and shaved and put on the clean shirt, and walked up with Hostetter to Sherman's house. The village seemed quiet, with not many people around. He got the feeling that they were watching him from inside the windows of the houses, but he did not mention it.

The wedding was short and plain. Amity was wearing a dress somebody must have loaned her. She looked smug. Esau did not look any way at all. He was just there. The minister was a young man and quite short, with an annoying habit of bobbing up and down on his toes as though he were trying all the time to stretch himself. Sherman and his wife and Hostetter stood in the background, watching. When it was over Mary Sherman put her arms around Amity, and Len shook hands rather stiffly with Esau, feeling silly. He was ready to go then, but Sherman said, "If you don't mind, I'd like you to stay awhile. All of you."

They were in a small room. He crossed it and opened the door into the living room, and Len saw that there were seven or eight men inside.

"Now there's nothing to worry about," Sherman said, and motioned them through the door. "Those three chairs right there at the table—that's right. Sit down. I want you to talk to some people."

They sat down, close together in a row. Sherman sat next to them, with Hostetter just beyond him, and the other men crowded in until they were all clumped around the table. There were pens and paper on it, and some other things, and in the middle a big wicker basket with the lid down. Sherman named over the men, but Len could not remember them all, except for Erdmann and Gutierrez, whom he already knew. They were nearly all middle-aged, and keen-looking, as though they were used to some authority. They were all very polite to Amity.

Sherman said, "This isn't an inquisition or anything, we're just interested. How did you first hear of Bartorstown, what made you so determined to come here, what happened to you because of it, how did it all start. Can you start us off, Ed? I think you were in on the beginning."

"Well," said Hostetter, "I guess it began the night Esau stole the radio."

Sherman looked at Esau, and Esau looked uncomfortable. "I guess that was wrong to do, but I was only a kid then. And they killed this man because they said he was from Bartorstown—it was an awful night. And I was curious."

"Go on," said Sherman, and they all leaned forward, interested. Esau went on, and pretty soon Len joined in, and they told about the preaching and how Soames was stoned to death, and how the radio got to be a fixation with them. And with Hostetter nudging them along here and there, and Sherman or one of the other men asking a question, they found themselves telling the whole story right up to the time Hostetter and the bargemen had taken them out of the smoke and anger of Refuge. Amity had something to tell about that too, and she made it graphic enough. When they were all through it seemed to Len that they had put up with a terrible lot for all they had found when they got here, but he didn't say so.

Sherman got up and opened another door on the far side of the room. There was a room there with a lot of equipment in it, and a man sitting in the midst of it with a funny-looking thing on his head. He took this off and Sherman asked him, "How did it go?" and he said, "Fine."

Sherman closed the door again and turned around. "I can tell you now that you've been talking to all of Fall Creek, and Bartorstown." He lifted the lid of the wicker basket and showed what was inside. "These are microphones. Every word you said was picked up and broadcast." He let the lid fall and stood looking at them. "I wanted them all to hear your story, in your own words, and this seemed like the best way. I was afraid if I put you up on a platform with four hundred people staring at you you'd freeze up. So I did this."

"Oh my," said Amity, and put her hand over her mouth.

Sherman glanced at the other men. "Quite a story, isn't it?"

"They're young," said Gutierrez. He looked sick enough to die with it, and his voice was weak, but still bitter. "They have faith, and trust."

"Let them keep it," said Erdmann shrilly. "For God's sake, let *somebody* keep it."

Kindly, patiently, Sherman said, "You both need a rest. Will you do us all a great favor? Go and take one."

"Oh no," said Gutierrez, "not for anything. I wouldn't miss this for the world. I want to see their little faces shine when they catch their first glimpse of the fairy city."

Looking at the microphones, Len said, "Is this the reason you said you had for letting us come?"

"Partly," said Sherman. "Our people are human. Most of them have no direct contact with the main work to keep them feeling important and interested. They live a restricted life here. They get discontented. Your story is a powerful reminder of what life is like on the outside, and why we have to keep on with what we're doing. It's also a hopeful one."

"How?"

"It shows that eighty years of the most rigid control hasn't been able to stamp out the art of independent thinking."

"Be honest, Harry," said Gutierrez. "There was a measure of sentiment in our decision."

"Perhaps," said Sherman. "It did seem like a betrayal of everything we like to think we stand for to let you get hung up for believing in us. Everybody in Fall Creek seemed to think so, anyway."

He looked at them thoughtfully. "It may have been a foolish decision. You certainly aren't likely, either one of you, to contribute anything to our work, and you do constitute a problem out of all proportion to your personal importance. You're the first strangers we've taken in for more years than I can remember. We can't let you go again. We don't want to be forced to do what I warned you we would do. So we'll have to take pains, far more than with any of our own, to see that you're thoroughly integrated into the fabric of our living, our thoughts, our particular goal. Unless we're to keep a watch on you forever, we have to turn you into trustworthy citizens of Bartorstown. And that means practically a complete re-education."

He cast a sharp, sardonic glance at Hostetter. "He swore you were worth the trouble. I hope he was right."

He leaned over then and shook Amity by the hand. "Thank you, Mrs. Colter, you've been very helpful. I don't think you'd find this trip interesting, so why don't you come and have some lunch with my wife? She can help you on a lot of things."

He led Amity to the door and handed her over to Mary Sherman, who always seemed to be where she was wanted. Then he came back and nodded to Len and Esau.

"Well," he said, "let's go."

"To Bartorstown?" asked Len. And Sherman answered, "To Bartorstown."

21

THE EXPLANATION was simple when you knew it. So simple that Len realized it was no wonder he hadn't guessed it. Sherman led the way up the canyon, past the mine slope and on to the other side of the little dam. Gutierrez was with them, and Erdmann, and Hostetter, and two of the other men. The rest had gone about their business somewhere else. The sun was hot down here in the bottom of the valley, and the dust was dry. The air smelled of dust and cottonwoods and pine needles and mules. Len glanced at Esau. His face was kind of pale and set, and his eyes roved restlessly, as though they didn't want to see what was in front of them. Len knew how he felt. This was the end, the solid inescapable truth, the last of the dream. He should have been excited himself. He should have felt something. But he did not. He had already been through all the feelings he had in him, and now he was just a man walking.

They turned up the disused slope that the rocks had rolled on. They walked between the rocks in the hot sun, up to the hole in the face of the cliff. It had a wooden gate across it, weathered but in good repair, and a sign above it saying

DANGER MINE TUNNEL UNSAFE Falling Rock Keep Out. The gate was locked. Sherman opened it and they went through, and he locked it again behind him.

"Keeps the kids out," he said. "They're the only ones that ever bother."

Inside the tunnel, as far as the harsh reflected sunlight showed, there was a clutter of loose rock on the tunnel floor and a crumbly look about the walls. The shoring timbers were rotted and broken, and some of the roof props were hanging down. It was not a place anybody would be likely to force his way into. Sherman said that every mine had abandoned workings, and nobody thought anything about it. "This one, naturally, is perfectly safe. But the mock-up is convincing."

"Too damn convincing," said Gutierrez, stumbling. "I'll break a leg here yet."

The light shaded off into darkness, and the tunnel bent to the left. Suddenly, without any warning, another light blazed up ahead. It was bluish and very brilliant, not like any Len had seen before, and now for the first time excitement began to stir in him. He heard Esau catch his breath and say, "Electric!" The tunnel here was smooth and unencumbered. They walked along it quickly, and beyond the dazzle of the light Len saw a door.

They stopped in front of it. The light was overhead now. Len tried to look straight into it and it made him blind like the sun. "Isn't that something," Esau whispered. "Just like Gran used to say."

"There are scanners here," said Sherman. "Give them a second or two. There. Go on now."

The door opened. It was thick and made of metal set massively into the living rock. They went through it. It closed quietly behind them, and they were in Bartorstown.

This part of it was only a continuation of the tunnel, but here the rock was dressed very smooth and neat, and lights were set all along it in a trough sunk in the roof. The air had a funny taste to it, flat and metallic. Len could feel it moving over his face, and there was a soft, soft hushing sound that seemed to belong to it. His nerves had tightened now, and he was sweating. He had a brief and awful vision of the outside of the mountain that was now on top of him, and he thought he could feel every pound of it weighing down on him. "Is it all like this?" he asked. "Underground, I mean."

Sherman nodded. "They put a lot of places underground in those days. Under a mountain was about the only safe place you could get."

Esau was peering down the corridor. It seemed to go a long way in. "Is it very big?"

Gutierrez answered this time. "How big is big? If you look at Bartorstown one way it's the biggest thing there is. It's all yesterday and all tomorrow. Look at it another way, it's a hole in the ground, just big enough to bury a man in."

About twenty feet away down the corridor a man stepped out of a doorway to meet them. He was a young fellow, about Esau's age. He spoke with easy respect to Sherman and the others, and then stared frankly at the Colters.

"Hello," he said. "I saw you coming through the lower pass. My name's Jones." He held out his hand.

They shook it and moved closer to the door. The rock-cut chamber beyond was fairly large, and it was crammed with an awful lot of things, boards and wires and knobs and stuff like the inside of a radio. Esau looked around, and then he looked at Jones and said, "Are you the one that pushes the button?"

They were all puzzled for a minute, and then Hostetter laughed. "Wepplo was joshing them about that. No, Jones would have to pass that responsibility on."

"Matter of fact," said Sherman, "we've never pushed that button yet. But we keep it in working order, just in case. Come here."

He motioned them to follow him, and they did, with the cautious tenseness of men or animals who find themselves in a strange place and feel they may want to get out of it in a hurry. They were careful not to touch anything. Jones went ahead of them and began casually doing things with some of the knobs and switches. He did not quite swagger. Sherman pointed to a square glass window, and Len stared into it for a confused second or two before he realized that it could hardly be a window at all, and if it were it couldn't be looking into the narrow rocky cut that was away on the other side of the ridge.

"The scanners pick up the image and transmit it back to this screen," Sherman said, and before he could go on Esau cried out in a child's tone of delighted wonder, "Teevee!"

"Same principle," said Sherman. "Where'd you hear about that?"

"Our grandmother. She told us a lot of things."

"Oh yes. You mentioned her, I think—talking about Bartorstown." Smoothly, but with unmistakable firmness, he drew their attention to the screen again. "There's always somebody on duty here, to watch. Nobody can get through that gateway unseen, in—or out."

"What about nighttime?" asked Len. He supposed Sherman had a right to keep reminding them, but it made him resentful. Sherman gave him a sharp, cool glance.

"Did your grandmother tell you about electric eyes?"

"No."

"They can see in the dark. Show them, Jones."

The young man showed them a board with little glass bulbs on it, in two rows opposite each other. "This is like the lower pass, see? And these little bulbs, they're the electric-eye pairs. When you walk between them you break a beam, and these bulbs light up. We know right where you are."

If Esau got the byplay, he didn't show it. He was staring with bright envious eyes at Jones, and suddenly he asked, "Could I learn to do that too?"

"I don't see why not," said Sherman, "if you're willing to study."

Esau breathed heavily and smiled.

They went out and down the corridor again, under the brilliant lights. There were some other doors with numbers on them that Sherman said were storerooms. Then the corridor branched into two. Len was confused now about direction, but they took the right-hand branch. It widened out into a staggering series of rooms, cut smooth out of the rock with heavy columns of it left in regular rows to bear the weight of the low roof. The rooms were separate from each other but interconnecting, like the segments of a wheel, and they seemed to have smaller chambers opening from their outer edges. They were full of things. Len did not try, after the first few minutes, to understand what he saw because he knew it would take him years to do that. He just looked, and felt, and tried to get hold of the full realization that he had entered into a totally different world.

Sherman was talking. Sometimes Gutierrez, too, and sometimes Erdmann, and sometimes one of the other men. Hostetter didn't say much.

Bartorstown had been made, they said, as self-supporting as such a place could be. It could repair itself, and make new parts for itself, and there were still some of the original materials it had been supplied with for that purpose. Sherman pointed out the various rooms, the electronics lab, the electrical maintenance shop, the radio shop, rooms full of strange machines and strange glittering shapes of glass and metal, and endless panels of dials and winking lights. Sometimes a man or several men would be in them, sometimes not. Sometimes there were chemical smells and unfamiliar sounds, and sometimes there was nothing but an empty quiet, with the hush-hush of the moving air making them seem even quieter and lonelier. Sherman talked about air ducts and pumps and blowers. Automatic was a word he used over and over, and it was a wonderful word. Doors opened automatically when you came to them, and lights went on and off. "Automatic," said Hostetter, and snorted. "No wonder the Mennonites got to be such a power in the land. Other folks were so spoiled they could hardly tie their shoelaces any more by hand."

"Ed," said Sherman, "you're a poor advertisement for Bartorstown."

"I don't know," said Hostetter. "Seems I was good enough for some."

Len looked at him. He knew Hostetter's moods pretty well now, and he knew he was worried and ill at ease. A nervous chill crawled down Len's back, and he turned to stare again at the strange things all around him. They were wonderful, and fascinating, and they didn't mean a thing until somebody named a purpose for them. Nobody had.

He said so, and Sherman nodded. "They have a purpose. I wanted you to see all of Bartorstown, and not just a part of it, so you would realize how important the government of this country thought that purpose was, even before the Destruction. So important that they saw to it that Bartorstown would survive no matter what happened. Now I'll show you another part of their planning, the power plant."

Hostetter started to speak, and Sherman said quietly, "We'll do this my way, Ed." He walked them a little way more around the central corridor that Len had come to think of as the hub of a wheel, and with a sidelong glance at Len and Esau he said, "We'll use the stair instead of the elevator."

All the way down the echoing steel stair, Len tried to remember what an elevator might be, but couldn't. Then he stopped with them on a floor, and looked around.

They were in a cavernous place that echoed with a deep and mighty throbbing, overtoned and undertoned with other sounds that were strange to Len's ear but that blended all together into one unmistakable voice, saying a word that he had heard spoken before only by the natural voices of wind and thunder and flood. The word was power. The rock vault had been left rougher here, and all the space was flooded with a flat white glare, and in that glare a line of mighty structures stood, squat, bulbous, Gargantuan, dwarfing the men who worked around them. Len's flesh picked up the throbbing and quivered with it, and his nose twitched to the smell of something that was in the air.

"These are the transformers," Sherman said. "You can see the cables there—they run in sunken conduits to carry power all over Bartorstown. These are the generators, and the turbines——"

They walked in the bright white glare under the flanks of the great machines.

"—the steam plant——"

Here was something they could understand. It was enormously bigger than any they had dreamed of, but it was steam, and steam they knew as an old friend among these foreign giants. They clung to it, making comparisons, and one of the two men whose names Len was not sure of patiently explained the differences in design.

"But there's no firebox," said Esau. "No fire, and no fuel. Where's the heat come from?"

"There," said the man, and pointed. The steam plant joined onto a long, high, massive block of concrete. "That's the heat exchanger."

Esau frowned at the concrete. "I don't see——"

"It's all shielded, of course. It's hot."

"Hot," said Esau. "Well, sure, it would have to be to make the water boil. But I still don't see——" He looked around, into the recesses of the cavern. "I still don't see what you use for fuel."

There was a moment of silence, as silent as it ever was in that place. The thrumming beat on Len's ears, and somehow he knew that he stood on a moment's edge before some unguessable pit of darkness, he knew it from the schooled and watchful faces of the men and the way Esau's question hung loud and echoing in the air and would not die away.

"Why," said Sherman, very gently, very casually, and Hostetter's eyes were sharp and anguished in the light, "we use uranium."

And the moment was gone, and the pit gaped wide and black as perdition, and Len shouted, but the shout was swallowed up and drowned until it was only the ghost of a whisper, saying, "Uranium. But that was—that was——"

Sherman's hand rose up and pointed to where the concrete structure heightened and widened into a great thick wall.

"Yes," he said. "Atomic power. That concrete wall is the outer face of the shield. Behind it is the reactor."

Silence again, except for the throbbing of that great voice that never stopped. The concrete wall loomed up like the wall of hell, and Len's heart slowed and the blood in him turned cold as snow water.

Behind it is the reactor.

Behind it is evil and night and terror and death.

A voice screamed in Len's ears, the voice of the preaching man, standing on the edge of his wagon with the sparks flying past him on the night wind—*They have loosed the sacred fire which only I, the Lord Jehovah, should dare to touch—and God said—Let them be cleansed of their sin——*

Esau's voice spoke in shrill denial. "No. There ain't any more of that left in the world."

Let them be cleansed, said the Lord, and they were cleansed. They were burned with the fires of their own making, yea, and the proud towers vanished in the blazing of the wrath of God, and the places of iniquity were made not——

"You're lying," Esau said. "There ain't any more of that, not since the Destruction."

And they were cleansed. But not wholly——

"They're not lying," Len said. He backed slowly away from that staring wall of concrete. "They saved it, and it's there."

Esau whimpered. Then he turned and ran.

Hostetter caught him. He spun him around and Sherman caught his other arm and they held him, and Hostetter said fiercely, "Stand still, Esau."

"But it'll burn me," Esau cried, staring wild-eyed. "It'll burn me inside, and my blood will turn white and my bones will rot and I'll die."

"Don't be a fool," said Hostetter. "You can see it hasn't hurt any of us."

"He's got a right to be afraid of it, Ed," said Sherman, more gently. "You ought to know their teaching better than I. Give them a chance. Listen, Esau. You're thinking of the bomb. This isn't a bomb. It isn't hurtful. We've lived with it here for nearly a hundred years. It can't explode, and it can't burn you. The concrete makes it safe. Look."

He let go of Esau and went up to the shield and put his hands on it.

"See? There's nothing here to fear."

And the devil speaks with the tongues of foolish men and works with the hands of the rash ones. Father, forgive me, I didn't know!

Esau licked his lips. His breath came hard and uneven between them. "You go and do it too," he said to Hostetter, as though Hostetter might be of a different flesh from Sherman, being a part of the world that Esau knew and not solely of Bartorstown.

Hostetter shrugged. He went and put his hands on the shield.

And you, thought Len. This is what you wouldn't tell me, what you wouldn't trust me with.

"Well," said Esau, choking, hesitant, sweating and shaking like a frightened horse but not running now, standing his ground, beginning to think. "Well——"

Len clenched his icy fists and looked at Sherman standing against the shield.

"No wonder you're so afraid," he said, in a voice that did

not sound like his own at all. "No wonder you shoot people if they try to leave. If anybody went out and told what you've got here they'd rise up and hunt you out and tear you to pieces, and there wouldn't be a mountain in the world big enough to hide yourselves under."

Sherman nodded. "Yes. That's so."

Len shifted his gaze to Hostetter. "Why couldn't you have told us about this, before we ever came here?"

"Len, Len," said Hostetter, shaking his head. "I didn't want you to come. And I warned you, every way I could."

Sherman was watching, intent to see what he would do. They were all watching, Gutierrez with a weary pity, Erdmann with embarrassed eyes, and Esau in the middle of them like a big scared child. He understood dimly that it had all been planned this way and that they were interested in what words he would say and how he would feel. And in a sudden black revulsion of all the hopes and dreams and childhood longings, the seeking and the faith, he shouted at them, "Wasn't one burning of the world enough? Why did you have to keep this thing alive?"

"Because," said Sherman quietly, "it wasn't ours to destroy. And because destroying it is the child's way, the way of the men who burned Refuge, the way of the Thirtieth Amendment. That's only an evasion. You can't destroy knowledge. You can stamp it under and burn it up and forbid it to be, but somewhere it will survive."

"Yes," said Len bitterly, "as long as there are men foolish enough to keep it going. I wanted the cities back, yes. I wanted the things we used to have, and I thought it was stupid to be afraid of something that was gone years and years ago. But I never knew that it wasn't all gone——"

"So now you think they were right to kill Soames, right to kill your friend Dulinsky and destroy a town?"

"I——" The words stuck in Len's throat, and then he cried out, "That isn't fair. There was no atom power in Refuge."

"All right," said Sherman reasonably. "We'll put it another way. Suppose Bartorstown was destroyed, with every man in it. How could you be sure that somewhere in the world, hidden under some other mountain, there wasn't another Bartorstown? And how could you be sure that some forgotten professor of nuclear physics hadn't hoarded his textbooks—you had one in Piper's Run, you said. Multiply that by all the books there must be left in the world. What chance have you got to destroy them all?"

Esau said, slowly, "Len, he's right."

"Book," said Len, feeling the blind fear, feeling the crouching of the Beast behind the wall. "Book, yes, we had one, but we didn't know what it meant. Nobody knew."

"Somebody, somewhere, would figure it out in time. And remember another thing. The first men who found the secret of atomic power didn't have any books to go by. They didn't even know if it could be done. All they had was their brains. You can't destroy all the brains in the world, either."

"All right," cried Len, driven into a corner and seeing no escape. "What other way is there?"

"The way of reason," said Sherman. "And now I can tell you why Bartorstown was built."

22

THERE WERE three levels in Bartorstown. They climbed now to the middle one, below the laboratories and above the cavern where the old evil hid behind its concrete wall. Len walked ahead of Hostetter, and the others were all around him, Esau still trembling and wiping his mouth over and over with the back of his hand, the Bartorstown men silent and grave. And Len's mind was a wild dark emptiness like a night sky without stars.

He was looking at a picture. The picture was on a long curving piece of glass taller than a man and lit from inside someway so that the picture was like real, with depth and distance in it, and color, and every tiny thing sharp and clear to see. It was a terrible picture. It was a blasted and fragmented desolation, with one little lost building still standing in it, leaning over as though it was tired and wanted to fall.

"You talk about the bomb and what it did, but you never saw it," said Sherman. "The men who built Bartorstown had, or their fathers had. It was a reality, a thing of their time. They put this picture here to remind them, so that they wouldn't be tempted to forget their job. That was what the first bomb did. That was Hiroshima. Now go on, around the end of the wall."

They did, and Gutierrez was already ahead of them, walking with his head down. "I've already seen them too often," he said. He disappeared, through a door at the end of a wide passageway that had more pictures on either side. Erdmann started after him, hesitated, and then dropped back. He did not look at the pictures either.

Sherman did. He said, "These were some of the people who survived that first bombing, after a fashion."

Esau muttered, "Holy Jesus!" He began to shake more violently, hanging his head down and looking sidelong out of the corners of his eyes so as not to see too much.

Len did not say anything. He gave Sherman a straight and smoldering look, and Sherman said, "They felt very strongly about the bomb in those days. They lived under its shadow. In these victims they could see themselves, their families. They wanted very much that there should not be any more victims, any more Hiroshimas, and they knew that there was only one way to make sure of that."

"They couldn't," said Len, "have just destroyed the bomb?"

It was a stupid thing to say, and he was angry with himself instantly for saying it, because he knew better; he had talked about those times with Judge Taylor and read some of the books about them. So he forestalled Sherman's retort by saying quickly, "I know, the enemy wouldn't destroy his. The thing to have done was never to get that far, never to make a bomb."

Sherman said, "The thing to have done was never to learn how to make a fire, so no one would ever get burned. Besides, it was a little too late for that. They had a fact to deal with, not a philosophical argument."

"Well, then," said Len, "what was the answer?"

"A defense. Not the imperfect defense of radar nets and weapon devices, but something far more basic and all-embracing, a totally new concept. A field-type force that could control the interaction of nuclear particles right on their own level, so that no process either of fission or fusion could take place wherever that protecting force-field was in operation. Complete control, Len. Absolute mastery of the atom. No more bombs."

Quiet, and they watched him again to see how he would take it. He closed his eyes against the pictures so that he could try to think, and the words sounded in his head, loud and flat, momentarily without meaning. Complete control. No more bombs. The thing to have done was never to build them, never build fires, never build cities——

No.

No, say the words again, slowly and carefully. Complete control, no more bombs. The bomb is a fact. Atomic power is a fact. It is a living fact close down under my feet, the dreadful power that made these pictures. You can't deny it, you can't destroy it because it is evil and evil is like a serpent that dieth not but reneweth itself perpetually——

No. No. No. These are the words of the preaching man, of Burdette. Complete control of the atom. No more bombs. No more victims, no more fear. Yes. You build stoves to hold the fire in, and you keep water handy to put it out with. Yes.

But——

"But they didn't find the defense," he said. "Because the world got burned up anyway."

"They tried. They pointed the way. We're still following it. Now go on."

They passed through the door where Gutierrez had gone, into a space hollowed like the other spaces out of the solid rock, smoothed and pillared and reaching away on all sides under a clear flood of light. There was a long wall facing them. It was not really a wall, but a huge panel as big as a wall and set by itself, with a couple of small machines linked to it. It was nearly six feet high, not quite reaching the roof. It had a maze of dials and lights on it. The lights were all dark, and the needles of the dials did not move. Gutierrez was standing in front of it, his face twisted into a deep, sad, pondering scowl.

"This is Clementine," he said, not turning his head as they came in. "A foolish name for something on which may hang the future of the world."

Len dropped his hands, and it was as though in that dropping he cast from him many things too heavy or too painful to be carried. Inside my head there is nothing, let it stay that way. Let the emptiness fill up slowly with new things, and old things in new patterns, and maybe then I'll know—what? I don't know. I don't know anything, and all is darkness and confusion and only the Word——

No, not that Word, another one. Clementine.

He sighed and said aloud, "I don't understand."

Sherman walked over to the big dark panel.

"This is a computer. It's the biggest one ever built, the most complex. Do you see there——"

He pointed off beyond the panel, into the pillared spaces that stretched away there, and Len saw that there were countless rows of arrangements of wires and tubes set all orderly one after the other, interrupted at intervals by big glittering cylinders of glass.

"That's all part of it."

Esau's passion for machines was beginning to stir again under the fog of fright.

"All one machine?"

"All one. In it, in those memory banks, is stored all the knowledge about the nature of the atom that existed before the Destruction, and all the knowledge that our research teams have gained since, all expressed in mathematical equations. We could not work without it. It would take the men half their lifetimes just to work out the mathematical problems that Clementine can do in minutes. She is the reason Bartorstown was built, the purpose of the shops upstairs and the reactor down below. Without her, we wouldn't have much chance of finding the answer within any foreseeable time. With her—there's no telling. Any day, any week, could bring the solution to the problem."

Gutierrez made a sound that might have been the beginning of a laugh. It was quickly silenced. And once more Len shook his head and said, "I don't undertand."

And I don't think I want to understand. Not today, not now. Because what you're telling me is not a description of a machine but of something else, and I don't want to know any more about it.

But Esau blurted out, "It does sums and remembers them? That don't sound like any machine, that sounds like—a—a——"

He caught himself up sharp, and Sherman said with no particular interest, "They used to call them electronic brains."

Oh Lord, and is there no end to it? First the hell-fire and now this.

"A misnomer," said Sherman. "It doesn't think, any more than a steam engine. It's just a machine."

And now suddenly he rounded on them, his face stern and cold-eyed and his voice as sharp as a whiplash to bring their attention to him, startled and alert.

"I won't push you," he said. "I won't expect you to understand it all in a minute, and I won't expect you to adjust overnight. I'll give you reasonable time. But I want you to remember this. You kicked and clawed and screamed to be let into Bartorstown, and now you're here, and I don't care what you thought it was going to be like, it's what it is, so make your peace with it. We have a certain job to do here. We didn't particularly ask for it, it just happened that way, but we're stuck with it and we're going to do it, in spite of what your piddling little farm-boy consciences may feel about it."

He stood still, regarding them with those cold hard eyes, and Len thought, He means that just the way Burdette meant it when he said, There shall be no cities in our midst.

"You claim you wanted to come here so you could learn," said Sherman. "All right. We'll give you every chance. But from here on, it's up to you."

"Yes, sir," said Esau hastily. "Yes, *sir*."

Len thought, There is still nothing in my head, it feels like a wind was blowing through it. But he's looking at me, waiting for me to say something—what? Yes, no—and oh Lord, he's right, they did everything under the sun to keep us out and we would bull our way in, and now we're caught in a pit of our own digging——

But the whole world is caught in a pit. Isn't that what we wanted out of, the pit that killed Dulinsky and nearly killed us? The people are afraid and I hated them for it and now—I don't know what the answer is, oh Lord, I don't know, let me find an answer because Sherman is waiting and I can't run away.

"Someday," he said, wrinkling his brows in a frown of effort, so that he looked once more like the brooding boy who had sat with Gran on that October day, "someday atomic power will come back no matter what anybody does to stop it."

"A thing once known always comes back."

"And the cities will come back too."

"In time, inevitably."

"And it will all happen over again, the cities and the bomb, unless you find that way to stop it."

"Unless men have changed a lot by tomorrow, yes."

"Then," said Len, still frowning, still somber, "then I guess you're trying to do what ought to be done. I guess it might be right."

The word stuck to his tongue, but he got it off, and no bolt of lightning came to strike him dead, and Sherman did not challenge him any further.

Esau had moved toward the panel, magnetized by the lure of the machine. He reached hesitantly out and touched it, and asked, "Could we see it work?"

It was Erdmann who answered. "Later. She's just finished a three-year project, and she's shut down now for a complete overhaul."

"Three years," said Gutierrez. "Yes. I wish you could shut me down too, Frank. Pick my brain to pieces and put it together again, all fresh and bright." He began to raise and lower his fist, striking the panel each time, lightly as a feather falling. "Frank," he said, "she could have made a mistake."

Erdmann looked at him sharply. "You know that isn't possible."

"A vagrant charge," said Gutierrez. "A speck of dust, a relay too worn to function right, and how would you ever know?"

"Julio," said Erdmann. "You know better. If the slightest thing goes wrong with her she stops automatically and asks for attention."

Sherman spoke, and the talking stopped, and everybody began to move out into the passageway again. Gutierrez came close behind Len, and even through the doubt and fear that clouded in so thick around him Len could hear him muttering to himself, "She *could* have made a mistake."

23

Hostetter was a lamp in the darkness, a solid rock in the midst of flood. He was the link, the carry-over from Piper's Run to Bartorstown, he was the old friend and the strong arm that had already reached out twice to save him, once at the preaching, once at Refuge. Len clung to him, mentally, with a certain desperation.

"You think it's right?" he asked, knowing the inevitable answer, but wanting the assurance anyhow.

They were walking down the road from Bartorstown in the late afternoon. Sherman and the others had lingered behind, perhaps deliberately, so that Hostetter was alone with Len and Esau. And now Hostetter glanced at Len and said, "Yes, I think it's right."

"But," said Len softly, "to *work* with it, to keep it going——"

He was out in the open air again. The mountain was away from over his head, and the rock walls of Bartorstown no longer shut him in, and he could breathe and look at the sun. But the horror was still on him, and he thought of the destroyer crouched in a hole of the rock, and he knew he did not want ever to go back there. And at the same time he knew that he would have to go whether he wanted it or not.

Hostetter said, "I told you there'd be things you wouldn't like, things that would jar against your teachings no matter how much you said you didn't believe them."

"But you're not afraid of it," said Esau. He had been thinking hard, scuffing his boots against the stones of the road. Up above them on the east slope was the normal, comforting racket of the mine, and ahead the village of Fall Creek drowsed quietly in the late sun, and it was very much like Piper's Run if there had been a devil chained in the hills behind it. "You went right up and put your hands on it."

"I grew up with the idea of it," said Hostetter. "Nobody ever taught me that it was evil or forbidden, or that God had put a curse on it, and that's the difference. That's why we don't take strangers in but once in a coon's age. The conditioning is all wrong."

"I ain't worrying about curses," said Esau. "What I worry about is, will it hurt me?"

"Not unless you find some way to get inside the shield."

"It can't burn me."

"No."

"And it can't blow up."

"No. The steam plant might blow up, but not the reactor."

"Well, then," said Esau, and walked on awhile in silence, thinking. His eyes got bright, and he laughed and said, "I wonder what those old fools in Piper's Run, old Harkness and Clute and the rest, would think. They were going to birch us just for having a radio, and now we've got *that.* Jesus. I bet they'd kill us, Len."

"No," said Hostetter somberly, "*they* wouldn't. But all the same, you'd wind up like Soames, at the bottom of a pile of stones."

"Well, I ain't going to give them a chance. Jesus! Atom power, the real thing, the biggest power in the world." His fingers curled with greedy excitement and then relaxed, and he asked again, "Are you *sure* it's safe?"

"It's safe," said Hostetter, getting impatient. "We've had it for nearly a century, and it hasn't hurt anybody yet."

"I guess," said Len slowly, leaning his head against the cool wind and letting it blow some of the darkness out of him, "we don't have any right to complain."

"You sure don't."

"And I guess the government knew what it was doing when it built Bartorstown."

They were afraid too, whispered the cool wind. *They had a power too big for them to handle, and they were afraid, and well they should have been.*

"It did," said Hostetter, not hearing the wind.

"Jesus," said Esau, "just think if they had found that thing to stop the bomb."

"I've thought," said Hostetter. "We all have. I suppose every man in Bartorstown has a guilt complex a mile wide from thinking about it. But there just wasn't time."

Time? Or was there another reason?

"How long will it take?" asked Len. "It seems like in almost a hundred years they should have found it."

"My God," said Hostetter, "do you know how long it took to find atomic power in the first place? A Greek named Democritus got the basic idea of the atom centuries before Christ, so you can figure that out."

"But it ain't going to take them that long now!" cried Esau. "Sherman said with that machine——"

"It won't take them that long, no."

"But how long? Another hundred years?"

"How do I know how long?" said Hostetter angrily. "Another hundred years, or another year. How do I know?"

"But with the machine——"

"It's only a machine, it's not God. It can't pull an answer out of thin air just because we want it."

"How about that machine, though," said Esau, and once more his eyes were glistening. "I wanted to see it work. Does it really——" He hesitated, and then said the incredible word. "Does it really think?"

"No," said Hostetter. "Not in the way you mean the word. Get Erdmann to explain it to you sometime." Suddenly he said to Len, "You're thinking that only God has any business building brains."

Len flushed, feeling like what Sherman had called him, a conscience-ridden farm boy in the face of these men who knew so much, and yet he could not deny to Hostetter that he had been thinking something like that.

"I guess I'll get used to it."

Esau snorted. "He always was a doubtful-minded kind, taking forever to make up his mind."

"Why, God damn you, Esau," cried Len furiously, "if it hadn't been for me you'd still be shoveling dung in your father's barn!"

"All right," said Esau, glaring at him, "you remember that. You remember whose fault it is you're here and don't go whining around about it."

"I ain't whining."

"Yes, you are. And if you're worried about sinning, you ought to have minded your pa in the first place and stayed home in Piper's Run."

"He's got you there," said Hostetter.

Len grumbled, kicking pebbles angrily in the dust. "All

right. It scared me. But it scared him, too, and I wasn't the one that tucked my tail and ran."

Esau said, "I'd run from a bear, too, till I knew it wouldn't kill me. I ain't running now. Listen, Len, this is important. Where else in the world could you find anything as important?" His chest puffed out and his face lit up as though the mantle of that importance had already fallen on him. "I want to know more about that machine."

"Important," said Len. "Yes, it is." That's true. There isn't any question about that. Oh God, you make the ones like Brother James who never question, and you make the ones like Esau who never believe, and why do you have to make the in-between ones like me?

But Esau is right. It's too late now to worry about the sinning. Pa always said the way of the transgressor was hard, and I guess this is part of the hardness.

So be it.

They left Esau at Sherman's to pick up his bride, and Len and Hostetter walked on together toward Wepplo's. The swift clear dusk was coming down, and the lanes were deserted, with a smell of smoke and cooking in them. When they came to Wepplo's Hostetter put his foot on the bottom step and turned around and spoke to Len in a strange quiet tone that he had never heard him use before.

"Here's something to remember, the way you remember that mob that killed Soames, and Burdette and his farmers, and the New Ishmaelites. It's this—we're fanatics too, Len. We have to be, or we'd drift away and live our own lives and let the whole business go hang. We've got a belief. Don't tangle with it. Because if you do, even I won't be able to save you."

He went up the steps and left Len standing there staring after him. There were voices inside, and lights, but out here it was still and almost dark. And then someone came around the corner of the house, walking softly. It was the girl Joan, and she nodded her head toward the house and said, "Was he trying to frighten you?"

"I don't think so," said Len. "I think he was just telling me the truth."

"I heard him." She had a white cloth in her hands, as though she might have been shaking it just before. Her face looked white, too, in the heavy dusk, blurred and indistinct. But her voice was sharp as a knife. "Fanatics, are we? Well, maybe he is, and maybe the others are, but I'm not. I'm sick of the whole business. What made you want to come here, Len Colter? Were you crazy or something?"

He looked at her, the shadowy outlines of her, not knowing what to say.

"I heard you talk this morning," she said.

Len said uncomfortably, "We didn't know——"

"They told you to say all those things, didn't they?"

"What things?"

"About what dreadful people they are out there, and what a hateful world it is."

"I don't know exactly what you mean," said Len, "but every word of what we said was true. You think it wasn't, you go out there and try it."

He started to push past her up the steps. She put a hand on his arm to stop him.

"I'm sorry. I guess it was all true. But that's why Sherman had you talk over the radio, so we'd all hear it. Propaganda." She added shrewdly, "I'll bet that's why they let you two in here, just to make us all see how lucky we are."

Len said, very quietly, "Aren't you?"

"Oh yes," said Joan, "we're very lucky. We have so much more than the people outside. Not in our everyday lives, of course. We don't even have as much, of things like food and freedom. But we have Clementine, and that makes up. Did you enjoy your trip to The Hole?"

"The Hole?"

"It's a name some of us have for Bartorstown."

Her manner and her tone were making him uneasy. He said, "I think I better go in," and started once more up the steps.

"I hope you did," she said. "I hope you like the canyon, and Fall Creek. Because they'll never let you leave."

He thought of what Sherman had said. He did not blame Sherman. He did not have any intention of going away. But he did not like it. "They'll learn to trust me," he said, "someday."

"Never."

He did not want to argue with her. "Well, I reckon to stay awhile, anyway. I've spent half my life getting here."

"Why?"

"You're a Bartorstown girl. You shouldn't have to ask."

"Because you wanted to learn. That's right, you said that this morning. You wanted to learn, and nobody would let you." She made a wide mocking gesture that took in the whole dark canyon. "Go. Learn. Be happy."

He got her by the shoulder and pulled her close, where he could see her face in the dim glow from the windows. "What's the matter with you?"

"I just think you're crazy, that's all. To have the whole wide world, and throw it all away for this."

"I'll be damned," said Len. He let her go and sat down on the steps and shook his head. "I'll be damned. Doesn't anybody like Bartorstown? Seems to me I've heard more griping since I got here than I ever heard in my lifetime before."

"When you've lived a lifetime here," she said bitterly, "you'll understand. Oh, some of the men get out, sure. But most of us don't. Most of us never see anything but these canyon walls. And even the men have to come back again. It's like your friend says. You have to be a fanatic to feel that it's all worth while."

"I've lived out there," said Len. "I think what it is now, and what it could be, if——"

"If Clementine ever gives them the right answer. Sure. It's been almost a century now, and they're no nearer than they ever were, but we've all got to be patient and devoted and dedicated—dedicated to what? To that goddamned mechanical brain that squats there under the mountain and has to be treated like it was God."

She leaned over him suddenly, in the faint glow of the lamplight.

"*I'm* no fanatic, Len Colter. If you want somebody to talk to, remember that."

Then she was gone around the corner of the house, running. Len heard a door open somewhere at the back. He got up, very slowly, and climbed the steps and went slowly into the house and ate his dinner at the Wepplos' table. And he did not hear hardly anything that was said to him.

24

THE NEXT MORNING Len and Esau were called again to Sherman's place, and this time Hostetter was not with them. Sherman faced them over the table in the living room, balancing two keys back and forth between his hands.

"I said I wouldn't push you, and I won't. But in the meantime you have to work. Now if I let you work at something you could do in Fall Creek, like blacksmithing or taking care of the mules, you wouldn't learn anything more about Bartorstown than if you hadn't left home."

"Well, no," said Esau, and then he asked eagerly, "Can I learn about the big machine? Clementine?"

"Offhand, I'd say she's always going to be beyond you, unless you want to wait until you're an old man. But you can take it up with Frank Erdmann, he's the boss on that. And don't worry, you'll get all the machine you want. But whatever you pick will mean a lot of studying before you're ready, and until then——"

He hesitated for only the fraction of a second, perhaps he didn't really hesitate at all, and perhaps it was only by pure and unmeaning chance that his eyes happened to rest then on Len's face, but Len knew what he was going to say before he said it and he set himself hard so that nothing would show.

"Until then you've been assigned to the steam plant. You've had some experience with steam, and it shouldn't take you too long to master the differences. Jim Sidney, the man you were talking to yesterday, will give you all the help you need."

He got up and came around the table and handed them the keys. "To the safety gate. Take care of them. Jim will tell you your hours and all that. In free time you can go anywhere you want to in Bartorstown and ask any questions you want so long as you don't interfere with work in progress. You can make arrangements with Irv Rothstein in the library. And you don't need to look so stony-faced, both of you. I can read your minds."

Len looked at him, startled, and he smiled.

"You're thinking that the steam plant is right next to the reactor and you would rather be anywhere else than there. And that is exactly why you're going to work on the steam plant. I want to get you so accustomed to the reactor that you'll forget to be afraid of it."

Is that the truth? thought Len. Or is it his way of testing us, to see if we *can* get over being afraid, to see if we can ever learn to live with it?

"Get along now," Sherman said. "Jim's expecting you."

So they went, walking in the early morning up the dusty road and across the slope between the rocks to Bartorstown. And at the safety gate they stopped and fidgeted, each one waiting for the other one to open it, and Len said, "I thought you weren't afraid."

"I ain't. It's just that—oh, hell, those other men work around it. It's all right. Come on."

He jabbed his key savagely in the lock and wrenched it open and went in. And Len closed it carefully, thinking, Now I am locked in with it, the fire that fell from the sky on Gran's world.

He walked after Esau down the tunnel and through that inner door, past the monitor room where young Jones nodded at them. And isn't he afraid? No, he's like Ed Hostetter, he's never been taught to be afraid. And he's alive, and healthy. God hasn't struck him down. God hasn't struck any of them down. He's let Bartorstown survive. Isn't that a proof right there that it's all right, that this answer they're trying to find is right?

But the ways of the Lord are past our understanding, and the wicked man is given his day upon the earth——

"What are you mooning about?" snapped Esau. "Come on." There was a line of sweat across his upper lip, and his mouth was nervous. They went down the stairs again, the steel treads ringing hollow under their feet, past the level where the big computer was, down and down to the lowest step and then off that and out into the great wide cavern with the throb of power beating through it, past the generators and the turbines, and there it was, the concrete wall, the blank and staring face. And the sins of our fathers are still with us, or if not their sins their follies, and they should never, never have——

But they did.

Jim Sidney spoke to them. He spoke twice before they heard him, but this was their first time there and he was patient. And

Len followed him toward the looming mass of the steam plant, feeling dwarfed and small and insignificant among all that tremendous power. He set his teeth and shouted silently inside himself, It's only because I'm afraid that I feel this way, and I'll get over it like Sherman said. The others aren't afraid. They're men, just like any other men, good men, men who believe they're doing right, doing what the government trusted them to do. I'll learn. Gran would want me to. She said Never be afraid of knowing, and I won't be.

I won't be. I'll be a part of it, helping to free the world of fear. I'll believe, because I am here now and there is nothing else I can do.

No. Not that way. I will believe because it is right. I will learn to see that it is right. And Ed Hostetter will help me, because I can trust him, and *he* says it's right.

And Len went to work beside Esau on the steam plant, and all the rest of that day he did not look at the wall of the reactor. But he could feel it. He could feel it in his flesh and his bones and the tingling of his blood, and he could still feel it when he was back in Fall Creek and in his own bed. And he dreamed about it when he fell asleep.

But there was no escape from it. He went back to it the next day, and the day after that, and regularly on the days that followed, except Sunday, when he went to church and walked in the afternoons with Joan Wepplo. It reassured him to go to church. It was comforting to hear from a pulpit that God was blessing their efforts, and all they had to do was remain patient and steadfast and not lose heart. It helped him to feel that they really were right. And Sherman's treatment did seem to be working. Every day the shock of being close beside that dreadful wall grew less, perhaps because a nerve continually pricked and rubbed will become too callused to react. He got so he could look at it calmly, and think calmly, too, about what was behind it. He could learn a little about the instruments set into its face that measured the flow of force inside, and he could learn a little more, of layman's knowledge, about what that force was and how it worked, and how in this form it was so easily controlled. He would get along like that sometimes for several days, laughing and talking with Esau about how the folks in Piper's Run would feel if they could see them now—

Mr. Nordholt, the schoolmaster, who thought he knew so much and dealt his knowledge out so sparingly lest it should corrupt the young, and the other elders of the town, who would take off your hide with a birch rod for asking questions, and, yes, Pa and Uncle David, whose one answer was the harness strap. No, that wasn't true of Pa, and Len knew all too well what Pa would say, and he didn't like to think about that. So he would turn his thoughts to Judge Taylor, who got a man killed and a town burned up because he was afraid that it might sometime become a city, and he would think vindictively that he would like to tell Judge Taylor what was under the rock of Bartorstown and watch his face then. And I am not afraid, he would think. I was afraid, but now I am not. It is only a natural force like any other force. There is nothing evil in it, any more than there is evil in a knife, or in gunpowder. There is only evil in the way it is used, and we will see to it that no evil will ever be done with it again. We. We men of Bartorstown. And, oh Lord, the nights of cold and shivering along the misty creek beds, the days of heat and mosquitoes and hunger, the winters in strange towns, all the days and nights and years when we dreamed of being men of Bartorstown!

But the dream was different then. It was all bright and wonderful, like Gran used to tell about, and there was no darkness in it.

He would get along that way, and he would think, Now I really have got over it. And then he would wake up screaming in the night with Hostetter shaking his shoulder.

"What were you dreaming about?" Hostetter would ask.

"I don't know. A nightmare, that's all." He would get up and get a drink of water, and let the sweat on him dry. Then he would ask, casually, "Did I say anything?"

"No, not that I heard. You were just yelling."

But he would catch Hostetter looking at him with a brooding eye, and wonder if he did not know perfectly well what the nightmare was.

Esau's fear ran shallower than Len's. It was practically all physical, and once he was convinced that no unseen force was going to burn his bones to powder he got very casual and proprietory with the reactor, almost as though he had made it himself. Len would ask him sometimes, "Doesn't it ever worry you—I mean, don't you ever think that if this reactor thing hadn't been kept going here there wouldn't be any need to find an answer——"

"You heard what Sherman said. There could be other ones. Maybe enemy ones. Then where would you be?"

"But if it *was* the last one in the world?"

"Well, it ain't hurting anything. And anyway, Sherman said even if it was it wouldn't matter, somebody'd figure atoms out again."

Maybe not, maybe never. Maybe he's only saying that to justify himself. Hostetter had a word for it. Rationalizing. Anyway, it wouldn't be for a long time. A hundred years, two hundred, maybe longer. I'd never live to see it.

Esau laughed. "That woman of mine, she's sure a dandy."

Len didn't go around Amity much. There was a certain chill between them, a sort of mutual embarrassment that did not make for pleasant conversations. So he asked, "How's that?"

"Well, when she heard about this atom power being here she had a terrible fit. Swore she was going to lose the baby, it was so bad. And now do you know what? She's got it all fixed up in her mind that it's a big lie just to make her think everybody here is awfully important, and she can prove it."

"How?"

"Because everybody knows what atom power does, and if there'd ever been any here there wouldn't be any canyon left, but only a big crater like the judge used to tell about."

"Oh," said Len.

"Well, it makes her happy. So I don't argue. What's the use? She don't know anything about anything like that, anyway." He rubbed his hands together, grinning. "I sure hope that kid of mine's a boy. Maybe I can't learn enough to work that big machine, but he could. Hell, he might even be the one to find the answer."

Esau was fascinated by the big machine called Clementine. He hung around it every minute he could in his off hours, asking questions of Erdmann and the technicians who were working there until Erdmann began to talk up a tremendous enthusiasm for radio every time he even met Esau in the street. Often Len would go with him. He would stand looking at the dark face of the thing until a feeling of nervousness crept over him, as though he stood by the bed of a sleeper who was not really asleep but was watching him from under closed, deceitful lids. And he would think, It is not really a brain, it does not really think, it is only called a brain, and the things it knows and the mathematics it can do are only imitations of thought. But through the night hours a creature haunted him, a creature with a great throbbing heart of hell-fire and a brain as big as Pa's barn.

On the whole, though, he was trying hard and adjusting pretty well. But there were other hours, waking hours, in which another creature haunted him and left him little peace. And this was a human creature and no nightmare. This was a girl named Joan.

25

THREE DIFFERENT groups of strangers came into Fall Creek before snow, stayed briefly to trade, and went away again. Two of them were little bands of dark hardy men who followed the wild herds, hunters, and horse tamers, offering half-broken colts in exchange for flour, sugar, and corn whiskey. The third and last were New Ishmaelites. There were about twenty-five of them, demanding powder and shot as a gift to the Lord's anointed. They would not stay the night in Fall Creek, nor come in past the edges of the town, as though they were afraid of contamination, but when Sherman sent them out what they wanted they began to sing and pray, waving their arms and crying hallelujah. Half the people in Fall Creek had come out to watch them, and Len was there too, with Joan Wepplo.

"One of 'em will preach pretty soon," she said. "That's what everybody's waiting for."

"I've seen enough preaching," muttered Len. But he stayed. The wind was icy, blowing down the canyon from snow fields on the high peaks. Everybody was wearing cowhide or horsehide coats against it, but the New Ishmaelites had nothing but their shrouds and their goatskins to flap about their naked legs. They did not seem to mind it.

"They suffer terribly in the winters, just the same," said Joan.

"Starve to death, and freeze. Our men find their bodies in the spring, sometimes a whole band of them, kids and all." She looked at them with cold contemptuous eyes. "You'd think they'd give the kids a chance, at least. Let them grow up enough to make up their own minds about freezing to death."

The children, bony and blue with the chill, stamped and shouted and tossed their tangled mops of hair. They would never be able to make up their own minds about anything, even if they did grow up. Habit would have got too big a start on them. Len said, "I guess they can't afford to, any more than your people or mine."

A man stepped out of the group and began to preach. His hair and beard were a dirty gray, but Len thought that he was not as old as he looked. New Ishmaelites did not seem to get very old. He wore a goatskin, greasy and foul, with the hair worn off it in big patches. The bones of his chest stood out like a bird cage. He shook his fists at the people of Fall Creek and cried:

"Repent, repent, for the Kingdom of God is at hand! You who live for the flesh and the sins of the flesh, your end is near. The Lord has spoken in flame and thunder, the earth has opened and swallowed the unrighteous, and some have said, This is all, He has punished us and now we are forgiven, now we can forget. But I tell you that God in His mercy only gave you a little more time, and that time is nearly gone, and you have not repented! And what will you say when the heavens open, and God comes to judge the world? How will you beg and plead and cry out for mercy, and what will your luxuries and your vanities buy you then? Nothing but hell-fire! Fire and brimstone and everlasting pain, unless you repent and do penance for your sins!"

The wind made his words thin and blew them far away, repent, repent, like a fading echo down the canyon, as though repentance was already a lost hope. And Len thought, What if he knew, what if I was to go and shout it at him, what's up the canyon there not half a mile away? Then what good would it all be to him, his dirty goatskin and the murders he's done in the name of faith?

Get out. Get out, crazy old man, and stop your shouting.

He did, at last, seeming to feel that he had made sufficient payment for the gift. He rejoined the group and they all moved off up the winding road to the pass. The wind had got stronger, whistling cruelly past the rocks, and they bent a little under it and the steepness of the climb, their long hair blown out in front of them and their ragged garments lashing around their legs. Len shivered involuntarily.

"I used to feel sorry for them, too," Joan said, "until I realized that they'd kill us all in a minute if they could." She looked down at herself, at her coat of calfskin with the brown and white outside and her woolen skirt and her booted legs. "Vanity," she said. "Luxury." And she laughed, very short and hard. "The dirty old fool. He doesn't know the meaning of the words."

She lifted her eyes to Len. They were bright with some secret thought.

"I could show you, Len. What those words mean."

Her eyes disturbed him. They always did. They were so keen and sharp and she always seemed to be thinking so fast behind them, thoughts he could not follow. He knew now she was challenging him in some way, so he said, "All right, then, show me."

"You'll have to come to my house."

"I'm coming there for dinner anyhow. Remember?"

"I mean right now."

He shrugged. "Okay."

They walked back through the lanes of Fall Creek. When they reached the house he followed her inside. It was quiet, except for a couple of flies buzzing on a sunny windowpane, and it felt warm after the wind. Joan took off her coat.

"I guess my folks are still out," she said. "I guess they won't be back for a while. Do you mind?"

"No," said Len. "I don't mind." He took off his own coat and sat down.

Joan wandered over to the window, slapping vaguely at the flies. She had walked fast all the way, but now she did not seem in any hurry.

"Do you still like working in the Hole?"

"Sure," said Len warily. "It's fine."

Silence.

"Have they found the answer yet?"

"No, but as soon as Erdmann—— Now why ask a question like that? You know they haven't."

"Has anybody told you how soon they will?"

"You know better than that, too."

Silence again, and one of the flies lay dead on the floor.

"Almost a hundred years," she said softly, looking out the window. "It seems such an awful long time. I just don't know if we can stand it for another hundred."

She turned around. "I don't know if *I* can stand it for another one."

Len got up, not looking straight at her. "Maybe I better go."

"Why?"

"Well, your folks aren't here, and——"

"They'll be back in time for dinner."

"But it's a long time till dinner."

"Well," she said, "don't you want to see what you came for?" She showed him the edges of her teeth, white and laughing. "You wait."

She ran into the next room and shut the door. Len sat down again. He kept twisting his hands together, and his temples felt hot. He knew the feeling. He had had it before, in the rose arbor, in the judge's dark garden with Amity. He could hear Joan rummaging around in the room. There was a sound like the lid of a trunk banging against the wall. A long time went by. He wondered what the devil she was doing and listened nervously for footsteps on the porch, knowing all the time that her folks would not be back because if they were going to come she would not be doing this, whatever it was.

The door opened and she came out.

She was wearing a red dress. It was faded a little, and there were streaks and creases in it from having been folded away for a long time, but those were unimportant things. It was red. It was made of some soft, shiny, slithery stuff that rustled when she moved, and it came clear down to the floor, hiding her feet, but that was about all it hid. It fitted tight around her waist and hips and outlined her thighs when she walked forward, and above the waist there wasn't very much at all. She held out her arms at the sides and turned around slowly. Her back and shoulders were bare, white and gleaming in the sunlight that fell through the window, and her breasts were sharply outlined in the red cloth, showing above it in two half-moon curves, and her black hair fell down dark and glossy over her white skin.

"It belonged to my great-grandmother. Do you like it?"

Len said, "Christ." He stared and stared, and his face was almost as red as the dress. "It's the most indecent thing I ever saw."

"I know," she said, "but isn't it beautiful?" She ran her hands slowly down her front and out across the skirt, savoring the rustle, the softness. "This was real vanity, real luxury. Listen, how it whispers. What do you think that dirty old fool would say if he could see it?"

She was quite close to him now. He could see the fine white texture of her shoulders and the way her breasts rose and fell when she breathed, with the bright red cloth pressing them tight. She was smiling. He realized suddenly that she was handsome, not pretty like Amity had been, but dark-eyed handsome even if she wasn't very tall. He looked into her eyes and suddenly he realized that *she* was there, not just a girl, not just a Joan Wepplo, but *herself*, and something happened to him inside like when the electric lights came on in the dark tunnel that led to Bartorstown. And this feeling he had never had for Amity.

He reached out and took hold of her and she held up her mouth to him and laughed, a deep throaty little laugh, excited and pleased. A wave of heat swept over Len. The red cloth was silky, soft and rustling under his fingers, stretched tight over the warmth of her body. He put his mouth down over hers and kissed her, and kissed her again, and all by themselves his hands came up onto her bare shoulders and dug hard into the white skin. And this too was not like it had ever been with Amity.

She pulled away from him. She was not laughing now, and her eyes were as hard and bright as two black stars burning at him.

"Someday," she said fiercely, "you'll want a way out of this place, and then you come to me, Len Colter. Then you come, but not before."

She ran away into the other room again and slammed the door and shot the bolt in its socket, and it was no use trying to get in after her. And when she came out again in her regular clothes, a long time later, her folks were coming up the path and it was as if nothing had been said or done.

But it was Joan, in another place, at another time, who told him about Solution Zero.

26

WINTER CAME. Fall Creek became an isolated pocket of light and life in a vast emptiness of cold and rock and wind and blizzard snows. The pass was blocked. Nothing would move in or out of the canyon before spring. The snow piled high around the houses and drifted in the lanes, and the mountains were all white, magnificent on a clear day with the sun on them, ghostly in the dusk like the mountains of a dream, but too large and still to have in them any friendliness for man. And the air they breathed down across their icy slopes was bitter as the chill of death.

In Bartorstown there was neither winter nor summer, night nor day. The lights burned and the air went hushing through the rock rooms, never altering, never changing. The Power entrapped behind the concrete wall gave of its strength silently, untiring, the deathless heart beating and throbbing in the rock. Above in its chamber the brain slept, Clementine, the foolish name for the hope of the world, while men soothed and healed the frayed wires and the worn-out transistors of her being. And above that, in the monitor room, the eyes watched and the ears listened, on guard against the world. Len worked at his job, and sweated and struggled over the books he was advised to read, and thought how much he was learning and how few other people in the ignorant, fearful, guilt-ridden, sin-stricken world outside would have been able to do what he and Esau had done, and what they would do to make tomorrow different from the terrible yesterday. He wondered why the evil dreams still caught him unawares in the jungles of sleep, and he envied Esau his untroubled nights, but he did not say so. He hardly ever thought any more of the Bartorstown he had spent half his life to find, accepting the reality, and a little more of his youth slipped away from him. He thought about Joan, and tried to stay away from her, and couldn't. He was afraid of her, but he was even more afraid to admit that he was afraid of her, because then in some obscure way she would have beaten him, she would have proved that he did want to leave Fall Creek and run away from Bartorstown. She was a challenge that he didn't dare ignore. She was also a girl, and he was crazy about her.

Other people had work to do, too. Hostetter spent long hours with Sherman, doing what it seemed he had come home to do—giving the advice gained from his years of experience on how to make the system of outside trade work smoother and better. He was a different-looking Hostetter these days, with his beard trimmed short and his hair cropped, and the New Mennonite dress laid aside. Len had done this a long time ago, so he could not say why it seemed wrong, but it did. Perhaps it was only because he had grown up with one image of Hostetter firmly fixed in his mind, and it was hard to change it. They did not see very much of each other any more. They still shared the same room, but they each had their own work, and Hostetter had his own friends, and Len's spare time was pretty much taken up with Joan. After a while he got the feeling that the Wepplos figured they would probably get married any day. It made him feel guilty every time he went there, remembering what Joan had said, but not guilty enough to keep him away.

"Just girl talk," he would say to himself, "like Amity teasing me along when it was really Esau she wanted. They don't know what they're after. She's got an idea about outside just like I had about here, but she wouldn't like it."

And he told her over and over how she wouldn't like it, describing this and that about the great, quiet, sleeping country and the people and the life that was lived there. Over and over, trying to make her understand, until he got so homesick he would have to stop, and she would turn away to hide the satisfaction in her eyes.

Besides, that was crazy talk about a way out of the canyon. There wasn't any way. The cliffs were too steep to climb, the narrow gorge of the stream bed was too broken and treacherous with falls and rockslides, and beyond them was only more of the same. The site had been carefully picked, and it had not changed in a century. The eyes of Bartorstown watched, the ears listened, and the hidden death was always ready in that winding lower pass. There was a personal matter, too. Len knew, without having to be told, without having to see any overt signs of it, that every move he made was noted carefully by somebody and reported on to Sherman. The problem of finding Bartorstown would be easy compared with that of getting away from it again. And yet she sounded so sure, as if she had a way all planned. It kept nagging at him, wondering what it could be—just for curiosity. But he didn't ask her, and she didn't tell him, nor even hint at it again.

For everybody it was a dull and ingrown time, a time for peering too closely at your neighbors and getting too concerned with what they did, and talking about it too much. Before Christmas the whispers had started about Gutierrez. Poor Julio, he sure took that last disappointment hard. Well, his life's work—you know. Oh sure, but everybody gets disappointed, and they don't take to drink like that, couldn't he pull himself together and try again? I suppose a man gets tired, loses heart. After all, a lifetime—— Did you hear they found him passed out in a drift by Sawyer's back fence, and it's a wonder he didn't freeze to death? His poor wife, it's her *I* feel sorry for, not him. A man his age ought to know this life isn't all cakes and roses for anybody. I hear he's hounding poor Frank Erdmann nearly out of his mind. I hear——

I hear. Everybody heard, and nearly everybody talked. They talked about other people and other things, of course, but Gutierrez was the winter's sensation and sooner or later any conversation got around to him. Len saw him a few times. Some of those times he was obviously drunk, an aging man staggering with stiff dignity down a snowy lane, his face dark with an inner darkness above the neat white beard. At other times he seemed to be less drunken than dreaming, as though his mind had wandered off along some shadowy byway in search of a lost hope. Len saw him only once to speak to, and then it was only Len who spoke. Gutierrez nodded and passed on, his eyes perfectly blank of recognition. At night there was nearly always a lamp burning in a certain room in Gutierrez' house, and Gutierrez sat beside it at a table covered with papers, and he would work at them and drink from a handy jug, work and drink, until he fell asleep and his wife came and helped him to the bed. People who happened to be passing by at night could see this through the window, and Len knew that it was true because he, too, had seen it; Gutierrez working at a vast tangle of papers, very patient, very intent, with the big jug at his elbow.

Christmas came, and after church there was a big dinner at the Wepplos'. The weather was clear and fine. At one in the afternoon the temperature topped zero, and everybody said how warm it was. There were parties all over Fall Creek, with people trudging back and forth in the dry crunching snow between the houses, and at night all the lamps were lit, shining yellow and merry out of the windows. Joan got very passionate with the excitement, and when they were on the way to somebody else's place she led him into the darkness behind a clump of trees, and they forgot the cold for a few minutes, standing with their arms around each other and their mingled breaths steaming in a frosty halo around their heads.

"Love me?"

He kissed her so hard it hurt, his hand bunched in her hair at the back of her neck, under her wool cap.

"What does that feel like?"

"Len. Oh, Len, if you love me, if you really love me——"

Suddenly she was tight against him, talking fast and wild.

"Take me out of here. I'll lose my mind if I have to stay here cooped up any longer. If I wasn't a girl I'd have gone alone, long ago, but I need you to take me. Len, I'd worship you all the rest of my life."

He withdrew from her, slowly, carefully, as a man draws from the edge of a quicksand.

"No."

"Why, Len? Why should you spend your whole life in this hole for something you never heard of before? Bartorstown isn't anything to you but a dream you had once when you were a kid."

"No," he said again. "I told you before. Leave me alone."

He started away, but she scuffled through the snow and stood in front of him.

"They filled you up on all that stuff about the future of the world, didn't they? I've heard it since I was born. The burden, the sacred debt." He could see her face in the frosty pale snow glimmer, all twisted up with anger she had saved and hidden for a long time and now was turning loose. "I didn't make the bomb and I didn't drop it, and I won't be here a hundred years from now to see if they do it again or not. So why have I got any debt? And why have you got any, Len Colter? You answer me that."

Words came stumbling to his tongue, but she looked so fiercely at him that he never said them.

"You haven't," she said. "You're just scared. Scared to face reality and admit you've wasted all those years for nothing."

Reality, he thought. I've been facing it every day, reality you've never seen. Reality behind a concrete wall.

"Let me alone," he said. "I ain't going, I can't. So shut up about it."

She laughed at him. "They told you a lot of stuff up there in Bartorstown, but I bet there's one thing they never mentioned. I bet they never told you about Solution Zero."

There was such a note of triumph in her voice that Len knew he should not listen any more. But she jeered at him. "You wanted to learn, didn't you? And didn't they tell you up there always to look for the whole truth and never be satisfied with only part of it? You want the whole truth, don't you? Or are you afraid of that, too?"

"All right," he said. "What is Solution Zero?"

She told him, with swift, vindictive relish. "You know how they work, building theories and turning them into equations, and feeding the equations to Clementine to solve. If they work out, that's another step forward. If they don't, like the last time, that's a blind alley, a negative. But all the time they're piling these equations into Clementine, adding up these steps toward what they call the master solution. Well, suppose *that* one comes out negative? Suppose the final equations just don't work, and all they get is the mathematical proof that what they're looking for doesn't exist? That's Solution Zero."

"God," said Len, "is that possible? I thought——" He stared at her in the snowy night, feeling sick and miserable, feeling an utter fool, betrayed.

"You thought it was certain, and the only question was

when. Well, you ask old Sherman if you don't believe me. Everybody knows about Solution Zero, but you don't hear them talk about it, any more than they talk about how they're going to die someday. You ask. And then you figure how much of your life *that's* worth!"

She left him. She had a genius for knowing when to leave him. He did not go on to the party. He went home and sat alone, brooding, until Hostetter came in, and by that time he was in such a mean, low mood that he didn't give him a chance to shut the door before he demanded, "What's this about Solution Zero?"

There was a cloud on Hostetter's brow, too. "Probably just what you heard," he said, taking off his coat and hat.

"Everybody's kept mighty quiet about it."

"I advise you to, too. It's a superstition we've got here."

He sat down and began to unlace his boots. Snow was melting from them in little puddles on the puncheon floor. Len said, "I don't wonder."

Hostetter methodically unlaced his boots.

"I thought they knew," Len said. "I thought they were sure of it."

"Research isn't done that way."

"But how can they spend all that time, and maybe that much more again, if they know it might be all for nothing?"

"Because how would they know if they didn't try? And because there isn't any other way to do it." Hostetter flung his boots in the corner by the potbellied stove. Usually he set them there, neatly, and not too close to the heat.

"But that's a crazy way," said Len.

"Is it? When your pa put seed in the ground, did he have a guarantee it was going to come up and yield him a harvest? Did he know every calf and shoat and lamb was going to stay healthy and pay back all the feed and care?"

He began to pull off his shirt and pants. Len sat scowling.

"All right, that's true. But if his crop failed or his cattle died there was always another season. What about this? What if it does come out—nothing?"

"Then they try again. If no such force-field is possible, then they think of other ways. And maybe some part of the work they did will give them a clue, so it isn't all lost." He slapped his clothes over the hide-seated chair and climbed into his bunk. "Hell, how do you think the human race ever learned anything, except by trial and error?"

"But it all takes such a long, long time," said Len.

"Everything takes a long time. Birthing takes nine months, and dying takes you all the rest of your life, and what are you complaining about, anyway? You just got here. Wait till you're as old as the rest of us. Then you might have some reason."

He turned his back and covered his head with the blanket. After a while Len blew out the lamp.

The next day it was all over Fall Creek that Julio Gutierrez had got drunk at Sherman's and knocked Frank Erdmann down, and Ed Hostetter had stepped in and practically carried Gutierrez home. A brawl between the senior physicist and the chief electronics engineer was scandal enough to keep the tongues all wagging, but it seemed to Len that there was a darker, sadder note in the gossip, a shadow of discouragement. Or maybe that was only because he had dreamed all night of rust in the wheat and new lambs dying.

27

ESAU CAME banging at the door before it was light. It was the third morning in January, a Monday, and the snow was coming down in a solid desperate rush as though God had suddenly commanded it to bury the world before lunch. "Ain't you ready?" he asked Len. "Well, hurry up, this snow's going to slow us down enough as it is."

Hostetter stuck his head out of the bunk. "What's all the rush?"

"Clementine," said Esau. "The big machine. They're going to test her this morning, and Erdmann said we could watch before work. Hurry up, can't you?"

"Let me get my boots on," Len grumbled. "She won't run away."

Hostetter said to Esau, "Do you figure you can work with Clementine someday?"

"No," said Esau, shaking his head. "Too much math and

stuff. I'm going to learn radio instead. After all, that's what got me here. But I sure do want to see that big brain do its thinking. Are you ready now? You sure? All right, let's go!"

The world was white, and blind. The snow fell straight down, with hardly a vagrant breath of air to set it swirling. They groped their way through the village, still able to follow the deep-trodden lanes, and conscious of the houses even if they could not really see them. Out on the road it was different. It was like being in the fields at home when it snowed like this, with no landmark, no direction, and the same old dizzy feeling came over Len. Everything was gone but up and down, and presently even that would go, and there was not even any sound left in the world.

"You're going off the road," said Esau, and he floundered back from the drifted ditch. Then it was Esau's turn. They walked close together, making the usual comments on the cursedness of fate and the weather, and Len said suddenly, "You're happy here, aren't you?"

"Sure," said Esau. "I wouldn't go back to Piper's Run if you gave me the place."

He meant it. Then he asked, "Aren't you?"

"Sure," said Len. "Sure."

They plowed on, the chill feathery flakes patting their faces, trying to fill up their noses and mouths and smother them quietly, whitely, because they disturbed the even blankness of the road.

"What do you think?" asked Len. "Will they ever find the answer? Or will it come out zero?"

"Hell," said Esau, "I don't care. I got enough of my own to do."

"Don't you care about anything?" Len growled.

"Sure I do. I care about doing what I want to do, and not having a lot of damn fool old men telling me I can't. That's what I care about. That's why I like it here."

"Yes," said Len. "Sure." And that's true, you can do what you want and say what you want and think what you want—except one thing. You can't say you don't believe in what they believe in, and that way it isn't much different from Piper's Run.

They stumbled and blundered up the slope, between the artfully tumbled boulders. About halfway up to the gate Esau started and swore, and Len shied too as he sensed a dark dim shape moving, in all that whiteness, furtively among the rocks.

The shape spoke to them, and it was Gutierrez. The snow was piled up thick across the top of his shoulders and on his cap, as though he had been standing still in it for some time, waiting. But he was sober, and his face was perfectly composed, and pleasant.

"I'm sorry if I startled you," he said. "I seem to have mislaid my own key to the gate. Do you mind if I go in with you?"

The question was purely rhetorical. The three of them walked on together up the slope. Len kept glancing uneasily at Gutierrez, thinking of the long night hours spent with the papers and the jug. He felt sorry for him. He was also afraid of him. He wanted desperately to question him about Solution Zero, and why they couldn't be sure a thing existed before they spent a couple of hundred years in hunting for it. He wanted to so much that he was certain Esau would blurt the question out, and then Gutierrez would knock them both down. But nobody said anything. Esau, too, must have been awed into wisdom.

Beyond the safety gate there was a drift of snow, and then only the darkness and the dank, freezing chill of a place shut off forever from the sun. Gutierrez went ahead. He had stumbled that first time, but now he did not stumble, walking steadily, his head held high and his back very straight. Len could hear him breathing, heavy breathing like that of a man who had been running, but Gutierrez had not been running. Where the passage bent and the light came on, far down over the inner door, he had left them far behind, and Len had a curious cold feeling that the man had forgotten them entirely.

They stood side by side again under the scanners. Gutierrez looked straight ahead at the steel door until it swung open, and then he strode away down the hall. Jones came out of the monitor room and looked after him, wondering out loud, "What's he doing here?"

Esau shook his head. "He came in with us. Said he lost his key. I suppose he's got some work to do."

Jones said, "Erdmann won't be happy. Oh well. Nobody

told me to keep him out, so my conscience is clear." He grinned. "Let me know what happens, huh?"

"He was drunk the other night," said Len. "I don't reckon anything will happen."

"I hope not," said Esau. "I want to see that brain work."

They left their coats in a locker room and hurried on down to the next level, past the picture of Hiroshima, past the victims with their tragic impassive eyes. And the voices reached them from beyond the door.

"No, I am sorry, Frank. Please let me say it."

"Forget it, Julio. We all do things. Forget it."

"Thank you," said Gutierrez, with immense dignity, with great contrition.

Len hesitated outside, looking at Esau, whose face was a study in violent indecision.

"How does she go?" asked Gutierrez.

"Fine," said Erdmann. "Smooth as silk."

Their voices fell silent. Len's heart came up into his throat and stuck there, and a cold cord was knotted through his belly. Because there was now another voice audible in the room, a voice he had never heard before. A small, dry, busy whisper-and-click, the voice of Clementine.

Esau heard it, too. "I don't care," he whispered. "I'm going in."

He did, and Len followed him, walking softly. He looked at Clementine, and she was no longer sleeping. The many eyes on the panel board were bright and winking, and all through that mighty grid of wires there was a stir and a quiver, a subtle pulse of life.

The selfsame pulse, thought Len, that beats down there below. The heart and the brain.

"Oh," said Erdmann, almost with relief. "Hello."

The high-speed printer burst into a sudden chatter. Len started violently. The eyes on the panel board winked as though with laughter, and then it was all quiet, all dark again, with the exception of a steady light that burned as a signal that Clementine was awake.

Esau sucked in his breath. But he did not speak because Gutierrez beat him to it.

He had taken some papers out of his pocket. He did not seem to be aware that anyone was there but Erdmann. He held the papers in his hands and said, "My wife felt that I shouldn't come here and bother you today. She hid my key to the safety gate. But of course this was far too important to wait."

He looked down at the papers. "I've gone over this whole sequence of equations again. I found where the mistake was."

Something tightened and became wary behind Erdmann's face. "Yes?"

"It's perfectly plain, you can see for yourself. Here."

He shoved the papers into Erdmann's hand. Erdmann began to scan through them. And now there came into his face an acute discomfort, a sorrow, a dismay.

"You can see," said Gutierrez. "It's plain as day. She made a mistake, Frank. I told you. You said it wasn't possible, but she did."

"Julio, I——" And Erdmann shook his head from side to side and glanced in desperation at Len, and found no help there, and began to shuffle again through the papers in his hands.

"Don't you see it, Frank?"

"Well, Julio, you know I'm not mathematician enough——"

"Hell," said Gutierrez impatiently, "how did you get to be an electronics engineer? You know enough for that. It's all written out plain. Anybody should see it. Here." He fumbled at the papers in Erdmann's hands. "Here, and here, you see?"

Erdmann said, "What do you want me to do?"

"Why, run it through again. Correct it. Then we'll have the answer, Frank. The answer."

Erdmann moistened his lips. "But if she made a mistake once she might do it again, Julio. Why don't you get Wentz or Jacobs——"

"No. It would take them all winter, a year. She can do it right now. You've tested her. You said so. You said she was smooth as silk. That's why I wanted it to be today, while she's still fresh and unused. She can't possibly make the same mistake again. Run it through."

"I—well," said Erdmann. "Well, all right."

He went over to the input mechanism and began to transfer onto the tape. Gutierrez waited. He still had his heavy outdoor clothes on, but he did not seem to feel that he was hot or uncomfortable. He watched Erdmann, and from time to time he glanced at the computer and smiled and nodded, like a man who has caught someone else in an error and thereby vindicated himself. Len had withdrawn into the background. He did not like the look on Erdmann's face. He began to wonder if he should go, and then the lights on the panel began to glow and wink at him, and the dim voice hummed and murmured, and he was as fascinated as Esau and could not go.

He was startled when Erdmann spoke to them. "I'll be free in a bit. Then I'll answer your questions."

"Would you rather we'd come back later?" asked Len.

"No," said Erdmann, glancing at Gutierrez. "No, you stick around."

Clementine pondered, mumbling softly. Apart from that it was very still. Gutierrez was calm, standing with his hands folded in front of him, waiting. Erdmann fidgeted. There was sweat on his face and he kept wiping it off and running his hand over his mouth and looking at Gutierrez with an expression of utter agony.

"I think there were some circuits we missed on the overhaul, Julio. She hasn't been fully checked. She might still——"

"You sound like my wife," said Gutierrez. "Don't worry, it'll come out."

The output printer chattered. Erdmann started forward. Gutierrez knocked him out of the way. He snatched the paper out of the printer and looked at it. His face darkened, and then the color left it and it was gray and sick, and his hands trembled.

"What did you do?" he said to Erdmann. "What did you do to my equations?"

"Nothing, Julio."

"Look what she says. No solution, recheck your data for errors. No solution. No solution——"

"Julio. Julio, please. Listen to me. You've been working too long on this, you're tired. I put the equations just as they were, but they——"

"They what? Go on and say it, Frank. Go on."

"Julio, please," said Erdmann, with a terrible helplessness, and put out his hand to Gutierrez as one does to a child, asking him to come.

Gutierrez hit him. He hit him so suddenly and so hard that there was no way and no time to dodge the blow. Erdmann stepped back three or four paces and fell down, and Gutierrez said quietly, “You are against me, both of you. You had it arranged between you, so that no matter what I did she would never give me the right answer. I’ve thought of you all winter, Frank, in here talking with her, laughing, because she knows the answer and she won’t tell. But I’m going to make her tell, Frank.”

He had stones in his pockets. That was why he had kept his coat on, in the warmth of Bartorstown. He had a lot of stones, and he took them out and threw them one by one at Clementine, shouting with a wild joy, “I’ll make you tell, you bitch, you lying bitch, deceitful bitch, I’ll make you tell.”

Glass on the panel board crashed and tinkled. Circuit wires twanged. One of the big glass tanks that held a part of Clementine’s memory burst open. Frank Erdmann scrambled up unsteadily from the floor, yelling for Gutierrez to stop, yelling for help. And Gutierrez ran out of stones and began to beat on the panel with his fists and kick it with his boots, screaming, “Bitch, bitch, bitch, I’ll make you tell, you’ve got my life, my mind, my work stored up in you, I’ll make you tell!”

Erdmann was grappling with him. “Len. Esau, for God’s sake, help me. Help me hold him.”

Len went forward slowly, as a sleepwalker moves. He put his hands out and took hold of Gutierrez. Gutierrez was very strong, incredibly strong. It was hard to hold onto him, hard to drag him away from the ravaged panel, and now there were new lights winking and flashing on it, red lights saying I am wounded, help me. Len looked at them, and he looked into Gutierrez’ eyes. Erdmann panted. There was blood coming out of the side of his mouth. “Julio, please. Take it easy. That’s it, Len, back a little farther, now—— It’s all right, Julio, please be quiet.”

And Julio was quiet, all at once. There was no transition. One second his wiry muscles were straining like steel bars against Len’s grasp, and the next he was all gone, limp, sagging, a frail and hollow thing. He turned his face to Erdmann and he said with infinite resignation, “Somebody is against me, Frank. Somebody is against us all.”

Tears ran down his cheeks. He hung like a dying man between Len and Erdmann, weeping, and Len looked at Clementine, blinking her bloody eyes for help.

Find your limit, Judge Taylor said. Find your limit before it is too late.

I have found my limit, Len thought. And it is already too late.

Men came and relieved him of his burden. He went down with Esau into the belly of the rock, and he worked all day with a face as blank as the concrete wall, and as deceitful, because behind it there was violence and terror, and astonishment of the heart.

In the afternoon the whisper came along the line of the great machines. They took him back home, did you hear, and the doctor says he's clear gone. They say he'll have to stay there locked up, with someone to watch him.

As we are all locked up here in this canyon, Len thought, serving this Moloch with the head of brass and the bowels of fire. This Moloch who has just destroyed a man.

But he knew the truth at last, and he spoke it to himself.

There will be no answer.

And Lord, deliver me from the bondage of mine enemies, for I repent. I have followed after false gods, and they have betrayed me. I have eaten of the fruit, and my soul is sickened.

The fiery heart beat on behind the wall, and overhead the brain was already being healed.

That night Len floundered through the deep new-fallen snow to Wepplo's. He said to Joan, quietly so that no one else should hear, "I want what you want. Show me the way."

Her eyes blazed. She kissed him on the lips and whispered, "Yes! But can you keep it secret, Len? It's a long time yet till spring."

"I can."

"Even from Hostetter?"

"Even from him."

Even from him. For a lamp is set to guide the footsteps of repentance.

28

FEBRUARY, MARCH, APRIL.

Time. A tight passivity, a waiting.

He worked. Every day he did what was expected of him, under the very shadow of that concrete wall. He did his work well. That was the ironic part of it. He could become interested now in the whole chain of great machines that harnessed and transmitted the Power, and he could admit the fascination, the sense of importance it gave a man to hold those mighty brutes in check and guidance as you held a team of horses. He could do this because now he recognized the fascination for what it was, and the fangs of the serpent were drawn. He could think what power like that would do for places like Refuge and Piper's Run, how it would bring back the bright and comfortable things of Gran's childhood, but he understood now why people were savagely determined to do without them. Because once you set your feet on the path you went on and on until you couldn't go back again, and suddenly there was a rain of fire from the sky. You had to get back to where it was safe and stay there.

Back to Piper's Run, to the woods and the fields, to the end of doubt, the end of fear. Back to the time before the preaching, before Soames, before you ever heard of Bartorstown. Back to peace. He used to pray at night that nothing should happen to Pa before he came, because part of the salvation would be in telling him that he was right.

Things happened in that time. Esau's son was born, and christened David Taylor Colter in some obscure gesture of defiance or affection to both grandfathers. Joan made careful, scheming arrangements for a separate house and planned a marriage date. And these things were important. But they were shadowed over and made small by the one great drive, the getting away.

Nothing else mattered now to him and Joan, not even marriage. They were already bonded as close as two people could be by their hunger to escape the canyon.

"I've planned this way for years," she would whisper. "Night after night, lying awake and feeling the mountains around holding me in, dreaming about it and never letting my folks know. And now I'm afraid. I'm afraid I haven't planned it right, or somebody will read my mind and make me give it all away."

She would cling to him, and he would say, "Don't worry. They're only men, they can't read minds. They can't keep us in."

"No," she would answer then. "It's a good plan. All it needed was you."

The snow began to soften and thunder in great avalanches down the high slopes. In another week the pass would be open. And Joan said it was time. They were married three days later, by the same little teetering minister who had married Esau and Amity, but in the Fall Creek church with the spring sun brightening the dust on the flagstones, and Hostetter to stand up with Len and Joan's father to give the bride away. There was a party afterward. Esau shook Len's hand and Amity gave Joan a kiss and a spiteful look, and the old man got out the jug and passed it around and told Len, "Boy, you've got the finest girl in the world. You treat her right, or I'll have to take her back again." He laughed and thumped Len on the back until his spine ached, and then a little bit after Hostetter found him alone on the back stoop, getting a breath of air.

He didn't say anything for a time, except that it looked like an early spring. Then he said, "I'm going to miss you, Len. But I'm glad. This was the right thing to do."

"I know it was."

"Well, sure. But I didn't mean that. I mean that you're really settled here now, really a part of it. I'm glad. Sherman's glad. We all are."

Then Len knew it had been the right thing to do, just like Joan said. But he could not quite look Hostetter in the face.

"Sherman wasn't sure of you," said Hostetter. "I wasn't either, for a while. I'm glad you've made peace with your conscience. I know better than any of them what a tough thing it must have been to do." He held out his hand. "Good luck."

Len took his hand and said, "Thanks." He smiled. But he thought, I am deceiving him just as I deceived Pa, and I don't want to, any more than I did then. But that was wrong, and this is right, this I have to do——

He was glad that he would not have to face Hostetter any more.

The new house was strange. It was little and old, on the edge of Fall Creek, swept and scrubbed and filled with woman-things provided by Joan's mother and her well-wishing friends, curtains and quilts and tablecloths and bits of rag carpeting. So much work and good will, all for the use of a few days. He had been given two weeks for his honeymoon. And now they were all ready. Now they could cling together and wait together with no one to watch them, with all suspicion set at rest and the path clear before them.

"Pray for Ishmaelites," she told him. "They always come as soon as the pass is open, begging. Pray they come now."

"They'll come," said Len. There was a calmness on him, a conviction that he would be delivered even as the children of Israel were delivered out of Egypt.

The Ishmaelites came. Whether they were the same ones that had come last fall or another band he did not know, but they were gaunter and more starved-looking, more ragged and suffering than he would have believed people could be and live. They begged powder and shot, and Sherman threw in a keg of salt beef, for the sake of the children. They took it. Joan watched them start their slow staggering march back up to the pass before evening, with her hand clasped tight in Len's, and she whispered, "Pray for a dark night."

"It's already answered," he said, looking at the sky. "We'll have rain. Maybe snow, if it keeps getting colder."

"Anything, just so it's dark."

And now the house fulfilled its purpose, giving up the things it had hidden for them safely, the food, the water bags, the blanket packs, the two coarse sheets rubbed with ashes and artfully torn. Len wrote some painful words to Hostetter. "I won't ever tell about Bartorstown, I owe you that. I am sorry. Forgive me, but I got to go back." He left the paper on the table in the front room. They blew out the candles early, knowing they would not be disturbed.

But now Joan's courage failed her and she sat shivering on the edge of the bed, thinking what would happen if they were seen and caught.

"Nobody'll see us," Len said. "Nobody."

He believed that. He was not afraid. It was as though some

secret word had been given him that he was beyond harm until he got back to Piper's Run.

"We better go now, Len."

"Wait. They're weak and carrying the young ones. We can catch them easy. Wait till we're sure."

Dark, full night, and a drifting rain. Len's muscles drew tight and his heart pounded. Now it is time, he thought. Now I take her hand and we go.

The road to the pass is steep and winding. There is no one behind us. The rain pours down, and now it is sleet. Now the sleet has turned to snow. The Lord has stretched out his garment to hide us. Hurry. Hurry to the pass, over the steep road and the freezing mud.

"Len, I've got to rest."

"Not yet. Give me your hand again. Now——"

Into the black gut of the pass, with the snow falling and the winter's drifts still piled high where the sun can't reach. Now we can rest a minute, only a minute.

"Len, this looks like it might be a spring blizzard. It could close the pass again before morning."

"Good. Then they can't follow us."

"But we'll freeze to death. Hadn't we better turn back?"

"Haven't you any faith? Can't you see this is being done for us? Come on!"

On and up, across the saddleback and down the other side, going fast, much faster than the slow mule teams with the loaded wagons. Past the camping place, and onto the rocky slope beyond. There is a sound of singing on the wind.

"There. You hear that? Where's those sheets?"

I will put on the garment of repentance. The Ishmaelites have no wagons. They have no cattle to break their legs among the stones. They march all night, away from the haunts of iniquity and back to the clean desert where they do their lifelong penance for the sins of man. I have a penance too. I will do it when it is sent upon me.

Close now, but not too close, in the night and the falling snow. They sing and moan as they go along, into the lower pass, all straggled out in a ragged line. If they look back they will only see two Ishmaelites, two of their own band.

They do not look back. Their eyes are on God.

Down through the winding cut in the rock, and back there in Bartorstown in the monitor room someone is sitting. Not Jones, this isn't his time, but someone. Someone watching the little lights blinking on the board. Someone thinking, There go the crazy Ishmaelites back to the desert. Someone yawning, and lighting a pipe, waiting for Jones to come so he can go home.

Someone with a button close under his fingers, ready to use.

He does not use it.

It is dawn. The Ishmaelites have disappeared in the wind and the blowing snow.

Joan. Joan, get up. Joan look, we're out of the pass.

We're free.

Praise the Lord, who has delivered us from Bartorstown.

29

IT WAS a spring blizzard. They survived it, crouched in a hole of the rock like two wild things sheltering together for warmth. It stopped the high pass and covered their tracks, and afterward they fled south along the broken line of the foothills, watchful, furtive, ready to hide at the slightest sign of human life other than their own.

"They'll hunt for us."

"I left a letter. I swore——"

"They'll hunt for us. You know that."

"I reckon they'd have to. Yes."

He remembered the radios, and how the Bartorstown men had kept track of two runaway boys, a long time ago.

"We'll have to be careful, Len. Awfully careful."

"Don't worry." His jaw thrust out, stubborn, bristling with a growing beard. "They ain't going to take us back. I told you, the hand of the Lord is over us. He'll keep us safe."

Piper's Run and the hand of God. Those were the burden of the first days. There was a mist over the world, obscuring everything but a vision of home and a straight path to it. He could see the fields very green with the sun on them, the crooked apple trees with their old black trunks drowned in blossom, the barn and the dooryard, still, waiting, in a warm and golden peace. And there was a path, and his feet were on it, and nothing could stop him.

But there were obstacles. There were mountains, gullies, rocks, cold, hunger, thirst, exhaustion, pain. And it came to him that before he could reach that haven of peace there was a penance to be done. He had to pay for the wrong he had done in leaving it. That was fair enough. He had expected it. He suffered gladly and never noticed the look of doubt and amazement that came into Joan's eyes, shading gradually toward contempt.

The ecstasy of abasement and repentance stayed with him until one day he fell and hurt his knee against a rock, and the pain was pain merely, with no holiness about it. The world rocked around him and fell sharply into place with all the mist cleared out of it. He was hungry and cold and tired. The mountains were high and the prairies wide. Piper's Run was a thousand miles away. His knee hurt like the very devil, and an old growling rebellion rose up in him to say, All right, I've done my penance. Now that's enough.

That was the end of the first phase. Joan began to look at him like she used to. "For a while there," she said, "you weren't much better than a New Ishmaelite, and I began to get scared."

He muttered something about repentance being good for the soul, and shut her up. But secretly her words stung him and made him feel ashamed. Because they were more than partly true.

But he still had to get back to Piper's Run. Only now he realized that the path to it was very long and hard just as the path away from it had been, and that no mystical power was going to get him there. He was going to have to walk it on his own two feet.

"But once we get there," he would say, "we'll be safe. The Bartorstown men can't touch us there. If they denounced us they'd denounce themselves. We'll be safe."

Safe in the fields and the seasons, safe in the not-thinking, not-wanting. A contented mind and a thankful heart. Pa said those were the greatest blessings. He was right. Piper's Run is where I lost them. Piper's Run is where I will find them again.

Only when I think now of Piper's Run I see it tiny and far off, and there is a lovely light on it like the light of a spring evening, but I can't bring it close. When I think of Ma and Pa and Brother James and Baby Esther I can't see them clearly, and their faces are all blurred.

I can see myself, all right, running with Esau across a pasture at night, kneeling in the barn straw with Pa's strap coming down hard on my shoulders. I can see myself as I was then. But when I try to see myself as I will be, a grown man but a part of it again, I can't.

I try to see Joan wearing the white cap and the humility, but I can't see that, either.

Yet I have to get back. I have to find what I had there that I've never had since I left it. I have to find certainty.

I have to find peace.

Then one evening just at sundown Len saw the man driving a trader's wagon with a team of big horses. He crossed a green swell of the prairie, showing briefly on the skyline, and was gone so quickly that Len was not sure he had really seen him. Joan was on her knees making a fire. He made her put it out, and that night they walked a long way by moonlight before he would stop again.

They fell in with a band of hunters—this was safe because the Bartorstown men did not go with the hunters, and Joan made doubly sure. They told a tale of New Ishmaelites to account for their condition, and the hunters shook their heads and spat.

"Them murdering devils," one of them said. "I'm a believing man myself"—and he looked warily at the sky—"but killing just ain't no way to serve the Lord."

And yet you would kill us if you knew, thought Len, to serve the Lord. And he nagged Joan, who had never needed to guard her tongue so rigidly, until she was afraid to speak her name.

"Is it all like this?" she whispered to him, in the privacy of their blankets at night. "Are they all like wolves ready to tear you?"

"About Bartorstown they are. Never tell where you came from, never give them a hint so they could even guess."

The hunters passed them on to some freighters, joining up at a rendezvous point to go south and east with a load of furs and smelted copper. Joan made sure there were no Bartorstown men among them. She kept her tongue tightly between her teeth, looking with doubtful eyes at the tiny sun-baked towns they stopped in, the lonely ranches they passed.

"It'll be different in Piper's Run, won't it, Len?"

"Yes, it'll be different."

Kinder, greener, more fruitful, yes. But in other ways, no, not different. Not different at all.

What is it that lies on the whole land, in the dusty streets and the slow beat of the horse hoofs, in the faces of the people?

But Piper's Run is home.

On a clear midnight he thought he saw a solitary wagon tilt far off, glimmering under the moon. He took Joan and they scurried eastward alone, over river beds drying white in the summer sun, working their way from ranch to ranch, settlement to settlement.

"What do people *do* in these places?" Joan asked, and he answered angrily, "They live."

The blazing days went by. The long hard miles unrolled. The vision of Piper's Run faded, little by little, no matter how he clung to it, until it was so faint he could hardly see it. He had been going a long time on momentum, and now that was running out. And the man on the wagon hounded him all through the summer days, plodding relentlessly out of the vast horizon, out of the wind and the prairie dust. Len's going became more of a running from than a running to. He never saw the face of the man. He could not even be sure it was the same wagon. But it followed him. And he knew.

In September, in a little glaring town lost in a gray-green sea of bear grass and shinnery on the Texas border, he sat down to wait.

"You fool," Joan told him despairingly, "it isn't him. It's only your guilty conscience makes you think so."

"It's him. You know it."

"Why should it be? Even if it is someone from there——"

"I can tell when you're lying, Joan. Don't."

"All right! It is him, of course it's him. He was responsible for you. He was sworn for you to Sherman. What did you think?"

She glared at him, her thin brown hands curled into fists, her eyes flashing.

"You going to let him take you back, Len Colter? Aren't you a man yet, for all that beard? Get on your feet. Let's go."

"No." Len shook his head. "I never realized he was sworn."

"He won't be alone. There'll be others with him."

"Maybe. Maybe not."

"You are going to let him take you." Her voice was shrill, breaking like a child's. "He's not going to take me. I'm going on."

He spoke to her in a tone he had never used before. "You'll stay by me, Joan."

She stared at him, startled, and then came a look of doubt, a stirring of some dark apprehension.

"What are you going to do?"

"I don't know yet. That's what I got to decide." His face had grown stony and hard, impassive as flint. "Two things I'm sure of. I ain't going to run. And I won't be taken."

She stayed by him, quiet, frightened of she knew not what.

Len waited.

Two days. He has not come yet, but he will. He was sworn for me.

Two days to think, to stand waiting on the battlefield. Esau never fought this battle, nor Brother James. They're the lucky ones. But Pa did, and Hostetter did, and now it is my time. The battle of decision, the time of choice.

I made a decision in Piper's Run. It was a child's decision, based on a child's dreams. I made a decision in Bartorstown, and it was still a childish decision, based on emotion. Now I am finished with dreams. I am finished with emotions. I have fasted my forty days in the wilderness and I am through with penance. I stand stripped and naked, but I stand as a man. What decision I make I will make as a man, and there will be no turning back from it after it is made.

Three days, to tear away the last sweet sunlit hopes.

I will not go back to Piper's Run. Whichever way I go, it will not be there. Piper's Run is a memory of childhood, and I am finished with memories, too. That door is closed behind me, long ago. Piper's Run was a memory of peace, but no matter which way I go I know now that I will never have peace.

For peace is certainty, and there is no certainty but death.

Four days, to set the stubborn feet firmly on the ground, teaching them not to run.

Because I am finished with running. Now I will stop and choose my way.

Sooner or later a man has to stop and choose his way, not out of the ways he would like there to be, or the ways there ought to be, but out of the ways there are.

Five days, in which to choose.

There were people in the town. It was the time of the fall trading, the hot dead time when the shinnery stands gray and stiff and the bear grass rustles in the wind and every plank of wood is as dry as a cracked bone. They came in from the outlying ranches to barter for their winter supplies, and the traders' wagons were lined up in a row at the end of the one short, dusty street.

All over the land, he thought, it is the time of the fall trading. All over the land there are fairs, and the wagons are pulled up, and the men trade cattle and the women chaffer over cloth and sugar. All over the land it is the same, unchanging. And after the trading and the fair there is the preaching, the fall revival to stock the soul against the winter too. This is life. This is the way it is.

He walked the street restlessly, up and down. He stood by the traders' wagons, looking into the faces of the people, listening to their talk.

They have found their truth. The New Ishmaelites have found theirs, and the New Mennonites, and the men of Bartorstown.

Now I must find mine.

Joan watched him from under the corners of her eyelids and was afraid to speak.

On the fifth night the trading was all done. Torches were set up around a platform in the trampled space at the end of the street. The stars blazed bright in the sky and the wind turned cool and the baked earth breathed out its heat. The people gathered.

Len sat on the crushed dry shinnery, holding Joan's hand. He did not notice after all when the wagon rolled in quietly at the other side of the crowd. But after a while he turned, and Hostetter was sitting there beside him.

30

THE VOICE of the preacher rang out strong and strident. "A thousand years, my brethren. A thousand years. That's what we was promised. And I tell you we are already in that blessed time, a-heading toward the Glory that was planned for them that keeps the way of righteousness. I tell you——"

Hostetter looked at Len in the flickering light of the wind-blown torches, and Len looked at him, but neither of them spoke.

Joan whispered something that might have been Hostetter's name. She pulled her hand away from Len's and started to scramble around behind him as though she wanted to get to Hostetter. Len caught her and pulled her down.

"Stay by me."

"Let me go. Len——"

"Stay by me."

She whimpered and was still. Her eyes sought Hostetter's.

Len said to both of them, "Be quiet. I want to listen."

"—and except you go as little children, the Book says, you won't never get in. Because Heaven wasn't made for the unrighteous. It wasn't made for the scoffer and the unbeliever. No sir, my brothers and sisters! And you ain't in the clear yet. Just because the Lord has chose to save you out from the Destruction, don't you think for a minute——"

It was on another night, at another preaching, that I set my foot upon the path.

A man died that night. His name was Soames. He had a red beard, and they stoned him to death because he was from Bartorstown.

Let me listen. Let me think.

"—a thousand years!" cried the preacher, thumping on his

dusty Book, stamping his boots on the dusty planks. "But you got to work for it! You can't just set down and pay no heed! You can't shirk your bounden duty to the Lord!"

Let it blow through me like a great wind. Let the words sound in my ears like trumpets.

I can speak. A power has been given me. I can kill another man as that boy killed Soames, and free myself.

I can speak again, and lead the way to Bartorstown as Burdette led his men to Refuge. Many will die, just as Dulinsky died. But Moloch will be thrown down.

Joan sits rigid beside me. The tears run on her cheeks. Hostetter sits on the other side. He must know what I am thinking. But he waits.

He was part of that other night. Part of Refuge. Part of Piper's Run and Bartorstown, the one end and the other and in the middle.

Can I wipe it all away with his blood?

Hallelujah!

Confess your sins! Let your soul be cleansed of its burden of black guilt, so the Lord won't burn you again with fire!

Hallelujah!

"Well, Len?" said Hostetter.

They are screaming as they screamed that night. And what if I rise and confess my sin, offering this man as a sacrifice? I will not be cleansed of knowledge. Knowledge is not like sin. There is no mystical escape from it.

And what if I throw down Moloch, with the bowels of fire and the head of brass?

The knowledge will still exist. Somewhere. In some book, some human brain, under some other mountain. What men have found once they will find again.

Hostetter is rising to his feet.

"You're forgetting something I told you. You're forgetting we're fanatics too. You're forgetting I can't let you run loose."

"Go ahead," said Len. He stood up, too, dragging Joan with him by the hand. "Go ahead if you can."

They looked at each other in the torchlight, while the crowd stamped and raised the dust and shouted hallelujah.

I have let it blow through me, and it is just a wind. I have let the words sound in my ears, and they are nothing but words, spoken by an ignorant man with a dusty beard. They do not stir me, they do not touch me. I am done with them, too.

I know now what lies across the land, the slow and heavy weight. They call it faith, but it is not faith. It is fear. The people have clapped a shelter over their heads, a necessity of ignorance, a passion of retreat, and they have called it God, and worshiped it. And it is as false as any Moloch. So false that men like Soames, men like Dulinsky, men like Esau and myself will overthrow it. And it will betray its worshipers, leaving them defenseless in the face of a tomorrow that will surely come. It may be a slow coming, and a long one, but come it will, and all their desperation will not stop it. Nothing will stop it.

"I ain't going to speak, Ed. Now it's up to you."

Joan caught her breath and held it in a sob.

Hostetter looked at Len, his feet set wide apart, his big shoulders hunched, his face as grim and dark as iron under his broad hat. Now it was Len's turn to wait.

If I die as Soames died, it will not matter except to me. This is important only because I am I, and Hostetter is Hostetter, and Joan is Joan, and we're people and can't help it. But for today, yesterday, tomorrow, it is not important. Time goes on without any of us. Only a belief, a state of mind, endures, and even that changes constantly, but underneath there are two main kinds—the one that says, Here you must stop knowing, and the other which says, Learn.

Right or wrong, the fruit was eaten, and there can't ever be a going back.

I have made my choice.

"What are you waiting for, Ed? If you're going to do it, go on."

Some of the tightness went out of the line of Hostetter's shoulders. He said, "I guess neither one of us was built for murder."

He bent his head, scowling, and then he lifted it again and gave Len a hard and blazing look.

"Well?"

The people cried and shouted and fell on their knees and sobbed.

"I still think," said Len slowly, "that maybe it was the Devil let loose on the world a hundred years ago. And I still think maybe that's one of Satan's own limbs you've got there behind that wall."

The preacher tossed his arms to the sky and writhed in an ecstasy of salvation.

"But I guess you're right," said Len. "I guess it makes better sense to try and chain the devil up than to try keeping the whole land tied down in the hopes he won't notice it again."

He looked at Hostetter. "You didn't get me killed, so I guess you'll have to let me come back."

"The choice wasn't entirely mine," said Hostetter.

He turned and walked away toward the wagons. Len followed him, with Joan stumbling at his side. And two men came out of the shadows to join them. Men that Len did not know, with deer rifles held in the crooks of their arms.

"I had to do more than talk for you this time," said Hostetter. "If you had denounced me, these boys might not have been able to save me from the crowd, but you wouldn't have grown five minutes older."

"I see," said Len slowly. "You waited till now, till the preaching."

"Yes."

"And when you threatened me, you didn't mean it. It was part of the test."

Hostetter nodded. The men looked hard at Len, clicking the safeties back on their guns.

"I guess you were right, Ed," one of them said. "But I sure wouldn't have banked on it."

"I've known him a long time," said Hostetter. "I was a little worried, but not much."

"Well," said the man, "he's all yours."

He did not sound as though he thought Hostetter had any prize. He nodded to the other man and they went away, Sherman's executioners vanishing quietly into the night.

"Why did you bother, Ed?" asked Len. He hung his head, ashamed for all that he had done to this man. "I never made you anything but trouble."

"I told you," said Hostetter. "I always felt kind of responsible for the time you ran away."

"I'll pay you back," said Len earnestly.

Hostetter said, “You just did.”

They climbed up onto the high seat of the wagon.

“And you,” Hostetter said to Joan. “Are you ready to come home?”

She was beginning to cry, in short fierce sobs. She looked at the torchlight and the people and the dust. “It’s a hideous world,” she said. “I hate it.”

“No,” said Hostetter, “not hideous, just imperfect. But that’s nothing new.”

He shook out the reins and clucked to the big horses. The wagon moved out across the dark prairie.

“When we get a ways out of town,” said Hostetter, “I’ll radio Sherman and tell him we’ve started back.”

THE SHRINKING MAN

Richard Matheson

To
Harry Altshuler
for faith, hope and clarity.

*I also wish to thank Dr. Sylvia Traube
for her generous assistance.*

Chapter One

FIRST HE thought it was a tidal wave. Then he saw that the sky and ocean were visible through it and it was a curtain of spray rushing at the boat.

He'd been sunbathing on top of the cabin. It was just coincidence that he pushed up on his elbow and saw it coming.

"Marty!" he yelled.

There was no answer. He scuttled across the hot wood and slid down the deck. "Hey, Marty!"

The spray didn't look menacing, but for some reason he wanted to avoid it. He ran around the cabin, wincing at the hot planks underfoot. It would be a race.

Which he lost. One moment he was in sunlight. The next he was being soaked by the warm, glittering spray.

Then it was past. He stood there watching it sweep across the water, sun-glowing drops of it covering him. Suddenly he twitched and looked down. There was a curious tingling on his skin.

He grabbed for a towel and dried himself. It wasn't so much pain as a pleasant stinging, like that of lotion on newly shaven cheeks.

Then he was dry and the feeling was almost gone. He went below and woke up his brother and told him about the curtain of spray that had run across the boat.

It was the beginning.

Chapter Two

THE SPIDER rushed at him across the shadowed sands, scrabbling wildly on its stalklike legs. Its body was a giant, glossy egg that trembled blackly as it charged across the windless mounds, its wake a score of sand-trickling scratches.

Paralysis locked the man. He saw the poisonous glitter of the spider eyes. He watched it scramble across a loglike stick, body mounted high on its motion-blurred legs, as high as the man's shoulders.

Behind him, suddenly, the steel-encased flame flared into life with a thunder that shook the air. It jarred the man loose. With a sucking gasp, he spun around and ran, the damp sand crunching beneath his racing sandals.

He fled through lakes of light and into darkness again, his face a mask of terror. Beams of sunlight speared across his panic-driven path, cold shadows enveloped it. Behind, the giant spider scoured sand in its pursuit.

Suddenly the man slipped. A cry tore back his lips. He skidded to a knee, then pitched forward onto outstretched palms. He felt the cold sands shaking with the vibration of the roaring flame. He pushed himself up desperately, palms flaking sand, and started running again.

Fleeing, he glanced back across his shoulder and saw that the spider was gaining on him, its pulsing egg of a body perched on running legs—an egg whose yolk swam with killing poisons. He raced on, breathless, terror in his veins.

Suddenly the cliff edge was before him, shearing off abruptly to a gray, perpendicular face. He raced along the edge, not looking down into the vast canyon below. The giant spider scuttled after him, the sound of its running a delicate scraping on the stone. It was closer still.

The man dashed between two giant cans that loomed like tanks above him. He threaded, racing, in between the silent bulks of all the clustered cans, past green and red and yellow sides all caked with livid smears. The spider had to climb above them, unable to move its swollen body rapidly enough between them. It slithered up the side of one, then sped across their metal tops, bridging the gaps between them with sudden, jerking hops.

As the man started out into the open again, he heard a scratching sound above. Recoiling and jerking back his head, he saw the spider just about to leap on him, two legs slipping down a metal side, the rest clutching at the top.

With a terrified gasp, the man dived again into the space between the giant cans, half running, half stumbling back along the winding route. Behind him, the spider drew itself back up to the top and, backing around in a twitching semicircle, started after him again.

The move gained seconds for the man. Plunging out into the shadow-swept sands again, he raced around the great stone pillar and through another stack of tanklike structures. The spider leaped down on the sand and scurried in pursuit.

The great orange mass loomed over the man now as he headed once more for the edge of the cliff. There was no time for hesitation. With an extra springing of his legs, he flung himself across the gulf and clutched with spastic fingers at the roughened ledge.

Wincing, he drew himself onto the splintered orange surface just as the spider reached the cliff's edge. Jumping up, the man began running along the narrow ledge, not looking back. If the spider jumped that gap, it was over.

The spider did not jump it. Glancing back, the man saw that and, stopping, stood there looking at the spider. Was he safe now that he was out of the spider's territory?

His pale cheek twitched as he saw thread-twined cable pour like shimmering vapor from the spider's tubes.

Twisting around, he began running again, knowing that, as soon as the cable was long enough, air currents would lift it, it would cling to the orange ledge, and the black spider would clamber up it.

He tried to run faster, but he couldn't. His legs ached, breath was a hot burning in his throat, a stitch drove dagger points into his side. He ran and skidded down the orange slope, jumping the gaps with desperate, weakening lunges.

Another edge. The man knelt quickly, tremblingly, and, holding tight, let himself over. It was a long drop to the next level. The man waited until his body was swinging inward, then let go. Just before he fell, he saw the great spider scrabbling down the orange slope at him.

He landed on his feet and toppled forward on the hard wood. Pain drove needles up his right ankle. He struggled to his feet; he couldn't stop. Overhead, he heard the spider's scratching. Running to the edge, he hesitated, then jumped into space again. The arm-thick curve of the metal wicket flashed up at him. He grabbed for it.

He fell with a fluttering of arms and legs. The canyon floor rushed up at him. He *had* to miss the flower-patched softness.

And yet he didn't. Almost at the edge of it, he landed feet first and bounced over backward in a neck-snapping somersault.

He lay on his stomach and chest, breathing in short, strangled bursts. There was a smell of dusty cloth in his nostrils, and fabric was rough against his cheek.

Alertness returned then and, with a spasmodic wrenching of muscles, the man looked up and saw another ghostlike cable being spun into the air. In a few moments, he knew, the spider would ride it down.

Pushing up with a groan, he stood a moment on trembling legs. The ankle still hurt, breathing was a strain, but there were no broken bones. He started off.

Hobbling quickly across the flower-splotched softness, the man lowered himself across the edge. As he did so, he saw the spider swinging down, a terrible, wriggling pendulum.

He was on the floor of the canyon now. He ran, limping, across the wide plain of it, his sandals flopping on the leveled hardness. To his right loomed the vast brown tower in which the flame still burned, the very canyon trembling with its roar.

He glanced behind. The spider was dropping to the flower-covered softness now, then rushing for the edge. The man raced on toward the great log pile, which was half as high as the tower itself. He ran by what looked like a giant, coiled serpent, red and still and open-jawed at either end.

The spider hit the canyon floor and ran at the man.

But the man had reached the gigantic logs now, and, falling forward on his chest, he wriggled into a narrow space between two of them. It was so narrow he could hardly move; dark, damp, cold, and smelling of moldy wood. He crawled and twisted in as far as he could, then stopped and looked back.

The black, shiny-cased spider was trying to follow him.

For a horrible moment, the man thought it was succeeding. Then he saw that it was stuck and had to pull back. It could not follow.

Closing his eyes, the man lay there on the canyon floor, feeling the chill of it through his clothes, panting through his opened mouth, wondering how many more times he would have to flee the spider.

The flame in the steel tower went out then, and there was

silence except for the spider's scratching at the rock floor as it moved about restlessly. He could hear it scraping on the logs as it clambered over them, searching for a way to get at him.

When at last the scratching sounds had gone, the man backed himself cautiously out from the narrow, splinter-edged passage between the logs. Out on the floor again, he stood with wary haste and looked in all directions to see where the spider was.

High up on the sheer wall he saw it climbing toward the cliff edge, its dark legs drawing its great egg of a body up the perpendicular face. A shaking breath trickled from the man's nostrils. He was safe for another while. Lowering his gaze, he started toward his sleeping place.

He limped slowly past the silent steel tower, which was an oil burner; past the huge red serpent, which was a nozzleless garden hose clumsily coiled on the floor; past the wide cushion whose case was covered with flower designs; past the immense orange structure, which was a stack of two wooden lawn chairs; past the great croquet mallets hanging in their racks. One of the wickets from the croquet set had been stuck in a groove on the top lawn chair. It was what the man, in his flight, had grabbed for and missed. And the tanklike cans were used paint cans, and the spider was a black widow.

He lived in a cellar.

Now he walked past the towering clothes tree toward his sleeping place, which was underneath a water heater. Just before he reached it, he twitched sharply as, in its concrete cave, the water pump lurched into spinning motion. He listened to its labored wheezing and sighing, which sounded like the breathing of a dying dragon.

Then he clambered up the cement block on which the looming, enamel-faced heater rested and crawled under its protective warmth.

For a long time, motionless, he lay on his bed, which was a rectangular sponge around which a torn handkerchief was wrapped. His chest rose and fell with shallow movements, his hands lay limp and curled at his sides. Without blinking, he stared up at the rust-caked bottom of the heater.

The last week.

Three words and a concept. A concept that had begun in a

flash of incomprehensive shock and become the intensely intimate moment-by-moment horror it now was. The last week. No, not even that now, because Monday was already half over. His eyes strayed briefly to the row of charcoal strokes on the wood scrap that was his calendar. Monday, March the tenth.

In six days he would be gone.

Across the vast reaches of the cellar, the oil-burner flame roared up again, and he felt the bed vibrate under him. That meant the temperature had fallen in the house above and that the thermostat had kicked a switch and now heat was flowing again through the floor grilles.

He thought of them up there, the woman and the little girl. His wife and daughter. Were they still that to him? Or had the element of size removed him from their sphere? Could he still be considered a part of their world when he was the size of a bug to them, when even Beth could crush him underfoot and never know it?

In six days he would be gone.

He'd thought about it a thousand times in the past year and a half, trying to visualize it. He'd never been able to. Invariably, his mind had rebelled against it, rationalizing: the injections would start to work now, the process would end by itself, *something* would happen. It was impossible that he could ever be so small that . . .

Yet he was; so small that in six days he would be gone.

When it came on him, this cruel despair, he would lie for hours on his makeshift bed, not caring whether he lived or died. The despair had never really gone. How could it? For no matter what adjustment he thought he was making, it was obviously impossible to adjust, because there had never been a tapering or a leveling off. The process had gone on and on, ceaseless.

He twisted on the bed in restless agony. Why did he run from the spider? Why not let it catch him? The thing would be out of his hands then. It would be a hideous death, but it would be quick; despair would be ended. And yet he kept fleeing from it, and improvising and struggling and existing.

Why?

68″

When he told her, the first thing she did was laugh.

It was not a long laugh. Almost instantly it had been choked off and she stood mutely before him, staring. Because he wasn't smiling, because his face was a taut blankness.

"Shrinking?" The word was spoken in a trembling whisper.

"Yes." It was all he could manage to say.

"But that's—"

She'd been about to say that was impossible. But it wasn't impossible, because now that the word had been spoken, it crystallized all the unspoken dread she'd felt since this had begun, a month before; since Scott's first visit to Dr. Branson, when he'd been checked for possible bowing of the legs or dropping of the arches, and the doctor's first diagnosis of loss of weight due to the trip and the new environment and his pushing aside of the possibility that Scott was losing height as well.

The dread had grown through the passing days of tense, frightened suspicion while Scott kept growing shorter; through the second visit to Branson and the third; through the X-rays and the blood tests; through the entire bone survey, the search for signs of bone-mass decrease, the search for a pituitary tumor; through the long days of more X-raying and the grim search for cancer. Through today and this moment.

"But that's impossible."

She had to say it. They were the only words her mind and lips would form.

He shook his head slowly, dazedly.

"It's what he said," he answered. "He said my height's decreased more than half an inch in the last four days." He swallowed. "But it's not just my height. I'm losing. Every part of me seems to be shrinking. Proportionately."

"No." There was adamant refusal in her voice. It was the only reaction she could make to such an idea. "That's *all?*" she asked, almost angrily. "That's all he can *say?*"

"Honey, it's what's *happening*," he said. "He showed me X-rays—the ones he took four days ago and the ones he took today. It's true. I'm shrinking." He spoke as though he'd been kicked violently in the stomach, half dazed, half breathless with shock.

"No!" This time she sounded more frightened than resolute. "We'll go to a specialist," she said.

"He wants me to," Scott said. "He said I should go to the Columbia Presbyterian Medical Center in New York. But—"

"Then you will," she said before he could go on.

"Honey, the *cost*," he said painfully. "We already owe—"

"What has that got to do with it? Do you think for one moment—"

A nervous tremor broke her words off. She stood trembling, arms crossed, her hands clutched at her goose-fleshed upper arms. It was the first time since it had started that she'd let him see how afraid she was.

"Lou." He put his arms around her. "It's all right, honey, it's all right."

"It isn't. You have to go to that center. You *have* to."

"All right, all right," he murmured, "I will."

"What did he say they'd do?" she asked, and he could hear the desperate need for hope in her voice.

"He . . ." He licked his lips, trying to remember. "Oh, he said they'd check my endocrine glands; my thyroid, pituitary—my sex glands. He said they'd give me a basal metabolism. Some other tests."

Her lips pressed in.

"If he knows that," she said, "why did he have to say what he did about—about shrinking? That's not good doctoring. It's thoughtless."

"Honey, I asked him," he said. "I established it when I started all the tests. I told him I didn't want any secrets. What else could he—"

"All *right*," she broke in. "But did he have to call it . . . what he did?"

"That's what it *is*, Lou," he said in anguish. "There's evidence for it. Those X-rays . . ."

"He could be wrong, Scott," she said. "He's not infallible."

He didn't say anything for a long moment. Then, quietly, he said, "Look at me."

When it had begun, he was a six-footer. Now he looked

straight across into his wife's eyes; and his wife was five feet, eight inches tall.

Hopelessly he dropped the fork on his plate.

"How can we?" he asked. "The cost Lou, the *cost*. It'll take at least a month's hospitalization; Branson said so. A month away from work. Marty's already upset as it is. How can I expect him to go on paying me my salary when I don't even—"

"Honey, your health comes first!" she said in a nerve-flaring voice. "Marty knows that. *You* know it."

He lowered his head, teeth clenched behind drawn lips. Every bill was a chain that weighed him down. He could almost feel the heavy links forged around his limbs.

"And what do we—" he began, stopping as he noticed Beth staring at him, her supper forgotten.

"Eat your food," Lou told her. Beth started a little, then dug her fork into a mound of gravy-topped potatoes.

"How do we pay for it?" Scott asked. "There's no medical insurance. I owe Marty five hundred dollars for the tests I've already taken." He exhaled heavily. "And the GI loan may not even go through."

"You're going," she said.

"Easily said," he answered.

"All right, what would you rather do?" she snapped with the temper of fear in her voice. "Forget it? Accept what the doctor said? Just sit back and—" A sob swallowed her words.

The hand he put over hers was not a comforting one. It was as cold and almost as shaky as hers.

"All right," he murmured. "All right, Lou."

Later, while she was putting Beth to bed, he stood in the darkened living room watching the cars drive by on the street below. Except for the murmuring voices in the back bedroom, there was no sound in the apartment. The cars swished and hummed past the building, their headlights probing ahead at the dark pavement.

He was thinking about his application for life insurance. It had been part of the plan in coming East. First working for his brother, then applying for a GI loan with the idea of becoming a junior partner in Marty's business. Acquiring life and medical insurance, a bank account, a decent car, clothes, eventually a house. Building a structure of security around himself and his family.

Now this, disrupting the plan. Threatening to destroy it altogether.

He didn't know at what precise second the question came to him. But suddenly it was terribly there and he was staring fixedly at his upheld, spread-fingered hands, his heart throbbing and swollen in an icy trap.

How long could he go on shrinking?

Chapter Three

FINDING WATER to drink was not a problem for him. The tank near the electric pump had a minute leak on its bottom surface. Beneath its dripping he placed a thimble he had carried once from a sewing box in a cardboard carton underneath the fuel-oil tank. The thimble was always overflowing with crystal well water.

It was food that was the problem now. The quarter loaf of stale bread he'd been eating for the last five weeks was gone now. He'd finished the last crunchy scraps of it for his evening meal, washed it down with water. Bread and cold water had been his diet since he'd been imprisoned in the cellar.

He walked slowly across the darkening floor, moving toward the white, cobwebbed tower that stood near the steps leading up to the closed cellar doors. The last of the daylight filtered through the grime-streaked windows—the one that overlooked the sand hills of the spider's territory, the one over the fuel tank, and the one over the log pile. The pale illumination fell in wide gray bars across the concrete floor, forming a patchwork of light and darkness through which he walked. In a little while the cellar would be a cold pit of night.

He had mused for many hours on the possibility of somehow managing to reach the string that dangled over the floor and pulling down on it so the dust-specked bulb would light, driving away the terror of blackness. But there was no way of reaching the string. It hung, for him, a hundred feet above his head, completely unattainable.

Scott Carey walked around the dull white vastness of the refrigerator. It had been stored there since they'd first moved to the house—was it only months before? It seemed a century.

It was the old-fashioned type of refrigerator, one whose coils were encased in a cylindrical enclosure on its top. There was an open box of crackers beside that cylinder. As far as he knew, it was the only food remaining in the entire cellar.

He'd known the cracker box was on the refrigerator even before he'd become trapped down there. He'd left it there himself one afternoon long before. No, not so long before, as time went. But, somehow, days seemed longer now. It was as if hours were designed for normal people. For anyone smaller, the hours were proportionately magnified.

It was an illusion, of course, but, in his tininess, he was plagued by manifold illusions: the illusion that he was not shrinking, but the world enlarging; the illusion that objects were what they were thought to be only when the person who thought of them was of normal size.

For him—he couldn't help it—the oil burner had virtually lost its role of heating apparatus. It was, almost actually, a giant tower in whose bowels there roared a magic flame. And the hose was, almost actually, a quiescent viper, sleeping in giant, scarlet coils. The three-quarter wall beside the burner *was* a cliff face, the sands a terrible desert across whose hills crawled not a spider the size of a man's thumbnail, but a venomous monster almost as tall as he was.

Reality was relative. He was more forcefully aware of it with every passing day. In six days reality would be blotted out for him—not by death, but a hideously simple act of disappearance.

For what reality could there be at zero inches?

Yet he went on. Here he was scanning the sheer face of the refrigerator, wondering how he might get up there and reach the crackers.

A sudden roar made him jump and spin around, his heart thudding.

It was only the oil burner leaping into life again, the rumble of its mechanism making the floor beneath him tremble, sending numbing vibrations up his legs. He swallowed with effort. It was a jungle life he led, each sound a warning of potential death.

It was getting too dark. The cellar was a frightening place when it was dark. He hurried across the chilled expanse of it, shivering under the tentlike robe he had made by poking a head hole in a piece of cloth, then ripping the edges into dangling strips and tying them into knots. The clothes he had been wearing when he had first tumbled into the cellar now lay in dirty heaps beside the water heater. He had worn them as long as he could, rolling up sleeves and cuffs, tightening the waistband, keeping them on until their sagging volume hampered movement. Then he had made the robe. He was always cold now except when he was under the water heater.

He broke into a nervous, hopping walk, suddenly anxious to be off the darkening floor. His gaze flew for a moment to the cliff edge high above and he twitched again, thinking he saw the spider clambering over. He'd started to run before he saw that it was only a shadow. His run slowed again to the erratic, jerky walk. Adjust? he thought. Who could adjust to this?

When he was back under the heater, he dragged a box top over his bed and lay down to rest underneath its shelter.

He was still shivering. He could smell the dry, acrid odor of the cardboard close to his face, and it seemed as if he were being smothered. It was another illusion he suffered nightly.

He struggled to attain sleep. He'd worry about the crackers tomorrow, when it was light. Or maybe he would not worry about them at all. Maybe he'd just lie there and let hunger and thirst finish what he could not finish, despite all dismays.

Nonsense! he thought furiously. If he hadn't done it before this, it wasn't likely that he could do it now.

64"

Louise guided the blue Ford around the wide, graded arc that led from Queens Boulevard to the Cross Island Parkway. There was no sound but the valve-knocking rumble of the motor. Idle conversation had faded off a quarter-mile after they'd emerged from the Midtown Tunnel. Scott had even jabbed in the shiny radio button and cut off the quiet music. Now he sat staring glumly through the windshield, vision glazed to all but thought.

The tension had begun long before Louise came to the Center to get him.

He'd been building himself up to it ever since he'd told the doctors that he was leaving. For that matter, the blocks of anger had been piling up from the moment he'd entered the Center. Dread of the financial burden had constructed the first one, a block whose core was the dragging weight of further insecurity. Each nerve-spent, fruitless day at the Center had added more blocks.

Then to have Louise not only angrily upset at his decision, but unable to hide her shock at seeing him three inches shorter than herself—it had been too much. He'd scarcely spoken from the moment she'd entered his room, and what he had said had been quiet, withdrawn, each sentence shackled by reserve.

Now they were driving past the understated richness of the Jamaica estates. Scott hardly noticed them. He was thinking about the impossible future.

"What?" he asked, starting a little.

"I said, did you have breakfast?"

"Oh. Yes. About eight, I guess."

"Are you hungry? Shall I stop?"

"No."

He glanced at her, at the tense indecision apparent on her face.

"Well, *say* it," he said. "Say it, for God's sake, and get it off your chest."

He saw the smooth flesh on her throat contract in a swallow.

"What is there to say?" she asked.

"That's right." He nodded in short, jerky movements. "That's right, make it sound like my fault. I'm an idiot who doesn't want to know what's wrong with himself. I'm—"

He was finished before he could get started. The undertow of nagging, unspoken dread in him swallowed all attempts at concentrated rage. Temper could come only in sporadic bursts to a man living with consistent horror.

"You know how I feel, Scott," she said.

"Sure I know how you feel," he said. "You don't have to pay the bills, though."

"I told you I'd be more than willing to work."

"There's no use arguing about it," he said. "Your working wouldn't help any. We'd still go under." He blew out a tired breath. "What's the difference anyway? They didn't find a thing."

"Scott, that doctor said it might take *months!* You didn't even let them finish their tests. How can you—"

"What do they think I'm going to do?" he burst out. "Go on letting them *play* with me? Oh, you haven't *been* there, you haven't *seen*. They're like kids with a new toy! A shrinking man, Godawmighty, a shrinking man! It makes their damn eyes light up. All they're interested in is my 'incredible catabolism.' "

"What difference does it make?" she asked. "They're still some of the best doctors in the country."

"And some of the most expensive," he countered. "If they're so damned fascinated, why didn't they offer to give me the tests free? I even asked one of them about it. You'd've thought I was insulting his mother's virtue."

She didn't say anything. Her chest rose and fell with disturbed breath.

"I'm tired of being tested," he went on, not wanting to sink into the comfortless isolation of silence again. "I'm tired of basal-metabolism tests and protein-bound tests; tired of drinking radioactive iodine and barium-powdered water; tired of X-rays and blood cultures and Geiger counters on my throat and having my temperature taken a million times a day. You haven't been through it; you don't know. It's like a—an inquisition. And what the hell's the point? They haven't found a thing. Not a *thing!* And they never will. And I can't see owing them thousands of dollars for nothing!"

He fell back against the seat and closed his eyes. Fury was unsatisfying when it was leveled against an undeserving subject. But it would not disappear for all that. It burned like a flame inside him.

"They weren't finished, Scott."

"The bills don't matter to you," he said.

"*You* matter to me," she answered.

"And who's the 'security' bug in this marriage, anyway?" he asked.

"That's not fair."

"Isn't it? What brought us here from California in the first place? Me? Because I decided I just had to go into business with Marty? I was happy out there. I didn't—" He drew in a shaking breath and let it empty from his lungs. "Forget it," he said. "I'm sorry, I apologize. But I'm not going back."

"You're angry and hurt, Scott. That's why you won't go back."

"I won't go back because it's pointless!" he shouted.

They drove in silence for a few miles. Then she said, "Scott, do you really believe I'd hold my own security above your health?"

He didn't answer.

"*Do* you?"

"Why talk about it?" he said.

The next morning, Saturday, he received the sheaf of application papers from the life-insurance company and tore them into pieces and threw the pieces in the wastebasket. Then he went for a long, miserable walk. And while he was out he thought about God creating heaven and earth in seven days.

He was shrinking a seventh of an inch a day.

It was quiet in the cellar. The oil burner had just shut itself off, the clanking wheeze of the water pump had been silenced for an hour. He lay under the cardboard box top listening to the silence, exhausted but unable to rest. An animal life without an animal mind did not induce the heavy, effortless sleep of an animal.

The spider came about eleven o'clock.

He didn't know it was eleven, but there was still the heavy thudding of footsteps overhead, and he knew Lou was usually in bed by midnight.

He listened to the sluggish rasping of the spider across the box top, down one side, up another, searching with terrible patience for an opening.

Black widow. Men called it that because the female destroyed and ate the male, if she got the chance, after the mating act.

Black widow. Shiny black, with the constricted rectangle of scarlet on its egg-shaped abdomen; what was called its "hourglass." A creature with a highly developed nervous system, possessing memory. A creature whose poison was twelve times as deadly as a rattlesnake's.

The black widow clambered over the box top under which he was hiding and the spider was almost as big as he. In a few days it *would* be as big; then, in another few days, bigger. The thought made him sick. How could he escape it then?

I have to get out of here! he thought desperately.

His eyes fell shut, his muscles clamping slowly in admission of his helplessness. He'd been trying to get out of the cellar for five weeks now. What chance had he now, when he was one sixth the size he'd been when he had first been trapped there?

The scratching came again, this time *under* the cardboard.

There was a slight tear in one side of the box top; enough to admit one of the spider's seven legs.

He lay there shuddering, listening to the spiny leg scratching at the cement like a razor on sandpaper. It never came closer than five inches from the bed, but it gave him nightmares. He clamped his eyes shut.

"Get out of here!" he screamed. "Get out of here, get *out* of here!"

His voice rang shrilly underneath the cardboard enclosure. It made his eardrums hurt. He lay there trembling violently while the spider scratched and jumped and clambered insanely around the box top, trying to get in.

Twisting around, he buried his face in the rough wrinkles of the handkerchief covering the sponge. If I could only kill it! his mind screamed in anguish. At least his last days would be peaceful then.

About an hour later, the scratching stopped and the spider went away. Once more he became conscious of his sweat-dewed flesh, the coldness and the twitching of his fingers. He lay drawing in convulsive breaths through his parted lips, weak from the rigid struggle against horror.

Kill it? The thought turned his blood to ice.

A little while later he sank into a troubled, mumbling sleep, and his night was filled with the torment of awful dreams.

Chapter Four

HIS EYES fluttered open.

Instinct alone told him that the night was over. Beneath the box it was still dark. With an indrawn groan in his chest, he pushed up from the sponge bed and stood gingerly until he shouldered the cardboard surface. Then he edged to one corner and, pushing up hard, slid the box top away from his bed.

Out in the other world, it was raining. Gray light sifted through the erratic dripping across the panes, converting the shadows into slanting wavers and the patches of light into quiverings of pallid gelatine.

The first thing he did was climb down the cement block and walk over to the wooden ruler. It was the first thing he did every morning. The ruler stood against the wheels of the huge yellow lawnmower, where he'd put it.

He pressed himself against its calibrated surface and laid his right hand on top of his head. Then, leaving the hand there, he stepped back and looked.

Rulers were not divided into sevenths; he had added the markings himself. The heel of his hand obscured the line that told him he was five-sevenths of an inch tall.

The hand fell, slapping at his side. Why, what did you expect? his mind inquired. He made no reply. He just wondered why he tortured himself like this every day, persisting in this clinical masochism. Surely he didn't think that it was going to stop now; that the injections would begin working at this last point. Why, then? Was it part of his previous resolution to follow the descent to its very end? If so, it was pointless now. No one else would know of it.

He walked slowly across the cold cement. Except for the faint tapping, swishing sound of the rain on the windows, it was quiet in the cellar. Somewhere far off there was a hollow drumming sound; probably the rain on the cellar doors. He walked on, his gaze moving automatically to the cliff edge, searching for the spider. It was not there.

He trudged under the jutting feet of the clothes tree and to the twelve-inch step to the floor of the vast, dark cave in which the tank and water pump were. Twelve inches, he thought, lowering himself slowly down the string ladder he'd made and fastened to the brick that stood at the top of the step. Twelve inches, and yet to him it was the equivalent of 150 feet to a normally sized man.

He let himself down the ladder carefully, his knuckles banging and scraping against the rough concrete. He should have thought of a way to keep the ladder from pressing directly against the wall. Well, it was too late for that now; he was too small. As it was, he could, even with painful stretching, barely reach the sagging rung below, the one below that . . . the one below that.

Grimacing, he splashed icy water into his face. He could just about reach the top of the thimble. In two days he would be unable to reach the top of it, probably unable, even, to get down the string ladder. What would he do then?

Trying not to think of ever-mounting problems, he drank palmfuls of the cold well water; drank until his teeth ached. Then he dried his face and hands on the robe and turned back to the ladder.

He had to stop and rest halfway up the ladder. He hung there, arms hooked over the rung, which to him was the thickness of rope.

What if the spider were to appear at the top of the ladder now? What if it were to come clambering down the ladder at him?

He shuddered. Stop it, he begged his mind. It was bad enough when he actually had to protect himself from the spider without filling the rest of the time with cruel imaginings.

He swallowed again, fearfully. It was true. His throat hurt.

"Oh, God," he muttered. It was all he needed.

He climbed up the rest of the way in grim silence, then started on the quarter-mile journey to the refrigerator. Around the hulking coils of the hose, by the tree-thick rake handle, the house-high lawn-mower wheels, the wicker table that was half as high as the refrigerator, which was, in turn, as high as a ten-story building. Already hunger was beginning to send out lines of tension in his stomach.

He stood, head pulled back, looking up at the refrigerator. If there had been clouds floating by its cylinder top, its mountain-peak remoteness could not have been more graphically apparent to him.

His gaze dropped. He started to sigh, but the sigh was cut off by a twitching grunt. The oil burner again, shaking the floor. He could never get used to it. It had no regular pattern of roaring ignition. What was worse, it seemed to be growing louder every day.

For what seemed a long time he stood indecisively, staring at the white piano legs of the refrigerator. Then he stirred himself loose from bleak apathy and drew in a quick breath. There was no point in standing there. Either he got to those crackers or he starved.

He circled the end of the wicker table, planning.

Like a mountain peak, the top of the refrigerator was attainable by numerous routes, none of them easy. He might try to scale the ladder, which, like the lawn mower, lay against the fuel-oil tank. Reaching the top of the tank (an Everest of achievement in itself), he could move to the huge cardboard boxes piled beside it, then across the wide leather face of Louise's suitcase, then up the hanging rope to the refrigerator top. Or he could try climbing the red cross-legged table, then jump across to the cartons, move across the suitcase again, and up the rope. Or he could try the wicker table which was right next to the refrigerator, achieve its summit, then climb the long, perilous length of the hanging rope.

He turned away from the refrigerator and looked across the cellar at the cliff wall, the croquet set, the stacked lawn chairs, the gaudily striped beach umbrella, the olive-colored folding canvas stools. He stared at all of them with hopeless eyes.

Was there no other way? Was there nothing to eat but those crackers?

His gaze moved slowly along the cliff edge. There was the one dry slice of bread remaining up there; but he knew he couldn't go after it. Dread of the spider was too strong in him. Even hunger couldn't drive him up that cliff again.

He thought suddenly, Were spiders edible? It made his stomach rumble. He forced the thought out of his mind and turned again to face the immediate problem.

He couldn't manage the climb unaided, and that was the first hurdle.

He walked across the floor, feeling the chill of it through his almost worn sandals. Under the shadows of the fuel tank, he climbed between the ragged edges of the split carton side. What if the spider is in there waiting? he thought. He stopped, heartbeat jolting, one leg inside the box, the other leg out. He drew in a deep, courage-stiffening breath. It's only a spider, he told himself. It's not a master tactician.

Climbing the rest of the way into the musty depth of the carton, he wished he could really believe that the spider were not intelligent, but driven only by instinct.

Reaching for thread, his hand touched icy metal and jerked back. He reached again. It was only a pin. His lips twitched. Only a pin? It was the size of a knight's lance.

He found the thread and laboriously unrolled about eight inches of it. It took an entire minute of pulling, jerking, and teeth gnawing to separate it from its barrel-sized spool.

He dragged the thread out of the carton and back to the wicker table. Then he hiked over to the pile of logs and tore from one of them a piece the size of his arm from elbow to fingertips. This he carried back to the table and fastened to the thread.

He was ready.

The first throw was an easy one. Twisting vinelike around the main leg of the table were two narrower strips about the thickness of his body. At a point three inches below the first shelf of the table these two strips flared out from the leg, angling up to the shelf, then turning again and, three inches above the shelf, twining about the main leg again.

He flung the wood up at the space where one of the strips began jutting out from the leg. On his third attempt the wood sailed through the opening and he pulled it back carefully so that it was wedged between leg and strip. He then climbed up, feet braced on the leg as he ascended, body swung out at the end of the tautened thread.

Reaching the first point, he hauled up the thread, worked the wooden bar loose, and prepared for the next stage of his climb.

Another four throws and the wooden bar caught between two strips of the latticework shelf. He pulled himself up.

Stretched out limply on the shelf, he lay there panting.

Then, after a few minutes, he sat up and looked down at what to him was a fifty-foot drop. Already he was tired, and the climb had barely started.

Far across the cellar the pump began its sibilant chugging again, and he listened to it while he looked up at the wide canopy of the tabletop a hundred feet above.

"Come on," he muttered hoarsely to himself then. "Come on, come on, come on, come on."

He got to his feet. Taking a deep breath, he flung the stick up at the next joining place of leg and twining strip.

He had to leap aside as the throw missed and the wood fell toward him heavily. His right leg slipped into a gap in the latticework and he had to clutch at the crosspieces to keep from plunging to the floor below.

He hung there for a long moment, one leg dangling in space. Then, groaning, he pulled and pushed himself to a standing position, wincing at the pain in the back muscles of his right leg. He must have sprained it, he thought. He clenched his teeth and hissed out a long breath. Sore throat, sprained leg, hunger, weariness. What next?

It took twelve muscle-jerking throws of the wooden bar to get it into the proper opening above. Pulling back until the thread grew taut in his grip, he dragged himself up the thirty-five-foot space, teeth gritted, breath steaming out between them. He ignored each burning ache of muscle while he climbed; but when he reached the crotch, he wedged himself between the table leg and strip and half lay, half clung there, gasping for air, muscles throbbing visibly. I'll have to rest, he told himself. Can't go on. The cellar swam before his eyes.

He had gone to visit his mother the week he was five-feet-three. The last time he'd seen her, he'd been six feet tall.

Dread crawled in him, colder than the winter wind, as he walked up the Brooklyn street toward the two-family brownstone where his mother lived. Two boys were playing ball in the street. One of them missed the other's throw. The ball bounced toward Scott, and he reached down to pick it up.

The boy shouted, "Throw it here, kid!"

Something like an electric shock jolted through his system. He flung the ball violently.

The boy shouted, "Good throw, kid!"

He walked on, ashen-faced.

And the terrible hour with his mother. He remembered that.

The way she kept avoiding the obvious, talking about Marty and Therese and their son, Billy; about Louise and Beth, about the quietly enjoyable life she was able to live on Marty's monthly checks.

She had set the table in her impeccable way, each dish and cup in its proper place, each cookie and cake arranged symmetrically. He sat down with her, feeling hollowly sick, the coffee scorching his throat, the cookies tasteless in his mouth.

Then, finally, when it was too late, she had spoken of it. This thing, she said—he was being treated for it?

He knew exactly what it was she wanted to hear and he mentioned the Center and the tests. Relief pressed out the extra worry lines in the rose-petal skin of her face. Good, she said, good. The doctors would cure him. The doctors knew everything these days; everything.

And that was all.

As he went home, he felt dazedly ill, because of all the reactions she might have shown to his affliction, the one she had shown was the last one in the world he could have imagined.

Then, when he got home, Louise cornered him in the kitchen, insisting that he go back to the Center to finish the tests. She'd work, they'd put Beth in a nursery. It would work out fine. Her voice was firm in the beginning, obdurate; then it broke and all the withheld terror and unhappiness flooded from her.

He stood by her side, arm around her back, wanting to comfort her but able only to look up at her face and struggle futilely against the depleted feeling he had at being so much shorter than she. All right, he'd told her, all right, I'll go back. I will. Don't cry.

And the next morning the letter arrived from the Center, telling him that "because of the unusual nature of your disorder, the investigation of which might prove of inestimable value to medical knowledge," the doctors were willing to continue the tests free of charge.

And the return to the Center; he remembered that. And the discovery.

Scott blinked his eyes back into focus.

Sighing, he pushed himself to a standing position, one supporting hand holding onto the table leg.

From that point on, the two twining strips left the leg entirely and flared up at opposing angles, paralleled by bolstering spars until they reached the bottom side of the tabletop. Along each upward sweep, three vertical rods were spaced like giant banisters. He would not need the thread any more.

He started up the seventy-degree incline, first lurching at the vertical rod and, catching hold of it, pulled himself up to it, sandals slipping and squeaking along the spar. Then he lunged up at the next spar and pulled himself to it. By concentrating on the strenuous effort he was able to blank away all thoughts and sink into a mechanical apathy for many minutes, only the gnawing of hunger tending to remind him of his plight.

At last, puffing, breath scratching hotly at his throat, he reached the end of the incline and sat there wedged between the spar and the last vertical rod, staring at the wide overhang of the tabletop.

His face tightened.

"No." The mutter was a crusty, dry sound as his pain-smitten eyes looked around. There was a three-foot jump to the bottom edge of the tabletop. But there was no handhold there.

"No!"

Had he come all this way for nothing? He couldn't believe it, wouldn't let himself believe it. His eyes fell shut. I'll push myself off, he thought. I'll let myself fall to the floor. This is too much.

He opened his eyes again, the small bones under his cheeks moving as he ground his teeth together. He wasn't going to push himself off anything. If he fell, it would be in jumping for the edge of the tabletop. He wasn't going down by his own volition under any circumstances.

He clambered along the top of the horizontal spar just below the tabletop, searching. There had to be a way. There *had* to be.

Turning the corner of the spar, he saw it.

Running along the under edge of the tabletop was a strip of wood about double the thickness of his arm. It was fastened to the tabletop with nails a trifle shorter than he was.

Two of these nails had pulled out, and at that point the strip sagged about a quarter of an inch below the tabletop edge. A quarter of an inch—almost three feet to him. If he could jump to that gap he could catch hold of the strip and have a chance to pull himself up to the top of the table.

He perched there, breathing deeply, staring at the sagging strip and at the space he'd have to jump. It was at least four feet to him. Four feet of empty space.

He licked his dry lips. Outside, the rain was falling harder; he heard its heavy splattering at the windowpanes. Swirls of graying light swam on his face. He looked across the quarter-mile that separated him from the window over the log pile. The way the rain water ran twistingly over the glass panes made it appear as if great, hollow eyes were watching him.

He turned away from that. There was no use in standing here. He *had* to eat. Going back down now was out of the question. He had to go on.

He braced himself for the leap. It may be now, he thought, strangely unalarmed. This may be the end of my long, fantastic journey.

His lips pressed together. "So be it," he whispered then, and sprang out into space.

His arms banged so hard on the wooden bar that they were almost numbed beyond the ability to hold. I'm falling! his mind screamed. Then his arms wrapped themselves around the wood and he hung there gasping, legs swinging back and forth over the tremendous void.

He dangled there for a long moment, catching his breath, letting feeling return to his arms. Then, carefully, with agonizing slowness, he turned himself around on the bar so that he faced the spar arrangement. That done, he dragged himself up to a sitting position on the bar, holding on overhead for support. He sat there, limbs palsied with exhaustion.

The last step to the tabletop was the hardest.

He'd have to stand up on the smooth, circular top of the bar and, lurching up, throw his arm over the end of the tabletop. As far as he knew, there would be nothing there to hang onto. It would be entirely a matter of pressing his arms and hands so tightly to the surface that friction would hold him there.

Then he'd have to climb over the edge.

For a moment the entire grotesque spectacle of it swept over him forcibly—the insanity of a world where he could be killed trying to climb to the top of a table that any normal man could lift and carry with one hand.

He let it go. Forget it, he ordered himself.

He drew in long breaths until the shaking of his arm and leg muscles slackened. Then slowly he eased himself up to a crouch on the smooth wood, balancing himself by holding onto the bottom edge of the tabletop.

The bottoms of his sandals were too smooth. He couldn't grip the wood well enough. As cold as it was, he'd have to take them off. Gingerly he shook them off one at a time and, after a moment, heard the faint slap as they struck the floor below.

He wavered for a moment, steadied himself, then drew in a long, chest-filling breath. He paused.

Now.

He lunged up into empty air and slapped his arms across the end of the tabletop. A broad vista of huge, piled-up objects met his eyes. Then he began slipping, and he clutched at the wood, digging his nails into it. He kept sliding toward the edge, his body moving into space, dragging him.

"No," he whimpered in a strangled voice.

He managed to lurch forward again, fingertips scraping at the wood surface, arms pressing down tightly, desperately.

He saw the curving metal rod.

It was hanging a quarter of an inch from his fingers. He had to reach it or he'd fall. Leaving one hand down, splinters gouging under its nails, he raised the other hand toward the rod.

Look out!

His raised hand slapped down again and clawed frantically at the wood. He began slipping back again.

With a last, frenzied lunge, he grabbed for the curving rod and his hands clamped over its icy thickness.

He dragged himself, kicking and struggling, over the edge

of the tabletop. Then his hands dropped from the metal—which was the hanging handle of a paint can—and he collapsed heavily on his chest and stomach.

He lay there for a long time, unable to move, shaking with the remains of dread and exertion, sucking in lungfuls of the cold air. I made it, he thought. It was all he could think. I made it, I made it!

As exhausted as he was, it gave him a warming pride to think it.

Chapter Five

AFTER A WHILE he got up shakily and looked around.

The tabletop's expanse was littered with massive paint cans, bottles and jars. Scott walked along their mammoth shapes, stepping over the jagged-toothed edge of a saw blade and racing acrosss its icy surface to the tabletop again.

Orange paint. He strode past the luridly streaked can, the top of his head barely as high as the bottom edge of the can's label. He remembered painting the lawn chairs during one of the many hours he'd spent in the cellar before his last, irrevocable, snow-caked plunge into it.

Head back, he gazed up at an orange-spotted brush handle sticking out of an elephantine jar. One day—not so long ago—he'd held that handle in his fingers. Now it was ten times as long as he was; a huge, knife-pointed length of glossy yellow wood.

There was a loud clicking noise and then the ocean-like roar of the oil burner filled the air again. His heartbeat raced, then slowed once more. No, he'd never get used to its thundering suddenness. Well, there'd be only four more days of it, anyway, he thought.

His feet were getting cold; there was no time to waste. Between the barren hulks of paint cans he walked until he'd reached the body-thick rope that hung down in twisted loops from the top of the refrigerator.

A stroke of fortune. He found a crumpled pink rag lying next to a towering brown bottle of turpentine. Impulsively he drew part of it around himself, tucked it under his feet, then sank back into the rest of its wrinkled softness. The cloth reeked of paint and turpentine, but that didn't matter. The held-in warmth of his body began surrounding him comfortingly.

Reclining there, he squinted up at the distant refrigerator top. There was still the equivalent of a seventy-five foot climb to make, and without footholds except for those he could manage to find on the rope itself. He would, virtually, have to pull himself all the way up.

His eyes closed and he lay there for a while, breathing slowly, his body as relaxed as possible. If the hunger pangs had not been so severe, he might have gone to sleep. But hunger was a wavelike pressure at his stomach walls, causing it to rumble emptily. He wondered if it could possibly be as empty as it felt.

When he discovered himself beginning to dwell on thoughts of food—of gravy-dripping roasts and broiled steaks inundated with brown-edged mushrooms and onions—he knew it was time to get up. With a last wiggle of his warmed toes, he threw off the smooth covering and stood.

That was when he recognized the cloth.

It was part of Louise's slip, an old one that she'd torn up and thrown into the rag box. He picked up a corner of it and fingered its softness, a strange, yearning pain in his chest and stomach that was not hunger.

"Lou." He whispered it, staring at the cloth that had once rested against her warm, fragrant flesh.

Angrily he flung away the cloth edge, his face a hardened mask. He kicked at it.

Shaken, he turned from the cloth, walked stiffly to the edge of the table, and grabbed hold of the rope. It was too thick to get his hands around; he'd have to use his arms. Luckily, it was hanging in such a way that he could almost crawl up the first section of it.

He pulled down on it as hard as he could to see if it was secure. It gave a trifle, then tautened. He pulled again. There was no further give. That ended any chance of dragging the cracker box off the refrigerator. The box was resting on top of the rope coils up there, and he'd thought it a vague possibility that he might pull it down.

"Well," he said.

And, taking a deep breath, he started climbing again.

He modeled his ascent on the method South Sea natives use in climbing coconut trees—knees high, body arched out, feet gripping at the rope, arms curled around it, fingers clutching. He kept himself moving upward steadily, not looking down.

He gasped and stiffened against the rope spasmodically as it slipped down a few inches—to him, a few feet. Then it stopped and he hung there trembling, the rope swinging back and forth in little arcs.

After a few moments the motion stopped and he began climbing again, this time more cautiously.

Five minutes later he reached the first loop of the hanging rope and eased himself into it. As if it were a swing, he sat there, holding on tightly, leaning back against the refrigerator. The surface of it was cold, but his robe was thick enough to prevent the coldness from penetrating to his skin.

He looked out across the broad vista of the cellar kingdom in which he lived. Far across—almost a mile away—he saw the cliff edge, the stacked lawn chairs, the croquet set. His gaze shifted. There was the vast cavern of the water pump, there the mammoth water heater; underneath it one edge of his box-top shield was visible.

His gaze moved and he saw the magazine cover.

It was lying on a cushion on top of the cross-legged metal table that stood beside the one whose top he'd just left. He hadn't noticed the magazine before because the paint cans had blocked it from view. On the cover was the photograph of a woman. She was tall, passably beautiful, leaning over on a rock, a look of pleasure on her young face. She was wearing a tight red long-sleeved sweater and a pair of clinging black shorts cut just below the hips.

He stared at the enormous figure of the woman. She was looking at him, smiling.

It was strange, he thought as he sat there, bare feet dangling in space. He hadn't been conscious of sex for a long time. His body had been something to keep alive, no more—something to feed and clothe and keep warm. His existence in the cellar, since that winter day, had been devoted to one thing—survival. All subtler gradations of desire had been lost to him. Now he had found the fragment of Louise's slip and seen the huge photograph of the woman.

His eyes ran lingeringly over the giant contours of her body—the high, swelling arches of her breasts, the gentle hill of her stomach, the long, curving taper of her legs.

He couldn't take his eyes off the woman. The sunlight was glinting on her dark auburn hair. He could almost sense the feeling of it, soft and silklike. He could almost feel the perfumed warmth of her flesh, almost feel the curved smoothness of her legs as mentally he ran his hands along them. He could almost feel the gelatinous give of her breasts, the sweet taste of her lips, her breath like warm wine trickling in his throat.

He shuddered helplessly, swaying on his loop of rope.

"Oh, God," he whispered. "Oh, God, God, God."

There were so many hungers.

49″

When he came out of the bathroom, damply warm from a shower and shave, he found Lou sitting on the living-room couch, knitting. She'd turned off the television set and there was no sound but the infrequent swish of cars passing in the street below.

He stood in the doorway a moment, looking at her.

She was wearing a yellow robe over her nightgown. Both garments were made of silk, clinging to the jut of her rounded breasts, the broadness of her hips, the smooth length of her legs. Electric prickling coursed the lower muscles of his stomach. It had been so long, canceled endlessly by medical tests and work and the weight of constant dread.

Lou looked up, smiling. "You look so nice and clean," she said.

It was not the words or the look on her face; but, suddenly he was terribly conscious of his size. Lips twitching into the semblance of a smile, he walked over to the couch and sat down beside her, instantly sorry that he had.

She sniffed. "Mmm, you smell nice," she said. She was referring to his shaving lotion.

He grunted quietly, glancing at her clean-featured face, her wheat-colored hair drawn back into a ribbon-tied horse's tail.

"You *look* nice," he said. "Beautiful."

"Beautiful!" she scoffed. "Not me."

He leaned over abruptly and kissed her warm throat. She raised her left hand and stroked his cheek slowly.

"So nice and smooth," she murmured.

He swallowed. Was it just ego-flattened imagination, or was she actually talking to him as if he were a boy? His left hand, which had been lying across the heat of her leg, drew back slowly, and he looked at the white, glazed-skinned band across the bottom of its third finger. He'd been forced to take the ring off almost two weeks before because the finger had become too thin.

He cleared his throat. "What are you making?" he asked disinterestedly.

"Sweater for Beth," she answered.

"Oh."

He sat there in silence while he watched her skillful manipulation of the long knitting needles. Then, impulsively, he laid his cheek against her shoulder. Wrong move, his mind said instantly. It made him feel even smaller, like a young boy leaning on his mother. He stayed there, though, thinking it would be too obviously awkward if he straightened up immediately. He felt that even rise and fall of her breathing as he rested there, a tensed, unresolved sensation in his stomach.

"Why don't you go to sleep?" Lou asked quietly.

His lips pressed together. He felt a cold shudder move down his back.

"No," he said.

Imagination again? Or was his voice as frail as it sounded to him, as devoid of masculinity. He stared somberly at the V-neck of her robe, at the flesh-walled valley between her breasts, and his fingers twitched with his repressed desire to touch her.

"Are you tired?" she asked.

"No." It sounded too harsh. "A little," he amended.

"Why don't you finish up the ice cream?" she asked, after a pause.

He closed his eyes with a sigh. Imagination it might be, but that didn't prevent him from feeling like a boy—indecisive, withdrawn, much as though he'd conceived the ridiculous notion that he could somehow arouse the physical desire of this full-grown woman.

"Shall I get it for you?" she asked.

"No!" He lifted his head from her shoulder and fell back heavily against a pillow, staring morosely across the room. It was a cheerless room. Their furniture was still stored in Los Angeles and they were using Marty's attic castoffs. A depressing room, the walls a dark forest green, pictureless, only one window with ugly paper drapes, a pale, thread-worn rug hiding part of the scratched floor.

"What is it, darling?" she asked.

"Nothing."

"Have I done something?"

"No."

"What, then?"

"*Nothing*, I said."

"All right," she said quietly.

Was she unaware of it? Granted it was torture for her to be living with terrible anxiety, hoping each second to get that phone call from the Center, a telegram, a letter, and the message never coming. Still . . .

He looked at her full body again, feeling breath catch in him uncontrollably. It wasn't just physical desire; it was so much more. It was the dread of tomorrows without her. It was the horror of his plight, which no words could capture.

For it wasn't a sudden accident removing him from her life. It wasn't a sudden illness taking him, leaving the memory of him intact, cutting him from her love with merciful swiftness. It wasn't even a lingering sickness. At least then he'd be himself and, although she could watch him with pity and terror, at least she would be watching the man she knew.

This was worse; far worse.

Month after month would go by—almost a year of them still if the doctors didn't stop it. A year of living together day by day, while he shrank. Eating meals together, sleeping in the same bed together, talking together, while he shrank. Caring for Beth and listening to music and seeing each other every day, while he shrank. Each day a new incident, a new hideous adjustment to make. The complex pattern of their relationship altered day by day, while he shrank.

They would laugh, unable to keep a long face every single moment of every single day. There would be laughter, perhaps, at some joke—a forgetful moment of amusement. Then suddenly the horror would rush over them again like black ocean across a dike, the laughter choked, the amusement crushed. The trembling realization that he was shrinking covering them again, casting a pall over their days and nights.

"Lou."

She turned to face him. He leaned over to kiss her, but he couldn't reach her lips. With an angry, desperate motion he pushed up on one knee on the couch and thrust his right hand into the silky tangle of her hair, fingertips pressing at her skull. Pulling back her head with a tug, he jammed his lips on hers and forced her back against the pillow.

Her lips were taut with surprise. He heard her knitting thud on the floor, heard the liquid rustle of silk as she twisted slightly in his grip. He ran a shaking hand across the yielding softness of her breasts. He pulled away his parted lips and pressed them against her throat, slowly raking teeth across the warm flesh.

"Scott!" she gasped.

The way she said it seemed to drain him in an instant. A barren chill covered him. He drew back from her, feeling almost ashamed. His hands fell from her body.

"Honey, what *is* it?" she said.

"You don't know, do you?" He was shocked by the trembling sound of his own voice.

His hands went up quickly to his cheeks and he saw in her eyes that she suddenly knew.

"Oh, *sweetheart*," she said, bending forward. Her warm lips pressed at his. He sat there stiffly. The caress and the tone of voice and the kiss—they were not the passionate caress and tone and kiss of a woman who craved her husband's want. They were the sounds and touches of a woman who felt only loving pity for a poor creature who desired her.

He turned away.

"Honey, don't," she begged, taking hold of his hand. "How could I know? There hasn't been a bit of lovemaking between us in the last two months; not a kiss or an embrace or—"

"There wasn't exactly time for it," he said.

"But that's the whole point," she said. "How could I help but be surprised? Is it so odd?"

His throat contracted with a dry, clicking sound.

"I suppose," he said, barely audible.

"Oh, honey." She kissed his hand. "Don't make it sound as if I—turned you away."

He let breath trickle out slowly from his nostrils.

"I guess it . . . would be rather grotesque, anyway," he said, trying to sound detached. "The way I look. It'd be like—"

"Honey, please." She wouldn't let him finish. "You're making it worse than it is."

"Look at me," he said. "How much worse can it get?"

"Scott. *Scott.*" She pressed his small hand to her cheek. "If only I could say something to make it all right."

He stared past her, unable to meet her eyes. "It's not your fault," he said.

"Oh, why don't they *call*? Why don't they *find* it?"

He knew then that his desire was impossible. He'd been a fool even to think of it.

"Hold me, Scott," she said.

He sat motionless for a few seconds, chin down, the fixed dullness of his eyes sealing the mask of defeat that was his face. Then he drew back his right hand and slid it behind her; it seemed as if the hand would never reach her other side. His stomach muscles flexed in slowly. He wanted to get up from the couch and leave. He felt puny and absurd beside her, a ludicrous midget who had planned the seduction of a normal woman. He sat there stiffly, feeling the warmth of her body through the silk. And he'd rather have died than tell her that the weight of her arm across his shoulders was hurting him.

"We could . . . work it out," she suggested in a different voice. "We—"

His head twisted back and forth in erratic motions as though he were looking for escape. "Oh, stop it, will you? Let it go. Forget it. I was a fool to . . ."

His right hand pulled back and clamped tensely on the knuckles of his left hand. He squeezed until it hurt. "Just let it go," he said. "Let it go."

"Honey, I'm not just saying it to be nice," she protested. "Don't you think I—"

"No, I *don't!*" he answered sharply. "And you don't, either."

"Scott, I know you're hurt, but . . ."

"Please forget it." His eyes were shut, and the words came softly, warningly through clenched teeth.

She was still. He breathed as though he were suffocating. The room was a crypt of futility to him.

"All right," she whispered then.

He bit his lower lip. He said, "Have you written your parents?"

"My parents?" He knew she was staring at him curiously.

"I think it might be wise," he said, holding his voice in careful check. He shrugged ineffectually. "Find out about staying with them. You know."

"I *don't* know, Scott."

"Well . . . don't you think it's a good idea to make some recognition of the facts?"

"Scott, what are you trying to do?"

He lowered his chin to hide the quick swallowing movement in his throat. "I'm trying," he said, "to plan some disposition of you and Beth in the event—"

"Disposition! What are we—"

"Will you stop interrupting me?"

"You said disposition! What are we—bric-a-brac to be disposed of?"

"I'm trying to be realistic about this!"

"You're trying to be cruel about it! Just because I didn't know that you—"

"Oh, stop it, stop it. I can see there's no point in trying to be realistic."

"All right, we'll be realistic," she said, face tense with repressed anger. "Are you suggesting that I leave you and take Beth with me? Is that your idea of being realistic?"

His hands twitched in his lap.

"And what if they don't find it?" he said. "What if they *never* find it?"

"You think I should leave you, then," she said.

"I think it might be a good idea," he said.

"Well, I don't!"

And she was crying, hands spread across her face, tears trickling out between the fingers. He sat there feeling numbed and helpless, looking at her trembling shoulders.

"I'm sorry, Lou," he said. He didn't sound it.

She couldn't answer; her throat and chest were too tight with breath-shaking sobs.

"Lou. I . . ." He reached out a lifeless hand and put it on her leg. "Don't cry. I'm not worth that."

She shook her head as if at a great, unanswerable problem. She sniffed and brushed at her tears.

"Here," he muttered, handing her the handkerchief from his robe pocket. She took it without a word and pressed it against her wet cheeks.

"I'm sorry," she said.

"You have nothing to be sorry for," he said. "It's me. I got angry because I felt foolish and—stupid."

And now, he thought, he was inclined in the other direction—toward self-castigation, toward self-indulgent martyrdom. The mind troubled was capable of manifold inversions.

"No." She pressed his fingers briefly. "I had no right to—" She let the sentence hang. "I'll try to be more understanding."

For a moment her gaze rested on the white-skinned patch where his wedding ring had been. Then, with a sigh, she rose.

"I'll get ready for bed," she said.

He watched her walk across the room and disappear into the hallway. He heard her footsteps, then the clicking of the lock on the bathroom door. With slow-motion actions he got on his feet and went into the bedroom.

He lay there in the darkness, staring at the ceiling.

Poets and philosophers could talk all they wanted to about a man's being more than fleshly form, about his essential worth, about the immeasurable stature of his soul. It was rubbish.

Had they ever tried to hold a woman with arms that couldn't reach around her? Had they ever told another man they were as good as he—and said it to his belt buckle?

She came into the bedroom, and in the darkness he heard the crisp rustle of her robe as she took it off and put it across the foot of the bed. Then the mattress gave on her side as she sat down. She drew her legs up and he heard her head thump back softly on her pillow. He lay there tensely, waiting for something.

After a moment there was a whispering of silk and he felt her reaching hand touch his chest.

"What's that?" she asked softly.

He didn't say.

She pushed up on her elbow. "Scott, it's your *ring*," she said. He felt the thin chain cutting slightly into the back of his neck as she fingered the ring. "How long have you been wearing it?" she asked.

"Since I took it off," he said.

There was a moment's silence. Then her love-filled voice broke over him.

"Oh, darling!" Her arms slipped demandingly around him, and suddenly he felt the silk-filmed heat of her body pressing against him. Her lips fell searchingly on his, and her fingertips drew in like cat claws on his back, sending icy tingles along the flesh.

And suddenly it was back, all the forced-down hunger in him exploding with a soundless, body-seizing violence. His hands fled across her burning skin, clutching and caressing. His mouth was an open shiver under hers. The darkness came alive, a sabled aura of heat crawling on their twining limbs. Words were gone; communication had become a thing of groping pressures, a thing felt in their blood, in the liquid torments rising, sweetly fierce. Words were needless. Their bodies spoke a surer language.

And when, too soon, it had ended and the night had fallen black and heavy on his mind, he slept, content, in the warm encirclement of her arms. And for the measure of a night there was peace, there was forgetfulness. For him.

Chapter Six

He clung to the edge of the open cracker box, looking in with dazed, unbelieving eyes.

They were ruined.

He stared at the impossible sight—cobweb-gauzed, dirty, moldy, water-soaked crackers. He remembered now, too late, that the kitchen sink was directly overhead, that there was a faulty drainpipe on it, that water dripped into the cellar every time the sink was used.

He couldn't speak. There were no words terrible enough to express the mind-crazing shock he felt.

He kept staring, mouth ajar, a vacuous look immobile on his face. I'll die now, he thought. In a way, it was a peaceful outlook. But stabbing cramps of hunger crowded peace away, and thirst was starting to add an extra pain and dryness to his throat.

His head shook fitfully. No, it was impossible, impossible that he should have come so far to have it end like this.

"No," he muttered, lips drawing back in a sudden grimace as he clambered over the edge. Holding on, he stretched out one leg and kicked a cracker edge. It broke damply at his touch, jagged shards of it falling to the bottom of the box.

Reckless with an angry desperation, he let go of the edge and slid down the almost vertical glossiness of the wax paper, stopping with a neck-snapping jolt. Pushing up dizzily, he stood in the crumb-strewn box. He picked up one and it disintegrated wetly in his hands like dirt-engrained mush. He picked it apart with his hands, searching for a clean piece. The smell of rot was thick in his nostrils. His cheek puffed out as a spasm shook his stomach.

Dropping the rest of the scraps, he moved toward a complete cracker, breathing through his mouth to avoid the odor, his bare feet squishing over the soaked, mold-fuzzed remains.

Reaching the cracker, he tore off a crumbling fragment and broke it up. Scraping green mold from one of the pieces, he bit off part of it.

He spat it out violently, gagging at the taste. Sucking in breath between his teeth, he stood shivering until the nausea had faded.

Then abruptly his fists clenched and he took a punch at the cracker. His vision was blurred by tears, and he missed. With a snarled curse he swung again and punched out a spray of white crumbs.

"Son-of-a-bitch!" he yelled, and he kicked the cracker to bits and kicked and flung the pieces in every direction like soggy rocks.

He leaned weakly against the wax-paper walls, his face against its cool, crackling surface, his chest expanding and contracting with short, jerking breaths. Temper, temper, came the whispered admonition. Shut up, he answered it. Shut up, I'm dying.

He felt a sharp-edged bulge against his forehead and shifted position irritably.

Then it hit him.

The other side of the wax paper! Any crumbs that had fallen there would have been protected.

With an excited grunt he clawed at the wax paper, trying to tear it open. His fingers slipped on the glossy smoothness and he thudded down on one knee.

He was getting up when the water hit him.

A startled cry lurched in his throat as the first drop landed on his head, exploding into spray. The second drop smashed across his face with an icy, blinding impact. The third bounced in crystalline fragments off his right shoulder.

With a gasp, he lunged backward across the box, tripping over a crumb. He pitched over onto the carpet of cold white mush, then shoved up quickly, his robe coated with it, his hands caked with it. Across from him the drops kept crashing down in a torrent, filling the box with a leaping mist that covered him. He ran.

At the far end of the box he stopped and turned, looking dizzily at the huge drops splattering on the wax paper. He pressed a palm against his skull. It had been like getting hit with a cloth-wrapped sledge hammer.

"Oh, my God," he muttered hoarsely, sliding down the wax-paper wall until he was sitting in the mush, hands pressed to his head, eyes closed, tiny whimperings of pain in his throat.

He had eaten, and his sore throat felt much better. He had drunk the drops of water clinging to the wax paper. Now he was collecting a pile of crumbs.

First he had kicked an opening in the heavy wax paper, then squeezed in behind its rustling smoothness. After eating, he'd begun to carry dry crumbs out, piling them on the bottom of the box.

That done, he kicked and tore out handholds in the wax paper so he could climb back to the top. He made the ascent carrying one or two crumbs at a time, depending on their size. Up the wax-paper ladder, over the lip of the box, down the handholds he had formerly ripped in the paper wrapping of the box. He did that for an hour.

Then he squeezed his way behind the wax-paper lining, searching for any crumbs he might have missed. But he hadn't missed any except for one fragment the size of his little finger, which he picked up and chewed on as he finished his circuit of the box and emerged from the opening again.

He looked over the interior of the box once more, but there was nothing salvageable. He stood in the middle of the cracker ruins, hands on hips, shaking his head. At best, he'd got only two days' food out of all his work. Thursday he would be without any again.

He threw off the thought. He had enough concerns; he'd worry about it when Thursday came. He climbed out of the box.

It was a lot colder outside. He shivered with a hunching up of shoulders. Though he'd wrung out as much as possible, his robe was still wet from the splattering drops.

He sat on the thick tangle of rope, one hand on his pile of hard-won cracker crumbs. They were too heavy to carry all the way down. He'd have to make a dozen trips at least, and that was out of the question. Unable to resist, he picked up a fist-thick crumb and munched on it contentedly while he thought about the problem of getting his food down.

At last, realizing there was only one way, he stood with a sigh and turned back to the box. Should use wax paper, he thought. Well, the hell with that; it was going to last only two days at the most.

With a straining of arm and back muscles, feet braced against the side of the box, he tore off a jagged piece of paper about the size of a small rug. This he dragged back to the edge of the refrigerator top and laid out flat. In the center of it he arranged his crumbs into a cone-shaped pile, then wrapped them up until he had a tight, carefully sealed package about as high as his knees.

He lay on his stomach peering over the edge of the refrigerator. He was higher off the floor now than he'd been on the distant cliff that marked the boundary of the spider's territory. A long drop for his cargo. Well, they were already crumbs; it would be no loss if they became smaller crumbs. The package wasn't likely to open during the fall; that was all that mattered.

Briefly, despite the cold, he looked out over the cellar.

It certainly made a difference, being fed. The cellar had, for the moment anyway, lost its barren menace. It was a strange, cool land shimmering with rain-blurred light, a kingdom of verticals and horizontals, of grays and blacks relieved only by the dusty colors of stored objects. A land of roars and rushings, of intermittent sounds that shook the air like many thunders. His land.

Far below he saw the giant woman looking up at him, still leaning on her rock, frozen for all time in her posture of calculated invitation.

Sighing, he pushed back and stood. No time to waste; it was too cold. He got behind his bundle and, stooping over, pushed the dead weight of it to the edge and shoved it over the brink with a nudge of his foot.

Momentarily on his stomach again, he watched the package's heavy fall, saw it bounce once on the floor, and heard the crunching noise as it came to rest. He smiled. It had held together.

Standing once more, he started around the top of the refrigerator to see if there were anything he might use. He found the newspaper.

It was folded and propped against the cylindrical coil case. Its lettered faces were covered with dust and part of the sink's leaking had splashed water across it, blotting the letters and eating through the cheap paper. He saw the large letters OST and knew it was a copy of the New York *Globe-Post*, the paper that had done his story—at least as much of it as he had been able to endure.

He looked at the dusty paper, remembering the day Mel Hammer had come to the apartment and made the offer.

Marty had mentioned Scott's mysterious affliction to a fellow Kiwani, and from there the news had drifted, ripple by ripple, into the city.

Scott refused the offer, despite the fact that they needed the money desperately. Although the Medical Center had completed the tests free of charge, there was still a sizable bill for the first series of examinations. There was the five hundred owed to Marty, and the other bills they'd accumulated through the long, hard winter—the complete winter wardrobe for all of them, the cost of fuel oil, the extra medical bills because none of them had been physically equipped to face an Eastern winter after living so long in Los Angeles.

But Scott had been in what he now called his period of furies—a time when he experienced an endless and continuously mounting anger at the plight he was in. He'd refused the newspaper offer with anger. No, thank you, but I don't care to be exposed to the morbid curiosity of the public. He flared up at Lou when she didn't support his decision as eagerly as he thought she should have, saying, "What would you like me to do—turn myself into a public freak to give you your security?"

Erring, off-target anger; he'd known it even as he spoke. But anger was burning in him. It drove him to depths of temper he had never plumbed before. Strengthless temper, temper based on fear alone.

Scott turned away from the newspaper and went back to the rope. Lowering himself over the edge with an angry carelessness, he began sliding down the rope, using his hands and feet. The white cliff of the refrigerator blurred before his eyes as he descended.

And the anger he felt now was only a vestigial remnant of the fury he'd lived with constantly in the past; fury that made him lash out incontinently at anyone he thought was mocking him. . . .

He remembered the day Terry had said something behind his back; something he thought he heard. He remembered how, no taller than Beth, he'd whirled on her and told her that he'd heard what she'd said.

Heard what? she asked. Heard what you said about me! I didn't say anything about you. Don't lie to me, I'm not deaf! Are you calling me a liar? Yes, I'm calling you a liar! I don't have to listen to talk like that! You do when you decide to talk about me behind my back! I think we've had just about enough of your screaming around here. Just because you're Marty's brother— Sure, sure, you're the boss's wife, you're the big cheese around here! Don't you talk to me like that!

And on and on, shrill and discordant and profitless.

Until Marty, grim, soft-spoken, called him into the office, where Scott had stood in front of the desk, glaring at his brother like a belligerent dwarf.

"Kid, I don't like to say it," Marty told him, "but maybe—

till they get you fixed up—it'd be better if you stayed home. Believe me, I know what you're going through, and I don't blame you, not a bit. But . . . well, you can't concentrate on work when you're . . ."

"So I'm being fired."

"Oh, come on, kid," Marty said. "You're not being fired. You'll still be on salary. Not as much, of course—I can't afford that—but enough to keep you and Lou going. This'll be over soon, kid. And—well, Christ, the GI loan'll be coming through any day now anyway, and then—"

Scott's feet thudded on the top of the wicker table. Without pausing, he started across the wide expanse, lips set tightly in the thick blond wreathing of his beard.

Why did he have to see that newspaper and go off on another fruitless journey to the past? Memory was such a worthless thing, really. Nothing it dealt with was attainable. It was concerned with phantom acts and feelings, with all that was uncapturable except in thought. It was without satisfaction. Mostly it hurt. . . .

He stood at the edge of the tabletop, wondering how he was going to get down to the hanging strip. He stood indecisively, shifting from leg to leg, wriggling the toes of the lifted foot gingerly. His feet were getting cold again. The ache in his right leg was returning, too; he'd almost forgotten it while he was collecting crumbs, the constant movement loosening and warming him. And his throat was getting sore again.

He walked behind the paint can whose handle he had grabbed before and, bracing his back against it, pushed. The can didn't move. Turning around, he planted his feet firmly and pushed with all his strength. The can remained fixed. Scott walked around it, breathing hard with strain. With great effort, he was able to draw the handle out slightly so that it protruded over the edge of the table.

He rested for a moment, then swung out over the space and dangled there until his searching feet found the strip and pressed down on it.

Cautiously he put one hand on the tabletop. Then, after a moment of feeling for balance, he let go of the paint-can handle and lowered himself quickly. His feet slipped off the ledge, but his convulsively thrusting arms caught hold of it and he clambered back on.

After a few seconds he leaped across to the spar arrangement.

The descent along the rod-spaced incline was simple; too simple to prevent the return of memories. As he slid and edged down the length of the incline, he thought of the afternoon he'd come home from the shop after the talk with Marty.

He remembered how still the apartment was, Lou and Beth out shopping. He remembered going into the bedroom and sitting on the edge of the bed for a long time, staring down at his dangling legs.

He didn't know how long it had been before he'd looked up and seen a suit of his old clothes hanging on the back of the door. He'd looked at it, then got up and gone over to it. He'd had to stand on a chair to reach it. For a moment he held the dragging weight of it in his arms. Then, not knowing exactly why, he pulled the jacket off the hanger and put it on.

He stood in front of the full-length mirror, looking at himself.

That's all he did at first, just stood looking—at his hands, lost deep in the sagging hollow of the dark sleeves; at the hem of the coat, far below his calves; at the way the coat hung around him like a tent. It didn't strike him then; the disparity was too severe. He only stared at himself, his face blank.

Then it did strike him, as if for the first time.

It was his own coat he wore.

A wheezing giggle puffed out his cheeks. It disappeared. Silence while he gaped at his reflection.

He snickered hollowly at the child playing grownup. His chest began to shake with restrained laughs. They sounded like sobs.

He couldn't hold them back. They poured up his throat and pushed out between shaking lips. Sobbing laughter burst out against the mirror. He felt his body trembling with it. The room began to resound with his taut, shrill laughter.

He looked at the mirror again, tears raining down his cheeks. He did a little dance step and the coat puffed out, the sleeve ends flapping. Screeching with a deranged appreciation, he flailed spastic blows against his legs, doubled over to ease the pain in his stomach. His laughter came in short, explosive, throat-catching bursts. He could hardly stand.

I'm funny!

He swung the sleeve again and flopped over suddenly on his side, laughing and kicking at the floor with his shoes, the thumping sounds making him even more hysterical. He twisted around on the floor, limbs thrashing, head rolling from side to side, the choked laughter pealing from his lips, until he was too weak to laugh. Then he lay there on his back, motionless, gasping for breath, his face wet with tears, his right foot still twitching. I'm funny.

And he thought, quite calmly it seemed, about going into the bathroom and getting his razor blade and cutting his wrists open. He really wondered why he went on lying there, looking up at the ceiling, when it would solve everything if he went into the bathroom and got a razor blade and—

He slid down the rope-thick thread to the shelf of the wicker table. He shook the thread until the stick came loose and fell. He fastened it again and started down toward the floor.

It was strange; he still didn't know why he hadn't committed suicide. Surely the hopelessness of his situation warranted it. Yet, although he had often wished he could do it, something had always stopped him.

It was difficult to say whether he regretted this failure to end his life. Sometimes it seemed as if it didn't matter one way or the other, except in a vague, philosophical way; but what philosopher had ever shrunk?

His feet touched the cold floor, and quickly he gathered up his sandals and put them on—the sandals he had made of string. That was better. Now to drag the package to his sleeping place. Then he could strip off his wet robe and lie in the warmth, resting and eating. He ran to the package, anxious to get it over with.

The package was so heavy that he could move it only slowly. He pushed it a dozen yards, then stopped and rested, sitting on it. After he got his breath, he stood up and pushed it some more—past the two massive tables, past the coiled hose, past the lawn mower and the huge ladder, across the wide, light-patched plain toward the water heater.

The last twenty-five yards he moved backwards, bent over at the waist, grunting as he dragged his bundle of food. Just a few more minutes and he'd be warm and comfortable on his bed, fed and sheltered. Teeth clenched in suddenly joyous effort, he jerked the bundle along to the foot of the cement block. Life was still worth struggling for. The simplest of physical pleasures could make it so. Food, water, warmth. He turned happily.

He cried out.

The giant spider was hanging across the top edge of the block, waiting for him.

For a single moment their eyes met. He stood frozen at the foot of the cement block, staring up in heart-stilled horror.

Then the long black legs stirred, and with a strangled groan Scott lunged into one of the two passages cut through the block. As he started running along the damp tunnel, he heard the spider drop heavily to the floor behind him.

It's not fair! his mind screamed in desolate fury.

There was time for no more thought than that. Everything was swallowed in the savage maw of panic. The pain in his leg was gone, his exhaustion was washed away. Only terror remained.

He leaped out through the opening on the other side of the cement block and cast back a glance at the shadowy lurching of the spider in the tunnel. Then, with a sucked-in breath, he started racing across the floor toward the fuel tank. There was no use trying to reach the log pile. The spider would overtake him long before he could make it.

He sped toward the big split carton under the tank, not knowing what he would do when he got there, only instinctively heading for shelter. There were clothes in the carton. Maybe he could burrow under them, out of the black widow's reach.

He didn't look back now; there was no need to. He knew the great swollen body of the spider was wobbling erratically over the cement, carried by the long black legs. He knew that it was only because one of those legs was missing that he had any hope of reaching the carton first.

He ran through viscid squares of light, sandals thudding,

robe flapping about his body. Air scorched rawly down his throat, his legs pumped wildly. The fuel tank loomed over him.

He darted into the vast shadow of it, the spider skimming the floor less than five yards behind. With a grunt Scott leaped off the cement and, grabbing hold of a hanging string, dragged himself up, then swung in feet first through the opening in the side of the carton.

He landed in a limb-twisting heap on the soft pile of clothes. As he started up he heard the rasping of the spider's legs up the carton's side. He shoved to his feet but lost his balance on the yielding cloth and fell. Sprawling, he saw the black, leg-fluttering bulk of the spider appear in the V-shaped opening. It lunged through.

With a sob, Scott pushed up, then fell again on the uneven hill of clothes. The hill gave twice; once under his weight, again under the impact of the spider's wriggling drop. It spurted through the shadows at him.

There was no time to struggle to his feet. He shoved desperately with his legs and sent himself flailing backward. He flopped heavily again, hands clawing for an opening between the clothes. There was none. The spider was almost on him now.

A high-pitched whining flooded in his throat. Scott flung himself back again as one of the spider's legs fell heavily across his ankle. He grunted in shock as he fell into the open sewing box, hands still groping. The huge spider jumped down and clambered over his legs. He screamed.

Then his hand closed over cold metal. The pin! With a sucking gasp, he kicked back again, dragging up the pin with both hands. As the spider leaped, he drove the pin like a spear at its belly. He felt the pin shudder in his grip under the weight of the partially impaled creature.

The spider leaped back off the point. It landed yards away on the clothes, then, after a second's hesitation, rushed at him again. Scott pushed up on his left knee, right leg back as a supporting brace, the pinhead cradled against his hip, his arms rigidly tensed for the second impact.

Again the spider hit the pinpoint. Again it sprang back, one of its flailing spiny legs raking skin off Scott's left temple.

"Die!" he heard himself scream suddenly. "Die! Die!"

It did not die. It stirred restlessly on the clothes a few yards away as if it were trying to understand why it couldn't reach its prey. Then suddenly it leaped at him again.

This time it had barely touched the pinpoint before it stopped and scuttled backward. Scott kept staring at it fixedly, his body remaining in its tense crouch, the heavy pin wavering a little in his grip, but always pointing at the spider. He could still feel the hideous clambering weight of it across his legs, the flesh-ripping slash of its leg. He squinted to distinguish its black form from the shadows.

He didn't know how long he remained in that position. The transition was unnoticeable. Suddenly, magically, there were only the shadows.

A confused sound stirred in his throat. He stood up on palsied legs and looked around. Across the cellar the oil burner roared into life and, heart pounding jaggedly, he twisted around in a panic, thinking that the spider was going to leap on him from behind.

He kept circling there for a long time, the weight of the lancelike pin dragging down his arms. Finally it dawned on him that the spider had gone away.

A great wave of relief and exhaustion broke over him. The pin seemed made of lead, and it fell from his hands and clattered down on the wooden bottom of the box. His legs gave way and he slipped down into a twisted heap, head fallen back against the pin that had saved his life.

For a while he lay there in limp, contented depletion. The spider was gone. He'd chased it away.

It was not too long, however, before the knowledge that the spider was still alive dampened all contentment. It might be waiting outside for him, ready to spring as soon as he came out. It might be back under the water heater again, waiting for him there.

He rolled over slowly on his stomach and pressed his face against his arms. What had he accomplished, after all? He was still virtually at the spider's mercy. He couldn't carry the pin everywhere he went, and in a day or so he might not be able to carry it at all.

And even if (he didn't believe it for a second) the spider would be too frightened to attack him again, there was still the food that would be gone in two days, still the increasing difficulties in getting to the water, still the constant altering of his clothes to be made, still the impossibility of escaping the cellar, still—worst of all, always there, constantly nagging—the dread of what was going to happen to him between Saturday night and Sunday morning.

He struggled to his feet and groped around until he found the hinged cover of the box. He pulled it over and lowered it into place, then sank back into the darkness. What if I smother? he thought. He didn't care.

He'd been running since it had all started. Running physically, from the man and the boys and the cat and the bird and the spider, and—a far worse kind of flight—running mentally. Running from life, from his problems and his fears; retreating, backtracking, facing nothing, yielding, giving in, surrendering.

He still lived, but was his living considered, or only an instinctive survival? Yes, he still struggled for food and water, but wasn't that inevitable if he chose to go on living. What he wanted to know was this: Was he a separate, meaningful person; was he an individual? Did he matter? Was it enough just to survive?

He didn't know; he didn't know. It might be that he was a man and trying to face reality. It might also be that he was a pathetic fraction of a shadow, living only out of habit, impulse-driven, moved but never moving, fought but never fighting.

He didn't know. He slept, curled up and shivering, no bigger than a pearl, and he didn't know.

Chapter Seven

HE STOOD UP and listened carefully. The cellar was still. The spider must have gone. Surely, if it were still intent on killing him, it would have ventured into the carton again. He must have been asleep for hours.

He grimaced, swallowed, as he realized that his throat hurt again. He was thirsty, hungry. Did he dare go back to the water heater? He blew out a hissing breath. There was no question. It had to be done.

He felt around until his hands closed over the thick, icy shaft of the pin. He picked it up. It was heavy. Amazing that he had been able to handle it so well. Fright, probably. He lifted the pin in both hands, then shifted it to his right side and held it there. It dragged at his arm muscles as he climbed out of the sewing box and moved up the shifting hill of clothes toward the opening in the side of the carton. If the spider appeared, he could easily grab the pin with both hands and use it as he had before. It gave him the first definite sense of physical security he had had in weeks.

At the opening, he leaned out cautiously, looking up first, then sideways, and finally down. The spider was not to be seen. His breathing eased a little. He slid the pin out through the opening, then, after letting it dangle a moment, dropped it. It clanged on the floor and rolled a few feet before stopping. Hastily he slid out of the carton and let himself drop. As he landed, the water pump began its chugging wheeze, making him jump to the pin, grab it up, and hold it poised as if to ward off attack.

There was no attack. He lowered the gleaming spear and shifted it to his side again, then began walking across the floor toward the water heater.

He moved out from beneath the mountainous shadow of the fuel tank into the grayish light of late afternoon. The rain had stopped. Out beyond the filmed windows was utter stillness. He walked by the vast lawn-mower wheels, glancing up warily to see if the spider were crouching up there.

Now he was on the open floor. He began the short hike to the water heater. His eyes went to the refrigerator, and in his mind he saw the newspaper up there, and he endured again the agony of the photographer's invasion of his home. They had posed him in his old shoes, which were five sizes too large, and Berg said, "Look like ya was rememberin' when ya could wear 'em, Scotty." Then they posed him beside Beth, beside Lou, beside a hanging suit of his old clothes; standing beside the tape measure, Hammer's big, disembodied hand sticking out from the edge of the photograph, pointing at the proper mark; being examined by the doctors appointed by the *Globe-Post*. His case history had been rehashed for a million readers, while he suffered a new mental torture each day, thrashing in bed at night, telling himself that he was going to break the contract he'd signed whether they needed the money or not, whether Lou hated him for it or not.

He had gone on with it anyway.

And the offers came in. Offers for radio and television and stage and night-club appearances, for articles in all kinds of magazines except the better ones, for syndication of the *Globe-Post* series. People started to gather outside the apartment, staring at him, even asking for his autograph. Religious fanatics exhorted him, in person and by mail, to join their saving cults. Obscene letters arrived from weirdly frustrated women—and men.

His face was blank and unmoving as he reached the concrete block. He stood there a moment, still thinking of the past. Then he refocused his eyes and started, realizing that the spider might be up there waiting to spring.

Slowly he climbed the block, pin always ready for use if necessary. He peered over the edge of the block. His sleeping place was empty.

With a sigh, he slung the pin over the edge and watched it roll to a stop against his bed. Then he climbed down again for the crackers.

After three trips he had all the cracker bits in a pile beside his bed. He sat there crunching on a fist-size piece, wishing he had some water. He didn't dare go down to the pump, though; it was getting dark, and even the pin was not enough assurance in the dark.

When he'd finished eating, he dragged the box top over his bed, then sank back on the sponge with a soft groan. He was still exhausted. The nap in the carton had done little to refresh him.

He remembered and, reaching around, he searched for the wood and charcoal. Finding them, he scratched a careless stroke. It would probably cross another stroke, but that hardly mattered. Chronology became less of a concern each day. There was Wednesday and there was Thursday, there were Friday and Saturday.

Then nothing.

He shuddered in the darkness. Like death, his fate was impossible to conceive. No, even worse than death. Death, at least, was a concept; it was a part of life, however strangely unknown. But who had ever shrunk into nothingness?

He rolled on his side and propped his head on an arm. If only he could tell someone what he felt. If only he could be with Lou; see her, touch her. Yes, even if she didn't know it, it would be a comfort. But he was alone.

He thought again of the newspaper stories, and of how sick it had made him to become a spectacle, how it had driven him into nerve-screaming wrath, making him maniacal with fury against his plight.

Until, at the peak of that fury, he had sped to the city and told the paper he was breaking his contract, and stormed away in a palsy of hatred.

42″

Two miles beyond Baldwin, a tire blew out with a crack like the blast of a shotgun.

Gasping, Scott froze to the wheel as the Ford lurched off balance, scouring wide tire marks across the pavement. It took all the strength in his arms to keep the car from ramming the center wall. The steering wheel shuddering in his grip, he guided the car off the highway.

Fifty yards farther on, he braked the car and twisted off the ignition. He sat there for a moment, wordless, glaring straight ahead with baleful eyes. His hands were white-ridged fists quivering in his lap.

At last he spoke. "Oh, you son-of-a—" Fury sent a jolting shudder down his back.

"Go ahead," he said, rage crouching behind the patience of his tone. "Go ahead. Pour it on. Sure. Go ahead; why not?" His teeth clicked together. "Don't just stop with a flat tire, though," he said, words thumping at the closed gates of his teeth. "Kill the generator. Tear out the spark plugs. Split the radiator. Blow up the whole goddam son-of-a-bitch car!" Apoplectic rage sprayed across the windshield.

He thudded back against the seat, spent, his eyes shut.

After a few minutes, he pulled up the door handle and pushed the door open. Cold air rushed over him. Drawing up the collar of his topcoat, he shifted his legs and slid down off the raised seat.

He landed on gravel, spilling forward, hands out for support. He got up quickly, cursing, and fired a stone across the highway. With my luck it'll break a car window and put out an old lady's eye! he thought furiously. With my luck.

He stood shivering, looking at his car, hunched blackly over the collapsed tire. Great, he thought, just great. How in the hell was he supposed to change it? His teeth gritted. He wasn't even strong enough for *that*. And, of course, Terry couldn't watch the children today and Lou had to stay home. It figured.

A spasm shook him beneath the topcoat. It was cold. Cold on a May night. Even that figured. Even the weather was against him. He closed his eyes. I'm ready for a padded cell, he thought.

Well, he couldn't just stand there. He had to get to a phone and call a garage.

He didn't move. He stared at the road. And after I call the garage, he thought, the mechanic will come and he'll talk to me and look at me and recognize me; and there'll be guarded stares, or maybe even open ones, the kind Berg always gave him—blunt, insulting stares that seemed to say, Jesus, you *are* a creep! And there would be talk, questions, the kind of withdrawn camaraderie a normal man offers to a freak.

His throat muscles drew in slowly as he swallowed. Even rage was preferable to this; this complete negation of spirit. Rage, at least, was struggle, it was a moving forward against something. This was defeat, static and heavy on him.

Weary breath emptied from him. Well, there was no other way. He had to get home. He might have called Marty under any other circumstances; but he felt awkward about Marty now.

He slid his hands into the slash pockets of his coat and started trudging along the roadside gravel.

I don't care, he kept telling himself as he walked. I don't care if I *did* sign a contract. I'm tired of playing guinea pig for a million readers.

He walked on quickly in his little-boy clothes.

Moments later, headlight beams bleached across him and he stepped farther away from the road and kept on walking. He certainly wasn't going to try to get a ride.

The dark car hulk rolled past him. Then there was a slowing of the tires on the pavement and, looking up, Scott saw that the car was stopping. His mouth tightened. I'd rather walk. He formed the words with his lips, getting them ready.

The door shoved open and a fedora-topped head appeared.

"You alone, my boy?" the man asked huskily. The words came out from one side of his mouth. The other side was plugged with a half-smoked cigar.

Scott trudged toward the car. Maybe it was all right; the man thought he was a boy. He might have expected it. Hadn't they refused to let him in the movie one afternoon because he wasn't accompanied by an adult? Hadn't he been forced to show his identification before that bartender would serve him a drink?

"You alone, young fellow?" the man asked again.

"Just walking home," Scott said.

"Have you far to go?" An intelligent voice, somewhat thickened. Scott saw the man's head bobbing. So much the better, he thought.

"Just to the next town," he said. "Could you give me a ride, mister?" Deliberately he raised the already raised pitch of his voice.

"Certainly, my boy, certainly," the man said. "Just climb aboard and it's bon voy-*age* for you and me and Plymouth, vintage fifty-five." His head drew in like that of a startled turtle. It disappeared into the shell of his car.

"Thanks, mister." It was a form of masochism, Scott knew, this playing the role of boy to its very hilt. He stood outside the car until the heavy-set man had pushed up awkwardly and was sitting behind the steering wheel again. Then he slid onto the seat.

"Just sit right here, my boy, just— Caution!"

Scott jumped up as he sat on the man's thick hand. The man drew it away, held it before his eyes.

"You have injured the member, my boy," he said. "Wreaked havoc to the knuckles. Eh?" The man's chuckle was liquid, as if it came up through a throatful of water.

Scott's smile was nervously automatic as he sat down again. The car reeked of whisky and cigar smoke. He coughed into his hand.

"Anchors, so be it, Od's blood, aweigh," the man declared. He tapped down the shift to drive position and the car jerked a little, then rolled forward. "*Fermez la porte*, dear boy, *fermez la* goddam *porte*."

"I have," Scott told him.

The man looked over as if he were delighted. "You understand French, my boy. An excellent boy, a most seemly boy. Your health, sir."

Scott smiled thinly to himself. He wished he were drunk too. But a whole afternoon drinking in a darkened barroom booth had done nothing to him at all.

"You reside in this humid land, my boy?" the heavy man asked. He began slapping himself about the chest.

"In the next town," Scott said.

"In the next town, the following city," the man said, still slapping at himself. "In the adjacent village, the juxtaposed hamlet. Ah, *Hamlet*. To be or not to be, that is the— God damn it, a match! My kingdom for a match!" He belched. It was like a drawn-out leopard growl.

"Use the dashboard lighter," Scott said, hoping to get both of the man's unsteady hands back on the wheel.

The man looked over, apparently astounded. "A brilliant boy," he said. "An analytic fellow. By God, I love an analytic fellow." His bubbly chuckle rippled in the stale-smelling car. "*Mon dieu*."

Scott tensed suddenly as the heavy man leaned over, ignoring the highway. The man knocked in the lighter, then straightened up again, his shoulder brushing Scott's.

"So you live in the next town, *mon cher*," he said. "This is . . . fascinating news." Another leopard-growl belch. "Dinner with old Vincent," said the man. "Old Vincent." The sound that came from his throat might have indicated amusement. It might, as well, have indicated the onset of strangulation. "Old Vincent," said the heavy man sadly.

The cigarette lighter popped out and he snatched it from its electric cavity. Scott glanced aside as the man relit his dark-tipped cigar.

The man's head was leonine beneath the wide-brimmed fedora. Glows of light washed his face. Scott saw bushy eyebrows like awnings over the man's darkly glittering eyes. He saw a puffy-nostriled nose, a long, thick-lipped mouth. It was the face of a sly boy peering out through rolls of dough.

Clouds of smoke obscured the face. "A most seemly boy, Od's bodkins," said the man. He missed the dashboard opening and the lighter thumped on the floor boards. "God's hooks!" The man doubled over. The car veered wildly.

"I'll get it," Scott said quickly. "Look out!"

The man put the car back in its proper lane. He patted Scott's head with a spongy palm. "A child of most excellent virtues," he slurred. "As I have always said—" He drew up phlegm, rolled down the window, and gave it to the wind. He forgot what he had always said. "You live around here?" he asked, belching conclusively.

"In the next town," Scott said.

"Vincent was a friend, I tell you," the man said remorsefully. "A *friend*. In the truest sense of that truest word. Friend, ally, companion, comrade."

Scott glanced back at the service station they had just passed. It looked closed. He'd better ride into Freeport and make sure he could get hold of someone.

"He insisted," the man said, "in donning the hair shirt of matrimony." He turned. "You *comprends*, dear boy? Do you, bless your supple bones, *comprends?*"

Scott swallowed. "Yes, sir," he said.

The man blew out a puff of smoke. Scott coughed. "And what," the man said, "was a *man*, dear boy, became, you see, a creature of degradation, a lackey, a serf, an automaton. A—in short—lost and shriveled soul." The man peered at Scott dizzily. "You see," he asked, "what I mean to say, dear boy? *Do* you?"

Scott looked out the window. I'm tired, he thought. I want to go to bed and forget who I am and what's happening to me. I just want to go to bed.

"You live around here?" asked the man.

"Next town."

"Quite so," said the man.

Silence a moment. Then the man said, "Women. Who come into man's life a breath from the sewer." He belched. "A pox on the she." He looked over at Scott. The car headed for a tree. "And dear Vincent," said the man, "lost to the eye of man. *Swallowed* in the spiritual quicksands of—"

"You're going to hit that tree!"

The man turned his head.

"There," he said. "Back on course, Cap'n. Back in the saddle again. Back where a friend is a—"

He peered at Scott again, face aslant as though he were a buyer examining merchandise. "You are—" he said, purse-lipped and estimating. He cleared his throat violently. "You are twelve," he said. "First prize?"

Scott coughed a little at the cigar smoke. "First prize," he said. "Look out."

The man repointed the car, his laugh ending in a belch.

"An age of pristine possibility, my dear," he said. "A time of untrammeled hope. Oh, dear boy." He dropped a portly hand and clamped it on Scott's leg. "Twelve, twelve. Oh, to be twelve again. Blessed be twelve years of age."

Scott pulled his leg away. The man squeezed it once more, then reached back to the steering wheel. "Yes, yes, yes, yes, yes," he said. "Still to meet your first woman." His lips curled. "That experience which is analogous to turning your first rock and finding your first bug."

"I can get off at—" Scott started, seeing an open gas station ahead.

"Ugly they are," stated the heavy man in the dark, wrinkled suit. "Ugly with an ugliness that worries the fringes of phenomena." His eyes moved, peering out at Scott over banks of crow-lined fat. "Do you intend to marry, dear boy?" he asked.

If I could laugh at anything these days, Scott thought, I could laugh at that.

"No," he said. "Say, could I get off at—"

"A wise, a noble decision," said the heavy man. "One of virtue, of seemliness. *Women.*" He stared wide-eyed through the windshield. "Append them to cancer. They destroy as secretly, as effectively, as—speak truth, O prophet—as *hideously.*" The man looked at him. "Eh, boy?" he said, chuckling, belching, hiccuping.

"Mister, I get off here."

"Take you to Freeport, my boy," said the man. "To Freeport away! Land of jollities and casual obliterations. Stronghold of suburban ax-grindings." The man looked directly at Scott. "You like girls, my boy?"

The question caught Scott off guard. He hadn't really been

paying attention to the drift of the man's monologue. He looked over at the man. Suddenly the man seemed bigger; as if, with the question, he had gained measurable bulk.

"I don't really live in Freeport," Scott said. "I—"

"He's *dif*fident!" The heavy man's heretofore husky chuckle suddenly erupted into a cackle. "O diffident youth, belovèd." The hand again went to Scott's leg. Scott's face tensed as he looked up at the man, the smell of whisky and cigar smoke thick in his nostrils. He saw the cigar tip glow and fade, glow, fade.

"I get off here," he said.

"Look thee, young chap," said the heavy man, watching the road and Scott at the same time, "the night hath yet a measure of youth. It's only a trifle past nine. Now," his voice fell to cajoling, "in the icebox of my rooms there squats a squamous quart of ice cream. Not a pint, mind you, but—"

"Please, I get *off* here." Scott could feel the heat of the man's hand through his trouser leg. He tried to draw away but he couldn't. His heartbeat quickened.

"Oh, come along, young dear," the man said. "Ice cream, cake, a bit of bawdy badinage—what more could two adventurers like you and me seek of an evening? Eh?" The hand tightened almost threateningly.

"Ow!" Scott said, wincing. "Get your hand off me!"

The man looked startled at the adult anger in Scott's voice, the lowering of pitch, the authority.

"Will you stop the car?" Scott asked angrily. "And look out!"

The man jerked the car back into its lane.

"Don't get so excited, boy," he said, beginning to sound agitated.

"I want to get *out*." Scott's hands were actually shaking.

"My dear boy," the man said in an abruptly pitiful voice, "if you knew loneliness as *I* know it—black solitude and—"

"Stop the car, damn it!"

The man stiffened. "Speak with respect to your superior, lout!" he snapped. His right hand drew back suddenly and smashed against the side of Scott's head, knocking him against the door.

Scott pushed up quickly, realizing, with a burst of panic, that he was no stronger than a boy.

"Dear boy, I apologize," the man said instantly, hiccuping. "Did I hurt you?"

"I live down the next road," Scott said tensely. "Stop here, please."

The man plucked out his cigar and threw it on the floor.

"I offend you, boy," he said, sounding as if he were about to cry. "I offend you with distasteful words. Please. *Please.* Look behind the words, behind the peeling mask of jollity. For there is utter sadness, there utter loneliness. Can you understand that, dear boy? Can you, in your tender years, know my—"

"Mister, I want to get out," Scott said. His voice was that of a boy, half angry, half frightened. And the horror of it was that he wasn't sure if there was more of acting or of actuality in his voice.

Abruptly the man pulled over to the side of the highway.

"Leave me, leave me, then," he said bitterly. "You're no different from the rest, no, not at all."

Scott shoved open the door with trembling hands.

"Good night, sweet prince," said the heavy man, fumbling for Scott's hand. "Good night and dreams of plenteous goodness bless thy repose." A wheezy hiccup jarred his curtain speech. "I go on—empty, empty . . . empty. Will you kiss me once? For good-by, for—"

But Scott was already out of the car and running headlong toward the service station they had just passed. The man turned his heavy head and watched youth racing away from him.

Chapter Eight

THERE WAS a thumping sound, like that of a hammer on wood; like the sound of a huge fingernail tapping, falsely patient, on a blackboard. The tapping pounded at his sleeping brain. He stirred on the bed, rolling over on his back with a fitful toss of arms. *Thump—thump—thump.* He moaned. At his sides, his hands raised up a trifle, then dropped again. *Thump. Thump.* He groaned irritably, still not fully conscious.

Then the water drop burst across his face.

Gagging and coughing, he reared up on the sponge, hearing a loud squishing noise. Another drop splashed off his shoulder.

"What!" His brain struggling to orient itself, his wide-eyed, startled gaze fled around the darkness. *Thump! Thump!* It was a giant's fist beating at a door; it was a monster gavel pounding on a rostrum.

Sleep was gone. He felt his chest jerk with staggering heart-beats. "Good God," he muttered. He threw his legs over the side of the sponge.

They landed in lukewarm water.

He jerked his legs back with a gasp. Overhead the noise seemed to be coming faster. *Thump-thump-thump!* Breath caught in his throat. What in God's name . . .

Grimacing at the brain-jolting sound, he let his legs over the side of the bed again and let them sink in the warm water. He stood hastily, rigid hands clamped over his ears. *Thump thump thump!* It was like standing inside a fiercely beaten drum. Gasping, he lurched for the edge of the box top. He slipped on the water-slick surface, crying out as his right knee banged down on the cement. He pushed up with a groan, then slipped again.

"Damn it!" he screamed. He hardly heard his voice; the noise was almost deafening. Frantic, he braced his feet and, reaching up, lifted the box-top edge and ducked out under it.

He slipped again, crashing down on an elbow. Pain knifed up his arm. He started up. A drop of water slammed across his back, sending him sprawling again. He twisted over like a fish and saw the water heater leaking.

"Oh, my God," he muttered, wincing at the pain in his knee and elbow.

He stood up, watching great drops splatter off the box top and cement. The water ran warmly across his ankles; there was a minor waterfall of it flowing over the edge of the block, splashing on the cellar floor.

For a long moment he stood there indecisively, staring at the falling water, feeling the robe cling warm and wet to his body.

Then he cried out suddenly. "The crackers!"

He lunged at the box top again, sliding and struggling for balance. He lifted the top and carried it over the bed, feet almost slipping out from under him all the way. He dropped it, then flung himself across the sponge, hearing water burst out from its swollen pores.

"Oh, *no*."

He couldn't drag the package up, it was so waterlogged. Face wild with frightened anger, he tore it open, the soggy paper parting like tissue in his hands.

He stared at the water-soaked cracker bits molded together into an ashen paste. He picked up a handful and felt the sodden drag of it, like day-old porridge.

With a curse he flung the dripping mass away. It flew over the edge of the block and splattered into a hundred pale scraps on the floor.

He knelt there on the sponge, oblivious now of the water that poured around and over him. His eyes were fastened to the pile of crumbs, his lips pressed into a blood-pinched, hating line.

"What's the use?" he muttered. His fists snapped shut like jaws. "What's the *use*?" A water drop fell in front of him and he took a savage punch at it, losing balance and toppling over, face first, on the sponge. Water flooded from the compressed honeycomb.

He jolted to his feet on the block, hard with fury.

"You're not going to beat me," he said, he hadn't the slightest idea to whom. His teeth jammed together and it was defiance and a challenge that he hurled. "You're not going to *beat* me!"

He grabbed up handfuls of the soggy cracker and carried it up to the dry safety of the first black metal shelf of the water heater. What good are soaked crackers? asked his brain. They'll dry! he answered. They'll rot first, said his brain. Shut up! he answered.

He yelled it. "Shut up!" God! he thought. He flung a cracker snowball at the water heater and it spatted off the metal.

Suddenly he laughed. Suddenly the whole thing seemed hilarious—him four-sevenths of an inch tall, in a tentlike robe, standing ankle-deep in lukewarm water and throwing soggy cracker balls at a water heater. He threw back his head and laughed loudly. He sat down in the warm water and slapped his palms at it, splashing geysers of it across himself. He pulled off his robe and rolled around in the warm water. A bath! he thought. I'm having my goddam morning bath!

After a while he got up and dried himself on what was left of the handkerchief around the sponge. Then he squeezed the water from the robe and hung it up to dry. My throat is sore, he told himself. So what? he said. It'll have to wait its turn.

He didn't know why he felt so exhilarated and stupidly amused. He was certainly in a fix. It was just, he guessed, that when things got so bad they were absurd, you couldn't take them straight any more; you had to laugh or crack. He almost imagined that if the spider came lumbering over the edge of the block now, he'd laugh at it.

He ripped up the handkerchief with teeth, nails, and hands, and made a flimsy robe of it, tying up the sides as he had done with the other robe. He put it on hastily. He had to get over to the sewing box.

Picking up the heavy pin, he threw it to the floor, then climbed down the cement block and retrieved it. I'll have to find another sleeping place now, he thought. It was amusing. He might even have to go up the great cliff face after that slice of dry bread. That was amusing, too. He shook his head as he jogged across the floor toward the carton, sunlight streaming through the windows over him.

It was like the time after he'd broken the contract. There were all the bills, the pitiless insecurity, the problems of adjustment. He'd tried to go back to work. He'd begged Marty, and Marty had reluctantly agreed. But it hadn't worked. It had got worse and worse until one day Therese had seen him trying to climb onto a chair and had picked him up like a boy and set him on it.

He'd screamed at her and gone storming to Marty's office; but before he could say a word Marty had shoved a letter across the desk at him. It had been from the Veterans Administration. The GI loan had been turned down.

And that afternoon, driving home, when the same tire had gone flat a second time, half a block from the apartment, Scott had sat in the car shrieking with laughter, so hysterical that he'd fallen off his special seat, bounced off the regular one, and landed in a laughter-twitching heap on the floor boards.

It was the way. Self-defense; a mechanism the brain devised to protect itself from detonation; a release when things became wound up too tightly.

When he reached the carton, he climbed in, not even caring if the spider was waiting in there for him. He walked in long strides to the sewing box and found a small thimble. It took all the strength in him to push it up the hill of clothes and shove it out through the opening.

He rolled the thimble across the floor like a giant empty hogshead, the pin stuck through his handkerchief robe and scraping behind him on the cement as he moved.

At the heater he thought first of trying to lift the thimble to the top of the cement block, then realized it was much too heavy and pushed it up against the base of the block, where the torrent of water quickly filled it.

The water was a little dirty, but that didn't matter. He picked up palmfuls of it and washed his face. It was a luxury he'd not experienced for many months. He wished he could shave off his thick beard, too; that would really feel good. The pin? No, that wouldn't work.

He drank some of the water and made a face. Not too good. Well, it would cool. Now he wouldn't have to climb all the way down to the pump.

Straining, he managed to drag the thimble a little bit away from the waterfall and let the quivering surface still itself. Then, propping the pin against the side of the thimble, he shinnied up its slanting length to the lip. There, amidst the faint spray, he looked into the mirror-like water at his face.

He grunted. Truly, it was remarkable. Small, yes, a particled fraction of its former self; yet still the same, line for line. The same green eyes, the same dark-brown hair, the same broad taper of nose, the same jawline, the same ears and full lips. He grimaced. And the same teeth, though likely rotted after so long a time without being brushed. Yet they were still white; rubbing on them with a moistened finger had accomplished that. Amazing. He would be a poor testimonial for a toothpaste concern.

He stared a while longer at his face. It was unusually calm for the face of a man who lived each day with dread and peril. Perhaps jungle life, despite physical danger, was a relaxing one.

Surely it was free of the petty grievances, the disparate values of society. It was simple, devoid of artifice and ulcer-burning pressures. Responsibility in the jungle world was pared to the bone of basic survival. There were no political connivings necessary, no financial arenas to struggle in, no nerve-knotting races for superior rungs on the social ladder. There was only to be or not to be.

He ruffled the water with a hand. Begone, face, he thought, you matter nothing in this cellar life. That he had once been called handsome seemed stupid. He was alone, with no one to please or cater to or like because it was expedient.

He let himself slide down the pin. Except, he thought, wiping spray from his face, that he still loved Louise. It was a final standard. To love someone when there was nothing to be got from that person; that was love.

He had just measured himself at the ruler and was walking back to the water heater when there came a loud creaking noise, a thunderous crash, and a glaring carpet of sunlight flung across the floor. A giant came clumping down the cellar steps.

Paralysis locked him.

He stood horror-rooted to the spot, staring up at the mammoth figure bearing down on him, its plunging shoes raised higher than his head, then slamming down and shaking the floor beneath him. It was double shock that froze him into heart-leaping petrifaction: seeing the mountainous being so abruptly and, at the same time, realizing despite numb terror that he had once been that very size himself. Head thrown back, he stared, open-mouthed, at the giant's approach.

Then thought and immobility were torn away by a bolt of instinct and with a gasp he sprinted toward the edge of the engulfing shadow. The floor shook harder; he heard the bat squeak of gigantic shoes about to mash him like a bug. With a sucked-in cry, he lunged another yard, then dived headlong toward the light, arms out to brace himself.

He landed hard, rolling on his shoulder to break the fall. The vast shoe, like a whale leaping, slammed down inches from his body.

The giant stopped. From the tunnel of a pocket it withdrew a screw driver as long as a seven-story building, then billowed out its black shadow like a spreading pool as it crouched before the water heater.

Scott ran, splashing, around its right shoe, the top of his head level with the lip of the sole. Standing beside the cement block, he peered up at the colossus.

Far up—so far he had to squint to see—was its face: nose like a precipitous slope that he could ski on; nostrils and ears like caves into which he could climb; hair a forest he could lose himself in; mouth a vast, shut cavern; teeth (the giant grimaced suddenly) he could slide an arm between; eye pupils the height of him, black irises wide enough to crawl through, lashes like dark, curling sabers.

He stared mutely at the giant. That was what Lou looked like now—monstrously tall, with fingers as thick as redwood trees, feet like elephants that never were, breasts like pliant, hill-peaked pyramids.

Suddenly the vast shape wavered before the colorless gelatine of tears. It had never struck him so hard before. Not seeing her, his own physique the norm, he had imagined her as someone he could touch and hold, even knowing it wasn't so. Now he knew it completely; and the knowing was a cruel weight that crushed all memory beneath itself.

He stood there crying silently, not even caring when the giant picked up his sponge and, with a dinosaur grunt, tossed it aside. Moods had come with quicksilver indistinction that morning—panic to misery to hilarity to peacefulness to terror, now to misery again. He stood by the block watching the giant remove the skyscraper side of the water heater and set it aside to poke the screw driver into the heater's belly.

A cold wind fogged across him then and his head snapped around so quickly it sent painful twinges down his neck. The door!

"Oh, my God," he muttered, astonished at his own stupidity. To stand here in disconsolate gloom when all the time his escape route was waiting.

He almost dashed straight across the floor. Then, with a rocking lurch, he realized that the giant might see and think him an insect, being conscious only of smallness and movement.

Eyes on the looming figure, he backed along the side of the block until he reached the wall. Then, turning, he raced along its base to the great shadow of the fuel tank. Eyes still on the giant, he ran underneath the tank, past the fifty strides of the ladder, under the red metal table, the wicker table, hardly starting at all when the oil burner flared once more into sound. Behind, the giant tapped and probed at the machinery of the water heater. Scott reached the foot of the steps.

The first one loomed fifty feet above him. He paced in the chilly shadow of it, looking up its sheer face at the sunlight pouring overhead like a golden canopy. It was still early morning, then; the back of the house faced east.

Abruptly he ran along the block-long distance of the step, looking for a place to climb. But there was nothing except a narrow vertical passage at the far right end where mortar between two cement blocks had contracted, leaving a three-sided chimney about the thickness of his body. He'd have to climb it as mountaineers did—braced rigid between back and sandal bottoms, inching himself up by leg tension. It was a terribly difficult way, and there were seven steps to the back yard. Seven fifty-foot faces to climb. If he were exhausted after the first one . . .

The thread. It might help. He ran back to the wicker table and shook loose the bar from its place. He glanced over at the giant, still crouching in front of the heater, then ran back to the step, dragging the thick thread behind him. There was just a chance.

He flung the bar up. But it wouldn't reach the top of the step, and even if he could throw it that high, there wasn't likely to be any niche for it to catch in. He dragged the thread to the three-sided chimney and stood there searching its narrow height for a crevice in which he might lodge the bar. There was none.

He threw the bar down and, half walking, half running, moved restlessly along the base of the steps. He turned like a trapped animal and ran back again. There had to be a way. He'd been waiting for this opportunity for months; through half a winter in the cellar, waiting for someone to open that vast door so he could climb to freedom.

But he was so *small*. "No, no." He wouldn't let himself think about that. There was a way; there always was a way. No matter how difficult, there always was a way. He had to believe that. Nervously he cast another glance back at the crouching giant. How long would he stay there? Hours? Minutes? There was no time to waste.

The broom.

Whirling again, Scott raced across the floor, shivering in the wind. He should have put on the heavier robe. But there had been no time. Besides, it was probably still wet. The thimble; he wondered whether the giant's monstrous feet had knocked it over, perhaps even crushed it.

It doesn't matter! he yelled at himself. I'm getting out of here! He skidded to a halt in front of the broom that leaned against the refrigerator.

There was a spider web across the top of the bound bristles. He knew it wasn't the black widow's work, but it reminded him that his pin was back at the water heater. Should he go back and try to get it?

He shook that off too. It doesn't *matter!* He was going to get out of there. That was all he'd let himself concentrate on. I'm going to get out, that's all; I'm going to get out.

He grabbed one of the club-thick straws and pulled at it with all his strength. It stuck. He pulled again, with the same result. He grabbed the next straw and jerked at it. It stuck fast. With an impatient curse, he grabbed the next straw and pulled and the next and the next. They all stuck fast.

He tried another. He pulled as hard as he could, carelessly, bracing his feet against the bristles. When one finally did pull out, it came loose so easily that it sent him flying over on his back on the cement floor. He cried out sharply, then had to roll out of the way quickly to keep the toppling straw from crashing down on his skull.

He struggled to his feet, wincing at the pain in his back. Squatting, he grabbed hold of the straw and dragged it slowly over to the step, laying it perpendicular to the face. Then he let it drop and stood there panting, hands on hips. The sunlight overhead was like a bolt of shimmering cloth, so thick and brilliant it seemed that he could run right up it to the yard.

He closed his eyes and drank in fast lungfuls of the cold March air. Then he ran back to the other end of the straw and lifted it. Bracing the end against the rough cement face, he kept lifting it, drawing in the far end so that the straw rose at a steeper and steeper angle against the step. Wouldn't the giant hear the scraping? No, of course not. Those vast ears could never pick up such a tiny sound.

When the straw was leaning against the step at approximately a seventy-degree angle, he dropped his arms and let them hang aching at his sides. His head fell forward, mouth open, gasping at the air. As cold as it was, he leaned against the cement. The cellar swam in shadowy ripples before his exhaustion-glazed eyes. The oil burner had stopped. In the void of silence, he could hear the clatter of the giant's tools in the water heater.

When normal sight returned and his arms had stopped throbbing so badly, he looked up at the straw. He groaned. It wasn't nearly as long as he had expected; and shorter yet because, reared, it sagged limply in the middle. Even if he reached its very top, there would still be a good eight to ten feet for him to scale before he reached the top of the step. Eight to ten feet of vertical cement with no handholds to help him up.

He ran a shaky hand through his hair. You're not going to beat me, he thought, addressing unknown powers again. His face was a tense mask of lines and ridges. He was going to get up there, that was all there was *to* it.

He looked around.

Against the wall near the log pile there was a hill of stones, leaves, and wood scraps. Long ago, in a life that seemed now more imaginary than real, he had swept them all there in a spurt of atypical neatness.

He ran to the pile. It rose above him like a hill of boulders and giant logs, some as high as houses. Could he hope to drag some of them to the base of the step, at least enough to prop the straw on and make up five of those eight to ten feet? The rest of the footage he could chance with an upward spring, as he had done in climbing to the tabletop. But you almost fell from the tabletop, he reminded himself. If it hadn't been for that paint-can handle . . .

He ignored the recollection. This was beyond argument. Every action since his plunge into the cellar had been dedicated to the hope of getting up those steps. In the beginning, he'd been up and down them a hundred times, always stopped by the closed door. When he thought of how easily he'd been able to mount the steps then, it made him sick. It was cruel that now, when the door was finally opened, the steps should be no longer walls to him, but cliffs.

The first stone he tried to move was so heavy he couldn't budge it. He stumbled over the uneven surface of the hill looking for smaller stones, his restless gaze pausing momentarily on various of the dark cave openings formed by the piled rock. What if the spider were hiding in one of them? Heart thudding in slow, heavy beats, he moved over the broken slope until he found a flat stone he could move.

This he pushed with agonizing slowness across the floor, jamming it up against the step. He straightened up and stepped back. The stone was a little higher than his knees. He'd need another one.

Returning to the hill of rocks, he continued searching until he'd found a similar stone plus a piece of bark. Added to the original stone, these two extra pieces would just about make up the needed height. Moreover, there was a groove in the bark onto which the end of the straw might fit.

Grunting with satisfaction, he pushed the dead weight of the second stone back to the step. There, teeth clamped, body shaking with taut-muscled exertion, he managed to lift it to the top of the first stone, something giving in his back as he did it. Straightening up, he felt a flare of pain in his back muscles. You're coming apart, Carey, he told himself. It was amusing.

The second stone teetered a little on the first, he discovered. He had to cram pieces of torn cardboard into the gaps between the two facing surfaces. That done, he climbed up on top of it and jumped up and down. So far, his little platform was secure.

Worriedly he looked over at the giant, still working on the water heater—but for how long? He jumped down off the top stone, gasping at the pain in his back, and limped back to the hill. Sore throat, aching back, twitching arms. What next? A cold wind blew over him and he sneezed. Pneumonia next, he thought. It was—well, almost—amusing.

The scrap of bark was easier to transport. He carried the thin end of it on his shoulder and walked, bent over, dragging the bark behind him. It was getting colder. It suddenly occurred to him that he didn't know what he was going to do when he got out in the yard. If it was so cold, wouldn't he freeze to death? He pushed the thought aside.

He slid the bark over the top of the two stones, then stood leaning against his structure, looking at it.

No, now that they were close together, he could see that the straw end was too thick to fit into the groove in the bark. He blew out a breath through gritted teeth. Troubles, troubles. Another anxious glance at the giant. How could he tell how much time there was? What if he got up two steps and the giant finished and went back up? If he weren't crushed to death by those monstrous shoes, he would be, at the very least, stranded on the high, darkened step, unable to see well enough to get down again.

But he wasn't going to think of that. This was it, the end, the finale. He got out now or— No, there was no *or*. He wouldn't let there be one.

Picking up a tiny scrap of rock, he climbed to the top of his platform and scraped at the groove, tearing away stringy fibers until the slot was wide enough to accommodate the end of the straw. He threw down the piece of rock and, lifting the hem of his robe, mopped his sweaty face dry.

He stood there for a few minutes, breathing deeply, letting his muscles unknot. There's no *time* for rest, his brain scolded. But he answered it, I'm sorry, I've got to rest or I'll never make the top. He'd have to take a chance on the length of time the giant would be working. He'd never make the summit in one all-out effort, that was clear.

That was when the thought occurred to him. What am I doing all this for?

For a moment it stopped him cold. What *was* he doing it for? In a matter of days it would all be over. He would be gone. Why all this exertion, then? Why this pretense at continuing an existence that was already doomed?

He shook his head. It was dangerous to think like that. Dwelling on it could end him. For in the final analysis, everything he had done and was doing was illogical. Yet he couldn't stop. Was it that he didn't believe that everything would be over on Sunday? How could he doubt it? Had the process faltered once—*once*—since it had begun? It had not. A seventh of an inch a day, as precise as clockwork. He could have devised a mathematical system on the absolute constancy of his descent into inevitable nothingness.

He shuddered. Strange, thinking about it was debilitating. Already he felt weaker, more exhausted, less confident. If he pursued it long enough he would be finished.

He blinked his eyes and, deliberately ignoring his rise of hopeless weariness, moved to the straw. He wouldn't let it happen to him. He'd lose himself in work.

Lifting the straw to the top of the bark proved extremely difficult. It was one thing to lift an end of it, using the floor as a fulcrum. It was one thing to slide the straw to a leaning position against the step. It was another entirely to lift the whole weight of it from the floor and prop it on the base he had erected.

The first time he lifted the straw, it slipped from his grasp and banged down on the cement, crushing one edge of a sandal. He remained pinned until he lifted the straw again and pulled his foot away.

He leaned against the platform, chest throbbing with agitated breath. If the straw had landed on his foot . . .

He closed his eyes. Don't think about it, he warned himself. Please. Don't think about the things that *could* have happened.

The second time he tried, he managed to get the straw propped on the edge of the first stone. But while he was resting the straw fell over and almost knocked him down. Cursing with desperate anger, he dragged the straw to a leaning position, then, with a surge of energy, lifted it once more, this time making sure it was secure before letting go.

The next lift was harder yet. Leverage would be bad because he'd have to start raising the straw at waist level, and then up to the top of the second stone, which was at the level of his shoulders. His legs would be of no service. All the strength would have to come from his back, shoulders, and arms.

Drawing in breath through his mouth, he waited till his chest was swollen taut, then cut off air abruptly and lifted the heavy straw, setting it down on the second stone. It wasn't until he let go that he realized how much of a lift it had been. There was a painful tension through his back and groin that loosened very slowly, as if the muscles had been twisted like wrung-out cloths and were unraveling now. He pressed a palm against the soft area on his back.

A few moments later he climbed to the top of the platform. With one more short lift, he slid the end of the straw into the groove. He shook the straw until it was in the most advantageous position, then sat down to gather strength for the climb. The giant was still working. There would be time. Of course there would.

Then he stood and tested the straw. Good, he thought. He inhaled quickly. Now to get out of there. He felt at the coil of thread over his right shoulder. Good. He was ready.

He began inching up the straw, shinnying along it carefully to keep it from sliding over. It sagged even more under his weight. Once it began to slip a little to the side, and he had to stop and, with body jerks, shake it back into position.

After a pause, he started climbing again, legs wrapped around the straw, lips drawn back from clenched teeth, eyes looking straight ahead at the dead gray of the cement face. When he got to the top of the step, he'd lower a thread loop and pull up the straw. There would be no stones to prop it on up there, but he'd manage something. Now he was twenty feet up, now twenty-five, now thirty, now . . .

A gigantic shape slid over him, blotting the sun from view.

He almost fell off the straw. Losing his grip, he spun around to the underside of the straw, arms hugging wildly at its smooth surface. He jerked himself to a halt, and found himself looking into the green lantern eyes of the cat.

Shock drained breath from him. He felt even more helplessly petrified than when the giant had come down the steps. He clung to the straw, staring at the cat as if hypnotized.

The spearlike whiskers twitched. The huge cat edged forward in wary curiosity, belly near the floor, front legs flattened, back slightly arched. Scott felt the warm wind of its breath misting over him, and he almost retched.

Unconsciously he let himself slide down a few inches. There was a liquid rumbling in the cat's throat and he stopped abruptly, hanging there motionless. The cat's whiskers twitched again. Its breath was sickening. Turning his head from side to side, he saw its protruding side teeth like giant, yellow-edged daggers that could pierce his body in an instant.

An electric shuddering ran down his back. He slid down the straw a little more. The cat hunched forward. No! his mind screamed. He froze to the quivering straw, heartbeat like a fist pounding at his chest.

If he tried to descend, the cat would attack. If he jumped, he'd break a leg and be eaten. Yet he couldn't stay there. His throat contracted with a dry clicking. He hung there impotently under the bland surveillance of the huge cat.

When it raised its right paw twitchingly, his breath stopped.

In a fascination of absolute horror, he watched the huge, gray, scythe-clawed paw rise up slowly, coming closer and closer to him. He couldn't move. Unblinking, stark-eyed, he hung there waiting.

Just before the paw was going to touch him, everything shook loose at once.

"Get out!" he screamed into the cat's face. It jumped back, startled. With a lurch, he flung the straw to the side, and it began sliding raspingly along the cement face, faster and faster. Not looking at the cat, he hung on till the toppling straw was about five feet from the floor. Then he leaped.

Landing, he twisted himself in a somersault. Behind him the cat glided forward, growling. Get *up!* his mind shrieked. He found his feet again and lurched forward, falling.

As he skidded to his knees, the cat jumped, great paws banging down on each side of him, claw ends raking sparks from the cement. The mouth yawned open, a cave of scimitars and hot winds.

Twitching back against the step, Scott felt the thread coil slip off his shoulder. Grabbing it, he flung it deep into the cat's mouth and it jumped back, spitting and gagging. Pushing off from the step, Scott raced to the hill of stones and dived into a cave.

A second after, the cat's paw raked across the spot where he had entered. A cuffed stone rattled away. Scott crawled to the back of the cave and down a side tunnel as the cat scratched wildly at the rocks.

"Hey, puss."

Scott stopped abruptly, head cocked, as the deep voice thundered.

"Hey, what're you after?" asked the voice. Scott heard chuckling like a threat of distant thunder. "Got yourself a mouse in there?"

The floor shook as the giant's shoes thudded across it. With an indrawn cry, Scott ran down the sloping tunnel, off into another one, again into yet another, until he skidded to a halt before a blank wall.

There he crouched, shivering and waiting.

"Got yourself a mouse, have you?" the voice asked. It made Scott's head hurt. He covered up his ears. He still heard the fierce meowing of the cat.

"Well, let's see if we can't find 'im, puss," the giant said.

"No." Scott didn't even know he spoke. He shrank against the wall, hearing the boulders being shoved aside by the giant's hands, the sound a grating, screeching rasp that plunged like a knife into his brain. He pressed both palms against his ears as hard as he could.

Suddenly, light speared across him. With a cry, he dived headlong into a newly opened tunnel. Clawing wildly at the air, he fell seven feet to a hard rock shelf, landing on his side and raking skin off his right arm. In the darkness, a boulder slammed down beside him, tearing skin from the heel of his right hand. He cried out in terror.

The giant said, "We'll find 'im, puss, we'll find 'im."

Light again. With a rasping sob, Scott lurched up and dived into the darkness again. A stone bounced off the floor and knocked him down. He rolled over and up again, running across the floor of the collapsing cavern, mute with panic. Another bouncing rock sent him flailing across the floor to smash head-on into a rock wall.

As deeper blackness blotted out his mind, he felt blood trickling warmly down his cheek. His legs went limp, his hands uncurled like flowers dying, and falling rocks reared up a tomb around him.

Chapter Nine

AT LAST he stumbled into light.

He stood at the mouth of the cave, looking around the cellar with dull, unwitting eyes.

The giant was gone. And the cat. The side of the water heater was fastened back in place. Everything was as it had been; the vast, piled objects, the heavy silence, the imprisoning remoteness of it all. His gaze moved slowly to the steps and up them. The door was shut.

He stared at it, feeling empty with desire. He had struggled in vain once more. All the pushing of boulders, the endless crawlings and climbings through inky tunnel twists had been in vain.

His eyes closed. He swayed weakly on the hill of rocks, one throbbing length of pain. It seemed to well over him; his arms, his hands and legs and trunk. Inside, too, in his throat and chest and stomach. He had a dull, eating headache. He didn't know if he were starving or nauseous. His hands shook fitfully.

He shuffled back to the heater.

The thimble had been knocked on its side. The few drops remaining in it he drank like a thirsty animal, sucking them up from the cuplike indentations. It hurt to swallow.

When he had finished the water, he climbed with slow, exhausted movements to the top of the cement block. His sleeping place was completely barren, the sponge, handkerchief, cracker bundle, the box top all gone. He stumbled to the edge of the block and saw the box top across the floor. It looked big and heavy. He hadn't the strength to lift it.

He remained in the shadowy warmth for a long while, just standing, weaving a little, staring out at the darkening cellar. Another day ending. Wednesday. Three days left.

His stomach gurgled hungrily. Slowly he tilted his head back and looked up to where he put the few soggy cracker crumbs. They were still there. With a groan he moved to the leg of the water heater and climbed up to the shelf.

He sat there, legs dangling, eating the cracker pieces. They were still damp, but edible. His jaws moved with rhythmless lethargy, his eyes staring straight ahead. He was so tired he could hardly eat. He knew he should go down and get the box top to sleep under in case the spider came. It came almost every night. But he was too weary. He'd sleep up here on the shelf. If the spider came . . . Well, what did it matter? It reminded him of a time, long before, when he had been with the Infantry in Germany. He'd been so tired that he'd gone to sleep without digging a foxhole, knowing it might mean his death.

He plodded along the shelf until he came to a walled-in area, then climbed over the wall and sank down in the darkness, his head resting on a screw head.

He lay there on his back, breathing slowly, barely able to summon the strength to fill his lungs. He thought, Little man, what now?

It occurred to him then that, instead of fighting with the stones and the straw, he might simply have climbed into the giant's slack cuff and been carried from the cellar in a moment. The only indication of the self-fury he felt was a sudden bunching of skin around his closed eyes, a moist clicking sound as his lips pulled back suddenly from clenched teeth. Fool! Even the thought seemed to rise wearily.

His face relaxed again into a mask of sagging lines.

Another question. Why hadn't he tried to communicate with the giant? Oddly enough, that thought didn't anger him. It was so alien it only surprised him. Was that because he was so small, because he felt that he was in another world and there could be no communication? Or was it that, as in all decisions now, he counted on only himself for any desired accomplishment?

Surely not that, he thought bitterly. He was as helpless and ineffectual as ever, maybe a little more blundering, that was all.

In the darkness he felt experimentally around his body. He ran a hand over the long, raw-fleshed scrape on his right forearm. He touched the torn flesh on the heel of his right hand, nudged an elbow against the swelling, purplish bruise on his right side. He ran a finger over the jagged laceration across his forehead. He prodded at his sore throat. He reared up a trifle and felt the shoot of pain in his back. Finally he let the separate aches sink back again into the general, coalescent pain.

His eyes opened, the lids seeming to fall back of their own accord, and he stared sightlessly at the darkness. He remembered regaining consciousness in the sepulcher of rocks; remembered the horror that had almost driven him insane until he realized that there was air to breathe and he had to keep his mind if he wanted to get out.

But that first instant of realizing that he was sealed in a black crypt and still alive had been the lowest point.

He wondered why the phrase occurred to him. How did he know it was his lowest point? There might be others much worse waiting around the next corner—if he stayed alive.

But he couldn't think of anything else. It *was* the lowest point, the nadir of his existence in the cellar.

It made him think of another lowest point, in the other life he had once led.

35″

When they got home from Marty's, he stood at the living-room window while Lou carried Beth to bed. He didn't offer to help. He knew he couldn't lift his daughter now.

When Lou came out of the bedroom he was still standing there.

"Aren't you going to take off your hat and coat?" she asked.

She went into the kitchen before he could answer. He stood in his boy's jacket and his Alpine hat with the red feather stuck in the band, hearing her open the refrigerator. He stared out at the dark street and heard the nerve-twisting crunch of ice cubes being freed in their tray, the muted pop of a bottle cap being pried off, the carbonated gurgle of soda being poured.

"Want some Coke?" she called to him.

He shook his head.

"Scott?"

"No," he said. He felt a throbbing at his wrists.

She came in with the drink. "Aren't you going to take off your things?" she asked.

"I don't know," he said.

She sat down on the couch and kicked off her shoes. "Another day," she said. He didn't reply. He felt as if she were trying to make him feel like a boy for getting dramatic over something inconsequential, while she patiently humored him. He wanted to burst out angrily at her, but there wasn't any opening.

"Are you just going to stand there?" she asked.

"If I choose," he said.

She looked at him for a moment, blank-faced. He saw the reflection of her face in the window. Then she shrugged. "Go ahead," she said.

"No skin off *your* nose," he said.

"What?" There was a sad, weary smile on her lips.

"Nothing, nothing." Now he *did* feel like a boy.

Her drinking and swallowing sounded noisy to him. He grimaced irritably. Don't *slurp*, his mind rasped. You sound like a pig.

"Oh, come on, Scott. Brooding won't help." She sounded faintly bored.

He closed his eyes and shuddered. It has come to this, he thought. The horror was gone; she was inured. He had expected it, but it was still a shock to find it happening.

He was her husband. He had been over six feet tall. Now he was smaller than her five-year-old daughter. He was standing in front of her, grotesque in his little boy's clothes, and there was nothing but a faint boredom in her voice. It was a horror beyond horror.

His eyes were bleak as he stared out at the street, listening to the trees rustle in the night wind like a woman's skirts descending an endless stairway.

He heard her drink again and he stiffened angrily.

"Scott," she said. Falsely applied affection, he thought. "Sit down. Staring out the window won't help Marty's business."

He spoke without turning. "You think that's what I'm worried about?"

"Isn't it? Isn't it what we're both—"

"It *isn't*," he cut her off coldly. Coldness in a little boy's voice sounded bizarre—as if he were acting out a part in a grade-school play, unconvincing and laughable.

"What, then?" she asked.

"If you don't know by now . . ."

"Oh, come on, darling."

He picked on that. "Takes a little straining to call me darling now, doesn't it?" he said, skin tight across his small face. "Takes a little—"

"Oh, *stop* it, Scott. Aren't there enough troubles without your imagining more?"

"Imagining?" His voice grew shrill. "Sure! I'm imagining everything! Nothing has changed. Everything's just the same. It's all just my imagination!"

"You'll wake Beth up."

Too many enraged words filled his throat at once. They choked each other and he could only stand fuming impotently. He turned back to the window and stared out again.

Then, abruptly, he headed for the front door.

"Where are you going?" she asked, sounding alarmed.

"For a walk! Do you mind?"

"You mean down the street?"

He wanted to scream. "Yes," he said, his voice shaking with repressed anger, "down the street."

"You think you should?"

"Yes, I think I should!"

"Scott, I'm only thinking of you!" she burst out. "Can't you see that?"

"Sure. Sure you are." He jerked at the front door, but it stuck. Color sprouted in his cheeks and he jerked harder, a curse muffled on his lips.

"Scott, what have *I* done?" she asked. "Did I make you this way? Did I take that contract away from Marty?"

"Damn this goddam—" His voice shook. Then the door opened and banged against the wall.

"What if someone sees you?" she asked, starting up from the couch.

"Good-by," he said, slamming the door behind him. And even that was ineffective because the jamb was too warped and the door wouldn't slam, only crunch into its frame.

He didn't look back. He started down the block with quick, agitated strides, heading for the lake.

He was about twenty yards from the house when the front door opened.

"Scott?"

He wasn't going to answer at first. Then, grudgingly, he stopped and spoke over his shoulder.

"What?" he asked, and he could have wept at the thin, ineffectual sound of his voice.

She hesitated a moment, then asked, "Shall I come with you?"

"No," he said. It was spoken in neither anger nor despair.

He stood there a moment longer looking back in spite of himself, wondering if she would insist on coming. But she only stood there, a motionless outline in the doorway.

"Be careful, darling," she said.

He had to bite off the sob that tore up through him. Twisting around, he hurried quickly down the dark street. He never heard her close the door.

This is the bottom, he thought, the very bottom. There is nothing lower than for a man to become an object of pity. A man could bear hate, abuse, anger and castigation; but pity, never. When a man became pitiable, he was lost. Pity was for helpless things.

Walking on the treadmill of the world, he tried to blank his mind. He stared at the sidewalk, walking quickly through the patches of street light and into darkness again, trying not to think.

His mind would not co-operate; it was typical of introspective minds. What he told it not to think about it dwelt on. What he demanded it to leave alone it clung to, doglike. It was the way.

Summer nights on the lake were sometimes chilly. He drew up the collar of his jacket and walked on, looking ahead at the dark, shifting waters. Since it was a week night, the cafés and taverns along the shore were not open. Approaching the dark lake, he began to hear the slapping of water on the pebbled beach.

The sidewalk ended. He moved out across rough ground, the leaves and twigs crackling under his tread like things alive. There was a cold wind blowing off the lake. It cut through his jacket, chilling him. He didn't care.

About a hundred yards from the sidewalk, he came to an open area beside a dark, rustic building. It was a German café and tavern, next to it a few dozen tables and benches for outdoor eating and drinking. Scott threaded his way among them until he overlooked the lake. There he sank down on the rough, pocked surface of a bench.

He sat staring grimly at the lake. He tried to imagine sinking down in it forever. Was it so fantastic? The same thing was happening to him now. No, he would hit bottom and that would be the end of it.

He was drowning in another way.

They had moved to the lake six weeks before, because Scott had felt trapped in the apartment. If he went out, people stared at him. With the first week and a half of the *Globe-Post* series already in print and reprint, he had become a national celebrity. Requests still poured in for personal appearances. Reporters came endlessly to the door.

But mostly it was the ordinary people, the curious, staring people who wanted to look at the shrinking man and think, Thank God, *I'm* normal.

So they had moved to the lake, and somehow they had managed to get there without anyone's finding out.

Life there, he discovered, was no improvement.

The dragging of it was what made it so bad. The way shrinking went on day by day, never noticeable, never ceasing, an inch a week like hideous clockwork. And all the humdrum functions of the day went on along with it in inexorable monotony.

Until anger, crouching in him like a cornered animal, would spring out wildly. The subject didn't matter. It was the opening that counted.

Like the cat:

"I swear to God, if you don't get rid of that goddam cat, I'll kill it!"

Fury from a doll, his voice not manlike and authoritive, but frail and uncompelling.

"Scott, she's not hurting you."

He dragged up a sleeve. "What's that? Imagination?" He pointed to a ragged scar.

"She was frightened when she did that."

"Well, I'm frightened too! What does she have to do, rip open my throat before you get rid of her?"

And the two beds:

"What are you trying to do, humiliate me?"

"Scott, it was your idea."

"Only because you couldn't stand to touch me."

"That's not true!"

"Isn't it?"

"No! I tried to do everything I could to—"

"I'm not a boy! You can't treat my body like a little boy's!"

And Beth:

"Scott, can't you see she doesn't understand?"

"I'm still her father, damn it!"

All his outbursts ended alike; him rushing to the cool cellar, standing down there, leaning on the refrigerator, breath a rasping sound in him, teeth gritted, hands clenched.

Days passed, one torture on another. Clothes were taken in for him, furniture got bigger, less manageable. Beth and Lou got bigger. Financial worries got bigger.

"Scott, I hate to say it, but I don't see how we can go on much longer on fifty dollars a week. With all of us to feed and clothe and house . . ." Her voice trailed off; she shook her head in distress.

"I suppose you expect me to go back to the paper."

"I didn't say that. I merely said—"

"I know what you said."

"Well, if it offends you, I'm sorry. Fifty dollars a week isn't enough. What about when winter comes? What about winter clothes, and oil?"

He shook his head as if he were trying to shake away the need to think of it.

"Do you think Marty would—"

"I can't ask Marty for more money," he said curtly.

"Well . . ." She said no more. She didn't have to.

And if she forgot and undressed without turning out the light, perhaps thinking he was asleep, he would lie in bed staring at her naked body, listening to the liquid rustle of her nightgown as it undulated down over her large breasts and stomach and hips and legs. He'd never realized it before, but it was the most maddening sound in the world. And he'd look at her as if he were a man dying of thirst looking at unreachable waters.

Then, the last week in July, Marty's check didn't come.

First they thought it was an oversight. But two more weeks went by and the check still didn't come.

"We can't wait much longer, Scott," she said.

"What about the savings account?"

"There isn't more than seventy dollars in it."

"Oh. Well . . . we'll wait one more day," he said.

He spent that day in the living room, staring at the same page of the book he was supposedly reading.

He kept telling himself he should go back to the *Globe-Post*, let them continue their series. Or accept one of the many offers for personal appearances. Or let those lurid magazines write his story. Or allow a ghost writer to grind out a book about his case. Then there would be enough money, then the insecurity that Lou feared so desperately would be ended.

But telling himself about it wasn't enough. His revulsion against placing himself before the blatant curiosity of people was too strong.

He comforted himself. The check will come tomorrow, he kept repeating, it'll come tomorrow.

But it didn't. And that night they'd driven over to Marty's and Marty had told him that he'd lost his contract with Fairchild and had to cut down operations to almost nothing. The checks would have to stop. He gave Scott a hundred dollars, but that was the end.

Cold wind blew across him. Across the lake a dog barked. He looked down and watched his shoes swinging above the ground like pendulum tips. And now no money coming in. Seventy dollars in the bank, a hundred in his wallet. When that was gone, what?

He imagined himself at the paper again, Berg taking pictures, ogling Lou, Hammer asking endless questions. Headlines fluttered across his mind like banners. SMALLER THAN TWO-YEAR-OLD! EATS IN HIGH CHAIR! WEARS BABY CLOTHES! LIVES IN SHOEBOX! SEX DESIRE STILL SAME!

His eyes shut quickly. Why wasn't it really acromicria? At least then his sex desire would be almost gone. As it was, it got worse and worse. It seemed twice as bad as when he had been normal, but that was doubtless because there was no outlet at all. He couldn't approach Louise any more. The drive went on burning in him, banking higher and higher each day, adding its own uniquely hideous pressure to everything else he was suffering.

And he couldn't talk to Louise about it. The night she'd made that obvious offer, he'd felt almost offended. He knew it was over.

"Laughin' at the blues!
Laughin' till I'm crazee!"

He twitched up on the bench, his head snapping around. Squinting into the darkness, he saw three shadowy figures strolling a short distance away, their youthful voices thin as they sang.

"My life is nothin' but a stumblin' in the dark.
I lost my way when I was born."

Boys, he thought, singing, growing up and taking it for granted. He watched them with a biting envy.

"Hey, there's a kid down there," one of them said.

At first Scott didn't realize they were talking about him. Then he did and his mouth tightened.

"Wonder what he's doin' there."

"Prob'ly—"

Scott didn't hear the rest of it, but from the burst of coarse laughter he could guess what had been whispered. With a tensing of muscles, he slid off the bench and started walking back toward the sidewalk.

"Hey, he's goin'," one of the boys said.

"Let's have some fun," said another.

Scott felt a jolt of panic, but pride would not allow him to run. He kept steadily on toward the sidewalk.

Now the footsteps of the three boys grew faster.

"Hey, where ya goin', kid?" he heard one of the boys call to him.

"Yeah, kid, where ya goin'?" said another.

"Where's the fire, kid?"

There was a general snicker. Scott couldn't help it; he walked faster. The boys walked faster.

"I don't think Kiddo likes us," said one of them.

"That ain't nice," said another.

It was a race. Scott knew it with a hanging tautness in his stomach. But he wouldn't run. Not from three boys. He'd never be small enough to run from three boys. He glanced aside as he started up the slope toward the sidewalk. They were gaining on him. He saw the glowing tips of their cigarettes moving toward him like hopping fireflies.

They caught up to him before he reached the sidewalk. One of them grabbed his arm and held him back.

"Let go of me," he said.

"Hey, kid, where ya goin'?" asked the boy who held him. His voice was insolent with pretended friendliness.

"I'm going home," he said.

The boy looked about fifteen, sixteen maybe. He had a baseball cap on. His fingers dug into Scott's arm. Scott didn't have to see his face; he could almost imagine it—thin, mean, the jawline and brow peppered with pimples, the cigarette drooping from one corner of a lean, almost lipless mouth.

"The kid says he's goin' home," said the boy.

"Izzat wot the kid says?" said another.

"Yeah," said the third. "Ain't that somethin'?"

Scott tried to push by them, but the boy in the cap drew him back into their surrounding circle.

"Kid, you shouldn't do that," he said. "We don't like kids that do that, do we, fellas?"

"Naw, naw. He's a fresh kid. We don't like fresh kids."

"Let go of me," Scott said, shocked at the tremble of his voice.

The boy released his arm, but he was still penned in.

"I wantcha t'meet my pals," said the boy. No face. Just the flash of a pale cheek, the glitter of an eye in the tiny flaring glow of the cigarette. A black, shadowy figure leaning over him.

"This is Tony," he said. "Say hello to 'im."

"I have to go home," Scott said, moving forward.

The boy pushed him back. "Hey, kid, you don't understand. Fellas, this kid don't understand." He tried to sound gentle and reasonable.

"Kid, don't you unnerstand?" said one of the other boys. "That's funny, y'know? The kid should unnerstand."

"You're very funny," Scott said. "Now will you—"

"Hey. The kid thinks we're funny," said the boy with the baseball cap on. "D'ya hear that, fellas? He thinks we're funny." His voice lost its banter. "Maybe we oughta show 'im how funny we are," he said.

Scott felt a crawling sensation in his groin and lower stomach. He looked around at the boys, unable to keep down the fear.

"Listen, my mother expects me home," he heard himself saying.

"Awwwww," said the boy with the cap. "His mother's waitin'. Jesus, ain't that sad? Ain't that sad, fellas?"

"That makes me cry," said one of the others. "Boo-hoo-hoo. I'm cryin'." A vicious chuckle emptied from his throat. The third boy snickered and punched his friend playfully on the arm.

"Live around here, kid?" asked the boy with the cap. He blew smoke into Scott's face and Scott coughed. "Hey, the kid's croakin'," said the boy, with mock concern. "He's chokin' 'n croakin'. Ain't that sad?"

Scott tried to push past them again, but he was shoved back, more violently this time.

"Don't do that again," warned the boy in the cap. His voice was friendly and amiable. "We wouldn't wanna hurt a kid. Would we, fellas?"

"Naw, we wouldn't wanna do *that*," said another.

"Hey, let's see if he has any dough on 'im," said the third.

Scott felt himself tightening with a weird mixture of adult fury and childlike dread. It was even worse than it had been with that man. He was smaller now, much weaker. There was no strength in him to match his man's anger.

"Yeah," said the boy in the cap. "Hey, ya got any dough on ya, kid?"

"No, I haven't," he said angrily.

He gasped as the boy in the cap hit him on the arm.

"Don't talk t'me like that, kid," said the boy. "I don't *like* fresh kids."

Dread overwhelmed anger again. He knew he'd have to play it different to get out of this.

"I don't have any money," he said. His neck was beginning to arch from looking up at them. "My mother doesn't give me any."

The boy in the cap turned to his friends. "The kid says his mother don't give him none."

"Cheap bitch!" said another.

"I'll give her a good cheap—" said the third, breaking off with a convulsive forward jerk of his lower frame.

The boys laughed loudly. "Ya hear that, kid?" said the boy in the cap. "Tell yer old lady that Tony'll give 'er a good cheap one."

"Cheap? I'll do it fer nothin'," Tony said, humor submerged in a sudden surge of angry desire. "Hey, kid, has she got a big pair on 'er?"

Their raucous laughter broke off as Scott lunged between two of them. The boy in the cap grabbed him by the arm and spun him around. The heel of his palm slammed across Scott's cheek.

"I *told* ya not t'do that," snarled the boy.

"Son-of-a—!" Scott raged, spitting blood. The last word was swallowed in a grunt as he drove his small fist into the boy's stomach.

"Bitch!" snapped the boy in a fury. He shot a fist into Scott's face. Scott cried out as the blow drove a wedge of pain into his skull. He fell back against one of the other boys, blood streaming darkly from his nose.

"Hold 'im!" snarled the boy, and the two other boys grabbed Scott's arm.

"Hit me in the belly, will ya, ya little son-of-a-bitch?" the boy said. "I'll . . ." He seemed undecided as to what revenge to take. Then he made a sound of angry decision and pulled out a book of matches from his trouser pocket.

"Maybe I'll give ya a coupla brands, kiddo," he said. "How d'ya like *that?*"

"Let me go!" Scott struggled wildly in the boys' grip. He kept on sniffing to keep the blood from running across his lips. "Please!" His voice cracked badly.

The match flared in the darkness and Scott saw the boy's face as he'd imagined it.

The boy leaned in close.

"Hey," he said, suddenly fascinated. "Hey!" a crooked smile lifted the corner of his mouth. "This ain't no kid." He stared into Scott's twisted face. "Ya know who this *is?*"

"Whattaya talkin' about?" asked one of the boys.

"It's that guy! That shrinkin' guy!"

"What?" they said.

"Look at 'im, *look* at 'im, for God's sake!"

"Damn it, let me go or I'll have you all in jail!" Scott stormed at them to hide the burst of agony in him.

"Shut up!" ordered the boy in the cap. His grin returned. "Yeah, don't ya see? It's—"

The match sputtered out and he lit another one. He held it so close to Scott's face that Scott could feel the heat of it.

"Ya see now? Ya *see?*"

"Yeah." The two other boys stared, open-mouthed, into Scott's face. "Yeah, it's him. I seen his picture on TV."

"And he tried t'make us think he was a kid," the boy said. "The freakin' son-of-a-bitch."

Scott couldn't speak. Despair had toppled anger. They knew him, they could betray him. He stood drained, his chest rising and falling with convulsive breath. The second match was thrown on the ground.

"Uh!" His head snapped over as the boy in the cap backhanded him.

"That's fuh lyin', Freako," the boy said. His laugh was thin and strained. "Freako, that's ya name. What d'ya say, freako? What d'ya say?"

"What do you *want* of me?" Scott gasped.

"What d'we want?" mimicked the boy. "Freako wants t'know what we want." The boys laughed.

"Hey," said the third boy, "let's pull down his pants and see if *all* of him shrunk!"

Scott surged forward in their grip like a berserk midget. The boy in the cap drove a palm stingingly across his face. The night was a spiraling blur before Scott's eyes.

"Freako don't understand," said the boy. "He's a dumb freako." He was breathing quickly through clenched teeth.

Dread was the knife in Scott now. He knew there was no reasoning with these boys. They were hating angry with their world and could express it only through violence.

"If you want my money, take it," he said quickly, buying desperate time.

"Bet ya shrinkin' *butt* we'll take it," sneered the boy. He laughed at his own joke. "Hey, that's pretty good." The humor left again. "Hold 'im," he said coldly. "I'll get his wallet."

Scott tensed himself in the darkness as the boy in the cap started around one of his friends.

"Ow!" One of the boys howled as Scott's shoe tip flashed up against his shin. The restraining hands on Scott's left arm were dropped.

"Ow!" The other boy's cry echoed the first; his hands dropped. Scott lunged forward in the darkness, heartbeat like a fist driving at his chest.

"Get 'im!" cried the boy in the cap. Scott's short legs pumped faster as he darted up the broken incline. "Bastard!" the boy shouted, and then he started after him.

Scott was gasping for breath before he reached the sidewalk. He almost tripped across its edge, went flailing forward, palms out, legs racing, then, finally, caught his balance and ran on. A stitch jabbed hotly at his side. Behind him, rapid shoe falls spattered onto the cement. "Lou," he whimpered, and ran on, open-mouthed.

Fifty yards up, he saw his house. Then, suddenly he realized he couldn't go there, because they'd know then where he lived, where the shrinking man lived.

His teeth jammed together and he turned impulsively into a dark alley.

He reached out, thinking he might open a side screen door and, still running, slam it shut so they'd think he'd gone in there. But that house was too close to his own. He ran on, gasping. Behind him the boys swept into the alley, their shoes crunching on the gravel.

Scott dashed around the back edge of the darkened house and raced across the yard.

There was a fence. Panic leaped in him. He knew he couldn't stop. Running at top speed, he jumped at it, clutching wildly for the top. He began scrambling up, slipped, started up again.

"Gotcha!"

A fist of dread pounded at his temples as he felt rough hands clutching at his right foot. His head snapped around and he saw the boy in the cap dragging him down.

A half-mad sound filled his throat. His other foot flailed out and drove into the boy's face. With a cry the boy let go and went staggering back, clutching at his face. Scott dragged himself over the fence, shoe tips scraping at the wood. He dropped down on the other side.

Jagged lances of pain shot up his ankle. He couldn't stop. Pushing up with a groan, he ran on, limping. Behind, he heard the two boys join their friend.

He scuttled painfully across the uneven ground until he came to the next street. There, finding a cellar door open, he half slipped, half jumped down the high steps, turned, and pulled the heavy door shut. It landed on his head and knocked him sideways against the cold concrete wall. He clutched out for a handhold as he rolled down two steps and landed on the dirt floor of the cellar.

He sat hunched over on the first step, trying to catch his breath. The step was cold and damp. He could feel it through his trousers. But he was too dizzy and weak to get up.

Breath wouldn't come. His thin chest kept jerking spasmodically as his lungs labored for air. There was a hot burning in his throat. The stitch was razor-tipped, a knife stabbing at his side. His head throbbed and ached. The inside of his mouth felt raw and smarting, and there was blood still running across his lips. The muscles of his legs were cramping in the coldness of the cellar. He was sweaty and shivering.

He began to cry.

It was not a man's crying, not a man's despairing sobs. It was a little boy sitting there in the cold, wet darkness, hurt and frightened and crying because there was no hope for him in the world; he was beaten and lost in a strange, unloving place.

Later, when it was safe, he limped home, chilled to the bone.

A frightened, wretched Lou put him to bed. She kept asking him what had happened, but he wouldn't answer. He just kept shaking his head, face expressionless, his small head rustling slowly on the pillow, back and forth, endlessly back and forth.

Chapter Ten

WAKING WAS a gradual itemization of pains.

His throat felt scraped and dry, feeling like a raw, juiceless wound. His face contorted as he swallowed. Whimpering softly, he twisted on his side. The pain of rubbing his lacerated temple against the screw head stabbed him into wakefulness.

He started to sit up, then sank back with a gasp, hot barbs ripping across the muscles of his back. He lay staring up at the dust-coated insides of the water heater. He thought: It's Thursday; there are three days left.

His right leg was throbbing. The knee felt swollen. He flexed the leg experimentally and winced when the dull ache flared into needling pain. He lay there quietly a moment, letting the pain ebb. He felt his face, his fingers stroking over the blood-caked scratches and tears.

Finally, with a groan, he shoved himself up and stood shakily, holding on to the black wall for support. How could he have got so mauled in such a few days? He'd been in the cellar for almost three months and it had never been like this before. Was it his size? Was it because the smaller he got, the more perilous life became for him?

He climbed over the wall slowly and he walked along the metal shelf to the leg. He kicked aside the few tiny scraps of crackers left there, then climbed down the leg with slow, careful movements until he stood dizzily on top of the cement block. Thursday. Thursday. His tongue stirred like a piece of thick, dry cloth in his mouth. He needed water.

He climbed down the block and looked into the thimble. Empty. And all the water on the floor had dried up or flowed into the small holes drilled in the cement. He stood there staring dully into the thimble cave. That meant he'd have to climb down the endless thread to the other thimble under the water tank. He sighed drearily and shuffled over to the ruler.

Three-sevenths of an inch.

Stolidly, as if it were something he had planned and not sudden disgust, he pushed the ruler over, and it clattered onto its side. He was sick of measuring himself.

He started walking toward the cavern in which the water

pump clanked and chugged. Then he stopped, remembering the pin. His gaze moved slowly over the floor, searching. It was not in sight. He went over to the sponge and looked under it. He looked under the box top. There was no pin. The giant must have kicked it away, or else the head of it had become embedded in the sole of those gargantuan shoes.

His gaze moved over to the house-high carton under the fuel tank. It looked miles away. He turned from it. He wasn't going to get another one. I don't care, he thought. It doesn't matter; let it go. He started again for the water pump.

There was another point, he decided, a point below that at which a man either laughed or broke. There was one more step down to the level of absolute negation. He was there now. He didn't care about anything. Beyond the simple plane of bodily function, there was nothing.

As he moved from beneath the mammoth legs of the clothes tree, his gaze slid up the cliff wall. He wondered if the spider were up there. Probably it was, crouching seven-legged and silent in its web, perhaps sleeping, perhaps chewing up some bug it had killed.

It might have been himself.

Shuddering, he looked back at the floor. He'd never resign himself to the spider, no matter how depleted his spirit became. It was too alien a form to adjust to. Horror and revulsion toward it were too deeply engrained in him. It was better not to think of it at all. Better not to think that today the spider was as tall as he was, its body three times the volume of his, its long, black legs the thickness of his legs.

He reached the edge of the cliff and looked down into the vast canyon. Was it really worth it? Maybe it would be better just to forget about water altogether.

His throat labored dryly. No, water was not something you could forget about. Shaking his head like a sorrowing old man, he got on his knees and lowered himself over the edge of the step, then began easing himself down the thread. Fifty feet, two days before. Seventy-five today, probably. Tomorrow?

What if the spider is waiting down there? he thought. It frightened him to think it, but he kept descending, too weak to stop himself. He tried not to think about climbing back up. Why hadn't he had the foresight to make knots at regular intervals in the thread? It would have made ascent so much easier.

His sandals finally touched bottom and he let go of the thread-rope. At least his fingers had not been scraped as badly, now that they were so small.

The thimble loomed over him like a giant vat, the lip of it a good six feet above his head. If it had been overflowing, he might have caught water in his palms. As it was, he would have to climb to the top.

But how? The side, even with its indentations, was smooth and slightly overhanging. He pushed at the thimble, thinking he might knock it over, but it was too heavy, filled with water. He stood staring at it.

The thread. He limped back to the wall and picked up the heavy end of it, lugging it as far as it would go. It didn't reach. He let go of it and it slid back to the wall.

He shoved at the thimble again. His arms fell. It was too heavy. No use. He started back for the thread. It's no use, he thought. I'll just forget about it. His face was martyred. I'm going to die anyway, what's the difference? I'll die. Who cares?

He stopped, biting his lip savagely. No, that was the old way. It was the childish way, the "I'll punish the world by dying" attitude. He needed water. The thimble had the only water available. Either he got it or he would die, and no one the wiser or the stupider or the worse for it.

Gritting his teeth, he walked around, looking for pebbles. Why do I go on? he asked himself for the hundredth time. Why do I try so hard? Instinct? Will? In many ways it was the most infuriating thing of all, this constant bewilderment at his own motivations.

At first he found nothing. He moved in the shadows, muttering to himself. What if there are other spiders here? What if there are . . .

It would have been so much better if his brain had lost its toxic introspections long before. Much better if he could have concluded life as a true bug instead of being fully conscious each hideous, downward step of the way. Awareness of the shrinking was the curse, not the shrinking.

Even thirsty, hungry, the thought stopped him. He stood in the cold shadows, turning it over in his mind.

It was true. He had realized it once, fleetingly, then forgotten it again, sinking into the physical. But it was true. So long as he had his mind, he was unique. Even though spiders were larger than he, even though flies and gnats could shade him with their wings, he still had his mind. His mind could be his salvation, as it had been his damnation.

He almost left the floor when the pump began.

With a hoarse cry, he slammed back against the wall of the cavern, hands clutching up at his ears. The noise seemed to come in physically tangible waves, pinning him there. He thought his eardrums would burst. Even through his pressing palms the thunderous, shrieking clatter penetrated, hammering jagged spikes into his head. He couldn't think. Like a mindless beast, he cringed against the wall, drowning in noise, his face twisted, his eyes stark with pain.

When the pump finally shut off, he slumped down bonelessly into a heap, his eyes slitted, his mouth hanging open. His brain felt numb and swollen. His limbs still shook.

Oh, yes, his mind mocked faintly. Yes, so long as you can think, you're unique.

"Fool," he muttered weakly. "Fool, fool, fool."

After a while he stood up and looked for a pebble again. Finding one at last, he pushed it back beside the thimble, then climbed up on it. There were three feet left. He crouched down a little, braced himself, then jumped.

His fingers clawed at the edge of the thimble and caught. His feet kicked out and slipped on the smooth edge as he pulled himself up. Water, he thought, almost tasting it in his mouth. Water. He didn't notice at first that the thimble was tipping.

Panic speared through him as the thimble started to topple. Seeking lost balance, he tightened his grip spasmodically instead of loosening it. Let go! his mind cried shrilly. He released his hold and dropped heavily, landing on the edge of the pebble, losing balance a second time and falling backward, arms flailing. He flopped back on the cement, the breath knocked from him. The thimble kept falling. With a cry he flung an arm across his face and went rigid, waiting for the thimble to crash on him.

Only cold water poured across him, blinding and gagging him. Sucking air into his lungs, he struggled to his knees. Another wave of water dashed over him, almost knocking him on his back again. Coughing and spluttering, he stood up, rubbing at his eyes.

The thimble was rocking back and forth, water flooding across its lip and splattering on the cement. Scott stood there shivering, catching his breath, his tongue licking the cold drops from his mouth.

Finally, when the thimble was rocking less violently, he moved up to it warily and caught the spilling water in his palms. It was so cold it numbed his hands.

When he had finished drinking, he backed away and sneezed. Oh, God, now comes the pneumonia, he thought. His teeth were beginning to chatter. The cotton robe was cold and clammy on his flesh.

With jerky, impulsive movements he dragged the robe over his head. Cold air flooded over him. He had to get out of there. Throwing down the dripping robe, he ran to the thread and started climbing as rapidly as he could.

After he'd gone up ten feet he felt exhausted. Every upward movement became more difficult than the last. Pain seesawed in his muscles, a taut, drawing sharpness as he dragged himself up, a dull, throbbing ache as he hung resting.

He couldn't rest for more than a few seconds. With every pause he grew more chilled. His white body covered with goose flesh, he kept climbing, gasping at the air between clenched teeth. Half a dozen times he thought he was going to fall as exhaustion welled up in his arms and legs, every muscle seeming to go slack. His hands clutched desperately at the ropelike thread, his legs curled around it. He pressed against the cement face, panting.

Then, in a moment, he began climbing again, not looking up because he knew that if he looked up, even once, he would never reach the top.

He stumbled across the floor, waves of heat and coldness breaking over him. He pressed a shaking hand against his forehead. It was hot and dry. I'm sick, he thought.

He found his old robe lying behind the cement block, crusted with dirt, but dry. He brushed it off and put it on. It helped a little. Shaking with weariness and anger, and still shivering with cold, he circled around the floor collecting the few damp pieces of cracker left and throwing them on top of the sponge.

It took all the strength he had remaining to drag the box top over the sponge. Then he lay in the darkness, his breath a thin, rasping sound that faltered in his throat like steam. The cellar was without sound.

After a few minutes he tried to eat. But swallowing hurt too much. Already he was thirsty again. He rolled over on his stomach and pressed his burning face into the soft sponge, his hands opening and closing in weary, ceaseless movements. After a moment he felt moisture on his face, and he started squeezing hard, remembering that the sponge had been soaking wet the morning before. But the little water he got was so brackish it almost made him lose the food he'd managed to eat.

He rolled onto his back again. What do I do now? he thought despairingly. There was no food left but the pitiful scraps under the box top with him; no water except at the bottom of a cliff he'd never have the strength to climb again; no way of getting out of the cellar. And now, added to everything else, fever.

He rubbed fiercely at his hot forehead. The air felt close and heavy. Heat pressed down on him like a hand. I'm suffocating, he thought. He sat up abruptly, looking around with hot eyes, head lolling on his neck. Unaware, his right hand picked a cracker crumb to bits and flung the shreds aside.

"I'm sick," he groaned. His thin voice ballooned around him. He sobbed, digging teeth into the knuckles of his left hand until the skin broke. "I'm sick. I'm sick!"

He fell back with a groan and lay there limply, staring up through fever-slitted eyes.

Half-conscious, he thought he heard the spider walking on the box again. One, two, three, his twisting mind began to chant. Four, five, six. Seven legs my true love has.

Distortedly, he remembered the day when he had been twenty-eight inches tall, the height of a one-year-old child—a china doll that shaved real whiskers and bathed in a dishpan and used a baby's potty chair and wore made-over baby clothes.

He had stood in the kitchen yelling at Lou because he'd

suggested that she put him in a sideshow to make some money and she hadn't insisted that he shouldn't say such things; she'd only shrugged.

He'd yelled and ranted, his little face red, stamped his cunning high-topped shoes, glared up at her, until suddenly she'd turned from the sink and shouted back, "Oh, stop squeaking at me!"

In a fury so complete it blinded him, he spun and lurched for the doorway, only to trip over the cat and get badly clawed.

Lou had run to him and tried to make it up. She'd cleaned the jagged scratch on his arm and apologized. But he'd known it wasn't a woman apologizing to a man, but a woman apologizing to a midget she felt sorry for.

And when she'd finished bandaging him, he'd gone down to the cellar again; the last refuge to which he always fled in those days. And he'd stood there by the steps staring through anger and hurt at the cellar.

He'd squatted down and picked up a rock that was lying on the floor and he'd rocked there on his heels, thinking of all the things that had happened to him in the past few weeks. He'd thought of the money almost gone, of Lou unable to find a job, of Beth's increasing disrespect, of the Medical Center never calling, of the endless shrinking of his body. And while he thought of them, his mind had grown angrier, his lips whitening on each other, his hand closed like a steel trap over the rock.

When he saw the spider walking on the wall across from him, he reared up suddenly and fired the rock at it with all his might. Fantastically the rock had pinned one of the spider's black legs to the wall and it had fled, leaving the leg behind. Scott had stood in front of the wall watching the leg twitch like a living hair. And, blank-faced, he'd thought, Someday my leg will be that small.

It had been impossible to believe.

But now his leg *was* that small, and the insane descent of his existence was bearing down toward inevitable conclusion.

He wondered what would happen if he died now. Would his body keep shrinking? Or would the process cease? Surely it could not go on if he were dead.

Far across the floor, the oil burner began its hurricane roar again, shaking the air with deafening vibrations. With a moan he pressed his hands over his ears and lay there shivering without control, feeling as if he were in a buried coffin while an earthquake shook the cemetery.

"Leave me alone," he muttered feebly. "Leave me alone." He drew in a whining breath. His eyes closed.

He twitched, woke.

The oil burner still roared. Was it the same roaring on which he had closed his eyes? Had seconds passed, or hours?

He sat up slowly, lightheaded and shaking. He lifted a trembling hand and touched his forehead. It was still hot. He rubbed the hand across his face, groaning deeply. Oh, God, I'm sick.

Weakly he pushed himself to the rim of the sponge and slid over the edge. His grip was so weak that it broke instantly and he thudded down on his feet, sitting down heavily with a startled grunt.

He sat on the cold cement a long moment, blinking, his torso weaving. His stomach rumbled with hunger. He tried to stand up. He had to lean against the sponge. Breath came from his nostrils in short, hot bursts. He swallowed. I need water. Tears ran down his cheeks. There was no water he could get. He hit the sponge with an impotent fist.

After a few minutes he stopped crying and, turning slowly, stumbled through the darkness until he collided with the box-top wall. It knocked him down. Muttering, he crawled to the box-top side again and, lifting it first with his hands and then with his back, he squeezed out from under.

It was like crawling into a refrigerator. A shudder rippled down his back. He stood up and leaned back against the box top.

It was afternoon; he *had* slept. Rays of sunlight were visible through the window over the log pile, the window that faced south. Two, three o'clock, he estimated. Another day was half gone; more than half.

He spun around and drove a strengthless punch into the cardboard wall. Pain stung his knuckles. He hit again. Damn you! He leaned his head against the side and rained in enervated blows, feeling the impact of each one leap up his arms, across his shoulders, down his back.

"Pointless, pointless, pointless, pointless, point—" In a wild, croaking voice he chanted the word on one breath until no sound came from him. Then his arms flopped to his sides like lengths of wood and he fell against the cardboard, eyes closed, twitching with jerking breaths.

When he finally turned, it was with a mind blanked to everything except water. He started across the floor slowly. I can't go down to the tank, but I need water, he thought. But there isn't any water anywhere else. There's water that drips in the cracker box, but I can't climb that high. But I need water. He walked, eyes down, hardly seeing. I need water.

He almost fell in the hole.

For a frightening instant, he wavered on the very edge of it. Then he caught himself and stepped back.

He got down on his knees and peered into the dark cavity drilled through the cement floor. It was like looking down a well, except that the well broke off about fifteen feet down and there was nothing but lightless void.

He poised his tilted head over the hole, listening. At first there was only the sound of his own labored breathing. Then, holding his breath, he began to hear another sound. The sound of softly dripping water.

It was a nightmare to lie there on his stomach, racked with thirst, and listen to the drip of unreachable water. His tongue kept stirring in his mouth, seeking to escape the imprisonment of his lips. He kept swallowing endlessly, hardly noticing the jabs of pain it caused.

For one moment he almost dived headfirst into the hole. I don't care! he thought in a fury. I don't care if I die!

What kept him from it he didn't know. Whatever it was, it was below consciousness, for on the surface he was angrily determined to plunge into the well-like hole and find that water.

But he drew back from the hole and got on his knees again. He hesitated. Then he fell forward again and listened to the sound, almost inhaling it like air. He moaned. He pushed to his knees once more, stood dizzily, and then began walking away from the drainage hole. He turned and walked back to the brink of it. He swung a foot over it, staring down into its unseeable depths.

"Oh, God, why don't you . . ."

He turned and walked away from the hole on rigid legs, hands clenched into fists at his sides. There's no point! he wanted to scream. Why *shouldn't* he go down the hole? Why not, like some grotesque, latter-day Alice, plunge into yet another world?

He thought it was a red wall at first. He stopped in front of it, staring at it. He prodded it. Not stone or wood. It was the hose.

He walked around its serpentine bulk until he came to one end of it. There he stared into the long, shadowy tunnel curving away from him. He stepped up onto the metal ring and stood in a groove, thinking. Sometimes when you picked up a hose water dripped from the end of it.

With a gasp, he started running clumsily down the smooth-floored tunnel, banging into hard walls where the hose twisted abruptly, racing as fast as he could along the winding labyrinth of it. Until, curving to the right for what seemed to be the hundredth time, he found himself ankle-deep in cold liquid. With a grateful sob, he squatted down and lifted trembling palmfuls of the water to his lips. It tasted stale and it hurt his throat to swallow, but he had never gulped the finest wine so eagerly.

Thank God! he kept thinking. Thank God! All the water I need now. All I need! He grunted, almost in amusement, thinking of the many times he'd climbed down that fool thread to the water tank. What an ass he'd been! Well, it didn't matter now. He was all right now.

It wasn't until he began walking back along the tunnel that he realized it had been, at best, a reactive triumph. How different did it make the situation, how better off? His minuscule existence was preserved a little longer, yes. He would see the end of it intact; but the end would come. Was that a triumph?

Or would he see the end of it?

As he emerged into the cellar again, he realized how weak with sickness he was; worse, how weak with hunger. The sickness he might alleviate with rest and sleep, but to hunger there was only one answer.

His gaze moved to the towering cliff.

He stood there in the shadow of the hose, looking up at the place where the spider lived. One piece of food remained in the cellar; he knew that much for sure. One slice of dried-up bread; more than enough to keep him for the last two days. And it was up there.

It came upon him with annihilating simplicity. He hadn't the strength to climb up there. Even if he could, by some incredible extension of will power, make it up the cliff, there was the spider. And he hadn't the courage to face the spider again. Not a black, scuttling horror three times the size of him.

His head fell forward. Then that was it; that was the decision he must accept. He stepped away from the hose and started across the floor toward the sponge. What decision was there but that? Was there, after all, a choice? Wasn't it out of his hands, inexorable? He was three-sevenths of an inch tall. What could he hope to do?

Something made him look again at the cliff face.

The giant spider was running down the wall.

With a body-jarring gasp, Scott fled across the floor. Before the spider had reached the bottom of the cliff, he had squeezed beneath the edge of the box top and climbed onto the sponge. When the spider clambered, black and bulbous, onto the box top, he was waiting for the sound of it, his teeth jammed so hard together that his jaws ached.

There could be no hope of food, then; not with that quivering black cannibal guarding it. He closed his eyes, sobs dragging at his throat, hearing overhead the scratching, scrabbling movements of the spider.

Chapter Eleven

As in a dream, delirium-driven, he was back again at the Columbia Presbyterian Medical Center, being tested.

Voice a crispness, voice a hollow waver, Dr. Silver told him that no, he did not have acromicria, as had first been suspected. Yes, there was the bodily shrinkage, but no, his pituitary gland was not diseased. There was no loss of hair, no cyanosis of extremities, no bluish discoloration of skin, no suppressed sexual function.

There were urinary-excretion tests to establish the amounts

of creatin and creatinine in his system; important tests, because they would tell much about the functioning of his testes, his adrenals, about the balance of nitrogen in his body.

Discovery: You have a negative nitrogen balance, Mr. Carey. Your body is throwing off more nitrogen than it is retaining. Since nitrogen is one of the major building blocks of the body, consequently, we have shrinkage.

An imbalance of creatinine was causing further involution. Phosphorus and calcium were being thrown off, too, in the precise proportion in which those elements were found in his bones.

ACTH was administered, possibly to check the catabolic breakdown of tissue.

ACTH was ineffective.

There was much discussion about a possible dosage of pituitary extract. "It might enable his body to retain nitrogen and cause the disposition of new protein," they murmured.

It seemed there was danger, though. The response of the human body to administered growth hormone is not ascertainable; even the best extracts are poorly tolerated and often give aberrant results.

"I don't care. I want it. Can I be worse off?" he said.

Dosage administered.

Negative.

Something was combatting the extract.

At last the paper chromatography; the capillary trailing of body elements across paper, the specific gravity of each one causing it to stain a different part of the paper.

And a new element was found in his system. A new toxin.

Tell us something, they said. Were you ever exposed to any kind of germ spray? No, not bacterial warfare. Have you, for instance, ever been accidentally sprayed with a great deal of insecticide?

No remembrance at first; just a fluttering amorphous terror. Then sudden recollection. Los Angeles, a Saturday afternoon in July. He had come out of the house, heading for the store. He had walked through a tree-lined alley, between rows of houses. A city truck had turned in suddenly, spraying the trees. The spray misted over him, burning on his skin, stinging his eyes, blinding him momentarily. He yelled at the driver.

Could *that* possibly be the cause of all this?

No, not that. They told him so. That was only the beginning of it. Something happened to that spray, something fantastic and unheard of; something that converted a mildly virulent insecticide into a deadly growth-destroying poison.

And so they searched for that something, asking endless questions, constantly probing into his past.

Until, in a second, it came. He remembered the afternoon on the boat, the mist washing over him, the acid sting on his body.

A spray impregnated with radiation.

And that was it; the search was over at last. An insect spray hideously altered by radiation. A one-in-a-million chance. Just that amount of insecticide coupled with just that amount of radiation, received by his system in just that sequence and with just that timing; the radiation dissipating quickly, becoming unnoticeable.

Only the poison left.

A poison that, without destroying the pituitary gland, destroyed, little by little, its ability to maintain growth. A poison that day by day forced his system to convert nitrogen into excess waste matter; a poison that affected creatinine and phosphorus and calcium and left them as waste to be thrown off. A poison that decalcified his bones so that, soft and pliant, they could shrink, little by little. A poison that nullified any administered hormone extract by causing antihormone action in direct opposition.

A poison that made him, little by little, the shrinking man.

The search over at last? Not really. Because there was only one way to fight a toxin, and that was with an antitoxin.

So they'd sent him home. And while he waited there, they sought the antitoxin that might save him.

At his sides, hands folded into gnarled fists. Why, asleep or waking, did he have to think about those days of waiting? Those days when his very body was continuously tensed for the sound of a knock on the door, the sudden stridency of the telephone ringing. It had been a free fall of the mind, taut consciousness never finding a base to settle on, but hanging in constant suspense, waiting.

The countless trips to the post office, where he'd rented a

box so he could get two and three deliveries a day, instead of only one. That cruel walk from the apartment to the post office, wanting to run and still walking, his body twitching with his desperate desire to run. Entering the post office, hands numb, heart pounding. Crossing the marble floor, stooping and looking into the box. And, when there were letters, his hands shaking so badly that he could barely slide the key into the lock. Jerking out the letters, gaze stabbing at the return addresses. No letter from the Center. The sudden feeling that life was gone from him, that his feet and legs were running into the floor like candle wax.

And when they'd moved to the lake the suffering was even worse, because then he had to wait for Lou to go to the post office—standing at the front window, hands shaking when he saw her come walking back down the street. He would know she had no letter because she walked so slowly, and yet he would be unable, until she actually said so, to believe that no letter had come.

He pitched over on his stomach and bit into the sponge savagely. It was so horribly true that thought was his undoing. To be unaware; dear God, to be joyously unaware. To be able to rip the tissues of his brain away and let them drip like clouded paste from his fingertips. Why couldn't—

His breath stopped. He reared up sharply, ignoring the sudden throb of pain in his head.

Music.

"Music?" He murmured faintly. How could there be music in the cellar?

Then he knew; it wasn't in the cellar, but upstairs. Louise was playing music on the radio: Brahms' First Symphony. He leaned on his elbows, lips parted, holding his breath and listening to the sturdy beat of the symphony's opening phrase. It was barely audible, as though he stood in the lobby of a concert hall hearing the orchestra through closed doors.

Breath escaped finally, but he did not move. His face was still, eyes unblinking. It was still the same world, then, and he was still a part of it. The connecting sound of music told him so. Upstairs, gigantically remote, Louise was listening to that music. Below, incredibly minute, he was listening too. And it was music to both of them, and it was beauty.

He remembered how, toward the end of his stay in the house, he had been incapable of listening to music unless it was played so low that Lou couldn't even hear it. Otherwise the music was magnified into a clubbing noise at his ears, giving him a headache. The clatter of a dish was a knife jab at his brain. The sudden cry or laughter of Beth assailed him like a gun fired beside his ear, making his face contort, making him cover his ears.

Brahms. To lie like a mote, an insignificance in a cellar, listening to Brahms. If life itself were not fantastic, that moment could be labeled so.

The music stopped. His gaze jerked up as if he might see, in the darkness, the reason for its stopping.

He lay there, silent, listening to the muffled voice of the woman who had been his wife. His heart seemed to stop. For a moment he was really part of that old world again.

His lips formed the name Lou.

21″

Because the summer ended, the teen-aged girl who had worked at the lake grocery store had to return to school. The opening had been given to Lou, who had applied for it a month before.

Vaguely she'd thought that Scott would take care of Beth when she got a job. But now it was painfully clear that, barely reaching the height of Beth's chest, he couldn't take care of her at all. Moreover, he refused to try. So she made arrangements with a neighborhood girl who had left high school. The girl agreed to take care of Beth while Lou was working.

"Lord knows, we won't have much money left after paying her," Lou had said, "but I guess there's no alternative."

He'd said nothing. Not even when she told him that, as much as she hated to say it, he'd have to stay in the cellar during the day unless he wanted the girl to know who he was; for, obviously, he couldn't pass for a child. He'd only shrugged his dainty shoulders and left the room without a word.

Before Lou left for work the first morning, she prepared sandwiches and two thermos bottles—one of coffee, one of water—for Scott. He sat at the kitchen table, propped up on two thick pillows, his pencil-thin fingers partially curled around a mug of steaming coffee, his face giving no indication that he heard a word she was saying to him.

"This should last you easily," she was saying. "Take a book with you; read. Take naps. It won't be so bad. I'll be home early."

He stared at the circles of cream floating like oil drops on the coffee. He twisted the cup very slowly on its saucer. It made a squeaking sound that he knew irritated Lou.

"Now remember what I told you, Beth," Lou said. "Don't say a word about Daddy. Not a *word*. Do you understand?"

"Yes." Beth nodded.

"What did I say?" Lou demanded.

"I don't say a word about Daddy."

"About the freako," Scott mumbled.

"What?" Lou asked, looking at him. He stared into the coffee. She didn't pursue it; he had fallen into the habit of muttering to himself since they'd moved to the lake.

After breakfast, Lou went down to the cellar with him, carrying one of the lawn chairs for him to sit on. She pulled down her suitcase from a pile of boxes between the fuel tank and the refrigerator and set it on the floor. She put two chair cushions in it.

"There, you can take a nice nap there," she said.

"Like a dog," he muttered.

"What?"

He looked at her like a bellicose doll.

"I don't think the girl will try to come down," she went on. "Then again, she might be nosy. Maybe I'd better put the lock on the door."

"No."

"But what if the girl comes down?"

"I don't want the door locked!"

"But, Scott, what if—"

"I don't want the door locked!"

"All right, all right," she said, "I won't put the lock on. We'll just have to hope the girl doesn't decide she wants to see the cellar."

He didn't speak.

While she made sure he had everything he needed, bent far

over to give him a dutiful peck on the forehead, went back up the steps and lowered the door into place, Scott stood motionless in the middle of the floor. He watched her walk past the window, the skirt of her dress windblown around her shapely legs.

Then she was gone, but he remained unmoving, staring out the window at the spot where she had passed. His small hands kept flexing slowly against his legs. His eyes were motionless. He seemed engrossed in somber thought, as if he might be contemplating the relative merits of life and death.

At last the expression slipped from his features. He drew in a long breath and looked around. He lifted his palms briefly in a gesture of wry surrender, then let them slap down on his thighs.

"Swell," he said.

He climbed up on the chair, taking his book with him. He opened the book to the fringe-bottomed leather marker that read, "This Is Where I Fell Asleep," and started to read.

He read the passage twice. Then the book fell forward in his lap and he thought about Louise, about the impossibility of his touching her in any way. He reached her kneecaps and a little more. Somewhat short of manliness, he thought, teeth gritted. His expression did not change. Casually he shoved the book off the chair arm and heard it slap down loudly on the cement.

Upstairs he heard Lou's footsteps moving toward the front of the house, then fading. When they returned they were accompanied by another set of footsteps and he heard the voice of the girl, typically adolescent, thin, fluttery, and superficially confident.

Ten minutes later Lou was gone. In front of the house he'd heard the sputtering cough, the sudden gas-fed roar of the Ford being warmed up. Then, after a few minutes, the gunning sound had gradually disappeared. Now there were only the voices of the girl Catherine and Beth. He listened to the rise and fall of Catherine's voice, wondering what she was saying and what she looked like.

Bemused, he put the indistinct voice to distinct form. She was five feet six, slim-waisted and long-legged, with young, uptilted breasts nudging out her blouse. Fresh young face, reddish-blonde hair, white teeth. He watched her moving lightly as a bird, her blue eyes bright as polished berries.

He picked up the book and tried to read, but he couldn't. Sentences ran together like muddy rivulets of prose. The page was obscured with commingling words. He sighed and stirred uncomfortably on the chair. The girl stretched to the urging of his fancy, and her breasts, like firm-skinned oranges, forced out their silken sheathing.

He blew away the picture with an angry breath. Not that, he ordered.

He drew his legs up and wrapped both arms around them, resting his chin on his knees. He sat there like a child musing on the case for Santa Claus.

The girl had half taken off her blouse before he shut the curtain on her forcibly imposed indelicacy. The taut look was on his face again, the look of a man who has found effort unrewarding and has decided on impassivity instead. But, far beneath, like lava threatening in volcanic bellies, the bubbling of desire went on.

When the screen door of the back porch slapped shut and the voices of Beth and the girl floated into the yard, he slid off the chair with sudden excitement and ran to the pile of boxes beside the fuel tank. He stood there for a moment, his heart jolting. Then, when his mind came up with no authoritative resistance, he clambered up the pile and peered through a corner of the cobweb-streaked window.

Lines of pain shriveled in around his eyes.

Five feet six had become five feet three. The slim waist and legs had become chunky muscle and fat; the young, uptilted breasts had vanished in the loose folds of a long-sleeved sweat shirt. The fresh young face lurked behind grossness and blemishes, the reddish-blonde hair had been dyed to a lackluster chestnut. There was, feebly remaining, white teeth and movements like a bird's; a rather heavy bird's. The color of her eyes he couldn't see.

He watched Catherine move around the yard, her broad buttocks cased in faded dungarees, her bare feet stuck in loafers. He listened to her voice.

"Oh, you have a cellar," she said.

He saw the look on Beth's face change obviously and felt his muscles tightening.

"Yes, but it's just empty," Beth said hastily. "Nobody lives there."

Catherine laughed unsuspiciously.

"Well, I hope not," she said, looking toward the window. He shrank back, then realized that the cellar could not be seen through any of the windows because of the glare of light on them.

He watched them until they disappeared around the back end of the house. His eyes caught the fleeting sight of them as they moved past the window over the log pile. Then they were gone. Grunting, he climbed back down the pile of boxes and went back to the chair. He put one of the thermos bottles on the arm of the chair and retrieved the book. Then, sitting down, he poured smoking coffee into the red plastic cap and sat there, the book open and unread on his lap, sipping slowly.

I wonder how old she is, he thought.

He started up on the chair cushion, eyes jerking open.

Someone was lifting the cellar door.

With a gasp, he flung his legs over the edge of the suitcase just as the person's hold slipped and the door crashed down. He struggled to his feet, looking frantically toward the steps. The door started to rise again; a spear of light shot across the floor, widening.

With two distinct lunges, Scott grabbed the coffee thermos and the book and almost dived under the fuel tank. As the opened door slammed down, he slid himself behind the big carton of clothes. He clutched the book and thermos bottle to his chest, feeling sick. Why did he have to be so vitriolically stubborn about having the lock put on the door? Yes, it was the idea of being imprisoned that he hadn't liked. But at least in prison, others could not come in.

He heard the cautious descent on the stairs, the clicking of loafers, and he tried to stop breathing. As the girl entered he shrank back into the shadows.

"Hmm," the girl said. She moved around the floor. He heard her kick the chair experimentally. Would she wonder why it was there? Wasn't it an odd place for a chair, right in the middle of a cellar floor? He swallowed dryly. And what about the suitcase with the pillows in it? Well, that might be where the cat slept.

"Jesus, what a mess," said the girl, her shoes scuffing over the cement. For a moment he saw her thick calves as she stood by the water heater. He heard her fingernails tapping on the enameled metal.

"Water heater," she said to herself. "Uh-huh."

She yawned. He heard the straining sound in her throat that accompanied tense stretching. It broke off with a loud grunt. "Boop-dee-doodle-oodle," said the girl.

She moved around some more. Oh, my God, the sandwiches and the other thermos, he thought. Damn nosy bitch! his mind snapped. Catherine said, "Hmm. Croquet."

Then, in a few minutes, she said, "Oh, well," and went back up the steps and the cellar shook with the crash of the dropped door. If Beth were taking a nap, that would end it.

As Scott crawled out from under the fuel tank, he heard the back screen door slam shut and Catherine's footsteps overhead. He got up and put the thermos bottle back on the chair arm. Now he'd have to let Lou put the lock on the door.

"Damn the stupid little . . ."

He paced the floor like a caged animal. Nosy bitch! You couldn't trust one of them. First damn day and she had to see the whole house. She'd probably gone through every bureau, cabinet, and closet in the house.

What had she thought about seeing male clothing? What lie might Lou have to tell—or already told? He knew that she'd given Catherine a false last name. Since no mail was delivered to the house, there was not too much danger of the girl's discovering the lie.

The only danger was that Catherine might have read those articles in the *Globe-Post* and seen the pictures. Yet if that were so, surely she already suspected that he must be hiding in the cellar and would have searched more carefully. Or *had* she been searching?

It was ten minutes later when he decided to have a second sandwich and discovered that the girl had taken them.

"Oh, *Christ!*" He slammed an infuriated fist on the arm of

the chair and almost wished she'd hear him and would come down so he could berate her for a stupid pryer.

He sank back on the chair and shoved the book off the arm again. It slapped loudly on the floor. The hell with it, he thought.

He drank all the coffee and sat there, sweating, glaring straight ahead. Upstairs, the girl walked around and around.

Fat slob, he called her in the jaded smallness of his head.

"Sure, go ahead," he said. "Lock me in."

"Oh, Scott, *please*," she begged. "It was your decision. Do you want to take a chance on her finding you?"

He didn't answer.

"She may come down again if the door's open," Lou said. "I don't think she thought anything one way or the other about finding that bag of sandwiches here yesterday. But if she finds another one . . ."

"Good-by" he said, turning away.

She looked down at him for a moment. Then she said quietly, "Good-by, Scott," and she kissed him on the top of the head. He drew away.

While she went up the steps he stood on the floor, rhythmically slapping the folded newspaper against the calf of his right leg. Every day it's going to be the same, he thought; sandwiches and coffee in the cellar, a good-by peck on the head, exit, door lowering, lock snapping shut.

When he heard it, a great suction of terror pulled the breath from him and he almost screamed. He saw Lou's moving legs, and suddenly he shut his eyes, pressing his lips together to block the cry wavering in his vein-ridged throat. Oh; God, dear God, a *prisoner* now. A monster that good and decent people lock into their cellars so the world may not know the awful secret.

After a while the tension ran out of him and passive withdrawal came back again. He climbed up on the chair and lit a cigarette, drank coffee, and thumbed carelessly through the previous evening's *Globe-Post* that Lou had brought home.

The short article was on page three. Head: WHERE IS THE SHRINKING MAN? Subhead: *No Word Since Disappearance Three Months Ago.*

"New York: Three months ago Scott Carey, the 'Shrinking Man', so called because of the strange disease he had contracted, disappeared. Since then, no word about him has been received from any quarter."

What's the matter, you want more pictures? he thought.

"Authorities at the Columbia Presbyterian Medical Center, where Carey was being treated, said they could make no comment as to his present whereabouts."

They also can't make antitoxin, he thought. One of the top medical centers in the country, and here I sit, shriveling away while they fumble.

He was going to shove the thermos bottle off the chair, but then he realized it would only be hurting himself. Compulsively he gripped one hand with the other and squeezed until the fingernails went bloodless, until his wrists began to ache. Then he let his hands flop on the arms of the chair and stared morosely at the orange wood between his spread fingers. Stupid color to paint lawn chairs, he thought. What an idiot the landlord must have been!

He wriggled off the chair and began pacing. He had to do something besides sit and stare. He didn't feel like reading. His eyes moved restlessly about the cellar. Something to do, something to do . . .

Impulsively he stepped over to a brush leaning against the wall and, grabbing it, began to sweep. The floor needed sweeping; there was dirt all over, stones, scraps of wood. He cleared all of them from the floor with quick, savage motions; he swept them into a pile beside the steps, and flung the brush against the refrigerator.

Now what?

He sat down and had another cup of coffee, kicking nervously at the chair leg.

While he was drinking, the back screen door opened and closed, and he heard Beth and Catherine. He didn't get up, but his gaze moved to the window, and in a moment he saw their bare legs move past.

He couldn't help it. He got up and went to the pile of boxes and climbed up.

They were standing by the cellar door in bathing suits, Beth's red and frilly, Catherine's pale blue and glossy, in two pieces.

He looked at the round swell of her breasts in the tight, pulled-up halter.

"Oh, your mother locked the door," she said. "Why did she do that, Beth?"

"I don't think I know," Beth answered.

"I thought maybe we could play croquet," said Catherine.

Beth shrugged ineffectually. "I don't know," she said.

"Is the key in the house?" asked Catherine.

Another shrug. "I don't know," said Beth.

"Oh," said Catherine. "Well . . . let's have a catch, then."

Scott crouched on top of the boxes, watching Catherine as she caught the red ball and threw it back to Beth. It wasn't until he'd been there five minutes that he realized he was rigidly tensed, waiting for Catherine to drop the ball and bend over to pick it up. When he realized that, he slid off the boxes with a disturbed clumsiness and went back to the chair.

He sat there breathing harshly, trying not to think about it. What in God's name was happening to him? The girl was fourteen, maybe fifteen, short and chubby, and yet he'd been staring at her almost hungrily.

Well, is it my fault? he suddenly flared, letting fury take over. What am I supposed to do—become a monk?

He watched his hand shake as he poured water. He watched the water spill over the sides of the red plastic cup and dribble down his wrist. He felt the water like a trickling of ice down his hot, hot throat.

How old *was* she? he wondered.

Flesh pulsed over his jaws as he kept biting. He stared through the grimy window at Catherine, who was lying on her stomach, reading a magazine.

She lay sideways to him, stretched out on a blanket, her chin propped up by one hand, the other hand idly turning the pages.

His throat was dry but he didn't notice it; not even when it tickled and he had to clear it. His small fingers pressed for balance against the rough surface of the wall.

No, she couldn't be less than eighteen, he commented to himself. Her body was too well developed. That bulge of breast as she lay there, the breadth of her hips. Maybe she was only fifteen, but if so she was an awfully advanced fifteen.

His nostrils flared angrily and he shuddered. What the hell difference did it make? She was nothing to him. He took a deep breath and prepared to return to the floor but just then Catherine bent her right knee and the leg wavered lazily in the air.

His eyes were moving, endlessly moving over Catherine's body—down her leg and across the hill of her buttock, up the slope of her back and around her white shoulder, down to the ground-pressing breast, back along the stomach to her leg, up her leg, down her—

He closed his eyes. He climbed down rigidly and went back to the chair. He sank back in it, ran a finger over his forehead, and drew it away dripping. His head fell back against the wooden chair.

He got up and went back to the boxes. He climbed up without a thought. Yes, that's it, have another look at the back yard, mocked his alien mind.

At first he thought she had gone into the house. A betraying groan began in his throat. Then he saw that she was standing by the cellar door, lips pursed estimatingly, looking at the lock.

He swallowed. Does she know? he thought. For one wild instant he thought he would run to the door and scream, "Come down, come down here, pretty girl!" His lips shook as he fought the desire.

The girl walked past the window. His eyes drank her in thirstily, as if it were the final view for all time. Then she was gone and he sat down on the top of the boxes, back to the wall. He stared at his ankles, the thickness of a policeman's club. He heard the back door shut and then the footsteps of the girl moving around overhead.

He felt drained. He felt that if he relaxed an iota more, his body would run down over the boxes like sirup on a hill of ice cream.

He didn't know how long he'd been there when the back door whined open and slammed shut again. He twitched, startled, and rose up again.

Catherine walked past the window, a key chain dangling from her fingers. His breath caught. She'd been in the bureau drawers and found the extra keys!

He half slid, half jumped down the stacked boxes, wincing

as he landed on his right ankle. He grabbed the sandwich bag and shoved the thermos bottles into it. He tossed the half-finished box of crackers on top of the refrigerator.

His eyes fled around. The paper! He darted to it and snatched it up, as he heard the girl experimenting with the keys at the door. He stuck the folded newspaper on the shelf of the wicker table, then grabbed his book and the bag and ran for the dark, sunken room where the tank and water pump were. He'd decided beforehand that if Catherine ever came down again, that was where he'd hide.

He jumped down the step to the damp cement floor. At the door, the lock clicked open and was pulled out of the metal loop. He stepped gingerly over the network of pipes and slid in behind the high, cold-walled tank. He set down the bag and book and stood there panting as the door was pulled up and Catherine came down in the cellar.

"Locking the cellar," he heard her say in slow disgust. "Think I was gonna steal somethin' or somethin'."

His lips drew back in a teeth-clenched, soundless snarl. Stupid bitch, he thought.

"Hmmph," said Catherine. He heard her loafers clicking over the floor. She kicked the chair again. She kicked the oil burner and it resounded hollowly. Keep your goddam feet to yourself! his brain exploded.

"Croquet," she said. He heard a mallet being slid out of the rack. "Hmmph," she said again, a little more amusedly. "Fore!" The mallet clicked loudly on the cement.

Scott edged cautiously to the right. His shirt back scratched over the rough cement wall and he froze. The girl hadn't heard. "Uh-huh," she was saying. "Hoops, clubs, balls, stakes. Yowza."

He stood looking at her.

She was bending over the croquet rack. She'd loosened her halter while she'd been lying in the sun, and it hung down almost off her breasts as she leaned over. Even in the dim light, he could see the distinct line of demarcation where tanned flesh became milk-white.

No, he heard someone begging in his mind. No, get back. She'll see you.

Catherine leaned over a little more, reaching for a ball, and the halter slipped.

"Oops," said Catherine, putting things to order. Scott's head fell back against the wall. It was damply cool in there, but wings of heat were buffeting his cheeks.

When Catherine had gone and locked the door behind her, Scott came out. He put the bag and book on the chair and stood there feeling as if every joint and muscle were swollen and hot.

"I can't," he muttered, shaking his head slowly. "I can't. I *can't*." He didn't know what he meant exactly, but he knew it was something important.

"How old's that girl?" he asked that evening, not even glancing up from his book, as though the question had just, idly and unimportantly, occurred to him.

"Sixteen, I think," Lou answered.

"Oh," he said, as if he had already forgotten why he asked.

Sixteen. Age of pristine possibility. Where had he heard that phrase?

He shook it off, crouching on the boxes, a delicately limbed dwarf in corduroy rompers, looking out bleakly at the rain, watching the drops spatter on the ground, splashing freckles of mud on the windowpanes. His face was a mask of expressionless defeat. It shouldn't have precipitated, thought his mind. Oh, it shouldn't have.

He hiccuped. Then, with a tired sigh, he climbed down the pile and walked unsteadily to the chair. O orange chair beloved! he saluted the chair. He jolted back in it and—whoops!—he caught the whisky bottle as it almost toppled off the arm. O bottle of booze beloved! He snickered.

The cellar was a haze of gelatine around his bobbing head. He tilted back the bottle and let the whisky trickle hot in his throat, burning in his stomach.

His eyes watered. I am drinking Catherine! his mind cried fiercely. I have distilled her, synthesizing loins and breasts and stomach and sixteen years of them into a conflagrating liquor, which I drink—*so*. His throat moved convulsively as the whisky gurgled down. Drink, drink! And it shall make thy belly bitter, but it shall be in thy mouth sweet as honey.

Drunk I am and drunk I mean to stay, he thought. He

wondered why it had never occurred to him before. This bottle that he held before him now had stood in the cupboard for three months and, before that, two months in the old apartment. Five months of suffering neglect. He patted the brown glass bottle; he kissed it fervently. I kiss thee, Catherine liquefied. I buss the distillation of thy warm, sugared lips.

Simple, came the thought, because she is so much smaller than Lou, that's why I feel like this.

He sighed. He swung the empty bottle over his lap. Catherine gone. Down the hatch with Catherine. Sweet girl, you swim now in my veins, a dizzying potion.

He jumped up suddenly and flung the bottle with all his might against the wall. It exploded sharply and a hundred whisky-fragrant scraps of glass danced across the cool cement. Good-by, Catherine.

He stared at the window. Why'd it have to rain? he thought. Oh, why'd it? Why couldn't it be sunny so the pretty girl could lie outside in her bathing suit and he could stare at her and lust in secret, sick vicariousness?

No, it had to rain; it was in the stars.

He sat on the edge of the chair swinging his legs. Upstairs there were no footsteps. What was she doing? What was the pretty girl doing? Not pretty—*ugly*. What was the ugly girl doing? Who cared whether she was pretty or ugly? What was the girl doing?

He watched his feet swinging in the air. He kicked out. Take that, air; and *that*.

He groaned. He got up and paced around. He stared at the rain and the mud-spattered windows. What time was it? Couldn't be more than noon. He couldn't take this much longer.

He went up the steps and pushed at the door. It was locked, of course, and Louise had taken all the keys this time. "Fire her!" he'd yelled that morning. "She's dishonest!" and Lou had answered, "We can't, Scott. We simply can't. I'll take the keys. It'll be all right."

He braced his back against the door and reared up. It hurt his back. He gasped angrily at the air and butted his head against the door. He fell down on the step, dizziness clouding his brain.

He sat there mumbling, hands pressing at his skull. He knew why he wanted the girl discharged. It was because he couldn't stand to look at her, and it was far beyond his ability to tell Lou about it. The most she could do would be to make one more insulting offer. He wouldn't take that.

He straightened up, smiling in the shadows.

Well, I fooled her, he said. I fooled her and sneaked a whisky bottle down, and she never knew.

He sat there, breathing heavily, thinking about Catherine leaning over the croquet rack, about her halter slipping.

He stood abruptly, banging his head again. He jumped down the steps, ignoring the pain. And I'll fool her again!

He managed to feel grimly justified as he climbed the box pile clumsily. A drunken, crooked grin on his face, he knocked up the hook on the window and shoved at the bottom of its frame. It stuck. His face got red as he pushed at it. Get out, goddam your stupid bones!

"Son-of-a—"

The window flew out and he flopped across the ledge. The window flew back in and banged the top of his head. The hell with it! His teeth were gritted. *Now*, he dizzily told the world. Now we'll see. He crawled out into the rain, not fighting at all against the vicious dredging of heat in him.

He stood up and shivered. His eyes fled up to the dining-room window and the rain drizzled in his eyes and ran across his face and spattered on his cheeks. What now? he thought. The cold air and rain were cooling off the surface of impulsion.

Deliberately he walked around the house, staying close to the brick base until he'd reached the porch. Then he ran to the steps and up them. What are you *doing*? he asked. He didn't know. His mind was not conducting the tour.

He stood on tiptoe and cautiously looked into the dining room. No one was there. He listened but didn't hear anything. The door to Beth's room was shut; she must be taking a nap. His gaze moved to the bathroom door. It was shut.

He sank back on his heels and sighed. He licked raindrops from his lips. Now what? he asked again.

Inside the house, the bathroom door opened.

With a start, Scott backed away from the window, hearing

footsteps pad across the kitchen floor, then fade. He thought she'd gone into the living room and edged to the window again, pushed up on his toes.

His breath stopped. She was standing at the window looking out at the yard. She was holding a yellow bath towel in front of her.

He couldn't feel the rain splattering off him, crisscrossing like cold, unrolling ribbons across his face. His mouth hung open. His gaze moved slowly down the smooth concavity of her back, the indentation of her spine a thin shadow that ran down and was lost between the muscular half-moons of her white buttocks.

He couldn't take his eyes from her. His hands shook at his sides. She stirred and he saw the glitter of water drops on her, quivering like tiny blobs of gelatine. He sucked in a ragged, rain-wet breath.

Catherine dropped the towel.

She put her hands behind her head and drank in a heavy breath. Scott saw her left breast swing up and stand out tautly, the nipple like a dark spear point. Her arms moved out. She stretched and writhed.

When she turned he was still in the same tense, muscle-quivering pose. He shrank back, but she didn't see him because the top of his head was barely higher than the window sill. He saw her bend over and pick up the towel, her breasts hanging down, white and heavy. She stood up and walked out of the room.

He sank down on his heels and had to clutch at the railing to keep his legs from going limp beneath him. He half hung there, shaking in the rain, a stark look on his face.

After a minute he stumbled weakly down the steps and around the house to the cellar window. He crawled through and locked the window behind him. He climbed down the hill of boxes, still shuddering.

He sat on the lawn chair, an old sweater wrapped around himself. His teeth were chattering, and he shivered uncontrollably.

Later he took his clothes off and hung them on the oil burner to dry. He stood by the fuel tank in his brown, high-topped shoes, holding the sweater around his shoulders, staring up at the window. And finally, when he couldn't bear the stillness or the pressure or the thoughts a second longer, he began to kick the cardboard carton. He kicked it until his leg ached and the cardboard side was split almost to the floor.

"But how did you get a cold?" Lou asked, her voice carrying a note of exasperation.

His voice was nasal and thick. "What do you expect when I'm stuck in that damn cellar all day!"

"I'm sorry, darling, but . . . well, shall I stay home tomorrow so you can stay in bed all day?"

"Don't bother," he said.

She didn't mention that she'd noticed that the whisky bottle was gone from the kitchen cupboard.

If Lou had been able to lock the windows, too, it would have been all right. But knowing he could get out any time he wanted; knowing that he could spy on Catherine, made it an impossible situation.

Hours dragged in the cellar. He might manage to absorb himself in a book for an hour or two, but ultimately the vision of Catherine would flit across his mind and he would put down the book.

If Catherine had come out in the yard more often, it would have been all right. Then, at least, he could look at her through the window. But days were getting colder as September waned, and Catherine and Beth stayed in the house most of the time.

He had taken to bringing a small clock to the cellar. He'd told Lou he wanted to be able to keep track of the time, but what he really wanted was to be able to know when Beth was napping. Then he could go out and peer through the windows at Catherine.

One day she might be on the couch reading a magazine, and there would be no satisfaction. But the next day she might be ironing, and, for some reason, when she ironed she always took off part of her clothes. Another time she might take a shower and, afterward, stand naked at the back window. And once she had lain naked in the bedroom under the skin-purpling glare of Lou's portable sun lamp. That had been one cloudy afternoon and she hadn't drawn the shades all the way down. He'd stood outside for thirty minutes and never budged.

Days kept passing. Reading was almost forgotten. Life had become one unending morbid adventure. Almost every afternoon at two o'clock, after having sat in shaking excitement for an hour or more, he would crawl out into the yard and walk secretively around the house, climbing up and peering over the sills of every window, looking for Catherine.

If she were partly or completely nude, he counted the day a success. If she was, as was most often the case, dressed and engaged in some dull occupation, he would return angrily to the cellar to sulk out the afternoon and snap at Louise all evening.

Whatever happened, though, he would lie awake at night, waiting for the morning to come, hating and despising himself for being so impatient, but still impatient. Sleep grew turgid with dreams of Catherine; dreams in which she grew progressively more alluring. Finally he even gave up scoffing at the dreams.

In the mornings he would eat hastily and go down to the cellar for the long wait until two o'clock, when, heart pounding, he would crawl out through the window again to spy.

The end of it came with shocking suddenness.

He was on the porch. In the kitchen, Catherine was standing naked under Lou's open bathrobe, ironing some clothes.

He shifted his feet, slipped, and thumped down on the boards. Inside, he heard Catherine call out, "Who's there?"

Gasping, he jumped down the steps and started running around the house, looking over his shoulder in fright, to see a frozen-faced Catherine standing at the kitchen window, gaping at his fleeing childlike form.

All that afternoon he stood shivering behind the water tank, unable to come out because, even though she hadn't seen him go into the cellar, he was sure she was looking in through the window. And he cursed himself and felt sickly wretched thinking about what Lou would say to him and how she would look at him when she knew.

He lay still under the box top, listening to the scratching clamber of the spider over the cardboard.

He moistened his lips with a sluggish tongue and thought of the pool of cold water in the hose. He felt around with his hand until it closed over a fragment of damp cracker; then he decided he was too thirsty to eat and his hand drew back again.

For some reason the sound of the spider's crawling didn't bother him too much. He sensed that he was beyond stark disruption, lying in the shallows of emotion, spent and quiescent. Even memory failed to hurt. Yes, even the memory of the month they'd discovered the antitoxin and injected him three times with it—to no avail. All past laments were undone by the drag of present illness and exhaustion.

I'll wait, he told himself, until the spider is gone, and then I'll go through the cool darkness and walk over the cliff and that will be the end of it. Yes, that's what I'll do. I'll wait until the spider's gone and then I'll go over the cliff and that will be the end of it.

He slept, heavily, motionlessly. And, in his dream, he and Lou were walking in September rain, talking as they went. And he said, "Lou, I had an awful dream last night. I dreamed I was as small as a pin."

And she smiled and kissed his cheek and said, "Now, wasn't that a foolish dream?"

Chapter Twelve

THUNDER WOKE HIM. His fingers shriveled in abruptly, his eyes jerked open. There was an instant of blank suspension, consciousness hanging submerged beneath the shock of sudden awakening. His eyes stared mindlessly; his face was a pale, unmarked tautness, mouth a dash embedded in beard.

Then he remembered; and the scars of worry and defeat gouged across his brow and around his eyes and mouth again. Staring became sightlessness behind fallen lids, his hands uncurled. Only the faint murmur in his throat acknowledged the pain it was to lie in thunder.

In five minutes the oil burner clicked off, and the cellar became a vast, heavy silence.

With a grunt he sat up slowly on the sponge. The headache

was almost gone. Only when he grimaced did it flare minutely. His throat still hurt, his body felt encrusted with aches and twinges, but at least the headache was gone and—he felt his forehead—the fever had abated somewhat. The able ministrations of sleep, he thought.

He sat weaving a little, licking his dry lips. Why did I sleep? he wondered. What had drugged him when he'd decided to end it all?

He worried his way across the sponge and, holding on to the edge, dropped to the floor. Pain shot up his legs, faded. If only he could believe there had been purpose in his helpless sleep; that it might have been the act of a watching benevolence. He could not. More than likely it had been cowardice that had sent him off to sleep instead of to the cliff's edge. Even wanting to, he could not honor it with the title "will to live." He had no will to live. It was simply that he had no will to die.

At first he couldn't lift the box top, it had become so heavy. That told him what he'd meant to verify at the ruler; that overnight he had shrunk another fraction and was now only two-sevenths of an inch tall.

The cardboard edge scraped across his side as he dragged himself out from beneath it. It pinned his ankle so that he had to bend over and work at it with his hands. Free at last, he sat on the cold cement, letting the waves of dizziness settle. His stomach was a flagon of air.

He didn't measure himself; there was no point in it. He walked slowly across the floor looking to neither one side nor the other. On unsteady legs he headed for the hose. Why had he slept?

"No reason." He framed the words with his cracked lips.

It was cold. Gray, cheerless light filtered through the windows. March fourteenth. It was another day.

After the half-mile walk, he clambered over the metal lip of the hose and trudged along the black tunnel, listening to the echo of his scuffing sandals. His feet kept coming loose from the strings, and the robe dragged heavily along the rubber floor.

Ten minutes of walking through the twisting, lightless maze brought him to the water. He crouched in its shallow coldness and drank. It still hurt to swallow, but he was too grateful there was water to care.

As he drank, there crossed his mind a brief vision of himself holding a hose much like this one, carrying it outside, connecting it to the faucet, playing a glittering stream of water across his lawn. Now, in a similar hose, he crouched, less than one fifth of its width, a mote man sipping driblets of water from a hand no bigger than a grain of salt.

The vision passed. His size was too common now, too much a reality. It was no longer a phenomenon.

When he had finished drinking, he walked back out of the hose, shaking his feet to get the water off his sandals. March forth, he thought, march forth to nothingness. March fourteenth, he thought. In a week the first day of spring would come upon the island.

He would never see it.

Out on the floor again, he walked back to the box top and stood beside it, one palm braced against it. His gaze moved slowly over the cellar. Well? he thought. What happened now? Did he crawl under the box top, lie down again and sleep once more, a surrendering sleep? His teeth raked slowly across his lower lip as he looked at the cliff that went up to the spider's land.

Avoid it.

He started walking around the cement block, searching for cracker crumbs. He found a dirty one, scraped off its surface, and kept walking, chewing ruminatively. Well, what was he going to do? Go back to his bed, or—

He stopped and stood motionless on the floor. Something in his eyes caught minor fire. His lips drew back from his teeth as he grimaced.

All right. He had a brain. He'd use it. After all, wasn't this his universe? Couldn't he determine its values and its meanings? Didn't the logic of a cellar life belong to him, who lived alone in that cellar?

Very well, then. He had planned suicide, but something had kept him from it. Call it what you will, he thought—fear, subconscious desire to survive, action of outside intelligence maintaining him. Whatever it was, it had happened. He lived still, his existence unbroken. Positive function was still possible; decision was still his.

"All right," he muttered. He may as well act alive.

It was like the clearing of a mist in his brain, like a rush of cool wind across a parched desert of intentions. It made—absurdly, perhaps—his shoulders draw back, made him move with more certainty, ignoring the pain of his body. And, as if in instant reward, he found a large chunk of cracker behind the cement block. He cleaned it off and ate it. It tasted horrible. He didn't care. It was nourishment.

He walked back across the floor. What did his decision mean? He knew, really, but he was afraid to dwell on it. Rather, he let himself drift surely toward the giant carton under the fuel tank, knowing what had to be done; knowing that he would do it or perish.

He stopped before the looming mass of the carton. Once, he thought, he had kicked open its side himself. At the time, it had been an act of rage, of frustration turned to acid fury. How odd that an ancient fury was making it easier for him now; that it had, indeed, saved his life more than once.

For hadn't he got two thimbles from that carton, one that he'd put under the water tank, and another that he'd put under the dripping water heater? Hadn't he got the material for his robe from the carton? Hadn't he got there the thread that enabled him to reach the top of the wicker table and get the crackers? Finally, hadn't he actually fought off the spider in there, discovering in a flash of astonishment that he did have some efficacy against its horrible seven-legged blackness?

Yes, all these. And all because, one day long ago, he had burned with a terrible, angry desire and kicked open the side of the carton.

He hesitated for a moment, thinking he should search for the needle he'd taken from the carton before and lost. Then he decided he might not find it and the fruitless search would waste not only time, but valuable, needed energy.

He jumped up the carton side and dragged himself through the opening. It was difficult to get in. The difficulty pointed up, disconcertingly, how hard it was going to be to get up to the cliff, much less fight the—

No. He wasn't going to let himself think about that. If anything could stop him, it was thoughts about the spider. He blanked his mind to them. Only far behind the conscious barrier did they move.

He slid down the hill of clothes until he went over the edge and fell down into the sewing box. For a moment panic jarred him as he thought that he might not be able to get out of the box. Then he remembered the rubber cork into which the pins and needles were inserted. He could push that to the edge of the box and then be able to climb out.

He found a cool needle lying on the bottom of the box and picked it up.

"God," he muttered. It was like a harpoon made of lead. He let it fall and it clanked loudly. He stood there a moment, lines of distress around his eyes. Was he to be defeated already? He couldn't possibly carry that needle up the face of the cliff.

Simple, said his mind. Take a pin.

He closed his eyes and smiled at himself. Yes, yes, he thought. He searched around in the shadows for a pin, but there were none loose. He'd have to get one from the rubber cork.

First he had to knock the cork over. It was four times as high as he was. Gritting his teeth, he shoved at the rubber cork until it toppled. Then he moved around it and jerked out a pin, hefted it in his hands. That was better. Still heavy, but manageable.

How could he carry it, though? Sticking it into his robe was no good; it would dangle, bang against surfaces, impede his climb, maybe cut him. He'd fasten a thread sling on the pin and carry it across his back. He looked around for thread. No point in going after the thread he'd flung into the cat's mouth; it was probably lost.

He cut himself a short length of rope-heavy thread by dragging the sharp pin point across it until the fibers were weakened enough to be torn apart. Panting in the dark, shadowy cavern, he tied one end of the thread around the pinhead, then tied the other end near the point. The second loop slid a little, but it would hold well enough. With a grunt he slung the pin across his back, then flexed on his toes to test the weight. Good enough.

Now. Was that all he needed? He stood indecisively, brow lined, but not with worry. He didn't actually acknowledge it, but it gave him a good feeling to be calculating positively. Maybe there was something to the theory that true satisfaction was based on struggle. This moment was certainly the antithesis of the hopeless, listless hours of the night before. Now he was working toward a goal. True, it might be self-induced emotion, but it gave him the first definite pleasure he could remember experiencing for a long time.

All right, then, what was needed? The climb was too difficult to be attempted unaided. He was simply too small; he needed apparatus. Very well, then. Since it was a cliff, that made him a mountaineer. What did mountaineers use? Cleated shoes. He couldn't manage that. Alpenstocks. Nor that. Grappling hooks. Nor—

Yes, he could! What if he got another pin and managed somehow to bend it into a semicircle? Then if he attached it to a long thread, he could fling it at openings in the lawn chairs, hook it in, and climb the thread. It would be perfect equipment.

Excited he pulled another pin from the rubber cork, then unrolled about twenty feet—to him—of thread. He threw the pins and thread out of the box, climbed out by using the cork, and dragged his prizes up the hill, throwing them out onto the floor.

He slid out of the carton and dropped down. He started toward the cement block, dragging the pins and thread behind. Now, he thought, if only I could take a little food and water with me . . .

He stopped, squinting at the box top. Suddenly he remembered, there were still pieces of cracker on the sponge! He could put them inside his robe somehow and take them with him.

And water? On his face there was a look of concentration bordering on exultation. The sponge itself! Why couldn't he tear off a small piece of it, soak it with water from the hose, and carry it with him? Certainly it would drip, it would run, but some of the water would stay in it, enough to see him through.

He didn't let himself think about the spider. He didn't let himself think about the fact that there were only two days left to him, no matter what he did. He was too absorbed in the small triumphs of conquered detail and in the large triumph of conquered despair to let himself be dragged down again by crushing ultimates.

That was it, then. The pin spear slung across his back, the cracker crumbs and water-soaked sponge in his robe, the pin hook for climbing.

In half an hour he was ready. Although he already felt tired from the tremendous effort required to bend the pin (which he had done by shoving the point under the cement block and lifting at the head), hacking and tearing off a fragment of sponge, getting the water and the crackers and carrying everything to the foot of the cliff, he was too pleased to care. He was alive, he was trying. Suicide was a distant impossibility. He wondered how he could ever have considered it.

Excitement faded, almost died when he tilted back his head and looked up toward the soaring top of the lawn chairs as they leaned against the Everest heights of the wall. Could he possibly climb that high?

He lowered his eyes angrily. Don't look, he ordered himself. To look at the entire journey all at once was stupidity. You thought of it in segments; that was the only way. First segment, the shelf. Second, the seat of the first chair. Third, the arm of the second chair. Fourth—

He stood at the very bottom of the cliff. Never mind anything else, he told himself. He had the resolve to get up there; that was what mattered.

He remembered another time in the past when resolution had come. Thoughts of it ran through his mind as he flung up the hook and began to climb.

18″

It was a giant's toy; a glowing, moving, incredible toy. The Ferris wheel, like a vast white-and-orange gear, turned slowly against the black October sky. Scarlet-lit Loop-the-Loop cages blurred across the night like shooting stars. The merry-go-round was a bright, cacophonous music box that turned and turned, the grimacing, wild-eyed horses rising and falling, endlessly rising and falling, frozen in their galloping postures. Tiny cars and trains and trolleys, like merry bugs, raced around in their imprisoning circles, overflowing red-faced children who waved and screamed. Aisles were sluggish currents of doll people who clustered like filings around the magnetism of barker stands, food concessions, and booths where balloons could be exploded with broken-feathered darts, wooden milk bottles toppled with scratched and grimy baseballs, and pennies tossed upon mosaics of colored squares. The air pulsed with a many-tongued clamor and spotlights cast livid ribbons across the sky.

As they drove up, another car pulled away from the curb and Lou eased the Ford into the opening, pulling out the hand brake, and turned off the engine.

"Mamma, can I go to the merry-go-round, *can* I?" Beth asked excitedly.

"Yes, dear." Lou spoke distractedly, her gaze moving to where Scott was sitting, dwarfed in a shadowy corner of the back seat, the carnival glare splashed across his pale cheek, his eye like a tiny, dark berry, his mouth a pencil gash.

"You *will* stay in the car," she said worriedly.

"What else can I do?"

"It's for your own good," she said.

It was a phrase she used all the time now; spoken with a hopeless patience, as if she could think of nothing better to say.

"Sure," he said.

"Mother, let's *go*," Beth said with determined anxiety. "We'll *miss* it."

"All right." Lou pushed open the door. "Push down your button," she said, and Beth punched down the knob-topped rod that locked the door on her side, then scrambled across the seat.

"Maybe you'd better lock yourself in," Lou said.

Scott didn't speak. His baby shoes thudded down slowly on the seat. Lou managed a smile.

"We won't be long," she said, and she closed the door. He stared at her shadowy figure as she twisted the key in the lock; he heard the button clicking down.

Lou and Beth moved across the street, Beth tugging eagerly at her mother's hand, and entered the crowded carnival grounds.

He sat for a while, wondering why he'd been so insistent on coming when he'd known all along he couldn't go into the carnival with them. The reason was obvious, but he wouldn't admit it to himself. He'd yelled at Lou to hide the shame he felt at forcing her to give up her job at the lake store; the shame he felt because she had to stay home, because she didn't dare get another sitter, because she'd had to write her parents and borrow money. That's why he'd yelled and insisted on going with them.

After a few minutes he stood up on the seat and walked over to the window. Dragging a pillow over, he stepped on its yielding surface and pressed his nose against the cold window. He stared at the carnival with hard, unenjoying eyes, looking for Lou and Beth; but they had been ingested by the slowly moving crowd.

He watched the Ferris wheel revolving, the little pivoted seats rocking back and forth, passengers holding on tight to the safety bars. His gaze shifted to the Loop-the-Loop. He watched it flip over, the two cage-tipped arms flashing past each other like clock hands gone berserk. He watched the merry-go-round's rhythmic turn and heard faintly the clash-grind-thump of its machinelike music. It was another world.

Once, long ago, a boy named Scott Carey had sat on another Ferris-wheel seat, transfixed with delicious terror, white-knuckled hands clutched over the bar. He had ridden other toy cars, twisting the steering wheel like a chauffeur. He had, in a perfect agony of delight, flipped over and over in another Loop-the-Loop, feeling the frankfurters and popcorn and cotton candy and soda and ice cream homogenized in his stomach. He had walked through the glittering unreality of another carnival, overjoyed with a life that built such wonders overnight on empty lots.

Why *should* I stay in the car? The question came minutes later, belligerently, demanding satisfaction. So what if people saw him? They'd think he was a lost baby. And even if they knew who he was, what difference did it make? He wasn't going to stay in the car, that's all there was to it.

The only trouble was that he couldn't open the door. It was hard enough to push one of the front seats forward and clamber over it. It was impossible for him to get the door handles up. He kept jerking at them, angrier and angrier, until he kicked the gray-lined door and butted it with his shoulder.

"Well, the *hell* . . ." he muttered then, and, impulse-driven, rolled down the window.

He sat on the thin ledge a few moments, legs kicking restlessly. The cold wind blew up his legs. His shoes drummed on the door. I'm going, I don't care. Abruptly he turned, lowered himself over the window edge, and hung suspended above the ground. Carefully he reached down one hand and caught hold of the outside door handle. After a moment he swung down.

"Oh!" His fingers slipped off the smooth chrome and he fell in a heap on the ground, banging against the side of the car. Momentary fear nibbled coldly at his insides when he realized he couldn't get back; but it passed quickly. Louise would return soon enough. He walked to the end of the car, jumped down the steep curb, and moved into the street.

He flinched back as a car roared by. It passed at least eight feet away from him, but the noise of its motor was almost deafening. Even the crisp sound of its tires on the pavement was inordinately loud in his ears. When it was past he darted across the street, leaped up the knee-high curb, and raced around to a deserted area behind a tent. He walked beside the dark, wind-stirred canvas wall, listening to the din of the carnival.

A man came around the corner of the tent and started toward him. Scott froze into immobility and the man walked by without noticing him. It was a thing about people. They did not look down expecting to see anything but dogs and cats.

When the man was out on the sidewalk, Scott moved on again, ducking through the triangles the ropes made with the ground and the tent side.

He stopped before a pale bar of light that poked out from beneath the tent, blocking his path. He looked at the loosened canvas, delicate excitement mounting in him. Impulsively he got on his knees, then fell forward on his chest on the cold ground, lifted the flap, and, wriggling forward a little, peered in.

He found himself looking at the hind end of a two-headed

cow. It was standing in a hay-strewn, rope-enclosed square, staring at the people with four glossy eyes. It was dead.

The first smile Scott had managed in more than a month eased his tight little face. If he had jotted down a list of all the things in the world he might have seen in this tent, somewhere near the bottom of the list he might conceivably have put a dead two-headed cow pointed the wrong way.

His gaze moved around the tent. He couldn't see what was on the other side of the aisle; clustering people hid the view. On his side, he saw a six-legged dog (two of the legs atrophied stumps), a cow with a skin like a human being's, a goat with three legs and four horns, a pink horse, and a fat pig that had adopted a thin chicken. He looked over the assemblage, the faint smile wavering on his lips. Monster show, he thought.

And then the smile faded. Because it had occurred to him how remarkable an exhibit he would make, posed, say, between the chicken-mothering pig and the dead two-headed cow. Scott Carey, *Homo reductus.*

He drew back into the night and stood up, brushing automatically at his corduroy rompers and jacket. He should have stayed in the car; it had been stupid to leave.

Yet he didn't start back; he couldn't make himself start back. He trudged past the end of the tent and saw people walking, heard the clatter of wooden bottles being struck by flying baseballs, the pop of rifles, and the tiny explosions of burst balloons. He heard the dirgelike grind of the merry-go-round music.

A man came out through the back doorway of one of the booths. He glanced at Scott. Scott kept walking, moving quickly behind the next tent.

"Hey, kid," he heard the man call.

He broke into a run, looking for a place to hide. There was a trailer parked behind the tent. He raced to it and crouched behind a thick-tired wheel, peering around the edge.

Fifteen yards away he saw the man appear at the corner of the tent and, fists poked on hips, look around. Then, after a few seconds, the man grunted and went away. Scott stood up and started to leave the shadow of the trailer, then stopped. Someone was singing overhead.

Scott's face grew taut-browed with attention. "If I loved you," sang the voice, "time and again I would try to say . . ."

He moved from under the trailer and looked up at the white-curtained window glowing with light. He could still hear the singing, faint and sweet. He stared at the window, feeling a strange restlessness.

The happy screams of a girl in the Loop-the-Loop shook him loose from his reverie. He started away from the trailer, then turned and went back. He stood beside it until the song was ended. Then he walked slowly around the trailer, looking up first at one window, then at the other, and wondering why he felt so drawn to that voice.

Then he became fully conscious of the steps that led up to the windowed door of the trailer, and convulsively he jumped up on the first one.

It was just the right height.

His heart began to throb suddenly, his hand clamped rigidly on the waist-high railing. Breath shook in his shallow chest. It couldn't be!

He moved slowly up the steps until he stood just below the door that was only a little higher than he was. There were some words painted under its window, but he couldn't read them. He felt his skin alive with strange, electric pricklings. He couldn't help himself; he moved up the last two steps and stood before the door.

Breath stopped. It was his world, his very own world—chairs and a couch that he could sit on without being engulfed; tables he could stand beside and reach across instead of walk under; lamps he could switch on and off, not stand futilely beneath as if they were trees.

She came into the little room and saw him standing there.

His stomach muscles jerked in suddenly. He wavered there, staring blankly at the woman, sounds of disbelief hovering in his throat.

The woman stood rooted to the floor, one hand pressed against her cheek, her eyes round and still with shock. Time stood stricken and apart while she stared at him. It's a dream, his mind insisted. It *is* a dream.

Then the woman slowly, stiffly started for the door.

He shrank away. He almost slipped off the step edge. He

flailed out at the railing and jerked himself rigidly upright as the woman opened the tiny door.

"Who are you?" she asked in a frightened whisper.

He couldn't take his eyes from her fragile face; her doll-like nose and lips, her irises like pale-green beads, her ears like faded rose petals barely seen through hair of fine-spun gold.

"Please," she said, holding the bodice of her robe together with tiny alabaster hands.

"I'm Scott Carey," he said, his voice thin with shock.

"Scott Carey," she said. She didn't know the name. "Are you . . ." She faltered. "Are you . . . like me?"

He was shivering now. "Yes," he said. "*Yes.*"

"Oh." It was as if she breathed the word.

They stared at each other.

"I . . . heard you singing," he said.

"Yes, I—" A nervous smile twitched her pale lips. "Please," she said, "Will you . . . come in?"

He stepped into the trailer without hesitation. It was as though he'd known her all his life and had come back from a long journey. He saw the words that were on the door: "Mrs. Tom Thumb." He stood there staring at her with a strange, black hunger.

She closed the door and turned to face him.

"I'm . . . I was surprised," she said. She shook her head and once more drew together the bodice of her yellow robe. "It's such a surprise," she said.

"I know," he said. He bit his lower lip. "I'm the shrinking man," he blurted, wanting her to know.

She didn't speak for a long moment. Then she said, "Oh," and he didn't know what it was he heard in her voice, whether it was disappointment or pity or emptiness. Their eyes still clung.

"My name is Clarice," the woman said.

Their small hands clasped and did not let go. He couldn't breathe right; air faltered in his lungs.

"What are you doing here?" she asked, drawing back her hand.

He swallowed dryly. "I . . . came," was all he could say. He kept staring at her with stark eyes that would not believe. Then he saw a darkening flush creep into her cheeks and he sucked in a calming breath. "I'm—I'm so sorry," he said. "It's just that I haven't—" he gestured helplessly—"haven't seen anyone like *me*. It's . . ." He shook his head in little twitching movements. "I can't tell you what it's like."

"I know, I know," she answered quickly, looking intently at him. "When—" She cleared her throat. "When I saw you at the door, I didn't know what to think." Her laugh was faint and trembling. "I thought maybe I was losing my mind."

"You're alone?" he asked suddenly.

She stared at him blankly. "Alone?" she asked, not understanding.

"I mean your—your name. On the door," he said, not even realizing that he had alarmed her.

Her face relaxed into its natural soft lines. She smiled a sad smile. "Oh," she said, "it's what I'm called." She shrugged her small round shoulders. "It's just what they call me," she said.

"Oh." He nodded. "I see." He kept trying to swallow the hard, dry lump in his throat. He felt dizzy. His fingertips tingled like frozen fingers being thawed. "I see," he said again.

They kept staring at each other as if they just couldn't believe it was true.

"I guess you read about me," he said.

"Yes, I did," she answered. "I'm sorry that . . ."

He shook his head. "It's not important." A shudder ran down his back. "It's so good to—" He stood motionless, looking into her gentle eyes. "Clarice," he murmured. "So good to . . ." His hands twitched as he repressed the desire to reach out and touch her. "It was such a surprise seeing the—the room here," he said hastily. "I'm so used to—" he shrugged nervously—"*vast* things. When I saw those steps leading up here . . ."

"I'm glad you came up," Clarice said.

"So am I," he answered. Her gaze dropped from his, then rose instantly as if she feared he might disappear if she looked away too long.

"It's really an accident I'm here," she said. "I don't usually work the off seasons. But the owner of this carnival is an old friend who's feeling the pinch a little. And—well, I'm glad I'm here."

They looked at each other steadily.

"It's a lonely life," he said.

"Yes," she answered softly, "it can be lonely."

They were silent again, looking. She smiled restively.

"If I'd stayed home," he said, "I wouldn't have seen you."

"I know."

Another shudder rippled down his arms.

"Clarice," he said.

"Yes?"

"You have a pretty name," he said. The hunger was tearing at him now, shaking him.

"Thank you—Scott," she said.

He bit his lips. "Clarice, I wish . . ."

She looked back at him a long moment. Then, without a word, she stepped close to him and laid her cheek against his. She stood quietly as he put his arms around her.

"Oh," he whispered, "Oh, God. To—"

She sobbed and pressed against him suddenly, her small hands catching at his back. Wordlessly they clung to each other in the quiet room, their tear-wet cheeks together.

"My dear," she murmured, "my dear, my dear."

He drew back his head and looked into her glistening eyes.

"If you knew," he said brokenly. "If you—"

"I *do* know," she said, running a trembling hand across his cheek.

"Yes. Of course you do."

He leaned forward and felt her warm lips change under his from soft acceptance to a harsh, demanding hunger.

He held her tensely. "Oh, God, to be a man again," he whispered. "Just to be a man again. To hold you like this."

"Yes. *Do* hold me. It's been so long."

After a few minutes, Clarice led him to the couch and they sat there holding tightly to each other's hands, smiling at each other.

"It's strange," she said, "I feel so close to you. And yet I never saw you in my life before."

"It's because we're the same," he said. "Because we share the pity of our lives."

"Pity?" she murmured.

He looked up from his shoes. "My feet are touching the floor," he said wonderingly. His chuckle was melancholy. "Such a little thing," he said, "but it's the first time in so long that my feet have touched the floor when I've sat down. Do you—" He squeezed her hand. "You do know; you *do*," he said.

"You said pity," she said.

He looked a moment at her concerned face. "Isn't it pity?" he asked. "Aren't we pitiful?"

"I don't . . ." Distress flickered in her eyes. "I never thought of myself as pitiful."

"Oh, I'm sorry, I'm *sorry*," he said. "I didn't mean to—" His face was contrite. "It's just that I've become so bitter. I've been alone, Clarice. All alone. Once I was past a certain height, I was absolutely alone." He stroked her hand without consciousness. "It's why I feel so—so strongly toward you. Why I . . ."

"Scott!"

They pressed against each other and he could feel her heartbeat hitting at his chest like a little hand.

"Yes, you *have* been alone," she said. "So alone. I've had others like me—like us. I was even married once." Her voice faded to a whisper. "I almost had a child."

"Oh, I—"

"No, no, don't say anything," she begged. "It's been easier for me. I've been like this all my life. I've had time to adjust."

A shuddering breath bellowed his lungs. He said—he couldn't help saying it—"Someday even you'll be a giant to me."

"Oh, my dear." She pressed his face to her breasts, still stroking his hair. "How terrible it's been for you; to see your wife and child magnifying every day—leaving you behind."

Her body had a clean, sweet smell. He drank in the perfume of it, trying to forget everything except her presence and her soothing voice, the blessing of each moment as it was.

"How did you get here?" she asked him, and he told her. "Oh," she said, "won't she be frightened if—"

His urgent whisper cut her off. "Don't make me go."

She drew him more securely against the yielding swell of her breasts. "No, no," she said quickly. "No, stay as long as—"

She stopped. He heard her swallowing again and he asked, "What is it?"

She hesitated before answering. "Just that I have to give another show in—" she twisted slightly, looking at the clock across the room—"ten minutes."

"No!" He clung to her desperately.

Her breathing grew heavier. "If only you could stay with me a little while. Just a *little* while."

He didn't know what to say. He straightened up and looked at her tense face. He drew in a shaky breath.

"I can't," he said. "She'll be waiting. She'll—" his hands stirred fitfully in his lap, grew immobile once again. "It's no use," he said.

She bent forward and pressed both palms gently to his cheeks. She put her lips on his. He ran shaking hands over her arms, his fingertips scratching delicately at the silk robe. Her arms slid around his neck.

"Would she be so frightened if—" she began, breaking off as she kissed his cheek. He still couldn't answer. She drew back and he stared at her flushed face. Her eyes fell.

"You mustn't, please, you mustn't think I'm just an—an *awful* person," she said. "I've always lived—decently. I just . . ." Nervously she ran smoothing fingers over the lap of her robe. "I just feel, as you said, so *strongly* toward you. After all, it's not as if we were just two people in a world of people all alike. We're—we're only *two* of us. If we went a thousand miles we wouldn't find another. It just doesn't seem the same as if—"

She stopped abruptly as a heavy shoe sounded on the trailer steps and there was a single knock on the door. A deep voice said, "Ten minutes, Clar."

She started to answer, but the man was already gone. She sat there shivering, looking toward the door. Finally she turned to him. "Yes, she would be frightened," she said.

Suddenly his hands tightened on her arms, his face grew hard. "I'm going to tell her," he said. "I won't leave you. I *won't*."

She threw herself against him, her breath hot on his cheek. "Yes, tell her, *tell* her," she begged. "I don't want her to be hurt, I don't want her to be frightened, but tell her. Tell her what it's like, how we feel. She couldn't say no. Not when . . ."

She pulled away and stood, breathing harshly. Her trembling fingers ran down the front of her robe, undoing buttons. The robe slid, hissing, from her ivory shoulders, catching in the crook of her bent arms. She wore pale underthings that clung to the contours of her body.

"Tell her!" she said almost angrily. Then she turned and rushed into the next room.

He stood up, staring at the half-open door that led to the room she had entered. He could hear the quick rustle of clothes as she dressed for her performance. He stood there motionless until she came out.

She stood apart from him, her face pale now.

"I was unfair," she said. "Very unfair to you." Her eyes fell. "I shouldn't have done what I did. I—"

"But you'll wait," he interrupted. He grabbed her hand and squeezed it until she winced. "Clarice, you'll wait for me."

At first she wouldn't look at him. Then suddenly her head jerked up, her eyes burned into his. "I'll wait for you," she said.

He listened to the faint clacking of her high heels as she ran down the trailer steps. Then he turned and walked around the small room, looking at the furniture, touching it.

Finally he went into the other room and, after a hesitant moment, sat down on her bed and picked up the yellow silk robe. It was smooth and yielding in his fingers; it still smelled of her flesh.

Suddenly he plunged his face into its folds, gasping in the perfume of it. Why did he have to ask? There was nothing left between Lou and him; nothing. Why couldn't he just stay with Clarice? It wouldn't matter to Lou. She'd be glad to get rid of him. She'd . . .

. . . be frightened, he concerned.

With a weary sigh, he put aside the robe and pushed to his feet. He walked through the trailer, opened the door, moved down the steps, and started back across the cold, night-shrouded earth. I'll tell her, he thought. I'll just tell her and come back.

But when he reached the sidewalk and saw her standing by the car, a heavy despair fell over him. How could he possibly tell her? He stood hesitantly; then, as some teenaged boys started out of the carnival grounds, he darted into the street.

"Hey, ain't that a midget?" he heard one of the boys say.

"Scott!"

Lou ran to him and, without another word, snatched him up, her face both angry and concerned. She walked back to the car and pulled open the door with her free hand.

"Where have you *been?*" she asked.

"Walking," he said. No! cried his mind. Tell her, *tell* her. The vision flitted across his mind; Clarice unrobed, saying it to him. Tell her!

"I think you might have considered how I'd feel when I got back and found you gone," Lou said, pushing forward the front seat so he could get in the back of the car.

He didn't move. "Well, get in," she said.

He sucked in a fast breath. "*No*," he said.

"What?"

He swallowed. "I'm not going," he said. He tried not to be so conscious of Beth staring at him.

"What are you talking about?" Lou asked.

"I—" He glanced at Beth, then back again. "I want to talk to you," he said.

"Can't it wait till we get home? Beth has to go to bed."

"No, it can't wait." He wanted to scream out in fury. The old feeling was coming back—the feeling of being useless, grotesque, a freak. He should have known it would return the moment he left Clarice.

"Well, I don't see—"

"Then leave me here!" he yelled at her. There was no strength, no resolution now. He was the stringless marionette again, pulling for inconsequential succor.

"What's the matter with you?" she asked angrily.

He choked on a sob, cut it off. Abruptly he turned and started across the pavement.

"Scott!"

A mind-jarring flurry of sights and sounds; the roar of an oncoming car, a blinding glare of headlights, the crunch of Lou's running heels, the bruising of her fingers on his body, the head-snapping jerk as she pulled him out of the car's path and around to the back of the Ford, the screeching of the other car's tires as it lurched across the center line, then back into the proper lane.

"What in God's name!" Her voice was furiously agitated. "Have you lost your mind?"

"I wish it had hit me!" Everything flooded out in his voice, all the anguish, the fury, and the shattered hopes.

"Scott!" She crouched down so she could speak to him. "Scott, what is it?"

"Nothing," he said. Then, almost immediately, "I want to stay. I'm *going* to stay."

"Stay where, Scott?" she asked.

He swallowed quickly, angrily. Why did he have to feel like a fool, like an unimportant fool? It had seemed so vital before; now it seemed absurd and trashy.

"Stay *where*, Scott?" she asked in failing patience.

He looked up, stiff-faced, going on with it willessly.

"I want to stay with . . . her," he said.

"With—" She stared at him and his gaze fell. He looked along the broad length of her slack-covered leg. He gritted his teeth and pain flared along his jawline.

"There's a woman," he said, not looking up at her.

She was silent. He glanced up at her. In the light of a distant street lamp he could see the glow of her eyes.

"You mean that midget in the sideshow?"

He shuddered. The way she said it, the sound in her voice, made his desire seem vile. He dragged his teeth across his upper lip. "She's a very kind and understanding woman," he said. "I want to stay with her for a while."

"You mean overnight."

His head jerked back. "Oh, God, how you can—!" His eyes burned. "You can make it sound so—"

He caught himself. He stared down at her shoes. He spoke as distinctly as possible.

"I'm going to stay with her," he said. "If you'd rather not come back for me, all right. Leave me. I'll get by somehow."

"Oh, stop being so—"

"I'm not just talking, Lou," he said. "I swear to God I'm not just talking."

When she didn't reply, he looked up and saw her staring down at him. He didn't know what the expression on her face meant.

"You don't know, you just don't know any more," he said. "You think this is something . . . disgusting, something animal. Well, it isn't. It's more—much more. Don't you understand? We're not the same any more, you and I. We're apart now. But you can have companionship if you want. I can't. We've never spoken of it, but I expect you to remarry when this is done—as it *will* be done.

"Lou, there's nothing for me now, can't you see that? Nothing. All I have to look forward to is dissolution. Going on like this, day after day, getting smaller and smaller and—lonelier. There's nobody in the world who can understand now. Even this woman will one day be as . . . be beyond me. But now—for *now*, Lou—she's companionship and—and affection and love. All right, and love! I don't deny it, I can't help it. I may be a freak but I still need love and I still need—" He drew in a quick, rasping breath. "One night," he said. "It's all I ask. One night. If it were you and you had a chance for one night of peace, I'd tell you to take it. I would."

His eyes fell. "She has a trailer," he said. "It has furniture I can sit on. It's my size."

He looked up a little. "Just to sit on a chair as if I were a man and not . . ." He sighed. "Just that, Lou. Just *that*."

He looked up at her face finally, but it wasn't until a car drove by and the headlights flared across her face that he saw the tears.

"Lou!"

She couldn't speak. She stood biting at a fist, her body shaking with noiseless sobs. She struggled against them. She took a deep breath and brushed away the tears while he stood beside her, staring at her even though it hurt his neck muscles to look up so high.

"All right, Scott," she said then. "It would be pointless and—and cruel of me to stop you. You're right. There's nothing I can do."

She breathed in laboredly. "I'll come back in the morning," she blurted then, and ran to the car door.

He stood in the wind-swept street until the red taillights had faded out of sight. Then he ran across the street, feeling ill and miserable. He shouldn't have done it. It wasn't the same now.

But when he saw the trailer again, and the light in the window, and the little easy steps that led up to her, it all returned. It was like stepping into another world and leaving behind all the sorrows in the old one.

"Clarice," he whispered.

And he ran to her.

Chapter Thirteen

He was sitting on one of the broad slats that formed the seat of the lower lawn chair, leaning against a tree-thick arm support, and chewing on a piece of cracker. He hadn't touched the sponge except to squeeze a few drops from it halfway up the first stage of the climb. By his side lay the coils of thread, the pin hook attached to them, and the long, shiny pin spear.

Weariness eased slowly from his relaxing muscles. Slowly he reached down and rubbed at his knee. It was a little swollen again. While he was climbing the thread, he'd banged the knee against the chair leg. A wince drew back his lips as he rubbed. He hoped it wouldn't get worse.

It was quiet in the cellar. The oil burner hadn't roared on once in the past hour. It must be warm out, he thought. He glanced far across at the window over the fuel tank. It was a shimmering square of light. He closed his eyes. He wondered why Beth wasn't out in the yard playing. The water pump hadn't started lately, either. Lou and Beth probably weren't home. He wondered where they might be.

Warned by the stirring of uneasiness in his chest, he blanked his mind to thoughts of sunlight and outdoors, of his wife and child. They were not a part of his life now, and it was a senseless man who dwelt on things that were not a part of his life.

Yes, he was still a man. Two-sevenths of an inch tall and still a man.

He remembered the night he'd been with Clarice, and how, then too, it had come to him that he was still a man.

"You aren't pitiful," she'd whispered to him. "You're a man." She'd dragged tense fingers across his chest.

It had been a moment of decisive alteration.

Almost all night, lying beside her, feeling the warm flutter of her breath against his shoulder, he had lain awake, thinking of what she'd said.

It was true; he *was* still a man. Living beneath the degrading weight of his affliction, he had forgotten it. Looking at his marriage and his inadequacy in it, he had forgotten it. Looking at his life and the barrenness of that life's achievements, he had forgotten it. The diminishing effect that the size of his body had had on the size of his thoughts had made him forget it. It had not been just introspection. All he'd had to do was look into a mirror to know that it was so.

And yet it was not so. A man's self-estimation was, in the end, a matter of relativity. Here he lay in a bed in which he was full size and there was a woman held in his arms. It made all the difference. He could see again.

And he saw that size had changed nothing essential; he still had his mind, he was still unique.

In the morning, lying in the warm bed with her, bars of butter-colored sunlight across their legs, he'd told her of his thoughts and the change in his thoughts.

"I'm not going to fight it any more," he said. "No, I don't mean I'm giving up," he'd added hastily, seeing the look on her face. "I mean I'm going to stop struggling against the part of it I can't beat. I know I'm incurable now. I can say it; even that's an accomplishment. I've never really admitted it before. I was so afraid I'd find out I was incurable that I even left the doctors once. I said it was because of money, but it wasn't; I know that now. It was because I was terrified of finding out."

He'd lain there, staring at the ceiling, feeling Clarice's small hand on his chest, her eyes watching him.

"Well, I accept it," he'd finally said. "I accept it and I'm not going to scream at fate any more. I'm not going to go down hating." He'd turned to her suddenly. "You know what I'm going to do?" he'd asked, almost excitedly.

"What, dear?"

His smile had been quick, almost boyish. "I'm going to write about it," he said. "I'm going to follow myself as far as I can. I'm going to tell about everything that happened to me, and everything that's *going* to happen to me. This is a rare thing; I'm going to look at it as rare—as a thing of potential value, not just as a curse. I'm going to study it," he said. "I'm going to tear it apart, see what there is to see. I'm going to live with it and beat it. And I'm not going to be afraid. *I'm not going to be afraid.*"

He finished the bit of cracker and opened his eyes. Reaching into his robe, he drew out the piece of sponge and squeezed a few drops of water into his mouth. They were warm and brackish, but they felt good in his dry throat. He put the sponge back. There was still a long climb ahead.

He looked at the pin hook. It had been spread apart a little by the dragging weight of his body. He ran a hand over its smoothness. Well, he could probably rebend it somehow if it became necessary.

He thought he heard a noise overhead and his head jerked back.

There was nothing. But that didn't make his heartbeat any slower. It was a grim reminder of what was waiting up there for him.

He shuddered and a mirthless smile moved his lips. *I'm not going to be afraid.* The words mocked him. If I'd known, he thought. If he'd known the moments of rank terror he was still to experience, he'd never have made it. Only the blessing of an unknown future enabled him to keep the promise he had made to himself.

For he *had* kept it. Without telling Lou, he had gone to the cellar every day, armed with stubby pencil and thick school notebook. He'd sat there in the damp coolness, writing until his wrist ached so much that he couldn't hold the pencil.

Desperate, he would knead at his wrist and hand, trying to press strength back into them so he could go on. Because, more and more, his mind was becoming an uncontrollable powerhouse of memories and thoughts, generating them endlessly. If they were not written down, they would flow from his brain and be lost. He wrote so persistently that in a matter of weeks he had brought himself up to date on his life as the shrinking man. Then he'd begun to type it up, picking slowly and laboriously at the keys as the days fled by. When it had reached the typing stage, he hadn't been able to keep it a secret from Lou any longer. The typewriter had to be rented. At first he'd planned to tell her he just wanted the typewriter to pass the time. But the rental fee was high and he knew there wasn't enough money to pay for it if it were just a whim. So he'd told her what he'd done. She had been unexcited, but she had got the typewriter and paper.

When he wrote the letters to the magazines and book publishers, she said nothing, but he sensed a rising interest in her.

And, when, almost immediately, he'd received a flood of interested offers, she suddenly had to realize that, despite everything, he was giving her the security she'd already given up hoping for.

One glorious afternoon he'd received the first check for his manuscript along with a congratulatory letter, and Lou had sat with him in the living room and told him how sorry she was for having fallen into a state of withdrawal. It was protective, she said, but she regretted even that. She'd told him how proud she was of him. She'd held his tiny hand and said, "You're still the man I married, Scott."

He stood up. Enough of the past. He had to get on; there was still a long way to go.

Picking up the pin spear, he slung it across his back again. The added weight stirred up hot pressures in his knee, and he grimaced. Never mind, he told himself. Teeth gritted, he bent over and picked up the pin hook. He looked around.

Now if he stayed where he was, he would have approximately fifty feet to climb to the level of the chair arm. The only trouble was that there were no places to catch the hook there. He'd have to do as he'd done before; go up the back of the chair.

The shelf below ran in a downward slope parallel to the seat. This shelf almost touched the floor. He'd had to throw up the hook only a short way to make it catch onto one of the shelf's bottom slats. Ascending the shelf itself had been no more difficult than walking up a moderately steep incline, using the hook and thread to bridge the gaps between the slats. The only hard part had been the vertical climb to the seat where he was now.

No help for it, then; in order to get up higher, he had to descend again a short distance.

He started walking down the slope toward the back of the chair. The openings between slats were somewhat wider here than they had been on the shelf. All in all though, it looked simple enough.

He reached the first opening. Pulling in the ropelike thread, he coiled it and tossed it across the gap. It landed heavily and he heard the metallic ring as the hook struck the wood.

The thundering of the oil burner caught him by surprise. He staggered with shock, his lips jerking back from his teeth.

He jammed rigid hands over his ears and stood there trembling, eyes almost closed, feeling the thunderous shudder running through his frame.

When it finally stopped, he stood limply for a long while, staring ahead. Then, shaking his head, he took a running start and leaped across the opening between the slats.

It wasn't as easy as he'd imagined. He barely made the other side, and the pain of landing sharply on the leg with the swollen knee made him gasp. He sat down quickly, face contorted.

"Good God," he muttered. He'd better not do that again.

After a minute, he pushed up and limped down across the next wide slat, dragging the thread behind him.

At the next gap he tossed the rope thread across. Carefully he unslung the spear. He'd toss that across too, then follow without its dragging weight on him. He'd try to land on his good leg, too.

He threw the spear across the opening. Its point dug into the orange wood, then the pin flew over, the weight of it tearing the point loose. Scott was backing up to get his running start when he saw the pin start rolling down the slope.

It would fall through the next opening!

Thoughtlessly he ran to the edge of the slat and jumped into space. He landed on the bad leg again, lines of pain gashing across his face. He couldn't stop; the pin was gaining momentum, heading for the gap. He lunged after it, loose sandals flapping on the wood. One of the sandals came off and the bottom of his lurching foot dragged up a splinter from the wood. He still kept running, trying to gain on the pin.

Frantic, he dived forward to catch it as it started over the edge of the slat. Pain exploded in his knee. He almost went over the edge himself. He missed the pin.

But the pin was not going over parallel to the opening, and its spinning movement was suddenly checked as its point stuck into the slat on the far side and the head held it up on the side where Scott sprawled.

Gasping, he pulled the pin back and dug its point into the wood, standing it like a spear in sand. Then he twisted his foot around and, teeth clenched, picked at the brown leathery-skinned sole until he'd drawn out the long wood sliver. Drops of blood followed it. He pressed them out angrily. Not going to be afraid, not going to be afraid, he thought. Oh, sure.

He started to rub his knee, then jerked back his hand with a gasp. In falling, he'd scraped his hand. He blew out a short, heavy breath as he looked at it. He felt water trickling down his chest and across the creases of his stomach. In falling he'd also pressed water from the sponge.

He closed his eyes again. Never mind, he thought, it's all right.

He tore a strip of cloth from the hem of his robe and tied it around his hand. Better. He rubbed determinedly at the knee, biting down hard to fight the pain. There. That was better; much better.

Limping cautiously, he retrieved his sandal and tied extra knots in the strings to keep the sandal from slipping off again. Then he returned to the thread coil and carried it to the edge of the slat. This time he'd fasten the end of the thread to the spear. Then when he threw the spear over it would not only carry over the thread, but it would be prevented from rolling again.

It worked that way. He jumped over after the spear, landing on his good leg, then pulled in the thread and hook. Yes, that was much better. A little thought is all it takes, he told himself.

In this fashion he maneuvered across the sloping seat of the orange chair until he reached its back. There he rested, looking up the almost sheer back of the chair. Far up, he saw the croquet wicket sticking out in space. He could use that wicket now.

After he'd caught his breath and squeezed a couple more water drops into his mouth, he stood up and prepared to complete the next stage of the climb, to the arm of the top lawn chair.

It would not be too difficult. Spaced across the three boards that made up the back of the chair were bracing slats. He had only to throw up the hook, catch it over the first of these slats, climb up to it, throw the hook over the second slat, climb up to it, and so on.

He began throwing up the hook. On the fourth try it caught and, slinging the spear over his back, he climbed up to the first slat.

An hour later, when he reached the top slat, the pin hook was almost unbent. He tossed it up on the arm of the upside-down chair, climbed up beside it, and lay down, breathing heavily. God, I'm tired, he thought, rolling over. He looked down the vast face he had just climbed, and he couldn't help remembering that once his back could have covered that area completely. Once he could have carried this chair. He rolled on his back again. At least being exhausted cut down on thoughts. Ordinarily, he might have been thinking about the spider, about the past, about a good many purposeless things. Instead, he lay there almost stupefied, and that was good. . . .

He stood up on shaky legs and looked around. He must have fallen asleep for a while; a black, peaceful sleep, unmarred by dreams.

He put the spear across his back, picked up the hook, and hiked across the long orange plain of the chair arm, the thread trailing behind him like a lazy serpent.

For some reason he found himself able to think about the spider. It disturbed him vaguely that he hadn't seen any sign of it since he'd got up that morning. It was usually somewhere around when he was moving about. Night and day, it was never absent for long.

Was it possible it was dead?

For a second, an exultant feeling flooded through him. Maybe it had been killed somehow!

The excitement faded almost instantly. He just couldn't believe it was dead. That spider was immortal. It was more than a spider. It was every unknown terror in the world fused into wriggling, poison-jawed horror. It was every anxiety, insecurity, and fear in his life given a hideous, night-black form.

Before he started up on the next stage of the climb, he'd have to bend that pin again. He didn't like the way it was opening under his weight. What if it did that while he was hanging in space?

It *won't*, he told himself, jamming the point of it under the joining place of chair arm and leg and bending it around again. There.

He flung the hook up and it caught over the croquet wicket. He tested it, then began the swaying climb up to the wicket. In two minutes he was clinging to the smooth metal surface.

It took a long time for him to climb its cool, curving length. The weight of thread, hook, and spear made it difficult; it was too far to throw those things without risking their loss.

Time and again he lost balance and spun around to the underside of the sapling-thick wicket and hung there desperately, heart pounding. Each time it took him longer to get back. Finally, toward the end of the climb, he stayed under, pulling himself up with legs and arms, the thread hanging down from his body and swinging wildly beneath him.

By the time he'd reached the shelf of the upper chair, his muscles were starting to cramp. He crawled onto the shelf and lay there gasping, his forehead pressed against the wood. It hurt to have the scraped skin of his forehead against the rough wood, but he was too tired to move. His feet stuck out over the seven-hundred-foot drop.

It was twenty minutes later when he pulled himself around and looked across the edge. The cellar world lay beneath him. Far below, the red hose was a serpent once again, still asleep, still open-mouthed and motionless. The cushion was a flower-strewn plain again. He saw the well-like hole in the floor, the one he'd almost fallen into, then almost dived into when he'd heard the sound of water running deep in it. The hole was only a black dot now. The box top he slept under was only a small gray square, like a faded stamp.

He crawled over to the wide leg of the chair and leaned against it, discarding the hook, thread, and spear. Pulling the sponge and the last piece of cracker from his robe, he sat there eating and drinking, legs stretched out limply before him. He emptied about half the sponge. It didn't matter. He'd be at the top soon. And if he got the bread without any trouble, he could climb down very quickly. If he was barred from reaching the bread, he would no longer be in any position to eat it, anyway.

His sandal bottoms touched the clifftop. He shook the hook loose from the lawn chair, dodged its cartwheeling fall, picked it up hastily, and dashed behind the glass base of a giant, bell-shaped fuse. There he stood, panting, peering around its edge at the wide, shadowy desert.

In the pale shaft of light that transfixed the dust-filmed

window he could see nearby details: the vast pipes and ropy wires fastened under the overhead supports, the great scraps of wood, stone, and cardboard strewn across the sands; to his left, the towering hulks of paint cans and jars; in front of him, the rolling desert wastes, as far as his eye could see.

Two hundred yards off stood the slice of bread.

He licked his lips. He almost started out immediately across the sand. Then he twitched back sharply, head jerking from side to side as he looked in all directions, even behind. Where was it? He was beginning to get nervous wondering where it was.

Stillness, only stillness. The light shaft angled down like a shimmering bar leaning on the window, a bar alive with moving dust. The huge wood scraps, the stones, the concrete pillar, the hanging wires and pipes, the cans and jars and sand hills—all were motionless and still, as if they waited. He shuddered and unslung his spear. He felt a little better holding it in his hand, its head resting on the cement, its razor tip wavering high overhead.

"Well . . ." he muttered, and, swallowing dread, he started across the sand.

The hook dragged in the sand. He dropped it. I won't need it, he thought; I'll leave it here. He walked a few paces, stopped. He didn't like the idea of leaving it. Nothing could happen to it, and yet—what if something did? He'd be trapped, helpless.

Carefully he backed toward the hook, casting nervous glances over his shoulder to make sure nothing was behind him. He reached the hook and, hastily crouching, picked it up. If it came at him, he could drop the hook fast and grab the spear with both hands. Take it easy, he told himself. Nothing's happened yet.

He started across the sand again, walking slowly and warily, eyes always moving and searching. There was no help for it, of course, but it didn't help things much that the thread knots dragging in the sand behind him made a swishing, uneven sound that reminded him of—

He stopped and looked behind him in fright. There was nothing. Stop worrying, he ordered himself.

He looked around slowly, heartbeat still punching slowly at the walls of his chest. No, nothing. Just shadows and silence and waiting objects.

Maybe that was it. Maybe it was because none of the objects

were straight up and down or straight across. Everything tilted, angled, leaned, sagged, beetled. Every line was restless and fluid. Something was going to happen. He knew it. The very silence seemed to whisper it.

Something was going to happen.

He drove the spear point into the sand and began drawing in the thread, looping it so he could carry it over his shoulder and do away with that dragging, whispering sound behind him. As he pulled in the dark, sand-dripping thread he kept looking around, searching.

At a breath of sound the coil thumped down and he snatched the spear from its place again, throwing it out before him. His arm and shoulder muscles shook, his legs stood tensely arched, his eyes were wide and staring.

Breath shook from his lips. He stood listening carefully. Maybe it was the settling of the house he heard. Maybe . . .

A cracking sound, a thud, a roaring wave of sound.

With a flat cry, he jerked around, terror-stricken eyes searching; but, in the very same instant, he realized that it was the oil burner. Dropping the spear, he covered his ears with shaking hands.

Two minutes later the burner clicked off and silence fell across the shadow-pooled desert again.

Scott finished coiling the thread, picked up the heavy loops and the spear and started walking again, eyes still searching. Where was it. Where *was* it?

When he came to the first piece of wood he stopped. He dropped the coil of thread and extended the spear. It might be hiding behind that piece of wood. He licked dry lips, moving in a half crouch for the wood. It was becoming darker the farther he went into the dunes. It might be behind there; what if it's behind there?

He jerked back his head suddenly as it occurred to him that it might be overhead, floating down on a gossamer cable.

He ground together his chattering teeth and looked down again. The fear was a cold, drawing knot in his stomach now. All right, God damn it! he thought. I'm not going to just stand here like a paralytic. On shaking but resolute legs, he walked to the edge of the wood scrap and looked around it. There was nothing.

Sighing, he went back to the thread and picked it up. It's so heavy, he thought. He really ought to leave it behind. What could happen to it, anyway? He stood indecisively. Then it occurred to him that he'd need the hook to drag the slice of bread back to the cliff edge. That settled, he picked up the heavy coil and slung it over his shoulder again. He was glad he'd thought of a use for the thread. Now he had a definite reason to take it. Heavy as it was, he didn't feel right about leaving it behind.

Every time he came to a scrap of wood, a boulder-high stone, a piece of cardboard, a brick, a high mound of sand, he had to do the same nerve-clutching thing—put down the thread, approach the obstacle carefully, pin spear extended rigidly, until he'd found out that the spider was not hiding there. Then, each time, a great swell of relief that was not quite relief made his body sag, made the spear point drop, and he would return to his thread and hook and go on to the next obstacle; never really relieved because he knew that each reprieve was at best, only temporary.

By the time he reached the bread he wasn't even hungry.

He stood before the tall white square like a child standing beside a building. It hadn't occurred to him before, but how could he possibly drag that slice by himself?

Well, it didn't matter, he thought bluntly. He wouldn't need that much bread, anyway. It had to last only one day more.

He looked around carefully but saw nothing. Maybe the spider *was* dead. He couldn't believe it, but he should have seen it by now. On all other occasions it had seemed to sense his presence. Certainly it remembered him, and probably it hated him. He knew he hated it.

He drove the spear into the sand and broke off a hard piece of bread, bit off a chunk, and started to chew. It tasted good. A few moments of chewing seemed to restore appetite, and a few minutes of eating brought it to a point of voraciousness. Although he couldn't relax his tense caution, he found himself breaking off piece after piece of the bread and crunching rapidly on its crisp whiteness. He hadn't realized it before, but he'd missed that bread. The crackers hadn't been the same.

When he was filled as he hadn't been filled for days, he finished off the water. Then, after a moment's hesitation, he flung away the piece of sponge. It had served its purpose. He picked up the spear and hacked out a piece of bread about twice his size. More than enough, stated his mind. He ignored it.

He plunged the hook into the piece of bread and dragged it slowly back to the cliff, scraping out a road behind him in the sand. At the edge of the cliff he drew out the hook and, propping up the huge chunk, pushed it over the brink.

It fluttered through the air, tiny crumbs flaking off as it fell, settling after it like snow. It hit the floor, breaking into three parts, which bounced once, rolled a little way, then flopped onto their respective sides. There. That was that. He'd made the hard climb, got the bread he was after, and it was done.

He turned to face the desert again.

Why then the tension continuing in his body? Why didn't that knot of cold distress leave his stomach? He was safe. The spider was nowhere around; not behind the pieces of wood or the stones or the cardboard scraps, not behind the paint cans or the jars. He was safe.

Then why wasn't he starting down?

He stood there motionless, staring out across the dim-lit desert wastes, his heart beating faster and faster, as if it were grinding out a truth for him, sending it up and up the neural pathways to his brain, pounding at the doors and the walls of it, telling him that he hadn't only gone up for the bread, he'd also gone to kill the spider.

The spear fell from his hand and clattered on the cement. He stood there shivering, knowing now what that tension in him was, knowing exactly what it was that was going to happen —that he was going to *make* happen.

Numbly he picked up the spear and walked into the desert. A few yards out his legs gave way and he slumped down heavily, cross-legged on the sand. The spear fell down across his lap and he sat there holding it, looking out across the silent sands, an unbelieving look on his face.

He waited.

Chapter Fourteen

"Life in a Dollhouse." It had been the title of a chapter in his book; the last chapter. After he'd finished it, he'd realized that he couldn't write any more. Even the smallest pencil was as big as a baseball bat. He decided to get a tape recorder, but before that was possible, he was beyond communication.

That was later, though. Now he was ten inches tall and Louise came in one day with a giant doll house.

He was resting on a cushion underneath the couch, where Beth couldn't accidentally step on him. He watched Lou put down the big doll house and then he crawled out from under the couch and stood up.

Lou got on her knees and leaned forward to put her ear near his mouth.

"Why did you get it?" he asked.

She answered softly so the sound of her voice wouldn't hurt his ears. "I thought you'd like it."

He was going to say that he didn't like it at all. He looked at her profile for a moment; then he said, "It's very nice."

It was a de luxe doll house; they could afford it now, with the sales and resales of his book. He walked over to it and went up on the porch. It gave him an odd feeling to stand there, his hand on the tiny wrought-iron railing; the feeling he'd had the night he'd stood on the steps of Clarice's trailer.

Pushing open the front door, he went into the house and closed the door behind him. He was standing in the large living room. Except for fluffy white curtains, it was unfurnished. There was a fireplace of false bricks, hardwood floors, windows and a window seat, candle brackets. It was an attractive room, except for one thing: One of its walls was missing.

Now he saw Lou on that open side, peering in at him, a gentle half-smile on her face.

"Do you like it?" she asked.

He walked across the living room and stood where the missing wall should have been.

"Is there furniture?" he asked.

"It's in—" she began, then stopped, seeing him wince at the loudness of her voice. "It's in the car," she said, more softly.

"Oh." He turned back to the room.

"I'll get it," she said. "You look at the house."

She was gone. He heard and felt her move across the floor of the big living room, the tremble reflected through the floor. Then the other front door thudded shut and he looked around his new house.

By noon, all the furniture was in place. He'd had Lou push the house against the wall behind the couch so he could have the privacy as well as the protection of four walls. Beth, on strict orders, did not approach him, but occasionally the cat got into the house, and then there was danger.

He'd also had Lou put an extension cord into the house so he could have a small Christmas-tree bulb for light. In her enthusiasm, Lou had forgotten that he would need light. He would have liked plumbing too, but that, of course, was impossible.

He moved into the doll house, but doll furniture was not designed for comfort, dolls having no particular need for comfort. The chairs, even the living-room chairs, were straight-backed and uncomfortable because they had no cushions. The bed was without springs or mattress. Lou had to sew some cotton padding into a piece of sheet so he could sleep on the hard bed.

Life in the doll house was not truly life. He might have felt inclined to fiddle on the keyboard of the glossy grand piano, but the keys were painted on and the insides were hollow. He might wander into the kitchen and yank at the refrigerator door in search of a snack, but the refrigerator was all in one piece. The knobs on the stove moved, but that was all. It would take eternity to heat a pot of water on it. He could twist the tiny sink faucets until his hands fell off, but not the smallest drop of water would ever appear. He could put clothes in the little washer, but would remain dirty and dry. He could put wood scraps in the fireplace, but if he lit them, he'd only smoke himself out of the house because there was no chimney.

One night he took off his wedding ring.

He'd been wearing it on a string around his neck, but now it was too heavy. It was like carrying a great gold loop around. He carried it up the stairs to his bedroom. There he pulled out the bottom drawer of the little dresser and put in the ring and shut the drawer again.

Then he sat on the edge of the bed looking at the bureau, thinking about the ring; thinking that it was as if he'd been carrying the roots of his marriage all these months, but now the roots had been pulled up finally and were lying still and dead in the little dresser drawer. And the marriage, by that act, was formally ended.

Beth had brought him a doll that afternoon. She'd put it on his porch and left it there. He'd ignored it all day; but now, on an impulse, he went downstairs and got the doll, which was sitting on the top step in a blue sun suit.

"Cold?" he asked her as he picked her up. She had nothing to say.

He carried her upstairs and put her down on the bed. Her eyes fell shut.

"No, don't go to sleep," he said. He sat her up by bending her at the joining of her body and her long, hard, inflexible legs. "There," he said. She sat looking at him with stark, jewel-like eyes that never blinked.

"That's a nice sun suit," he said. He reached out and brushed back her flaxen hair. "Who does your hair?" he asked. She sat there stiffly, legs spread apart, arms half raised, as though she contemplated a possible embrace.

He poked her in her hard little chest. Her halter fell off. "What do you wear a halter for?" he asked, justifiably. She stared at him glassily, withdrawn. "Your eyelashes are celluloid," he said tactlessly. "You have no ears," he said. She stared. "You're flat-chested," he told her.

Then he apologized to her for being so rude, and he followed that by telling her the story of his life. She sat patiently in the half-lit bedroom, staring at him with blue, crystalline eyes that did not blink and a little red cupid's-bow mouth that stayed perpetually half puckered, as if anticipating a kiss that never came.

Later on, he laid her down on the bed and stretched out beside her. She was asleep instantly. He turned her on her side and her blue eyes clicked open and stared at him. He turned her on her back again and they clicked shut.

"Go to sleep," he said. He put his arm around her and snuggled close to her cool plaster leg. Her hip stuck into him. He turned her on her other side, so she was looking away from him. Then he pressed close to her and slipped his arm around her body.

In the middle of the night, he woke up with a start and stared dazedly at the smooth, naked back beside him, the yellow hair tied with a red ribbon. His heartbeats thundered.

"Who *are* you?" he whispered.

Then he touched her hard, cool flesh and remembered.

A sob broke in his chest. "Why aren't you real?" he asked her, but she wouldn't tell him. He pressed his face into her soft flaxen hair and held her tight, and after a while he went to sleep again.

He sat on the cool sand, staring blankly at the doll arm sticking up out of the huge cardboard box across the way from him. It had reminded him.

He blinked and looked around. How long ago had that been? He couldn't remember. More importantly, how long had he been daydreaming here? There was no way of telling. The shaft of sunlight still pierced the window.

He blinked, looked around. He hadn't much longer. If it started to get dark, he could never—

There; *there*—wasn't that indicative? That failure to finish the thought. In the dark he could never kill the spider; he wouldn't have a chance. That was the thought. Why hadn't his mind finished it?

Because the thought terrified him.

Why was he remaining, then? He didn't have to. He had to think about it; understand it. All right. He pressed his lips together, holding on to the spear with white-knuckled hands.

For some reason, the spider had come to symbolize something to him; something he hated, something he couldn't coexist with. And, since he was going to die anyway, he wanted to take a chance at killing that something.

No, it wasn't that simple. There was something else mixed in with it. Maybe it was that he didn't really think he was going to disappear tomorrow. But wasn't it the same way with death? What young, normal person could ever really believe he was going to die? Normal? he thought. Who's normal? He closed his eyes.

Then he stood up hastily, the blood throbbing at his temples.

Tomorrow had nothing to do with it, or, if it had, he would assume it hadn't. Now was what counted. And now he decided that, even if he died for it, that black monstrosity would also die. He let it go at that. It was enough.

He found himself moving across the sand on legs that felt like wood. Where are you going? he asked himself. The answer was obvious. I'm going after the spider and—

The whisper of his sandals on the sand ceased. And *what?*

He shivered. What could he do? What could he possibly do against a seven-legged giant spider? It was four times the size of him. What good was his little pin?

He stood there motionless, staring out across the still desert. He needed a plan, and soon. Already he was thirsty again. There was no time to waste.

Very well, he thought, struggling against the rising flutter of dread; very well, then, consider it a beast to be destroyed. What did hunters do when they wanted to destroy a beast?

The answer came quickly. A pit. The spider would fall into it and—

The pin! Sticking up like a long, sharp spike!

Quickly he took the thread coil from his shoulder and flung it down. Unslinging the spear, he began to scrape at the sand, using the pin as he would a hoe.

It took him forty-five minutes of constant digging to finish. Face and body dewed with sweat, his muscles shuddering, he stood in the bottom of the pit, looking up its sheer walls. If the thread weren't hanging down, he himself would be trapped.

After resting a while, he pushed the spear into the sand so the point stuck up at a slight angle. He pushed it in deep and packed hard, wet sand around it so it would be secure. Then he climbed up the thread, pulled it out after him, and stood by the side of the pit, looking down into it.

Almost immediately, doubts began to assail him. Would it work? Wouldn't the spider run up its sides as easily as it ran up a wall? What if it missed the pin? What if it jumped back before it touched the pin? Then he'd have nothing to fight it with. Wouldn't it be better to do as he had done in the carton that time—hold the pin out and let the spider impale itself on the point?

He knew he couldn't do it that way; not now. He was too

small. The impact would knock him over. He remembered the hideous sensation of that great black leg raking over him. He couldn't face that again. Then why stay? He wouldn't answer.

One thing more. He'd have to cover up the pit after the spider was in it. Could he possibly bury it in sand? No, that would take too long.

He walked around until he found a flat piece of cardboard that was wide enough to drop over the pit. He dragged it back.

That was it, then. He'd lure the spider here, it would fall in on the pin, and he would throw the cover over it, and sit on it until he was sure the spider was dead.

He licked his lips. There was no other way.

He stood quietly for a few minutes, catching his breath. Then, although still tired and still a little breathless, he started off. He knew that if he waited any longer, his resolve would go.

He walked across the desert, searching.

The spider must be in its web. That's what he'd look for. He walked in carefully measured strides, looking around anxiously. There was a cold stone lying in his stomach. He felt defenseless without the pin. What if the spider got between him and the pit? The stone dropped, making him gasp. No, no, he argued desperately, I won't let it happen.

Sound again. He started, then realized that it *was* the settling of the house and regained his stride, muscles at a constant anticipating tension.

It was getting darker. He was going deeper and deeper into the shadows, walking farther from the window light. Frightened breath made his chest jump a little. It was the way with black widows, he knew; naturally reticent and secretive, they built their webs in the most dark, secluded corners.

He went on in the deepening gloom, and there it was. High on its web it hung, a pulsing black egg, a giant ebony pearl with legs, clinging to the ghostly cables.

There was a dry, hard lump in Scott's throat. He wanted to swallow, but the throat seemed calcified. He felt as if he were choking as he stood there staring at the giant spider. It was clear now why he hadn't seen it all day; underneath its motionless bulk, hanging slackly from the web, was a fat, partially eaten beetle.

Scott felt a nauseous foaming in his stomach. He closed his

eyes and drew in a shuddering breath. The air seemed to reek of stale death.

His eyes jerked open. The spider hadn't moved. It was still immobile, its body like a glossy black berry hanging on a milky vine.

He stood shuddering, looking at it. Obviously he couldn't go up after it. Even if he had the courage for it, the web would doubtless snare him as it had the beetle.

What could he do? Immediately inclination told him to leave unobserved, as he had approached. He even backed away several yards before he stopped.

No. He *had* to do it. It was senseless, unreasonable, insane, and yet he had to do it. He crouched down, looking up blankly at the huge spider, his hands stroking unconsciously at the sand.

His hands twitched away from something hard. He almost fell back, gasping. Then, eyes fluttering up and down to see if the spider had heard his gasp and to see what it was he'd touched, he saw the fragment of stone on the sand.

He picked it up and juggled it in his palm, a knot in his stomach, tightening slowly. His chest rose and fell with quick, erratic breaths. His gaze was fixed again on the bloated body of the spider.

He stood up quickly, teeth clenched. He walked around a small area and found nine more pieces of stone like the first one. He put them all down before him on the sand.

Far across the desert, the oil burner suddenly began to roar. He braced himself against its thundering, hands over his ears. The sand trembled under him. Up on the wall, it seemed as if the spider moved, but it was only the web stirring slightly.

When the burner clicked off, Scott picked up a stone, hesitated for a long moment, then fired the stone at the spider.

It missed, whizzing over the dark round body and knocking a hole through the web. Filaments of the web stirred out from the edges of the hole like wind-blown curtains. The spider flexed its legs, then was still again.

You're still safe, his mind warned quickly. You're still safe; for Christ's sake, get out of here!

Stomach muscles boardlike, he picked up the second stone and hurled it at the spider.

He missed again. This time the stone stuck to the web,

swaying a little, then sagging heavily, pulling down the spider's perch. The spider oozed darkly up the gossamer cables. It twitched its legs, then was motionless once more.

With a half-sobbed curse, Scott snatched up the third stone and flung it. It bulleted through the air in a blurring arc and bounced off the spider's glossy back.

The spider jumped. It seemed to hang suspended in the air, then it was on the web again, spurting across the silken hatching like a giant egg running loose. Scott jerked up another stone and pitched it, another stone and pitched it, half horrified, half in a demented fury. The stones plowed into the gelatinous web, one striking, the other tearing a second hole.

"Come on!" he suddenly screamed at the top of his voice. "Come on, damn you!" Then the spider was skimming down the web, body trembling on its scrabbling legs. Another cry died in Scott's throat. With a sucked-in breath, he whirled and started racing across the sand.

Ten yards from where he'd started, he glanced back hurriedly across his shoulder. The spider was on the sand now, an inky bubble floating after him. Sudden panic clouded his brain. His legs seemed without strength. I'm falling! he thought.

It was an illusion. He was still running hard, mouth open. His gaze flew on ahead, searching for the pit, but he couldn't see it. A little farther yet. He jerked his head around again. It was gaining on him.

His eyes turned back quickly. Don't look! he thought. A stitch slashed up his side. His fleeing sandals pounded on the sand. He kept on searching ahead for the pit.

He couldn't help it, he looked back. It was closer still, quivering blackly on its leg stalks, scrambling almost sideways over the sand, eyes fixed on him. He sprinted, wild-eyed, through the shadows and the light.

Where was the pit?

For now he'd gone too far—he knew it—and was almost to the paint cans and jars. No, it was impossible! He'd planned it too carefully for it to happen like this. He glanced back. Still closer; scrabbling, hopping, bogging, fluttering, a horrible blackness running at him, higher than a horse.

He had to go back again! He started running in a wide semi-circle, praying that the spider would not cut across his path. The sand seemed to hold him back more and more, his sandals plowing into it, making quick sucking sounds.

He looked back again. It was following in his wake, but it was still closer. He thought he heard the wild scratching of its legs on the sand. The spider was twelve yards behind him, it was eleven yards behind him, ten yards . . .

Still running, he sprang into the air to see if he could locate the pit. He couldn't. His body jarred down heavily. A whining fluttered in his throat. Was it going to end like this?

No, wait! Ahead, to the right! He altered direction and dashed for the parapet of sand around his pit. Nine yards behind, the huge spider raced after him.

The pit grew larger now. He ran still faster, gasping through his teeth, arms pumping at the air. He skidded to a halt at the edge of the pit and whirled. It was the vital moment: he had to stand there until the spider was almost on him.

He stood petrified, watching the black spider bear down on him, getting taller and wider with every second. He saw its black eyes now, the cruel pincer-like jaws beneath it, the hair sprouts on its legs, the great body. It rushed closer and closer; his body twitched. No, wait—wait! The spider was almost on top of him; it blotted out the world. It reared up on its back legs to cover him.

Now!

With a tremendous spring, he leaped to one side and the lurching spider toppled into the pit.

The ghastly, piercing screech almost paralyzed him. It was like the distant scream of a gutted horse. Only instinct drove him to his feet to grab the cardboard and slide it rapidly toward the pit. The screeching continued, and suddenly he found himself screaming back at it. As he shoved the cardboard across the top of the pit, he saw the great black body vibrating wildly, the thick legs scraping and clawing at the sides of the pit, raking at the sand, kicking it up in clouds.

Scott flung himself across the cover. Immediately he felt it lurch and jump beneath him as the spider's body heaved up against it. Flesh cold and crawling, he clung to the jolting cardboard scrap, waiting for the spider to die. I did it! he exulted. I *did* it!

His breath choked off. The cardboard was tilting up.

Terror drove a steel-gloved fist into his heart. He started sliding off the cardboard as it tilted more steeply.

When the black leg flailed out like the twig-spiked branch of some living tree, he screamed. He began sliding toward the leg, sliding, sliding.

Instinct drove him to his feet. As the cardboard was flung up violently, he added the springing of his legs to the impetus and leaped high above the leg.

He landed in a heap beside his coil of thread and whirled on hands and knees, staring at the pit. The spider was crawling out, dragging the impaling pin behind.

His body was convulsed with a terrible shudder. His hands clutched at something as he struggled up and started backing away.

"No," he muttered flatly. "No. No. No."

The spider was completely out of the pit now, moving awkwardly toward him, the pin still in its body. Suddenly it leaped up, landed, then spun around in a sand-scouring circle, trying to dislodge the pin. *Do* something! screamed his mind. He stared, sickly fascinated, at the jerking spider.

Suddenly he was conscious of the pin hook in his hands, and then he was running with it, uncoiling the rest of the thread. Behind him, the spider still writhed and flung itself around, blood drops flying out from it and spattering in murky ribbons across the sand.

Abruptly the spear came loose. The spider whirled toward Scott.

He was swinging the hook around his head at the end of six feet of thread. It flashed around him like a glittering scythe, swishing at the air.

The spider ran right into it.

The point drove into its bulbous body like a needle plunged into a watermelon. It leaped back sharply, screeching again, and Scott raced around a heavy scrap of wood, looping the thread around it until it was secure. The spider rushed at him, the pin hook deep in its body. Scott turned and fled.

It almost caught him. Before the thread grew taut and jerked the spider back, one of its black legs flailed across his shoulder, almost dragging him back. He had to fall to the sand and tear away from it before he could scuttle backward to freedom.

He stood up shakily, hair dangling across his forehead, face grimy with dirt. The spider tried to leap at him, legs slashing, jaws spread wide to clamp on him. The pin jerked it back; the hideous screeching knifed into Scott's brain again.

He couldn't stand it. He fled across the sand, the spider following him as far as it could, leaping and dragging fiercely at its binding.

The pin was slick with blood. Teeth set on edge, Scott flung handfuls of sand across it, then grabbed it up and moved back quickly, spear extended and braced against his hip.

The spider leaped. Scott jabbed out quickly and the spear point pierced the black shell; another drip of blood began. The spider leaped again; again the spear point tore its hide and drew blood. Again and again the spider leaped into the spear point, until its body was a mass of punctures.

By then the screeching had stopped. The spider moved in slowly, rearing shakily on its weakened legs. Scott wanted it over suddenly. He could walk away and let it die now, but he wouldn't. For some fantastic reason swimming in mists of past morality, he felt sorry for the spider now and wanted to end its suffering. Deliberately he walked inside its circle of confinement, and with a final burst of violent effort the spider leaped.

The spear point pierced its body and the spider fell into a shuddering heap, its poison-dripping jaws clamping shut inches from Scott's body. Then it was dead, its body lying still and gigantic on the bloody sands.

Scott staggered away from it and pitched across the sand, unconscious. The last sound he remembered was the slow and awful scratching of the spider's legs—dead, but not at rest.

He stirred feebly, hands drawing in slowly, clutching at the sand. A groan wavered in his chest; he rolled over onto his back. His eyes opened.

Had it been a dream? He lay breathing carefully for a minute; then, with a grunt, he sat up.

No dream. Yards away from him the spider lay, its body like a great, dead stone, its legs like motionless spars bent in every direction. The stillness of death hung over it.

It was almost night. He had to get down the cliff before dark. Exhaling wearily, he struggled to his feet and walked across to the spider. It made him ill to stand beside its bloody hulk, but he had to have the hook.

When it was finally done, he stumbled across the desert, dragging the hook behind him so the sands would clean it.

Well, it's done, he thought. The nights of horror were ended. He could sleep without the box top now, sleep free and at peace. A tired smile eased his stark expression. Yes, it was worth it. Everything seemed worth it now.

At the cliff's edge, he flung out the hook until it bit into wood. Then slowly, wearily, he pulled himself up, drew in the thread, and started across the lawn chair's arm. A long descent yet. He smiled again. It didn't matter; he'd make it.

As he was swinging down to the lower chair, hanging in space, the hook broke.

In an instant he was plummeting through the air, turning in slow, arm-waving cartwheels. It was such an absolute shock to him that he couldn't make a sound. His brain was stricken and taut. The only emotion he felt was one of complete, dumfounded astonishment.

Then he landed on the flower-patterned cushion, bounced once, and lay still.

After a while he stood up and felt over his body. He didn't understand it. Even if he had landed on the cushion, he'd fallen many hundreds of feet. How could he still be alive, much less unhurt?

He stood a long time, feeling ceaselessly at himself, almost unable to believe that no bones were broken, that he was only bruised a trifle.

Then it came to him: his weight. He'd been wrong all the time. He'd thought that in a fall he'd suffer the same effects as he might have when he had his full size and weight. He was wrong. It should have been obvious to him. Couldn't an ant be dropped almost any distance and still walk away from the fall?

Shaking his head wonderingly, he walked to one of the pieces of bread and carried a big hunk of it back to the sponge. Then, after he'd got a long drink from the hose, he climbed to the top of the sponge with his bread and ate supper.

That night he slept in utter peace.

Chapter Fifteen

He reared up with a cry, suddenly awake. A carpet of sunlight glared across the cement floor; there was a drumlike jarring on the steps. Breath froze in him. Cutting off the sunlight, a giant appeared.

Scott flung himself across the yielding sponge, scrambling for its edge, then toppling over it. The giant stopped and looked around, its head almost touching the ceiling, far above. Scott dropped lightly to the cement, pushing to his feet, then pitching forward, tripping on the oversized robe. He jumped up a second time, eyes staring at the giant, who stood motionless, vast arms on hips. Grabbing up handfuls of his dragging robe, Scott raced barefoot across the cold floor, his sandals left behind.

After five yards, the folds of robe slipped from his hands and he went sprawling again. The giant moved. Scott gasped, recoiling, flinging up an arm. There was no chance to flee. The floor shook with the giant's coming. Horrified, Scott saw the Gargantuan shoes crash down on the cement. His gaze leaped up. The giant's body seemed to totter over him like a falling mountain. Scott threw the other arm across his face. The end! his mind screamed.

The thunder stopped and Scott drew down his arms.

Miraculously, the giant had stopped beside the red metal table. Why hadn't it gone on to the water heater? What was it doing?

A gasp tore back his lips as the giant reached across the plateau of the table, pulled over a carton bigger than an apartment house, and tossed it to the floor. The noise it made in landing drove an aural spear through Scott's brain. He clamped both hands over his ears and, struggling to his feet, backed off hastily. What was it doing? Another vast carton was flung across the cellar, landing deafeningly. Scott's frightened gaze followed its rocking descent, then jumped back to where the giant stood.

Now it was pulling something even larger from the pile between the fuel tank and the refrigerator. Something blue. It was Lou's suitcase.

Suddenly he knew it wasn't the same giant that had been

there Wednesday. His eyes fled up the cliff walls of its trousers. That blue-gray pattern of squares and lines, what was it? He stared at it. Glen plaid! The giant was a man in a glen-plaid suit, wearing black shoes that seemed a block long. Where had he seen that glen-plaid suit before?

It came to him an instant before a second, smaller giant jumped down the steps and, in a piercing voice, said "Can I help you, Uncle Marty?"

Scott stood rigid, only his eyes moving—from the immense form of his daughter to the even more immense form of his brother, then back again.

"I don't think so, sweetheart," Marty said. "I think they're too heavy." His voice rang out in Scott's ears with such a resonant volume that he could barely make out the words.

"I could carry the small one," answered Beth.

"Well, maybe you could, at that," said Marty. Cartons still flew through the air, bounced on the floor. Now two canvas chairs went flying. "There. And there," said Marty. They crashed against the lawn chairs and were still. "And *there*," said Marty. A net pole like a two-thousand-foot tree flashed across the floor and fell against the cliff, leaning there, its bottom end braced by the moonlike metal rim to which the net was fastened.

Now Scott was back against the cement block, head back, and he was gaping at the towering shape of his brother. He watched Marty's elephantine hand close over the handle of the second suitcase and drag it raspingly across the metal table, then drop it on the floor. What was Marty taking down the suitcases for?

The answer came: They were moving.

"No," he muttered, running forward impulsively. He saw Beth's gigantic form lurch across the floor in three strides, then bend over to grab the second suitcase.

"No!" His face was drawn with panic. "Marty!" he screamed, racing toward his brother. He tripped across the dragging hem of his robe again, pitched forward. He stood up, crying his brother's name again. She couldn't leave!

"Marty, it's me!" he shrieked. "Marty!"

With palsied fingers, he jerked the robe over his shoulders and head and flung it down. He ran berserkly at his brother's shoes.

"Marty!"

At the steps, he heard the sawing, teeth-setting din of Beth dragging the smaller suitcase over rough cement edges. He ignored it, still running toward his brother. He had to make him hear.

"Marty! Marty!"

With a sigh, Marty started for the steps.

"No! Don't go!" Scott yelled as loudly as he could. Like a pale white insect, he sprinted over the cold cement toward his brother's rapidly moving form.

"Marty!"

At the steps, Marty turned. Scott's eyes widened suddenly with excitement.

"Here, Marty! *Here!*" he shouted, thinking his brother had heard. He waved his thread-thin arms wildly. "I'm here, Marty! Here!"

Marty turned his giant head. "Beth?" he said.

"Yes, Uncle Marty." Her voice drifted down the steps.

"Does your mother have anything else down here?"

"Some things," Beth replied.

"Oh. Well, we'll come back, then."

By then Scott had reached the giant shoe and leaped up clawing at the high ridge of its sole. He caught at the hard leather and held on.

"Marty!" He screamed it again and dragged himself up onto the shelf. Standing hurriedly, he began to beat his fists against the shoe. It was like hitting a stone wall.

"Marty, please!" he begged. "Please! Oh, please!"

Abruptly the shelf lurched and swung around in an immense, brain-whirling circle. Scott lost his balance and fell back with a cry, arms flailing for balance.

He landed heavily on the cement and lay breathless, watching his brother move up the steps with Lou's suitcase.

Then Marty was gone and sunlight poured blindingly across him. Scott flung an arm across his eyes and twisted away. A sob tore through his chest. It wasn't fair! Why were all his triumphs undone so quickly, all his victories negated in the very next instant?

He lurched to his feet and stood trembling, his back to the

blazing sunlight. She was moving; Louise was moving away. She thought he was dead and she was leaving him.

His teeth grated together. He had to let her know he was still alive.

He looked sideways, shading his eyes with a cupped hand. The door was still open. He ran to the edge of the bottom step and looked up its sheer rise. Even if he made himself another hook, he couldn't throw it that high. He walked restlessly along the base of the step, muttering to himself.

What about the cracks between the cement blocks? Could he climb them now as he'd planned to do on Wednesday? He started toward the nearest one, then stopped, realizing that he had to have some clothes and food, some water.

It was then that the impossibility of the climb fell over him like a splash of molten lead.

He fell against the cold cement of the step and stood shivering, staring with dead eyes at the floor. His head shook slowly back and forth. It was no use trying. He'd never make the top. Not now; not at one seventh of an inch.

He'd stumbled halfway back to the sponge when the idea dispersed his despair. Marty had said he was coming back down.

With a gasp, he started running for the step again, then halted once more. Wait, wait, he cautioned, you have to prepare first. He couldn't just jump at the shoe again; there was no secure hold. Somehow he had to grab Marty's trouser leg, maybe even crawl inside the cuff, and cling there until he was carried into the house. Then he could get out, climb up on a table or a chair, anything, wave a piece of cloth, catch Lou's attention. Just to have her know that he was still alive, he thought excitedly. Just to have her know that.

All right, then. Quickly, quickly. He clapped his hands together with a nervous movement. What came first?

First came eating, drinking; a good meal under his—he laughed nervously—his belt? He glanced down at his white, goose-fleshed nakedness. Yes, that was first; but what could he wear? The robe was too big and its material too strong to tear up. Maybe . . .

He ran to the sponge and, after a wild tugging and jerking and gnawing of teeth, managed to tear away a big piece of it.

This he thinned as much as he could and pulled around himself, sticking his arms and then his legs through its pores. It pressed against him, rubber-like, and did not cover him very well; it kept springing open in the front. Well, it would have to do. There was no time to make anything better.

Food next. He jogged across the floor and broke a chunk of bread from one of the pieces by the cliff. He carried it quickly to the hose and sat there eating it, perched on the metal lip of the opening, legs dangling. His feet should have something on them, too; but what?

When he'd finished eating and made the long, cold trek through the black hose passage, he went back to the sponge and pulled off two small pieces for his feet. He ripped out the centers of them and jammed his feet in. The sponge didn't hold very well. He'd have to fasten them with thread.

Suddenly it occurred to him that the thread not only would fasten his improvised clothing to himself, but could also get him into Marty's cuff. If he could get another pin and bend it, and tie it to a length of thread, he could hook the pin into the trousers and hang on until he was upstairs in the house.

He started to run for the carton under the fuel tank. He stopped and whirled, remembering the piece of thread he'd had when he'd fallen the night before. It must still have a piece of pin fastened to it. He ran to find it.

It did; what was more, the piece of pin was still bent enough to hook onto Marty's trouser leg.

Scott ran on the pile of stones and wood by the bottom step, waiting for his brother to come down again.

Upstairs, he could hear restless, hurried footsteps moving through the rooms, and he visualized Lou moving about, preparing to leave. His lips pressed together until they hurt. If it was the last thing he did, he'd let her know he was alive.

He looked at the cellar. It was hard to believe that, after all this time, he might be getting out. The cellar had become the world to him. Maybe he'd be like a prisoner released after long confinement, frightened and insecure. No, that couldn't be true. The cellar had been no womb of comfort to him. Life on the outside could hardly be more onerous than it had been down here.

He ran his fingers lightly over his bad knee. The swelling

had gone down considerably; it ached only a little. He touched at the cuts and abrasions on his face. He unwrapped the bandage on his hand, tugged it off and dropped it to the floor. He swallowed experimentally. His throat felt sore, but that didn't matter. He was ready for the world.

Upstairs, he heard the back door shut and footsteps on the porch. He jumped from the boulder and shook loose the length of thread. Then, picking up the hook, he pressed back against the wall of the step, waiting, his chest wall thudding with heavy heartbeats. Up in the yard, he heard a crunch of shoes on the sandy ground, then a voice saying, "I'm not sure exactly what we have down there."

His face grew tautly blank, his eyes were like frozen pools. He felt as if his legs were rubber columns under him.

It was Lou.

He shrank against the cement as giant shoes stamped down the steps. "Lou," he whispered, and then the two of them blocked off the sun like dark clouds passing.

They moved around, their heads more than half a mile high. He couldn't see her face, only the great moving redness of her skirt.

"That box on the shelf is ours," she said, a voice in the sky.

"All right," said Marty, moving toward the cliff wall and pulling down the carton with the doll arm sticking from it.

Lou kicked aside the small sponge on the floor. "Let's see, now," she said. "I think . . ."

She crouched down, and abruptly Scott could see the massive features of her face as a billboard hanger might see the features of the woman's face he pasted up. There was no sense of over-all appearance; just a huge eye here, an enormous nose there, lips like a rosy-banked canyon.

"Yes," she said, "this carton under the tank."

"I'll get it," Marty said, moving up the steps with the first box.

He was alone with her.

His gaze leaped up as she stood again. She moved around slowly, giant arms crossed under the mountainous swell of her breasts. There was a twisting agony in Scott's chest and stomach. For there was no denying it; she was beyond him now. Thoughts of trying to tell her he was alive evaporated. They had disappeared the moment he saw her. He was an insect to her; he knew it now with hideous clarity. Even if he managed somehow to attract her attention, it would solve nothing, it would change nothing. He would still be gone tonight, and the only thing accomplished would be that he would have torn open an old wound that might be nearly closed by now.

He stood silent, like a tiny piece from a miniature charm bracelet, looking up at the woman who had been his wife.

Marty came down the steps again.

"I'll be glad to get out of here," Lou told him.

"I don't blame you," Marty said, walking to the fuel tank and crouching down before it.

Beth came down the steps, asking, "Can I carry something, Mamma?"

"I don't think there's anything. Oh, yes, you can take up that jar of paint brushes. I think they're ours."

"All right." Beth moved to the wicker table.

Suddenly Scott twitched out of his reverie. He didn't want to tell Lou, but he did still want to get out of the cellar. And he couldn't wait for Marty, he realized. Marty would pass by the step too quickly; there would be no time.

Pushing away from the step, he raced to the refrigerator, under its shadowing bulk, then under the wicker table. Marty was still squatting by the tank, pulling out the carton. Scott ran beneath the red metal table. Quickly! He ran faster, dragging the thread behind him. Marty stood up with the carton in his arms. He started for the steps.

There was no time. As Scott rushed out into the open, Marty's immense black shoe was already crashing down before him. With a muscle-jerking hitch, he flung the hook at the swishing trouser leg.

If he had caught a galloping horse, he couldn't have been torn off his feet more violently.

His cry choked off. Abruptly he was flying through the air, then dipping down, the floor rushing grayly at him. With a twisting of his legs, he flattened out his body, his sponge coat scratching the floor as he flashed over it. The vast leg moved again. Scott, caught in the apex of his swing, was jerked high into the air. The thread grew taut and he was snapped forward again, his arms almost wrenched from their sockets. The cellar whirled by, a flash of light and shadow blended. He wanted to scream but he couldn't. He was swinging again, rocking violently in the air, spun around, his tiny body bulleting toward the steps. A wall rushed at him, disappeared below as he was jerked above it. His feet skidded along the top of the first step, the sponge bits torn away. The violent impact tore him loose, and suddenly he was running at top speed across the cement, heading for the face of the second step. He flung out his arms to ward off the shock. He screamed.

Then he tripped over a grain of concrete and went sprawling. His legs flew up, his skull cracked against the cement. Pain exploded through his head, white and vivid, then drew in suddenly to a black core, which also exploded, splashing his brain with night. He lay there limply as the shoe of his wife slammed down an inch from his body, then was gone.

Later, while Marty was driving them to the railroad station, Beth saw the hook and thread sticking to his trouser leg, and, bending down, she plucked it out. Marty said, "I must have picked it up in the cellar," then forgot about it. Beth put it in the pocket of her overcoat, and she forgot about it too.

7"

"Put me down!" he screamed.

He could say no more. Her hand was clamped around his body, binding him from shoulder to hip, pinning his body, squeezing out his breath. The room blurred by; he started to black out.

Then the doll-house porch was under his feet, his hand was clutching at the wrought-iron railing, and Beth was looking down at him with half-frightened eyes.

"I gave you a ride," she said.

He jerked open the front door and plunged into the house, slamming the door behind him and snapping the tiny hook into its eye. Then he slumped down weakly in the living room, breath a dry rasping in his throat.

Outside, Beth said defensively, "I didn't hurt you."

He didn't answer. He felt as if he'd just been almost crushed in a vise.

"I didn't *hurt* you," she said, and she began to cry.

He'd known that the time would come, and finally it had. He could put it off no longer. He'd have to ask Lou to keep Beth away from him. She wasn't responsible.

He got up weakly and stumbled over to the couch. He heard Beth going outside again, the floor trembling with her exit. The crash of the front door made him start violently. She'd come in a few moments ago, seen him making the long walk to his house, and picked him up.

He fell back on the small cushions Lou had made for him. He lay there a long time, staring at the shadowy ceiling and thinking of his lost child.

She'd been born on a Thursday morning. Lou's labor had been a long one. She'd kept telling him to go home, but he wouldn't. Occasionally he'd go down to the car, curl up on the back seat, and catch a few minutes of shallow sleep, but most of the time he stayed up in the waiting room, thumbing sightlessly through magazines, the book he'd brought to read unopened on the table beside him. Oh, yes, he was going to be smart; no movie melodramatics for him, no floor pacing and mashing of butts beneath heels. For that matter, he couldn't pace the floor even though he would have liked to. The waiting room was only a small alcove at the end of the second-floor hall, and he couldn't walk in the hall because there was too much traffic there.

So he'd sat in the waiting room, feeling as if there were a bomb in his stomach, primed to explode shortly. There was one other man there, but it was his fourth baby and he was blasé. He actually read a book: *The Curse of the Conquistadores.* Scott still remembered the title. How could a man sit reading such a book when his wife was writhing and twisting in labor? Or maybe his wife was one of the easy deliverers. As a matter of fact, the man couldn't have read more than three chapters before the baby was born, about one in the morning. The man had shrugged, winked at Scott, and gone home. Scott had cursed softly after him, then sat alone in the waiting room, waiting.

At seven-one A.M., Elizabeth Louise had put in her appearance.

He remembered Dr. Arron coming out of the delivery room and starting down the hall toward him, soft-soled shoes squeaking on the tiles. A dozen different horrors had pulsed through Scott's brain. She's dead. The baby's dead. It's misshapen. It's twins. It's triplets. There was nothing in there.

Dr. Arron had said, "Well, you've got a daughter."

And he'd been led to the glass window and, inside, a nurse was holding up a blanket-wreathed child, and it had black hair and it was yawning, its red little fists twitching at the air. And he'd just managed to brush away the tears before anyone could see.

He sat up on the couch and stretched out his legs. The pain in his rib box was not so bad now. He'd had trouble breathing for a little while there. He ran exploring hands over his chest and sides. No bones broken; that was sheer luck. Beth had clutched him terribly. Doubtless she'd only meant to make sure she wouldn't drop him, but . . .

He shook his head. "Beth, Beth," he murmured. Unseen, he'd been losing her day by day ever since the shrinking began. The loss of his wife had been a clear and certain process; the divorce from his child had been something else again.

At first there had been the circumstantial separation from her. He was suffering a terrible, unknown affliction, going regularly to doctors, being examined, being installed in a hospital. He had no time for her.

Then he was home, and worry and dread and the failing of his marriage had kept him from seeing how he was losing her. Sometimes he would hold her in his lap, read her a story, or, late at night, stand beside her bed and look down at her. Mostly, though, he was too absorbed in his own state to see anything else.

Then physical size had entered into it. As he'd grown shorter and shorter, so had he grown less certain of his authority and her respect. It was not a thing to be lightly conquered. As his size affected his attitude toward Lou, so did it affect his attitude toward Beth.

The authority of fatherhood, he discovered, depended greatly on simple physical difference. A father, to his child, was big and strong; he was all-powerful. A child saw simply. It respected size and depth of voice. What physically overshadowed it, it almost always respected or at least feared. Not that Scott had gained Beth's respect by trying to make her fear him. It was simply a basic state that existed because he was six feet two and she was four feet one.

When he had sunk to her height, then gone below it, when his voice had lost depth and authority and become a high-pitched, ineffective sound, Beth's respect had slackened. It was merely that she could not understand. God knew they had tried to explain it to her—endlessly. But it wasn't explicable, because there was nothing in Beth's mental background comparable to a shrinking father.

Consequently, when he was no longer six feet two and his voice was no longer the voice she knew, she no longer actually regarded him as her father. A father was constant. He could be depended on, he did not change. Scott was changing. Therefore, he could not be the same; he could not be treated the same.

And so it had gone, each day her respect waning more. Especially when his jaded nerves began sending him into flurries of temper. She could not understand or appreciate. She was not old enough to sympathize. She could only see him baldly. And, in the actuality of pure sight, he was nothing but a horrid midget who screamed and ranted in a funny voice. To her he had stopped being a father and had become an oddity.

And now the loss was irreparable and final. Beth had reached the stage where she was a physical menace to him. Like the cat, she had to be kept away from him.

"She didn't mean it, Scott," Lou said that night.

"I know she didn't," he answered into the small hand microphone, so that his voice came clearly through the phonograph loud-speaker. "She just doesn't understand. But she'll have to stay away from me. She doesn't realize how frail I am. She picked me up as if I were an indestructible doll. I'm not."

The next day it ended.

He was standing, stooped over, in a hay-strewn stable, looking at the faces of Mary and Joseph and the Wise Men as they looked upon the infant Jesus. It was very quiet and, if he squinted, it seemed almost as if they were all alive and Mary's face was gently smiling and the Wise Men were wavering, awed and reverent, over the manger. The animals were stamping in their stalls and he could smell the acrid stable smells and there was the faint, beautiful sound of the infant's gurgling.

Then a cold wind blew over him, making him shudder.

He looked toward the kitchen and saw that the door had been blown open a little and the wind was blowing powdery snowflakes across the floor. He waited for Lou to close it, but she didn't. Then he heard the faint, distant drumming of water and knew she was taking a shower. He stepped out of the stable and walked across the crinkled cotton glacier under the Christmas tree, his tiny homemade shoes crunching on the artificial snow. The wind rushed over him again and he shivered fitfully.

"Beth!" he called, then remembered that she was outside playing. He muttered irritably to himself, then ran across the rug onto the wide expanse of green linoleum. Maybe he could shut it himself.

He'd barely reached the door when a throaty rumble sounded behind him.

Whirling, he saw the cat by the sink, head just lifted from a dish of milk, its furry coat wet and disheveled. There was a heavy sinking in his stomach.

"Get out of here," he said. Its ears pricked up. "Get *out* of here," he said again, more loudly.

Another growl wavered liquidly in the cat's throat and it slid forward a predatory paw, claws extended.

"Get out of here!" he yelled, backing off, the icy wind across his back, snowflakes buffeting like fragile hands at his shoulders and head.

The cat moved forward as smoothly as sliding butter, mouth open, saber teeth exposed.

Then Beth came in the front door and the sudden draft hurricaning across the floor flung the back door toward its frame, scooping Scott along with it. In an instant the door had slammed shut and he had landed in a bank of snow.

Scrambling up, his clothes feathered with snow, Scott charged back to the door and pounded his fists against it.

"Beth!" The sound was barely audible to him above the wailing of the wind. Cold snow blew across him in ghostlike clouds. A huge pile of it fell from the railing, crashing down nearby and splattering him with its freezing granules.

"Oh, my God," he muttered. Frantically he began kicking at the door. "Beth!" he howled. "Beth, let me in!" He pounded until his fists ached and throbbed, kicked until his feet felt dead, but the door remained closed.

"Oh, my God." The horror of the situation was billowing in his mind. He turned and looked out fearfully at the snow-swept yard. Everything was dazzling white. The ground was a livid desert of snow, the wind blowing powdery mists of it across the high dunes. The trees were vast white columns topped with skeleton-white branches and limbs. The fence was a leprous barricade, wind ripping off snowy flesh, exposing the bony pickets underneath.

Realization came bluntly: if he stayed out here very long, he'd freeze to death. Already his feet felt like lead, his fingers ached and tingled from the cold, his body was alive with shudders.

Indecision tore at him. Should he remain and try to get in, or should he leave the porch and seek shelter from the snow and wind? Instinct bound him to the house. Safety lay on the other side of the white, paneled door. Yet intelligent observation made it clear that to remain was to risk his life. Where could he go, though? The cellar windows were locked from the inside, the doors were much too heavy for him to lift. And it would be no warmer underneath the porch.

The front porch! If somehow he could climb the front-porch railing, he might be able to reach the bell. Then he could get in.

Still he hesitated. The snow looked deep and frightening. What if he were swallowed in a drift? What if he got so cold he never reached the front porch?

But he knew it was his only chance, and the decision had to be made quickly. There was no guarantee that his absence would be noted soon enough. If he stayed here on the back porch, Lou might find him in time. But she might not, too.

Gritting his teeth, he moved to the edge of the porch and jumped down to the first step. Piled snow cushioned his drop. He slipped a little, regained his balance, and scuffed to the edge of the step. He jumped again.

His feet slid out from under him and he spilled forward, arms plunging into the snow to his shoulders, face slapping into its flesh-numbing chill. He jerked up, gagging, and stood with a lurching movement, brushing at his face as if it swarmed with icicle-legged spiders.

There was no time to waste. Quickly he moved to the edge of the step, putting down his feet carefully. He poised at the brink a moment, looking down, then, with a quick breath, jumped.

Again he skidded, arms striking at the air. He slid to the side edge of the step, held on for a moment, then pitched into space.

Four feet down, his body plowed into a cone of snow like a knife driven into ice cream. Frost crystals floured across his face and down his neck. He pushed up, spluttering, then fell again, legs imbedded in the icy packing. He lay there, stunned, snow clouds powdering over him.

Then cold began creeping up his limbs and he pushed to his feet. He had to keep moving.

He couldn't run. The best he could manage was a sort of lurching, staggering walk, feet torn loose from the clinging snow, then put down again, his body hitching forward as his legs sank in. As he flopped across the yard, the wind whipped his hair to lashing ribbons and tore at his clothes, cutting through the material like frozen blades. Already his feet and hands were going numb.

At last he reached the corner of the house. In the far distance he saw the covered bulk of the Ford, its tarpaulin covered with scattered peaks of snow. A groan wavered in his throat. It was so far. He sucked in a mouthful of the lip-chilling air and lurched forward again. I'll make it, he told himself. I'll make it.

An object spilled across the sky like a plummeting stone.

One moment there was only wind and cold and thigh-deep snow. The next, a weight had crushed against him suddenly, knocking him down. His face a snow-cottoned mass of shock he flung himself over just in time to see the dark sparrow diving at him again.

Gasping, he flung up an arm as the bird flashed over him, swooping up on rigid wings. It shot into the air, circled sharply, and came at him again. Before he'd reached his feet, it was hovering before him, so close that he could smell its wet feathers. Its wings beat savagely at the air; the double sabers of its beak lunged at him.

He fell back again, snatching up a handful of snow and flinging it at the sparrow's head. It rose into the air, chattering fiercely, whirled about in a tight arc, then began to circle him in narrow, blurring sweeps, dark wings beating.

Scott's stark gaze jumped to the house, and he saw the cellar window and the missing pane.

Then the bird was at him again. He flung himself forward on the snow, and the dark, wing-flashing bulk shot over him. The sparrow swooped up, circled sharply, then bulleted back. Scott ran a few feet, then was knocked over again.

He stood up, flinging more snow at the bird, seeing the snow splatter off its dark, flaring beak. The bird flapped back. Scott turned and struggled a few more strides, then the bird was on him again, wet wings pounding at his head. He slapped wildly at it and felt his hands strike the bony sides of its beak. It flew off again.

It went on like that endlessly. He would leap through the icy snow until he heard its wing-drumming approach. Then, falling to his knees, he would whirl and fling a cloud of snow into its eyes, blinding it, driving it off long enough to push on a few more inches.

Until, finally, cold and dripping, he stood with his back to the cellar window, hurling snow at the bird in the desperate hope that it would give up and he wouldn't have to jump into the imprisoning cellar.

But the bird kept coming, diving at him, hovering before him, the sound of its wings like that of wet sheets flapping in a heavy wind. Suddenly the jabbing beak was hammering at his skull, slashing skin, knocking him back against the house. He stood there dazedly, waving his arms in panic at the bird's attack. The yard swam before him, a billowing mist of white. He picked up snow and threw it, missing. The wings were still beating at his face; the beak gashed his flesh again.

With a stricken cry, Scott whirled and leaped for the open square. He crawled across it dizzily. The leaping bird knocked him through.

He fell, clawing, his screams ending with a breathless grunt as he crashed down on the sand beneath the cellar window. He tried to stand, but he had twisted his leg in falling and it refused now to bear his weight.

Ten minutes later he heard running footsteps up above. The back door opened and slammed shut. And all the while he lay there in a snarl of limbs. Lou and Beth walked around the house and through the yard, trampling down the snow, calling his name over and over until darkness fell. And they didn't stop even then.

Chapter Sixteen

IN THE DISTANCE he could hear the thumping of the water pump. They forgot to turn it off. The thought trickled like cold honey across the fissures of his brain. He stared with vacant eyes, his face a blank. The pump clicked off, and silence draped down across the cellar. They're gone, he thought. The house is empty. I'm alone.

His tongue stirred sluggishly. Alone. His lips moved. The word began and ended in his throat.

He twisted slightly and felt a stirring of pain in the back of his skull. Alone. His right fist twitched and thumped once at the cement. Alone. After everything. After all his efforts, he was alone in the cellar.

He pushed up finally, then sank down instantly as pain seemed to tear open the back of his head. Lying there, he reached up gingerly and touched a finger to the spot. He traced the edges of the brittle lacework of dried blood; his fingertip ascended and descended the parabola of the lump. He prodded it once. He groaned and dropped his arm. He lay there on his stomach, feeling the cold, rough cement against his forehead.

Alone.

Finally he rolled over and sat up. Pain rolled sluggishly around the inside of his head. It did not stop quickly. He had to press the palms of his hands against his temples to cushion its stabbing rebound. After a long while it stopped and dragged down at the base of his skull, spikes sunk in his flesh. He wondered if his skull were fractured, then decided that, if it were, he would be in no condition to wonder about it.

He opened his eyes and looked around the cellar with pain-slitted eyes. Everything was still the same. His dismal gaze moved over the familiar landmarks. And I thought I was going to get out, he thought bitterly. He looked up over his shoulder with a wince. The door was closed again, of course. And locked too, probably. He was still trapped.

His chest shuddered with a long exhalation. He licked his dry lips. And he was thirsty again too, and hungry. It was all senseless.

Even the slight amount of tensing in his jaws sent pain gnawing through his head. He opened his mouth and sat limply until the aching had diminished.

When he stood, it came back again. He pressed one palm against the face of the next step and leaned against it, the cellar wavering before him as though he saw it through a lens of water. It took a while for objects to appear clearly.

He shifted on his feet and hissed, discovering that his knee was swollen again. He glanced down at its puffiness, remembering that it was the leg that had been injured in his original fall into the cellar. Odd that he'd never made the connection, but that was undoubtedly why that leg always weakened first.

He remembered lying on the sand, the leg twisted under him, while outside Lou was calling him. It was night and the cellar had been dark and cold. Wind had blown snow confetti through the broken pane. It had drifted down across his face, feeling like the timid, withdrawing touches of ghostly children. And, though he answered her and answered her, she never heard him. Not even when she came down into the cellar and, unable to move, he had lain there, crying out her name.

He walked slowly to the edge of the step and looked down the hundred-foot drop to the floor. A terrible distance. Should he labor down the mortar-crack chimney or—

Abruptly, he jumped.

He landed on his feet. His knee seemed to explode and a knife-edged club smashed across his brain as he fell forward to his hands. But that was all. Shaken, he sat on the floor, smiling grimly despite the pain. It was a good thing he'd discovered that he could fall so far without being hurt. If he hadn't discovered it, he would have had to climb down the chimney and wasted time. The smile faded. He stared morosely at the floor. Time was no longer something to be wasted, because it was no longer something to be saved. It was no longer a commodity to be spent or hoarded. It had lost all value.

He got up and started walking, feet padding softly over the cold cement. Should have got the sponge shoes, he thought. Then he shrugged carelessly. What did it matter, anyway?

He got himself a drink from the hose, then returned to the sponge. He didn't feel hungry, after all. He climbed to the top of the sponge and lay back with a thin sigh.

He lay there inertly, staring up at the window over the fuel tank. There was no sunlight visible. It must be late afternoon. Soon darkness would fall. Soon the last night would begin.

He looked at the twisted latticework of a spider web that blocked off one corner of the window. Many things hung from its adhesive weave—dust, bugs, bits of dead leaf, even a stubby pencil he had thrown up there once. In all his time in the cellar he'd never seen the spider that made that web. He didn't see it now.

Silence hung over the cellar. They must have turned off the oil heater before they left. There was that faint crackling, creaking sound of warping boards, but that couldn't even scratch the surface of the silence. He could hear his own breath, uneven and slow.

Through that window, he thought, I watched that girl. Catherine; was that her name? He couldn't even recall what she'd looked like.

He'd also tried to get up to that window after he'd fallen into the cellar. It had been the only one available. The window with the broken pane was too far above the sand, only a vertical wall beneath it. The window over the log pile was even less accessible. The only one that had presented the slightest possibility had been the one over the fuel tank.

But, at seven inches, he hadn't been able to climb the boxes and suitcases. And, by the time he'd found the means, he was too small. He'd gone up there once, but, without a stone, he'd been unable to break the pane and had had to go down again.

He rolled over on his side and turned away from the window. It was unbearable to see sky and trees and know he'd never be out there again. He breathed heavily, staring at the cliff wall.

And here I am, he thought, back to morbid introspection again; all action undone. This could have ended long ago. But he had had to fight it. Climb threads, kill spiders, look for food. He clamped his mouth shut and stared at the long net pole leaning against the cliff wall. His gaze moved along the pole leaning against the wall, the long pole leaning against the wall.

He jerked up suddenly.

With a breathless grunt, he scrambled to the edge of the sponge and jumped down, ignoring the pain in his knee and head. He started racing for the cliff wall, stopped. What about water and food? Never mind, he wouldn't need it; it wasn't going to take that long. He ran toward the pole again.

Before he reached the net, he ran into the hose and got a drink. Then, running out again, he began to shinny up the metal rim of the net, past the body-thick cords. He climbed until he'd reached the pole, then pulled himself up onto its wide, curving surface.

It was better than he'd imagined. The pole was so wide and it was leaning against the wall at such a low angle that he wouldn't have to clamber up, hands down, for support. He could almost run erect up the long, gradual slope. With an excited cry he started up the road to the cliff.

Was it possible, he wondered as he ran, that things had worked out in a definite manner? Was it possible that there was purpose to his survival? It was hard to believe, and yet, in a greater measure, hard to disbelieve. All the coincidences that had contributed to his survival seemed to go beyond the limits of probability.

This, for instance; this pole thrown here in just this way by his own brother. Was that only chance? And the spider's death yesterday providing the final key to his escape. Was that only chance? Most importantly, the two occurrences combining in just this way to make possible his escape. Could it be only coincidence?

He could hardly believe it. Yet how could he doubt the process going on in his body, which told him clearly that he had today and nothing more? Unless the very precision with which he shrank indicated something. But indicated what—beyond hopelessness?

Still he did not lose the shapeless feeling of excitement as he hurried up the broad pole. It was still rising when he passed the first lawn chair; rising when he passed the second; rising when he stopped and sat looking down at the vast gray plain of the floor; rising when, an hour later, he reached the top of the cliff and fell down, exhausted, on the sand. And it was still rising as he lay there, heart pounding, fingers clutching at the sand. Get up, he kept telling himself. Let's go. It will be dark soon. Let's get out before it's dark.

He got up and started running across the shadowy desert. After a while he passed the silent bulk of the spider. He didn't stop to look at it; it was not important now. It was only a step already taken, which provided the ground for the next step. He stopped only once, to pull loose a chunk of bread and shove it under his coat of sponge. Then he ran on again.

When he reached the spider's web, he rested a while, then began to climb. The cable was sticky. He had to pull his hands and feet loose from it before he could climb up to the next one. The web trembled and swayed beneath his weight as he climbed past the dead beetle, not looking, breathing through his mouth.

And still excitement rose. Suddenly everything seemed meaningful, as if things had to happen in just this way. He knew it might be the rationalizing of desire, but he couldn't help thinking it anyway.

He reached the top of the web and quickly climbed onto the wooden shelf that ran around the wall. He could run now, and he did, his feet pounding down with a strong rhythm. He ignored the throbbing of his knee; it didn't matter.

He ran as fast as he could. Three blocks this way along the shadow-dark path, around the corner at top speed, then a mile straight ahead. He skittered like a tiny bug along the beam, running until he could hardly breathe.

He ran into blinding light.

He stopped, chest lurching, hot breath spilling from his lips. He stood there, eyes closed, and felt the wind blowing across his face. He closed his eyes and sniffed at its sweet, clear coolness. Outside, he thought. The word ballooned in his brain until it crowded out everything else and was the only word left. Outside. Outside. Outside.

Quietly then, slowly, with a dignity befitting the moment, he pulled himself up the few inches to the open square of window, clambered over the wooden rim, and jumped down.

He stepped across the cement walk on trembling legs and stopped.

He stood at the edge of the world, looking.

He lay on a soft mattress of sere, crinkly leaves, other leaves pulled over him, the vast house behind him, blocking off the night wind. He was warm and fed. He'd found a dish of water underneath the porch, and had drunk from it. Now he lay there quietly on his back, looking at the stars.

How beautiful they were; like blue-white diamonds cast across a sky of inky satin. No moonlight illuminated the sky. There was only total darkness, broken by the flaring pin points of the stars.

And the nicest thing about them was that they were still the same. He saw them as any man saw them, and that brought a deep contentment to him. Small he might be, but the earth itself was small compared to this.

Odd that after all the moments of abject terror he had suffered contemplating the end of his existence, this night—which was the very night it would end—he felt no terror at all. Hours away lay the end of his days. He knew, and still he was glad he was alive.

That was the wonderful part of this moment. That was the thick blanket of contentment that warmed his toes. To know the end was close and not to mind. This, he knew, was courage, the truest, ultimate courage, because there was no one here to sympathize or praise him for it. What he felt was felt without the hope of commendation.

Before, it had been different. He knew that now. Before he had kept on living because he kept on hoping. That was what kept most men living.

But now, in the final hours, even hope had vanished. Yet he could smile. At a point without hope he had found contentment. He knew he had tried and there was nothing to be sorry for. And this was complete victory, because it was a victory over himself.

"I've fought a good fight," he said. It sounded funny to say it. He felt almost embarrassed. Then he shook away embarrassment. It was what was left to him. Why shouldn't he proclaim the bittersweetness of his pride?

He bellowed at the universe. "I've fought a good fight!" And under his breath he added, "God damn it to hell."

It made him laugh. His laughter was the faintest icy sprinkling of sound against the vast, dark earth.

It felt good to laugh, and good to sleep, under the stars.

Chapter Seventeen

As on any other morning, his lids fell back, his eyes opened. For a moment he stared up blankly, his mind still thick with sleep. Then he remembered and his heart seemed to stop.

With a startled grunt, he jolted up to a sitting position and looked around incredulously, his mind alive with one word:

Where?

He looked up at the sky, but there was no sky—only a ragged blueness, as if the sky had been torn and stretched and squeezed and poked full of giant holes, through which light speared.

His wide, unblinking gaze moved slowly, wonderingly. He seemed to be in a vast, endless cavern. Not far over to his right the cavern ended and there was light. He stood up hastily and found himself naked. Where was the sponge?

He looked up again at the jagged blue dome. It stretched away for hundreds of yards. It was the bit of sponge he'd worn.

He sat down heavily, looking over himself. He was the same. He touched himself. Yes, the same. But how much had he shrunk during the night?

He remembered lying on the bed of leaves the night before, and he glanced down. He was sitting on a vast plain of speckled brown and yellow. There were great paths angling out from a gigantic avenue. They went as far as he could see.

He was sitting on the leaves.

He shook his head in confusion.

How could he be less than nothing?

The idea came. Last night he'd looked up at the universe without. Then there must be a universe within, too. Maybe universes.

He stood again. Why had he never thought of it; of the microscopic and the submicroscopic worlds? That they existed he had always known. Yet never had he made the obvious connection. He'd always thought in terms of man's own world and man's own limited dimensions. He had presumed upon nature. For the inch was man's concept, not nature's. To a man, zero inches means nothing. Zero meant nothing.

But to nature there was no zero. Existence went on in endless cycles. It seemed so simple now. He would never disappear, because there was no point of non-existence in the universe.

It frightened him at first. The idea of going on endlessly through one level of dimension after another was alien.

Then he thought: If nature existed on endless levels, so also might intelligence.

He might not have to be alone.

Suddenly he began running toward the light.

And, when he'd reached it, he stood in speechless awe looking at the new world with its vivid splashes of vegetation, its scintillant hills, its towering trees, its sky of shifting hues, as though the sunlight were being filtered through moving layers of pastel glass.

It was a wonderland.

There was much to be done and more to be thought about. His brain was teeming with questions and ideas and—yes—hope again. There was food to be found, water, clothing, shelter. And, most important, life. Who knew? It might be, it just might be there.

Scott Carey ran into his new world, searching.

BIOGRAPHICAL NOTES

NOTE ON THE TEXTS

NOTES

Biographical Notes

Frederik Pohl Born Frederik George Pohl Jr. in Brooklyn, New York, on November 26, 1919, the only child of Frederick George Pohl, a salesman, and Anna Jane Mason Pohl, a secretary. Attended Brooklyn Technical and Thomas Jefferson High Schools, dropping out at 17. In 1934, at 14, joined the Brooklyn chapter of the Science Fiction League, a fan group, editing and writing for club magazine *The Brooklyn Reporter.* Beginning in 1936 was active in the Young Communist League, co-organizing a Committee for the Political Advancement of Science Fiction, but grew disillusioned after the 1939 Hitler-Stalin Pact. In 1937, with John Michel, Donald Wollheim, and Robert Lowndes, cofounded the Futurians, another science fiction fan group whose members included Isaac Asimov and Cyril Kornbluth. Worked as a freelance literary agent, and in 1939 was hired as editor for pulp magazines *Astonishing Stories* and *Super Science Stories.* Also published short stories, often under pseudonyms and with various collaborators, including C. M. Kornbluth, Dirk Wylie, Harry Dockweiler, and Robert Lowndes. Married fellow Futurian Doris Baumgardt in 1940. Joined the Army in 1943, serving with the 12th Weather Squadron in Italy and editing the squadron newspaper. Divorced Baumgardt in 1944 and married Dorothy LesTina. After the war worked in New York as an advertising copywriter and book editor for Popular Science Publishing; began a literary agency. With Lester del Rey, founded the Hydra Club for science fiction writers. Divorced, and married writer Judith Merril in 1948; they had a daughter. With Cyril Kornbluth, wrote *Gravy Planet* (1952), published in book form as *The Space Merchants* (1953). Edited *Star Science Fiction Stories* anthologies for Ballantine Books (1953–59) and other anthologies. Married Carol Stanton in 1953; they had three children. Assisted Horace Gold in editing *Galaxy* magazine. Published novels *Search the Sky* (1954, with Kornbluth), *Gladiator-At-Law* (1955, with Kornbluth), *Preferred Risk* (1955, with del Rey), *Slave Ship* (1957), *Wolfbane* (1959, with Kornbluth), *Drunkard's Walk* (1960), *A Plague of Pythons* (1965), and *The Age of the Pussyfoot* (1969), as well as stories, juvenile novels, and non–science fiction novels. In 1960, took over editorship of *Galaxy* and *If*, serving until 1969; began magazines *Worlds of Tomorrow* (1963–70), *International Science Fiction* (1967–68), and *Worlds of Fantasy* (1970), and travelled widely as a lecturer. Expanded audience with novels *Man Plus* (1976); the "Heechee" sequence (beginning with *Gateway* in 1977, winner of the Hugo and Nebula awards, and continuing through five more volumes); *JEM: The Making of a Utopia* (1979); and *The Years of the City* (1984). Married Elizabeth Anne Hull in 1984. Published non–science fiction novels, including *Terror* (1986) and *Chernobyl* (1987). Later science fiction included *Black Star Rising* (1985), *The Coming of the Quantum Cats* (1986), *Narabedla Ltd.* (1988), *Homegoing* (1989), *The World at the End of Time* (1990), and the "Eschaton" series: *The Other End of Time* (1996), *The Siege of Eternity* (1997), *The Far Shore of Time* (1999), and *All the Lives He Led* (2011). Completed Arthur C. Clarke's unfinished novel *The Last Theorem* (2008). Served as president of the Science Fiction Writers of America (1974–76) and World SF (1980–82), and was inducted into the Science Fiction Hall of Fame in 1998. His autobiography *The Way the Future Was* (1978) was continued and expanded online beginning in 2009 in "The Way the Future Blogs." Lives in Palatine, Illinois.

C. M. Kornbluth Born Cyril Kornbluth on July 2, 1923, in New York City, the second child of Samuel Kornbluth, an accountant, and Deborah Ungar Kornbluth, the daughter of a tailor. (Later added the initial "M." to some of his bylines, after his wife Mary.) Grew up in upper Manhattan, graduating from George Washington High School in 1940. While still in high school, attended Futurian Society fan meetings in New York, meeting Isaac Asimov, Frederik Pohl, Donald A. Wollheim, and others, and contributing poems and stories to Futurian-edited magazines. Began earning money for his stories, often writing collaboratively (with Robert Lowndes, Pohl, Wollheim, Dirk Wylie, and others) and publishing under pseudonyms, including S. D. Gottesman and Cecil Corwin. Enrolled at City College, but after a few months dropped out to write professionally. In 1942–43, apprenticed as a machinist under the National Youth Administration, worked in a Connecticut machine shop, and enrolled in a military training program; married Mary Byers, with whom he would later have two children. Called to active duty in the Infantry, he fought in the Battle of the Bulge, earning a Bronze Star; developed combat-related health problems, including chronic tinnitus and hypertension, that would persist until his death. After his Army discharge, moved briefly to a farm near Springfield, Ohio; wrote detective stories for *10 Story Detective*, *Black Mask*, and *Dime Detective*. Relocated to Chicago, enrolling at Wilson Junior College and then the University of Chicago, without earning a degree. Worked as a news writer for Transradio Press Service. Urged by Pohl, took up science fiction again, publishing "The Little Black Bag" (1950, later adapted for television three times), "The Silly Season" (1950), and "The Marching Morons" (1951). With Judith Merril, collaborated on *Outpost Mars* and *Gunner*

Cade; finished solo novel *Takeoff* (all 1952). Returned to the New York area, ultimately settling in the small town of Waverly. With Pohl, collaborated on *Gravy Planet* (1952; later retitled *The Space Merchants*, 1953), *Search the Sky* (1954), *Gladiator-At-Law* (1955), and *Wolfbane* (1959), as well as the non–science fiction novels *A Town Is Drowning* (1955), *Presidential Year* (1956), *Sorority House* (1956), and *The Man of Cold Rages* (1958), some under the pseudonym Jordan Park. Writing independently, he published *The Syndic* (1953) and *Not This August* (1955); story collections *The Explorers* (1954) and *A Mile Beyond the Moon* (1958); and non–science fiction novels *The Naked Storm* (1952, as Simon Eisner), *Valerie*, and *Half* (both 1953, also as Jordan Park). At the end of 1954, accepted position as assistant curator for Tioga Point Historical Society Museum, in nearby Athens, Pennsylvania; began Civil War novel *The Crater* (never published) using museum documents and records. Attended 1956 Newyorcon (14th World Science Fiction Convention) and the Milford Science Fiction Writers' Conference. At the latter, joined in an "oracular" all-night encounter with Algis Budrys, James Blish, Damon Knight, and Jane Roberts; profoundly moved, they later referred to each other as "The Five" and began a round-robin exchange of letters exploring their interconnectedness. Gave 1957 lecture on "The Failure of the Science Fiction Novel as Social Criticism" at the University of Chicago. Moved with family to Levittown, New York. Prepared to assume consulting editor role at *The Magazine of Fantasy and Science Fiction*, but died of a heart attack on March 21, 1958, in Levittown. Works collected posthumously in *The Wonder Effect* (1962) and *His Share of Glory: The Complete Short Science Fiction of C. M. Kornbluth* (1997), among other volumes.

Theodore Sturgeon Born Edward Hamilton Waldo on February 26, 1918, in Staten Island, New York, the second son of Edward Molineaux Waldo, a paint and dye manufacturer, and Christine Hamilton Waldo, a Canadian-born teacher. Name legally changed to Theodore Hamilton Sturgeon at age 11 following his mother's remarriage to William Dickie Sturgeon, who taught at Drexel College in Philadelphia. An unexceptional student who excelled in gymnastics, Sturgeon was stricken at age fifteen by rheumatic fever, ending his aspiration to become a circus acrobat. He entered Pennsylvania State Nautical School but dropped out after one term, shipping out as an engine room laborer on a freighter. During three years at sea, began writing stories and poems. Published crime stories and other short fiction with McClure's newspaper syndicate beginning in 1938. "Ether Breather," his first science fiction story, appeared in *Astounding Science Fiction* in September 1939. Married Dorothy Fillingame in 1940;

they had two daughters, divorcing in 1945. Published little between 1941 and 1946: managed a resort hotel in the West Indies, sold door-to-door, organized military mess halls, and operated a bulldozer in Puerto Rico (leading to the 1944 story "Killdozer!"). After returning to New York, became an advertising copywriter and literary agent; worked for *Time* and *Fortune*. Won a prize competition sponsored by British magazine *Argosy* with story "Bianca's Hands" (1947). Was married briefly to singer Mary Mair. In 1951, proposed "Sturgeon's Law" ("Ninety percent of SF is crud, but then, ninety percent of *everything* is crud"). In 1953, married Marion McGahan, with whom he had four children. His first story collection, *Without Sorcery* (1948), was followed by *E Pluribus Unicorn* (1953), *A Way Home* (1955), *Caviar* (1955), *A Touch of Strange* (1958), *Aliens 4* (1959), *Beyond* (1960), *Sturgeon in Orbit* (1964), *Starshine* (1966), *Sturgeon Is Alive and Well . . .* (1971), *The Worlds of Theodore Sturgeon* (1972), *Sturgeon's West* (1973), *Case and the Dreamer* (1974), *Visions and Venturers* (1978), and *Alien Cargo* (1984). His first novel, *The Dreaming Jewels* (1950), was followed by *More Than Human* (1953); *I, Libertine* (1956, under the pseudonym Frederick R. Ewing, in response to a radio hoax by Jean Shepherd, who invented the name and title); *The Cosmic Rape* (1958); *Venus Plus X* (1960); the vampire novel *Some of Your Blood* (1961); and two pseudonymous "Ellery Queen" novels, *The Player on the Other Side* (1963) and *The House of Brass* (1968). He also published a novelization (*Amok Time*, 1978) of one of three scripts he wrote for the television series *Star Trek*. (Two of these, "Shore Leave" and "Amok Time," aired in 1966–67; the third, "The Joy Machine," was later novelized by James Gunn.) From 1969 to 1974, he lived with journalist Wina Golden; they had a son. He subsequently lived with Jayne Tannehill Englehart. He died of pneumonitis in Eugene, Oregon, on May 8, 1985. His novel *Godbody* was published posthumously in 1986, followed by a 13-volume *Complete Stories* (1994–2010). In 2000 he was inducted into the Science Fiction Hall of Fame.

Leigh Brackett Born Leigh Douglass Brackett on December 7, 1915, in Los Angeles, California, the only child of William Franklin Brackett, an accountant and aspiring writer, and Margaret Douglass Brackett. Her father died in 1918 during the flu pandemic and she was raised by her mother and maternal grandparents in Santa Monica, where she attended a private girls' school. Declined a college scholarship because of family financial difficulties. In 1939, joined the Los Angeles Science Fiction Society, meeting Ray Bradbury, Robert Heinlein, Willy Ley, and others; attended gatherings of Heinlein's Mañana Literary Society. Published first story, "Martian Quest," in *Astounding Science Fiction* in 1940. Her first book, the detective novel *No Good from a Corpse* (1944), drew the attention of director Howard Hawks, who hired her to work with William Faulkner and Jules Furthman on screenplay of Raymond Chandler's *The Big Sleep* (released 1946). Busy with this screenplay, she asked Bradbury to complete her novella "Lorelei of the Red Mist," and it was published jointly in 1946. The same year, married author Edmond Hamilton; they bought a house in rural Kinsman, Ohio. Remained under contract with Hawks and Charles Feldman for more than two years, and would later earn screenwriting credit for *Rio Bravo* (1959), *Hatari!* (1962), *El Dorado* (1966), *Rio Lobo* (1970), *The Long Goodbye* (1973), *The Empire Strikes Back* (1980, with Lawrence Kasdan), and several works for television. Her first science fiction novel, *Shadow Over Mars*, had appeared in the magazine *Planet Stories* in 1944, but did not appear in book form until 1961, as *The Nemesis from Terra*; similarly, *Sea-Kings of Mars* was first serialized in 1949 and then published as *The Sword of Rhiannon* in 1953. In science fiction, she would go on to write *The Starmen* (1952), *Alpha Centauri or Die!* (1953; as book, 1963), *The Big Jump* (1955), and *The Long Tomorrow* (1955). Also wrote crime novels, Westerns, and other fiction, including *An Eye for an Eye* (1957, later basis for CBS series *Markham*, 1959–60), *The Tiger Among Us* (1957; filmed as *13 West Street*, 1962), *Rio Bravo* (1959, novelization of the film), *Follow the Free Wind* (1963), and *Silent Partner* (1969). Returned to science fiction themes in *The Ginger Star* (1974), *The Hounds of Skaith* (1974), and *The Reavers of Skaith* (1976). *The Best of Leigh Brackett*, edited by Edmond Hamilton, was published in 1977. She died of cancer in Lancaster, California, on March 18, 1978.

Richard Matheson Born Richard Burton Matheson on February 20, 1926, in Allendale, New Jersey, the third child of Bertolf Matheson and Fanny Swanson Matheson (nee Svenningsen), both Norwegian immigrants. Grew up without his father, who abandoned the family. Graduated from Brooklyn Technical High School in 1943. Served as an infantryman in Germany during World War II, then earned a journalism degree (1949) from the University of Missouri. Sold his first story, "Born of Man and Woman," to *The Magazine of Fantasy and Science Fiction* in 1950, followed by "Third from the Sun" (later adapted for the television series *The Twilight Zone*) and others the same year. Moved to Santa Monica, California, in 1951; married Ruth Ann Woodson, with whom he would have four children, in 1952. Worked as a postal clerk and at an airplane factory, writing stories and two suspense novels, *Fury on Sunday* and *Someone Is Bleeding* (both 1953), in his spare time. Published *Born of Man and Woman* (1954), the first of many story collections. His third novel, *I Am Legend* (1954; filmed as *The Last Man on Earth*, 1964; *The Omega Man*, 1971;

and *I Am Legend*, 2007), gained him wider attention. For his fourth, *The Shrinking Man* (1956), he also wrote the screenplay (a condition he insisted on when he sold the film rights), beginning a long-sought career as a film and television writer; it was filmed as *The Incredible Shrinking Man* (1957). Traveled to London to write a screenplay, ultimately blocked by the British censor, for a Hammer Studios version of *I Am Legend*. Published supernatural novel *A Stir of Echoes* (1958, filmed 1999), suspense novel *Ride the Nightmare* (1959), and semi-autobiographical World War II novel *The Beardless Warriors* (1960). From 1959 to 1964, wrote fourteen episodes for *The Twilight Zone*, with two more adapted from his stories, also contributed to many Western and fantastic television series, including *Star Trek* ("The Enemy Within," 1966), and wrote a number of screenplays, most notably adaptations of Edgar Allan Poe stories for director Roger Corman, 1960–63. His short story "Duel" (1971) became the basis of Steven Spielberg's first feature film, made for television the same year. Later novels, many adapted for film, include *Hell House* (1971), *Bid Time Return* (1975), *What Dreams May Come* (1978), and most recently *Other Kingdoms* (2011). His *Collected Stories* was published in three volumes in 2003–5. Won the World Fantasy Award for Life Achievement in 1984 and was inducted into Science Fiction Hall of Fame in 2010. Lives in Calabasas, California.

Note on the Texts

This volume collects four American science fiction novels of the 1950s: *The Space Merchants* (1953) by Frederik Pohl and C. M. Kornbluth, *More Than Human* (1953) by Theodore Sturgeon, *The Long Tomorrow* (1955) by Leigh Brackett, and *The Shrinking Man* (1956) by Richard Matheson. A companion volume in the Library of America series, *American Science Fiction: Five Classic Novels, 1956–1958*, includes five later works: *Double Star* (1956) by Robert A. Heinlein, *The Stars My Destination* (1957) by Alfred Bester, *A Case of Conscience* (1958) by James Blish, *Who?* (1958) by Algis Budrys, and *The Big Time* (1961) by Fritz Leiber. (Though it did not appear in book format until after the decade had ended, *The Big Time* was published in *Galaxy* magazine in 1958.) The texts of all of these novels have been taken from the first American book editions.

The Space Merchants. In his memoir *The Way the Future Was* (1978), Frederik Pohl claimed responsibility for the first piece of what would eventually become *The Space Merchants.* By the summer of 1951, after some earlier false starts, he had written about twenty thousand words of "the beginning of a science-fiction novel about advertising" titled *Fall Campaign*. "I didn't know where I was going with it," he confessed. But with the encouragement of Horace Gold—who would be the first to publish the novel, as *Gravy Planet*, in *Galaxy* in June, July, and August 1952—he enlisted Cyril Kornbluth's help as collaborator. Pohl and Kornbluth had collaborated extensively in the past, publishing their first joint efforts in 1940 under the pseudonym S. D. Gottesman, and Pohl served as Kornbluth's literary agent. Pohl showed Kornbluth his fragmentary *Fall Campaign* and they talked about possible directions for the book; Phil Klass, a fellow writer of science fiction who had also read Pohl's fragment, suggested "having the hero do the Haroun al Raschid bit, wandering around the planet as a plebeian instead of an upper-crust advertising executive." Kornbluth and Pohl later discussed the novel during one or more story conferences at Gold's apartment-office in New York. Gold reportedly disliked the title *Fall Campaign* and may have been responsible for *Gravy Planet.*

Gold would later say of Pohl and Kornbluth's collaborations that "it was impossible to tell who produced what parts of any story, so closely did they work." But the surviving contemporary correspondence and

Pohl's recollections indicate that Kornbluth substantially rewrote *Fall Campaign* and added at least the middle third, or more probably almost all of a new draft of *Gravy Planet.* Pohl remembered writing the last third of the novel "turn-by-turn," but his papers, now at the Syracuse University Library, include two undated letters from Kornbluth that show Kornbluth had advanced the novel up to its last chapter. (He left this for Pohl to write "for the good of your soul," he said, and "in the hope that you can wind up the thing with your own peculiar stamp on it.") Kornbluth urged further work on at least one section first written by Pohl ("You've *got* to change the scene in the basement of the Met"), noted parts of the novel he himself had written that might need more work, and conveyed new comments from Gold: "Horace also says some of the earlier touches are unclear, that it's not always self-evident . . . that public agencies have been supplanted by for-profit firms." After sending the last of these letters with his nearly complete draft, Kornbluth probably left all further revision to Pohl. As on other occasions when the pair worked together, Pohl finished a final typescript, putting "the whole thing through the typewriter one more time." ("After the rough draft . . . was done, he was out of it," Pohl said of their habitual division of labor; "I always did the final revisions . . . and I always did all the dealing with editors and publishers.")

On February 15, 1952, Pohl wrote Kornbluth with the news of "a kind of hitch" in their project: the novel was several thousand words shorter than they had agreed with Gold it would be, and he "promised to add enough" to bring it to contractual length. By the end of April these "added chapters," probably by Pohl, were complete and awaited Gold's review. In the interim, Pohl had submitted the novel to at least two book publishers, both of whom rejected it. At Doubleday (he explained to Kornbluth in March), Walter Bradbury complained: "There are holes in the story that put a strain on the credulity of the reader and the unshaded black-and-white political situation removes it even farther from reality and, for my part, interest." At Simon and Schuster (he wrote Kornbluth in April), Orrin Keepnews "liked GP as far as he got but is terribly worried because Lester del Rey once wrote a story about a midget rocket pilot." Finally in October, having shown the novel to at least one and probably several additional publishers, Pohl received a favorable response from Ian Ballantine of Ballantine Books, who was eager to publish it and within a few weeks had sent a contract.

Stanley Kauffmann, the Ballantine editor assigned to the novel, gave it an "immediate and careful line-by-line reading in preparation for a final story conference," Pohl recalled online (in a post on *The Way the Future Blogs*, "Great Subject, Really Lousy Book," November 7, 2010; accessed October 20, 2011). After a "long, friendly, and intelligent" conversation over the phone in which Kauffmann proposed and all three agreed on a number of revisions, Kauffmann "penciled the corrections onto the manuscript and sent it off to the printer." Pohl assumed both he and Kornbluth would have checked the proofs of the novel before it was published, but he had no particular memory of having seen them. "We were two kids with our first big break," he remembered, "and about all I am sure of is that whatever changes Ballantine Books asked us for, we agreed to." It was probably Kauffmann who suggested *The Space Merchants* as a new title for the novel; by mid-February 1953, Pohl was referring to it as "*The Space Merchants* née *Gravy Planet.*" Ballantine published the novel in a simultaneous hardcover and paperback edition in May 1953.

The *Galaxy* and Ballantine texts of the novel vary considerably at many points, but it would be mistaken to assume—as Mark Rich does in *C. M. Kornbluth: The Life and Works of a Science Fiction Visionary* (2010)—that the earlier text was necessarily altered to produce the later one. It is more likely that both published texts were prepared independently from copies of Pohl's final typescript—a typescript he would have used as he made multiple submissions to publishers, both before and after *Gravy Planet* appeared in *Galaxy.* Differences between the published *Gravy Planet* and *The Space Merchants* are most probably attributable to the varying editorial interventions of Horace Gold and Stanley Kauffmann rather than to either author's subsequent changes. In the absence of the final typescript of *Gravy Planet*—which is no longer known to exist—it may be impossible to determine in a given case which published text, if either one, most closely reflects the final typescript. (The ending of the novel stands as one exception to this observation: Only the *Galaxy* text includes the "added chapters" Gold requested. These final *Galaxy* chapters are reprinted in the Notes to the present volume.)

At *Galaxy*, Gold developed a reputation as a zealous and thoroughgoing reviser, and he is likely to have made extensive changes to the typescript *Gravy Planet*, beyond the suggestions he had offered while the novel was being written. (As the editor of Alfred Bester's *The Stars My Destination* a few years later, to cite a comparable case, Gold's alterations to Bester's typescript were far more extensive than those of Bester's English and American book publishers. "He could not keep his fingers off his writers' prose," Pohl recounted in his memoir *The Way the Future Was.*) Gold may or may not have given Kornbluth or Pohl an opportunity to review his editing, to the extent that they cared to. At Ballantine, Kauffmann probably had a lighter touch and was more likely to have offered Pohl proofs for review. *The Space Merchants* was subsequently reprinted many times by Ballantine and appeared under the imprints of a number of other publishers as well, but neither Pohl nor Kornbluth made further changes to the novel. The text of *The Space Merchants* in the present volume has been taken from the 1953 Ballantine Books first printing.

More Than Human. Theodore Sturgeon began *More Than Human* as a short story, "Baby Is Three," in the spring of 1952. Inspired by a minor character in Pearl S. Buck's novel *Pavilion of Women* (1946)—"a Chinese monk, who took care of a ragged passel of kids in a cave someplace in the wilderness"—he finished the story in "about eight days," he later recalled, and sent it to Horace Gold, who published it in *Galaxy* in October 1952. Soon afterward, Ballantine Books proposed that Sturgeon publish a novel with them. Accepting their offer, he found that "the only thing I wanted to write about at that length was something about where the people in 'Baby Is Three' came from, and where they went to." He "chuntered around with ideas for a few months" and then wrote the first and last sections of the novel, "The Fabulous Idiot" and "Morality," in about three weeks, also lightly revising "Baby Is Three." Farrar, Straus & Young, who had recently agreed to publish simultaneous hardcover editions of some of Ballantine's paperbacks on a title-by-title basis, signed on as copublisher. By early August 1953, Sturgeon had revised his initial draft in response to comments from Bernard Shir-Cliff (of Ballantine) and Sheila Cudahy (of Farrar, Straus). In many cases he chose not to follow these editors' suggestions: prepublication versions of the novel now among his papers at the Kenneth Spencer Research Library, University of Kansas—including galley proofs and two typescripts—suggest that he retained considerable control over the form in which his novel finally appeared. *More Than Human* was published by Farrar, Straus & Young and Ballantine Books in November 1953 from identical plates, the Ballantine Books edition omitting the hardcover contents page. The novel was reprinted on many occasions during Sturgeon's lifetime, but he did not alter the text. The present volume prints the text of the 1953 Farrar, Straus & Young first printing.

The Long Tomorrow. Leigh Brackett's husband Edmond Hamilton explained in his introduction to *The Best of Leigh Brackett* (1977) that her novel *The Long Tomorrow* began with her interest in the history of Kinsman, Ohio, near which they had bought an old farmhouse in 1950: "when she first came to Ohio, she was greatly intrigued by the Amish folk here who continue their old, simple way of life in the midst of the modern world. This led to her remark that if modern civilization disappeared, the Amish would be perfectly fitted to live in a non-mechanical world—and that remark grew into a novel." *The Long Tomorrow* was published by Doubleday & Company, without prior serialization, in September 1955. A subsequent book club printing (Garden City, NJ: Doubleday, 1956), paperback printing (New York: Ace, 1962), and first British printing (London: Mayflower, 1962) were prepared from the same plates, and Brackett did not revise the text for a later paperback edition (New York: Ballantine, 1974). The text in the present volume has been taken from the 1955 Doubleday first printing.

The Shrinking Man. The basement in which Scott Carey finds himself gradually disappearing in Richard Matheson's novel *The Shrinking Man* was closely based on the basement in which Matheson wrote the novel, over the course of about ten weeks in 1955, in his house in Sound Beach, Long Island. Matheson later explained that a scene in the movie *Let's Do It Again* (1953) had given him his initial inspiration for the book (the actor Ray Milland mistakenly puts on a hat several sizes too large for him), and that his publisher had added *The* to his original title, *Shrinking Man.* (*The Shrinking Man* was further expanded as *The Incredible Shrinking Man* for the 1957 film version. Universal Studios purchased the film rights to the novel in September 1955, before it had appeared in print, and Matheson, with the uncredited assistance of Richard Alan Simmons, wrote the screenplay.) *The Shrinking Man* was first published in May 1956 as a Gold Medal paperback by Fawcett Publications in New York. It has been reprinted often since and has appeared in several new editions—sometimes as *The Incredible Shrinking Man*—but Matheson has not revised the text. A new introduction he contributed to a special limited edition (Springfield, PA: Gauntlet Publications, 2001) is included in the Notes to the present volume. The text of *The Shrinking Man* has been taken from the first Fawcett printing of May 1956.

This volume presents the texts of the original printings chosen for inclusion here, but it does not attempt to reproduce nontextual features of their typographic design. The texts are reprinted without change, except for the correction of typographical errors. Spelling, punctuation, and capitalization are often expressive features and are not altered, even when inconsistent or irregular. The following is a list of typographical errors corrected, cited by page and line number: 24.20, get to; 56.10, 15, skiis; 59.14, Shocken; 64.34, Groby I; 89.18, the ike.; 89.26, noncommittally.; 91.10, minutes wait; 97.14, Sir, I; 98.34, me: Nobody; 106.12, 'way; 107.20–21, mike "Woman's; 119.26, breath; 130.22, Shocken; 137.28, onto; 139.14, way.; 152.32, "Um."; 154.31, "Uh."; 207.18, Bonnie; 207.19, Beanie; 207.21, Bonnie; 208.22, latter; 217.2, sighed. I'll; 261.26, hassel; 262.32, hassel; 270.33, said "I; 286.36, "Sure," she; 312.17, lauged; 335.34, *your're*; 344.35, What;

352.5, moisure; 366.14, to small; 374.4, projected; 410.22, plur; 495.3, "Hm?' "; 610.15–16, quater-mile; 620.6, He said.; 622.30, cobwed-gauzed; 626.22, ease.; 640.20, apparantly; 645.17, firecely; 658.11, sowly; 669.13, twiched; 675.3, filled this; 676.17, he could; 683.33, throught; 684.8, thought But; 687.21, abberant; 702.35, Scott We; 707.17–18, he had Lou; 717.10, dog; (two; 760.2, if off; 762.5, respect,.

Notes

In the notes below, the reference numbers denote page and line of the present volume; the line count includes titles and headings but not blank lines. No note is made for material found in standard desk-reference books. Quotations from the Bible are keyed to the King James Version. Quotations from Shakespeare are keyed to *The Riverside Shakespeare*, ed. G. Blakemore Evans (Boston: Houghton Mifflin, 1974). For additional information and references to other studies, see Rosemarie Arbur, *Leigh Brackett, Marion Zimmer Bradley, Anne McCaffrey: A Primary and Secondary Bibliography* (Boston: G. K. Hall, 1982); Mike Ashley, *Transformations: The Story of Science Fiction Magazines from 1950 to 1970* (Liverpool: Liverpool University Press, 2005); John L. Carr, *Leigh Brackett: American Writer* (Polk City, IA: Chris Drumm, 1986); Lahna F. Diskin, *Theodore Sturgeon: A Primary and Secondary Bibliography* (Boston: G. K. Hall, 1980); Damon Knight, *The Futurians: The Story of the Science Fiction "Family" of the 30s That Produced Today's Top SF Writers and Editors* (New York: John Day, 1977); Barry N. Malzberg, *Breakfast in the Ruins: Science Fiction in the Last Millennium* (Riverdale, NY: Baen Publishing, 2007); Lucy Menger, *Theodore Sturgeon* (New York: Frederick Ungar, 1981); Frederik Pohl, *The Way the Future Was: A Memoir* (New York: Ballantine, 1978); Mark Rich, *C. M. Kornbluth: The Life and Works of a Science Fiction Visionary* (Jefferson, NC: McFarland, 2010); Robert Silverberg, *Musings and Meditations: Reflections on Science Fiction* (New York: Nonstop Press, 2011); and *The Richard Matheson Companion*, ed. Stanley Wiater, Matthew R. Bradley, and Paul Stuve (Colorado Springs, CO: Gauntlet Publications, 2008).

THE SPACE MERCHANTS

6.38 V-2's] Rocket-powered ballistic missiles developed by Germany in World War II and deployed against England.

8.30–31 the Clive . . . John Jacob Astor] Robert Clive, 1st Baron Clive (1725–1774), credited with securing India for the British Empire through the East India Company; Simón Bolívar (1783–1830), Venezuelan political leader instrumental in winning independence for several nations from the Spanish Empire; John Jacob Astor (1763–1848), who established a major fur-trading empire following the American Revolution.

9.25 Nash-Kelvinator] A corporation formed in 1937 by the merger of automobile maker Nash Motors and appliance maker Kelvinator; in 1954, it became part of American Motors.

13.40 B.B.D. & O.] Batten, Barton, Durstine, & Osborn, a large advertising agency founded by merger in 1928.

21.18 G.C.A.] Ground-controlled approach, a radar-based air traffic control system widely used in the Berlin Airlift of 1948–49.

33.7 Power ennobles . . . absolutely.] A reversal of a famous remark (1887) by Lord Acton (1834–1902): "Power tends to corrupt, and absolute power corrupts absolutely."

36.10 Keats, Swinburne, Wylie] Poets John Keats (1795–1821), Algernon Charles Swinburne (1837–1909), and Elinor Wylie (1885–1928).

36.17–18 'Thou still unravish'd . . . slow Time—'] From Keats's "Ode on a Grecian Urn" (1820).

37.7 Tanagra figurine] A small, molded terra-cotta statue mass-produced in or around the village of Tanagra, near Athens, beginning around the last quarter of the fourth century BCE.

43.3 C.I.C.] The Counter Intelligence Corps, a U.S. Army espionage agency supplanted by U.S. Army Intelligence Corps in 1961.

43.3 A.E.C.] The Atomic Energy Commission, established in 1946 to oversee peacetime development of nuclear energy; it was replaced by other agencies in 1974.

43.21 O.N.I.] The Office of Naval Intelligence.

45.3–4 Victor Herbert's *Toyland* theme] The song "Toyland," from the operetta *Babes in Toyland* (1903), by popular composer Victor Herbert (1859–1924).

53.1 Thomas Cook and Son] Travel agency founded in England in the 1840s.

53.17 R.D.F.] Radio Direction Finder, an instrument for assisting navigation by finding the direction of a radio source.

72.8 "*Porque no, amigo?*"] Spanish: "Why not, friend?"

72.9 "*tu hablas . . . la lengua?*"] Spanish: "You speak Spanish! When did you learn the language?"

73.6 *Como 'sta*] Spanish: "How are you?"

77.29 San Lázaro] St. Lazarus; see John 11.

77.30 *pobrecita*] Spanish: Poor thing; pitiable.

84.15–17 "Do You Make . . . in a Carload"] Headlines from two highly successful advertising campaigns. The first, for the Sherwin Cody School of

English, ran with variations between 1919 and 1959; the second, for Old Gold cigarettes, began appearing around 1926.

99.4 Albert Fish] Albert Fish (1870–1936), a serial killer, cannibal, and masochist, executed for kidnapping and murder.

100.22 Gilles de Rais] Gilles de Montmorency-Laval (1404–1440), Breton knight and child-murderer executed by hanging; widely believed to be the inspiration for Charles Perrault's 1697 fairy tale "Bluebeard."

155.15 It didn't take that long.] When Pohl and Kornbluth's novel first appeared in print—as *Gravy Planet*, in the June, July, and August 1952 issues of *Galaxy* magazine—it concluded with three chapters not subsequently reprinted in *The Space Merchants* (1953). These final chapters, presented below, had to be added after the authors submitted the novel for publication to bring it to the contractually agreed-upon length:

20

So we landed. After the wild excitement wore off, I felt like sitting and writing a postcard to the little man back in Washington:

"Dear Mr. President, now I know what you mean. On special occasions they sometimes let me in, too. Sincerely, Mitchell (Superfluous) Courtenay."

We torpedoed the billowy cloud layer, roared incandescently down in the tangential orbiting approach, minced the final few hundred meters to the landing—and I was a bum.

They were nice enough about it. They said things like: "No, thanks, I can handle it myself," and, "Would you mind stepping back, Mr. Courtenay?" when what they should have said was: "Get the hell out of the way." And I wondered how long it would take before they began to put it that way.

You know what it's like being a lost soul?

It's wandering through a spaceship with busy people rushing here and there carrying incomprehensible things. It's people talking urgently and efficiently to each other and you understand maybe one word in three. It's offering a suggestion or trying to help and getting a blank stare and polite refusal.

It's Kathy: "Not right now, Mitch darling. Why don't you—" And her voice trailed off. The only appropriate, constructive, positive thing I could do was drop dead. But nobody said so. They would carry me on the books, a hero whose brief hour of service rendered, when balanced against the long years that followed, might or might not show a tiny net profit. You never could tell with ex-heroes, but you can't just gas them . . .

They were nice about letting me come along when fourteen of the really important people donned spacesuits and set foot on Venus. (Note for historians: it was completely unceremonious. We just went out the lock into the lee of the ship, anchored by cables. Nobody noticed who of the fifteen was first to step out—and be yanked by the burning wind as far as the cable slack would let him, or her.)

I reached for my wife and the wind sent her bobbing on the end of her cable out of my grasp. Nor did she notice me, a hulking and brutish figure in an oversized suit, trying to claw my way to her along the grab-irons welded to the hull. She had eyes only for the planet I had given her, the orange-lit, sandstorming inferno.

When they reeled us in and we took off our armor, I felt as though I had been flailed with anchor chains from Easter to Christmas. Aching, I turned to Kathy.

She was briskly rubbing her surgeon's fingers and conferring with somebody named Bartlow in words that sounded like these: "—then we'll clam the ortnick for seven frames and woutch green until sembril gills?"

"Yes," Bartlow said, nodding.

"Splendid. When the grimps quorn with the fibers, Bronson can fline dimethyloxypropyloluene with the waterspouts—"

I hung around and Kathy finally noticed me with a "Hello, dear" and plunged back into the important stuff. After a while I wandered off. I got in the way of the crews dismantling the ship's internal bulkheads. Then I got in the way of the commissary women, then in the way of the engineers who were already modifying our drive reactor to an AC electric pile. When I got in the way of the medics who were patching up passengers banged around in the landing, I took a sleepy-pill. My dreams were not pleasant.

Kathy was crouched over the desk when I woke up, pawing through stacks of green, pink and magenta-covered folders. I yawned. "You been up all night?"

She said absently, "Yes."

"Anything I can do to help?"

"No."

I rescued one of the folders from the floor. *Medical Supplies Flow Chart, 3d to 5th Colony Year, No Local Provisioning Assumed* was the heading. The one under it covered: *Permissible Reproductive Rate, 10th Colony Year.*

"That's real planning," I said. "Got one covering forecasted life-expectancy of third-generation colonists born of blue-eyed mothers and left-handed fathers?"

"Please, Mitch," she said impatiently. "I've got to find the planning schedules for the first two months. Naturally we planned far ahead."

I dressed and wandered out to the chowline. The man ahead of me, still wearing soft padded undershoes that went with donning a heat suit, was telling his friends about Venus. Not more than a tenth of the colonists had seen their new planet close up as yet; he had a large and fascinated audience.

"So we located the spot for the drilling unit," he said. "We moored it to a rock taller than me. We started bracing the unit. What happens? *Plop.* The damn rock explodes. The wind catches the drill and you should've seen that thing take off. Lucky we hadn't cast off the cables to the ship yet, it'd still been going. As it is, back to the shop. A whole day's work shot."

I listened through the story and the questions.

When he was hurrying off to another incomprehensible job, I said to him: "Wait a minute. I want to talk to you."

"Sure, Mr. Courtenay. What can I do for you?"

"Most of this stuff I don't get, but I understand a rock drill. You're a foreman. Can you put me on your crew?"

"You *sure* you understand a rock drill, Mr. Courtenay? It ain't easy to change a carbide tip out there in the wind. You got to unscrew the camber-flamber and wuldge it to the imbrie before the wind gets it, and that takes—"

There we were again. But this time I said: "I can handle it."

"That's great, Mr. Courtenay. I can use another man. Weiss, I guess you don't know him, he got smacked by a piece of flying something or other, so I'm one short." He measured me with his eye. "You can use his suit. It wasn't hurt a bit."

An ugly little chill went through me. "What about Weiss?"

"The work-suits are too rigid. Something hits you hard, it goes *clang* hard enough to burst your eardrums, drive your eyes into your head and rupture membranes all through your body. But the suit lives through it. Well, we go out with a replacement drill at 1730, Port Fourteen aft. I'll see you there, Mr. Courtenay."

I was there and proud of it. The drilling crew was big and tough—shock troops. They knew my name and face, of course, and were reserved. As we got into the armored work-suits, one of them asked apologetically: "Sure you can handle this, Mr. Courtenay? It's rough out there—"

I felt my blood pounding with anger I shouldn't put into words. He was only trying to be helpful. There was no use yelling at him that I was a man and could swing my weight with men, that I wasn't just a copysmith and as obsolete as the dinosaur. I nodded and we stepped out.

Whoosh! The wind hurled us five yards.

Crack! The cables held.

Three seconds outside and I was fighting for breath.

"Goddam it!" I gasped, hating my weakness.

I had forgotten that work-suits were wired for sound. The foreman's voice said inside my helmet: "Mr. Courtenay, please keep the circuit clear for orders. Guire! Slack off! More—hold it! Winters, haul your cable—hold it. Mr. Courtenay, work your way over to Winters and lay hold."

Clawing along the storm-swept rocks, I reached Winters and grabbed the cable. I wondered dimly if the suit's oxygen supply was functioning, if the dryer was working. It didn't feel as if they were. I could hardly breathe and I was soaked with sweat.

I made a feeble pretense of helping Winters, who had the build of a granite crag, jockey the drill.

It was like flying a kite—if it took five men to fly a kite, and if the kite had to be kept at ground level, and if the kite perpetually threatened to fly you instead of vice versa.

After two minutes outside, my leg and arm muscles were quivering uncontrollably from the mere effort of standing up and keeping balanced. It was the tremor of flexor pulling against extensor, the final fatigue that comes just before you let go, forgetting everything except that you can't keep it up any longer, that you'll die if you keep it up for another split-second.

But I hung on for one minute more, streaming sweat, sobbing air into my lungs and maybe—maybe—helping a little with a few extra foot pounds of heave-ho on the cable when it was ordered.

And then I let go, a little less than half-conscious, and the wind got me. My cable streamed and I dangled at the end of it, unable to do anything but listen to the voices in my helmet.

"Mr. Courtenay, can you make it back to the ship?"

"He don't answer. He must have blacked out."

"Stinking luck! Almost get the drill positioned and then—damn the stinking luck! Winters, work your way to him and see if he's all right."

"Hell, what can I see? Phone them to reel him in is all we can do."

"Winchman! Reel in Number Five. He's blacked out."

The cable thrummed and I began to scrape along the ground to the port.

And still they talked. "We can do it with four if it kills us, men. You all game?"

I heard the ragged chorus of yesses as I scraped helplessly over the rocks, like a fish on a hook.

"Shouldn't have let him come out at all," one of the crew said.

Shame was crowded out by terror. My suit clanged against something and motion stopped. A rock, I saw dazedly. A big rock. The six ring-bolts to which my cable was lashed began to creak and strain.

The fools at the winch, I realized with clear, pure horror, had not noticed I was snagged.

"Stop!" I screamed into the helmet. But I did not have a phone line through my cable to the ship.

The foreman understood instantly. "*Winchman! Ease off! He's snagged!*" The ring-bolts ceased to strain. "Mr. Courtenay, can you clear yourself or—or should we come to help you?" He was only human. There was bitterness in his voice.

I said rustily: "I can clear myself. Thanks."

But I didn't have to. The big, solid rock I had snagged on began to disappear. I don't mean it vanished, either with or without a thunderclap. Nor did it grow transparent and finally become invisible. But it began to melt from the top, like a ball of string unraveling or like an apple being peeled for a banquet before it's divided into servings—and yet it was something like gradually turning into powder and blowing away. Naturally, it isn't easy to describe.

It was the first Venusian anybody had ever seen.

21

They got me into the ship and patched me up. Kathy didn't tend me in the hospital—she was a surgeon and administrator, and all I had was R.N. stuff like bruises and scrapes, but plenty of them.

In three days I was discharged with the entire hospital staff suspecting I was psychotic. I could go them one better. I *knew* I was.

Item: I would wash and wash, but I never felt clean.

Item: Suicidal tendencies. I wanted to go into the nuclear reactor room so bad I could taste it—and the reactor room was sudden death.

Item: Claustrophobia. The giant ship wasn't big enough for me. I wanted to go outside into the flailing inferno.

The first night out of the hospital, I sat up in bed waiting and waiting for Kathy to come back from a staff meeting. I was dog-tired, but I didn't dare sleep. I had once found myself halfway to the reactor room before I stubbed my toe and woke up.

She came in blinking and red-eyed at 0245. "Still awake?" she yawned at me, plumping onto her hammock.

"Kathy," I said hoarsely. "I'm cracking up."

She looked at me without much interest. "Did I ever tell you I read a paper on malingering to the New York Academy of Medicine?"

I got up mechanically and started for the reactor room, grabbed hold of myself, turned around and sat down. I told her where I had been going.

She turned nasty. "Not you. I know you better than most doctors get to know their patients. I also know the exact science of psychiatry and I know that a person with your mental configuration could not possibly have the symptoms you describe. No more than two plus two can equal five. I presume you feel rejected—which, God knows, you have every right to—and are consciously trying to hoodwink me into thinking you're an interesting case that needs my personal attention."

"Bitch," I said.

She was too tired to be angry. "If I thought there were the smallest possible chance that your alleged symptoms are real and do spring from your unconscious, I'd treat you. But there isn't any such chance. I have to conclude that you're consciously trying to divert my energy from the job I have to do. And under the circumstances that is a despicable thing."

"Bitch," I said again, and got up and went out to go to the reactor room.

My feet moved as though they didn't belong to me, and I still felt the dirt on me that no soap and water or alcohol had been able to remove.

She had meant every word of it. She knew her trade. And it *was* an exact science. She thoroughly believed that I couldn't have the symptoms I had. If she'd said it about somebody else, I would have taken her word for it unquestioningly. Only I had the symptoms—

Or were they symptoms?

I stopped in the corridor, though my legs wanted to go on carrying me into the reactor room.

AGRONOMY SECTION, a sign over a door said. I went in. There was no microscope. I looked through three more rooms before I found one—and a knife that would do as a scalpel.

I meant only to flick a pinpoint specimen off the base of my thumb, but in my dull intoxication I gashed a minor blood vessel. I found some reasonably sterile-looking gauze and wound it around my hand.

I dropped the ragged little crumb of meat into the oil-lens objective, tapped it to shake free the bubbles, levered it into a turret chosen at random. There was some difficulty in getting the light source to function—I couldn't make out what I was supposed to do with the knob marked "polarizer"—but finally the stage appeared through the eyepiece, bathed in a greenish glow.

I saw:

Life.

Clustered around the fabric of the epidermis that loomed in the eyepiece like a decayed glacier were massive chunks of rock, the random dust particles of any atmosphere, the faint accretion that no washing will completely remove from the human skin. They were featureless, irregular blobs, most of them.

But not all.

Among the dust fragments were a dozen or so living things, sea-urchin-shaped. Under the flaring light of the microscope, they seemed spurred to action. The spines of one touched the spines of another; they flexed and locked. A third blundered into the linked pair, and they became a Laocoön trio.

They were no protozoans or bacilli of Earth. They glowed; they were utterly alien. And as I watched, the trio became six, then ten globes locked together. And at once the character of the action changed: The clustered spheroids seemed to beat their flagella in unison, driving the mass, like eggs trailing from a spawning trout, about the field of vision. Purposefully, the massed ten ran down the other globes and absorbed them, till all were joined.

That was the second time anyone had seen a Venusian.

This time, though, it was with awareness.

I didn't want to go into the reactor room. *I* didn't want to go outside. The Venusian did and somehow we had become . . . tangled.

Kathy, with the reflexes of a doctor, woke easily when I shook her shoulder. She stared fixedly at me.

"Come along," I said. "I want to show you something under a microscope. And I can't begin to tell you what it is because you won't believe me until you see it."

"You, with a microscope," she said scornfully.

But she came.

She looked, blinked, looked again. At last, not moving from the eyepiece, she said softly: "Good God! What in the world are they?"

"Now you prepare a slide from my skin," I told her.

She did, in seconds, and stared at it through the microscope. I knew the—cells?—were going through their outlandish linkup behavior.

"I'm sorry, Mitch," she said doubtfully. "Some sort of pathogenic organism, causing a paranoid configuration—" She swallowed. "I didn't mean to be unfair."

"It's all right." Forgiven, she was in my arms. "But they're—it's not a pathogenic organism. It's a Venusian." I told her about the rock that vanished. "Some of it got carried in with me on the suit, I suppose, and got on me, or into me—I don't know. *But I feel intelligence.* I can sort of isolate it, now that I can tell which is it and which is me. I can think of the reactor room in two ways. When it's me thinking, I know it's deadly. When it's *it* thinking, there's—hunger? Yes, I think hunger."

"It lives on plutonium? No, there isn't any on Venus. It has to be manufactured."

I was exploring, thinking of the reactor room, what was in it, what it looked like, what happened there, and noting my—no, its—no, call them *the* reactions that followed.

"Energy," I said softly. "Not material. It wants to be irradiated."

And I thought of the outside. The wind meant nothing to it, the heat meant mild comfort, like air to me or water to a minnow.

But lightning, free electrons and cosmic rays—ah, that was really living!

"Energy," I whispered.

And I thought of the rocks of Venus, the rocks that sometimes exploded and sometimes unwound like balls of string.

"Love," I said almost inaudibly. "Community. The whole that is greater than the sum of its parts. Without hate, without fear—"

Kathy told me later that I pitched forward onto my face in an old-fashioned faint.

22

Well, the grass is still not green. But Kathy and I walked the hundred yards from the ship's skeleton to our hut this morning with only oxygen masks on. The wind was no more than gale force, and it keeps dropping in velocity every week.

Once we found that the Venusians, those incongruous flurries of silicate life, were capable of something resembling thought, we learned what they needed and what they could do.

They needed energy. We gave them energy, from the hot-gas ends of our giant Hilsch Tubes. Maxwell's mythical demon picked the hottest molecules from Venus's air and flung them at the Venusians, who rejoicingly sucked them dry of high-level heat and used the energy so they could reproduce even more prolifically to absorb still more energy.

The water roared down from the upper atmosphere like an ocean falling out of the sky. Now we have seas, and the poisoned atmosphere is being locked in chemical bonds with the soil and the rocks.

We've saved a decade at least, the planners say. And the Venusians are doing it for us. They're feasting themselves into famine on the energy we ripped out of the air for them. They'll never vanish completely of course: as the amount of available energy grows less and less, they'll reduce their numbers and we'll have more and more of the planet for our use, but we'll keep some of them alive out of sheer gratitude.

We cannibalized the ship for our huts and shops, leaving only the giant structural members that we'll be able to work with later—melt them down, I suppose, or cut them up into useful shapes. It's a tidy little community, each couple with a plot of ground and furniture that doesn't have to be rolled or folded out of the way. We're scouting the terrain for sources of metals and minerals, which won't be senselessly scooped out of the ground, manufactured, used and thrown away: they'll be restored to the soil or scrupulously collected and reworked. We can't grow anything yet, but already we have plans for the protection of the rich loam we'll create.

It's a Conservationist world, all right, and it makes sense . . . you take what you need from the planet and put back when you're through. On Earth, that's the worst kind of radicalism, of course. Being a copysmith, trained in semantics, I keep wondering how I could get my concepts so tangled that I mistook the epitome of conservatism for wild-eyed sabotage, when I know now that any kind of purposeless destruction is almost physical anguish for a Conservationist.

You don't have to be a prophet to see how Venus is developing into a self-sustaining economy. Kathy figured it out: By the time our first-born is of age, Fowler Shocken's commercials will have come true.

MORE THAN HUMAN

158.2 NICHOLAS SAMSTAG] Samstag (1903–1968), director of promotion at *Time* from 1943 to 1960, was the author of a book of juvenile fiction, *Kay-Kay Comes Home* (1952); a novel, *Come and See My Shining Palace* (1966); and books and articles on advertising and public relations, including *Persuasion for Profit* (1957).

180.18–19 "Flow Gently . . . Home on the Range."] Popular songs "Flow Gently, Sweet Afton," composed by Jonathan E. Spilman (1812–1896) around 1837, with lyrics from a poem by Robert Burns (1759–1796), and "Home on the Range," composed by Daniel E. Kelley (1845–1905) in the mid-1870s, adapting lyrics from the poem "My Western Home," by Brewster M. Higley (1823–1911).

198.24 Heinies] Germans.

207.14–17 *Venus in Furs . . . Ivan Bloch*] *Venus in Furs*, an erotic novella by Leopold von Sacher-Masoch (1836–1895) first published in German in 1870; *My Gun Is Quick* (1950), a crime novel by Mickey Spillane (1918–2006); *The Illustrated Ivan Bloch*, an invented title that could describe any of several illustrated editions of the works of Ivan (or Iwan) Bloch (1872–1922), a German sexologist.

237.3 Eisenhower jacket] Military field jacket popularized by Gen. Dwight Eisenhower during World War II.

286.16 idio-savant] A now-obscure form of the phrase "idiot savant."

287.20 the Pekin man] Peking Man, a collection of fossil fragments discovered near Beijing, China, between 1929 and 1937 and identified as a subspecies of *Homo erectus*, regarded as providing substantial evidence of Darwinian evolution.

303.4 "Hippocrates."] Hippocrates of Kos (c. 460–370 BCE), a Greek physician widely viewed as the father of scientific medicine.

326.20 Fifties] Machine guns firing .50-caliber bullets.

326.24 Oerlikons!] Automatic anti-aircraft guns firing 20mm shells.

331.17 Toscanini] Arturo Toscanini (1867–1957), Italian-born conductor and director of the NBC Symphony Orchestra from 1937 to 1954.

346.19–20 'If thine eye . . . cast it from thee.] See Matthew 18:9.

347.31 Eohippus] Prehistoric horse-like animal, also known as Hyracotherium, which lived during the Eocene epoch.

347.33 Percheron] Breed of draft horse known for strength and intelligence.

365.20 Papa Haydn] Franz Joseph Haydn (1732–1809), Austrian classical composer.

365.21–22 introduced William to the Rossettis] Morris (1834–1896), a Victorian writer, artist, and designer, collaborated extensively with the Rossettis, a family of poets and artists associated with the Pre-Raphaelite Brotherhood, whose members included Dante Gabriel (1828–1882), William (1829–1919), and Christina (1830–1894).

365.22 Fermi] Enrico Fermi (1901–1954), Italian-born physicist who contributed to the development of the atomic bomb.

365.24 Landowska . . . Ford] Wanda Landowska (1879–1959), Polish-born harpsichordist; Henry Ford (1863–1947), American industrialist known for pioneering the manufacturing assembly line.

THE LONG TOMORROW

414.12–13 whited sepulchers . . . Bible] See Matthew 23:27.

424.12 Nahum . . . bloody city.] See Nahum 3:1 on the "bloody city," Nineveh.

469.15–16 Mine eyes have seen . . . Lord.] The opening line of "The Battle Hymn of the Republic" (1862), by Julia Ward Howe (1819–1910).

542.2–3 Democritus] Greek philosopher (c. 460–370 BCE) who with his tutor Leucippus first proposed the theory that all matter was composed of irreducibly small "atoms" in definable structures.

THE SHRINKING MAN

585.1 THE SHRINKING MAN] Matheson added the following introduction to the novel, addressed "To the Reader," when it was published in a new edition in 2001:

> While I have told this story many a number of times in past interviews, it has never been an introduction to the novel itself, which is appropriate at this time.
>
> How did I get the idea for this story? As in most cases in my early days of writing, I got it from a movie. The film starred Ray Milland and featured Aldo Ray. In one scene, Ray Milland leaves Ray's apartment angrily and, by mistake, puts on Ray's hat instead of his own. Ray's head being considerably larger than Milland's, the hat immediately comes down over Milland's ears and eyes. My immediate thought—and it *was* immediate—was "What if a man put on his own hat and had the same thing happen and realized that his head was smaller than it had been before?"

The rest followed in its course. I prepared an outline while my family and I were living in Gardena, California.

We moved to New York in 1954 and, after living briefly in Bay Shore on Long Island, rented a small house on the north shore of the island in a community called South Beach which was a little east of Port Jefferson. The house had a cellar in it reached by going down outside steps with folding doors over them. I decided that this would be an ideal location for the section of the novel—the major one—where my hero was imprisoned and getting smaller every day, his life endangered not only by the prospect of disappearing altogether but by the menace of being killed by a black widow spider *before* he disappeared.

It was down in this cellar that I actually wrote the novel. Not only was it quiet and isolated from the children but also it had an environment that I could use continuously. I did not have to keep notes on the environment. It was right there and all I had to do was imagine what my shrinking man would do from day to day. There was even the half stone wall with a piece of cake on it. There was no spider web since I knew that black widows did not display themselves at all but hid under things. I did not visualize a tarantula; I don't think one would find one on the north shore of Long Island. That came later in the movie.

Every morning, after breakfast, I would bundle up (it was cold in that cellar) and go down to where I had an old rocking chair I sat on with my pad and pencil and wrote what occurred to me that day. It was interesting for me to imagine how my protagonist would make use of what was in the cellar. I changed nothing in the environment, just used it for my story. I have used this method of writing a novel in *Hunger and Thirst* and what became *Somewhere in Time*. It is an intriguing way to write a novel; to actually be *there* in the environment you are writing about. Very stimulating to the imagination. Even more so to make use of unexpected occurrences. For instance, the first time I heard the furnace in the cellar kick on, I thought of how startling the sound would be to my little man. His reactions were, of course, my own, his thoughts my own. But, in a strange way, they were his; I was just an observer describing what he was doing and thinking.

After a brief submission, the book was purchased by Gold Medal and published.

Although I had grown up back east in Brooklyn, I had been (well, since I was old enough to be aware of them) fascinated with movies and had a dream about writing for them. When I was seventeen, I wrote a letter to Val Lewton praising his films and telling him that I figured out several methods he used to frighten people that were based on the craft of frightening people unexpectedly. He answered my letter graciously and told me that he and his editor Mark Robson, were "delighted" by my observing what they did in their films. I would have been overwhelmed to learn that, someday in the future, Jacques Tourneur would actually be directing a script of mine.

While living in Los Angeles from 1951–1954, I made various attempts to get script assignments none of which succeeded. I came to the conclusion that, the only way I would ever get such an assignment, would be to sell Hollywood a novel and demand the right to write the screenplay.

That is the way it worked out. I had an agent in Los Angeles named Al Manuel who submitted the manuscript of *The Shrinking Man* to a party [*sic*]. When we arrived, my mother, who was watching our two children, was lying on the couch in the small living room. She rose up on one elbow and said "Hollywood beckons."

I telephoned Al Manuel and discovered that I could, indeed, do the script. I'm sure they figured it would be an unsatisfactory first draft, which they could have re-written by one of their contract writers.

Fortunately, it did not work out that way. The script got me started in the movie business. To make use of Oliver Onions' title, I was ready for "The Beckoning Fair One."

When I went to the studio to watch them shooting the film, I met its director Jack Arnold (who became a friend) and was taken back by the unusual resemblance of the cellar set to the cellar I had written the book in. It was an intriguing *déjà vu*.

I hope you find the novel interesting to read. Structurally, it is different from the film, which, at the time, disturbed me. I now accept it since the film has come to be regarded as a minor science-fiction classic. But, if you have only seen the film, you may find its novel genesis interesting to examine.

586.2 Harry Altshuler] Altshuler (1913–1990) was Matheson's literary agent.

586.4 *Dr. Sylvia Traube*] Traube (1909–1989), a physician and psychiatrist, was a researcher in the field of somatotypology, which explored the relationships between physiognomy and character.

640.1 *Fermez la porte*] French: "close the door."

640.16 My kingdom for a match!"] See *Richard III*, V.iv.7.

641.2 Od's bodkins] British slang, probably from the Tudor period, meaning "God's body"; an oath.

641.3–4 "God's hooks!"] British slang, referring to the nails on the cross where Jesus was crucified; often contracted as *gadzooks*.

641.20 *comprends*] French: "understand."

644.19 "Good night, sweet prince,"] See *Hamlet*, V.ii.343.

669.1 acromicria] Condition characterized by abnormally small extremities.

687.12 ACTH] Adrenocorticotropic hormone, also referred to as corticotropin, a hormone produced in and released from the pituitary gland.

701.36–37 And it shall . . . sweet as honey.] See Revelation 10:9.

718.1–2 "If I loved you . . . say . . ."] Song from Richard Rodgers and Oscar Hammerstein III's popular stage musical *Carousel*, which premiered in 1945.

THE LIBRARY OF AMERICA SERIES

THE LIBRARY OF AMERICA, a nonprofit publisher, is dedicated to publishing, and keeping in print, authoritative editions of America's best and most significant writing. Each year the Library adds new volumes to its collection of essential works by America's foremost novelists, poets, essayists, journalists, and statesmen.

If you would like to request a free catalog and find out more about The Library of America, please visit www.loa.org/catalog or send us an e-mail at lists@loa.org with your name and address. Include your e-mail address if you would like to receive our occasional newsletter with items of interest to readers of classic American literature and exclusive interviews with Library of America authors and editors (we will never share your e-mail address).

1. Herman Melville: *Typee, Omoo, Mardi*
2. Nathaniel Hawthorne: *Tales and Sketches*
3. Walt Whitman: *Poetry and Prose*
4. Harriet Beecher Stowe: *Three Novels*
5. Mark Twain: *Mississippi Writings*
6. Jack London: *Novels and Stories*
7. Jack London: *Novels and Social Writings*
8. William Dean Howells: *Novels 1875–1886*
9. Herman Melville: *Redburn, White-Jacket, Moby-Dick*
10. Nathaniel Hawthorne: *Collected Novels*
11. Francis Parkman: *France and England in North America*, vol. I
12. Francis Parkman: *France and England in North America*, vol. II
13. Henry James: *Novels 1871–1880*
14. Henry Adams: *Novels, Mont Saint Michel, The Education*
15. Ralph Waldo Emerson: *Essays and Lectures*
16. Washington Irving: *History, Tales and Sketches*
17. Thomas Jefferson: *Writings*
18. Stephen Crane: *Prose and Poetry*
19. Edgar Allan Poe: *Poetry and Tales*
20. Edgar Allan Poe: *Essays and Reviews*
21. Mark Twain: *The Innocents Abroad, Roughing It*
22. Henry James: *Literary Criticism: Essays, American & English Writers*
23. Henry James: *Literary Criticism: European Writers & The Prefaces*
24. Herman Melville: *Pierre, Israel Potter, The Confidence-Man, Tales & Billy Budd*
25. William Faulkner: *Novels 1930–1935*
26. James Fenimore Cooper: *The Leatherstocking Tales*, vol. I
27. James Fenimore Cooper: *The Leatherstocking Tales*, vol. II
28. Henry David Thoreau: *A Week, Walden, The Maine Woods, Cape Cod*
29. Henry James: *Novels 1881–1886*
30. Edith Wharton: *Novels*
31. Henry Adams: *History of the U.S. during the Administrations of Jefferson*
32. Henry Adams: *History of the U.S. during the Administrations of Madison*
33. Frank Norris: *Novels and Essays*
34. W.E.B. Du Bois: *Writings*
35. Willa Cather: *Early Novels and Stories*
36. Theodore Dreiser: *Sister Carrie, Jennie Gerhardt, Twelve Men*

37a. Benjamin Franklin: *Silence Dogood, The Busy-Body, & Early Writings*

37b. Benjamin Franklin: *Autobiography, Poor Richard, & Later Writings*

38. William James: *Writings 1902–1910*
39. Flannery O'Connor: *Collected Works*
40. Eugene O'Neill: *Complete Plays 1913–1920*
41. Eugene O'Neill: *Complete Plays 1920–1931*
42. Eugene O'Neill: *Complete Plays 1932–1943*
43. Henry James: *Novels 1886–1890*
44. William Dean Howells: *Novels 1886–1888*
45. Abraham Lincoln: *Speeches and Writings 1832–1858*
46. Abraham Lincoln: *Speeches and Writings 1859–1865*
47. Edith Wharton: *Novellas and Other Writings*
48. William Faulkner: *Novels 1936–1940*
49. Willa Cather: *Later Novels*
50. Ulysses S. Grant: *Memoirs and Selected Letters*
51. William Tecumseh Sherman: *Memoirs*
52. Washington Irving: *Bracebridge Hall, Tales of a Traveller, The Alhambra*
53. Francis Parkman: *The Oregon Trail, The Conspiracy of Pontiac*
54. James Fenimore Cooper: *Sea Tales: The Pilot, The Red Rover*
55. Richard Wright: *Early Works*
56. Richard Wright: *Later Works*

57. Willa Cather: *Stories, Poems, and Other Writings*
58. William James: *Writings 1878–1899*
59. Sinclair Lewis: *Main Street & Babbitt*
60. Mark Twain: *Collected Tales, Sketches, Speeches, & Essays 1852–1890*
61. Mark Twain: *Collected Tales, Sketches, Speeches, & Essays 1891–1910*
62. *The Debate on the Constitution: Part One*
63. *The Debate on the Constitution: Part Two*
64. Henry James: *Collected Travel Writings: Great Britain & America*
65. Henry James: *Collected Travel Writings: The Continent*
66. *American Poetry: The Nineteenth Century*, Vol. 1
67. *American Poetry: The Nineteenth Century*, Vol. 2
68. Frederick Douglass: *Autobiographies*
69. Sarah Orne Jewett: *Novels and Stories*
70. Ralph Waldo Emerson: *Collected Poems and Translations*
71. Mark Twain: *Historical Romances*
72. John Steinbeck: *Novels and Stories 1932–1937*
73. William Faulkner: *Novels 1942–1954*
74. Zora Neale Hurston: *Novels and Stories*
75. Zora Neale Hurston: *Folklore, Memoirs, and Other Writings*
76. Thomas Paine: *Collected Writings*
77. *Reporting World War II: American Journalism 1938–1944*
78. *Reporting World War II: American Journalism 1944–1946*
79. Raymond Chandler: *Stories and Early Novels*
80. Raymond Chandler: *Later Novels and Other Writings*
81. Robert Frost: *Collected Poems, Prose, & Plays*
82. Henry James: *Complete Stories 1892–1898*
83. Henry James: *Complete Stories 1898–1910*
84. William Bartram: *Travels and Other Writings*
85. John Dos Passos: *U.S.A.*
86. John Steinbeck: *The Grapes of Wrath and Other Writings 1936–1941*
87. Vladimir Nabokov: *Novels and Memoirs 1941–1951*
88. Vladimir Nabokov: *Novels 1955–1962*
89. Vladimir Nabokov: *Novels 1969–1974*
90. James Thurber: *Writings and Drawings*
91. George Washington: *Writings*
92. John Muir: *Nature Writings*
93. Nathanael West: *Novels and Other Writings*
94. *Crime Novels: American Noir of the 1930s and 40s*
95. *Crime Novels: American Noir of the 1950s*
96. Wallace Stevens: *Collected Poetry and Prose*
97. James Baldwin: *Early Novels and Stories*
98. James Baldwin: *Collected Essays*
99. Gertrude Stein: *Writings 1903–1932*
100. Gertrude Stein: *Writings 1932–1946*
101. Eudora Welty: *Complete Novels*
102. Eudora Welty: *Stories, Essays, & Memoir*
103. Charles Brockden Brown: *Three Gothic Novels*
104. *Reporting Vietnam: American Journalism 1959–1969*
105. *Reporting Vietnam: American Journalism 1969–1975*
106. Henry James: *Complete Stories 1874–1884*
107. Henry James: *Complete Stories 1884–1891*
108. American Sermons: *The Pilgrims to Martin Luther King Jr.*
109. James Madison: *Writings*
110. Dashiell Hammett: *Complete Novels*
111. Henry James: *Complete Stories 1864–1874*
112. William Faulkner: *Novels 1957–1962*
113. John James Audubon: *Writings & Drawings*
114. *Slave Narratives*
115. *American Poetry: The Twentieth Century*, Vol. 1
116. *American Poetry: The Twentieth Century*, Vol. 2
117. F. Scott Fitzgerald: *Novels and Stories 1920–1922*
118. Henry Wadsworth Longfellow: *Poems and Other Writings*
119. Tennessee Williams: *Plays 1937–1955*
120. Tennessee Williams: *Plays 1957–1980*
121. Edith Wharton: *Collected Stories 1891–1910*
122. Edith Wharton: *Collected Stories 1911–1937*
123. *The American Revolution: Writings from the War of Independence*
124. Henry David Thoreau: *Collected Essays and Poems*
125. Dashiell Hammett: *Crime Stories and Other Writings*
126. Dawn Powell: *Novels 1930–1942*
127. Dawn Powell: *Novels 1944–1962*
128. Carson McCullers: *Complete Novels*
129. Alexander Hamilton: *Writings*
130. Mark Twain: *The Gilded Age and Later Novels*

131. Charles W. Chesnutt: *Stories, Novels, and Essays*
132. John Steinbeck: *Novels 1942–1952*
133. Sinclair Lewis: *Arrowsmith, Elmer Gantry, Dodsworth*
134. Paul Bowles: *The Sheltering Sky, Let It Come Down, The Spider's House*
135. Paul Bowles: *Collected Stories & Later Writings*
136. Kate Chopin: *Complete Novels & Stories*
137. *Reporting Civil Rights: American Journalism 1941–1963*
138. *Reporting Civil Rights: American Journalism 1963–1973*
139. Henry James: *Novels 1896–1899*
140. Theodore Dreiser: *An American Tragedy*
141. Saul Bellow: *Novels 1944–1953*
142. John Dos Passos: *Novels 1920–1925*
143. John Dos Passos: *Travel Books and Other Writings*
144. Ezra Pound: *Poems and Translations*
145. James Weldon Johnson: *Writings*
146. Washington Irving: *Three Western Narratives*
147. Alexis de Tocqueville: *Democracy in America*
148. James T. Farrell: *Studs Lonigan: A Trilogy*
149. Isaac Bashevis Singer: *Collected Stories I*
150. Isaac Bashevis Singer: *Collected Stories II*
151. Isaac Bashevis Singer: *Collected Stories III*
152. Kaufman & Co.: *Broadway Comedies*
153. Theodore Roosevelt: *The Rough Riders, An Autobiography*
154. Theodore Roosevelt: *Letters and Speeches*
155. H. P. Lovecraft: *Tales*
156. Louisa May Alcott: *Little Women, Little Men, Jo's Boys*
157. Philip Roth: *Novels & Stories 1959–1962*
158. Philip Roth: *Novels 1967–1972*
159. James Agee: *Let Us Now Praise Famous Men, A Death in the Family*
160. James Agee: *Film Writing & Selected Journalism*
161. Richard Henry Dana, Jr.: *Two Years Before the Mast & Other Voyages*
162. Henry James: *Novels 1901–1902*
163. Arthur Miller: *Collected Plays 1944–1961*
164. William Faulkner: *Novels 1926–1929*
165. Philip Roth: *Novels 1973–1977*
166. *American Speeches: Part One*
167. *American Speeches: Part Two*
168. Hart Crane: *Complete Poems & Selected Letters*
169. Saul Bellow: *Novels 1956–1964*
170. John Steinbeck: *Travels with Charley and Later Novels*
171. Capt. John Smith: *Writings with Other Narratives*
172. Thornton Wilder: *Collected Plays & Writings on Theater*
173. Philip K. Dick: *Four Novels of the 1960s*
174. Jack Kerouac: *Road Novels 1957–1960*
175. Philip Roth: *Zuckerman Bound*
176. Edmund Wilson: *Literary Essays & Reviews of the 1920s & 30s*
177. Edmund Wilson: *Literary Essays & Reviews of the 1930s & 40s*
178. *American Poetry: The Seventeenth & Eighteenth Centuries*
179. William Maxwell: *Early Novels & Stories*
180. Elizabeth Bishop: *Poems, Prose, & Letters*
181. A. J. Liebling: *World War II Writings*
182s. *American Earth: Environmental Writing Since Thoreau*
183. Philip K. Dick: *Five Novels of the 1960s & 70s*
184. William Maxwell: *Later Novels & Stories*
185. Philip Roth: *Novels & Other Narratives 1986–1991*
186. Katherine Anne Porter: *Collected Stories & Other Writings*
187. John Ashbery: *Collected Poems 1956–1987*
188. John Cheever: *Collected Stories & Other Writings*
189. John Cheever: *Complete Novels*
190. Lafcadio Hearn: *American Writings*
191. A. J. Liebling: *The Sweet Science & Other Writings*
192s. *The Lincoln Anthology: Great Writers on His Life and Legacy from 1860 to Now*
193. Philip K. Dick: *VALIS & Later Novels*
194. Thornton Wilder: *The Bridge of San Luis Rey and Other Novels 1926–1948*
195. Raymond Carver: *Collected Stories*
196. *American Fantastic Tales: Terror and the Uncanny from Poe to the Pulps*
197. *American Fantastic Tales: Terror and the Uncanny from the 1940s to Now*
198. John Marshall: *Writings*
199s. *The Mark Twain Anthology: Great Writers on His Life and Works*
200. Mark Twain: *A Tramp Abroad, Following the Equator, Other Travels*

201. Ralph Waldo Emerson: *Selected Journals 1820–1842*
202. Ralph Waldo Emerson: *Selected Journals 1841–1877*
203. *The American Stage: Writing on Theater from Washington Irving to Tony Kushner*
204. Shirley Jackson: *Novels & Stories*
205. Philip Roth: *Novels 1993–1995*
206. H. L. Mencken: *Prejudices: First, Second, and Third Series*
207. H. L. Mencken: *Prejudices: Fourth, Fifth, and Sixth Series*
208. John Kenneth Galbraith: *The Affluent Society and Other Writings 1952–1967*
209. Saul Bellow: *Novels 1970–1982*
210. Lynd Ward: *Gods' Man, Madman's Drum, Wild Pilgrimage*
211. Lynd Ward: *Prelude to a Million Years, Song Without Words, Vertigo*
212. *The Civil War: The First Year Told by Those Who Lived It*
213. John Adams: *Revolutionary Writings 1755–1775*
214. John Adams: *Revolutionary Writings 1775–1783*
215. Henry James: *Novels 1903–1911*
216. Kurt Vonnegut: *Novels & Stories 1963–1973*
217. *Harlem Renaissance: Five Novels of the 1920s*
218. *Harlem Renaissance: Four Novels of the 1930s*
219. Ambrose Bierce: *The Devil's Dictionary, Tales, & Memoirs*
220. Philip Roth: *The American Trilogy 1997–2000*
221. *The Civil War: The Second Year Told by Those Who Lived It*
222. Barbara W. Tuchman: *The Guns of August & The Proud Tower*
223. Arthur Miller: *Collected Plays 1964–1982*
224. Thornton Wilder: *The Eighth Day, Theophilus North, Autobiographical Writings*
225. David Goodis: *Five Noir Novels of the 1940s & 50s*
226. Kurt Vonnegut: *Novels & Stories 1950–1962*
227. *American Science Fiction: Four Classsic Novels 1953–1956*
228. *American Science Fiction: Five Classic Novels 1956–1958*
229. Laura Ingalls Wilder: *The Little House Books, Volume One*
230. Laura Ingalls Wilder: *The Little House Books, Volume Two*
231. Jack Kerouac: *Collected Poems*
232. *The War of 1812: Writings from America's Second War of Independence*
233. *American Antislavery Writings: Colonial Beginnings to Emancipation*

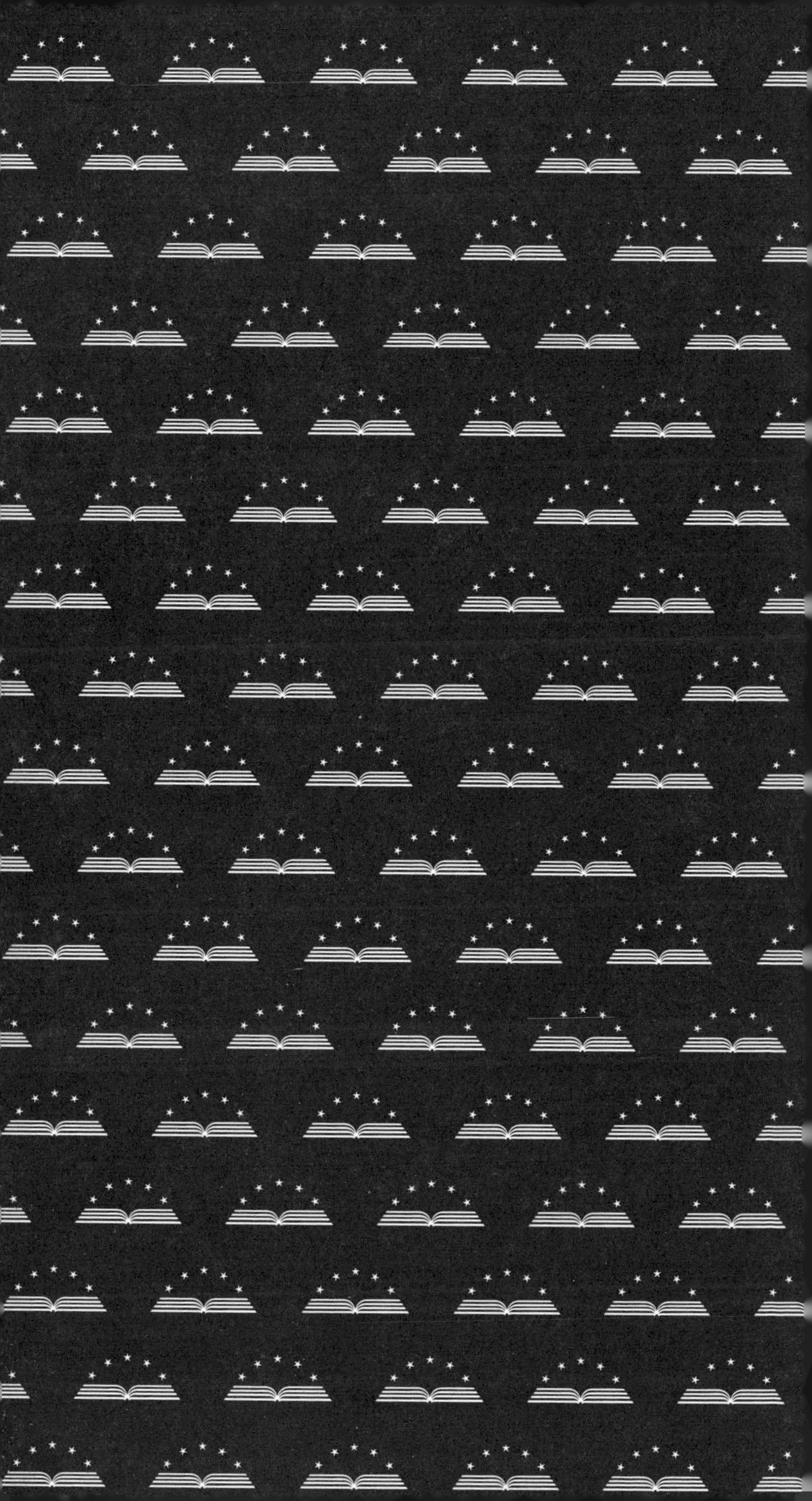